MMMMM000209160

MIKE Force

A Novel of Vietnam's Central Highlands War

Shaun Darragh

WARRIORS PUBLISHING GROUP
NORTH HILLS, CALIFORNIA

MIKE Force: A Novel of Vietnam's Central Highlands War

A Warriors Publishing Group book/published by arrangement with the author

PRINTING HISTORY
Warriors Publishing Group edition/November 2015
A previous version was published by Hellgate Press/Copyright © 2011 by Shaun Darragh

ISBN 978-0-9861955-3-2
Library of Congress Control Number: 2015954904

The name "Warriors Publishing Group" and the logo are trademarks belonging to
Warriors Publishing Group

PRINTED IN THE UNITED STATES OF AMERICA

10 9 8 7 6 5 4 3 2 1

For those who carried the rifles, radios, rucksacks, and medical kitbags in the II Corps Mobile Strike (MIKE) Force, whatever their race, ethnicity, or national origin. Though most of their names will not be found on any monument, they live on in the hearts of their clans and peoples.

And for Dick Chamberlain, who died as a result of hostile action, from wounds no one could see.

Cast of Characters

Lieutenant Galen Saint Cyr: A former Peace Corps volunteer who arrived home to find his draft notice waiting, and volunteered for Special Forces. As a lieutenant commanding an infantry company in Vietnam's Central Highlands, he runs into the MIKE Force and recognizes the place he always wanted to be.

Major Charlie Regter: A Korean War Ranger and career Special Forces officer who's been in and out of Vietnam since 1957. Regter's greatest fear is that continued service there will cost him his family, but his old friend and mentor Pappy Green has other ideas.

Lieutenant Colonel Loren 'Pappy' Green: One-time Special Forces officer, now CIA Paramilitary officer, serving as the 5th Special Forces deputy commander. Green's plan to expand the Mobile Strike (MIKE) Forces into Brigade sized units is being threatened by a revolt brewing in the II Corps MIKE Force. Green needs someone with an intimate knowledge of both the tribes and the war, and the latest batch of ticket punchers won't do.

Master Sergeant Marvin McElroy: Regter's radio operator from Korea, 'Mac' is an experienced and trusted Special Forces hand who has been in Vietnam's Central Highlands so long he has gone native and accepted a Major's commission in FULRO. Luckily or not, no one but Mac takes it seriously.

FULRO: The United Front for the Struggle of Oppressed Races. A Montagnard independence movement organized by Bahnar, Jarai, Rhade, and Koho tribal leaders in the 1950s. Crushed in 1957, it still managed a Highland revolt in September 1964, which the Americans—Regter among them—helped defuse. This time, they don't intend to let any Americans get in the way.

Me Sao: *Nom de guerre* of the chief MIKE Force FULRO agent who has taken the name of an early 20th century Rhade rebel whose punitive raids against French planters, Vietnamese settlers, and the Jarai, sparked numerous legends.

Major Ton That Ngoc: The Vietnamese commander of the MIKE Force whose clan are cousins to the former Imperial family. A well-decorated veteran of French paratroop units, and a Vietnamese nationalist, Ngoc dislikes Americans, and Regter in particular, but will he let that get in the way of the war?.

Rahlen H'nek: A Jarai tribal beauty destined to become her clan's leading matriarch or *Po Lan* based upon her reputation as a seer. H'nek aspires to unite all Highland tribes in a war against the Vietnamese, not only because they murdered her father, but because she sees it as necessary to keep her people from becoming just another thread in the Vietnamese mosaic.

Y B'Ham Enoul: The founder and president of FULRO, now living in exile in Cambodia's Moldolkiri province. His backing of Me Sao has split the FULRO leadership.

K'pa Doh: A radical Jarai FULRO leader who disputes Y B'Ham's authority and sends assassins after Me Sao.

The 212th MIKE Force Company: Three Americans, one Australian, one Ukrainian displaced person, two Vietnamese Special Forces, and 164 mostly Jarai tribesmen. They include:

> **Sergei 'Boris' Biloskirka,** who joined the Soviet Army in 1944 to clear his family's name after an older brother had joined the Germans. Tipped off that his family had been executed in 1945, Boris deserted later that year to make his way to the French sector, where he enlisted in the Foreign Legion. After hard years in Indochina, a chance encounter in a *Wolfratshausen gasthaus* put him into the U.S. Army Special Forces under the Lodge Act. Now back in Vietnam, he still has a few accounts to settle.

> **Warrant Officer Laurie Toller** left a hardscrabble cattle station in West Australia at the tender age of 14 to fend for himself. After knocking about for five years, he enlisted in the Royal Australian Regiment and saw service in Malaya. Though younger than Boris, Laurie views himself as his equal in knowledge and strength, if not height.

> **Specialist Five Morris Cohen**, the company radio operator, platoon leader, and joker. From St. Paul, Minnesota, the 'Superjew' originally joined Special Forces for the adventure. Now, he might even stick around for a career.

> **Sergeant Kevin Ryan**, the Afro-American medic, platoon leader, and Superjew's off-duty twin, Kev has dreams of attending Harvard Medical School and becoming a heart surgeon. Having done his pre-med at Tufts University, he is not particularly impressed with St. Cyr, whose own university was less prestigious. Still, the Army is the Army, however much it hurts to call someone 'Sir.'

Rahlen Blek: H'nek's older brother is 212th Company's senior interpreter and *de facto* commander. Blek is fearless in combat, and has much to teach anyone willing to observe, yet he is a political ingénue. He supports and loves his sister, but is fighting the war simply because that's what warriors do. He has no political ambitions, and his stoic silences are often mistaken for superior knowledge. His fellow tribesmen will follow him anywhere. In Regter's terms, he's a gang leader. But how well his gang will hold up once he's gone is anyone's guess.

Rchom Jimm: Young, handsome, muscled, intelligent, Jimm has ambitions of becoming H'nek's lover, or even husband. He is a rising star in the Jarai FULRO section. The only person standing in his way is Galen St. Cyr. Lucky for St. Cyr, Jimm genuinely respects him, and has been around long enough to know that not everyone who walks out of the wire will be walking back in. In war, sometimes all you have to do is wait.

Siu Dot Jhon Nie: A FULRO assassin. Dry leprosy has turned his hands into near claws, but it hasn't affected his marksmanship. Though loyal to Me Sao, Siu Dot is also ambitious. Fired from the II Corps MIKE Force for deserting with two companies at Dak To, he presently commands a company in the Nha Trang MIKE Force. He desires H'nek and would gladly kill St. Cyr, except for the fact that St. Cyr is blocking H'nek's gate to Rchom Jimm. The same chance of war that could remove St. Cyr at any moment, could just as easily remove Jimm. And if Siu Dot has anything to do with it, both of their removals are guaranteed.

Captain J.E.D. Saville: A young Australian Special Air Service officer who commands the 1st MIKE Force Battalion, Jed previously conducted secret raids against Indonesian forces in Borneo.

Y Bloom Nie, also Ney Bloom: Jed Saville's right hand man, interpreter, and shadow battalion commander. A Rhade tribesman, Bloom is the highest ranking known FULRO agent in the MIKE Force. If he knows Me Sao's true identity, he has never let on, and willingly allows others to presume he is Me Sao himself.

Romat Dat: A Jarai cattle raider and bandit turned rebel, Romah Dat is the FULRO Iron Brigade commander and an ally of K'pa Doh. He has been sent to the MIKE Force to uncover and kill Me Sao despite the reservations of his right-hand man, a half-French half-Jarai Métis named Glan Perr, who has some vague connection to the Rahlen clan.

Sergeant First Class Harry Perkins: Like Mac, Harry Perkins is an American who's all but gone native. As Regter's intelligence sergeant, his job is to ferret out Me Sao and keep his finger on FULRO's pulse, in addition to tracking all enemy forces in their area. Harry is where the rubber meets the road and he leaves no stone unturned in his search for Me Sao. But he also serves an important function as Regter's advisor and sounding board, as he has both allies and enemies in FULRO's senior ranks.

Ro'o Mnur: A rare Christian Jarai who comes into the MIKE Force with the Iron Brigade. Though St. Cyr's radio operator, Mnur also becomes his bodyguard. Oversized, easy going, and likeable, Ro'o Mnur will never run from a fight as long as anyone he knows is in danger.

Hong Klang: The evil "Wasp of the Bone." A malignant spirit greatly feared by the Highland tribes who resides in the hollow bones of their dead. Though he makes no known appearance, he is forever in the minds of the Montagnard troops.

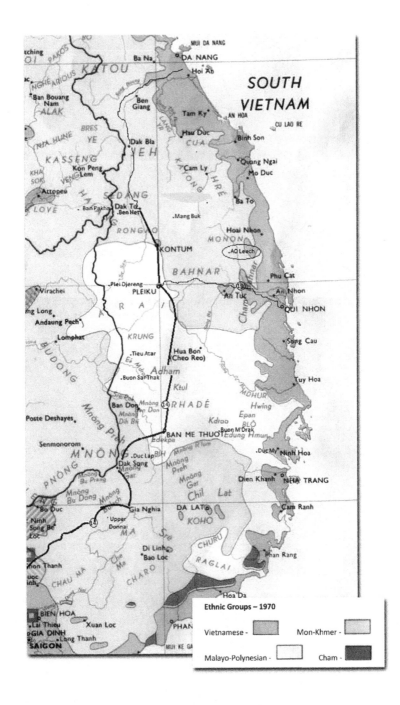

Chapter One

Buon Sar Thak, Rhade country, Montagnard High Plateaus of Champa, October, 1967:

Y SAR THAK'S EYES SHOT OPEN in the darkened longhouse. In the now familiar and unnatural silence, he felt it shimmy in barely perceptible waves. Beside him, wrapped in her own narrow polychromatic tribal blanket, his wife stirred.

"Why wake, Old Man?" The force of her breath sent an invisible wind rustling through the longhouse, like that of a spirit departing.

"Nothing." He whispered, as if there was someone else to hear.

"A lie," she snapped. "Men wake at night not healthy. Does memory of an old love disturb you?"

"Pah. Since the day we placed our feet on the ax-head, Old Woman, you have been my only love. It must be those under the bombs. Perhaps my spirits heard their cries."

"Of course," she muttered with a touch of sarcasm. "Go back to sleep. You leave in early morning."

"Yes, my Love," he sighed, shutting his eyes. This time he saw neither Bloom's face nor that of the shadowed specter behind him. Instead, he was a muscular and bronzed young man at the Ban Don elephant fair, eyeing a pretty young girl from the distant village of Tieu Atar.

Beside him that now much-older girl, Po Lan of the Mlo clan, closed her own eyes. His dreams had told him something that he wasn't going to say. And her third soul intuited it had something to do with the Jarai tribesman the Vietnamese had taken away. *Ai Die*, she invoked the Master of the Sky, *protect him.*

"Old man…"

"Mrmph…"

"I know you hear me. When you journey tomorrow, wear your old loincloth. I don't want you soiling the new one."

"Humph," visions of her full breasts and satin skin faded. "Why not wear? You wish save for my funeral?"

"Shhht, fool." Her eyes shot open.

"Shhht, yourself. We go to gather wood, not bones. Why would I wear my new loincloth?"

Y Thak's wood gathering party departed as the sun edged above the horizon, carrying axes, long handled *coup-coup* machetes, and the occasional crossbow. The few teenage boys were bare-chested and muscled. A few teenage girls went bare-chested, but most wore vests or narrow thin blankets wrapped around their upper torsos like the older women, though many came off as the sun climbed. After several hours of rapid march, they arrived at the gloomy hardwood forests of the northwestern mountains. It was an area Thak preferred to avoid, but the ironsmith needed hardwood charcoal if the village was to have more knives and hatchets, and no one knew the forest like Y Sar Thak.

Over two seasons ago bombs had dropped into a stand of mahogany and teak, barely missing his hiding place but catching several hundred North Vietnamese under their deadly carpet. The rolling thunder had ripped the trees apart, exposing their heartwood to the elements. And while there might be hungry ghosts present, with luck they'd gather enough heartwood shards to load everyone down and return home before sunset, earning him that pouch of promised Meerika—American—tobacco.

Under an early afternoon sun they moved into a strip of devastated forest near the edge of what had been a coffee plantation, and before that the *ray* of a tribal outlaw. After showing the women, boys, and children which pieces to gather, Thak settled into a sunlit clearing and lay back against an upturned trunk to allow his bad spirits to pass. They had become more frequent of late, with longer spells of nausea and chills. He had hoped that up here the teak spirits might drive them away. But as his chills grew more intense, he slipped around to the far side of the trunk, out of sight of the work party. *Village chiefs*, he chided himself, *should not set poor examples for the young.*

Clutching his knees in to his chest for warmth, he glanced across the small clearing. "Ai Die!"

At his shrill call, two boys with crossbows dropped to their haunches and sat. With practiced precision, they snagged their bows over their extended feet with one hand while extracting a bolt from their bamboo quivers with the other, placing it between their teeth. Bending at the waist, they used both hands to pull the elephant-hair bowstrings back into the trigger notch. Then, dipping their bolt points into a gummy poisonous resin pressed into the base of the firing channel, they reversed their bolts, pressing their nocks into that same resin to hold it in place. The maneuver took mere seconds, and they were back on their feet sprinting, trailed by two boys with razor-sharp *coup-coups* at the ready.

Y Sar Thak heard their approach, but his tongue was frozen with fear. The green and yellow 'Wasp of the Bone' had shot out of a skull's eye socket to hover within millimeters of his face.

You betrayed me, it buzzed. *Now is your time.*

"Not me," he screamed in his mind. "Not I."

Then who? Hong Klang hovered to and fro, seeking a spot to inject his venom.

"Uncle," the boys called. "Where are you?"

"Here," Thak gasped through the thumping in his chest. "I am here!" He glanced down at the skull, now just a skull. Hong Klang had flitted away.

"Mother's-uncle," the boys called as they closed in from two sides, crossbows at the ready. "What is it?"

Thak shook uncontrollably, adrenalin and malaria coursing through his veins. Squeezing his eyes shut, he invoked the spirit prayer. The first boy uncocked his crossbow, giving Thak a sympathetic smile.

"It is just a skeleton, Mother's-uncle. From your scream, we thought it Sir Tiger."

"If you had thought it Sir Tiger," scoffed a slightly older boy, "you would have run in other direction. What was it, Uncle?"

Thak stared into the empty eye sockets of the skull lying above a crumpled skeleton festooned with shreds of faded tiger-striped cloth.

"Nothing," he croaked. He knew better than to name the wasp of the bone in its own lair. "I should not have brought you all here. This was Bloom the Soldier's..."

"What, this?" The first boy nudged a shinbone with his toe.

"Fool." Thak's tone turned harsh. "Disturb those bones not. In my youth, Bloom lived here after being exiled for spilling blood. The French left him unmolested because he was their soldier. That," he dropped his voice to a bare whisper, "is the abode of he I cannot name. Let us warn the village."

At the wasp's reference, the boys made the spirit sign. Quickly, they rounded up the wood gatherers. Within minutes, their small column was wending its way home, weighted down with as much heartwood as they could carry. No one breathed a word until they had cleared the forest and regained the rolling hills that undulate towards Ban Me Thuot. Even then no one dared say much until they were back among the upland rice, corn, banana, tuber, and coffee fields of home. Work ceased as word of Hong Klang's sighting spread. Soon everyone was in their longhouses. The village gates were closed and spirit warnings posted.

Y Sar Thak lay in his longhouse, wrapped in myriad blankets, while his wife supervised the preparation of an herbal tea. Nearby, a gaggle of village elders bickered over sending for the *M'jao* at Ban Don, who was reputed to have some power over Hong Klang. Thak protested the expense that such a sacrifice would entail, but they sent for the M'jao anyway. You could never be too careful with spirits, though Hong Klang more often used human agents. No sooner had the runner departed than a voice hailed them from below. Booted feet were heard ascending the male log-steps.

"Father's Uncle," a voice called. "May we enter?"

"Ney Bloom," called a neighbor, "you are welcome."

Y Sar Thak shot his neighbor an alarmed look, but motioned for him to slide the door open. A muscular young man wearing a green military uniform stepped in. He had close-cropped black hair and Thai eyes. Respectfully greeting the Po Lan, he leaned over to take both of Thak's hands in his own, nodding a greeting to the neighbors as he did so.

"Uncle," said Ney Bloom, "with the Po Lan's permission, some guests would like to remain here tonight."

Thak glanced over at his wife, who ignored him to speak directly. Though Ney Bloom had been one of her favorite nephews, the uniform disturbed her.

"Are you on the Front's business?" she asked.

"Yes," Ney Bloom nodded gravely.

"So how can we refuse? Bid them enter."

Ney Bloom stepped to the door and motioned two men to mount the stepped log. They too were young, dressed in the same tiger striped camouflage that Thak had seen that afternoon. The first was a tribesman known to all by his clan name, and the second was vaguely familiar. A broad shouldered and handsome youth, the second carried a canvas case clutched in the claw-like hands of a leper. As he greeted everyone in Jarai, his unflinching gaze sent the neighbors on their way.

The Po Lan called in several clanswomen. They spread mats on the longhouse floor and set to work preparing the evening meal as night fell.

Despite his chills, Y Sar Thak sat with the men. Bloom lifted one of the oil lamps. Sweat beads glistened on his bronzed forehead as he lit the long crooked pipe he'd spent the past few minutes cramming with tinder-dry mountain tobacco. A young clanswoman stepped around him to place a large earthenware jar of *m'nam pay* rice wine in their midst. After the women had carefully arranged the drinking straws, meat, and rice bowls, the Po Pan thanked them and asked that they depart. Then the Po Lan, in whom the real village and clan power resided, sat back and nodded to Y Sar Thak.

"Much time has passed since we last saw you, Nephew."

"Too much, Uncle. I often dream of the longhouses of my childhood. How is everyone?"

"Pah!" the old man restrained himself from spitting. "As you see, not well. Too many young men leave to be soldier. Too few remain to plant and harvest. We are becoming a village of the old, the widowed, and the orphaned."

"This war is hard..."

"Hard?" Thak grunted, "Yes, killing hard. It kills our bodies, and our souls. Let's not talk of war. Maybe you can talk of plantings; of elephants, and gaur, and barking deer, and the taste of wild honey. Do you remember those?"

"Of course," Bloom answered, "every night in my dreams." Staring into the lamp flame, he felt the Po Lan's disapproval boring into him from the darkness. "Do you know Siu Dot and B Rob Ya, Uncle?"

"I am aging. Their names I had forgotten almost as soon as they entered. Rob Ya's father is respected. This claw-hands," he nodded at Siu Dot, "I know from those pictures the Viets put up in Ban Don. Jarai," he spat.

"If you know Siu Dot, Father's-Uncle, then you know why we have come."

"Yes..." The old man lowered his head.

"Some months ago," Bloom continued, "a brother from the Front came here seeking refuge. I myself personally assured his safety. He was Jarai, so we reasoned that the Viets would not seek him here in our country."

The old man nodded.

"And yet they did. In this village. My village. Where someone pointed him out."

Y Sar Thak nodded again.

"He was a Jarai, Uncle, but he was here on orders from our United Front. We have learned he is dead. Thrown from an 'up-away' for refusing to betray us."

"It is true," Thak whispered, "I myself have seen his bones."

"Where?" asked Rob.

The old man waved his hand northwestwards.

"Up near the old French coffee plantation. Molest them not, for a certain wasp resides in those bones."

"Thus the spirit signs?"

The old man nodded, and fell into a gloomy silence. At length, he fixed Bloom with an earnest stare.

"I was the M'jao at your naming ceremony. It was I who touched the sacred dew to your lips. We already knew who you were, yet your father prayed we were mistaken. I remember calling up your third soul, the *Yun*, and asking of it all the names that your father so wanted you to be. But you were none of those. Finally, when we could think of no more, he said: It is no use, call him Bloom. So I placed the last dewdrop on your lips, and called you Bloom. You stopped crying and smiled up at me. You were Bloom."

"I have heard…"

"And have you heard what your father said?"

Bloom gazed down at the floor and nodded.

"When the ceremony was over," Y Sar Thak continued, "your father took me outside the longhouse. 'Pah,' he spat, 'I wanted a daughter who would be a Po Lan for my first born. Not a son who will be a soldier.' And I said to him: 'In the days that are coming, this clan may well need a soldier.' We thought perhaps you would protect us from the Viets and Jarai."

"From the Jarai?" hissed Siu Dot. "How interesting."

Bloom shot his companion a withering stare.

"Your father's mother's father," continued the old man, "founded this village. They named it in his honor."

"Yes."

"It was he who brought the French administrator."

"I have heard…"

"It was he who showed us new ways to plant rice so that village would not have to move so often. He also brought French doctors when the plague came. It was only their priests he would not allow in, and still he was on good terms with those. He and my own father drove away that other malevolent spirit, Yang Brieng Pong. Those were good days."

Bloom said nothing.

"It was his sister's husband Bloom who led the fight against the Jarai raiding parties. The French promised much, but with the Great War they could do little. So Bloom took up raiding. Within two harvests, he put a stop to Nights of the Jarai. And by third harvest, they had reason to fear Nights of the Ede. And Days of the Ede as well, for he was bold. Many harvests later, they killed him, on his last raid; the one to bring Me Sao's daughter home. I was just a boy then, but I grew up hearing his name. This village could pass hours speaking his deeds. But as time passed, Bloom became less legend and more story. A hero of yesteryear, tales of whom served to instruct the youth. Peace was on the land then. Our tomorrows were hopeful. Not even the Japanese bothered us. Then, you were born and we began to hear rumors of war. And we knew that the spirit who had spent long years wandering the Jarai country had found its way home."

"Father's-Uncle," Bloom's voice was soft, "the Jarai are no longer enemies. Do you remember their raiding parties?"

"No, the French stopped the last of them while I was young. But I have the musket your Father's-father gave mine. Bloom taught him to use it. Would you like to see?"

"Yes."

They heard the matriarch moving about in the back of the longhouse. Presently she handed Y Sar Thak his father's musket, which he passed to Ney Bloom. It was percussion trade musket, manufactured around 1912 for sale in colonial possessions. After looking it over respectfully, Bloom passed it around.

"You call this a firearm?" scoffed Siu Dot. "Soon, old man, you will see a firearm."

Rob's eyebrows knit together. "This *pow-fusil* has killed many Jarai," he smirked.

"How would you know, little brother?" Siu Dot coolly returned Rob's stare. "Does it speak to you? I can make it speak to you with a little powder and ball."

Rob turned his eyes away as Bloom handed the musket back to Y Sar Thak.

"No," protested the old man. "It is yours. Bloom carried that firearm. Your third soul has a claim."

Ney Bloom hesitated, then lay the musket at his side.

"Old man," Siu Dot's voice cut through the night air as he fixed Thak with a cobra's gaze. "Did you betray our brother because he was Jarai? Or had you other reasons?"

Thak returned Siu Dot's glare while he carefully refilled his pipe. Without averting his eyes, he lifted the oil lamp for a light, its flame glinting off his pupils.

"I fear you not, Jarai. Nor do I fear why you have come. All my sons are dead. Worse, only two daughters live. I have had no sons-in-law to help me work my ray since our daughters went to Ban Me Thuot. If you doubt me, look at this my wife's longhouse. Must a Po Lan of the Mlo clan live like this? This is what your war has done. Look around."

Only Rob turned, and found the Po Lan's solitary form glaring back from the empty darkness.

"When this was her mother's longhouse, you could not step around at night without landing on someone. We were many and made much noise. Now, we live in a shell. Look at this our village. Our horned ladders are trod only by old men, male termites, and mangled soldiers. Listen! Where are the sounds of children? Tell me. Where are the cries, and gurgle, and laughter that every village must have?"

They listened, but all they heard was a faint thundering rumble far to the west.

"Yes. The forest thunders and flashes. And when the thunder is gone, not one thing lives as before where it has touched. It is you who have brought this upon us. In my youth, the forest sang. We feared Sir Tiger, rutting gaur, and rogue elephants, not forests that thunder and kill."

For long minutes, he wept in silence, before an angry rumble sounded from his throat.

"Pah! I am a village chief? Chief of what? Our young men have all gone off to be soldier. They are with MIfors, or camp strike force, or with the Front. Many are now in their tombs. Hong Klang abides in their bones. Of what use is a man now bone? What woman opens her legs to a memory? How does this memory fertilize the womb? That is why your 'friend' was denounced..."

Bloom took a long draw on the m'nam pay.

"The skies (times) have changed, Father's-Uncle..."

"Skies never change. We have ignored their warnings and are now a dying people. The Viets kill us. The Meerika kill us. Even the Khmer kill us. Worst of all, we kill ourselves. We who are the sons of Y Ad'ham, the father of all men, are dying. How can Ai Die permit this? What great drum can we crawl into this time to save us from the flood? A flood of fire and thunder."

"This time, Uncle, our drum is the Front. Within the United Front for the Struggle of Oppressed Races, we can become powerful enough to make it stop. Then we will be free."

"Free? Free from what? What must we do to have this free, nephew? Must we build metal birds and machines of death? Must we fly in the skies and dive beneath the great waters? We had that power in our previous world, and we destroyed it..."

"Legends," counseled Ney Bloom softly, "those are legends..."

"And your MIfors is legend? These Meerika are legend? The Viets are legend?"

"Those, Uncle, are real."

"Yes, and so were we."

The old man rocked back and forth on his haunches, crying to himself.

"I still don't understand," murmured B Rob Ya. "Was it you yourself who betrayed our brother. If so, why? Surely they didn't pay you?"

Y Sar Thak shot Rob a withering glare.

"Insult me, and I shall think you Jarai. I have told you it was done."

"Then you did not do so yourself."

The old man's shoulders slumped. "I am chief of this village. I alone am responsible. Two Tiep-zap came in an up-away searching for him. They said that they knew he was here, and that they only wished to talk to him. They said that if we did not point him out, they would send planes to bomb our village. Besides, he was Jarai and had caused enough scandal..."

"Scandal?"

"With all the widows in this village, he chose to sneak off into the bamboo with a married woman..."

"Whose husband betrayed him to the Viets?"

"Her husband is not here. Hah, he is a soldier like you. I have told you. This is my village. You must hold me responsible."

"We can find out," murmured Siu Dot.

Bloom looked into the earnest stare of his father's uncle. No, he whispered back, too many were dead already. If the old man wished to protect someone, they would respect his decision. Siu Dot shrugged and did not reply. In his own way, he felt a grudging admiration for the old Ede. Reaching into his fatigue shirt, he carefully removed a slip of paper which he passed to Ney Bloom. Bloom unfolded it and leaned near the lamp.

"Can you still read, Uncle?"

"Not like before. These days my eyes tire."

"This paper is in French. Do you wish for me to read it? Or shall I translate?"

"Read slowly. I still remember much French."

Bloom paused to catch his breath. When he did speak, his words reverberated through the longhouse in a voice he barely recognized as his own.

"Y Sar Thak, village chief of Buon Sar Thak, Ban Don district, Republic of the High Plateaus of Champa: Be it known that on this date you have been duly tried by a council of justice of the United Front for the Struggle of Oppressed Races, and found guilty of the charge of treason in that you knowingly betrayed an agent of this government to the Vietnamese occupational authorities. This sentence has been reviewed, and is without appeal. You will receive the ultimate punishment at a time and place as directed by a committee of this Front duly constituted for such purpose."

For several minutes there was silence, as Y Sar Thak pondered the meaning of the words.

"Beautiful words, Nephew. But they cannot hide an ugly deed. If memory has not betrayed me, you are here to murder me."

"No, Uncle. We are here for your execution."

Glistening rivulets traced a track down the old man's cheeks.

"My own nephew..."

"Uncle," Bloom's voice choked. "I was ordered to come. Do not assume that I have been held blameless. Ko'pa Jhon married into an important Jarai clan. He commanded the Eagle Flight and was the Front's highest ranking military officer in Pleiku. To speak truth, Siu Dot may well have such a paper with my name."

"Then why bring him?"

"Because, Uncle, I am a soldier. As such, my loyalty to the nation is above that which I owe my clan. It is only from such discipline, freely accepted and borne, that our Republic will be made reality. As well," Bloom nodded at Siu Dot, "I am here to guarantee his safety so no more will die. Do you have a coffin?'

"We both do. They are under the house. I have yet to purchase burial poles."

"I will do that for you. Here," Ney Bloom indicated a space on the paper and handed the old man his pen, "make your mark."

The old man placed the paper on the floor and leaned forward to pose a trembling hand over it.

"I can't. My bad spirits..."

"Uncle, I have never doubted your courage," Ney Bloom reached forward, took up the old man's hand in his own, and traced out Y Sar Thak's signature in a wobbly script.

"What about your daughters, Uncle?"

"Your cousins are at the training center in Ban Me Thuot. They learn to care for the sick and infirm."

"Send word of your funeral. Do not mention particulars. You know what will happen if anyone else from the Front is betrayed."

"Exactly what, Nephew? Would you kill a Po Lan of your father's clan?"

"I would," sneered Siu Dot, as he unsnapped his canvas case. With a sardonic grin and surprisingly smooth movements, he removed and assembled the components of a silenced Sten gun. Once the magazine had been inserted, he snapped back the bolt with a well-oiled click.

Above his glistening cheeks, Y Sar Thak's stare hardened into unrelenting hatred. Siu Dot returned an opaque stare of his own. Visibly trembling, Y Sar Thak leaned closer.

"I weep for what is happening to my race, fool. Not from any fear of you."

For once, it was Siu Dot's gaze that turned away. The old man grinned in triumph, rose, and hobbled back into the darkness. After long minutes consoling his wife, he returned to the lamp.

"You must forgive our Po Lan. She is ill. I will get your sleeping mats. You may use my daughters' quarters if you wish. That includes you, Jarai."

"My mat goes over there, old man," said Siu Dot, pointing to the door. "So you do not wander in your sleep."

"Sleep where you wish," Y Thak retorted. "Once those who slept near the door feared Sir Tiger. Now, Sir Tiger has become so lazy gorging himself on bodies, he no longer molests the living."

"How unfortunate," mused Rob, glancing at Siu Dot.

That night, Bloom lay awake until dawn. He remembered the first time he had seen this longhouse, after his father had fled Ban Me Thuot for killing a Vietnamese. The contrast between his mother's clan of Rhade-French civil servants and his father's clan of backwoods Ede had stunned him. These were hunters of elephants, gaur, and tiger. Men who bowed to no human, but paid close attention to the spirits. For the first few months he'd been a pariah. The finicky boy from Ban Me Thuot with the funny speech. And then one day, the village boys had decided to play soldier. With the help of an old crossbow stock, Bloom demonstrated the basic drills he'd seen the Montagnard Tirailleurs use in Ban Me Thuot. Suddenly, he had friends. Truly, noted the elders, this was Bloom. But as the village boys drew closer, his father and uncle became more distant.

Out in the darkness, he heard a steady rhythmic creaking from the Po Lan's quarters as two bodies came together to tremor and give life to the entire house. The spirit of the house, his father would have said, and the following day they would have gone into the forest to search for new stilt-posts to replace those that the termites had damaged.

Smiling at the thought, he raised himself on one elbow, and looked over to see Siu Dot's faintly illuminated form in the dim orange glow of a cigarette.

Siu Dot smiled, and gave a nonchalant wave of his claw. Not the sardonic grin of the 'centipede', but a genuine smile. For a brief moment, Bloom remembered the Siu Dot of old. His laughing, joking, shy friend from the days before the 1964 Revolt and the leprosy. The first friend he'd ever made outside his own tribal group. But when the smile faded, Bloom found that the spirits had played a trick. The old Siu Dot was dead. Buried in the bombed out rubble of a Jarai village where some unnamed Vietnamese pilot had casually dumped his unused bombs.

Buon Sar Thak was up well before first light. Though no one had actually spread the news, everyone knew. Three high ranking members from the Front didn't just happen through. Their visit had to be related to the Jarai the Po Lan had turned over to the Vietnamese. Y Sar Thak busied himself in the back of the longhouse while the matriarch served their guests chicken and warm rice. Siu Dot hesitated over the rice.

"Perhaps mine is poisoned," he mused.

"Twice you have insulted the hospitality of this clan," Ney Bloom scowled. "I wonder if you are not *Sedang*.[1] Or are you so afraid of poison?"

"It would spare me the rot," grinned Siu Dot, popping a clump into his mouth. "But I was wondering: If I were to die, who would carry out his sentence? You his kinsman? Or Rob his tribesman? You look down your noses at me, little brothers, but executioners have their purpose."

With breakfast finished, they wrestled a heavy log coffin from under the house. While Y Sar Thak put on his best ceremonial loincloth and shirt, Bloom rounded up a party of villagers to help with the labor. Though most knew Bloom, they were sullen and reluctant. When he called for Y Sar Thak, the old man stepped out onto the porch with Siu Dot.

"Where is our Po Lan," Bloom asked.

"She has bad spirits," Thak answered. "This Jarai has given her medicine."

"Morphine," Siu Dot whispered as he stepped down the ladder. "It should keep her quiet until mid-day. We have already been here too long."

They departed Buon Sar Thak with the morning sun two hands above the horizon. Friends, and even old enemies, had shown up to see Y Sar Thak off. Bloom noted, nevertheless, that they took the precaution of shutting the spirit gates behind them. In a land filled with hostile spirits, those loosed from Y Sar Thak would not be welcomed home.

They trudged out past the village rays, past the cemetery with its miniature longhouses, kepied sentry poles and revelers woven in *tranh* grass, up to where the valley merged into hilltop. Two hours into the march, they

---

[1] Sedang, a tribe living north of the Jarai who are often at odds with them.

reached a forest intermittently marked with the abandoned rays of the slash and burn agriculture that existed at the fringes of Ede society. Here, Ney Bloom called a halt. As the coffin bearers moved off to prepare their mid-day pipes, Y Sar Thak sat down on the lid of his coffin.

"Last night," he said to no one in particular, "I lay with my wife as a man should. When we were finished, I pleaded with Ai Die to loose my souls within the confines of my own village. It is not death I fear, but the strangeness of this death which you visit upon me. You condemn me to wander these Highlands forever."

"Old man," rasped Siu Dot, "I knew a Jarai who would have preferred an elder's death among his own clan and village. But he came to you seeking help. Better you pray that his wandering spirits do not find your own."

As they resumed the march, the trail narrowed and the forest closed in. Bloom pushed on for another hour, but could not put it off any longer. Finally, he ordered the coffin placed in the middle of a small clearing. While Siu Dot waved the bearers off to the side, Rob searched in his pack for the hammer and nails. Y Sar Thak looked hopelessly around. The village men avoided his gaze. He was fumbling in his pouch for his tobacco and pipe when Bloom offered a cigarette. He accepted with trembling hands. Bloom cupped his own hands over the old man's to shield the flame. Then he handed Y Sar Thak the rest of the pack. Thak gave him a quizzical look.

"Keep them—for the journey, Father's-Uncle."

Thak's hands trembled violently. Ashes tumbled from the end of his cigarette. His eyes searched for Bloom's, but Bloom looked away. It was getting late, Siu Dot noted, they had to hurry. Bloom sidled over to the bearers. Pulling out a fistful of Vietnamese bank notes, he handed them to the oldest.

"Give this to the M'jao. See that he is buried as befits a village chief."

The elder mumbled an oath that it would be so.

Bloom looked back into Siu Dot's eyes before walking off. He did not see Siu Dot raise the Sten gun, nor see the nearly invisible bronze and green hornets that shot out from its ugly black snout to tear into the old man's chest. But he did hear it whisper his name: Bloo huh huh huh oom...Bloo huh huh oom.

Chapter Two

THE APPROACH TO THE FORD was strewn with large boulders which the North Vietnamese negotiated with ease. As the file of troops emerged from the forest shadows, Senior Sergeant Trang raised his hand. Behind him, men froze as the dull scream of F-4 fighter-bombers loaded with napalm, slowing down for their run into Dak To, resonated above the trees. Only when the chilling sound had faded did the knot in Trang's stomach loosen ever so slightly.

"Goddess of Mercy," he whispered, "protect comrades ours from the fire. Amida Buddha, accept those who do not escape into your Pure Land of the West."

Gazing into the eyes of infantry-soldier Diep, Trang recognized the mix of fear and relief mirrored in his own, which turned hard as he looked past Diep to the American prisoner in a green flight suit. That this was a mere helicopter crewman mattered little. How many comrades had fallen to his guns?

Motioning his squad forward, Trang jabbed the muzzle of his AK-47 sharply into the prisoner's ribs. The tow-headed kid skidded on the rocks, but managed to stay upright as he plunged into the swift cold water. Behind him came a tall Black trooper from the 173rd Airborne, followed by a young Latino wearing a painfully new 4th Division patch. Though the river was not wide and only thigh deep, its swift current made crossing hazardous for prisoners whose arms and wrists were bound tightly behind them.

"*Di mau len di,*" Trang snapped. The prisoners did their best to comply. Every GI in Vietnam knew the words "go faster," and who could tell where the next Phantom might dump its load? A column of Gooks fording a river was as good a target as any.

Trang prodded his 'pilot' towards the trail at the far bank, where two Main Force Viet Cong privates were refilling a squad's empty canteens.

One, a highland savage *"Moi,"* piqued Trang's suspicions. His index finger felt for the trigger of his AK-47.

"Who goes?"

"Reconnaissance troops, regional Battalion 810, Senior Sergeant. Our section screens fords on this river." The reply was voiced with an aggressive pride. Trang chided himself for his suspicions as the Moi flashed the prisoners an evil-smiling glare. "These, you can leave with us. We have not eaten running-dog liver for much time."

"Gladly," grunted Trang, "but some certain commander mine has other idea. When these reach Ban Pakha, they go north. Perhaps to die on journey from napalm."

"Like so many comrades coming south," gritted the Moi.

"Just so…," Trang's voice choked, "…like so many comrades ours."

As the reconnaissance troops stepped aside to let Trang's column pass, they spotted the lead elements of a larger unit approaching the ford. Hurriedly, they filled their canteens and departed.

"How Many?"

To this question, whispered in English, the *Moi* held up three fingers. "Two soldier, one army pilot suit," he whispered back.

"Headed where"

"Ban Pakha."

"Shit, we don't have much time."

Specialist Five Randy Weber fished the radio handset out from the side pocket of his rucksack. His tiger-striped pants and olive green sleeping shirt contrasted sharply with the Main Force VC uniforms of the four men hunkered down around him.

Nearby, Specialist Four Dave Ferry stared up through the foliage canopy at a fading November sky.

"They won't make it today," Ferry whispered hoarsely. "The prisoners will slow 'em down. Tomorrow night—maybe. The day after tomorrow's more likely."

"Yeah, well that ain't our problem. Once that NVA sergeant gets to where he's going, maybe sooner, he's going to tell somebody that he ran into some recon troops from the 810th Regional Battalion."

"So? They're around here someplace."

"So since he's got prisoners, that somebody's likely to be some NVA Intel puke who knows exactly where the 810th Battalion's supposed to be. You wanna bet your gonads on some MACV pukes weeks old information?"

"No, but Faubacher'll want us to stay."

"Faubacher ain't the One-Zero of this team! We've got hot Intel and we're likely to be compromised. We need to get out of here while we can."

Ferry felt the pit in his stomach shrink to the size of a small cave. It was only slightly relieved by the sound of Weber's whispered call for a team extraction.

Captain Jim Fry hurried through the darkened Forward Operational Base or FOB at the edge of Kontum. Unlike FOBs at Danang and Ban Me Thuot, military compounds built from scratch, the Kontum FOB had grown up around a hamlet lying just outside Kontum town. Despite defensive trenches, berms, and landing pads, it still resembled a small village. Unknown to the Americans, it had once been a base for French G.C.M.A. Special Forces.

As he approached a small stucco building at the east corner of the crossroads near the center of the compound, Fry flicked away his cigarette. Pushing open the door, he nodded to the poker players seated around a large table in the smoke-filled room. Major Jack Faubacher looked up from his cards and read the urgent gleam in Fry's eyes. His hand froze.

"What's up, Jim?"

"Sir, Weber's team just spotted three American prisoners."

Minutes later, the poker players had reassembled around a mapboard in the operations center. While the recon company commander worked out details of Recon Team Minnesota's extraction, Faubacher and his crew agonized over aerial photos of Ban Pakha. The village's bucolic appearance was deceptive. Several major enemy installations were hidden in the Karst hills lying east and southeast of the hamlet, and all outlying roads were well used.

"Any known POW locations?"

His intelligence officer leafed through the Ban Pakha target folder with shaking hands.

"None, Major. We've had two reports of POWs being taken through the area, but no specifics on where they were held."

"Nothing?"

"Nossir. Just one other thing, though."

"What's that?"

"According to recent reporting, the place is filled with a shitpot of anti-aircraft artillery."

"What kind?"

"Uh…I'll check…"

"ZSU-23," chimed in the nearby S-2 sergeant, covering the mouth-piece of his phone. "They've got a single battery southeast of town, and 12.7 millimeter all over the place. An arc-light can take care of the ZSU-23s, but the 12.7mm and small arms will be a major problem."

"Only if they're expecting us," Faubacher growled. "Otherwise, it should be a surprise."

"They're always expecting us, sir."

Faubacher ignored the sergeant's muttered reply to pull Fry closer. "Jim, I want every available recon team inserted east of Ban Pakha as soon as possible after first light. And get the Hatchet Force ready. If we find a target, they're going in."

Fry was loyal, but no fool. "Sir, we've only got three recon teams available. They don't have time to prepare for this mission."

A steel glint crept into Faubacher's eye. "I'm not asking what they've got time for, Captain. I'm telling you what to do. Look, this is a tactical recon mission. I want them screening the trails. When we spot the group with the POWs, the hatchet force will helicopter into the nearest LZ."

"Sir, it'll be a massacre."

"Not if we get to them before they get to Ban Pakha. And," Faubacher's eyes narrowed, "if it's still just a squad, the Recon Teams may be able to handle them on their own. In the meanwhile, we need to give those bastards up at Ban Pakha something to worry about. Something that'll keep all that anti-aircraft artillery in place for a while…" his finger absent-mindedly traced a river valley running south from Ban Pakha into a small finger of Cambodia. "…like here, for example."

"We don't have the troops."

"No, but the MIKE Force does."

"We've got other problems, like airlift, and where we're going to stage out of."

"Captain, that's what you get paid to figure out. What the hell's this up here?" Faubacher's finger settled on a small map-splotch of jungle between Polei Klang and Ben Het.

"A 4th Division FARP. As best I can figure, they're using it to rearm and refuel their aerial scouts. They've got an infantry company guarding it. We thought it might be bait to divert some NVA from Dak To. Bad place for a FARP. I don't know why they didn't use Polei Klang."

"Yeah," Faubacher nodded. "I see what you mean. Damned near outside their own artillery range, and damned near inside Charlie's. Must be using it for bait, or deception. It'd make a great location if someone was going to make an end run past Polei Jar Sieng up to Ban Pakha. Since Charlie knows it's there, why not use it? Never mind calling the MIKE Force. I'll do that myself."

As Faubacher picked up the phone, Fry vaguely wondered who the poor bastard was commanding the 4th Division company at the FARP.

Lieutenant Galen Saint Cyr had just finished checking his mortars when a call came from Brigade that he was to expect some unexpected visitors. Having been in country for eight months, and in command of Delta Company, 1st Battalion, 35th Infantry for the past two, this was his first independent mission, operating directly under Brigade control. He'd been told its purpose was to draw off enemy units headed for Dak To. The rest of his battalion was standing by at Kontum, ready to launch in and reinforce them as needed, but most of Death Dealin' Delta had other ideas. They saw the FARP as punishment for the fragging that had killed Captain Davis, and left St. Cyr's ears ringing with a high-pitched whine that still gave him migraines. Their lieutenant's refusal to be medevaced for a bit of grenade shrapnel, and his face to face confrontation with Lieutenant Colonel

Love over the causes of the incident, had earned him their respect. And though company cynics grumbled that this FARP mission was a ploy to get them all wiped out, St. Cyr's steady manner and easy sense of humor had been successful in laying most rumors to rest. Rumors were what had killed CPT Davis in the first place. Rumors, plus a suspicion that their new battalion commander cared more for his career than the lives of his men, and an incident over pot smoking. Among the officers, some whispered that LTC Love had used a distorted version of Davis's death to prop up a request for an Air Medal with 'V' device, which he hoped to carry away from his six months of battalion command, along with a Silver Star and Legion of Merit.

St. Cyr had been at odds with Love ever since being fined a month's pay for taping a playboy poster under his foot locker lid. To Love, the poster violated his directive against displaying pornographic materials in common areas. The common area in question being a bare wooden room that St. Cyr and his fellow lieutenants used perhaps three nights a month. And the poster had come into 'public view' as Love rifled through their foot lockers while they were in the field. Friends at brigade had advised St. Cyr to appeal the punishment, but he had shrugged it off. He wasn't going to make the army a career anyway. Interpreting this as loyalty, Love had left him in temporary command.

At mid-morning, an unmarked helicopter touched down to unload a major and two captains. Clad in camouflage fatigues and black nylon jackets, they affected a mysterious air. St. Cyr's attempt to welcome them was met with icy instructions to stay the hell away. Later that afternoon, waves of helicopter troopships thundered in. Delta Company stopped digging trenches and bunkers long enough to see taut, muscular, tiger-striped bodies climb down from the slicks. These were no ordinary Gooks. In fact, they didn't look Vietnamese at all. Montagnard probably and definitely a whole cut above the camp strike forces the company occasionally saw. As Delta stared out, ebony eyes set in mahogany faces gazed back in cool appraisal. Their oiled and spotless weapons were obvious, even from a distance. Hand grenades had been taped to prevent premature explosions. And the same green hundred-mile-an-hour tape had been liberally applied to all hooks, buttons, straps, and anything else that might rattle or hang while on the move. Extra water and munitions were in evidence. A large white shoulder patch, depicting a fire breathing green dragon rampant on thin bands of clouds, proclaimed them the Airborne MIKE Force.

Delta Company grinned back, as sporadic thumbs-up signs flashed on both sides. These guys had it, all right. The look that, despite their M-2 carbines and BARs, told experienced infantrymen more than any record or reputation. These dudes were bad, and they had come to party with Victor Charles, which meant that somehow Death Dealin' Delta would be involved. That prospect exited the younger kids, but it put the veterans' nerves on edge.

St. Cyr kept his men at a distance. Brigade wanted no contact between the groups, and he wanted no problems. As he ordered Delta back to their picks and shovels, he was hailed by a tall Caucasian dressed in tiger fatigues wearing triple diagonal pips on each epaulet and a multi-hued blue and white cloth parachute badge on his upper right sleeve.

"G'day Mate. Would you be the man in charge?"

"Only for now. Lieutenant Tyrell went into Kontum. My company's on security."

"Bloody impolite of him, yeah? You'll do then. I'm Roo Rexburg and this is Marvin McElroy."

He gave St. Cyr a bone crushing handshake while nodding at a medium sized American sporting a bushy mustache, large silver coil necklace, a wrist full of tribal bracelets, and green beret. Although he wore no insignia of rank, he seemed to be a sergeant of sorts.

"We need a place to set up our radios," Rexburg continued.

"How big?"

The sergeant jerked his thumb and bracelets in the direction of a short blond American and two Montagnards wrestling large containers from a helicopter.

"I mean the place. How big do you need it?"

"B-big enough for those," McElroy countered. "At least a b-bunker, maybe two, b-back away from everybody else. Someplace where no one'll screw with us. How 'b-bout there," he motioned to St. Cyr's command bunker.

"That's mine."

"Got any others back off of the line, Mate?" asked Rexburg.

"No…"

"Well," Rexburg flashed a brotherly grin, "it'll have to do then, Leftenant. How long will it take you to clear out?"

St. Cyr's enthusiasm for the Australian Special Air Service faded long before he had cleared his bunker. Who the hell did this MIKE Force they think they were? They had enough goddamned manpower to dig their own damned bunkers. He complained to Tyrell when the pudgy little aviator returned from Kontum, but to no avail. If the MIKE Force wanted his command bunker, there was nothing Tyrell could do. Besides, who was going to contradict a captain, even if he was Australian? Tyrell was also certain that his own bunker was too small for them both. St. Cyr's men would have to get started on a new command bunker; the sooner the better.

Darkness brought a chill. Common enough at this time of year, it felt doubly cold after the day's exertions and heat. Third platoon was back inside the wire, having finished their patrolling duties. Listening posts were out and alert. The general feeling was that something would happen.

Sometime after midnight, as the sliver of a November moon dipped below the horizon, chopper blades sounded in the distance. Red lights lit up the FARP. Those who had been asleep sat up, rubbed their eyes, and cursed. Victor Charlie sure as hell wasn't going to miss this. Fingers tightened on triggers and checked selector switches. Two hundred plus eyes stared out across the wire.

St. Cyr stepped out from his new command bunker to find McElroy's dark form gazing up at a line of helicopter running lights descending into the FARP. He checked his watch with a red-lens flashlight.

"Almost midnight," McElroy grunted, focusing his attention on the dark forms rushing to board the troop ships. After the troop slicks had lifted off to rejoin the gunships, the fleet reassembled like some great dragon. Through clouds of dust, Delta Company watched the head of the dragon turn westward. Death Dealin' Delta held its collective breath. This was the tri-border area. West was off limits to U.S. forces. The column should be turning soon. But as the running lights extinguished, the receding whupper continued to snake westerly.

Cambodia! An electric thrill coursed through Delta. Men half asleep sat up to listen, while others climbed out on the bunkers to stare after fading chopper sounds. There were murmurs, then a rebel yell, as a staccato burst of machinegun fire arced out to patter into distant trees.

"Ain't going to no Dak To," someone yelled. Motherfuckers are heading for Cam—bodia!" There was more cheering as St. Cyr ducked into the bunker to warn his platoon leaders that the firing and noise had better cease. When he stepped out, McElroy had gone.

Delta didn't sleep much that night. There were whispered conversations that the invasion of Cambodia had begun. That the United States was finally going in to stamp out the Viet Cong in their sanctuaries. Saner heads argued that such an invasion would hardly kick off with forces as miniscule as these. And why invade Cambodia? They had all the NVA they could handle right up at Dak To. Others argued that the MIKE Force had actually entered Laos. Sitting in the black emptiness, everyone waited for the expected attack or probe.

From his new bunker, St. Cyr called for reports. Two platoons had suspicious movement; Haskell's platoon had nothing. Suspecting that Haskell had thrown the burden of running the platoon at night on his platoon sergeant, he demanded that Haskell confirm it himself. Then he passed the microphone to his field first sergeant and crashed for two hours sleep. He was still trying to fall asleep when Sergeant First Class White nudged him for his relief.

The day passed quietly. Following Love's radioed advice, St. Cyr had two platoons patrol west of the FARP while the other two worked on FARP defenses. Reports of no visible enemy presence were greeted with relief, but warning lights flashed in the veteran's minds. A well-run NVA battalion would not likely tip its hand, and there were reports of one in the area. By late afternoon, the assistant Brigade S-3 stopped by to check on their progress, and promised a platoon of engineers to help. Dinner was a hot meal, helicoptered in courtesy of LTC Love, who had undoubtedly found some means of communicating his largess to the brigade commander. With dinner came the unwelcome news that St. Cyr was wanted at battalion headquarters first thing in the morning. His first thought was that Love had been going through his foot-locker again, but any really graphic letters were in French. More likely, their welcomed semi-independence was coming to an end.

Darkness brought another bout of collective nerves. Aside from the occasional chopper, whose approach was greeted with dread, the radios and voices from the MIKE Force bunker set the men's teeth on edge. Too damned much noise, the platoon leaders complained. Charlie could hear that shit a mile away!

St. Cyr checked with his listening posts and forward positions. They heard nothing, but the tension was working its way into the men's neuroses. He decided to complain for form's sake, before any of Delta's dudes opted for action on their own. Feeling his way through the darkness to the MIKE Force bunker, he lifted the poncho draped over the entrance and stepped inside.

McElroy, an unidentified captain in a black jacket, and a Montagnard radio operator were hunched over a red-illuminated map board talking into different handsets. Only McElroy looked up.

"You gotta g-get outa here, *Tieu-oui*," he said, using the word for Second Lieutenant.

"Sure, Sarge, but you need to turn down the volume on your radios…"

"Who the fuck says so?" The captain glared up.

"I do. Perimeter security is my responsibility."

The captain started to reply with something obscene, but McElroy rose, put his hand on St. Cyr's shoulder, and guided him outside.

"Look, Tieu-oui, our guys are so close to C-Clyde they c-can hear 'em fart. They can't do nothing but whisper, understand? So the only way we c-can hear 'em is by keepin' the volume turned up to the max. Tell your guys we're sorry 'bout that, but we g-gotta take the chance."

The captain lifted the flap to call McElroy inside. As he did, St. Cyr heard the Montagnard say something like *h'reng taha nan*. The captain wanted coordinates for an arc-light, code for a B-52 strike. Blackjack Two-Six needed an arc-light and he needed it fast! McElroy called out coordinates which the captain repeated over his handset. There was a pause before a voice came back to say that they wouldn't have another arc-light for two hours. When the sergeant relayed this to the other side of the darkness, an Australian voice replied they didn't have that bloody fucking long. Were the geese bloody moving? McElroy switched into a Montagnard dialect and asked about the *h'reng taha nan*. There were three, he was told, making a run for the up-away zone. Switching back to English, Mac asked Blackjack Two-six if he could hold. He could not, not without the bloody arc-light. Although St. Cyr heard this clearly, McElroy did not pass the word to the Jarai. Instead, he recommended that the captain order in the extraction force. Then, seeing St. Cyr outside the partially closed poncho flap, he pulled the entrance shut.

Back in his command bunker, St. Cyr hooked up a conference call on the field telephone. After explaining the situation, with instructions to pass the word down, he checked the perimeter. The whispered banter made him proud of his men. *Yeah, man, what's a little noise? Poor Yards up to their assholes in alligators—tryin' to find the plug to that swamp! Glad we ain't with them dudes!*

He swung by his mortar pits. Illumination and High Explosive rounds stood fused and ready. By the time he finished, it was past 0300 hours. Sergeant White volunteered to take the first watch.

He crashed down onto his deflated air mattress nearly too tired to sleep. Closing his eyes, he remembered that Love wanted to see him in the morning, and found himself back in Sarawak. He'd been lying naked with Ha-mei when they were discovered. He was forced into a bamboo cage that resembled a large shoe box and had no room to either sit up or stretch. Ha-mei's moronic slobbering mean-eyed Chinese husband stood over it with a long wooden stave. Each time he struck the top of the cage, pain coursed down through the bamboo and into the marrow of St. Cyr's bones. The Chinese screamed barely intelligible epithets in pidgin Malay. One word caught his attention. A word that sounded like *hreng tanan*.

St. Cyr awoke in a cold sweat. The MIKE Force, the arc-lights, and helicopters that flew in the night. Suddenly it all made sense.

"*Oreng Tahanan*," he said aloud. "They're after prisoners." He sat up to rub sand grains from his stinging eyes, and glanced across the red-bulbed lantern into the face of Master Sergeant Marvin McElroy.

"That's right, Tieu-oui, and you ain't s'posed to know shit ab-bout it."

"What're you doing here, Sergeant?"

McElroy gave a tired smile. "Call me Mac, Tieu-oui. Everyb-body does. Where'd you learn Jarai?"

"I didn't. I learned Pasar Malay and a bit of Iban in the Peace Corps. It's close enough to what your people speak that I can understand some of what they say. How'd you find out?"

"Spielman told me. He said you two went through Training Group together."

"Paul's here? I'll have to stop by and say hello."

"Do that, b-but right now we're busy. G-got some choppers coming in. G-gonna need all the help your medics can give us."

"All right, Mac, but I need some help from you."

"Sure, what?"

"Around the company, or around my NCOs, forget the 'Tieu-oui' shit. It's either lieutenant, or sir."

"G-goddam," Mac grimaced. "Nothin' like losin' a little sleep to m-make a man testy."

The helicopters came in from the west, their running lights extinguished. Approaching the FARP, they lit up with an obscene brilliance. Down on the pads, men rushed forward as bay doors slid back. Inside the dimly lit slicks, dead, dying and wounded sprawled everywhere. Delta's medics, who spoke nothing more than English, could only shoot them up with morphine, replace blood-soaked bandages, release and retie tourniquets, and hook up bottles of albumin while the gas jockeys conducted hot refueling. For panicked minutes, turbines whined, fuel handlers cursed, medics screamed instructions, and the wounded moaned and gasped in agony. Only the dead were silent, among them a pale blond cadaver. Mac took one long look at Rexburg's body, and walked off into the darkness cursing.

And then they were gone, the sound of their liftoff lingering long after running lights had disappeared over nearby hills. Back at the landing pad, St. Cyr hung on, waiting for more choppers.

"El Tee," Sergeant White's voice called out from the distance, "you'd better get some sleep. Helicopter'll be here at 0700 to take you to battalion."

Once again, he lay down in the darkness. This time he saw neither Ha-mei nor the hills and forests of Sarawak. This time he was in the Victory restaurant in Caribou, Maine, where he'd driven down to meet the army recruiter.

"Galen," the recruiter was saying, "you aced the Special Forces test, but the army's working on a regulation to bar former Peace Corps workers from Special Forces. I can sign you up. But once that reg goes into effect, they'll pull you out. You'd do better to sign up for officer candidate school."

"Thanks but no thanks, Sarge. I either get drafted and do whatever the army wants me to for two years, or take my chances with Special Forces for three. Between the two, I'll take Special Forces."

"You're sure?"

"I'm damned sure."

"All right; let me ask you one more question: Why Vietnam?"

He glanced up past the recruiter into the eyes of his brother, Alcide, and Aurore Pelletier, an old girlfriend, who were waiting for the same answer.

Because my parents busted their asses all their lives on a northern Maine potato farm to send me to college, he wanted to say, *so I could do something with my life. So I went into the Peace Corps, where I thought I was the Raja of Sarawak. But my miracle rice failed, my pigs all caught swine flu, and I ended up with the unhappy Peranakan second wife of a local merchant, and got fired from the Peace Corps.*

Except he hadn't been fired. Ha-mei's husband kept things quiet, and the country Peace Corps Rep merely moved him to Kuching, where he taught English and managed office accounts for the next year.

Looking into the recruiter's eyes, he grasped for noble excuses and found none. What he couldn't say was that the Peace Corps had opened up far more interesting horizons than the St. John River Valley ever could. He wanted a career in international banking with a home in Penang, Singapore, or Hong Kong, a yacht at the nearby marina, and a Jaguar sedan, which he would park at the tennis club on those afternoons he played with clients. And he wanted a silk-skinned, jasmine-scented, jade-and-gold accoutered Asian wife or mistress who would direct the servants and keep his home fit for entertaining clients. A girl who would, when evening came, draw the curtains, let slip her clothing, and make such orgiastic love to him as to surpass even Aurore Pelletier, now sitting back on her counter stool, a cool eyebrow raised, waiting for his reply.

So he looked out at late autumn leaves whipping past the windows and mumbled banalities about French newsreels on Indochina he'd seen as a kid. About a young infantry captain from Maine named Lew Millett, who'd won a Medal of Honor in Korea. Millett was an old Yankee name, but it sounded French enough to inspire every kid in Madawaska. They would throw up snow forts, split the gang in two, and with the smaller kids defending, the older kids under Zeus Fongemie, playing *Capitaine Millette*, would charge the fort using hockey sticks for rifles. About northern Aroostook county's infamous winters and never-ending snow…

"Snow? You say something 'bout snow, sir?"

Sergeant White's voice jarred him awake. He sat up in the darkness, rubbed the stiffness in his shoulders, and wondered how much he'd said in his sleep.

"Just thinking, Top. Feel's so goddam cold you'd think it'd snow."

"Yessir. But it's better'n dry season. Cain't stand when it gets so hot we can't sleep. Hey, better get rolling! Stand-to's in fifteen minutes."

"Damn, Top! You let me sleep in again!"

"Only by an hour, El Tee. Figured you'd need that extra shut-eye to face the colonel."

"Thanks, Top, I'll pay you back tonight. Pass the word down. No firing at stand-to. No use giving away our positions any more than we already have."

"Funny you should say that, El Tee, I already passed that word down. Guess great minds think alike."

"I'd say it's more like you've got me well trained."

A genuine smile lit up Sergeant White's ebony face. "Jus' doin' mah job, El Tee. Jus' doin' mah job."

At 0800, St. Cyr sauntered into Love's field command post in Kontum where a tall slim captain in starched jungle fatigues and impeccably clean web equipment was waiting. Branch insignia identified him as the commanding general's aide-de-camp. St. Cyr didn't have to look at the ring finger to know that there was a star ruby West Point ring on it. The captain flashed St. Cyr a frank, open smile as the adjutant ushered them into Love's office. Love invited them to sit, and insisted that they have a cup of coffee.

"Galen, you've been doing a good job with Delta Company. The Brigade commander's called me twice to compliment you."

"Thank you, sir."

"I'll admit that I had my doubts, but you've come along very well. You've got the age we need in company commanders, and with more exposure, you'll have the experience. My problem is that you're only a second lieutenant…"

"I should get promoted in January, sir."

"Yes, and if I have anything to do with it, you will. But you're missing the point. I've no doubt you'll make an outstanding company commander, Galen, but you need more seasoning. Captain Reagan has just finished a tour as the commanding general's aide, and the CG's promised him a company. He's asked for Delta, and frankly there's a lot you could learn as his understudy."

St. Cyr heard the rest through a rush in his ears. He knew that there were still captains in division looking for command, but he desperately wanted to hold on. Delta was his now, and he wouldn't trade it for any unit in the world, even under Love. The colonel went on to say something about leaving him in charge for another few weeks, so as to ease the new commander in after a full blown steak-and-beer change of command party. Something dignified enough for the commanding general to attend. Maybe the CG would even pull him up to some plush job on the division staff. Love then formally introduced the two officers, and excused them to get acquainted.

Reagan suggested that they find a place to talk, as he only had an hour before he had to get back to division base. Thoroughly prepared to dislike this interloper, St. Cyr found himself drawn to Reagan's frank, friendly manner. An airborne-ranger West Pointer who'd done all the right things, Reagan had even had previous company command with the division at Fort Lewis. He didn't need to get his ticket punched to land a battalion S-3 job.

"So," St. Cyr wondered, "why Delta?"

"Because I want combat command, Galen. Not just peacetime. And I want a company with human beings who have real problems. The CG offered me the Long Range Reconnaissance Company, but when I heard about the fragging I turned down the Lurps and asked for Delta. You see Galen, I have the leadership skills to deal with that. I can make men respect and follow me, even when their instincts tell them not to…"

"They respected and followed Captain Davis…"

"I don't doubt that, Galen. Look, I respect your loyalty to Davis just as I respect the company's loyalty to you. And I want you to stay on. I'd like you to be my executive officer until I get my feet on the ground, but I'll send you back to a platoon if that's what you want. I'd even support a request to go elsewhere. But first, I'm asking you to give me a chance."

"I'll stay."

"Good!" Reagan extended a firm handshake. "I'll consider that a personal favor. We're going to do great things with Delta, Galen—you wait and see." And he said it with such sincerity that St. Cyr walked off feeling a profound sense of relief.

The battalion executive officer found him a ride back on a Light Observation Cargo Helicopter from the division's air cavalry troop, a pair of which was headed out to scout around the FARP. As they slip-slid along, his thoughts alternated between Love, Reagan, and the terrain flashing beneath him. The pilot was demonstrating nap-of-the-earth flying, which was nothing like going in on a Huey. St. Cyr suspected that the kid warrant officer really wanted to see his breakfast come up, and was grimly determined to keep it down. He'd always hated roller-coasters.

This particular pilot was a waterfall freak, and from time to time they dipped down to observe some waterfall judged of interest, while the trailing Loch lifted up in overwatch. On their third waterfall, the ship suddenly went into a tight spin.

"Blue Saber One-Three-alpha, this is One-Three…I've got commo wire. Repeat, commo wire strung across this little river just below the falls…over."

"Roger Saber One-Three, I'll pass to Blue Saber. Break…Let me know what else you see…out."

They were making a lower pass when the headphones sputtered again.

"Blue Saber One-Three…you're to clear the area immediately… repeat..," the voice cut off as they lifted up in a steep climb. "…uh… more saber teams and snakes are on the way, One-Three," he said, referencing the Cobra gunships known as *snakes*. "Saber Three says to drop your pax and return to the area…break…I'm going to hang around…over."

St. Cyr's pilot rogered his mate's transmission, and shot up out of the forest to make a beeline northwest.

Fifteen minutes later the FARP rolled into view. Green smoke rose from bare red earth in welcome. Instead of swinging around to approach from downwind, the pilot shot straight ahead. As they intersected a series of ridge lines, a pattering static rattled their earphones. The Loch shuddered violently as the horizon dipped and swayed. Through the Plexiglas bubble, St. Cyr saw puffs of smoky dust pepper the FARP as finger-sized people scrambled frantically. The pilot's curses buzzed in his earphones as the gunner opened up on something from his rear side-seat. St. Cyr's testicles contracted into the pit of his stomach as he felt the chopper yaw and drop.

They hit with a force that sledge-hammered his kidneys. For long seconds, he lay stunned. Then the flash and smoke ignited a panicked horror in his soul. Frantically he fought the safety harness, convulsing into pain-wrenching spasms each time he tried to straighten his body. He was conscious long enough to feel the heat and hear the pilot's screams. And his last thought was *God, please don't let me burn!*

He awoke in a cold faint grey half-darkness, feeling strangely detached and floating. A crystal blob on the periphery of his vision focused to become a plasma IV bottle. Turning his head slightly, he made out a dark shadow. He took it for a coat, but it moved.

"B-bout goddam time."

"Mac, that you?" his eyes focused on the heavy bandages around Mac's left arm and shoulder. "What happened?"

"Wrenched my arm out'a its socket p-pulling you free. Then caught some shrapnel just as we were g-getting you under cover…"

"The crew?"

"Nothin' we c-could do. Incoming mortars touched off the avgas. One of your kids got fried with 'em."

St. Cyr shuddered and closed his eyes, remembering the screams.

"Sergeant White?"

"He was helpin' m-me with you. Took some b-burns on his hands and forearms, but I suspect he'll be back with the company soon." Mac paused, a faint smile in his deep-set tired eyes. "G-goddam, Tieu-oui, I never saw so many people runnin' round tryin' to pull someone out of a fire in my life. Specially a lieutenant. Most times, everybody's trying to make damn sure they stay in. You must've been doing something right."

A bitter chuckle sent sharp pains coursing through St. Cyr's ribs, back, and chest. "That's Delta company, Mac. Finest sonsabitches in the army. And I'm going back just as soon as I get out of here. Where are we?"

"Eighth Field Hospital, Nha Trang. But you ain't g-gonna be here long. They're sending you to C-camp Zama tomorrow."

"Japan? What for?"

"Surgery, Tieu-oui. They say you've g-got some crushed vertebrae and kidney damage. From there, it's probably b-back to the States."

"The States? I need to get back to my company!"

"Yeah" Mac gave a sardonic smile. "Well it ain't exactly up to you, Tieu-oui. B-besides, by the time you do get back, it won't be yours. You'll be lucky if there's anyone left who remembers you. T-tell you what, though."

"What?"

"If you do g-get back in country, and you're lookin' for a job? Give me a call. We can use someb-body who speaks Jarai."

Mac slipped a business card into his free hand. St. Cyr held it up to a small glimmer of light. The left side showed a dagger and green beret, the right had the MIKE Force crest. The legend below Mac's name read: wars fought, revolutions started, armies organized, assassinations arranged, alcohol evaluated, and virgins converted. At the bottom right corner were the words: Have MIKE Force, Will Travel, followed by a telephone number and radio frequency.

"That's all there is to it, hunh? Call you?"

"Or send a message. Hey, us master sergeants g-got connections. You should'a learned that back when you were humpin' a radio for Jerzy Jake." Mac grinned at the flash of recognition. "Yeah, Spielman told me all about ya. Frenchy, the kid who was gonna be a banker."

"That was the plan."

"So, what happened?"

St. Cyr lowered his eyes. "Tri Chuc."

"You were at Tri Chuc?"

"Yeah. Me, Mike Foote, Jerzy Jake, Lamarr Edge…"

"Edge was a g-good man," Mac nodded.

"We all were. Edge is why most of us survived. Edge and Jerzy Jake, and a few Cambodes. After that, I figured banking could wait."

"Well, if you do get back here, m-make sure you let me know."

"I will, but you're wasting your time, Mac. That assignment limitation's in my records: Former Peace Corps volunteer, Special Forces duty prohibited."

"Oh yeah? That reg don't say nothin' about the MIKE Force, does it? We operate under a different set o' rules. So if you do get back and don't call me, I'll track you down, and the ass whipping won't be pleasant."

St. Cyr cracked a smile through a cloud of dull pain, and closed his eyes. The next time he opened them, he was staring into the friendly smile of an Air Force nurse on his flight to Japan. She whispered something in a sexy voice, adjusted the drip of his IV bottle, and watched him slip back into a cold sleep. He dreamed of Maine. Every time he was cold, he dreamed of Maine.

Chapter Three

CHARLIE REGTER SAT IN THE cold dark womb of a C-130 aircraft hurtling earthward and braced for the impact of its landing gear on the Nha Trang airfield tarmac. Pulled from the field after 18 days, he could barely stand his own smell. He would have stopped by Marble Mountain for a quick shower and a change of clothes, but when the deputy commanding officer of the 5th Special Forces Group wanted you immediately, that was what he meant.

The plane slammed onto the runway and taxied through several sharp turns. As the rear loading ramp dropped halfway down, Regter caught sight of a late afternoon sun wedged between purple-tinted clouds and distant shadowed mountains. Below them, Long Son Hill's enormous white Buddha cast its benevolent gaze over a forest of tin-roofed houses as evening mists rose from the Song Cai River plain. For the briefest of seconds, Regter felt at peace.

As the aircraft rolled to a stop, he shouldered his rucksack and made his way through the hot prop blast to a bare wooden shack on the 5th Special Forces side of the airfield marked *LSC control.*

"You Major Regter, sir?" A Private First Class in green beret and starched jungle fatigues snapped to casual attention.

"How'd you guess?"

"The jacket, sir. Besides, Colonel Green said you'd be coming in straight from the field."

A faint smile creased Regter's lips. It wasn't the smell of jungle and a two-week growth of beard that impressed the headquarters troops. It was the black nylon recon jacket with its embroidered snarling red-eyed green-beret-clad skull.

"OK. Get me to the best steam bath. I need about twenty minutes."

"No dice, sir. Colonel Green wants you ASAP."

"Even if it's a legitimate steam bath?"

Now it was the PFC's turn to smile. "I didn't know we had any of those left, but nossir."

"It's his nose..."

A short rushed ride later, Regter climbed down at a long low building fronted with a covered walkway. A billboard-sized sign proclaimed it the Headquarters, 5th Special Forces Group (Airborne). Glancing across the quadrangle, he gave the Green Beret Ice Cream shack and Silver Wings Souvenirs shop a disgusted shake of his head. Stepping inside, he found a solitary Nung trooper in starched tiger-striped fatigues wrestling a large buffer across a floor whose mirrored shine was painful to behold. Past the disapproving glare of the Nung, Regter knocked on a polished wooden door whose burnt-wood master parachutist badge-shaped plaque identified it as belonging to the DCO.

"Goddammit, Charlie. Get the hell in here! We haven't got all night!"

He found Lieutenant Colonel "Pappy" Green wedged back in a leather executive easy chair, his feet on a polished teak desk, thumbing through a stack of papers. Self-consciously, Green removed his reading glasses. He waved Regter to a chair with an unlit cigar.

"Want one? Genuine Upmann Havanas! I have them sent down from Laos where they cost twenty-five cents apiece. It's the one good thing the goddam Cubans have done up there."

"Sure. Mind if I light up?"

"Not at all."

Regter unscrewed a gold tube, removed the cigar, inhaled its cedar aroma, and carefully toasted its end with a match. He had first met Pappy Green in Korea, on the day his 4th Airborne Ranger Company had been disbanded. Green had shown up looking for volunteers to lead guerrillas in North Korea. Of those who stepped forward, only Regter and two others had made the grade. Green had put the other two out on an island in the Yellow Sea, and kept Regter for himself. Soon, they were slipping ashore from junks with pirate bands of North Korean guerrillas. Later, Green had nominated Regter for a battlefield commission. Very few officers wanted guerrilla duties, and their project was always short-handed. Besides, they didn't give out medals in the United Nations Partisan Forces like they did in the Regular Army regiments.

Following Korea, Regter was posted to the fledgling 77th Special Forces Group, and then to what became the 1st Special Forces Group. In Hawaii and Okinawa, he again ran into his old commander. Together they had conducted Special Forces' first training mission to Vietnam, at the Nha Trang commando training center, with what became the Vietnamese Special Forces. In 1957, Nha Trang had been pleasant. Morning swims in the ocean, late afternoon tennis at the *cercle sportif,* followed by dinners at the Neptune or Frégate where Pappy plied his wiles on the various French wives and daughters who made Nha Trang their Riviera. Green was aided in these nocturnal endeavors by his impeccable French and casually elegant manner. On occasion, he would affect a Tropical White dress uniform replete with French parachute badge and the stripes and anchor of an honorary corporal of the 8th Colonial Parachute Shock Battalion, souvenirs of his time as liaison officer to the French G.C.M.A. and the Vietnamese Airborne Battle Group.

But upon their return to Okinawa, Green had been riffed from the army. Patted on the back for past wars, he was put out on the street because no new ones were in sight. Years later, Regter ran into his Green in Guatemala, where Pappy claimed to work for a petroleum research firm. When they both ended up in the same camp training Cuban exiles, Pappy confessed that he might be a CIA paramilitary officer. And despite Green's protests to the contrary, Regter suspected that Pappy's civilian and military careers had somehow merged to place him in the seat he now occupied.

"That," Green tossed a thick file on his desk, "is Sam Theriault's recommendation for the Medal of Honor. Tell me, Charlie. Did he really do all that shit?"

"I'd have to read it."

"You didn't write it up?"

"Vanderveld did..."

"Vanderveld? So what's the consensus at Command and Control North?"

"Opinions are split. Some agree with the CMH but some others feel he really earned the Distinguished Service Cross. I'd go with the DSC myself."

"So why is Vanderveld pushing for a CMH?"

"Well, he and Sam were teammates back when the Mad Dutchman had a detachment at Bad Tolz. Sam was Vanderveld's Team daddy there, and then served as his B Team operations sergeant in the 6th Group before coming over here. Sam was headed for an A Team down in III Corps when Vanderveld talked him into CCN..."

"Goddam New Hampshire Canuck! I told him to keep his ass down and stay out of recon. Sonuvabitch kept trying to prove he was a twenty-year-old stud. He should've taken a staff job, but not Theriault. Did you know he was two months past retirement eligibility?"

"He never mentioned it."

"Well, I'm going to outvote you this one, Charlie, but there's politics involved. The Group's already gotten four Medals of Honor, and there are folks down at U.S. Army Vietnam who think awards are supposed to be evenly allocated among divisions and brigades. Tell Vanderveld that Colonel Ladd will give it his best try."

Regter nodded.

Pappy Green scrawled a note across the cover sheet and dropped the papers into his out-basket. Leaning back into his chair, he lit his own cigar, and sent up a plume of smoke.

"So, how's the war?"

Regter grinned. "You mean: how's Vanderveld doing?"

Pappy grimaced. Vanderveld was another Korean War guerrilla hand. A lieutenant who'd never left the Kangwha Island training base, he'd managed to make the army a career over Pappy Green's pointed objections. Now Vanderveld was up for full colonel, and the prospect of possibly working for him was not altogether pleasant.

"All right, how's Vanderveld doing?"

"Damned good so far. Broke up a fight among my people a while back, and they're not too anxious to tangle with him again. Now he's raising hell with the Marines up at Khe Sanh over their reconnaissance efforts."

"Thinks he can do better?"

"Why not? Marine recon kids are good, but our indigenous teams have the edge. Not only do they look and smell like Charlie, they think like him. Once the Marines wake up to that fact, they'll be able to use us."

"So I've heard. In fact, General Walt's asked SOG for a specialized reconnaissance unit that can be integrated into the Khe Sanh effort. Naturally it would come out of CCN..."[2]

Regter felt an old worm churning inside his intestines. "And naturally, I'd be the best man for the job."

"You would be, Charlie. After all you're an ex-Marine."

"Former Marine, '46 to '50. And Walt won't miss the fact that I did Korea with the army."

"A minor sin of omission..."

"Not to a Marine."

"Maybe, but that's not the job I have in mind."

Regter's worm subsided, but refused to go away.

"It had better be a short one, Pappy. I've only got four months left in country."

Pappy took a long draw on his cigar and studied his friend's red-rimmed eyes. It wasn't like Regter to shut him out so quickly.

"You tired, Charlie?"

"Tired? No. But I'm goddam disgusted. I've lost five lieutenants in as many months in a three platoon Hatchet Force and—Goddamit—Sam Theriault was a friend of mine. I knew Sam back when he was a buck sergeant. Anyway, I've been in country for eighteen months straight now. Off and on, I must have forty months since '57. So...," Regter shrank back into his chair, the military bearing draining from his body. "...if Vanderveld doesn't get me killed, I'm going back to Fort Bragg, find myself a staff job, and see what Marge and the kids are up to."

"How are Marge and the kids?"

---

[2] SOG—The Studies and Observation Group. CCN—Command and Control North, the SOG element for covert operations unit responsible for I Corps, Central Laos, and North Vietnam.

"'Bout time you asked! You were always their favorite house guest. Not so good. I had them in Hawaii on R&R a couple of months back, and Marge kept dropping hints of a divorce. The boys are getting to that age where they're difficult, and she's having a hard time."

"Think she's serious about a divorce?"

"I sure as hell hope not. But if I stay here much longer, she will be."

The two men fell silent: Regter thinking about a wife and three kids who'd done so much growing up without him, and Green plotting his next opening. As a friend, he would have liked to pat Regter on the back, wish him an easy assignment at Fort Bragg, and drag him off to get drunk and talk about old times. But the newer times were urgent. Green directed another plume of smoke to the ceiling and fixed Regter with a stare.

"You know, Charlie, Sam Theriault had a wife and kids..."

"So did a lot of others I've sent home in boxes."

"Sam was no tourist. No ticket puncher. He could've been back in New Hampshire, fishing..."

"Florida."

"What?"

"Sam was always going to retire in Florida. He hated cold weather."

"Look, dammit, the principle's the same! Remember Buon Enar?"

"Buon Enar?" Regter snorted. Green was pulling out all the stops. Buon Enar was why Regter had almost stayed a captain. In 1964, it was the showplace of Special Forces. Though he wasn't regular army yet, he'd been given command of Buon Enar over several well connected West Pointers. Despite pressure from the top, the Commander of United States Army Special Forces Vietnam held firm. Regter, he was fond of telling folks at MACV, had been in country back when their fair-haired protégés had been plebes at the Point.

At first, things went well: A raid into Cambodia to rescue downed airmen. A long range patrol that netted an important Viet Cong commander. The ambush of several well-known Viet Cong political agents. Regter's star rose quickly, as did the price on his head. The Viet Cong wanted revenge, and certain South Vietnamese officers wanted him out of the way. But Regter seemed immune. He had befriended two Montagnards, Y B'ham and K'pa Doh, who were desperately seeking allies in their struggle against the lowland Vietnamese. After Regter placed himself between them and certain Vietnamese officials, they placed their men between Regter and the Viet Cong.

Meanwhile, the war in the Highlands kept growing. The Diem government had resettled North Vietnamese refugees onto prime Montagnard lands, and the new arrivals brought in an open animosity towards the Highlanders, and no small number of clandestine Viet Cong cadres. Shortly afterwards, Montagnard communists who had gone north in 1954 began showing up in their native villages. To counter these, the tribal leaders had banded together in a movement of their own.

It all seemed comic opera until 24 September 1964, when the blue, red, and green flag of the United Front for the Struggle of Oppressed Races, FULRO for short, rose over Buon Enar. While Regter tried to defuse the revolt, his troops lined up 12 Vietnamese Special Forces in front of a pit that had been the camp latrine. When the guns went off, Regter's star came crashing down. No one bothered to credit either Regter or a young Australian named Barry Petersen for avoiding far greater bloodshed, mainly because a certain colonel in Ban Me Thuot had carefully worded all reports to cast himself in that role.

"You know damned well I remember Buon Enar, Pappy! Are you getting ready to do me another favor?"

"I most certainly am."

"Then forget it. I'm going home."

"In a pig's ass you are, Charlie. Look, you got passed over on your first go-around for major. And you almost missed it this time despite the war. Hell, they could have made you a staff sergeant this trip! So here you are, an experienced Special Forces officer commanding a one company reaction force, while majors junior to you are commanding virtual brigades. Oh, the jacket'll look nice at your funeral, and you have that cachet of belonging to the one command whose very initials make most of our young fair haired regular army types shit their pants. Hell, I asked the group commander to find me a replacement for you last month. Ladd interviewed three of 'em, and our courageous airborne-ranger-pathfinder heroes opted for staff jobs with their favorite lieutenant colonels instead. Don't forget that your predecessor went home in a body bag, Charlie. It tends to put your own chances in perspective."

Regter shrugged. "It's what we get paid to do."

"Yeah, Charlie. Look, I've watched you through two wars and a few almost-wars. One of these days we're going to wrap up what's left of you in a poncho and ship it back to Marge and the kids, while a bunch of clowns like myself stand around and cry crocodile tears at your memorial service, then sneak off to get drunk. I can live with that. But what I can't live with is sticking you down on some here-comes-the-cavalry job that any captain with a pair of testicles and four months in grade can handle. I need you in charge of those captains, Charlie, not running around trying to prove you're still one of them...Am I boring you?"

Regter flashed a hint of a smile. "Sounds suspiciously like the you've-gotta-take-this-commission speech I once heard."

"You're damned right it does." Pappy glanced at his watch. "Tell you what..."

Green was interrupted by a knock on the door. He looked up as a scruffy head poked cautiously in.

"Sorry I'm late, B-boss. Ran into the g-goddam group sergeant major."

"You're just in time, Mac. I take it he didn't approve of your necklace?"

Marvin McElroy stepped into the room in painfully new jungle fatigues two sizes too large, with newly sewn chevrons marking him as a master sergeant.

"S'matter of fact, he didn't say nothin' except to ask what it was. It was the tiger suit p-pissed the SMAJ off. Says I ain't s'posed to wear 'em in Nha Trang."

"Group policy, Mac. The SMAJ was only doing his job."

"Yeah, well I ain't in his goddam g-group, an' we got better things to do in the MIKE Force than worry 'bout small shit. Anyway, he was decent enough to give me a pair of his own when he found out supply was closed. I know a big Yard who'll just love this shit."

Mac paused long enough to give both men a warm Montagnard style handshake. He'd known both in Korea, and had been Regter's senior communications sergeant in Okinawa. Deployed to Vietnam in 1962, Mac had never left. The fact that he'd gone native was more than compensated for by his extensive knowledge of the Darlac Plateau tribes. When it came to clan and tribal histories, mores, and customs, Mac was a walking encyclopedia who spoke three Highland languages and several minor dialects. He could tell a Bru from a Bahnar from a Hodrung or Arap Jarai. His only drawback was that he did not get along with Vietnamese.

"So, Boss," he looked at Regter, "you g-gonna take the job?"

"What job?"

"The II Corps MIKE Force," Green cut in. "Charlie, I'm handing you command of the largest MIKE Force in country. It's up to six companies now, on its way to ten. Your job is to recruit and organize six battalions within a year. Three of those will be under your personal command."

"Pappy, I need to go home..."

"You need to listen to me and Mac, Charlie. Things up there are going to hell in a hand-basket, and you're the best chance of I have of stopping it. Mac's down here to give Ladd the real skinny on the problems we're having, and you're the only man I've got to throw into the breach. Ladd respects you. He remembers you from Okinawa. And he was the staff weenie up in the Pentagon who read our report on the First Observation Group. If I just drag Mac in there to drop the dime on the idiot we've got there now, Ladd will just fire him."

"Isn't that what you want?"

"It's only half of what I want. If I go in there without a strong candidate, Ladd will let Cox name his replacement. Cox is OK, but he's like a lot of lieutenant colonels we're getting these days. Preppy school SFers who've spent their entire careers in the conventional army until they smelled promotion in Special Forces. Then they wangled a spot in the SF Officers Course, spent a couple of months in some stateside group, and are now over here to get their tickets punched."

"And your MIKE Force commander is one of these preppie school SFers?"

"No. In fact, he looked pretty good…"

"So, what's the problem?"

Green glanced over at Mac. "It started with the eat-a-broad nights, sir," Mac stuttered. "You know, the unit parties. At first it wasn't bad, because they were s'posed to give the guys in from the field a little break, and the Teamhouse seemed like the safest place to do it. But the parties kept getting wilder, and we kept having more of 'em, until we had eat-a-broad nights, followed by beat-a-broad nights, followed by brown-a-broad nights. And it was always the same guys. McSweeney and his clique. They'd get all dressed up in black VC pajamas with the MIKE Force patch, and get guzzling drunk while they took turns with whatever whores they could scrounge up down in Pleiku. The night the shit hit the fan up at Dak To, McSweeney was too drunk to do anything about it. We let him sleep it off while our S-3 launched up there with a few guys to take control of the situation. Didn't do much good. Siu Dot walked off with two companies after the 173rd tried to turn 'em into line infantry..."

"Siu Dot 'Johnny?'" Regter cut in.

"Yessir. Of c-course," Mac gave a bitter laugh, "we fired him for that. Anyway, when McSweeney sobered up he decided that he'd better show everyone what Special Forces was all about, so he loaned us to FOB 2.[3] To g-give 'em credit, they didn't have a whole lot of time for plannin' before they hadda launch the company that was left 'cross the border. They got the shit shot out of 'em, we got the shit shot out of us, and I lost my captain."

"An Aussie named Rexburg," Green added. "Luckily, we got the body back. Needless to say, Brigadier Hughes was not pleased. We'd just had an Australian assassinated in the I Corps MIKE Force. So now he's wondering just what kind of risks he's exposing his people to by sending them here."

"You know me, sir," Mac continued. "I don't like officers, b-but Rexburg was okay. Still, gettin' greased is part of the job. Then a few days ago, McSweeney got smart with my daughter."

Regter raised an eyebrow.

"It's a long story," Mac shrugged. "Anyway she's Jarai, and you know how Jarai women are. She took a liking to my c-company commander and

---

[3] Forward Operational Base 2, later Command and Control Central. The site responsible for covert operations in Northern Cambodia and Southern Laos.

decided to take off her skirt for him. Well, that's her business, and there was nothin' that Blek and me could do about it. B-besides, Lieutenant Grey treats her pretty well. So I told 'em to keep it out of the village, you know, to avoid problems and all that. So she'd come up to the Teamhouse to see him. She was up there the other night when McSweeney c-came out of the club and decided that he hadda get in her drawers..."

"He raped her?"

"He didn't get the chance. But he d-did p-push her up against a wall and got a liplock on her tits. Asshole was tryin' to g-get his pants down when she called out the Yards. Only thing that saved his ass was his rank. The g-guards that came runnin' were reluctant to shoot him. If I'd have been there," Mac suddenly lost all trace of stutter, "they wouldn't have had any fucking problem at all. And if the son of a bitch ever lays another hand on her..."

"Your *step*daughter. Right, Mac?" Green said.

"Same difference," Mac grumbled.

"Yes," Green agreed. "Well it's better we don't hear any more. And Mac, forget any threats when I send you in to see the group commander."

"Whatever..."

"There's no whatever about it, Sergeant. That's an order. Look, I have to ask you to leave for now. Are you going to meet us for dinner? It's on me."

"Nossir. I g-got some business I gotta take care of."

"You sure? The best lobster in Vietnam, I guarantee it."

"No offense, Colonel," Mac chuckled, "b-but it takes more than food to keep a man going, and I don't get down here that often."

"Oh?" Pappy's tone turned conspiratorial. "Headed downtown? We can drop you off…"

"No thanks, sir. You know the old rule: Never leave witnesses."

With a sly wink and a grin Mac rose, pocketed one of Green's cigars, gave Regter a nod, and departed.

"OK," said Regter, "so McSweeney's a drunk and his parties get out of hand. So what?"

"So what? Charlie, if McSweeney was the real problem, I wouldn't need you. But what I do need is someone who not only understands Vietnam, but also FULRO, and that narrows my options."

Green pulled a single sheet of typewritten paper from his desk. "Read and sign. It says that you've never heard of Project Gamma, and if you ever breathe a word about it, we'll have your ass."

Regter scrawled a perfunctory signature and pushed the sheet back across the desk.

"You see, Charlie, radio research detachments have their use. Those companies at Dak To didn't just quit. Siu Dot made radio contact with the camp at Polei Klang, who radioed the camp at Plei Djereng, who contacted someone in Pleiku, stating that they expected heavy casualties and requested instructions. Someone named Me Sao ordered them to pull out."

"FM radio relay. They're not dumb."

"No they're not, Charlie. And Hell, I wish they could win—but they can't. There's no way a couple of hundred thousand Montagnards are going to liberate forty-six percent of South Vietnam from seventeen million South Vietnamese. Now you and I know that, but there are people here who don't. To put it bluntly, people like Mac, who've spent so much time in the Highlands they think they're Yards. Hell, even McSweeney thought FULRO was cute. He'd get up in the middle of his orgies and start screaming, 'Go FULRO, Ungh!' and when we asked him about Me Sao, we got some historical bullshit about a Rhade hero from a long time ago. That's the real reason he's being fired, Charlie. And that's why I need you."

"I'll think about it, Pappy."

"No you won't. You'll take the goddam job, and you'll extend to give me a year in the MIKE Force to do it. Charlie, I'm not asking you. This is a goddammed order! Look, you know more about FULRO than any officer in this Group. You know Y B'ham Enuol, K'pa Doh, Eban Y Kruit, Pierre K'pa, and Paul Nur personally! But have you ever heard of Me Sao?"

"Not until now."

"Neither has anyone else, and that's what has me worried. We're raising a six battalion airborne strike force, and we're going to arm it with the most modern small arms in country. The Vietnamese are already opposed to the idea, so God help us if the whole thing turns into FULRO's private army. You see, Gamma triangulated the order for Siu Dot's people to desert, and it came from right inside the MIKE Force dependent village."

"So this Me Sao's in the MIKE Force."

"Not just in it. He's close to running it. That's why I need you to get the MIKE Force reorganized, find out who this Me Sao is, and get word back to me. I'll take care of the rest."

"You're going to kill him?"

"I'm going to neutralize him. How we do it will depend on him. Sometimes a little money or the right job is all it takes. And hell, even if it doesn't, we won't do anything to him that he wouldn't do to us. We'll just do it first. Come on, Charlie, take the job. I'd consider it a personal favor..."

"It's not my line of business, Pappy."

"The Hell it isn't. Look, Charlie, I need you up there. This is important. So important I'm going to give up this job and move over to replace Cox when the new Group commander arrives. In three months, you'll be working directly for me. Will you take it?"

"I'll think about it. Now, how about that lobster?"

Green slid his feet from the desk and reached for his beret. "Oh, I should mention that the MIKE Forces are being upped to lieutenant colonel commands. That might be handy to have in your promotion packet when the next board meets..."

Outside in the darkness a light fog had drifted in. While Regter showered and shaved in Green's cabana, Mac's solitary figure threaded a meandering course down to the Nha Trang MIKE Force compound. As he drew abreast of the gate, a muscular young guard stepped forward.

"*Swas'm lai*," Mac greeted.

"*Swas'm lai*," the guard acknowledged. "You are who?"

"Rahlen Blek's father," replied Mac. "Of Viet soldiers, are there many?"

"No. They suppose be here in case of alert, but went to Nha Trang in search of their manhood."

"Then it will be a futile search."

The guard smiled his appreciation, the dark gap showing where he had filed off his two front teeth at his own manhood ceremony.

"Tell me," continued Mac, "do these Viets fight?"

"Among themselves, like old whores. The VC they leave to us."

McElroy spent a few minutes commiserating with the guard before entering the team house. He found Sergeant Dick Chamberlain sitting alone at the bar.

"G-goddam," grinned Mac, "helluva welcome for a b-brother!"

Chamberlain reached into the cooler and tossed him a beer. "I'm all you're gonna get, Mac. Most of the companies left for Seven Mountains this morning. We got back last night for three days stand-down. You'll find my Roundeyes down at the Project Delta club, trying to scrounge up some pussy."

"What 'b-bout the Indig?" asked Mac, referring to Chamberlain's Cham troopers.

"Probably in every whorehouse in Nha Trang by now."

"So what's with you?"

"I'm an old married man, Mac. Besides, I'm duty officer since I'm the only Roundeye left in the compound."

"Speakin' of officers, any word on your commission?"

"Group says I should have it by Tet. The Old Man is recommending me for a company in your MIKE Force."

"You'll be welcome," grunted Mac, "b-but I still say they're ruinin' a fine NCO."

"Thanks for the vote of confidence," Chamberlain grinned.

"Don't thank me. B-be nice to have a lieutenant we don't hafta break in."

Following a few minutes of pleasant conversation, Mac drained his beer and excused himself on the pretext of "findin' a p-place to shit." Ducking out through the back of the team house, he made his way down through the indigenous barracks, taking care to see that he wasn't followed.

He found Y Nguu and the others waiting on the darkened second floor of the Rhade barracks where a large earthenware drinking jar, set beside a recently slaughtered chicken, gave mute evidence of the sacrifice that had preceded his arrival. A solitary oil lamp lit the room with a faint glow hardly brighter than that from the men's pipes. All rose to offer Mac the traditional highland handshake; right hand extended, the left hand grasping the right wrist. Y Nguu motioned him to a mat while an assistant handed him a previously prepared pipe.

"*Mnam Luu,*" Y Nguu greeted.

"Let's get drunk together," Mac agreed. The greeting stemmed from the highland belief that a pleasant alcoholic buzz appeased the myriad spirits inhabiting the world of men. The drink itself was called *mnam pay.*

"*Salaam alaykum,*" invoked a stranger, thereby identifying himself as a Cham Bani.

"*Wu alalaykum is'slam,*" Mac muttered in reply, wondering how much Arabic the Cham knew beyond a few simple words and phrases.

They smoked their pipes in silence, occasionally breaking into small talk about each other's villages, clans, and families, as if they still had such. Once the glow of the pipes had died, Y Nguu took up the bamboo straw from the *mnam pay* jar. Muttering an inaudible prayer, he sprayed several mouthfuls of the cool green liquid in the four cardinal directions around the chicken's corpse, and then passed the straw to McElroy, who as a Jarai deferred the honor to the Cham.

The Cham was pleased to accept as a son of the mighty Cham people, heirs to the kingdoms of Indrapura, Vijaya, Amaravati, Kauthara, and Panduranga. After downing the required two measures, he passed the straw to McElroy. When the ritual was finished, they sat back on their mats and let the warm glow of the rice wine circle through their bodies. As it wafted out into the spirits' nostrils, Mac pulled a pack of cigarettes from his breast pocket, passed them around, and flipped the remainder of the pack back to the assistants with instructions to share them.

The Cham was first to speak, explaining the history of Nha Trang. Kauthara had been one of the last surviving Cham states, and only fell to the Nguyen lords in 1653. Even then, the Nguyen had needed assistance from Dutch warships, and their victory was so costly they allowed the Cham to continue as vassals until the nineteenth century, inhabiting the coast from Nha Trang to Phan Thiet. Westerners, the Cham hissed, had often allied with their enemies.

"The Dutch," Mac corrected, thinking that Cham piracy might have prompted the Dutch to lend the Nguyen a hand.

After the fall of Kauthara's westernmost fortress, the Cham continued, thousands of his ancestors had been taken out to the sand dunes of Dien Khanh and massacred.

"Dien Khanh," Mac interrupted. "The old French fort?"

"That so-called French fort," snapped the Cham, "was built by my people to keep out the Viet. The Nguyen built over our ruins with the help of *Phap* engineers."

"French engineers? Are you sure?"

"Our memory is long..."

"Especially for those trained in Moscow."

"So," smiled the Cham, "you think you know me. Rahlen Blek's father, a man studies where he can. I would have preferred your own country, but Paris was nice."

"Paris?"

"You see? Not everything one reads in a *dossier* is true. Your government turned down my visa, as they didn't wish to offend that great 'democrat' Diem. I have heard of a dying Jarai matriarch with a similar problem..."

"You have sharp ears," Mac acknowledged.

"Yes. Would you tell me that your pathetic attempt to save her was any different?"

Mac stared down at the fourteen bronze and brass bracelets dangling from his wrist. They were a weight he would forever bear in her honor.

"I would not..."

"Then," the Cham leaned forward, his voice softening. "We understand each other, even if we cannot be friends."

"Good," interrupted Y Nguu. "Then we can speak of matters at hand. Mac, have you spoken with Ney Bloom or Rchom Jimm since the conference?"

"No," Mac lied, "I have not been to Pleiku for weeks."

"But you know of the decision," pressed the Cham.

"Why else am I here?" Mac asked irritably.

"To receive your orders," said the Cham.

"Receive orders?" Mac stroked his moustache. "I was told to come here and receive proposals. It is one thing to hear what certain politicians have decided, but any strategy for war must be fashioned by war leaders."

"Fashioned by whom?" The Cham's jaw tightened. "Since when does the military foot dictate to the political wing? Brothers Bloom and Jimm had best weigh their actions with care."

"Brothers Bloom, Jimm, and even Siu Dot have little to say about this, other than their vote."

"The Leper is in on this too?" The Cham frowned. Siu Dot headed the internal disciplinary committee, FULRO's assassination squads.

"Like everyone else," Mac smiled, "Siu Dot takes orders from Me Sao..."

"How is it that we have never heard of this Me Sao before?" growled the Cham. "Who is this person?"

"Someone known to very few, but whose authority has been acknowledged by Y B'ham himself. Whatever your politicians say, the MIKE Force now speaks with one voice."

"So, a front has risen within our Front. Tell me: What has Me Sao decided concerning our revolt?"

Mac hesitated. Although he spoke a competent Rhade, almost as well as Jarai, he had said more than he intended and did not wish to compound the error.

"The MIKE Force will lead this revolt with conditions."

"Conditions," the Cham's voice was edged with contempt. "Who is Me Sao with one pygmy battalion to speak of conditions? An internal enemy. One who should be destroyed before the contagion spreads. As we should have done in 1964." Carefully crushing out his cigarette on the sole of his boot, before dropping the butt in his pocket, the Cham looked up to fix Mac with a decidedly unfriendly stare.

"So, Pleiku MIKE Force talks of conditions? Old women farting in the wind! I could have told these brothers as much. Pah!" he spat, "I have endangered myself for nothing to come here. Now, my brother, you tell this Me Sao, and Ney Bloom, and Rchom Jimm, and that leper Siu Dot, as well as that son you claim, that the Cham have met and decided. The time for whispering revolt is past. We are not a people ruled by our women, as are our *brothers*. Or is it our *sisters*? This revolt will come with or without you. Nha Trang is ours by right. It shall again be ours in fact. Or you will number the Cham on fingers and toes."

The Cham abruptly rose and stalked from the room. As he did so, McElroy could not help but feel a grudging admiration.

"So," asked Y Nguu, after his assistants signaled that the Cham was indeed gone, "what are these conditions?"

"That Nha Trang be left to the Viets. We have not the force to take and hold it."

"Then the Cham will not help us"

"We do not need the Cham. They are already numbered on fingers and toes. They have but one company, and act as if an army."

"They have two more companies at Phan Thiet and another at Phan Rang. Units they have armed with stolen weapons."

"Wow," sputtered Mac, switching suddenly to English, "ain't that just g-great! A whole goddam b-battalion here in Nha Trang. Won't the 91st ARVN Rangers just love that. G-give 'em somebody to shoot up b-besides themselves. Look," he fixed Y Nguu with an earnest stare, switching back to Rhade, "Nha Trang can be taken, but cannot be held. Vietnam would never allow such, and America will never allow such. It is bad strategy."

"Bad strategy?"

"Yes. Because it is on the coast that the Viets are strongest."

"Which is why we need Cham support."

"Only for diversion that Nha Trang will cause. And as Colonel Kasem just said, they will do that anyway. As for our own forces, we will number twenty companies..."

"Twenty companies," Y Nguu marveled. Despite years of service with the French and Americans, he had yet to see a Montagnard force that large assembled in a single place.

"Yes, and your four companies make twenty-four. Twenty-four companies are eight battalions. Eight battalions are three brigades. Three brigades is a division. And this is only our mobile reserve..."

"And with camp strike forces and Iron Brigade from Cambodia..." Y Nguu's eyes shone. Visions of columns of young Rhade, Jarai, Koho,

Bahnar, Sedang, Stieng, Rengao, M'nong, and Raglai marched before him, their blue, red, and green battle flags floating under a free Highland sky.

Y Nguu's assistant handed them two glasses of cognac, a luxury acquired serving with the 52nd Indochinese Machinegun Battalion at Carcassonne in the late 1930s. As they took the glasses, Y Nguu stared into the amber liquid.

"Mac, what you think of this revolt?"

"What I think matters not. What matters is what president Y B'ham thinks. He was against it, but K'pa Doh and his radicals carried the vote. They have pledged that the Viet Cong will not interfere."

"Viet Cong! But who would trust their word?"

"More'n likely," murmured Mac, his eyes searching the darkness, "certain cadres trained in Hanoi."

The old man's vision of red, green, and blue banners began to fade.

"Then Colonel Kasem was right."

"About what?"

"About time for whispering revolt being past. Perhaps by Ninthmonth, we too will be numbered on fingers and toes."

"Maybe," Mac half-whispered staring into the oil flame. "But what other choice have we?"

"Rahlen Blek's father," Y Nguu nodded, "you have always kept faith with us. We thank you for that, no matter where our bones may fall." He lifted his glass. "To the *Front Unifié pour la Lutte des Races Opprimées.*"

"FULRO," chorused Mac. And they drained their glasses in silence.

Chapter Four

GAUNT AND PALE, BUT REJUVENATED, Galen St. Cyr trailed a line of 4th Infantry Division replacements off the quaking ramp of a C-123 aircraft. Beyond the wavering heat of the prop blast, a weathered sign welcomed all to Pleiku. As the troops trailed off behind their guides, St. Cyr angled towards a scruffy figure slouched by a waiting Jeep.

"B-bout time ya got here." Mac extended a warm handshake. "I see they made you a First Lieutenant. Keep that shit up and I'll hafta start salutin' ya. Any trouble?"

"No, Mac. You were as good as your word."

"I told ya! Us master sergeants got connections. Climb in, I'll g-get your gear."

Minutes later, Mac gunned their Jeep past a 4th Division replacement convoy of deuce-and-a-half trucks, barreled out the gate, and swung a sharp left onto a gravel road, spraying up a cloud of orange red dust. Midway down the road, he cocked his head and abruptly wheeled onto the shoulder to cut the engine. Explosions echoed in the distance.

"Hear that?" Mac grinned as whooshing swizzles passed overhead. "Charlie must be trying to g-get rid of his basic load of 122 rockets before the Tet truce goes into effect. G-gotta hurry, or we'll miss it!"

"Miss it?" As Mac fishtailed back out into the road in a cloud of dust. St. Cyr clutched the Jeep's side-strap with grim determination. The irony that he might die in an accident trying to avoid rockets flashed through his mind.

"Slow down, Mac..."

Mac ignored him to point out the distant C Team, MIKE Force, and Vietnamese Special Forces compounds. Swinging a sharp left at the helipad, they hurtled a hundred meters down another gravel road, then skidded into what felt like a two-wheeled left turn. St. Cyr caught sight of an old Montagnard in faded green fatigues snapping to the French version of present arms as they flashed under a barely raised gate.

Barrooooom. Screams sounded in the distance.

"Damn, Trung-oui, may b-be too late!" Mac pounded on the Jeep's horn as they careened past rows of single-story barracks. Visions of shattered bunkers and maimed bodies flashed in St. Cyr's mind.

Barrooooom. Closer now, the screams sounded almost like cheers.

"Too late...?" St. Cyr bit his tongue at a severe jolt.

"Yeah," Mac flashed a maniacal grin. "For b-bout the only chance you're g-gonna get to see the Air Force earn their combat pay on the ground just like the rest of us assholes."

Their Jeep skidded to a dust-clouded stop inside a wide quadrangle flanked by a weathered cement building marked 'Big Marty's Bar and Grill' and a line of sand-bag covered Conex containers whose tops were mobbed with tiger-striped bodies.

Barrooom.

"A C-130!" chortled a swarthy bearded American. "They got a goddam C-130!"

"Ho! Blek's father, climb up," greeted a chorus of Montagnard voices, as hands reached down for Mac. While the crowd turned their attention to the latest volley, Mac helped pull St. Cyr up.

From atop the Conex, he gazed across sandbagged trenches and perimeter wire to the distant runway and aprons. Black smoke rose from a clump of tangled debris at the far end of the airfield. More swizzles sounded overhead.

"Hey Clyde," called a voice, "left one, up four!"

Barooom, a C-123 mushroomed out in burning pieces. St. Cyr felt a pang of unease, wondering if it was the one he'd come in on.

"Another fucking plane," chortled the bearded one. "Man, has Charles got his shit together today."

"Esshole. Thet is one less texi we have to ride! You want we should walk?"

A giant Caucasian in tiger fatigues too small for his large frame glowered at the cheering section. His eyes came to rest on St. Cyr.

"Hey, Mec, who's this?"

"New man, Boris... "

"New men, hunh?" Boris thrust a half-empty vodka bottle in St. Cyr's direction. "Here, new men, have a drink."

St. Cyr took what he hoped was a healthy slug and offered the bottle back.

"Shit, buddy, you call thet drink? Mebbe in C Team thet is drink, but this is MIKE Force."

St. Cyr took a healthier swig and returned the bottle with an assuring snap. Boris nodded a smile as a lanky figure in safari-cut green fatigues edged between them to retrieve the bottle. St. Cyr noted a green shield-shaped patch depicting a boomerang and crossbow.

"Whad'ya say we go easy on the new Leftenant, Boris."

"Why not?" Boris drew himself to an exaggerated position of attention, threw an open-handed salute, and bellowed: *"Les plus beaux soldats de la France, sont les voici, devant vous..."*

"Don't mind Boris," confided the Aussie. "Half a bottle, and he thinks he back with the bloody Legion. Hang 'round til it's gone, and he'll be teaching you old Russian army songs."

"He's Russian?"

The giant glowered.

"No fear," chuckled the Aussie. "Ukrainian. But Boris did spend some time in the Russian army. Laurie Toller here," he extended a bone-crushing handshake, "and these magnificent bastards," he nodded at the mob, "are 205 MIKE Force company. That..," he indicated the head of the cheering section, a short, balding, dark-complexioned American of about twenty-two with an Uzi slung from his shoulder, "...is Specialist Five Morris Cohen. We call him the Superjew. Sergeant First Class Sergei Biloskirka, you've just met. Ryan, our team medic, is presently in hospital recovering from wounds. Leftenant Grey... Hey, Boris. Where's the Trungoui?"

"Down here." A slender muscled form stretched up his hand. Dick Grey had bright green eyes, close-cropped dirty blond hair, and a tan, freckled complexion with a familiar pallor. As he was lifted up, St. Cyr noted the tremble.

"Now there's a condition I recognize."

The smile he flashed in Grey's direction was met with an icy stare, which warmed as Grey spotted the combat infantryman's badge on his chest.

"New man, huh? You must be the one Mac was talking about. Sorry, but when I saw the new junglies I thought you were one of the C Team pukes. Welcome aboard. Just don't eat the dog. In fact, don't eat anything if you can help it."

As explosions played across the runway, Grey explained the fundamentals of VC rocket gunnery. The 122 millimeter was most effective when fired from a stable platform at maximum range from its intended target. It also helped if it was at roughly the same elevation. Charlie's launchers tended to be primitive. Propped up on crossed sticks about 16 kilometers southwest of Pleiku, they merely let fly in the general direction of the airbase. Considering the wet-thumb approach to rocket gunnery, they didn't do that badly. You could hear the motors as the rockets passed over the compound. If the motors were going strong, Charlie was overshooting. If they cut out just overhead, then Charlie was on target. But if they cut out down below, Grey nodded back beyond the helipad, then everyone just puckered up and waited. To quote Mac, "It was like the h-hand of G-god."

"Fuck you too, El Tee" growled Mac. "And sp-speakin' of God, we better get the new Trung-oui down to meet the major."

Charlie Regter sat behind a bare plywood desk, in a bare plywood office, in front of a wall-mounted olive-drab army wool blanket embroidered with the II Corps MIKE Force patch. St. Cyr had expected a tall, hawk-nosed, barrel-chested man with chiseled features and a piercing stare, but Regter was of medium height, slender but muscular and wiry in a steel cable sort of way. His cornflower-blue eyes were friendly with wrinkles that accentuated his smile, but you sensed that they could quickly turn unfriendly. He exuded strength, agility, and a resoluteness of purpose that St. Cyr immediately envied. For the moment, Regter was disarmingly warm. He came out from behind the desk, rising to shake St. Cyr's hand, before motioning him to a seat on the bare wooden bench. Then, a more judicial mien settled in.

St. Cyr sat in silence as Regter leafed through his file. His rehearsed litany played in his head: How he had come home from the Peace Corps to find a draft notice waiting, and had instead enlisted for Special Forces. How he'd trained in radios, served a short stint stateside, and then deployed to Vietnam's Seven Mountains for a six-month stint that ended with the camp being nearly overrun. How that had postponed his plans to enter international banking. Returning stateside, he found former Peace Corps workers barred from Special Forces, and so had reenlisted for officer candidate school. After graduating and completing ranger and mortar training, he'd served as a mortar platoon leader before ending up in Vietnam. He expected questions about how well he spoke Pasar Malay and maybe even French.

"Lieutenant," Regter look him in the eyes, "it says here you're still on profile; no heavy lifting, running, or prolonged standing..."

"It's only temporary, sir. I'm good enough to hump a ruck. They were supposed to review it next week."

"If you'd stayed back at Camp Zama..."

"Yessir."

"But you didn't you stay at Camp Zama."

"Nossir," St. Cyr gave an involuntary shrug.

"Why not?"

"Well, to tell the truth, I wanted to get back here."

"Why in hell would anybody want to get back here? There must be something you could be doing in Japan. As I recall, Camp Zama's pretty nice."

"Yessir, it is. And there were a couple of fine young nurses I could be doing it with. But I got tired of hearing people bitch. Not the troops, or the draftees, but the career officers and NCOs. All most of them talked about was how badly they wanted a medical board to put them on extended profile, so they wouldn't get sent back in country."

"Only natural, wouldn't you say?"

"Maybe, but I also noticed they all wanted some key command slot or cushy staff job once they got stateside."

"And you don't think they deserved one, after getting shot up for their country?"

Anger flashed in St. Cyr's eyes. An edge cut into his tone.

"Sir, I thought that getting shot at was what we got paid to do. I had that kind of leadership back in the 4th Division, and we lost some good men because of it. My men damned sure deserved better. If some sonuvabitch can have the balls to go around calling himself a professional infantry officer, then he can damned sure start acting like one."

"And how can he do that, Lieutenant?" A hint of warmth crept into Regter's stare.

"For starters, by putting in his whole tour in a combat zone. After all, this is where the war's at."

Regter gave a slight nod, while warning bells sounded in St. Cyr's subconscious. He was talking too much. It was time to shut up.

"So you want to join the MIKE Force. Well, you fit our profile. Most here have previous combat tours under their belt, and all have seen time on an A Team. Your six months at Tri Chuc, and ground time with the 4th Division counts here. But to be frank, I prefer people with more time in Special Forces. Why should I make an exception for you?"

For a panicked second, St. Cyr forgot what he wanted to say. But gazing into Regter's eyes, he felt his confidence return.

"Because my six months in the Delta was spent running a combat recon platoon of Khmer Kampuchea Krom troops. And because I know what an infantry company is all about. I kept the loyalty of my men under some very trying leadership conditions, Sir, and I saw what this MIKE Force does. I'm tired of trudging around Indian country feeling like I'm always lost. Like I'm someone else's target. I want to do like we did back in Recon 91: to get out and hunt the Viet Cong like they've hunted me. To get my chance to kill a few more of the sunsabitches."

Regter's smile faded. "And how many have you killed, Lieutenant?"

"I've never counted. Not counting air strikes or artillery, I've killed a few. And they sure as hell have killed a few of mine..."

"In Delta Company?"

"In Delta Company, in A-713, in Recon 91 . . ."

"So it's personal?"

"Nossir, it's professional, but—personal, too." St. Cyr's voice caught. He tried to stop, but the words blurted out. "Look, Major, I wanted to come back to Special Forces, but the Army screwed me. So I took the next best thing, a line infantry company. And I loved those kids, sir. I loved them as much as any 'Bodes in Recon 91. And I'd give anything to be back with them, but Delta Company isn't mine anymore. And most of the kids I knew are gone."

"So we're your second choice?"

"Nossir, you're not. But if I could walk back in there and take command, I would. I owe them that much. Sometimes I used to feel that I was the only thing standing between them and the biggest asshole in the U.S. Army. But that's not going to happen. Sir, from the first time I ever heard of the MIKE Force, I wanted to be here. Then, when I saw you at the FARP, I knew that this was where I could do the most good."

Regter's eyes, which had remained cautiously detached, warmed again. St. Cyr felt their glow. "So, another moth looking for a flame."

"Yessir, that's an apt description."

Regter reached into his desk drawer, withdrew a large enameled MIKE Force pin, and placed it on the desktop.

"Welcome to the MIKE Force, Galen. Right now all my command slots are filled, but I need a supply officer. It's not what you wanted, but it's what I've got. Once you're off profile, and you've proven yourself, we'll see about a company. You've made the right choice. Now it's up to you to prove to me that I have."

The handshake was warm, the smile frank and friendly. St. Cyr peered into the recesses of Charlie Regter's eyes and felt a pride and gratitude welling up inside him. He wanted to say something in return, but Regter cut him off.

"Get out of here, Lieutenant. I've got work to do."

St. Cyr drew himself to attention and saluted. Then, as he faced right to step out, Regter's voice caught him.

"One final word."

"Yessir. What's that?"

"In the end, all us moths fly into the flame. It's the price we pay. I don't mind killers, and I understand anger and rage, but I won't abide a sadist or a murderer." Regter's smile had faded, and for an instant St. Cyr was back at the FARP. Then, with a wink, Regter waved him out.

Outside, it was getting dark. Mac had left a note pinned to the entry door. *Your bags are in Toller's room. Yours is the extra bunk,* it read below a short strip-map to his quarters. *Meet us in Big Marty's Bar and Grill.*

He crumpled the note into his pocket and made his way down through the compound past a mob of Montagnard troops lining up for chow under a faded sign that read "indigenous mess." Somewhere inside Big Marty's, a chorus of rough voices was singing something that sounded like "Jingle Bells."

Rat atat TaT / rat atat TaT / Mow those Bas-tards down.
Oh what fun, it is to Have / the MIKE Force back in town.
Riding through the Streets / In a black Mercedes-Benz.
Shooting all the Slopes / Saving all our Friends.
Machineguns all a-Blaze / Oh what a beautiful Sight.
Oh what fun, it is to Have / the MIKE Force back to-Night.
Hey...Rat atat TaT, rat atat TaT, Mow those Bas-tards down...

The tune was still going strong when he stepped out of his barracks to make his way to Big Marty's Bar and Grill. With some hesitation, he stepped through the swinging wooden saloon doors and into a room filled with song and banter. 205 Company's cadre was gathered around a rough plywood table. Mac was nowhere in sight, but Dick Grey pushed out a chair and motioned for St. Cyr to approach.

He slid into an empty seat next to two Montagnards: Rahlen Blek, who Grey introduced as the real 205 company commander, was a lean young Jarai with a smiling honest face. K'sor Tlur, a wizened old veteran of the French 3rd Battalion, Far East Provisional Brigade, was the company first sergeant, or *adjutant chef*. As the two Montagnards passed comments between themselves, St. Cyr was surprised to note that their military terminology was French.

"Hey Hoa," Grey called. "Get over here you ugly bitch."

A squat, muscular Chinese in tight green fatigues and a man's haircut uncoiled from behind the bar. Scowling through a face that had been ravaged by smallpox, she swaggered over to their table.

"Hoa no ugly bitch, you stinking long-nose monkey shit-smell for-inah! Hoa beautiful chinee eurasia girl!"

"Nung mixed with Chinese don't count as Eurasian. Hoa, meet the new Trung-oui."

Hoa brushed aside St. Cyr's proffered hand to pirouette lightly, come up behind Grey, and lock her arms in a choke hold around his neck. Grey's muscles tensed as he fought to rise, but Hoa forced his head to the table, knocking over his drink. He arched his body, straining desperately to break her hold, but her biceps knotted, flexed, and held.

"OK, Hoa," he wheezed. "You more than beautiful China Eurasia girl..."

"Say it!" she hissed. "Say it, you somnabitch!"

"I love you too many! You my beautiful China princess!"

Smiling a triumphantly evil grin, Hoa dropped Grey into his chair, paused briefly to give him a long, wet kiss, and took St. Cyr's hand in painful grip.

"Meet Hoa," panted Grey, as the color returned to his face, "our bartender, bouncer, and all around feminine ideal. Even better'n Maryanne Barnes, aren't you Hoa?"

"Fuck you," she hissed.

"See? Even learned her English at missionary school."

"Goddam mu'fu..."

"Hey Hoa," Grey held up his hand. "You gonna buy the new Trung-oui his first drink?"

She stopped in midsentence to shoot St. Cyr an evil glare.

"New man nevah been MIKE fohce befo'?"

The Roundeyes grinned and nodded.

"OK, Suckah." Hoa sauntered back behind the bar while Cohen drew St. Cyr's attention to an overly endowed nude painted on the wall. Clad in a green beret, bandolier, and M-16 rifle, someone had adorned her crotch and underarms with steel wool pads.

"That's Maryanne Barnes. Next to Hoa, she's the MIKE Force sweetheart."

Hoa ignored the opportunity to display any further mastery of English, and continued mixing his drink. From time to time she cast an evil smirk in St. Cyr's direction. When she emerged from behind the bar, she had what looked like a glass of flat cola. Everyone stood while Hoa handed St. Cyr the concoction. Removing the MIKE Force pin from St. Cyr's left breast pocket, Grey dropped it into the glass.

"Galen, welcome to the II Corps Mobile Strike Force, a somewhat motley crew of forty-seven Americans, seventeen Australians, and almost two thousand Yards." He directed St. Cyr to face the bar. "Our mission is to conduct mobile guerrilla operations throughout the II Corps Tactical Zone and anywhere else they send us. To hit Charlie back where he least expects it, when he least expects it. We're also II Corps' only indigenous parachute reaction force. Whenever a camp gets overrun, or any Special Forces unit gets its ass in a crack, we're the ones they call. Those thirty-six plaques up over the bar are for the men who've paid the price. Live long enough, and you'll get one to take home. Don't live long enough, you get one anyway, hung up where you'll be under Hoa's tender loving care. So, bottoms up, buddy."

To a long chant of "Go—MIKE Force—Ungh!" he swallowed in a steady gulp. The taste was flat. It had a sweet burn. By the fourth gulp his temples were ringing. Biloskirka took the empty glass, fished the insignia out, centered it over his left chest, drove it home with his fist, and handed St. Cyr the nylon fasteners before planting a wet kiss in his ear. Cohen and Grey did the same, while Toller and the Montagnards gave him hearty handshakes. Hoa came out from behind the bar to give him a prolonged, muscular kiss on the mouth, sliding her hand down between his legs to squeeze his testicles in an iron grip while she did so. When she released him, they called for another round.

By 2100 he was drunker than he'd ever been in his life, and the party showed no sign of letting up. Tiger-striped figures kept piling in. Above the din, Grey explained that these companies were home for the Tet stand-down. The rest were in the field. Regter stopped by, grinned at St. Cyr's predicament, and retired to his room to work on reports. As a new group stormed in, Cohen eyed an enormous American pulling two tables together, and nudged Grey.

"Where'd Boris go?" asked Grey.

"Taking a shit," said Cohen, keeping his eyes on the new arrival.

"Then it's time we were going."

St. Cyr threw them a questioning look.

"That," Grey nodded at the big American, "is 'Big Knute.' Knuudsen's a Finlander who doesn't like Russians. Boris doesn't like being called a Russian. Knute stands six-foot-nine and weighs about two-forty-five. Boris stands six-foot-nine and weighs two-thirty. Big Knute's a mean drunk, but Big Boris is a cunning one. They don't mix well. Some years ago, they got into a fight down at Hurlburt Field and it became a Special Forces legend. You don't want to be around for the rematch, and tonight could be that kind of night."

"Amen," muttered Cohen, carefully eyeing Boris as he ambled back into the bar, throwing Knuudsen a friendly wave.

"Well, Galen," Grey winked, "what say we go down to Pleiku and scrounge up some pussy?"

St. Cyr cast a wary eye in Hoa's direction.

"Naw," giggled Cohen, "he means real pussy..."

"Watch your mouth," Grey cautioned. "She'll cut your balls off."

"I swear," laughed Cohen, "the El Tee's getting soft on Hoa."

Hoa farewelled them with a barrage of expletives as they guided him out the door. The thought that Pleiku was off limits did occur.

"Don' worry," Boris assured St. Cyr, "thet is for Americans."

"And what the hell are we?"

"Us, Buddy? We're the MIKE Force."

Madame Binh's was in an old French villa on the outskirts of Pleiku which had seen better days. As the Jeep carrying them pulled up in front, a slender Vietnamese in a silk *ao-dai* stepped out to greet them. Grey introduced her to St. Cyr with instructions that he was to address her as *Chi*, elder sister, and that anytime he was in Pleiku she would take care of his needs. No one had ever caught anything at Madame Binh's, and from time to time she was even known to extend the privilege of a loan.

Inside a parlor that had been converted to a bar was a garishly lit juke box at the far end, flanked on either side by cheap kitchen chairs. Stepping in, they were swarmed by girls who could have never claimed a beauty prize.

"Well," he laughed, "now I know why no one ever catches anything here."

"Naw," explained Boris. "Pretty girls made enough to go home for Tet. Since this is bad night, only poorest girls are here."

Except for Blek, they were all soon paired off. The remaining girls milled around the jukebox.

"Hey Blek," called Grey, "my treat! Which one do you want? Blek pointed to a slender girl with light skin and thick hair, who turned away muttering a stream of angry Vietnamese. At the words *Filthy Moi*, Blek rushed over to grab her hair. Her screamed invectives alerted Madame Binh, who gave a high pitched shout. An enormous Sikh stepped in through the bead curtains to balance a club in Blek's direction. Biloskirka stood to face the Sikh, the Chinese bartender brought up a shotgun, and Cohen thumped his Uzi on the table.

"*Dung Lai!*" Grey called. "Goddam, guys, this is supposed to be a party. Chi Binh, what's the problem?"

"She from North, *Nguoi Bac*. No like *Moi, Nguoi Thuong*!"

"I didn't know this was a dating service, Chi. My friend's only looking to rent, not buy."

"She say she no like. I already tell you."

"I'll pay double."

Madame Binh gave a half-hearted shrug.

"Goddam North Vietnamese," Grey played to his audience. "First they come south and steal everybody's land, now they look down on Central and Southern people. They say they only look down on Moi, but they think they better than *nguoi Trung* and *nguoi Nam* too."

The central and southern Vietnamese girls cast hostile glances at Blek's captive. They didn't get much choice, so why should Miss Hanoi?

"Go with him," ordered Madame Binh in her best Hue dialect.

"I not dirty myself with one savage," hissed the girl in Phat Diem Hanoi.

"You do so," purred Madame Binh, "if you want I pay money your family. Besides, little sister, all seed same color. All seed wash away."

A tear rolled down the girl's nose. She nodded through clenched teeth. As Blek released her, she pulled away. He reached into his pocket and counted out one thousand dong—about nine dollars.

"Here," he said in Vietnamese, "for your hair."

"For my mother," she replied coldly, "who die now from sickness. Because mother mine dies, you may go-fuck me."

Despite the bad start, the party soon warmed up, thanks to half a bottle of scotch that Madame Binh donated to make up for Blek's reception and an arm-wrestling contest with a 20 dollar greenback pot that Boris had let the Sikh win. St. Cyr turned the bottle over and noted the 4th Infantry Division NCO club decal. Chi Binh had connections, all right. Too bad she hadn't used them to get him a better looking date. This one's splayed feet, spaced teeth, skinny body, and *eau de nuoc mam* breath had rice paddy stamped all over. But she had a delightful giggle and mischievous eyes, and the necessary equipment which she let him feel as they stumbled around the dance floor to plaintive lowland ballads.

Boris kept handing him the bottle, so the rest he remembered only vaguely. Two black troops from the 4th Division came in armed with M-14s. Madame Binh had no objection to Blacks, but did object to the weapons. They picked their girls and headed straight for the rooms. Sometime later, Boris and Superjew carried him out. He was deposited on a GI issue bunk with instructions not to tear the mosquito netting, in the care of Miss Rice Paddy, who kept jarring him awake to complete his duties. After he'd sworn she'd climaxed twice, he drifted off, only to awaken to find her locked onto him like some obscene frog, clutching his shoulders and demanding satisfaction. When she had finished, she released him to fall back and bring down the mosquito net.

Sometime around three in the morning, Cohen awoke to a familiar crawling in his intestines. He lay back for several minutes, trying to read the face of his Rolex, but it refused to stand still. His head throbbed. The Vietnamese had been up all night setting off fire-crackers and bottle rockets. Even now he could hear occasional fireworks in the distance. Damn, it was cold.

Swinging his leg over his girl, he slid cautiously out through the mosquito netting. He scrambled into the bathroom at the far end of an outer passageway just as a double attack of vomiting and the runs hit home. Agonizing minutes spent squatting over a solitary hole in the floor later, he staggered to his feet. *Cheap old bitch. You'd think she'd break down and buy a real American toilet at the prices she was charging. There were enough of them on the black market.* When whatever he'd passed finished passing, he opted for a walk. Vietnamese toilets were hell on Western knees.

Madame Binh's villa consisted of an older main house with several cement additions joined in a horizontal E. Its location was marked by a street light, approximately 100 feet from the entrance up a clay road. Further away, hedges and fences marked the boundaries of other villas. A necklace of occasional streetlights stretched down the road to pass up over a rise and into the city.

Cohen wandered through the courtyard and out onto the road, where he spent long minutes gazing at rooftops and hedgerows. In its own way, the area under the streetlight reminded him of his native St. Paul after a snowfall, except that these softened outlines were dust-covered. He was clad in boxer shorts and tee shirt. For footwear, he'd borrowed the girl's rubber sandals. Their small size made him walk pigeon toed.

From somewhere beyond the light, he detected a hint of movement that made him uneasy. *Calm down*, he told himself, *you're too damned jittery.* No doubt from the vodka that Boris had been pushing on him all day. A twitch in his stomach sent him back towards the villa, but it proved a false alarm. Strolling back to the road, he felt a queer sensation that someone or something was watching from directly overhead. A chill brushed the nape of his neck. *Hong Klang*, screamed an inner voice. His mind's eye flashed visions of a large skull-faced luminescent green hornet with blood-drenched fangs. *Fuck you*, he chided himself. *Wasp of the bone, my ass! That's just some bullshit Blek believes in.*

But an inner voice asked if the legend were true. What if there really were nocturnal green and black hornets whose venom resulted in an excruciating death? Hadn't they been told that there were no such thing as bloodsucking bees by some scholarly entomologist, after they'd returned from a patrol that had been plagued by them? Maybe the Yards ascribed the legend to some reality found nesting in the rotting tombs of their dead. Resisting a voice that urged him to run, he looked carefully around, and saw only the same quiet street, a star-filled sky, and soft walls bathed in starlight. He chided himself, but the inner voice refused to shut up. All right, maybe it wasn't Hong Klang. But something was out there.

It was an instinct he'd spent to many nights on patrols and ambushes to ignore. He retraced his path through the courtyard to the room. *Too much booze*, he told himself: It put your nerves on edge and brought back the nameless terrors of childhood. Back in the room, he surveyed an ordinary world: Biloskirka snored, as he always did when drinking. Grey's white boxer shorts showed through the netting. Blek's date was sniffling. The new lieutenant stirred. And Cohen's own warm bunk beckoned. But Biloskirka's snore grated on his nerves. A faint twitch rumbled his lower intestine. *Better have a cigarette and wait. Yeah, a cigarette would do nicely.* Rummaging through his pants, he fished out his cigarettes and lighter. The flash bothered no one but himself and sent a gunmetal blue glint off his Uzi. As he stepped away, he lifted it and slung it lightly over his shoulder. *Hey Stupid, what the hell are you going to shoot with that? Bees? Hornets? Might as well crown the ridiculous.* He felt around in his pant leg pocket for his tiger-striped skullcap. *Man, don't you look every bit the mighty Hebrew warrior! Uzi, yarmulke, tee shirt, boxer shorts, and girl's shower shoes. Don't forget to dangle the cigarette from your lips, James Dean style.*

Out in the street, Cohen gazed up into the brilliant stars of a late January sky. He found the Southern Cross low on the horizon, but had to guess at other constellations. Blek knew them all, by different names. That was the way it was with Yards. They arrived at the MIKE Force maybe six months out of the loincloth, supposedly simple, rustic folk. But they knew the constellations, and the jungle, and...The breeze ruffled his back with a strange sensation. Fear clamped down on his heart. He turned slowly, and the breeze turned with him. He did an abrupt about-face, and the breeze spun behind him. An alarm sounded somewhere in his mind. At a distant streetlight, a group of men entered the road.

Well, well. Looks like some 4th Division troopies got lost looking for a whorehouse. Sorry 'bout that guys, but you're a little late. His hand shifted to the pistol grip of the Uzi. *Nah, some sort of Vietnamese. Probably the goddam Quan Canh military police.*

The Uzi came up. His left hand reached for the fore-grip. The Vietnamese were peering at him. He chuckled, wondering what it felt like to be out on some nightly patrol and come across an American standing in the middle of the street, dressed in his underwear and toting a submachinegun. The realization that he was shorter and darker than the average American and that Vietnamese often strolled around in what Americans considered underwear hit him like a hammer.

What if they didn't recognize him as American? With the Uzi, that could be fatal. He was tempted to call out, but opted instead for a cautious wave. They were just approaching the streetlight's arc when another group turned into the road. They appeared to be some kind of Vietnamese militia.

As the first group stopped just beyond the light, Cohen waved again. Two men detached themselves to advance cautiously towards him. The second wore a flop hat, while the first wore no headgear at all. Their eyes were squinting, trying to make out his features. Cohen's grin froze. The bush hat, chest web equipment, and AK-47s registered in his mind's eye with alarming clarity. He glanced obliquely to the side, judged the distance between himself and the villa walls, and squeezed off a burst which cut down the two pointmen as he took off at a dead run. Wild shots and a short burst followed him in.

"VC regulars!" he cried, ducking behind the wall of the middle extension to squeeze off another burst. "Everybody up!"

Adrenalin and alcohol pounded in his temples. He had only one magazine of 32 rounds, and he'd already fired two bursts. Any grenades and ammunition in the Jeep's security box were now light years across the courtyard. The thirty-eights that Grey and Boris carried wouldn't be of much help. Rounds thunked through the cement as he discovered it was mere cinderblock. Cursing Madame Binh's shoddy construction, he fired off another short burst and screamed that he was on his way in. Biloskirka, Grey, and St. Cyr met him at the door. Blek was busy getting into his boots.

"What the hell's going on?" Grey demanded.

"Goddam platoon of VC regulars, and there's more on the way."

The girls scrambled whimpering under the beds.

"Let's go," Grey ordered, "everybody out the back now. Move!"

Rounds cracked through the doorway as St. Cyr fumbled for his boots. Grey grabbed his arm and shoved him towards the back window. "I said now! Superjew, cover our ass!"

"What about the girls?"

"Bring 'em if they if they wanna come. Otherwise, *Xin fuckin' Loi.*"

They slipped out through a window as RPD light machinegun rounds snapped through the wall. A girl screamed in terror. Behind the villa they stumbled blindly over chunks of cement block to reach the dense shadow of a mango tree.

"Who we got?" Grey barked as he surveyed the corners of the villa.

"All of us," murmured Biloskirka. A slow burst from an M-14 was punctuated by more screams, the pop-pop-pop of AK-47s, and the muffled explosion of a grenade. Grey pointed to a field just across the barbed wire fence.

"See those bushes about two hundred meters down from the ridge line? That's where we meet up. Boris, take the new Trung-oui and Blek and get moving. We'll cover the rear."

St. Cyr took off at a running crouch with Blek and Boris close behind, slowing down only long enough to tear his pants on the barbed wire. Ignoring the pain inflicted on naked feet by sticks, prickers, and rocks, he plunged into the tall grass. Its coarse sawblades cut his bare chest and arms. A few hundred meters into the field, his foot hit a sharp stone.

"Damn." He slowed to a hobble.

"Keep moving," Boris commanded.

He made it another 50 meters. "I can't run," he gritted through the pain. "You and Blek go on. I'll meet you at the rendezvous point."

"No dice, buddy. We'll hold up here and wait for others."

Minutes later, the crashing of brush alerted them to pursuit. As Biloskirka raised his pistol, Cohen and Grey hobbled in.

Grey ordered them down into the chest-high grass and instructed everyone to count their ammunition. He had two rounds, Cohen eleven, and

Biloskirka five. He took a round from Boris and was about to order a continuation of the march when a rash of bursts, muffled explosions, and screams sounded from the Villa.

"Bastards!" hissed Boris, "they are going from room to room killing everybody. Even girls!"

"That means they've taken Pleiku," Grey muttered. "Right under our noses they've come in and taken the city. Must be the regiments that Recon's looking for up at Plei Djereng."

"But it's Tet." said Cohen. "They've broken the truce before, but never like this."

"My ess," cut in Biloskirka, "they did it to us all the time. Christmas 47, Tet 51, end they always promised a truce."

"Enough!" ordered Grey. "We've got to get back and alert everyone. The roads aren't safe, so we'll have to E & E back. If we escape and evade and stick to the trails, we're bound to run into Clyde, and if we hit a checkpoint we'll get it from the Arvins, so cross-country's the only way. Take it slow. Blek, can you get us back to the MIKE Force?"

"Shuah"

"Good. Move out."

Chapter 5

REGTER ROSE EARLY. Following stretching exercises and 20 full minutes on weights, he jogged down past the indigenous mess hall and out the gate. Passing the C Team compound, he turned at the helipads. From inside the MIKE Force compound, various security company troops raised their weapons in salute as he passed at a brisk pace. At the Pleiku Air Base main gate, he cut left towards National Highway 14 and distant Montagnard villages. Approaching the empty highway, he checked at his watch: 06:25. There should have been a string of lambrettas and the occasional Vietnamese army truck by now. It was Tet, but even in the Highlands the Lunar New Year brought more holiday traffic. Vietnamese military dependents and settlers should be coming in to visit relatives and friends. Jogging up onto the roadbed, he felt his senses sharpen.

Five minutes down the highway, a rising sun glinted off the copper shards of spent AK-47 brass. Careful not to visibly change pace, Regter angled left and up across the field. Nearing the helipads, he broke into a sprint. His chest was heaving as he reached the MIKE Force gate. Rahlen Blir's wizened face smiled a welcome from the guard shack. Regter pointed to the sound of distant firing.

"*Pow-fusil?*" he asked.

Blir nodded. "Vietnamee shoot pow-fusil at Tet evayear. Mebbee Vietnam guard shoot pow-karbin but...sound same AK-47." As Regter turned away, Blir called out. "No maid."

"What?"

"Montagnard maid no come. S'pose be here."

Regter paused, acknowledged with a grim nod, and made for the indigenous mess hall. A few Nung cooks were preparing the morning rice. They prevailed upon him to accept a bowl seasoned with chunks of yesterday's pork while they complained about absent comrades.

He pulled up a chair in front of Ney Bloom and Rchom Jimm. Bloom was taking his new duties as battalion interpreter cum commander seriously.

"You come in early?" Regter asked.

"No. Much work. Stay in barracks last night."

"How 'bout you, Jimm?"

"Duty Interpreter. I also stay."

Regter's smile vanished. "I want all companies up and armed immediately, and get me a complete status report of who's in the compound and who's in the village."

He wolfed down the rice with warm tea before stepping out to call for Rahlen Blir. A good guerilla, warned a voice in the back of his mind, always eats when he can. He ordered the old Montagnard to check with the village security detachment. After climbing up on the bunkers for another glance at the national highway, he made for the Teamhouse, where he found Lieutenant Brock.

"Brock, I want every Roundeye up, dressed, armed, and in the Teamhouse in fifteen minutes. Any questions?"

"Nossir."

Back at the interpreter's shack, Blir reported no contact with the MIKE Force village. Regter ordered Bloom to take a platoon from the alert company, make a reconnaissance as far as Pleiku, and report back. He then stepped into his office to call the C Team commander. Major Anderson answered the phone.

"Andy, Charlie Regter here. I need to talk to Cox."

"Ah, the boss is hung up right now. Our counterparts kept us up late last night..."

"I'm not asking for a social report. Put Cox on the phone!"

Anderson didn't care for the edge to Regter's voice. "Charlie, you can pass the message to me."

"I'll pass my own goddam message. Now get him on the phone."

"Yessir," Anderson gulped involuntarily.

A moment later Cox's angry voice came over the wire. "Regter, this had better be important!"

"Important enough. If I'm right, Charlie's in Pleiku. Probably moved in last night…"

"Where the hell did you get that idea?"

Regter launched into a brief description of his morning run. Halfway through, Cox cut him off.

"Goddammit, it's Tet! Things are always this quiet at Tet."

"No disrespect, Colonel, but this is your first time in country."

"Meaning…"

"Meaning I've seen a few Tets, and something about this one's not right."

"All right, Regter! I'll get a helicopter so you can go up and take a look. And I'll gear up my staff, but you'd damned sure better be right!"

"Let's hope I'm not."

Regter found his Roundeyes assembled in the kitchen and pool room just behind Big Marty's. Most were groggy-eyed, but everyone was busy checking web gear and weapons. Despite the hangovers, they had a businesslike air. He nodded to Captain J.E.D. Saville, his Australian S-3 operations officer.

"Jed, what's our status?"

"Grey, Cohen, Biloskirka, Davis, Brown, and the new leftenant are missing. We believe they're downtown."

Regter nodded. Davis and Brown lived in Pleiku with their Vietnamese wives and children, and he'd last seen St. Cyr with Grey's gang.

"All right, listen up." His voice was quiet but earnest. "Something's going on. Maybe it's just Tet, or maybe I'm just paranoid, but every morning for the past two weeks, the traffic's been heavy with people going into Pleiku. Today there's no traffic on the road. Some of our cooks who live in town haven't shown up for work. The maids haven't shown up. There's no commo with the MIKE Force village, and when I went out running this morning, there were fresh AK-47 rounds on the highway. As some of you know, we were predicting a big push for Tet up at CCN. Jed, get 'em ready to move. I'm going over to the C Team and see what they've found out."

Mac had pulled a Jeep up outside and was checking frequencies on the radio when Regter climbed in. As they roared towards the gate, Rahlen Blir popped out, gesturing wildly towards the helipads. Regter turned to see five partially naked figures limping up the road. As Mac dropped him in front of the C Team headquarters, he sent him back to get Grey into uniform and over to the C Team immediately.

Down in the C Team bunker the panic was deafening. Orders were shouted, questioned, remanded, and countermanded as the staff mob fought with and for each other. The S-2 intelligence officer hung in the back, wearing the expression of a man about to be hung. Amid the raucous tumult, his silence was ominous. A senior NCO stood patiently by a mapboard, grease pencil in one hand, the other resting on the butt of a holstered .45. At the sight of Charlie Regter, he nodded a quiet hello. Anderson shot Regter a venomous glare as Cox guided him over to the situation map with a friendly hand on the shoulder.

"You're right, Charlie. Last night the Viet Cong moved into Nha Trang, Qui Nhon, Ban Me Thuot, Kontum, and Phan Thiet. Colonel Khanh tells me something's going on over at Corps headquarters right now. It looks like a major highland offensive..."

"More like country-wide."

"Look, I know you used to be in on the secrets of the gods, but so far it's just us. The VC might have the force for a nationwide offensive, but they're not that stupid. I've ordered everyone on full alert. What's your status?"

"I've got three companies here, one at Kontum, one at Ban Me Thuot, and two attached to the 101st Airborne down at Phan Thiet. I've also had some people down in Pleiku this morning. They'll be over to brief you."

Cox nodded, as if he expected no less. "Three, get that posted. I want a full staff briefing at zero-eight, and make sure you've got the latest situation reports from IFFV and Corps."

Regter felt a pang of sympathy for the C Team S-3. Cox's many tours in the Pentagon were showing. He was gearing his staff up for a network-style news show that would have them gleaning multiple reports from higher headquarters, all to repeat what everyone already knew. The real answers to his questions lay with his own A and B Teams, and whatever he could pull from the Vietnamese. Regter opted to let the lesson pass.

"Sir, you wanted to see me?"

Regter glanced over his shoulder to find Dick Grey.

"Yeah, Dick. Bring the colonel up to date."

Cox motioned them upstairs to his office, where he closed the door.

"All right, Lieutenant. What's going on?"

"Sir, Charlie's taken Pleiku. We were over at Madame Binh's last night, when the Superjew got up to take a crap..."

"Dick, save the juicy details," Regter cut in." Who, what, where, and how many?"

"Yessir. Viet Cong and North Vietnamese army regulars. Near as we can figure, a couple of battalions on the north and west sides of town. Looks like they had guides and help waiting inside the city..."

Cox frowned. "How close did you get?"

Grey held up his thumb and forefinger. "This close, Colonel. We had to shoot our way out. A couple of Fourth Division troopies weren't so lucky. Charlie must have had specific objectives and timetables, because he didn't bother to come after us, and we'd have been an easy kill. Probably figured we'd run into more VC. Just about right, too. Spotted a couple of companies moving down the highway."

"Highway Fourteen?"

"Yessir, two files just as neat as you please on both sides of the tarmac. Watched what looked like an ARVN Jeep pass them by. As soon as they saw the lights, they skipped off the road and you couldn't see a thing. After the Jeep passed, they just up and moved out. We had to crawl through a damned culvert and stayed to the trails. Saw a Jeep headed back that way after we passed, and heard firing. They probably nailed the Jeep on its return. I suspect that they've dug in down at the Highway Nineteen intersection just this side of town. We heard firing from that direction. Also south of town near the Christian Missionary Alliance hospital, and there appears to be a company behind the Arvin POW compound."

"Have they taken it?"

Grey shrugged. "They seemed to be waiting when we passed. I think their general attack was timed to kick off sometime just before dawn. They fired a couple of bursts in our direction, then just let us go."

"You weren't part of their plan."

"Nossir. And they damned sure seemed to have one."

"How about between here and the village?" asked Regter.

"Can't be much. Took a few shots as we came by. Could have been a squad of local VC, or even our own guys. We weren't taking any chances. Stayed pretty much out of sight."

"So would Charlie," Cox observed.

"Not this time, Sir. This time Clyde's in the driver's seat."

Cox pondered this for a minute, then nodded. "You're dismissed, Captain."

As Grey stepped away, Regter caught him. "Dick, tell Jed Saville that I want your company to be the lead element into Pleiku. Be prepared to seize a toehold at the edge of the city just past the Highway Nineteen intersection and develop the situation. Bloom's already out on reconnaissance. I'll fill Jed in on the rest when I get back." As Grey departed, Cox pushed the door closed.

"Who's this Madame Dinh?"

"Binh, Sir. She runs a whorehouse."

"And one of your officers was down there with his men?"

"Colonel, they just got back from four hard weeks in the bush."

Cox shook his head in disbelief. "Regter, I thought we put you in there to straighten that shit out. I want that officer disciplined, and when this is over you and I are going to have a chat."

Back at the MIKE Force, Jed Saville had Ferris's 206th company sweeping below the airbase to link up with the dependent village. Grey's 205th company had just set off for the highway intersection, and Jim Moshlatubbee's 204th company was preparing to move out in their wake. Regter confirmed Saville's actions. Checking radio communications with both the companies and C Team, he queried Cox about artillery.

That would be up to the Vietnamese, according to Cox. Meanwhile, the Vietnamese Rangers up at Corps needed help. Regter had better get ready to reinforce them.

"What?" Saville was incredulous. "Reinforce the ARVN Rangers with our Yards. Isn't Cox aware of their history?"

The Vietnamese Rangers were a contingency force kept in reserve for any MIKE Force uprising. They made no secret of their mission or their contempt for Montagnards. There had been gunfights between the two in the past.

"I don't think he has much of a choice, Jed, but you're right," agreed Regter. "Round up every LLDB in the compound and attach them to Moshlatubbee. Then wait until we get the order. Jed, if you were Charlie and your mission was to take Pleiku, how'd you do it?"

"Well, if I were Charlie," the young Aussie scratched his fawn colored SAS beret into his scalp, "I'd take at least a battalion and seal off the city from the north, east, and south. Two of those intersections are on high ground, so that's to my advantage. Then I'd put a battalion in the very center of town, and order them to dig in and hold at all costs. Using those streets and alleyways as sectors of fire, we'd play hell with anyone who tried to dig us out."

"What about artillery and air?"

"Well, you Yanks have the advantage there. Still, we're better off inside the city than out. More cover. Besides, there's a good chance your Vietnamese puppet allies won't allow you to use either. After all, a lot of people in this city are their dependents. Create a lot of resentment if you Yanks started lobbing shells and dropping bombs every time you drew fire, which may be exactly what they want you to do."

"Good point. How do you view your opposing forces?"

"As NVA commander?"

"That's right."

"Well, there's a regiment officially garrisoned here, but it really amounts to a single battalion of mechanized infantry, plus some cavalry and a few companies of glorified MPs. The Arvins are unlikely to risk an elite mechanized unit in house to house fighting, and they'll leave the cavalry to the roads. That leaves the Fourth U.S. Division. But if this is as big as it appears, the Fourth is going to be tied down all over II Corps. I'd wager you Yanks will concentrate your efforts on Kontum and along Highway Nineteen between An Khe and the Mangyang pass. So that leaves Fourth Infantry Division with a few battalions to defend their base, and the MIKE Force with the nasty task of taking back Pleiku. Now Charlie respects us, but he's sure as hell not afraid of us. Killed too many of us for that... "

"So artillery's the key"

"It is unless you Yanks are willing to take casualties. The MIKE Force will eventually run me out of town, but when you sit back and tally up the bodies, I'll have killed enough Yards to see that you don't have much of a MIKE Force left. The survivors will just pack up and leave. After all, they're raiding and patrol artists, not professional infantry. So, how do I rate as a Viet Cong strategist?"

"Too good, if you ask me. How long've you been in country, Jed?"

"Eight months."

"Only eight months?"

"Right. Well I did do some time in Malaya and Borneo. Didn't have you Yanks as allies then…"

Saville was interrupted by a squawk on the radio. Cox's helicopter was inbound.

At the C Team, Regter joined Cox just as his helicopter touched down. His suggestion that Cox turn the chopper over to the MIKE Force was met with a stony glare. From the looks of the C Team staff, the battle of Pleiku was going to be a purely private affair.

They took fire from near the Arvin POW compound shortly after takeoff, prompting the pilot to throw the Huey into a continuous climb until they leveled out at 6,000 feet. Regter's suggestion that they drop lower to better view enemy dispositions was ignored. Even so, the city was obviously in enemy hands. Activity was visible in the commercial district, and blocking forces were located at all three major highway entrances. Smaller forces were scattered around artillery hill, engineer hill, and the Camp Holloway aviation complex. Cox wanted every MIKE Force company outside of Pleiku returned immediately.

"Yessir, but hadn't we better check with the Fourth Division and First Field Force (IFFV)?"

"Look, Regter," Cox scowled, "until someone tells me otherwise, this is our fight. We don't need American troops to do our fighting for us. They have their hands full right where they are."

As they turned back to the C Team helipad, the pilot motioned for Cox to switch channels. General Rock was inbound and wanted an immediate briefing on all Special Forces units in the Highlands. And as of now,

the 4th Division was responsible for all combat operations in sector. Cox
grumbled that he had been trying to schedule just such a briefing for General Rock for a month and a half, but the general never had time. Now he
wanted to command not only his own division, but Cox's men as well.
Well, maybe it wasn't too late. Cox reported back that he'd just completed
a reconnaissance, and had committed units to the city's relief. Rock was
pleased with the initiative. Should Cox continue his present course of action? Certainly, but effective immediately he was under operational control of the assistant division commander. He could expect to be assigned
the western and southern sectors of the city. Had this been cleared with
IFFV? Rock wanted to know if Cox was questioning his orders. He wasn't.
Did Cox have any other questions? Yessir, what about MIKE Force assets
deployed elsewhere? If he still had any that weren't committed, they were
to be held in place.

They met General Rock at the helipad some ten minutes later, and
ushered him down into the bunker, where radios crackled with messages
from all over II Corps. In Nha Trang, elements from detachment A-502
had been locked in combat with main force VC below the Buddha since
before dawn. The Nha Trang MIKE Force had lost one commander in
street fighting, and had just medevaced his replacement with a sucking
chest wound. At Phan Thiet, elements of the 101st Airborne were fighting
off two VC battalions. Kontum, home to an ARVN infantry brigade was
under heavy attack by numerous NVA and VC battalions, as was Ban Me
Thuot, headquarters for the 23rd ARVN Division.

As the reports poured in, Regter detected a subtle shift of attitude.
The C Team staff was transitioning from a mere dog and pony show pro-
ducer to a true battle staff. It was a change he was pleased to see.

Back at the MIKE Force, Regter found McElroy running the operations center as Saville had gone up in the chopper for a look of his own.
Mac's stutter was noticeably absent as he brought Regter up to date. A few
VC squads had been cleared from around the dependent village, and Ferris
was anxious to assist the Rangers at Corps. Regter nixed that idea, and ordered Ferris to stand by. When he called Cox about the Rangers, Cox ordered the company in. Regter passed the mission to Moshlatubbee. Grey
was meanwhile receiving fire from the POW compound and didn't feel it

could be bypassed. Regter ordered Grey and Ferris to relieve the POW compound as a task force under Jed Saville. He informed Cox, who now wanted to know about the roadblocks. They had a recon platoon in the vicinity, Regter told him, but no reports as of yet. Did Cox have any news on the artillery? A fire support coordination Team was enroute from artillery hill, but no authority to fire had been received.

Regter was reorganizing elements of the Security and Training companies into a provisional unit under their Aussie warrant officer and Rahlen Blir when St. Cyr appeared, all kitted up for combat.

"With your permission, Sir, I'd like to join two-oh-fifth company."

"Lieutenant," Regter shook his head, "the last thing I need right now is an over-ranked rifle carrier. These companies are going to need all the resupply they can get, so get the hell down to the S-4 and start learning your job."

The enormous plank, plywood and zinc sheeted S-4 building stood at the back end of the compound, nestled up against the airbase perimeter in direct line with the axis of the runway. This left about ten feet of space for bomb-laden VNAF marked Skyraiders to clear it. Inside, Lieutenant Brock was supervising a handful of pipe puffing Montagnards cleaning cosmoline from M-60 machineguns in a tub of diesel fuel. The fumes appeared to have little effect as the tribesmen puffed happily away.

"He didn't buy it, did he?" chuckled Brock.

"No," grimaced St. Cyr.

"OK, let me show you around. We'll get our crack at Charlie later."

Up on the loading dock, Brock had one group of Montagnards breaking down ammunition crates, while another loaded magazines and bandoleers. A smaller group of Nungs and Vietnamese loaded these into crates marked 201 through 209. These in turn were stacked into sectioned bays, also numbered, along with boxes of rations and water cans.

Brock pointed to the work gangs. "These are the guys you have to watch. A few companies have M-16 rifles and M-60 machineguns, but most still have M-2 carbines, BARs, and M-1919A6 machineguns. I've arranged for the companies at Phan Thiet to get their ammo and water resupply from the hundred and first. Since they've got 16s and 60s, ammo won't be a problem. I want you to coordinate to send them PIRs, though. They hate C rations..."

"PIRs?"

"Personnel Indigenous Rations. It's a ziplock bag of flavored rice with bits of fish, squid, or beef in it. I'll show you one later. Just make sure they get 'em. Now, red square painted behind the bay numbers means 'old issue weapons' and blue square means 'new issue weapons.' These clowns are supposed to know that, but some of 'em are color blind as well as illiterate. Stay on 'em! If they put the wrong ammo in the wrong lot, you're going to have a whole company lookin' to punch your lights out."

"I know the feeling..."

"Well it might be a feelin' over in the fourth foot, but these company commanders'll do it. Especially Ferris. Send him the wrong ammo, and you'll be lucky to get off with a broken nose..."

St. Cyr glanced at a nearby pen with a cow and pigs in it. "Some kind of civic action project?"

"No, today's chow. Normally it's beef and pig, with chicken and buffalo when the companies first get back from the field. After the medics check 'em out, the cooks butcher 'em. The cow's for a two-oh-fifth company sacrifice."

St. Cyr nodded. Sarawak's Dyak had also practiced animal sacrifice to appease the spirits. Stepping back inside, he nearly stumbled over several long wooden cases as his eyes readjusted to the darkness.

"Mortars," said Brock. "Four-point-two inch and eighty-one millimeter. All A Teams have them for camp defense, but we can't set 'em up because of the flight path. The companies have sixty millimeters, but only a few actually carry 'em. Most add their mortar squad to the recon platoons."

"Got any ammo?"

"All kinds. And since only Ferris's and Saville's companies take mortars to the field, we've got a lot on hand. I've been trying to work a trade with the Air Force combat security folks for an air conditioner, or something else we can use."

"Trade...?"

"Galen. If you're gonna replace me, you've got to learn to do business. It's called 'combat loss.'" Brock led him back to the office and poured them each a cup of coffee.

"What about radios..."

"Shit, I almost forgot. Know how to set up an antenna?"

"Of course. A two-niner-two?"

"Yep."

They were hooking up the radios when Sergeant Blanco rushed in to tell them that Moshlatubbee needed an ammo resupply at Corps. Brock cursed that most of his Vietnamese drivers were off for Tet, and went out to see if any Yards knew how to drive. St. Cyr was monitoring the radio when Brock returned. Saville's provisional battalion was at the roadblock on the northern edge of the city. Grey was receiving heavy small arms fire from his right flank, and occasional mortar rounds, but he wasn't sure he'd located the enemy's forward positions. Twenty minutes later, Ferris had done just that. Saville ordered Grey to move his company around the enemy's flank. Grey wanted artillery, as the ground was too open. Regter asked for specific coordinates. There was a delay while that request was relayed to province headquarters. Ferris meanwhile called on Grey to get his ass moving, he needed that help now. Grey gave an ominous "Wilco, we're on the way."

Brock cursed and mentally braced for the sound of firing. The Vietnamese were dragging their feet, and Brock didn't see why Montagnard lives should be put at risk for Slope civilians. Grey got up on Ferris's flank just as 4th Division helicopter gunships arrived to rake the area. Although the enemy was dug in, they kept their heads down while Ferris and Grey maneuvered against them. Saville reported the first roadblock cleared, and called for an ammo resupply.

St. Cyr rushed out to climb up into the cab. As the engine cranked to life, Brock stepped up on the running board and motioned him to move over.

"Shouldn't you stay back here, Brock?"

"And miss the fun?"

"One of us needs to…"

"Look, Galen, Sergeant Blanco can run this place far better than we can, so move over, or get the fuck out and stay here yourself."

They found Saville's command post in a smoking, newly gutted, stucco shell near the intersection of National Routes 19 and 14 on the northwestern edge of Pleiku. At the sight of Brock, Mac shook his head. He wanted 205th Company resupplied first, and asked Brock who was going to take the load down.

"We are. How bad is it?"

"Well, you can't go down now, b-but after this firefight's over you should be able to get close."

"What about mortars, just eighty-deuce?"

"So far. B-but he ain't used 'em much. Probably waiting for the ammo resupply truck."

"Tell Grey his ammo's on the way."

"Who's g-gonna drive?"

"Who do you think?"

"It ain't g-gonna be you, Brock."

"That's not your call, Mac."

"The hell it ain't!"

"The hell it is, Sergeant!"

For a second, Mac was tempted to let him try, but he wasn't going to let his ammo resupply get caught in the crossfire while Brock grappled with internal demons. Brock had guts, but he couldn't control his reactions under fire."

"My ass! Let the new Trung-oui drive."

"Makes no difference to me, Mac."

The hell it doesn't, thought Mac, as he climbed down from the cab. Brock, who'd frozen on him twice in firefights back at Ben Het, was one of the few officers he respected.

While Brock and St. Cyr waited for the firing to die down, Jed Saville gave them a quick rundown on the situation. They appeared to be up against the H-15 Main Force VC battalion and the 40th Sappers, though NVA regulars had been reported outside the city. Since Victor Charles had far more troops than the MIKE Force, Saville was playing it by ear. Main Force VC were better trained than the average MIKE Force trooper, but the MIKE Force had better firepower. Not the organic weapons they carried, which paled to that carried by Main force VC, but in the air and artillery strikes that could be called down over a radio. Provided they got clearance to use them. That authority was the unknown factor and Charlie was betting that it would be slow in coming. In the meanwhile, he would draw the MIKE Force into a bloody battle in the city's interior where he could cut it to pieces.

Saville would have liked to explain the situation further, if only to clarify it for himself, but as the firing died down another call from Grey demanded ammo. Mac pointed to a clump of bamboo some four hundred meters away and indicated 205th Company's left flank just beyond.

While St. Cyr cranked up the engine, Brock hoisted himself up stiff legged into the passenger's seat.

"You all right, Brock?"

"Yeah. G-goddam, I'm starting to sound l-like Mac."

"I wouldn't worry about it. Been shot at before?"

"Sh-shot at, and h-hit. Twice."

"You want to stay back on this one?"

"Fuck you," growled Brock. "G-get this goddam truck movin'!"

With a crunch of gears, the truck jerked off the gravel road and bumped across a field. St. Cyr pushed the gas pedal to the floor, but the truck bucked along in seeming slow motion as he waited for a stray round to crash through his skull. He could barely hear the firing over the angry whine of the gearbox. Brock kept shouting for him to shift, but the words didn't register. St. Cyr ploughed on, his eyes fastened on that single clump of bamboo. Only when prone figures in tiger stripes jumped up and waived for him to stop did he realize they'd made it.

Boris climbed up on the running board. "Hey, Brock, you guys bring water?"

"You out already?"

"Shit, buddy, when it gets hot, troops get thirsty."

St. Cyr jumped down to unload ammo cases and water cans. Biloskirka joined in with several Yards, while Brock sat in the cab. "Hey Brock! How about a hand?"

"He's OK where he is," grunted Boris.

When the truck was one third unloaded, St. Cyr ordered the Yards to stop. "That's all for now, Boris. I have to leave some for the others. Got enough rockets?"

"Sure. Hey, you guys bringing hot chow?"

"Not unless we're ordered to."

"Hah! See that? Goddam staff weenies don't care nothing 'bout us combat troops! See you heroes later." With an RPD chattering in the near distance, Boris walked off with the air of an NCO out on some peacetime firing range.

Back in the cab, St. Cyr found Brock idly poking his fingers into two bullet holes in the right upper corner of the wind-shield. Small flecks of blood colored his face. He flashed St. Cyr a maniacal grin.

"Good thing we didn't pull up any further..."

St. Cyr shook his head, and eased the gearshift into reverse. This time, he remembered to shift gears.

After resupplying Ferris, they set up an ammo and water resupply point behind the MIKE Force command post. Given the number of bullet holes in their truck, the next resupply would be done using work parties. As St. Cyr stepped in to notify McElroy, he heard Regter on the radio asking Saville to check on the American hospital.

"An American hospital. In Pleiku?" He looked at Mac.

"Yeah, the Christian Missionary Alliance hospital. Nobody's heard from 'em since yesterday. Can't do it now, though. G-gotta rescue the national police. Sorry b-bunch of bastards. Too bad we can't let Charlie finish 'em first. I gotta g-go look at the companies. Wanna come along?"

St. Cyr pulled his M-16 and BAR belted web equipment from the truck cab and told Brock he was going forward. Brock nodded. He had to get back and check on the companies down country, so St. Cyr was in charge of ammo and water resupply until he returned.

St. Cyr and Mac moved to the first company's position at a crouching run. They found Captain Ferris and Y Mlo hunkered down in a cluster of NVA skirmishing trenches dotted with enemy dead. A line of low stucco houses some hundred meters distant occupied their attention. Sporadic fire came from both sides.

"About a platoon of them in there," Ferris explained to Mac, "reinforced with a company heavy machinegun and a shitpot of B-40 rockets. They pulled the other platoons back. I've got most of my company here, with a platoon across the road to the right flank. My guess is they'll counterattack up the road to take advantage of the embankments. When they do, their shit's mine. Got two M-60s sited on it from different angles. Right now they're busy digging. Hear 'em?"

Mac shook his head no.

"Shit!" Ferris gritted his teeth. "Probably down into mother earth by now. The longer we wait, the deeper they get. Where the hell's that artillery?"

"Still waiting on the p-province chief."

"Why not go straight to Corps?"

"We did. C-corps says it's up to province."

"That's bullshit! It's grenades and rockets then. How're we fixed for LAWs?"

"I've got a pile of them back at the CP," St. Cyr chimed in. Ferris looked right through him to Mac.

"Who's the straphanger?"

"Ain't no straphanger. The Trung-oui here's the same g-guy who dropped off your ammo resupply a few minutes ago. G-gonna replace Brock until he gets a company."

"OK, asshole," Ferris's eyes bored into St. Cyr's. "You make goddam sure you keep that pile high. Get him outta here Mac! I need ammo and water more than I need a goddam strap-hanger. And chow. Don't forget the chow."

They dipped down to follow a culvert and stream bed up past Ferris's last platoon to where Grey's company lay behind a small hummock, facing another row of stucco and cinderblock houses. Although the gunships had played havoc with the roofs and walls, Grey was not enthused about a frontal assault across open ground without artillery.

"Can't be helped," Mac said, "on account of you g-gotta cover Ferris's flank. Gunships'll be back on station soon."

"How about mortars?" St. Cyr almost whispered as Mac and Grey discussed casualties.

"60s won't do much good, but it beats nothing."

"I was thinking of 81s."

"We don't have any."

"Yeah we do. A supply shed full of 'em. Also got some four point deuces we could use for illumination tonight."

Mac and Grey fixed him with inspired stares.

"What b-bout ammo?"

"Brock says we've got HE and illumination, but I haven't seen it yet. Can't tell you how much."

"Who'll fire 'em?"

"I will, if I can scrounge up some crews. We actually use those things over in the 'Fourth Foot'."

Mac threw a friendly arm around St. Cyr's shoulder. "Trung-oui, I knew I recruited you for a reason."

While Mac pleaded with Saville to delay the attack, St. Cyr careened back to the compound in a hastily commandeered Jeep. The first person he saw was Sergeant Blanco. It occurred to him that the supply NCO might know who was trained on mortars.

"Hey Blanco...!"

"El Tee, hear tell you lookin' for mortarmen!"

"Yeah, know any?"

"Lots of 'em. Problem is, they be down with the companies. But I used to be heavy weapons, an' so was Berry down at admin. Major Regter done sent me to check with the Yards. I'll get back to you."

Behind the loading dock, Brock was supervising a detail unpacking mortar crates.

"Word travels fast around here," St. Cyr marveled.

"It does when you're the man of the hour."

Berry came over to shake hands and explain that he'd been in heavy weapons for fourteen years before a hearing loss had forced him into admin. He could man the tubes or the fire direction center—FDC—but recommended the latter. St. Cyr had assumed that he would run the FDC himself. But if the gun crews were going to be Yards, they'd need someone who could make himself understood. He agreed. Berry and Blanco would set up the FDC adjacent to the MIKE Force command post.

It took nearly two hours to unpack six mortar tubes, verify the required sights, stakes, and aiming circles, scrounge the radios they needed, and load a motley crew of Nungs and Montagnards into a deuce-and-a-half truck with the mortars and ammunition. With the help of Berry and a Vietnamese LLDB sergeant, St. Cyr soon had his mortars set up at the far side of the C Team. Mac stopped by just long enough to assure himself that everyone knew what they were doing.

The first row of houses had been taken with the help of gunships, which had since left. The MIKE Force was now bogged down at a second row of houses, several hundred feet beyond the first. Charlie had bought time defending the first row to develop the second, and the bodies of MIKE Force dead were stacking up behind Saville's CP. Vietnamese authorities were still silent on the use of artillery, and had prohibited anything but helicopter gunship strikes in the city. It was time to unlimber the mortars.

With Berry providing the gun-target azimuth, fuse, and recommended charge, Saville called for a test shot, which fired over. Minor charge and elevation adjustments placed the next round on target. Saville held fire long enough to allow Charlie to stick his head back up. Then, the mortars cut loose. With flank platoons providing a base of fire, Grey and Blek led their men forward in a mad dash. They reached the houses to find that the mortars had done well. Grenades and short bursts finished the rest. With adrenalin, fear, and excitement pumping in their veins, the assaulting troopers took no chances. Saville wanted prisoners for interrogation, but bursts of fire greeted all enemy wounded and any not obviously dead. Few tried to surrender.

By late mid-afternoon the MIKE Force had a firm toehold on the edge of the city. Ferris had beaten back a counterattack on his left flank with the help of St. Cyr's mortars, and when no further counter-attacks came, Saville alerted Grey that it was time to relieve the national police. Regter showed up at the CP with the welcome news that Moshlatubbee's company had cleared the VC from around Corps headquarters. Except for a few friendly fire incidents, which had killed two Yards and several ARVN Rangers, the operation was a success.

"What about their mechanized infantry?" Saville wanted to know.

"They're holding it in reserve," Regter replied

"Fat lot of good that will do us."

"Like you said, they're not going to risk it in street fighting. Not yet, anyway. The real question is what's Charlie going to do tonight? Any prisoners?"

"Not a one. Any chance they'll bring in fresh NVA tonight? I'd hate to see another few battalions show up."

"They've got the force," Regter eyebrows knit together, "but if we read the tea leaves right, this is a nationwide offensive. Those other battalions are likely somewhere else."

"But so far, it's just II Corps…"

"Not anymore. Something's up in I Corps too, but Cox is convinced that this is a drive to the sea."

"And you think otherwise."

"If they wanted to cut South Vietnam in half, they sure as hell wouldn't do it here. And getting tied down in house to house fighting makes no sense. They've given up all their advantages."

"Let's hope you're right, Major," Saville grimaced. "Once he's finished digging in, he's going to counterattack to draw us in. Now that he knows we're not getting artillery, his best bet is to make us dig him out house by house."

"Who says we're not getting artillery?"

Saville flashed Regter a curious look. "I'd say that our notable lack of gun support speaks for itself…"

"Got those documents translated, Boss," said Regter's intelligence sergeant, stepping in. "Besides H-15 battalion and the Fortieth Sappers, we're up against the Nine-sixty-sixth battalion. They were expecting a popular uprising…"

"Any prisoners yet?"

"Nossir…"

"Get on the companies, Harry. I want prisoners."

Sergeant First Class Perkins mumbled a yessir and ducked back out.

"Nine-sixty-sixth. NVA, aren't they?"

"Yeah. H-15 and the Fortieth are mostly Bahnar VC, so don't expect any prisoners out of that bunch. But Ferris and Grey should be able to get us some NVA."

"Yessir..."

"What's the status of the national police?"

"They're holding out against an estimated company. Bloom's men have them under observation. Two-oh-five Company has the mission."

"Have Grey send Bloom a platoon, two if he thinks he can spare them. I want the police relieved before sundown. You stay here while I go up to take a look."

205th Company was in a sector of old colonial villas reminiscent of Madame Binh's when the order came down. The police compound lay some six hundred meters south. This would be a raid to clear enemy forces from the area. For safety's sake, Grey decided to send Bloom two platoons under Blek and Toller. After several minutes grousing by both at the prospect of relieving the hated 'white mice,' they moved out.

Toller's 'Recces' led the way while Blek followed with Ryan's platoon. Crossing a dirt roadway bordered by a hedge and slight embankment, they surprised a small party of NVA underneath a villa. The NVA fired first, killing one pointmen and creasing Toller's shoulder. Under cover of grenade launchers and a squad firing full automatic, the platoon took the villa in a mad rush. They counted eight NVA dead and as many civilians, an old man with women and children. While the platoon medic hastily bandaged his shoulder, Toller had the bodies searched. They turned out to be a warrant officer and signalmen. A search for signs of field telephones and radios led to a tree lined alleyway behind the villas. Two strands of field telephone wire passed through a hedge. Toller took a quick look down the alleyway and ordered a squad to check it out. Minutes after ghosting past trees, hedge, and walls, the squad leader signaled the all clear.

Heavy firing sounded in the distance as Biloskirka's voice on the radio reported that he was engaged with an estimated platoon. Toller held up to see if there would be any change in mission. When Grey told him to continue, he motioned his men forward. They slipped down a shadowed road-bed, painfully aware that any surprise meant death. Shallow embankments to either side offered little protection, while fences, hedges, and walls impeded effective reaction. Their ears strained for the sounds of shovel scoops, or the thump of ammo cans. But the only sound was distant firing. Jimm ghosted along behind Toller.

As the Aussie reached his point squad, he pulled Jimm in close enough to whisper. "We should be running into Bloom's people. See if you can raise him."

Jimm spoke softly into his HT-1 radio, but all that came back was static.

"All right," whispered Toller, "Tell Blek we're advancing as far as the end of the road. I want him to put squads out to both flanks. If anything goes wrong, we'll come right back through the middle while they provide covering fire. It'll be a 'herringbone,' got it?" Jimm nodded and whispered into the mouthpiece.

Toller crawled forward and motioned his pointmen to follow. He felt like a man tiptoeing into the bedroom of a dangerously irate wife. Behind him, Jimm led the remaining squads. It was strangely quiet, with squalls of distant fire to the south. The far end of the maintenance roadway shone obscenely bright. Each rattle and thump grated into Toller's nerves. Sweat trickled down his neck. His ears sang. The afternoon wind rustled lazily through overhead branches and leaves. Sweat stung the corners of his eyes. His vision swept back and forth, noting every detail; the vein patterns of the leaves, the wood grain of the fences beneath their whitewash, the stitching on the underside of his hat brim. Near what appeared to be a storage shed, he detected something. Sound or shadow, he wasn't sure. Melting down into the earth, he brought up his M-16.

Some 60 feet away, three North Vietnamese privates lounged in the shadow of a mango tree, whispering quietly as they passed around a cigarette. Their AK-47s were stacked casually against the trunk, festooned with web magazine pouches. *All I bloody well need*, Toller cursed. Three NVA fuck-ups who'd snuck off for a smoke break. Looking back at Jimm, he held up three fingers and pointed. Jimm gave an exaggerated shrug. Toller pursed his lips and feigned smoking. Jimm passed the signal on to Blek.

Seconds later, he turned back to Toller and drew a finger across his throat. Toller nodded. Both platoons tensed.

Toller looked back at the Vietnamese; boys of 16 or 17 who months earlier had been planting rice or attending the *lycee* up north. The image of a wrinkled old crone keening bitter tears over a long bare coffin flashed in his mind. He quietly flipped his selector switch to semiautomatic. He motioned to his pointmen that they were not to fire. Laurie Toller had been the Royal Australian Regiment's All-Army Champion with the Self-Loading rifle. Edging forward to a hole in the hedge, he mentally reviewed his shot sequence before welding the stock to his cheek. The M-16 exploded twice in quick succession. The third boy, in a flash of motion, had just reached his AK-47 as Toller laid the peephole square upon his back. The first two slumped back. The third was spinning, his face a grimace, as he pushed the safety down. He winced, and fell, as Toller's rifle barked again. The silence was deafening. Toller caught a flash of movement near the veranda. Both platoons were up and moving. As Toller crashed through the hedge, he peeled off his pack and bound around the house to catch sight of a fourth NVA private tearing through the gate. His lead squad burst in through the back of the house to find a cowering Vietnamese family. Up on the porch, Toller took a bead on the fleeing North Vietnamese, and squeezed the trigger. As the sharp report sent the kid sprawling to earth, the area behind his tumbling body came alive with green clad figures. Toller hit the floor and called for his radio. Jimm leaped out to take cover behind a cement portal and call to Toller.

"Ol' woman insi' say battalion cross street."

Gawd, thought Toller. *Let's hope it's just their CP.* Ragged fire snapped above his head. He made out what looked like the police compound in the distance. A burst of RPD fire smacked into the portal and stitched the facing woodwork. Jimm called for squads around both sides of the house. This was no time for textbook formations. While Blek directed fire, Toller unfolded his map and screamed for mortars. There was a flash of movement to their right.

Blek called for Jimm to get a squad over there. A spotting round dropped somewhere behind a row of small shops and working class houses further down the street. Toller lay eyeball to map sheet and calculated his adjustment.

"Right two zero, drop one."

The next round exploded in an adjacent yard, peppering the porch with bits of stone and spent shrapnel. An RPG rocket slammed into the portico, triggering a child's gut-wrenching scream.

"Gawd. Up point five and fire for effect."

Toller braced involuntarily, knowing only too well that the mortars were manned by an ad hoc crew. A storm of firing broke to their right some two villas over. Ney Bloom came up on Jimm's radio to report that he had surprised several squads sneaking up their flank. Toller flashed Bloom a mental welcome while he surveyed the area before them. The main road turned a sharp left to the villa's front. Across the road was a small side road forming a sharp vee. Some type of enemy CP had been set up in the shop inside the vee. Further down, he could make out the edge of the police compound. That, he decided as the mortars came crashing in, would mark the axis of their attack.

Crashing through the villa's front door, he ordered everyone out the back. His mind snapped quick mental photos. A whimpering old Vietnamese woman clutched a child by its legs. The child stared in wide eyed wonder as Y Bear, the platoon medic, rapidly adjusted the bandages he'd applied to its head and chest. Splinters and stone chips from the B-40 rocket, thought Toller, as he noted a partially used morphine syrette on the floor. Y Bear would answer for that later. There wasn't enough morphine to waste on civilians, and too damned many strikers had come into the house. Toller screamed for his squad leaders to get their men up on line and spread them out as far as possible, his platoon to the right, Blek's to the left. Grabbing his radio operator by the harness, Toller pulled him around to the right of the house where he found Jimm directing an M-79 gunner while rounds slapped into the side of the villa above their heads. It was only then that he realized that the mortar rounds had stopped. Switching to the company frequency, he called for another two salvos and pulled Jimm down under the house.

"Can Bloom see us?" He shouted.

Jimm fired a rapid stream of words into his radio.

"No. But heah fire, know we heah."

"Can he see that CP over at the intersection."

More static, then "He see good."

"Right! Tell Bloom to move up and support our attack. The objective is the back side of the police compound down that street. Once we're in, Bloom's to move up and take our flank. He's to be prepared to sweep around the front of the compound from there. Got that?"

Jimm smiled a friendly "Shuah," but at times like these Toller was painfully aware of the language difference.

"Right. Get word to Blek. We attack on red smoke."

Reaching for a smoke grenade, he suddenly remembered he'd dropped his pack. No time to get it now. He fished into his RTO's rucksack pouches and pulled out a smoke grenade. The mortars fell in a closer pattern, this time behind the shop. Toller wasn't sure of the two salvo point, but popped and threw the smoke when he detected a pause.

Bloody Hell! The damned smoke was green. But everyone was up and rushing while Bloom's platoon let loose with everything they had. They pushed forward in a frenzied mob. Sporadic fire sliced through their left flank. Some fell. Others screamed in pain, fury, or fear. Everyone was firing full automatic, some at fleeting glimpses of men, some into suspect shadows, and some anywhere and everywhere. Grenades from M-79s arced by dangerously close to sail through open windows and doors.

Blek's platoon swarmed up over dead NVA sprawled behind sandbags at the front of the shop. Then they were through. Toller led his men from alleyway to alleyway. He remembered pale Vietnamese faces as they tried to surrender, and the glares of the wounded, some terrified, some stoic, and some enraged when they realized that surrender was not to be. Saville wanted prisoners. Regter demanded prisoners. Toller would have liked a few prisoners. Even Jimm screamed something about prisoners. But this was neither the time nor place. After agonizingly long minutes, the firing trailed off. Toller managed to reestablish some semblance of order over the mob, getting squads and platoons reformed while medics and recovery parties went back to pull the wounded into cover.

Ney Bloom moved up on their flank just in time to beat back a weak counterattack. Toller motioned for his radio handset, and discovered his radio operator missing. Back-tracking to the main road, he found the kid sprawled face down in a pool of blood, a breeze ruffling a shiny black tuft of hair. Two rounds had ripped open the radio. A third had torn through his cervical vertebrae. Toller squatted down to tousle the dead boy's hair, absent-mindedly testing the handset.

"God bless yer, Mate. You were a helluva fine radio."

Ten minutes later, Toller strode cautiously up to the front of the national police compound to inform them that the MIKE Force had cleared the enemy to their front and flanks. The rest was up to them. Having been under siege since dawn, when a corporal stepping away from his post to relieve himself had surprised a squad of VC sappers, the hated "White Mice," were genuinely grateful. Their gratitude would not survive the discovery of dead family and friends in nearby shops and houses. Survival too had its price.

Chapter Six

WORD THAT TOLLER HAD broken through to the national police came as Regter was briefing Cox and Lieutenant Colonel Khanh, the Vietnamese LLDB commander. Khanh sighed with audible relief. Corps and province had made the rescue of the police a litmus test of his skill in handling Americans. On paper, Khanh commanded all Special Forces camps in the Highlands. In fact, the vaunted *Luc Luong Dac Biet* owned little beyond their personal weapons and the right to fly their flag over their camps. The fact that Americans controlled the machinery of war—and had the loyalty of the tribesmen—offended Khanh. As he watched Regter direct the real fighting, it became clear that Cox was nearly as superfluous as himself. What he needed was a Vietnamese MIKE Force commander. Someone courageous, ruthless, and cunning, with a vision of what the Highlanders could do. He remembered one such officer; an arrogant cousin to the Imperial family who had once challenged a superior to a duel.

If Khanh's main concern had been the national police, Regter's was the Christian Missionary Alliance hospital. They hadn't been heard from, and he feared that the staff had been killed or carted off into captivity. An attempt to overfly their compound had been met with 12.7mm machinegun fire. Harry Perkins had even tried dialing them up on the local phone system in hopes the Viet Cong had overlooked it: They hadn't. Regter now demanded permission to infiltrate a company as far as the hospital, which Cox was pleased to approve. Saville passed the mission to Dick Grey.

As night settled over Pleiku, masses of displaced civilians huddled in stark terror as tracer streams and illumination rounds pierced the night. Most remained in the rubble of their homes, but others scampered about in a desperate search for safe haven. Few moved for long. A hundred meters of earth and years of racial hatred separated the two killer bands. In the real battle for Pleiku, there were no innocent civilians.

The MIKE Force had seized a toehold, cleared the westernmost road-block, and thrust in to occupy a few rows of cinderblock structures housing bars, brothels, shops, and families. Civilian casualties mounted as teams of tribesmen shot, blasted, and burned their way from room to room and building to building. The tribesmen normally shunned close quarters combat, but this night was different. The companies were now dug in facing a broad, tree-lined park that an early French resident had bequeathed the town. Across that park, well into the business district, lay an enemy who had been told to hold Pleiku or die.

After seeing Cox and Khanh off, Regter sat down with Jed Saville. The young Aussie had aged considerably in the past eighteen hours. Under the glare of a red-lens flashlight, Saville outlined plans for his two assault companies. Ferris would attack across the park after Moshlatubbee maneuvered around the province high school to hit the enemy on the flank. It was risky, but Moshlatubbee should be able to handle any counterattacks.

Cox had brought welcome news that the 4th Division would provide tanks and gunships at daylight. More importantly, they would have C-47 Spooky gunships all night. Even now, they could hear Spooky circling in the distance, looking to hose down any targets with a mournful spray of lead and steel.

As they discussed their plans, St. Cyr stepped into the CP. Not wishing to interrupt, he hunkered down against a wall. Regter paused anyway.

"Good job today, Galen. How're our mortars doing?"

"That's what I came to see you about, sir. I'm told we can't fire any more High Explosive rounds."

"Colonel Cox's orders," Saville cut in.

"That's what he said," agreed Regter, "The national police say we killed some of their dependents this afternoon."

"Bloody shame, that."

"Frankly, it is, but I'm not sending anybody across that park without mortars. Once we get into the center, we'll see what develops. Until then, Galen, you fire whatever Jed tells you to. I'll take the responsibility."

Laurie Toller had been a reconnaissance man and tracker all his life. New to both the MIKE Force and Australian Army Training Team, he'd spent most of his career as a section commander and platoon sergeant with the Royal Australian Regiment. Intensely proud of his unit, he refused to be intimidated by the exotic qualifications of his SAS and Commando compatriots. And having grown up tough on a West Australian cattle station, his mates knew better than to press any claims of martial superiority in anything but good natured banter. In truth, Toller got along quite well with the SAS and Commando hands. It was certain RAR mates who set his teeth on edge. Those who called Montagnards *Wogs* soon learned that the gregarious former jackeroo had a low flash point when it came to his men.

Those men were sluggish now, but Toller pushed them on. Bloom's scouts had guided the remaining platoons in. They had arrived toting a welcome resupply of ammunition, and at a leader's conference Grey had threshed out his plan to relieve the hospital. Of no minor concern was the fact that a fresh NVA battalion was reported somewhere nearby. Toller and Blek had done at least one company substantial damage, but the rest were unaccounted for. One, perhaps two, would be manning the road-block south of the hospital. With luck, the blocking forces would stay in place. But Grey wasn't counting on luck. Sending Toller's platoon out front as a tripwire, he had the remaining platoons follow behind. If Toller tripped an ambush, Grey would lead the counterattack.

Toller took the same care with his Yards he would have on any RAR platoon assault course. After a brief respite for food and water, he had them clear out their packs in an abandoned house near the police compound. As they stripped down for night combat, each man was left with his harness, a poncho, two canteens of water, a first aid kit, and one ration. Everything else was grenades, ammunition, mines, radio batteries, pyrotechnics, and the occasional flashlight. This mission demanded agility and speed. After the men had removed their slings, been checked for noise, and acknowledged instructions that no one would fire unless he or Rchom Jimm did so first, Toller led them out through a field behind the police compound.

Fifteen minutes later they stumbled upon a shallow creek containing twenty-five to thirty bodies; likely national policemen and their families. Hardly unexpected, it augured ill for the CMA hospital staff. Upstream from the execution site, they followed the streambed for several hundred meters, then cut south on a narrow dirt track before turning east to the outskirts of town. Progress was slow, as Toller took care to slip his squads forward under the covering guns of their comrades. The trailing platoons likewise hampered his speed with constant demands they hold up. But after hours of slipping and crawling undetected through streets and alleyways, they drew in sight of the hospital.

If the past 24 hours had been hard on combatants, they had been terrifying for the Christian Missionary Alliance staff. They had learned of the invasion from a former patient, who had burst in the previous midnight with news that her son had just arrived with a Viet Cong battalion. They had orders to kill all U.S. personnel caught in the city. Yet the Buchanans and their four nurses refused to flee. They were reluctant to accept that the Viet Cong had indeed taken the city. But as that became clear, their mounting sense of panic was allayed by the realization that so many people were willing to risk their lives for them. This reinforced the spiritual certainty that had led them into medical missionary work. To make a run for one of the American bases was to abandon their patients. With God's help, troops imbued in the spirit of Uncle Ho's alleged clemency would see the advantage of sparing a hospital willing to tend to the wounded of both sides.

Despite their prayerful optimism, anxiety seeped in. Treat the wounded of both sides? In a European war, perhaps. But here? There were too many old grudges, and all that stood between them and the Viet Cong was an old Nung guard who doubled as janitor and handyman. He could hardly be expected to keep the wounded from either faction from killing each other off. Ignoring questions that gave painful answers, the hospital staff concentrated on their work. While distant fighting raged, they closed their shutters, did their best to stay out of sight, and made their rounds tending patients.

Their first fright was the roving bands of Viet Cong soldiers who occasionally passed within sight of the main house after daybreak. These took obvious note of the lettering on the compound gate, and one even ducked inside to urinate. In its own way, this minor incident had provoked a sense of relief, proving that the enemy too was human. But in late afternoon, more somber figures stopped by. These had humorless eyes, and cruel knowing smiles stretched across thin lips. Clad in black, they did not carry the kit and AK-47s of the infantry, but submachineguns and notepads into which they carefully scribbled annotations. The staff's second terror was a growing certainty that these human mongoose would return.

Just after midnight, as Reverend Buchanan gathered his staff for prayer, the sky erupted with distant flashes, explosions, and a banshee wail. Faraway streams of molten red fire arced earthwards through the spider web tangle of silkwood branches. Thoughts of Tennessee mountains and Georgia farms were interrupted with fervent prayers to Jesus that he accept the souls of all races and creeds at that minute dying. Only then, did they append to their prayers the hope that the American side emerge victorious, and that if the worst happened, the enemy would spare their patients.

The not so distant battle raged for over an hour. Beneath the eerie yellow glow of parachute flares, the commander of the 40th Sapper battalion launched his companies into interlocking bands of machinegun fire in a desperate attempt to crack the Saigon Puppet Rangers. Their mortars and deadly fires did not surprise him, and neither did the hasty appearance of the flying specter. The B-3 front had grossly miscalculated the resistance potential of their local cadres and now needed time to salvage what they could. So the political cadres were serving his battalion up to the Americans on a platter. If by any chance he survived this fight, he would ensure that some of those same political cadres did not.

As the firing died down, Reverend Buchanan insisted that everyone not on shift get some sleep. Linda volunteered for the first watch. After making her rounds through the wards with the aid of a penlight, she walked out to where the old Nung was standing guard with an even more ancient shotgun.

"*Ni how ma,*" she smiled.

"*Haw ni haw,*" he grinned back.

"*Waugh shr...,*" her voice trailed off. What was the term for 'frightened?' Or was 'concerned' better? She gave up. Having known the old Nung for nearly 18 months, this was the first time she had tried to speak his language.

"Missy speak very good Chinee," he whispered.

"*Haw* tell very many lies..."

The old man's ears caught a slight sound. His grin disappeared as he motioned for silence and peered intently into the darkness. She listened, but heard nothing.

"You go back insi', Missy. Vee Cee come."

Terror surged into her heart as Phantom figures stole across the roadway to take cover behind a low wall. More figures rushed in to join them, while others slithered off to their right. The cock of shotgun hammers made her wince.

"They know we heah, Missy. This time they come fo' shua. Betta you go insi'."

Inside the main building, she rushed frantically through the staff corridor, making every effort to control the volume of her whisper.

"They're here! They're outside!"

Buchanan's head jerked up from the desktop he'd fallen asleep at as Linda stepped past him to stare into the darkness. More figures were moving stealthily toward the adjacent wards.

"There's no way out," she whispered hoarsely.

Mrs. Buchanan placed her hand gently on Linda's shoulder. "Let's pray they spare the patients."

Seconds later, a stone sailed through the night to smack, then clatter down, the tiled roof. Startled, the old Nung spun and fired. The explosion made Linda gasp. She could hear the old man's curses as he drew back into the shadows, blinking rapidly to regain his night vision. Old fool, he berated himself. He had wasted one of two shots! Next time, there'd be a clear target. As if to test him, a second stone smacked into the front of the building and clattered to the steps. The old Nung gripped his shotgun tighter, and waited.

"Pssst!" It came from behind them. "Pssst!"

The staff held their breath. The Nung's ears strained as the muzzle of his shotgun searched the darkness. Old trick, he thought. Make noise in east, strike from west. He would not die a fool. Someone might be behind, but their attack would come from the front.

"Pst. Hey!"

More silence. The reverend cleared his throat. "Yes?" He could barely hear himself.

"Tell the old man to put down the gun!"

"Americans!" cried Linda.

"Cor, I'm Aussie, Miss," Toller corrected. "Who's in there with you?"

"Americans," cheered the reverend. "I'm Doctor Buchanan. My wife and staff are with me."

"They've been worried about you, Doctor. Tell whoever's got the gun to put it down."

"Mr. Haw," Buchanan called softly, "put down the gun. Do you understand? Put down the gun!" Reluctantly, the old Nung lowered the muzzle of his fowling piece, keeping his finger on the trigger. "Who are you?" Buchanan called back.

"Us?" Toller pushed the back door open slowly with the barrel of his M-16, looked carefully around, and stepped in followed by several Yards. "We're the MIKE Force..."

In an instant Buchanan was frantically pumping his hand while the women overwhelmed him with wild hugs and kisses.

"Gawd," grinned Toller. "I don't mind telling you that's the best reception I've had all day!"

Helicopters carrying a company from Kontum touched down just after first light. As it moved to its jump off position, the 4th Division sent in more gunships to join the fray. At Regter's command post, Cox arrived with Khanh in tow to rake him over the coals for his *indiscriminate* use of mortars. The ass-chewing appeared meant to appease the Vietnamese. Though Cox sputtered and fumed mightily, he never uttered the word *relieved*. Regter did his best to appear contrite, but his ears were tuned to the radios. The main attack made it across the park, where it degenerated into an insane butchery around the business district. Room to room, building to building, and block by block, both sides stubbornly clawed, stabbed, and ripped at each other, desperate to close in for the kill while some pant-wetting inner soul screamed in mindless fear. The agonized cries of the gut-shot mixed with those of terrified civilians. Fallen enemy were stitched with point-blank fire, at times to ensure they were dead, at times for the hateful pleasure of seeing their bodies disintegrate into bone and red spray.

Even that never-proven legend, grenade-throwing kids, made their appearance. Fearlessly dashing out of the rubble to toss a grenade, they were just as quickly gunned down. Whether caught up in the emotion or insanity of the moment, or merely imitating an older VC brother, no one knew or cared to ask. It just made life that much shorter for those trying to find a safer hide in the rubble.

Regter kept demanding prisoners. But the few wounded prisoners Harry Perkins had managed to evacuate to the CP hadn't even been interrogated when a wounded Montagnard trooper limped up and riddled them up with BAR fire in full view of the assistant 4th Division commander. When one magazine failed to satisfy, he reloaded another. The general's outraged protest stopped cold when the Yard gunner spun the BAR around to glare into his eyes over its smoking barrel. While the general's aide fidgeted with his M-16, Regter stepped between them and sent the kid back to the medics. The general sputtered and demanded Regter's name and service number, then stomped off to his helicopter in a blue-lipped fury.

By midmorning, heavy smoke hung over the city, obscuring the visibility of gunship pilots. Jed Saville abandoned all attempts to direct his companies' progress by radio. They knew the mission, and their objectives. As far as anything else was concerned, they simply had too much to do. And unlike American units, most of it had to be done by themselves. When the companies did come up on the radio net, it was usually a frantic call for support. Often, they all came up at once in a garble that few could understand.

One of the few intelligible responses was to Regter's demand for prisoners, still needed for interrogation. "Fuck you," came the reply, before someone realized that their handset was keyed. There was a moment of awkward silence, followed by a hasty "Sorry..." and they were off the air.

By 1100 the city center had been cleared and what remained of the enemy withdrew into the southwestern suburbs. Saville had just issued orders sending Ferris and the recently arrived company north, and Moshlatubbee south to link up with Grey, when the long awaited tanks appeared. Though only a three tank section, tanks were tanks. Following an impassioned argument with their commander over how they were to be used, Saville sent one to the northern suburbs and attached the other two to Grey for use against the southern roadblock.

When the tanks arrived in Grey's sector, he and a chubby blond kid tank commander became embroiled in a heated argument. Grey wanted the tanks to lead, while Chubby wanted the MIKE Force out front to screen for rockets. They scuffled over threats of fragging and a court martial, which Biloskirka broke up by pulling Grey aside.

"Buddy, he's right. Here infantry should clear way for tanks."

Grey dabbed at his bleeding lip. "I'll get that sonuvabitch!"

"Forget it. When we took Berlin, people kill each other over same shit. Is not worth it."

Contact was light once they maneuvered away from the hospital. But as they cleared a row of houses, and the first tank moved into the lead, a rocket arced out to explode on its gunshield. Shifting wildly into reverse, it crushed the leg of one MIKE Force trooper and scattered his squad-mates in panic.

As the tank lurched forward, a second rocket arced out to smash into a sponson box. Tool shrapnel felled a second Yard. Scattered fire poured in the rocket's direction, a low cinder block wall, while most troops kept a wary eye on the tank itself.

The second tank pulled past the first, and shredded the wall with a hail of coaxial machinegun and fifty caliber fire. Grey had just pulled the mangled trooper to safety when a third rocket glanced off the hull of the rear tank. It lurched to a stop as Chubby and crew abandoned ship. Once Grey had passed the mangled trooper off to the medics, he shot out to confront Chubby.

"Get the fuck back in there!"

Chubby pointed his M-3 submachinegun at Grey. "Fuck you. You want us back in there, get this area cleared!"

Blek and several nearby Yards drew down on the three tankers still on the deck as a blast from the other tank slammed their ears and bodies. The corner of an adjacent villa wall disappeared in a plume of dust. Fifty caliber rounds smashed baseball sized holes through the flimsy cinderblock.

"Let's go," called Biloskirka. "If these essholes won't fight, screw 'em."

Grey lowered the barrel of his M-16 and moved around to get a better view of the villa. An abbatis was barely visible on the far side where the provincial highway curved out of town. The lead tank traversed its turret, raised its gun, and fired an HE round into it. Chubby hesitated, then stepped around Blek, his face red but pale. As he passed Boris, the big Ukrainian drove his rifle barrel into Chubby's ribs. Chubby dropped to his knees, clutching his stomach, while Boris hovered over him.

"Let's see you use that greasegun, you sonuvabitch! Try it on me!"

Chubby clutched his side and groveled in the dirt.

Boris glanced up at the other crewmen. "You call thet U.S. soldier?"

"Not me," muttered a Black tanker, "I always thought he was yellow." Turning around he climbed up onto the tank and into the commander's cupola. The other crewmen followed into their own hatches.

As firing from the villa died down, Cohen's platoon took it in a rush. Grey moved up to the edge of the shattered wall, with Blek in tow, and glassed the abbatis and nearby hamlet with his binoculars. Two gun-ships circled overhead. Grey called for a recon of the abbatis. The pilots could see no one, but there was movement in the hamlet. Just to be safe, one made a gun pass on the abbatis.

Grey ordered the company forward, instructing Toller to watch their right flank. The tanks moved into the lead. Just past the rear of the villa, more rockets arced out to smash on the turret of the lead tank. As smoke billowed from the hatches, Cohen pushed his people forward, only to run into a hail of automatic fire. While Blek led Ryan's platoon to his support, Chubby's tank lumbered into the lead, traversing its main gun. Another volley of rockets shot out, this time from behind the abbatis. Two hit the deck, one hit the side of the turret. The Black tanker's torso jerked violently up, then disappeared into the cupola. A heavy clank hit the roadway as the driver dropped out through his escape hatch, screaming and writhing in the dirt.

Grey pulled his radio operator into a drainage ditch while a gunship raked the abbatis with rockets. Two Yards ran forward to pull the tank driver to safety. Grey watched to see if anyone else would appear. When no one did, he low-crawled up the ditch. Another rocket slammed into the tank, this time a dud. Stripping off his web equipment, Grey motioned for his radio operator to do the same. Agonizing seconds later, Grey was out of the ditch and up over the tank's rear sprocket wheel. The hot deck burned his hands. Rounds pinged and whined off the turret. Mentally, he cursed his machinegunners for not providing covering fire. The assholes were likely watching him. He rushed the few remaining feet in a crouch, stood up, and wrenched the Black tanker out of the commander's cupola. The warm body was still alive.

"Down here, buddy," Boris called.

Grey passed the tanker down to Boris and a radio operator, mentally braced himself, and disappeared down the cupola and into the turret. Acrid ammonia smoke blinded his eyes and stung his lungs. He banged his knee-cap on the gun breech and his head on an optic sight. Blindly, he groped for the gunner. Nothing. Sticking his head out for a quick breath of fresh air, he realized that the gunner must be on the loader's side. Back inside the turret, he felt blindly around the floor. A hot, mushy wetness inside a jagged crewman's helmet shocked him into expelling his breath. Choking, he dived up through brownish-yellow smoke and slithered out onto the hot deck. His knees unsteady, weakly nauseous, he fought to clear his head while clutching the basket-rail.

Another B-40 rocket minnow-tailed off the forward slope of the hull and glanced up to slam the turret and explode. A rocketeer's dream and a tanker's nightmare, Grey caught the full force of its blast and spalling. As it pitched him off the deck, time stood still. He lay stunned for long painful minutes, fighting to breathe while a burning hot chill raced through his lower body and shot searing flashes up his spine. Dirt kicked up around him. An invisible boot smashed into his stomach. He fought desperately to breathe. Somebody was screaming. *Goddammit, my insides are on fire! Please, God, help!*

Motherfucker, some inner voice cursed quietly under a scream. Huge hands dragged him across the roadway. He looked up into Biloskirka's contorted face. Goddam, Boris, help. He felt a prick, please God, and an-other. The pain was turning fuzzy, but he couldn't breathe. An eternity later, it was getting bearable. Somewhere, he heard the Superjew's voice, then Toller's, then Blek's. Goddam you clowns. Finest goddam soldiers in two and a half armies. He caught some breath, but not enough to breathe. He let it out in short puffs. Please God, please let me breathe. The dark shadow over his face focused. It was Boris. They had rolled him into a poncho and were manhandling him back to the CMA hospital at full speed.

"Boris," he choked hotly, "put me down. I can't feel a goddam thing. I can't breathe. I mean—I can breathe—but it's not breathing."

"Don't talk, buddy," the big Ukrainian's face contorted with grief as dirty tears coursed down his cheeks. "Save your strength. We're almost there. Why you stay up there so goddam long? You gonna be all right. Right, Superjew!"

"Goddam right," swore the Superjew.

Grey felt Cohen's hand close over his own. Two Montagnards pushed open the door to the CMA hospital and helped lift him to a table. Boris's face moved away. Blek's eyes stared down into his own.

"Blek, my brother, *Swas'm lai*, hunh?"

Boris cursed the chubby tanker, swearing to kill him at the first opportunity. Cohen mumbled something in Hebrew. Blek's hand grasped Grey's own as Buchanan cut away at his shirt. Linda frantically swabbed down his arm for an IV.

"Oh God," she moaned, "please show me a vein."

"*M'nam luu*," promised Blek. They'd get drunk again together.

"*M'nam luu*," swore Grey. "Brother, you're in charge now..."

Under a late afternoon highland sun they brought Dick Grey home. Out behind the dispensary, he was laid amid rows of Montagnard bodies. Cox ordered it removed to the Pleiku mortuary with the other Roundeye bodies, but Regter prevailed on him to leave it where it was. Wrapped in a polychromatic Jarai blanket, under a bright highland sky, Dick Grey looked far smaller and more fragile in death than he ever had in life. When Cox went back to pay his respects, he found a young woman keening over the body. She was attractive, bare breasted, with bronze skin, large almond eyes, and long raven hair. And though he took care not to stare, he was discomfited by the hostile manner in which she greeted his intrusion.

Removing his beret, Cox bowed his head in silent prayer before carefully retreating back to Regter's office.

"You were right," he confessed to Regter. "It's important that they see that we fight and die with them. We can always send the body to the mortuary later. Who's the girl?"

"Her name's Rahlen H'nek."

"Was she his lover?"

Regter glared up into Cox's eyes. There was something in the way Cox phrased it that offended him.

"His interpreter's sister. They were friends..."

"Just friends?"

"I never asked any more than that, Colonel. It wasn't my goddam business."

Chapter Seven

VIETNAMESE MECHANIZED FORCES caught the withdrawing enemy on a low grassy hill east of the city. What .50 and .30 calibers didn't rip to shreds, steel tracks mashed into pea green and blue/black uniformed roadkill. While vultures cartwheeled in a porcelain blue sky, U.S. headlines screamed of battles in Saigon and Hue. Pleiku, ever remote, had been eclipsed by the Tet offensive.

The city's post-combat reaction was cautious shock. Survivors pushed up from the rubble whimpering and wailing. Squatting wretchedly in the remains of their homes, they showed the presence of mind not to wander too far. Rumors abounded of Viet Cong squads lying in wait for the unwary, and MIKE Force troopers strolled by with their weapons at the ready. Not even children, as the battle had shown, were above suspicion.

Slowly, the Vietnamese army appeared on the streets, followed by the white-shirted visor-capped national police. Only then did Pleiku's occupation residents really stir. The sound of hammers, saws, and trowels soon rose above the cries of ambulatory vendors, punctuated by the beat of drums and clackers, as convoys of white-clad mourners wound their way through rubble-strewn streets. Joss sticks and gilt frames were in record demand.

The losers required less ceremony. Gathered up by gauze-masked sanitation workers, they were carted off to an enormous ditch outside the city and dumped in piled rows. After gasoline mixed with soap and diesel fuel had reduced these to smaller piles, bulldozers on loan from engineer hill finished the task.

Highland burials were more complicated affairs. St. Cyr had no sooner put his crews to cleaning and repacking the mortars when he got caught up in the logistics of returning MIKE Force dead to their villages. Custom demanded that a man be buried in the village of his birth, and coordination had to be made for a casket, tomb decorations, and burial poles. Also, settlements had to be paid to widows and clans, with funds carefully allotted for the requisite ceremonies. Much of this could be coordinated through the B Teams and A Camps, but some cases required direct MIKE Force involvement.

On the morning after Dick Grey went home, St. Cyr received a call from Regter.

"Galen, how do you feel about being the only American on a short mission?"

"I can handle it if the Indig are Jarai or Rhade, or speak French."

"These are Sedang, but you'll be going up with Ney Bloom. The normal rule is two Roundeyes, but we're shorthanded."

"No problem, sir. Ney Bloom will do fine."

The four dead were from Moshlatubbee's company. Since helicopters were in high demand for combat operations, they air hitch-hiked the bodies as far as the Mang Buk Special Forces camp, where the pilot set them down with the friendly advice that they were now on their own. A harried young captain commanding Mang Buk agreed to lend them a camp strike force platoon. When the local village refused to provide porters, he provided those as well. He then saw them off with the friendly advice that if they got hit on the way up or back, he'd call for choppers to lift in a reaction force. But if the 4th Division had anything going on at the time, well, they could figure that out for themselves. Anyway, it was clear trail all the way, and things had been quiet these past few weeks.

By late next afternoon, St. Cyr and Ney Bloom were seated in the cathedral shadows of a Sedang *H'ngay Rong* communal house. Distant chopping signaled four wooden coffins taking shape. While Bloom and St. Cyr conferred, the patrol guarded the bodies outside the village gate.

"Why do they not allow the bodies in?" St. Cyr wondered. "Is it this Hong Klang?"

"No," Bloom shook his head. This new lieutenant was a rapid learner, his Rhade was almost understandable. "Spirits are excuse. They fear to be seen with we ourselves."

"Why, do they favor the VC?"

"No, they hate VC as we do, but they fear them. Once these Sedang were great warriors, raiding Bahnar, Halang, Rengao, and even the Jarai. Some were French allies in the war against Viet Minh. Now, they would rather be slaves. You can be sure that there are Viet Cong nearby. Maybe not soldiers, but soldier's eyes."

"Then we should not stay?"

Bloom rolled his own eyes. "I see no choice. Unless we can get an up-away from Mang Buk, we cannot leave until tomorrow. Word has already spread of our presence. Did you notice the floor?"

St. Cyr glanced down at the split bamboo logs overlapping each other like Spanish tile.

"In Malaysia, the bamboo was split into smaller strips. You could see light between the spaces."

"So it is with Ede houses. But the Sedang must make it difficult for their enemies to locate their sleeping place at night, or someone might thrust up a sword. They have much of that in their history. Some tribes call nights without moon *Nights of the Sedang*."

"As Viet Nam people spoke of *Nights of the Jarai*?"

"Yes." Bloom laughed. "But do not say that around the Jarai. It makes their heads swell. Tomorrow, maybe day after, we depart with first daylight. Tonight we must rely upon guardian spirit of this house."

"Guardian spirit?"

"Yes. In days before the French, the Sedang gave their houses a guardian spirit. A great feast was held, at which they would drink much rice wine. Even the slaves. Then the tallest and strongest slave would be allowed to have his way with their women, while they offered him even more wine and the very best foods. Then, when everyone had had their fill, they would seize that slave, bind him, and push him down into a piling-hole. The men would then raise the first piling with ropes and poles, and drop it in on top of the slave. Thus he became its guardian spirit."

"But," wondered St. Cyr, "wouldn't the slave's spirit want revenge?"

"Not if the women and wine had done their work well," Bloom winked. He was about to explain that the Sedang were Dega of a different race when the village chief called that the coffins were ready.

They stepped down from the longhouse to follow him out behind a group of family dwellings where a small group of bare-chested men stood around four crude log coffins. Burial poles carved in the likeness of kepied soldiers lay scattered about. The word *MIfors* was carved on each pole.

"These have yet to be finished," said Bloom.

"Tomorrow, we will do so," said the headman. "Pay now and go."

"When the poles are finished and my brothers are in their tombs will we pay. If not tomorrow, we wait." Bloom's tone was sharp. With the Sedang you either bullied, or were bullied in turn.

"Best you not wait," the village chief returned Bloom's stare.

"Wait we will."

"Ede, best we go to my own longhouse and talk."

"Then take us there."

"Without this Meerika." He cast a contemptuous glance at St. Cyr.

"Without this Meerika, Sedang, I do not enter your home."

"Then the communal longhouse."

"We have seen your communal house. It is empty and cold. No one brings the guest a jar of wine or pipe. Have the Sedang forgotten Dega ways?"

"There will be wine."

"Good wine?"

"Aged and buried with greatest care: Two, maybe three moons in ground."

"Then show us your communal house again."

They reentered the longhouse. While the village chief made arrangements for the wine, Bloom hung close to the entrance listening to animated snippets of conversation from a nearby house. St. Cyr didn't need to understand Sedang to recognize the hostile tone. He was not reassured when Bloom leaned over to check that there was a round chambered in his carbine.

"What's going on?"

"Nothing. Put my pistol under your belt where you can reach it."

"Nothing?" St. Cyr mentally calculated the time it would take to reach his M-16, stacked casually back against the wall.

"Really. But best to be prepared."

The village chief stepped in as St. Cyr was adjusting his .45 to a more accessible position. The old man's eyes searched his own. He paused, then motioned for his wife to set a large ceramic wine jar before their guests.

"Your pardon, but I have been *Klang Pley* for only some short time," he explained, meaning his time as headman.

"Even a new Klang Pley must know how to welcome guests."

"We welcome guests. Even those forced upon us."

"If we have done so," Bloom scowled, "fear not. We will depart when our arrangements are complete."

The Klang Pley leaned in closer to Bloom. "I refer to other guests. It would be best for every person here if you leave now."

"We have brothers to bury."

"Brothers? One my own sister's son. My flesh and bone! They will be buried as befit Sedang warriors tomorrow on four-night-after, as custom demands. Do not forget, Ede, that you are in the Sedang nation."

"Given the courtesy you have shown us, I question that the Sedang still have a nation. Now what of this wine?"

The Sedang took the first pull on the straw before passing it to St. Cyr. Rather than some tribal protocol, he was showing Bloom that it wasn't poisoned. St. Cyr glanced at Bloom, who nodded. Unsure, he took a few pulls and passed the straw to Bloom.

"Hear me!" The village chief half-whispered in rapid-fire Sedang. "You must leave now. We know who you are. You are Bloom the soldier. See, even here we hear your name. But Bloom the soldier is no longer safe here. You are from the Front. The Front is no longer safe here. You are with MIfors! The MIfors is not safe here. As Klang Pley I cannot guarantee your safety. And you well know what will happen should any harm befall you. Please. I ask you as one who was himself once a soldier. Go. Take your chances in the forest."

Bloom stared into the headman's pleading eyes. For an instant, he imagined a once familiar Ede face, and though he tried to brush it away, it hung in his subconscious.

"If everything finished day after tomorrow, we leave."

But even as Bloom said it, he knew that he would order his men out at first light, no matter what the status of the coffins. He had heard enough to know that the living must take priority over the dead, even if the dead were comrades. Besides, chided an inner voice, they were not Ede. They were Dega, he rebuked the voice, as are we all.

With the wine ceremony ended, Bloom called in the platoon over the headman's objections. To avoid incidents with local belles, he forbade them from wandering about the village and put them to work scraping out fighting positions under the communal house.

Back with St. Cyr, he explained that the Sedang were a race related to the Khmer, while the Rhade and Jarai were related to the Cham and Malay.

"So, were the Cambodians Dega?" St. Cyr asked.

"Some," Bloom explained. Many Stieng, Koho, M'nong, Rhade, Jarai, and Sedang inhabited eastern Cambodia, where they were called *Khmer Loeu*, but lowland Khmer were not Dega.

"And the Vietnamese? St Cyr wondered.

"No," Bloom laughed and shook his head. "Perhaps long ago, before the people that became the *Kinh* had split from their *Muong* roots. But today's Vietnamese were Tiep-zap, just as Dega were human beings."

"What is a Tiep-zap?"

Bloom chuckled. Tiep-zap was a play on words. A combination of unmentionable words that sounded like the Vietnamese word for tank. It was their way of speaking ill of the Vietnamese when they were present.

Just before dark, Bloom led a small patrol on rounds through the village. He returned as the matriarch was laying out their sleeping mats. She took pains to ensure that St. Cyr's was the more comfortable. After she had gone, St. Cyr unrolled his poncho liner, inflated his sleeping mat, and began to settle in.

"Not yet," Bloom whispered. "After everyone is sleeping, we will go below to sleep on ground."

"You're right," St. Cyr grinned self-consciously. "The VC tend to shoot high at night."

"Yes, better they think we are up here. But also this platoon is not our own. Many among them are Sedang. They owe us no loyalty. If we are down among them, they must fight for their own lives, and we can shoot any who try to desert."

"All right, but we take turns on watch."

Bloom nodded in agreement, though he had expected no less. An hour later, they slipped quietly under the house. St. Cyr brought only his groundsheet and poncho liner, but Bloom had a complete sleeping bag. When he was satisfied that everything was quiet, he unrolled it. Already the Highland chill was seeping through his pores. *You are Bloom the soldier,* came a whisper. *Bloom the soldier...*

Bloom shivered. Above or below, this longhouse indeed had a spirit. Pah, he told the spirit, it is not my fault. I wanted to be Bloom the healer. You made me Bloom the soldier.

"Get some sleep," St. Cyr interrupted the voices, "I'll wake you after midnight."

Bloom wrapped himself in his sleeping bag and leaned back against a piling. The last thing he wanted now was sleep, But it was cold, and Bloom the soldier advised that sleep was best. Staring down at his form in the bag, he could not help but think of the bags in which the Meerika wrapped bodies. Shaking off the thought, he listened to village sounds: Sliding doors, a cough, the creak of a longhouse floor, even the distant spirit sounds sounded normal. He recalled another village. "Father's-uncle," he murmured half-sleep, "it was my duty."

St. Cyr tried to fathom the words as Bloom tossed and turned. He caught snippets, but the language and voices confused him. He shrugged it off as combat stress. After all, no one had slept more than a few hours over the past week. A week! He'd been in the MIKE Force barely a week, and already it seemed like years. But sitting under that house surrounded by people whose language he could not understand, he felt at home. He was no longer wandering around lost in Indian country. He had become an Indian.

He had little difficulty staying awake. He strolled out to check on listening posts, brewed up a cup of C ration coffee using a pinch of C-4, and drug three late night chatterers out on another round through the village. They returned just after midnight. He shook Bloom awake and crashed himself. Despite a sleeping shirt and poncho liner, he was cold. The next thing he heard was the sound of chopping. As he sat up in the foggy dawn to carefully scrape grit from the corners of his eyes, Bloom handed him a canteen cup of coffee.

"How are we doing?" St. Cyr asked.

"Very well. I have already conducted stand-to. The Klang Pley's disposition has not changed. In front of his people he is all bluster and strut, but alone he becomes reasonable. He advises that we leave by the elephant trail as soon as possible."

"Is everything ready for the funerals?"

"No. Tonight at earliest, tomorrow more likely. Better we leave now. With your permission, I will pay this Klang Pley."

"I thought we weren't leaving until everything was ready?"

"For us, everything is. Those who waited for us last night have gone, while those who believe that we shall leave after the funerals are resting. Now is the time."

St. Cyr nodded in agreement, and Bloom gave the order to pack up. Trooping out of the village they stopped long enough to run up a long antenna between two trees and alert Mang Buk that they were headed back. That done, they slipped into the forest and avoided the Elephant trail.

Chapter Eight

"HEY BROCK, WHAT HAPPENED to my desk?"

"You don't need a desk," Brock glared up from his latest company status reports. "It's down at the CIDG hospital. Make sure you've got all your field gear. I'm not laying on a goddam resupply run just because you forgot some shit."

"Hey, what's the problem?" St. Cyr asked, perplexed.

"No problem. I've been in this MIKE Force almost a year. Shit, you've been here what, two weeks, and you're getting a company?"

"What company?"

"It's not official yet, but Major Regter wants to see you when he gets back from Nha Trang. That's all anyone's supposed to know." Brock held out his hand. "Nothing personal, Galen, but when you get greased, two-oh-five company's mine. Ever seen a CAR-15?"

"What's that?"

"The carbine version of the M-16. I picked up a few conversion kits down in Nha Trang. If you're going to be runnin' through the jungle with a handset stuck in your ear, you're gonna want one."

Regter didn't get back until late that evening. Being in a sour mood, he passed up the old Nung cook's attempt at dinner, steered clear of Big Marty's, and was pumping weights in his room when a knock sounded on the door.

"It's open!"

St. Cyr's head poked through. "You wanted to see me, sir?"

"That was this morning," Regter sounded irritated. "How was Mang Buk?"

"Not good. Bloom thinks the Viet Cong have taken control of everything outside the camp. They damned sure had the villagers spooked where we were."

"That's the nature of the war. Control of the population equals control of terrain. Make sure you debrief Sergeant Perkins over at the S-Two shop before you leave."

"Yessir, where to?"

"Ban Me Thuot. There's a chopper going down in the morning. From there you'll catch another headed for the Upper Donnai. Ever heard of it?"

"No."

"It's a rough piece of terrain on the edge of Lam Dong province. Captain Saville's trying to get a fix on the NVA battalions that hit Phan Thiet at Tet. This is his first operation as a battalion, and he needs a competent operations officer."

"Operations...oh."

Regter fought back a smile. "Sergeant McElroy's handling that right now. You're there to run Dick Grey's old gang."

"Two-oh-fifth Company?" St. Cyr's eyes flashed from jubilant to pensive.

"That's right. Can I give you some advice?"

"Yessir."

"For what it's worth, don't try to run the company like Grey did. Dick was a commo man with four years in Special Forces and two tours in country before they ever made him an officer. Back in the First Group, he and Cohen and Ryan served in the same B Team. He could treat them like teammates, and still be their boss. Don't you try it. We're a lot more informal here than the conventional army, especially down in the companies, but this isn't an A Team. Some people forget that, and every time they do we have problems. As for the Montagnards, remember what you learned about guerrillas. You can give orders, but they won't always be obeyed. If they come to trust your judgment, they'll follow you anywhere, as long as they think it's in their interest to do so. But if you lose that trust, it's all over. In a U.S. division, as long as your commander backs you up, it makes little difference what the troops think. The worst they can do is frag you, and even then the system can send whoever did it away for a long time."

Regter paused.

"Here it's a little different. They might drive on, and just fail to show up for the next operation. Or you might just wake up some morning and find you and your Roundeyes all alone. Or your radio operator might spot that booby trap, and drop back to see if you can spot it, too. And if you've really pissed them off, someone might just take the shortcut and drop a grenade next to you. It's happened before, and not just in this war. I saw it in Korea, and some of the old World War Two Burma hands told me similar stories. It's an occupational hazard, because here you're not a commander in any conventional sense. You give them the guns and ammunition. You work out the concept of operations, lay on the helicopters, and talk strange gibberish into the radio. And when the shit hits the fan, you're the one who tells them how, when, and where to fight. And you're the man who pays them. You can fine them, and you can fire them, but that's the only real power you have. Because the man who really controls that company is some unnamed FULRO agent down in the ranks. He's their real commander, so be warned: He's got his own war, and his own agenda, and you're going to be in his way. It's a tough job, and frankly, I would have preferred you had more experience. But Dick Grey left a large void, and Toller and Biloskirka are at loggerheads over who should run the company. They're both good men. In fact, when you and I were enlisted, neither one of us would have made a pimple on their asses. But if I put one in charge, the other will feel slighted. So it's your company now."

"To win friends and influence people," said St. Cyr.

"Exactly. And if need be, grab them by the balls so their hearts and minds follow. Just make sure that if you do, they come out of it thinking it was their idea. Any questions?"

"Nossir."

"Then, if you'll excuse me, I've got work to do. Good night, Galen, and Good Luck."

As St. Cyr closed the door, Regter returned to his weights with savage intensity. He had arrived in Nha Trang that morning for the weekly briefing at First Field Force known as IFFV, the senior American headquarters for the Central Highlands. Green's cryptic call for his attendance had not prepared him for the sight of the new deputy ARVN Corps Commander for Minority affairs, Colonel Pham Van Phu, or the youthful looking major he had in tow.

Green had climbed down from a chopper with the Vietnamese as Regter waited on the helipad. Even before he turned his face from the rotorwash, Regter had recognized a pair of French pattern paratroop fatigues. As everyone filed into First Field Force headquarters, the major turned and said, "Com Mang Do, Captain Regter. You remember me, no?"

"Lieutenant Ton, isn't it?"

Regter's impolite use of the family name was deliberate.

"It is Ngoc, *Major* Ngoc. No matter. We'll have time to get reacquainted."

Regter was about to ask Green what that meant when the room was called to attention.

If thoughts of old Nha Trang evoked fond memories, the sight of former Lieutenant Ton That Ngoc did not. In 1957, Regter's team had arrived in Vietnam with a well-rehearsed plan. As they saw it, the problem with the Vietnamese Com Mang Do (commando) course was its reliance upon French methods gleaned from their World War II SAS service. Even there, something seemed lost in transition. Instead of focusing on patrolling, as in the American ranger course, the Vietnamese version turned on a series of masochistic exercises whose sole purpose appeared to be to drive out or injure as many as possible. The American course lasted nine weeks. Its Vietnamese equivalent ran twelve. The first weeks were at the apparent whim of the instructors without any fixed training schedule. Three days of calisthenics and hand-to-hand combat were followed by three days in the bush. An entire day on the obstacle course was capped with a night jump by small teams into unprepared drop zones with orders to infiltrate back to camp. After one student had been killed, and several injured, Regter refused to let Americans accompany the Vietnamese on blind night drops. Ngoc was arrogantly disdainful. It was a commando's job, he informed Regter, to accept all risks, even in training.

The matter was kicked up to Captain Green, who backed Regter. But when the course moved out of Nha Trang and up to the mountain camp on Grand summit, Green stayed behind. Ngoc now gloried in his role as the mountain camp commander. His Vietnamese uniforms disappeared, replaced by French paratroop dress complete with the winged sword of St.

Michael on his beret. A Buddhist from Hue, and a member of the Ton That branch of the royal family, Ngoc had turned down appointment to the ARVN Military academy to enlist in the 3rd Colonial Paracommando Battalion's Indochinese Paratroop Company in 1950. His education and a fearless talent won him a place in the battalion's NCO student platoon, but his time with the 3rd BCCP was short-lived. A mine near Sam Neua, Laos, sent him to hospital, where he was recuperating when the battalion was annihilated at That Khe. Assigned to the Airborne Base Company in Hanoi, he ended up in De Lattre's commando formations. Eighteen months leading former Viet Minh on ambushes and raids in the Tonkin Delta earned him a return to parachute duty with the 6th Colonial Paratroops. Seriously wounded after the Tu Le combat jump, he missed the Langson raid, but rejoined the battalion for the early stages of Dien Bien Phu, only to be hospitalized for a combination of wounds and severe malaria. Assigned to the reconstituted 2nd Foreign Legion Paratroop Battalion after Dien Bien Phu, Ngoc left French service in protest after the division of Vietnam, and volunteered for the ARVN. An uncle on the General Staff had him sent to France's prestigious St. Cyr military academy, where in recognition of his French service he was placed in the advanced class, receiving his lieutenant's commission in the ARVN a year later.

Ngoc had greeted Regter's mobile training team with public contempt. There was little, he said openly, that the Americans could teach them. Regter was patient, but without Green it was hard to keep Ngoc under control. The open break came up on the peaks when Ngoc dragged out the school's mildewed ropes for rappelling. Regter called a halt to the training. Ngoc stormed up and demanded to know why. Regter showed him the damaged ropes. Too dangerous, he said. Ngoc shrugged. This was not the United States Army, and Vietnam was a poor country. These ropes would do.

Not for his training course, Regter replied.

It was not Regter's course, Ngoc exploded. It was a Vietnamese course for Vietnamese soldiers which the Americans were monitoring. Ngoc walked over to the edge of the precipice. If Americans were so timid, why had they bothered to come?

Now it was Regter's turn to explode. He had men on his team who had fought in World War II and Korea. Men far older than Ngoc who had seen other men die needlessly.

Older in years, Ngoc sneered, did not mean older in experience. Besides, it was a soldier's job to take risks, and what separated the Com Mang Do from the common draftee was his willingness to do so. Perhaps the American Ranger course was for pimps who strutted about the officers mess impressing girls. With that, Ngoc tied a quick Swiss seat, snapped himself onto a rope, and went over the side. Well, he called up from 70 feet below. Where the hell were their American monitors?

Sergeant Mansfield stepped up to the rope. He was, he noted to Regter, the lightest man on the team. Regter nodded, but his inner voice was screaming even as Mansfield went over the edge. The rope broke just over half way down. Sergeant First Class Stan Mansfield, a veteran of two wars, was evacuated to a hospital in Hawaii and went home an invalid.

Ngoc shrugged it off. At least there was one real Ranger in the American army. Besides, Mansfield would get a pension. At best, Vietnam's crippled veterans could only hope for a clean street to beg on.

Regter's anger with Ngoc was only slightly greater than his anger with Pappy Green. Green had chewed him out for allowing Mansfield on the rope in the first place, but insisted that Ngoc had been right. It was a Vietnamese course. The Americans had no right to intervene. Besides, Ngoc probably did have more combat experience than the whole team put together. It was only when Regter had demanded to send a priority message back to the group commander that Green had let him in on the full implications of their training.

"Charlie," he asked. "Doesn't it strike you as odd that we're over here running a ranger course for something called the First Observation Group?"

"Not really. It seems to be their way of saying long range reconnaissance," Regter shrugged.

"You mean like our LRRPs?"

"Yeah."

"That's what I thought. But do you remember our pre-mission training, when I talked about the difference between North, Central, and South

Vietnamese? Nearly every man in this so-called observation group is North Vietnamese. Now, most Vietnamese army units are regionally based, but this is supposed to be a national organization. And it just so happens that I met their commander, Major Dinh Ngo, when he was a captain in the French G.C.M.A. And the term I keep hearing them use among themselves, besides *Com Mang Do*, which is officially proscribed in today's Vietnamese army, is *mat kho*, or *maquis*. And when the assholes slip into French, they talk about interior commandos, exterior commandos, and special contact missions. They're not here to learn American ranger methods, Charlie. They're here to select men for secret missions in North Vietnam. And what we're seeing is the weeding out process. They're separating the faint hearted from the true hard core."

"Maybe. But I don't have to put Americans through those same risks, especially when their equipment doesn't meet our safety standards. We're not at war."

"Legally, neither are they. But how the hell do we not take the same risks and keep their respect? And as for a war, don't fool yourself. There's a war on, all right. It's just quiet now. Charlie, they lied to us in Hawaii, and those Embassy assholes lied to us in Saigon. The truth is, if we get anyone killed in training, if we get anyone killed in combat, they're just going to shrug it off as the cost of doing business."

"I still want a report on this to go out."

"I'll send the report, Charlie, but it's going to be the standard serious incident report. And you're going to write it for me. And for Mansfield's sake, it had better look like that rope break was a complete surprise. Otherwise, some asshole in the Pentagon will deny his pension."

"Then you'll have to sign it..."

"No! You'll sign it, junior Captain, and I'll endorse it. And that's an order."

"Pappy, with all due respect, I will not sign any report to that effect."

"Charlie, you're a friend. But for Mansfield's sake, you're fired."

Regter had been replaced by a Chinese-speaking West Pointer. Reporting in to Okinawa, he whiled his time away shuffling papers in the headquarters. Then word came that his replacement had been killed. The rumor mill said it was a Viet Cong ambush, but the official report deemed it a training accident involving an unstable coast artillery propellant called melanite.

While Regter wrestled with the ghosts of Nha Trang past, Colonel Phu was introduced to the IFFV staff and given the floor. He made the obligatory remarks of appreciation for U.S. military assistance, then launched into a drawn-out discussion on how the Vietnamese armed forces were going to "pass to the offensive" in the wake of Tet. No small part of his plan hinged upon an increased use of Vietnamese Special Forces to replace their American counterparts. Lieutenant Colonel Khanh nodded vigorously. The Americans, Phu noted, were expanding the MIKE Forces. The LLDB would be partners in that expansion. Proof of their intent was the selection of Major Ton That Ngoc as the first Vietnamese MIKE Force commander.

Regter sat bolt upright. Pappy Green shot him a nothing-I-could-do-about-it shrug. *At the least*, thought Regter, *you could have given me a goddam courtesy warning.* Ngoc got to his feet, made a brief reference to Dong Khe, Dong Trieu, the Bamboo canal, the Day river, Laos, and Dien Bien Phu, before moving on to his recent company command in Project Delta's 91st Airborne Rangers. The Vietnamese were impressed. The Americans began to doze off. Ngoc concluded by stating that he had never considered the Montagnards savages, and had worked intimately with Major Regter before. He welcomed his assignment with great anticipation.

Green broke away from Phu's party as they headed for his chopper. "Charlie, I know what you're thinking, but they pulled this on us just yesterday!"

"Come off it, Pappy. That goddam briefing of theirs wasn't put together in one afternoon."

"No, but they didn't drop it on us until yesterday morning. Colonel Ladd's still recovering from the shock. I think they were waiting for the new Group commander, but Tet pushed them ahead."

"Then it's cosmetic, for public consumption?"

"I'd be lying if I said that. You know Ngoc as well as I do. He intends to close this war out as a general, and he sees an expanded MIKE Force as a step in that direction. I think he dreamed this up to get around the fact that he can't get a command in the regular Vietnamese airborne. The northern clique considers him too pro-French."

"He hates the French. It's their army he worships. What was that he said about a Ranger Brigade?"

"Rescue Rangers, Charlie. As we phase out the camp strike forces, they'll be converted into ARVN Rangers."

"Pappy, you know a whole lot more Vietnamese than I do, so you damned well know the difference between a *Biet Doan Quan* ranger and a *Biet Kich Quan* special attack force. I don't know what the hell a *Tiep Ung* is, but the Yards will recognize that as 'you take the risks and casualties, and we'll take the credit.' They won't buy it. The Yards'll walk off."

"Then it's your job to see that they don't. Besides, we'll both be out of here by then."

"Not if they pull another one like this."

"Then it's still your job to see that the Yards stay."

"Pappy, if I was wearing my green tabs, I'd hand them to you."

"Don't give me that shit, Charlie. You're too professional. And don't pull any dumb stunts either. We already lost one MIKE Force commander today."

"Who?"

"Dick Clark, right here in Nha Trang. This morning some Vietnamese officer walked into Clark's office and notified him he was taking over. Dick ran him out of the compound. When the Group commander heard about it, he fired Dick on the spot. When Dick left, two Yard companies followed him out. Rumor has it they're headed up to join you. I'm supposed to tell you not to recruit them."

"Well, as long as I'm wearing those green tabs I'm not wearing, who I recruit is my business."

"I didn't hear that, Charlie. Look, a new wind's blowing. Westmoreland's about to be packed off, and Abrams is his replacement. You know Abrams: If it doesn't have tracks and high velocity cannon, he doesn't understand it. Still, he'll come in with a plan, and what you just heard may be part of it."

"What the hell does Abrams know about Vietnam?"

"What the hell did any of us know before we got here? Don't knock him, Charlie. He's got two sons in country and they're both in combat assignments."

"Great! Maybe one of them will get captured so we can raid up north and bring him home."

"You know Abrams better than I thought," Green grinned. "But raids don't win wars, Charlie. And neither do mercenary elites commanded by foreigners. That's why I need you in the MIKE Force. Sooner or later the Vietnamese have to take command."

"That's not what FULRO was told back in sixty-four and sixty-six. They were promised a Montagnard force with Montagnard commanders. And that's what I've been telling Bloom and the rest of the crew."

"Things have changed, Charlie. Look, Phu may only be a colonel, but he'll be a general soon. And General Phu expects to see Montagnards commissioned into these Rescue Rangers as reserve Vietnamese officers. But it won't be overnight. The Vietnamese army is no different than our own."

"Not up at your level, it isn't. But it's a hell of a lot different down at mine. For one thing, my people know how to fight. That's more than I can say for this overrated, over-ranked, and over-advised bunch of clowns you're running with."

"Major," Green's forefinger shot to within inches of Regter's face, "you're out of order!"

"My apologies," Regter said with a grimace. "Now if the Colonel will excuse me."

As St. Cyr crammed his rucksack with rations, grenades, claymores, parachute flares, star clusters, and ammunition, Regter sat in his room curling weights. The din from Big Marty's grated on his nerves. He wanted to stroll over, sit down, and get blind drunk. But in his current frame of mind that was likely to lead to comments that were nobody's business but his and Pappy Green's. And since Regter never drank alone, he pumped iron and prayed. If the gods of war were kind, Major Ton That Ngoc would climb on the wrong helicopter, draw the wrong parachute, step in front of the wrong truck, or run into the wrong VC patrol before reporting in as the

Vietnamese MIKE Force commander. But when had the gods of war ever
been kind?

Chapter Nine

THE SINGLE HUEY BARRELED IN over a ridgeline, dipped sharply into a tight circle, and zeroed in on a plume of violet smoke rising from an empty Montagnard village. Boris's huge frame braced against the rotor blast as smokestreams snaked through his legs. To his side, the tiger-striped taciturn figure of K'sor Tlur leaned into his slung American M-2 paratroop carbine, puffing away on a radically angled pipe. As St. Cyr and Bloom alighted from the chopper, K'sor Tlur's right hand snapped up to the edge of a tiger-striped beret, wrapped turban-like around his skull.

"*Soyez le bienvenue, mon Commandant!*"

St. Cyr returned the salute before realizing it was not for him.

"*Ah, Mon Adjutant-Chef. Ça marche bien avec le bataillon?*" replied Ney Bloom.

St. Cyr blinked in surprise. Bloom had never mentioned speaking French. He was equally sure he'd just heard what the French called sergeant majors.

"The only battalion commander here is Captain Saville," muttered Boris.

Bloom nodded and pulled K'sor Tlur aside to converse in rapid-fire patois while Boris guided St. Cyr into the village. Copper-faced troopers smiled up from fighting positions dug outside a large log enclosure. Stepping through this vestige of the old west, they followed a second log wall down 100 meters to another opening. The actual village lay within. Unlike the stilted Rhade longhouses Ney Bloom had pointed out in Ban Me Thuot, these nuclear family structures rested on solid ground. Cables running from several antennas led to the battalion CP.

Jed Saville steered St. Cyr over to the operations map with a hearty handshake. They were in western Lam Dong province, Saville explained, in the M'nong tribal area. To the south lay Bao Loc, which was Koho, and Ma territory. A forty kilometer flight due north would get them back into Rhade country.

The region's relatively small size was deceiving. The mountains erupting from the southern edge of the Darlac Plateau were covered with tropical rain forest. Contrary to the monsoon forest found in much of the M'nong tribal territory, it was extremely difficult to traverse, and the occasional bottle-necked valleys were no easier than the mountains. Most were filled with marshes. A Gaullist resistance unit had wandered into one in mid-1945. When its skeletal survivors finally stumbled out, they were met by motorized infantry from Leclerc's 2d Armored Division driving north to occupy Ban Me Thuot. They had spent months wandering within 12 air miles of a colonial highway. The lower Donnai, which stretched down to Bien Hoa, was rubber and timber country, The wilder Upper Donnai was a region most tribesmen avoided. Thus the Viet Cong should find it handy.

Intelligence believed the battalions that had attacked Phan Thiet had withdrawn here to rest and reorganize. Saville's job was to find and destroy them while they were still weak. To this end, two companies pounded the bush while a third stood ready to insert by helicopter once the enemy was located. This reaction company also guarded the battalion command post, and was available for other missions. Toller's platoon was presently out on reconnaissance with McElroy, trying to find out why the village had been abandoned, and where the villagers had gone.

There," Saville nodded. "You know as much as I do. Any questions?"

"How much longer will we be guarding the CP?"

"What, anxious to leave so soon?"

"It's a good way to get a feel for the company."

"Well, your mob replaces Ferris's in three days' time. That'll give the company a good chance to get a feel for you, if you get my drift."

Down at the company command post, St. Cyr found Blek, Boris and Cohen with a short intense-looking African-American. "Well, bad news travels fast," he smiled.

"No surprise, El Tee," grinned Cohen. "The major asked for our opinion."

"And you two figured that of all the lieutenants in the MIKE Force, I'd be the easiest to handle?"

"Mebbe," confessed Boris. "Better you then Toller. When the major called him down, he was sure it was to be company commander."

"I thought you and Toller were friends..."

"We are! But I was in Soviet army when he was in diapers..."

"Tell him what you did in the Russian army, Boris," chimed in the Black.

"Shaddup! Thet bellerina shit he has heard already from Superjew. Sir," Boris beamed. "Meet Kevin Ryan, best medic in all Special Forces. We call him 'the doc.' He is just got beck from Japan."

Ryan's handshake was tepid. "Whatsamatter, El Tee, you expected someone a little more Irish?"

"Does it show?"

"No, but most people do."

"Probably has something to do with the name Kevin. You're the first non-Irish Kevin I've met."

"Well, I am Irish. The other twenty-three parts Black and Creek Indian don't change that. And Kevins are common enough in South Carolina."

The accent was neither Gullah nor any other recognizable Carolina Black dialect, and Ryan's tone was that of someone addressing an equal.

"Where'd you drop out of medical school?"

Ryan's eyes warmed. "Tufts in Boston. But I didn't drop out, I did premed there. Figured I'd make this my ticket to Harvard Medical School."

"Yeah," cut in Cohen, "Ryan's going to have Sam pay his way through Harvard."

"Goddem right," beamed Boris, "and someday when he is famous surgeon, we can tell everybody thet we were his guinea pigs."

"Harvard Medical? What's the chance you'll get in?" The words slipped out just as St. Cyr realized that Ryan had been good enough to get into Tufts.

"I only had a 3.17 GPA, Lieutenant, but with two purple hearts and over eighteen months combat experience as both a Special Forces medic and MIKE Force platoon leader, I should make the cut. If not, there's always Johns Hopkins. Boris and the Superjew have written me letters of recommendation. Lieutenant Grey was supposed to write one too. I'm going to take his draft and send it in with a copy of his death certificate. I'd like to get one from you when this operation's over."

"OK, but I'm not qualified to judge your medical talents just yet."

"It's your call, Lieutenant." Ryan glanced away. He didn't need St. Cyr's recommendation. Hell, he already had one from Regter. Just who the hell did this newbie think he was? Some asshole from the Fourth Foot, the worst goddam division in Vietnam.

Ryan said as much to Boris, when he joined him for lunch. "Thinks he's in charge, doesn't he?"

"He is in charge, buddy," shrugged Boris, "as much as any of us. Besides, listen..."

From inside the M'nong house, they heard St. Cyr grilling Blek and the indigenous platoon leaders in his Malay. From the occasional laughs and grunts, it was going well.

"How meny of us can do thet?"

"So he speaks the language. Big deal. So does every Yard in the company."

"It is big deal, Buddy. Besides, Lieutenant Grey liked him from first minute they met."

"Yeah? Well that's because they're both officers. He still wouldn't have made a pimple on Grey's skinny white ass."

"We don't know that yet. Buddy. Like everyone else, he deserves his chance. No one is esshole until he has proven to be esshole!"

"OK, Boris," Ryan agreed. "The new Trung-oui will get his chance."

"One other thing, buddy."

"What's that, Big B?"

Just as soon as you get letter from Harvard," Boris' eyebrows knit together, "get the hell out of field. Go back and work at dispensary in Pleiku."

"You need to take your own advice, Boris. How long you been here?"

"With me is different, Buddy. I am displaced person. As long as communists hold Ukraine, I can never go home. When my wife divorce me, she took our daughter back to Berlin. For me, United States is citizenship. Don't get me wrong; I am proud American. But Ukraine is home to my blood. God willing, I will die there killing communists. You, you have bright future. Someday I know I will be very proud to say I knew you. Which is why you need to get your ass back to Pleiku to work in dispensary."

"Don't worry, Boris. Doctor Ryan, the well-known Boston cardiologist, will be waked at the Black Rose some fifty or sixty years from now. Maybe by that time they'll let us real Black Irish in."

"The Bleck Rose?"

"An Irish pub up in Boston. I used to go there for Saint Paddy's night. Got thrown out every time."

"Why they threw you out?"

"Some Irishman would sooner or later take offense at my name. They'd swear I was putting them on."

"And this is when Saint Peddy's night?"

"C'mon, Boris, March 17th. Everybody knows that. Why?"

"Because, buddy, on March 17th, 1969, you, me, and Superjew are going to Bleck Rose. I want to see somebody throw us out! I will swear to them my name is Boris...What is good Irish name?"

"Brannigan."

"Boris Brannigan. Hah, this I want to see!"

Ryan spooned the last of his rice and brine shrimp into his mouth, chuckling at the image of Boris swaggering into the Black Rose on Saint Patrick's Day.

"You've got a deal, Boris. Hey, I'd better check up on my platoon." As Ryan stepped out of the hut, Boris emptied another packet of coffee into his canteen cup.

"Frau Müller?" The voice in his mind was his own, speaking over a Wolfratshausen telephone in 1954. "I was with Rolf in Indochina. He gave me something for you. May I come by, or is there someplace we can meet?"

She did not trust his accent, and asked if he was Russian. Russians were unpopular in Germany then, and Rolf had never been much for writing. She demurred at first, but he insisted. Something in his voice was sincere. There was a gasthaus, at a brewery, just across the stone bridge at the Issar River. Did he know it?

He did not, but he would find it.

She agreed to meet him there. She was a small, mousy woman. Not the tall Aryan blond he had expected. The war and post-war years had been hard, and Rolf had been the last of her children. Boris did not tell her how he died, and she never asked, although he had the feeling that she wanted to. It was October, and the American Army was on maneuvers. The gasthaus was filled to capacity, with a waiting line outside. She could barely hear him above the din. He looked around. As he gave her the envelope, he noted two men watching them.

She glanced inside the envelope, flashed a startled look, and broke into a nervous smile. It was from Rolf, he lied, always saving money for his mother. Tears rolled down from the corners of her eyes. Boris waited, his own eyes coldly appraising the two men watching them while she dried her eyes and fought to keep her grief bottled up inside.

"You were Rolf's friend," she choked, "and I have treated you like this. Please come home with me, I should make you some coffee, and we can get some cake."

Tomorrow, perhaps, he promised. He walked her to the door, while she kept trying to thank him, and stood there as she darted off into the darkness. Their two watchers also rose, but Boris glared menacingly into their eyes and motioned for them to sit. As they did so, he pulled a stool up to their table.

"You two are not going anywhere. Not yet. Waiter, three coffees with Jaegermeister!"

The two men exchanged glances. The smaller one broke into a grin. "Whiteshirt. Sergei Whiteshirt. You do not remember me?" Boris shook his head no, but the larger man looked faintly familiar.

"It's me, Yacov. Remember? Yacov, the Jew!" Boris did remember. Berlin, 1945. Lieutenant Yacov, the political officer, had whispered to him that back in the Ukraine the families of those who'd served in the German army were being rounded up and shot. But I am in Red Army, he protested. Yes, Whiteshirt, but your brother was not. Whiteshirt, do not go home. You will not find your mother. Understand?

"Yakov," Boris mused. "You don't look the same."

"Is my job not to look the same. Now I am Corporal Ivanov, Ivan B., in American Army. You would be surprised how many Ivan B. Ivanovs we have in American Army right now." Ivanov once Yacov nodded to his companion. "Last

time I see this Cossack, we send him to Berlin with regimental dance troupe. Funny thing, he did not come back. This is Jacoweicz, a Pole. He says you look like legionnaire he knew."

Boris nodded. He remembered now. Jacoweicz had been with the Legion security service, tracking down war criminals. And the ones he found had a habit of going on patrol and never coming back.

"But," Boris looked over Yacov's clothes, "if you are American Army, why you are not in uniform like rest of soldiers here?"

"We are partisans, spying on these American soldiers as part of exercise. What about you, Whiteshirt?"

"Your Pole is right. I am in Legion."

"Dien Bien Phu?"

"I should have been, but no."

"So why not join us?" Yakov said. "You were partisan before you joined Red Army, No? We need men like you. So much so that American Congress has passed special law. Lodge Act it is called. You can join us right here, right now."

"I am French citizen now," Boris said. "Besides, I have been in Legion eight years."

"And I am American? This Polski here is American? Whiteshirt, I did you favor once. Now I do you second. Next week, come see us at Bad Tolz, Flint Kaserne, it will interest you, I promise. Ask for Ivanov, Ivan B., Russian Number Four. Important you say Russian Number Four, or you will end up with some other Ivanov, and not all of us are pleasant gentlemen. Look, you believe we will be fighting soon the communists, no?"

"I have been fighting them in Indochina."

"I mean real communists. Russians."

"Is matter of time."

"This is why you must come see us, Whiteshirt. If you stay in Legion, you will get yourself killed fighting communists who don't know what communism is. But in American Army, we will fight real communists, in Ukraine. Then, you can kill those bastards who had your mother shot."

Boris's eyebrows knit together. "You were political officer. How is it that these Americans trust you?"

"I was communist whiteshirt. I believed in the cause. But I was also Ukrainian Jew. After what they did to Ukraine, the communist in me died.

Americans had the genius to see that. Come see Bad Tolz, and you will see the kind of men who make me proud American."

Five days later, he traveled to Bad Tolz to discover the 10ᵗʰ Special Forces Group. One out of every seven were displaced persons like himself, and many had served in the Legion as well as a host of other armies. He signed up that afternoon. A little over a year later, he was back in Flint Kaserne as junior weapons man on Yacov's team. Yacov was wrong. He never did get back to the Ukraine. But he did get back to Indochina.

The flame in the pinch of C-4 explosive under Boris' canteen cup had died out. The cup was hot, the coffee barely warm enough to drink. As the metal rim burned his lips, he drank a silent toast to Yacov the Jew, his brother Ukrainian, killed two years later in a nighttime parachute drop over Corfu in the Ionian Sea.

McElroy thumped his rucksack to the ground as Toller signaled a halt for a 20-minute break to allow time for leech removal. As men slipped off to both sides of the trail, Rchom Jimm flashed the 'no smoking' sign. Whispered complaints rustled the humid stillness. For two days they had been moving up a valley formed in the horseshoe bend of an old river. Over time, the river had changed course. A small stream fed a marsh that clogged the lower reaches of the valley. McElroy guessed that the marsh again became part of a river once the monsoons arrived, reverting back to swamp in the dry season.

In true recon fashion, they had tried to avoid the trails. But dense undergrowth made movement difficult, and Toller soon lost patience with the sound of machetes. They had taken to a series of game trails when they stumbled across this manmade trail. The M'nong maintained such trials between villages and water sources in particularly rough country.

Mac rummaged through a side pocket of the rucksack for his toilet paper and insect repellent. Unfolding his entrenching tool, he walked straight into the brush, taking care to keep his back to the platoon's position. Forcing open a hole in the humid earth, he dropped down, visually inspecting his privates. McElroy hated leeches and was constantly concerned with getting them in his eyes, ears, nose, or penis while in the bush. None were visible, but a familiar squish in his boot warned him to check his feet and ankles. He scanned the area to his front and sides: Ants scurried up and down a small trail they had cut in the reddish-brown jungle floor. Vines as thick as a man's calf snaked across the earth to climb cathedral sized tree trunks.

Below a nearby tree, green leafed fronds waved lightly in the humid air. Mac was cursing his inability to feel that breeze when he suddenly rose, drew his pistol from the left side of his harness, and fired three shots into the waving fronds from a two-handed stance.

The shots echoed through the forest as Toller and Jimm came crashing up.

"Behind the tree," Mac grunted.

Jimm motioned a squad to fan out into the jungle and sweep back towards their position while Mac hastily buttoned his fly. Behind the fronds lay a crumpled Viet Cong regular in blue and black garb spiked with camouflage, rapidly sliding into shock. Two rounds had hit him center body mass. While Jimm barked instructions into the indigenous radio, the Montagnard RTO covered Toller, who knelt to speak to him.

"Not much we can do out here, Mate. Fancy a durry?" Toller fished a cigarette pack out of his ammo pouch, lit it, and held it out to the VC. The kid stared through uncomprehending eyes, but his lips closed on the butt. A short burst of fire down the trail distracted them. When Toller turned back to their prisoner, he was dead.

"One moah," called Jimm. "They get one moah. Also get prisoners."

"Not b-bad, hunh?" grinned Mac. "Specially for a g-guy with other things on his mind."

"Must've been your mind," mused Toller dryly, "I distinctly heard five shots, but the dead man took only two rounds."

"Three shots," Mac corrected.

Their report came over the battalion radio as St. Cyr was updating the companies' positions to the battalion operations map. Two trail watchers from a VC Main Force battalion KIA, and several male children from the village recovered. From what Jimm could glean from the oldest, who spoke a halting Rhade, the entire village had been conscripted at gunpoint to assist in the construction of a new VC base camp. The boys had slipped away and were on their way back to the village when they had been caught by trail watchers. They were being herded back to the base camp when one of the trail watchers had stumbled across signs of Toller's platoon. Deciding to check further, they had followed the sign as far as McElroy's cat-hole, where the smell stopped them cold. Good initiative on their part had been bested by blind luck and good shooting on Mac's.

Did Jimm think that the boys were trustworthy? Saville asked. Jimm replied that they were. One claimed to have a maternal uncle serving with the Bao Loc camp strike force, and the M'nong had no love for ethnic Vietnamese.

How far was to the base camp? Here communications broke down. Back at battalion, Bloom sent for a Rhade radio operator who spoke M'nong. The boy, however, refused to speak on the radio, believing the device would steal his spirits. The radio operator who showed up spoke M'nong Preh, happily related to M'nong Prong. He asked the questions into the handset while Jimm stood by the boy and repeated his responses. The boy wasn't sure how far it was. This was the first time that he had been that far from the village. But it was up on a plateau above a waterfall. The M'nong liked neither plateaus nor waterfalls. Both attracted evil spirits.

"Thank God for evil spirits," muttered Saville, pulling out his pocket glass to scan the map near Toller's position.

"Ask them how many rivers they crossed."

"Many."

"Was it the same river many times, or many rivers?"

There was a pause while the boy sorted this out. Saville pushed his boonie hat back and scratched madly at his dandruff. "Maybe three rivers, one river many times," came the answer.

"Did they stay on the same trail?"

"Yes. Once they had got free of the camp, they stayed to the trail, trusting in their ability to blend swiftly into the brush."

Saville spent another ten minutes agonizing over the map. The trail information was hopelessly outdated, but if he followed the ridge line up from Toller's position, dropped down into a draw, and crossed up over the spur into the next valley, there was a long hooking stretch that moved up into a dog-leg shaped plateau which might contain a waterfall. About nine kilometers straight line distance, it was probably closer to 24 by trail, mostly uphill. It lay seven kilometers from Ferris's last reported position, but the contour lines on that side were far more rugged.

Saville instructed Toller and Jimm to stand by, and bounced his train of thought off of St. Cyr. Talking mostly to himself, he wondered what trail watchers were doing so far down the trail. And if these were Main Force troops, where were their Montagnard regional counterparts? Who'd been their guides? Were they expecting another unit, or know for sure that the MIKE Force was in the area? He'd assume the latter, since the companies had been resupplied by helicopter some three days earlier. Then why hadn't the VC come down to take on them on?

"Well, it's either a logistics battalion, or elements of those Main force units we've been looking for," Saville said to himself through St. Cyr, "and I'll wager they're loggies. Bloom, ask Jimm if the boys are willing to lead us back there. Galen, get on the horn to Detachment B-23 and ask that they relay a request for an immediate red haze report. What's our transmit time for today's sitrep?"

The shade of the M'nong house came alive with the spirit of the hunt. Jimm radioed that the boys would lead them back up the trail, but Saville had changed his mind. Toller was to return with the boys immediately. St. Cyr was to ensure that the red haze mission understood that it was to make a single pass over the target. The infrared heat recording would give them an idea as to what was on the plateau, and roughly where it had been at the time of the pass. Ferris was to move his company up to the edge of the plateau and recon the area near the dog-leg.

"You," Saville looked at St. Cyr, "are the first blow of the hammer. Ferris is the anvil. Moshlatubbee will be prepared to follow you in. The question is when. I prefer first light, but everything depends upon how fast Ferris can move into position, assuming that they end up where we think they will. How well do you know Captain Ferris?"

"We...ah...exchanged a few words at Tet, sir."

"Not exactly warm and cuddly, is he?" Saville chuckled. "Right about now he's running a temperature of a hundred-and-four and glowing bright red. We've got five-and-a-half hours of daylight left. That'll put Ferris...," he circled his finger around the map, poking it into a mass of brown squiggles, "...here. Doesn't look like much, does it?"

"Nossir, but that's a helluva climb for anyone who's ever humped a rucksack. I'd want at least a full day for my old company."

"American, weren't they?"

St. Cyr nodded.

"Right. Well, let's hope Ferris doesn't kill off any more Yards. He's done it, you know. Killed two off from heat exhaustion up near Plei Djereng. It undermines their morale when they don't understand what killed a man. Where'd Bloom go?"

As the hours rolled by, Saville grew more intense. His greatest fear was that he'd picked the wrong piece of terrain. Toller failed to close by nightfall, and requested permission to remain in place until morning. Saville had to agree. If the trail was mined or booby-trapped, there was no reason to send Toller stumbling around in the dark. He checked with St. Cyr for form's sake. St. Cyr agreed that he could conduct the assault with three platoons. Besides, they'd have helicopter gunships, fighters on call, and Moshlatubbee standing by to reinforce them.

Ferris had pushed his company to almost where Saville had predicted when word came from the red haze aircraft, relayed from camp A-236 at Lac Thien, that they had a reading indicating somewhere between two and three hundred people in the small portion of the dog-leg. That, or a medium sized herd of wild elephants. Red haze reported body heat, nothing more. Saville passed the information to Ferris with orders to establish blocking positions, while St. Cyr called Ban Me Thuot to confirm the air mission. Pickup would be just outside the village. They would be landed in the center of the dog-leg under cover of gunships and assault the narrow end. The gunships would hold their fire until given specific targets by St. Cyr. Tactical air would be standing by.

After double-checking his coordinates, call signs, and frequencies, St. Cyr found Blek, Biloskirka, Cohen, and Ryan huddled with K'sor Tlur and the indigenous platoon leaders going over the airlift plan. Ryan was quick to grill him on medevac availability. He wanted it in the air over the near horizon. St. Cyr calculated that given the relative proximity of the Pickup and Landing Zones, flight time would be no more than 10 to 12 minutes, assuming there were no antiaircraft weapons along the flight paths. Once Clyde saw or heard anything more than a single chopper, he'd know what was up. Surprise was the key. They had to load up and get there before the enemy had any chance to react. The rest was up to Ferris.

Ferris was driving everyone as expected, but he was no mindless martinet. His company could not work miracles in the dark. The men, mostly Rhade under Y Mlo Duan Du, included thirty Koho and some M'nong, but no one from this area, so no one knew the trails. They had shot a cross country azimuth from a ridge line, where evaporation had cleared much of the undergrowth, but down in the draws they ran into heavy vegetation.

Barging through the darkness behind the point man, Ferris heard the young Rhade let out a yelp. Something had hit him in the leg. A few more steps and the boy complained that his leg was burning. Soon it was growing numb. Ferris inspected the leg under the light of a red lensed flashlight but could see nothing. The boy was visibly starting to shake. Unscrewing the red lens cover, Ferris crouched in close. Two fang marks showed in the obscene white light; some kind of snake. Cold chills ran down Ferris's back and legs. Snakes were his worst nightmare, and this one was nearby.

While the rest of the point element took up defensive positions, he alerted his team medic that they had a snakebite victim. Knapp rushed in with his medical kit and was soon cup-pumping blood and venom from two incisions cut in the leg. Ferris and Y Mlo were agonizing over a medevac when the pointman went into uncontrollable seizures. While Knapp cursed, the young Montagnard died. Y Mlo added one of his bracelets to the dead man's, and ordered the point to move on. When they held back, Ferris pushed into the lead, slamming his feet onto the ground, silently cursing snakes every step of the way. He kept that pace up for over an hour. Sometime after 0300 hours the next morning, an exhausted 206th Company settled in to await first light.

In the inky blackness, Ferris assembled Y Mlo Duan Du and his platoon leaders. They had lost a man. But somewhere up ahead, people were being held prisoner by the hated Viets. These were M'nong; Dega just like themselves. This was a battle that both the MIKE Force and FULRO needed badly. When daylight came, there could be only one thought in each man's mind: Push forward to close with and kill the hated Tiep-zap. Liberate the M'nong. Ferris made them repeat those words until the light of true believers shone in their eyes.

Dawn broke, but the sun was slow in burning off the morning haze. As it climbed into the sky, clouds clung to the edges of the plateau. Men cursed. While Toller and Jimm pushed their men down, Ferris and Y Mlo pushed theirs up, and Jed Saville paced back and forth in front of his radios. St. Cyr frittered between his men set up along the Pickup Zone (PZ), and the battalion CP. Back in Ban Me Thuot, pilots and doorgunners stood by, cursing the incompetence of whatever asshole had put this operation together.

At 0820, Toller and Mac emerged from a trail on the far side of the PZ with the boys in tow. By 0853 Ferris was below the dog-leg of the plateau in blocking positions. As soon as the haze lifted, Saville called for the choppers. At 1025 hours the first wave of 205th MIKE Force Company touched down in chest high *tranh* grass to begin the mad scramble for the wood line. St. Cyr noted with relief that far more rounds were going out than coming in. Blek led Cohen's platoon in the following wave.

Fighting on the objective was short, intense, and one sided. 205th Company pushed into a battalion sized base camp occupied only by caretaker elements who quickly disappeared. Ten minutes later, the sounds of a series of sharp firefights rumbled up from Ferris's blocking positions. St. Cyr left Toller and Ryan with the villagers, while he pushed Biloskirka's and Cohen's platoons towards the firing. Moshlatubbee's company stood by.

By 1430 all resistance had ceased. Five MIKE Force troopers, to include the snakebite victim, had died. Another twelve were wounded, among them an American from Ferris's company. But twenty-three enemy lay dead, two had been captured, and blood trails marked where others had fled. More importantly, over a hundred grateful M'nong villagers had been rescued. The rest had taken to the bush and were making their way home. Ferris celebrated by planting a wet kiss in St. Cyr's ear. Knuudsen gave Boris a friendly hug. And Saville went back to his maps.

Victory is a dance on your enemy's grave.

Chapter Ten

"I MAY ENTER, NO?"

Regter looked up to find Ngoc, who entered without waiting for a reply. Ngoc slouched down onto the wooden bench, flashed Regter an intent gaze, and lit a cigarette.

"That was good work we do near Gia Nghia. I may ask one question, no?"

Regter fought back the urge to ask Ngoc what the hell he'd done at Gia Nghia. "Go ahead."

"Why Companies return early? Mission to locate and destroy elements of one Viet Cong Main Force regiment. Instead find element of NVA Logistic Battalion Two-Fifty. They should move west to continue mission."

"Ngoc, those companies have been on operations since early January. They need rest and retraining to keep their edge."

"Of course," Ngoc shot a plume of smoke in Regter's direction. "But must explain in my report. So, office next door is whose?" he glanced through the door at the empty office across from Regter's.

"My new executive officer. He's due in next week."

"Perhaps he should find new office. You and I must locate together."

"It's not very large for a MIKE Force commander."

"As large as yours. No?"

"Yes, but I spend a lot of time away. Administration is what I have a staff for."

"My own philosophy. When I can brief you on plans for MIKE Force?"

"What plans for the MIKE Force?"

"My plans as MIKE Force commander."

Regter stared down at his desktop before raising his eyes. He had scheduled a flight to Nha Trang to have some unkind words with his old mentor, and didn't wish to offend Ngoc until he had cleared things up with Pappy Green.

"Look Ngoc. You're the Vietnamese commander, and I'm the American commander. As of now…"

"You are my American advisor…"

"Yes. But I am the de facto MIKE Force commander. And however unpleasant that 'facto' may be to you, I command every American, Australian, and Montagnard here. No Montagnard in this compound will follow you unless I tell them to, and even then some will quit…"

"Some certain major can be replaced…"

"Yes. But you have no control over who replaces me, and not a single one of your men will survive their first contact in the field if word gets out you had me fired. We're a long way from Nha Trang, Ngoc. You might remember that."

"Precisely why we should work together."

"The key word there, elder brother Ngoc, is *together*."

"Good." Ngoc sat back to puff his cigarette in triumph. Regter waited for him to leave, but instead he smiled and cleared his throat.

"There is one small matter of twenty new Luc Luong Dac Biet personnel. Men chosen by me based upon their combat records. As you know, none here were stellar performers. These new leaders must integrate into units as soon as possible."

Regter fought back the urge to throw Ngoc bodily out of his office. A higher quality LLDB soldier was in both their interests.

"I must discuss that with Nha Trang."

"Decision made in Nha Trang already. At LLDB high command."

"Ngoc," the corners of Regter's mouth tightened. "I'll gladly hear your proposal if you agree that nothing happens until I get back from Nha Trang. When can you brief me?"

"This same afternoon. In new LLDB staff building, just across street."

"All right. How does fourteen-hundred sound? I have a sacrifice at fifteen-thirty."

"OK. At fifteen-thirty I see you."

Regter stepped out to watch Ngoc leave, and caught sight of the Vietnamese evicting the security company from the facing building.

"Wait a minute, Major Ton! Who told you to move the security company out of their barracks?"

Ngoc ignored the insulting use of his family name and turned to mimic Regter's voice.

"As commander of Viet Nam Special Forces here, I own earth under this camp, no?"

"You own the land. You don't own the buildings yet."

"If earth is Vietnam, then buildings on it belong to Vietnam."

"That's not what the status of forces agreement says. Ngoc, you get one building. You will not do anything further until I return from Nha Trang. Is that understood?"

"For now, we need only one building," Ngoc smiled, and walked off.

St. Cyr was relaxing under a stream of hot water when Moshlatubbee stepped into an adjacent shower stall.

"Greatest goddam invention since pussy!" grunted the Choctaw. "Gotta get gussied up. Ferris and me are headed over to the Seventy-First Evac Hospital later. It's time those nurses met some real war heroes, instead of those sniveling 'I-could-be-making-seventy-thou-a-year' Doctor Kildares."

"Hey," St. Cyr protested, "docs are OK..."

"Tell me about it, I've been there. But when they start crying that 'Oh God, I've-seen-so-much-blood-and-gore' bullshit, I like to remind them that we're the poor bastards up on the table, giving them that once in a lifetime surgical training opportunity that's going to make them rich. Which is usually about the time some sweet young nurse decides to dump Doc Kildare and do her utmost to relieve the sufferings of our more mundane slice of humanity."

"Damn, Choctaw, you're cold hearted!"

"Like Daddy told me: do anything you can to get even with the White Eyes, or Lady White Eyes. Watchin' the docs get all up tight makes it even more fun. They'd gladly throw us out, but Ferris positively scares them to death."

St. Cyr grinned his appreciation. Further down the row, Ferris barged into a stall.

"Hey, ain't you two done a little early? You get all the weapons and ammo inventoried and turned in?"

"That's what we've got platoon leaders for."

"Oh yeah?" Ferris scowled. "What platoon leaders you got inventorying the ammo?"

"Roundeye and Indig," shot back the Choctaw.

"You still ought'a be there to supervise. If you don't keep an eye on 'em, a lot of that shit'll end up in FULRO stocks."

"Gooooo, FULRO, ungh!" grinned the Choctaw.

"Ain't no goddam joke, Lieutenant! When tracer rounds start zippin' through the barracks, you'll see what I mean. Speakin' of which, you two see what's going on down the compound?"

Moshlatubbee looked at St. Cyr, who shrugged. "What?"

"Goddam Zipperheads, that's what!"

"Surely you don't refer to our gallant Vietnamese allies?"

"Yeah. Came to the MIKE Force to get away from those dildo heads. Now they show up here."

"Can't do much harm," mused Moshlatubbee, "as long as they stay out of the field."

"Think so? Just watch 'em! Sonsuvbitches can screw up a wet dream."

"Captain Ferris," confided the Choctaw with mock seriousness, "commanded the A Team down at Vinh Thanh. One day he discovered that his counterpart had built a series of false agent networks to siphon off funds, so he turned him in. Big scandal! Fifth Group had to do something, so they fired our good captain. Couldn't fire the LLDB, you know. Oriental face and all that."

"Hey Blanketass," cut in Ferris, "when we goin' over to the Seventy-First Evac?"

"Nineteen hundred should do. I was thinking of dragging our new blood brother along."

"Who, that Canuck? Shit, it's his first sacrifice. He ain't goin' nowhere."

"S'pose you're right," laughed Moshlatubbee. "I still can't remember most of mine."

"Maybe not," chuckled Ferris, "but I sure as hell can. Wish I'd taken pictures."

St. Cyr stepped out of the shower hut to find Biloskirka and Toller waiting in a Jeep. They motioned for him to get a move on. Twenty minutes later, they were speeding past the MIKE Force dependent village towards a Jarai village on a distant rolling hill. Slowing down to pass through the gate, the Jeep threaded its way carefully among the longhouses until they spied Mac seated on a porch.

"Hey, Toller! When you g-gonna teach that Uke how to drive?"

"Shit," shot back Boris, "I was in combet when you were in grade school."

"Skip the war stories, B-boris. You t-tell the Trung-oui here about his sacrifice?"

"Nah," cut in Toller, "we left that for you."

"What about the sacrifice," St. Cyr wondered.

"Nothing to it, Trung-oui. You're about to g-get drunk on your ass, and you ain't g-gonna disgrace us. Hey Blek! Your brother company commander's here."

A bamboo slat door slid open. Blek stepped out wearing a black shirt with red piping on the shoulders, fringes, and chest, over a wide ceremonial loincloth. While St. Cyr negotiated the steps of the horned log ladder, Blek extended a Jarai handshake.

"*Mnam luu*, my brother. We must eat before sacrifice."

"Why? Isn't there enough meat for all?"

"Uangh. But you must armor yourself for battle. As new Meerika company commander you will be first on jar. My 'Father' will explain."

"Yeah," Mac grunted in English, "the boys just g-got paid, so they'll be betting heavy. And it'll all be on you to be the last commander standing."

As Mac explained the ceremony, there was a flurry of soft voices from the other side of the door. It slid open for a young woman, who stepped out carrying several bowls. She was followed by a girl of about fourteen. Two pairs of shapely legs stretched taught against ankle length black sateen skirts. The younger girl wore a green sateen blouse, while the woman's dusky breasts hung free. Her skin had neither blemish nor mole.

St. Cyr noted that Boris and Cohen took care to avoid staring at her breasts as she handed each a bowl. Ryan reached for the third bowl, but she offered it to St. Cyr.

"For you, Meerika, I prepared it myself. It is spicy, but will help you drink. They say you speak our language." She squatted down, demurely soft and feminine, and stared deep into his eyes. As he took the bowl, she wrapped her arms around her knees in an incredibly fluid gesture, and sat back. She had liquid, black, hypnotic eyes, full lips that accentuated high cheekbones in an oval face, and handsome Polynesian features grafted to the willow slenderness of a Malay. He fumbled for words as he stared at her dusky gold skin.

"It is an honor to meet so beautiful a woman who is my brother's wife."

"He speaks," giggled the girl. The woman returned St. Cyr's stare with a frank appraisal of her own.

"I am my brother's sister, Meerika, not his wife. And you are this *Sanseer* I have heard he and his father talk about?"

"I am. Did Rahlen Blir speak well of me."

"Blir?" She flashed Mac a puzzled look.

"She's talkin' b-bout me," Mac mumbled between bites. "Blir's her uncle, not her father. It's a long story. One of these days I'll exp-plain."

"So this Meerika does not know we call you Rahlen Blek's father?"

"He thinks Blir your father."

Slender fingers covered her mouth. As she smiled, her eyes toyed with St. Cyr's.

"Meerika, when I am Po Lan of this clan, you will be always welcome in my own long house." Her eyes flashed. The girl covered her mouth with both hands in a fit of giggles.

Everyone smiled: The girls at their own private joke: Blek, because he'd understood. St. Cyr, mostly out of relief. And the others because they thought it was expected. Only Mac's face was grim.

"Eat up and g-get movin'," Mac growled. "We got a sacrifice waitin'."

They met Saville, Moshlatubbee, and Ferris outside the dependent village longhouse with Ney Bloom, Rahlen Blir, and Y Mur Thak, the old Rhade who served as village priest. Most wore tiger fatigues, but Moshlatubbee, like Blek and Rchom Jimm, sported a highland shirt and loincloth. Nearby, carved wooden stakes and blood splotches marked the sacrifice. Blir's clothes also had blood stains.

"Mother's-brother," laughed Blek, "what happened to your clothes?"

"Pah. *Cabao* broke free. We had to run him down. He was angry and turned to fight. Luckily, I caught him in his haunch near the knee with my coup-coup. Thak says we have offended the spirits."

"Not you," snorted Y Mur Thak, "the idiot who partially severed the rope. Bad spirits will find him."

"From what company?" Blek asked in an edged tone.

"Big Meerika-Montagnard's," Y Mur Thak whispered, nodding at Moshlatubbee. "A bad sign, but it is done. Let us begin."

The old man stepped up to St. Cyr and stared carefully into his eyes and nostrils. His gnarled hands turned St. Cyr left and right, inspecting his hair and ears. When Y Mur Thak was satisfied no hostile spirits had followed the new man in, he stepped back to offer the guests his formal handshake. As they climbed the log steps, Y Thak spoke in French.

"They say you speak French as well as our Dega tongue. Have you ever visited Carcassonne? I was there with the 52nd Colonial Machinegunners."

"When?"

"In the years Thirty, before the Second War. We will talk about it sometime. Now as guest of honor, follow me."

The ceremonial longhouse was larger than those St. Cyr had seen in the Sedang and M'nong countries, and like all Jarai and Rhade houses, it was set above the ground on pilings. The interior was an enormous hall, with small rooms at the back end. Shields, spears, drums, cymbals, and gongs hung along the sides.

"Don't t-touch nothin' less they tell you," Mac cautioned. "Clan totems and all that. Only members of the clan can touch 'em. And when you g-go outside, don't piss on the bamboo."

"Right about that," murmured Toller "Cost me two pigs my first sacrifice."

Y Mur Thak motioned Jed Saville, St. Cyr, Moshlatubbee, and Ferris to their respective places in front of some eight rows of *mnam pay* jars.

Once the Roundeyes were seated, their Montagnard counterparts joined them. Centered in front of the jars was a metal wash pan containing the water buffalo's head. The buffalo's still moist eyes stared at the flies swarming across his muzzle. Bronze and brass bracelets hung from his horns.

Once everyone was seated, Y Mur Thak nodded to the musicians. The takataka taktak of cymbals and gongs broke out, spreading through the longhouse. Raising his voice in a wail, he called to the spirits and asked them to accept the buffalo and pigs whose merits he described in glowing terms. When he had finished a long series of incantations, invoking both Ai Die, who knew all men, and H'Ba Dung Dai, the goddess creator, he asked who would speak for the Rahlen clan.

"I speak for Rahlen clan," stated Blek.

"And who will speak for MIfors?"

"He speaks for MIKE Force," said Mac, nodding at Saville.

"This Meerika? Is he worthy of Rahlen clan protection?"

"He is," answered Blek.

"And has he been judged worthy of MIfors?"

Mac nodded to Jed Saville, who stated formally in English that he had been.

"Then he is henceforth a Dega," said Y Mur Thak.

Taking up the first bracelet from the buffalo's horn, Y Thak intoned another long incantation. Slipping the bracelet over St. Cyr's wrist, he took up the nearest straws. Bunching them together, he drew light sips which he sprayed in the cardinal directions about the buffalo head. His assistants then stepped forward to pass the end of a long bamboo straw to each man. St. Cyr glanced at Mac.

"Not yet," Cohen whispered from behind.

Thak took up four more bracelets. Starting with St. Cyr, he held one over the head of each guest of honor and mumbled a secret prayer of bestowal before placing one on each wrist. As he stepped back, the musicians abruptly changed their beat. Now, the longhouse shook with an orgiastic rhythm.

"All right, Trung-oui," murmured the Superjew, "see that tee shaped stick hanging down in the *mnam pay*?"

St. Cyr stared into the cool green liquid and nodded.

"When I nudge you, suck on that straw until the bottom swings free. That's when they'll pour in more water. Drink two measures as fast as you can, and get back to the end of the line."

"*M'nam Luu!*" Cohen poked him in the ribs.

St. Cyr and his fellow commanders sucked desperately on their straws. As the liquid level dropped, the watchers took up a chant to the tune of the music. Ryan leaned over from behind Blek. "Glad I'm not first man on that jar, Trung-oui. Great honor and all that, but who wants all that nasty shit in their mouth..."

St. Cyr's brow furrowed. The wine was cool, sweet, and had a slightly chlorophyll taste.

"You know," Ryan continued, "dried blood, fly larvae, mosquito larvae, various and sundry yeasts both known and unknown to medical science..."

"Ya rootin' for him, or f-fuckin' with him?" snapped McElroy.

"Just doing my duty as his medical advisor, Mac. Don't worry. I brought along the old medical kitbag just for our Trung-oui. God knows why this shit never gives you the squirts."

"The spirits like me," Mac grunted.

Within seconds, St. Cyr felt a warm pale glow spread up from his stomach to swirl around inside his body and nuzzle his brain. His eyes locked on the tee stick as the liquid level drooped down. His bladder warned that it was getting full, but he strained to keep the level dropping: An inch. Half an inch. A quarter of an inch to go. A peak of liquid that grew smaller and smaller until it was a tiny globule suspended just below the bottom of the tee. As he gasped for air, the downstroke swung free. Somewhere, a mob was cheering.

"Goddam," he observed to no one in particular, "I think I'm blown away already."

"That's *mnam pay*, Trung-oui, and you ain't seen nothin' yet."

St. Cyr stared around, owl-eyed, trying to identify the voice.

An assistant to Y Mur Thak refilled the jar to the cross-bar. St. Cyr hesitated.

"Get going," screamed Cohen, "you're falling behind."

"OK, but do I have to keep squatting?"

"No, sit down."

He dropped down on his buttocks to stretch out his cramped legs, taking care not to kick the buffalo head. The buffalo's eyes stared into his. A strange affinity for the animal welled up in his heart. From somewhere in his brain, he watched flashbacks of a solid, hard-working beast who'd liked his master's children. A little Vietnamese girl with long black hair came up and threw her arms around the buffalo's neck. Later, he felt the heels and toes of a teenage girl as she balanced herself on his back in a pond. A boy carefully picked ticks from his ears. A plow that got harder to pull, and then, a sense of fear as Y Mur Thak's assistants led him away. Tear tracks of betrayal glistened in the buffalo's eyes as its spirit bayed softly for a life left behind.

St. Cyr shook himself into the present. Cymbals and drums clanged dimly above the ringing in his ears. Globule by globule the *mnam pay* crept downwards. At the halfway point, the cheers ringing in his skull began to oscillate. Focusing his eyes on the wooden measure, his inner self calmly took in its grain, finish, and color. As this same self examined slivers held together by invisible molecules, his eyes flashed out of focus and his bladder wired frantic signals to the brain. Enough, it screamed; but the circuit had shorted out. A quarter of an inch. Another eternity. The damned stuff was standing still. He sucked and heaved. The liquid crawled down. The peak of a mountain showed. A mountain, a goddam mountain of...what was this stuff? *Mnam pay*! as in *M'nam Luu*, let's get drunk together. Said only to men, right? The liquid clung desperately to the bottom of the stick. A cheer thundered through the room. Down, damn you! Down! He braced and gave another mighty pull.

Thousands of microscopic fingers were torn from the tee stick to tumble down into a sea of cool milky green liquid. The tee stick shuddered with relief. More cheering sounded in the background. St. Cyr slumped back into Cohen's arms.

"Not now, Trung-oui. As guest of honor, you've got to set the example: Back to the end of the line."

"What for?"

"The next round. C'mon, Boris and Jimm are beating me."

The cheers had turned to laughter. Friendly laughter. Someone couldn't hold their *mnam pay* and the Yards were having a laugh at his expense. He crawled to the end of the line and sat behind a trooper he remembered from the dogleg.

"*M'nam luu*," he smiled.

The trooper mnam luu'd him back as Mac's face floated into focus.

"Welcome to the real MIKE Force, Trung-oui. Goooooo MMI-IIffforrrss..."

Above the frenzied takataktak takatak came a low, throaty, animal roar from what seemed like a thousand voices. "UuunnnGGGhhh!!!"

"Goooo miiike force!" he screamed.

"UuunnnGGGhhh!!!" grunted the longhouse.

Goddam, this was fun! He edged himself closer to the *mnam pay* jar and screamed again. "Goooooo MIKE forrcce!"

The entire longhouse grunted with violent resonance. He caught a deep breath, but was cut off by another chant. Maybe it came from Mac, or maybe from someone else. He couldn't be sure. But come it did, with a passion and violence that shot out through the bamboo slats.

"GGoooo, FfffuuuLLLrrrooo, UuunnnGGGhhh!!!"

FULRO? Hey, wasn't FULRO illegal? It was his turn on the jar again. Go FULRO, yeah!

Sometime later, unseen arms pulled him over to where he could be propped up against the woven bamboo wall. He stared vaguely at the beams and intricate thatching patterns on the underside of the roof. Though the musicians had quit playing to take their turn on the jars, their rakataktak takatak echoed in his brain.

He sneezed, and something at once misty and silvery hung suspended between lattice beams of fading sunlight. He chuckled. There were three of him. Well, not exactly him, but there were three, and they all resembled him. He giggled. They giggled back. The *M'ngat*, which after death becomes the *Yang Atao*, looked down at him and nudged the *M'ngah*, or giver of life soul, who cackled insanely and called for the *Tlang Hia*, or third soul, to take a close look at this asshole, who was most definitely crocked.

"You're full of shit," he told them, "I'm stone cold sober."

"You think?" sneered the M'ngat, "Watch!" It floated up into the air to turn slow somersaults.

St. Cyr felt his stomach churn. The Tlang Hia leaned forward until their noses almost touched, smiling insidiously. "Look at the pores of your skin, stupid! You're crocked!"

He sat stock still to gaze in newfound wonder at the fantastically porous screen of translucence which held in his tissue and muscle. Tiny rivulets of pale green mist rose from his pores. Someone nudged him. He looked down to see Toller standing over his inert body. It was time to go back inside. The spirits agreed.

"Time for another crack," grinned Toller. "Are you on?"

"Go FULRO," he mumbled.

Toller wrestled him into the line behind Regter.

"Major...?"

"Hello, Galen. I see you're getting broken in. Better here than at Madame Binh's."

"Uh...yessir. When d'you get here?"

"About a half hour ago. You don't remember? You were trying to explain something about a M'ngat or something, but you kept switching back into Yard."

"Oooh."

"Don't feel bad. You've made a lot of friends here today. I've never seen anybody get accepted so quickly, especially by the Jarai."

"Good sacrifice," the Montagnard trooper to St. Cyr's right smiled through the gap in his teeth. "The spirits are pleased."

"That they are," St. Cyr agreed. "What happened to your teeth?"

"These?" The tribesman bit down on his thumb through the gap.

"Yes."

"Why, I filed them off at my manhood ceremony, like everybody else. But maybe now I MIfors, I buy new ones like Blek's father..."

"Mac?"

"As Meerika call him."

"What happened to his teeth?"

"He file off, same as everybody. Now he not look like Tiep-zap or monkey. But since he live with Meerika, he buy teeth he can put in. That way, he can put in to be Meerika and take out to be Jarai. Maybe I do same."

"Too much talk," growled Mac. "Come on, Trung-oui, your turn back on the jug."

The third, fourth, maybe fifth jugs were milkier and decidedly milder. Only his kidneys felt the pain. As he drank down the taste of rice milk, he stared at the bronze bracelets dangling from his wrist. So this was what they stood for.

"Bullshit!" huffed Cohen, "Those bracelets mean more than that, Trung-oui. You'll find out soon enough."

"C'mon, buddy. Pump thet straw."

There was no cheering this time. The sacrifice had broken up into smaller circles of men huddled around their own *mnam pay* jars. By the time he passed the straw, his kidneys and bladder had found a trunk-line that flashed urgent messages to his brain.

"Where can I piss?" somebody asked in French.

"Outside," answered Biloskirka. "*Tu peut pisser* anywhere, but not on the bamboo."

He stepped out into a blinding late afternoon sun. Squinting, he made out some 20 or so Montagnards emptying their bladders on the grass below. Children played in front of an adjacent house. Passing village women paid scant attention. He climbed carefully down the log stairway and glanced up at the afternoon sky. The horizon twisted and dipped like the deck of a ship. What the hell was happening to the earth?

That's you, asshole, some inner voice chided. The M'ngat was still with him. Moosehead Ale, said an inner voice, was never like this. The pale afternoon quarter moon spun around two darker moons which focused to become the faces of Biloskirka and Cohen.

"Don't piss on me," he pleaded. "It wouldn't be dignified and I'd have to whip both your asses."

"Listen to that shit, Boris. Our new Trung-oui here can't even hold his *mnam pay.*"

"End he thinks he'll be as good as Grey."

"Yeah, that's what he thinks."

"Well, he'll get the chance."

"Hey, guys, I'm sorry..."

"For what? You and Blek did pretty good, finishing up first. And you didn't try to skydive from longhouse like Ferris did, first time..."

"I mean Grey. I didn't want to get the company like that..."

"Nobody does. Listen! Nothing heppened to Lieutenant Grey thet isn't going to heppen to us. You just be sure you are as good as he was."

"I'll try, Boris..."

"You'd better more then try. C'mon Superjew, let's take our Trung-oui someplace to sleep this shit off. Maybe Blek's house."

"All right! Nothing like a little hard tongue to cure the *mnam pay*. I'll get his feet."

"Why you get feet?"

"Because the torso is heavier and you're a whole lot goddam bigger'n I am."

"So, just because I em big person, I get heaviest load?"

"Makes sense..."

"Bullshit! I em Mester Sergeant and you are Spec Five."

"More reason you should get the torso. The torso is closer to the head. This is Vietnam and the highest ranking man always gets the head."

"Head of table; yes. Not head of torso!"

"C'mon Boris. When's the last time you were at a Slope ceremony? The highest ranking man always gets the head parts."

They trundled him out through the gate and over to the village, arguing every step of the way. At length, they dumped him on the porch of Blek's longhouse.

"Blir! Rahlen Blir!"

He managed to open one eye, and saw Blir's weather-beaten face staring down at his own. Biloskirka was explaining in his best pidgin Jarai that Blek had extended the hospitality of the house to his brother commander. As if to emphasize the point, St. Cyr waved his newly won bracelets under Blir's nose. Blir gave a hearty gap-toothed smile and motioned them in.

"Buddy, be beck to get you first thing in the morning."

"My ass, I've got a company to run."

"Not for five days you don't," laughed Cohen. "And Boris and I have some unfinished business downtown."

"Take plenty of ammo, and sleep with your boots on."

"Don't worry 'bout us, Trung-oui. Just make sure you're on your good behavior. Hate to come back and find out they cut off something no man should be without."

The interior of the longhouse was smaller than the Rhade structure in which the sacrifice had been held. Among the Jarai, the clan matriarch usually lived with only one or two married daughters. The remainder of her daughters and granddaughters and their husbands lived in adjacent longhouses. St. Cyr insisted on entering the house under his own power. He had barely sat back on a raised wooden pallet before he dropped off to sleep.

He slept a cool, green, liquid sleep which let the sounds of his surroundings ooze in through his pores. Their language was neither classical Malay, nor the harsher dialects of Sarawak, or even the formal sacred language used by Y Mur Thak at the sacrifice. This Nak'drai as they called it was rich in trilled rs and aspirated stops that gave the letters b, k, and t a sensuality of their own. He heard the voices of at least two children, and two woman named H'pak, and H'nek. The last voice was one he strained to hear. A sensual sound: H'nek. When spoken, it appeared to have a glottal pause immediately after the H, making it Hu'Nek. He wondered if all the women of this tribe had names that began with the aspirated H. H'nek, he whispered.

There was sudden silence."Blir," said a woman's voice.

"Blir," he repeated. Children giggled.

"H'pak," said a voice with an impish tinge.

"H'pak," he repeated, opening his eyes. Instead of the expected ceiling, he was staring at the weave in the floor mat. H'pak was a nice sound, but H'nek was more pleasing.

"H'nek," he said. The sound caressed his vocal chords.

"I am H'nek," said the speaker. And though he'd heard the voice before, it was delightfully musical. As it drew closer, turning softer and more subtle, he could feel her heat. Something rose within him. A brown foot stepped softly into his field of vision. His eyes wandered up the black sateen skirt, over her flat dusky stomach, and up through the cleavage showing between the edges of a cotton vest, to find the soft black pools of Rahlen H'nek's eyes staring down into his soul.

"Meerika," She crouched down to fold her arms softly around her knees, "welcome to my longhouse. But you have yet to enter my true long house."

"Where I learned the people's language," he grinned, "they would have taken a cane to any woman so brazen with her tongue."

Shrieks of laughter broke out. "He understands," the children chortled. "This Meerika can talk."

Rahlen H'nek merely smiled, and he was pleased to see that her smile was full and white.

"I have never known a Meerika who could understand our tongue so well. And you have not been here two moons."

"Your brother should have told you."

"Hah. If any Meerika can say ten words, they swear he is Jarai. I did not believe him."

"He's a good man..."

"Good men come from better women. He was my mother's favorite son. And her youngest. As I am last of her daughters still living. But she left many granddaughters."

"So McElroy. Her husband?"

"Yes and no. Mac and my father together in Eagle Flight. When my mother fell sick, Mac made up papers to say she was his wife. He wanted her sent to h'Meerika to get well. But neither Vietnamese nor h'Meerika government would allow her to leave Dega Highlands. She was our Po Lan. Before she died, she adopted Mac as her brother. Among Jarai, that is a great honor. When my father was killed, Mac moved in and took to calling himself our father. He is only Meerika we love, because he would die for us."

"Why they call him Blek's father and not H'nek's father?"

"Because my father commanded Twenty-Five MIfors Company before it was Two-Oh-Five Company. Blek became commander when Tiepzap killed my father. They threw him from up-away in the Rhade country."

"Why?"

"My father was officer in United Front for Struggle of Oppressed Races. Highest ranking FULRO officer in MIfors. When discovered, he went into hiding..."

"I am grieved for you."

"I accept your...grief." She stared at the floor in silence. And as she did so he detected a subtle change, as if some steel door had slid into place. When she raised her now distant eyes to his, he cursed himself for having asked too many questions. She turned away, letting the shine of the lamp show through her skirt as his eyes played across the bottom of her full breasts. But her walk was neither coy, nor sensual, and as she blew out the lamp, he felt something cold and resolute in her dark receding form.

Sometime during the night, he awoke in a sweat to find himself on his back. Above in the rafters, floated a form soft, feminine and sensual. It had a smell, and a taste, and a silky feel as it reached down to unbutton his pants and softly caress his aching erection. His first soul surged up to meet it, and as it did so they disappeared through the walls along with all sense of feeling.

When the M'ngat returned, the other souls were angry. "She is worth a soul or two," chortled the M'ngat. "Do what you can to sleep with her."

"She will get you killed," cautioned the second. "You would be better served at Madame Binh's."

"Pah," snorted his third soul. "I like her aura. No challenge is without risk."

He fell asleep to the muffled chatter of his bickering souls just as the first hints of dawn appeared.

Chapter Eleven

SUNLIGHT SPECKLED THROUGH the wall weave and across a shadowed floor. Outside, the muffled ebb and flow of children's voices punctuated the dull rhythmic pounding of rice mortars. As light darts touched his eyelids, he sat up to find himself alone. His temple throbbed, and a yeasty rice aftertaste clung to the roof of his mouth. God, the stuff had tasted so deceptively mild on its way down. How the hell did they make it so strong? Pushing himself to his feet, he heard the door slide open. Mlo H'pak stepped inside.

"So, K'sor Meerika awakes! Blek's father at MIfors. He will return at midday meal."

"K'sor? Is that not a clan name?"

"It is also given to Dega from other tribes accepted among we Jarai."

"And I have been so accepted?"

"As Rahlen Blek's brother, no one will stand against you while you wear his bracelet. Not from here to Plei Djereng, for you now command Ko'pa Jhon's company."

"Ko'pa Jhon?"

"Blek's father."

"Then you take your names from your mother's clan?"

"Of course. Fathers give life, but it is the mother's clan who gives flesh. Take this!" she pulled a western-style toilet kit from one of the baskets. On a guess, it was McElroy's. "H'nek will not see you until you wash. There is a well three houses over." H'pak smiled at some private joke.

"Not until I wash?" he chuckled. "She has been among the Meerika too long."

H'pak gently prodded him towards the door.

The sun blinded him as he negotiated his way past screeching children, suspicion-eyed swaybacked pigs, papaya trees and banana plants to a small cement and stonework well. Women of varying ages were drawing water, which some poured over giggling naked children. A faded wooden sign identified the well as some engineer unit's project. As he approached, several of the younger women turned away.

"Swas'm lai," he greeted.

"Lik jakk'a eh," replied one young woman, smiling shyly to her companions. "He talks funny."

"So, a Meerika who talks," harrumphed an old matriarch.

"Yes," he smiled. "But still I learn the people's language."

"You do well already. So, you have come to help in our war against the Viets," she said in both question and statement.

"I come to fight the Viet Cong," he agreed.

"Vietnam people same Viet Cong. Young warrior," her eyes challenged his own, "were I young and unmarried, I would teach you what only Jarai men should know."

Her companion giggled something to the younger girls in a rapid staccato he couldn't catch. There were laughs, and an awkward silence. Above the snaggle-toothed smile, the crone's eyes were studying him carefully. She was, he realized, waiting for a reply. He looked past her withered drooping breasts and slightly stooped frame, and found something in her stance and the fire in her eyes that hinted of a lost beauty whose hair, thighs, eyes, and lips had once set young men to dreaming.

"To have found you young and unmarried," he replied, "would have been a great honor."

The old matriarch's back straightened ever so slightly as she surveyed her companions. Her lightly mocking smile faded.

"This one truly speaks our tongue," she said. "He is welcome in our village, and among our clan."

As he set about washing up and shaving, the women drifted away. Mac's taste in aftershave was limited to Old Spice, which he absent-mindedly splashed on before realizing that he would have to use his finger as a toothbrush. The *mnam pay* aftertaste retreated only slightly before the dentifrice rubbed vigorously over teeth and gums. Afterwards, he walked back to the longhouse glorying in the feel of the highland sun. Only the sight of drying tiger suits strung out on village bushes and lines reminded him of another purpose in life.

He found the longhouse deserted. After long minutes of waiting, he decided that his status as Blek's fellow commander would permit entry. Carefully placing McElroy's toilet kit on the pallet, he turned to find H'nek watching from the doorway.

"*Swas'm lai*," he greeted.

She smiled, but said nothing. As her eyes searched his face and body, he was suddenly aware that the morning's chill was now a midday heat. The intensity of her stare silenced any further words. Stepping softly inside, she slid the door shut. He needed to get out, warned a voice in the far corner of his mind. An indignant Peace Corps official berated him for fornicating with a 'native woman' and disgracing his country. This native's nipples were showing dark and hard beneath a white sateen blouse. As she walked towards him, she undid the buttons.

"It is hot, no?"

"Much too hot," he agreed. "Blek and McElroy should arrive soon."

She said nothing as she slipped by, carefully removing and folding her blouse. Arching up on her toes to reach a suspended basket, she smiled at him from the corner of mischievous eyes.

"You find me attractive, yes Meerika?"

"Very," he stammered. "Were I that blouse, that I might cradle such breasts."

An impish smile played across her lips.

"Why Meerika like breasts? Breasts are for children. Would it not be better to be my lover? Then you could cradle all of me, and I all of you."

Reaching down, she undid the knot in her skirt and let it drop softly to the floor. An erection struggled up inside his pants.

"I am not the first woman you have seen."

She wasn't. But the pounding inside his chest drove away any memory of the others. His eyes wandered down across her nipples, past the tantalizing muscular wave of her naval, into the lightest tuft of hair between cinnamon colored thighs.

"You are...brazen."

She laughed, and reached up through his arms to sniff delicately at his neck, and cheeks and nose. It tickled, and he would have laughed, except for the urgent closing of her thighs over his leg and the silky feel of her skin beneath his hands. He inhaled her scent, playing his lips across her forehead, cheeks, and neck before parting her lips to let his tongue eagerly seek her mouth. Her own tongue played up and over his, and then back into his throat as her fingers slipped down across his buttocks. Somewhere in the distance, he heard the warning crash of silence. He was fumbling with his belt buckle when she stopped him.

"Not here," she whispered. "It would offend the spirits of this house."

He noted that her own breathing was now labored. "Then where?" he whispered.

"We have a place. Follow me."

Gladly, he chortled silently, as he watched her deftly retie her skirt. As if in response, she playfully squeezed his erection.

They hurried past a row of houses to a small ceremonial longhouse hidden in shadows of tall bamboo.

"The lover's house," she explained, "for unmarried couples."

Picking up a small teak baton, she rapped on a suspended section of bamboo. When there was no reply, she led him up the adjacent log steps and into a shadowed interior. He cupped his hands over her breasts, sniffed gently at the nape of her neck, and played his hands down her stomach to her thighs and buttocks, letting her aroma waft to the very bottom of his souls. She shuddered with pleasure as he ran his lips and nostrils up and down her tautly muscled back. Then she turned to nibble at his chest and neck, and pulled him down beside her. Their lips brushed, and touched, and kissed, until she was sucking wildly at his tongue while his fingers frantically ripped away his trouser buttons.

When they were finished, they lay tangled in each other's arms and legs, while he ran his fingers through her hair and continued to smell and taste her cinnamon skin. She listened to his heart and gently drew her fingernails across his chest. As he savored her soft, wet, salted codfish taste on his tongue, she turned pensive.

"Meerika, how are you named?"

"Galen."

"G'len?"

"No, Gay-Len."

"G'hlen?" It sounded better when she said it.

"Good enough."

"G'hlen. It is pretty. What does it mean?"

"Galen was a famous healer," he shrugged. "My mother picked it. What does H'nek mean?"

"The words?"

"Yes."

"H' means I am woman. 'Nek are eyes of a young deer."

"So you were named for the eyes of a fawn."

"That is the meaning. It is not my name."

"I do not understand."

"Because you are not Dega. We do not pick our names, G'hlen. Those who were our names pick us."

"So you are named for an ancestor."

"Not like you think. The spirit of an ancestor lives within me. Because she does so, I am recognized as H'nek. Do you understand?"

"I think so. Who was this H'nek?"

"The daughter of a great Ede warrior taken in a raid and brought to our country as a slave. My mother's grandmother's husband gave her to his wife, who had lost her only daughter to a cobra. Mother's grandmother grew to love her so greatly, that among Jarai people who were her captors, she rose to become a great Po Lan and had many famous lovers and two husbands. The first, my mother's grandmother's son, was killed by the Rhade when they came to take her back. But even so, she returned to the longhouse of my mother's grand-mother. I have lost a husband, she told our *Po Lan*, and under Jarai law I claim his first unwed brother. Mother's grandmother agreed, and gave her my mother's father as a husband. They were together many years, until he was killed by Sir Tiger. Upon my mother's grandmother's death, she was elected Po Lan of Rahlen clan. Her fame was so great, that many smaller clans came to live around her. And when she died, and time came to abandon her tomb, the procession stretched across many hills. Both the P'teo of Fire and P'teo of Water took care to offer condolences. My mother was her youngest daughter."

"Does each Dega have such a spirit living within them?'

"Each Dega has three such spirits. She is one of mine."

"And who are the others?"

"It is not for you to know their names, unless they tell me so."

Her eyes and tone turned melancholy, and he regretted having asked the question. There was a rapping of teak on bamboo, to which they ceded the lover's house. As they walked back to the longhouse, he reached for her hand. She let him take it, but as they approached some village women, she let it drop.

"G'hlen, do not misunderstand. I do this because I like you. I have had other lovers."

"As have I," he whispered into her ear. "But from today I remember only you."

"I cannot lie. My last lover went to an early tomb. I yet feel his emptiness within."

He wisely attempted no reply. Out of sight of the village women, she slipped her fingers back between his.

Mac and Blek were waiting in the longhouse, where H'pak was serving rice and chicken. Mac took one look at St. Cyr and scowled.

"Ya fucked up, Trung-oui. Might of b-been better if you'd stayed with the Fourth Foot."

"C'mon, Mac, we were just out walking..."

"Yeah, that's why the two of you keep r-rubbin' up against each other."

"Mac, I know you're close to the family, but what we were doing is our own damned business."

"Not here, it ain't. But we'll talk 'b-bout that later, 'cause this definitely ain't the place."

After the meal, they drove back to the compound in silence. When Mac wheeled up next to Big Marty's, St. Cyr climbed out with a friendly "See you later."

"That you will," growled Mac.

For a brief instant, he was tempted to call Mac aside for a sergeant, let's-you-and-I-have-a-talk-type talk. But he merely nodded and pushed open his door to find a note from Toller. The company Roundeyes were at Madame Binh's for the night. He was finishing a letter home when he heard a knock. He opened the door to find a red-eyed McElroy, casually clutching a bottle of 151-proof rum. Before he could say anything, Mac pushed his way in.

"Care for some?" Mac offered the bottle.

St. Cyr shook his head.

"Suit yourself, Trung-oui, but you and me need to have a talk."

"It's your dime, Mac."

"It ain't that kind of talk. It's the 'I need to give you some advice, and you need to shut the fuck up and listen' kind."

St. Cyr nodded in agreement. Mac's lack of stutter had caught his attention.

"Look," Mac continued, "I can't blame you for hoppin' in the sack with H'nek. Ain't a man in this compound wouldn't do the same if he could. But you're fuckin' up if it ever goes beyond a little roll in the lover's house. What you don't understand, Trung-oui, is that she's about to become a Po Lan. You know what that means?"

"She sort of explained it. They're the clan matriarchs."

"Yeah, but they're a little more than just old ladies who boss around their daughters' husbands. The Po Lans are the real political power of the Rhade, and certain subgroups of the Jarai. Most of 'em are withered old crones who've managed to outlive their aunts and sisters, but occasionally one comes up young. Guess it happens 'bout once every fifty years in the whole Jarai nation. Looks like it's going to happen this year, Only this is going to be big 'cause both the Jarai and Rhade are involved."

"How did the Rhade get involved?"

"You don't need to know. What you do need to know is that H'nek is two years past marrying age, and there's more than one Jarai buck who'd kill just for the chance to marry her. Two I know of are one nasty character named Siu Dot, and Rchom Jimm, one of your platoon leaders. Those two have been after H'nek for as long as I've been in country. Jimm, 'cause she can't walk upwind of 'em without giving him a hard-on, and Siu Dot because he's got political ambitions to be the P'teos of fire and water combined. You don't want either one of those coming after you."

"Mac, it's not something I'm going to walk around bragging about."

Mac took a long draw on the bottle, and slowly shook his head.

"Goddam, Trung-oui, you sure are dumb. Up here, you're livin' in a goddam fish bowl. Every time you fart. Every time you beat off. Every time you take some sweet young thing to the lover's hut. Word gets around. My people are primitive, but they ain't dumb. You take off some girl's skirt too many times, or go to the hut one time with the wrong woman, and you'll be out in the bush takin' a dump when some jealous young buck counts to three and rolls a grenade under your ass. Understand?"

"I understand."

"You'd better. Look," for a brief minute, Mac seemed to lose his focus. "Me an' Magnuson are headed downtown. Wanna tag along?"

"No thanks, Mac. I promised the Choctaw I'd help him terrorize the Seventy-First Evac."

"Suit yerself," he grunted, and rose to go. "Look. You don't know Siu Dot…"

"No. Who is he?"

"Used to b-be one of our company commanders, 'til we found out he was a FULRO hitman. G-got dry leprosy that's turned his hands into claws. You see a real muscular good lookin' Yard kid with c-claw hands following you, or lookin' at you real strange, kill him!"

"Just like that?"

"Choice is yours. Once he hears she's unwrapped her skirt for you, it'll b-be him or you. Check with the interpreter shack, they should have his p-picture on file."

After Mac left, he wandered over to Big Marty's to join Moshlatubbee and Ferris. At the 71st Evac officer's club, in lieu of legions of nubile young nurses, he found himself cornered by a peroxide blond major of at least 35, who politely ordered him to bed her. The situation grew more comical as she grew more serious. Ferris and the Choctaw had better luck, latching on to two plain nurses being desperately chased by two obnoxious doctors. This brought out their best behavior as each vied to personify the courage, candor, and gentlemanly behavior of the Special Forces warrior taking a

brief repose from the horrors of war. When this drew the expected response, the party drove back to Ferris's room minus an offended female
major.

While the two swains danced clumsily with their nurses to old country
tunes, St. Cyr perused the photographs on the walls. Prominent among
them was an intense young Montagnard with bulging muscles and claw
shaped hands.

"That's Johnny," announced Ferris, as he unclenched his nurse to
show her the photo. "Finest Yard company commander we ever had. And
the handiest sonuvabitch you ever seen with a gun. He could draw a thirty-
eight and put five shots into a paper plate at twenty-five feet so fast you'd
swear it was a burst of fire. And I've seen him hit a running man at two-
hundred-fifty meters with an M-79."

"Glad I got my boots on," grinned the Choctaw, nuzzling his nurse's
neck.

"Smart-assed blanket-ass! Ask anybody who's been here more'n a few
months. He had 'em all scared. His favorite weapon was a silenced Sten
gun. Brock gave it to him. Up at Dak To, I saw him kill two Viet Cong with
a short burst and pivot over ninety degrees to put another burst into a third
before the first two had hit the ground."

"And what were you doing all that time," asked the Choctaw.

"Shit," Ferris glared. "Callin' for fire support. What the hell d'ya think
I was doin', lieutenant? If you doubt my word on that, I suggest you check
with any of the interpreters before your alligator mouth overrides your canary ass, and I find myself obliged to whip it. Just make sure you get the
name right. Siu Dot. Us roundeyes called him Johnny."

"Johnny?" St. Cyr wondered, "As in Siu Dot Jhon Nie?"

Ferris's sense of wounded indignation subsided. "Naw, I don't think
so. Johnny, as in some old gangster movie he'd seen about a teenaged kid
forced to become a hitman for the mob. Sort'a like that Sedang we've got
who calls himself Elvis."

Moshlatubbee was about to comment on the chances of Elvis Presley
being a Sedang hitman for the mob when St. Cyr flashed a warning wink.
While Ferris steered his nurse back out to dance, his furrowed brow
stamped with the determination of a bull rhinoceros in rut, the Choctaw's

date announced in a stage whisper that she wanted to see his room. St. Cyr helped himself to a liberal dose of Ferris's Johnny Walker Black, took another look back at the barrel-chested claw-handed Yard in the photos, and stumbled out into the darkness. If Siu Dot was gone, he thought, why was Mac worried?

It was probably just a ruse to keep him away from H'nek.

Chapter Twelve

REGTER WAS ON A BUNK in the Nha Trang BOQ, glancing over the names on the latest Army Times casualty list, when someone knocked.

"It's open."

"Sir," Pappy Green's driver poked his head in. "Colonel Green's back from Can Tho. He'll meet you in the officer's club for dinner at six."

Regter nodded and checked his watch. He had time for a drink.

Ambling down the boardwalk past Group Headquarters, he noted hundreds of bullet holes pock-marking the inner wall of the small arms berm on the SFOB perimeter. Tet souvenirs, bragged the headquarters troops, when an NVA assault had nearly penetrated the compound. Visitors were impressed. On an impulse, Regter strolled out through the main gate to look in. There was a conspicuous absence of reciprocal bullet holes on the outside. Regter smiled. The Nha Trang gang must have been in a real panic. Staff officers, clerks, and drivers now sported combat infantryman's badges.

Up in the second floor bar of the officers club, a crowd was building in anticipation of a strip show. What was it Dick Grey used to say? War is swell, combat's hell. The war looked swell enough from Nha Trang. Despite his years in Special Forces, Regter didn't recognize many faces. His tribal bracelet, rank, and MIKE Force insignia gave them the advantage. If he hung around long enough, he'd start getting plaintive petitions from ambitious staff types eager to cap their Vietnam tour with a month or so in the MIKE Force. Several were already glancing his way. Affecting his least-friendly mein, he found a seat in a corner and enjoyed a quiet drink.

Down in the dining room, a pert Cambodian waitress ushered him to a table in the back, where Pappy Green was waiting.

"Filet mignon on the menu tonight, Charlie. I recommend it."

"To tell the truth, I was hoping for prawns at the Frégate."

"I'd love to, but the First Group commander's in town and I have a later engagement."

"Oh. A little politicking?"

"It's part of the job. Aaron will be replacing Ladd, and I need to make sure that I'm still replacing Cox. You have a dog in that fight. Aaron's all right, but I'm not too keen on his camp followers. Most are worried the war will be over before they can get their tickets punched."

"Hasn't anyone given them a reality check?"

"That happy task is my own. The S-Two's updating them on the war, and I'm briefing them on our programs. A protracted war requires long term solutions."

"Like our so-called Rescue Rangers?"

"Yes," Pappy Green chuckled. "You sound pissed."

"I am. I was hoping to get you down to the Frégate so I could punch your lights out. You owe me that much."

"It's not the first one I owe you, Charlie, and it won't be the last. I heard rumors of that rescue ranger proposal before Westmoreland's staff got it. But I didn't know it was going to get dropped on us so quickly, or that Ngoc was to be part of the package. As Colonel Phu and General Quang explained it, the MIKE Forces, specifically Nha Trang, Danang, and Pleiku, are to become part of an expanded airborne division. Nguyen Cao Ky wants the airborne beefed up to corps size."

"Why not the III and IV Corps MIKE Forces? Wouldn't the Vietnamese prefer ethnic Cambodians to Yards?"

"They do..." Green glanced uncomfortably around, "but those boys might be going home soon."

"Home? They are home. You mean Cambodia?"

"Possibly. Some Cambodians are tired of seeing large chunks of their country under North Vietnamese control. Which is all I'm going to say."

"Pappy," Regter shook his head. "There's no way in hell that the Vietnamese Airborne are ever going to accept Yards. I think your old buddies are sandbagging you."

"That's because you don't know their history, Charlie. The paras were originally recruited by region, like everybody else. But in fifty-four, the survivors were all regrouped here and filled with commandos from north and central Vietnam. The Airborne were Vietnam's first all Vietnam-

ese force in the sense that people from various regions could be found serving together, to include small numbers of tribesmen from both the north
and south. Quang and Phu remember those days. And they'll soon have
the position and punch to make that policy. If the MIKE Force can prove
itself under Ngoc, then the Airborne Mafia will welcome them in. And that
will complete the task we set for ourselves when we first got involved in
this country."

"What about all these Yard leaders I've been training?"

"They'll be offered reserve commissions in the ARVN with concur-
rent call to active duty. Ngoc is read on to this. He'll make the pitch to your
FULRO boys once we get rid of Me Sao."

"So everyone goes home happy."

"Yeah," Green sounded tired. "Great, isn't it?"

"Sure." Regter cocked an eye. "But what happens when my troops
walk out the gate?"

"They won't..."

The waitress arrived with their meal. Contrary to instructions, the
steaks were well done. What the hell, shrugged Green, this was Vietnam.
At least these didn't chew like rubber. They were the real thing, shipped in
frozen from the States. After the meal was finished, Pappy Green pulled
out an eel-skin cigar holder and offered Regter an Uppman. Checking his
watch, he announced there was still time for drinks at his quarters.

At Green's bungalow, Regter slid into a leather armchair while Pappy
poured two brandies from a flask-shaped green bottle bearing a hand-
lettered parchment label. Regter's French was limited to reading the date:
1941.

"You know, Pappy—when this is over, I need to get a plush job as
some deputy group commander. Havana cigars, fancy French cognac..."

"Armagnac," Green corrected, "and it's a gift from a friend who's now
French consul in Singapore. He was with the Vietnamese Airborne when I
advised them."

"That's what I mean. A job where I can make important friends and
contacts."

"That's what you've got now."

"It's what I had, until you foisted Ngoc off on me."

"Goddammit, Charlie," Green's voice turned angry, "we've been over that. Now if it's too much of a burden, I can put somebody in there who'll work with Ngoc."

"Bingo, Pappy. And those are the exact same words Ngoc dropped on me."

"Meaning?"

"Meaning I can't help but think that during one of your little poker games with Quang and Phu, the subject somehow came up."

"And if it did?"

"Then you could've at least done me the goddam courtesy of a heads-up."

"What for? So you could turn the job down?"

Regter shot up from his chair, eyes glaring. "You sonuvabitch! You knew about this from the beginning!"

Green sat back and stared into his brandy snifter.

"Maybe I did. So what? It doesn't change the facts. I need you there, Goddammit, Charlie, hear me out! I brought you down so I could snivel and cry on your shoulder. Not to have you snivel and cry on mine. Look, I like the Yards as much as you do, but Vietnam needs fighters. Whether the Yards like it or not, their future is tied to Vietnam's. They fought in the Nguyen armies. They fought in the Tay Son armies. Hell, they even helped put Gia Long on his throne. So they can damned sure fight for the ARVN. The last thing we need is another FULRO revolt. MACV won't stand for it, and neither will the Vietnamese. They'll slam the Yards, and they'll slam them hard. And you know what I'm talking about."

Green paused, and Regter nodded. He did know. The Vietnamese wouldn't waste any time tracking down units in the jungle. They'd target the villages, which would have to be abandoned. To save their families, FULRO would have to splinter and take to the bush. At best, they might make it to Cambodia, where the North Vietnamese would turn them into slave labor along the Ho Chi Minh trail.

"Look," Green continued. "We're building the Yards up to a military force that could do serious damage to Vietnam's cause, and create a second front in the Highlands. That's neither in Special Forces' nor our national interest. However short, it will only benefit North Vietnam. Hell, think of the field day the anti-war crowd would have. That's why whatever is going on in your MIKE Force worries us. Whoever this Me Sao is, he's come out of left field and appears to have more power than any of them. Meanwhile, we've got an army of galvanized career officers just dying to run up there and get a bunch of people killed so they can go back to the real army with a Silver Star and dynamite efficiency report. People who don't give a shit for the Yards, Special Forces, or Vietnam. So I did what any good officer would do. I suckered the best man I knew into taking the job. What's the difference between that and ordering you to take and hold some useless hill I know you're going to die on?"

"The difference," growled Regter, "is that you're supposed to give me all the information you have on that goddam hill before you send me up there."

"Well, la-di-da." Green sat back, and took a deep draw on his cigar. "Now you've got it. Remember those words, Charlie. Someday you're going to be sitting in my chair. Let's see how they sound then. So until then, shut up and soldier on."

"All right," Regter shrugged. "I've got that off my chest."

"Good. Know why I was a day late in getting back?"

"Not really," Regter grinned. "I figured you were having a good time."

"No such luck. Colonel Ladd had me sit in on a meeting at MACV headquarters. It was all about how long we're going to be here. Do you know how many actual French troops they had in Indochina?"

"No. I never gave it any thought."

"Well, apparently Abrams did, because he brought it up just after they went over the latest casualty figures. A bit over fifty-five thousand. In a total French force of two hundred-and-fifty thousand. Subtract the difference and you've got the number of Vietnamese, Cambodians, Legionnaires, North Africans, and Black Africans who fought in their cause." Green leaned forward, pointing his cigar at Regter. "Abe's point was that at the rate we're going, the United States is likely to lose more men killed in Vietnam than the number of Frenchmen they had here. And once anyone in Congress connects those two points, there's going to be a mad scramble to cut our losses and bow out. Abe's bottom line: We need to be ready to turn this war over to the Vietnamese now."

"They're not ready."

"I know that. But time is running out. Vietnam needs all the troops it can get, and the Yards have to accept the fact that their only real choice is a southern government or a northern one. Your job's not just to build the MIKE Force, but to professionalize it to the point that we can hand it over to Ngoc and the Vietnamese."

"Pappy, you should've told me that when you gave me the job."

"I know I should've. I thought we had more time." Green glanced at his watch. "Look, I've got to run. A last word—a plea, really, for you to work with Ngoc. If events outrun us. If the MIKE Force ends up fighting a conventional battle before it's time, it's going to get destroyed. Here, help yourself to my cigars, but take it easy on the Armagnac. Once I see our guests from Okinawa off, I have to catch a plane for Danang. So I won't be around for a couple of weeks."

"What's going on in Danang?"

"They're picking up signs of another offensive. You know how it is. No one wanted to listen before Tet. Now, every recon team after-action report is scrutinized twenty times over."

Pappy Green flashed a wan smile and extended his hand. For brief seconds, he appeared to age before Regter's eyes. "Take care, Charlie. No matter what."

"What's that supposed to mean?"

"Hell," Green shrugged. "I dunno. Maybe it just means I'm getting old. Have a good trip back."

Chapter Thirteen

ST. CYR HUDDLED IN THE dark shivering cabin of a C-130 aircraft, wedged against the fuselage wall as Blek, Jimm, and K'sor Tlur moved up and down the two aisles, calling out encouragement to the men. A longer retraining period had allowed time for an airborne operation. As no Montagnard had ever jumpmastered, it had taken several nights of instruction in a Pleiku Air Base C-123 hanger-queen before Blek and his crew felt comfortable in the role. Here, one of their new Vietnamese cadre had come in handy.

Pham Van Xuan and Nguyen Van Dung were both *Trung-si* platoon sergeants in the LLDB. Xuan, a tall lanky Buddhist from the Mekong Delta, had never served with Montagnards but was genuinely enthused with his new charges. His infectious smile, boyish demeanor, and affinity for U.S. rations prompted Cohen to nickname him Spam. Dung, by contrast, was a short pale Catholic from North Vietnam who affected a permanent sneer. His name was properly pronounced *Zung*, but among the Roundeyes and Yards he quickly became Dung once its English meaning spread through the ranks. Senior of the two, Dung had first carried a rifle at the age of ten in Ben Tre's Committee for the Defense of Christianity, a Catholic militia loyal to Diem. He wore an ornate crucifix and had the words *vi chua va to quoc* tattooed on his chest. Spam's tattoo was a tiger's head on his forearm emblazoned with the words *danh chet viet cong*.

At least, chuckled Boris, neither had plans of getting captured. 'For God and country' and 'Kill commies' were hardly mottos to endear you to your local VC. Cohen and Ryan were unimpressed.

The two Vietnamese had hung on the sidelines in retraining, disdaining to even fire their weapons at the range. But when St. Cyr ran into difficulty translating Boris's class on jumpmaster procedures, Spam had waded in. Patiently, he explained the signals, postures, and their purpose in Vietnamese, gesticulating and pantomiming as he went. The questions came back in Vietnamese, Jarai, and broken English. Spam's own English was heavily accented, but he was quick to pick up Jarai and regarded the Yards as racial equals, if inferior in rank. That attitude sparked its own response. Major Ngoc warned Spam against getting too familiar with the *Moi*, while on the night their training finished, Jimm pulled St. Cyr aside.

"What platoon Trung-si Pham go?"

"I send Boris platoon."

"Where Dung go?"

"Ryan or Cohen platoon. I not yet decide."

"Better I take Pham."

"Why? Are you and Pham become friends?"

"Friends?" Jimm snorted. "He is Tiep-zap. But he stay with me, better he stay alive."

"Then he is yours."

Rchom Jimm and Blek now scrutinized the troop bay of the lurching aircraft from the near edge of the ramp. It squealed open, air rushing in. Their arms shot rigidly out toward the center aisle. Dusky sweaty faces stared back. Rivulets of sweat trickled down under Jimm's helmet, but Blek's face was powder dry.

"Get ready!" Their voices were scarcely heard above the roar of engines.

"Inboah per snell, stan up!" Under the weight of parachutes, weapons, and equipment, the center row troops huffed, puffed, and heaved themselves into position. With over 60 pounds of chute and equipment, no man was truly light. Biloskirka and K'sor Tlur motioned those on the sides of the aircraft to remain seated. St. Cyr fought down the urge to step in. They were doing fine without him.

"Hook up!" Blek and Jimm made a circle with their thumbs and forefingers. Jumpers struggled desperately to reach the taut steel cable. Boris weighted it down while Spam dodged in and out, snapping fumbled static line hooks into place. St. Cyr noted that Spam had taken off his own parachute. So much the better, he thought. It would be easier to fire him for refusing to jump. Too bad it was Spam, and not Dung.

"Check Static Line!"

Steel cables resonated as the men jerked on their static lines. One hook sprang loose, clattering off a trooper's helmet to the floor. Within seconds Spam had darted in to re-attach the hook to its cable.

"Check Quip Men!" Blek and Jimm made a great show of checking equipment, while each Roundeye eyed the jumpers in their assigned sectors, searching for loose equipment or a misrouted static line.

"Soun off foah Quip Men check!" Another strange Roundeye incantation muttered to drive away bad spirits. Watching the men slap and push each other from the rear forward, St. Cyr recalled Boris's suggestion that they adopt the much simpler French commands of stand up, hook up, and go.

The Crew Chief shot Blek the six-minutes signal as shouts of "ghokay" rolled up the troop bay, hesitant at first, then full throated. As the propeller changed pitch, experienced jumpers felt the aircraft slow down. The crew chief held up two fingers as the ramp dropped behind him. While the Roundeyes held their collective breath, Blek and Jimm stepped out to the very edge, wind whipping their tiger fatigues skin tight about their legs as Pleiku's rolling plains yawed and slipped below.

The jumpmasters ignored the panorama to peer through the crack between ramp and fuselage. They'd been told not to expect to see much with the wind blasting their eyes at 180 miles an hour, but it reminded the troops that the jumpmasters were in charge. They weren't. Both had been ordered to go on the green light, and switching that light to green was the pilot's job. And yet through the v-shaped crack between ramp and fuselage, Blek made out the road that ran past the drop zone. He had yet to see the panels, or the green smoke, but he had seen enough. Triumphantly, he stood and swaggered back into the troop bay, motioning for Jimm to take his place. Jimm would lead the right side stick out the aircraft, as Blek would lead the left.

"MIfors," screamed Blek.

"Mifors," chorused the voices.

"Gooo, MIfors!" Blek yelled, spittle flying from his lips.

"MIfors!" came the refrain.

"MI-fors...MI-fors...MI-fors..."Blek stamped his feet on the metal deck in a simple one-two rhythm.

The jumpers took up the chant, stomping their feet and jerking their static lines to the rhythm. As the vibrations of 45-odd pairs of stomping boots passed up into the cabin, the crew cursed. What the hell was going on back there? "Close enough," grinned the pilot as he switched the light to green. "Let's get rid of these assholes."

Blek caught the light, but gave it a doubtful look.

"Go," called St. Cyr. The one-two stomp rhythm was reaching a crescendo. "Go!" he repeated, trying to be heard above the din.

Blek flashed a 'wait' signal, and motioned for Jimm to stand by. Squatting on the ramp, he looked down to see the marking panels slide into view. They formed an E. With a triumphant smile, he signaled to Jimm, who screamed an order to his stick, lowered his head, lumbered forward, and disappeared into the slipstream.

Men to both sides of the aircraft stared in wonder as their comrades shuffled past to be whipped off the ramp, appearing seconds later as a trail of descending green mushrooms in the sky. Cold air rushed into the troop bay. As the last man disappeared, St. Cyr was up with K'sor Tlur to manhandle the deployment bags back to the forward end of the bay. They had barely finished when the crew chief flashed the five-minute sign. K'sor Tlur trundled to the ramp while St. Cyr returned to the end of the trail stick. K'sor Tlur now gave the jump commands, assisted by Spam, who nonchalantly buckled on his parachute and equipment at the edge of the yawing void. Brief glimpses of Spam made St. Cyr's skin crawl. If they hit the slightest air pocket, Spam was history.

His thoughts blurred as the outboard personnel staggered to their feet. The rushing air and cabin noise were deafening. Blindly following those to his front St. Cyr stood up, hooked up, checked his static line and equipment, and felt the pit of his stomach began to crawl. Despite his advantage in height, he could barely make out what was going on.

K'sor Tlur motioned the lead stick to follow him, and disappeared. The aircraft rocked and swayed. St. Cyr counted in his mind, reviewing his safety checks. The left side of the aircraft was clear. He should be moving, he told himself. Fixing his eyes above the helmet of the Yard to his front, he pushed. The light brightened as they approached the ramp. Walk off at an angle, an inner voice advised, not too close to this guy in front. Wait until his bag deploys. The ramp shimmied beneath his feet. The helmet in front of him disappeared. He tried not to look at the earth rolling under the ramp-edge as a voice warned him to wait a split second. Bowing his head, he thrust forward, the last man in the aircraft. A thrill coursed through his veins. *Oh God, St. Jean Baptiste, blessed be thy name. Blessed— shit!* The pit of his stomach lurched upwards. *Maudit Christ du Tabonacle!*

He spun down into the void, locking a strangely detached gaze over his boot toes, as earth, mountains, horizon, and other jumpers flashed over their edges. One thousand, two thousand, three thousand; what in hell was he counting for? His parachute had deployed. Grassy plains, wooded knolls, villages, streams, and fields spread out below. Above him, a brilliant green canopy shone in the sun.

As his string of green mushrooms floated earthwards, he reveled in the sight. A voice inside reminded him of his equipment. He reached down, feeling around with his hands for panicked seconds. Then, relief, as his fingers found the quick release straps. Jerking out and up, he felt his rucksack drop to the bottom of its tether. The green and red earth was coming up fast. Diminutive figures scrambled about. Locking his gaze on the horizon, he winced, bent his knees slightly, pointed his toes down, and prayed that everyone below was clear.

He hit, driving his heels up into his buttocks and falling over backwards. As he struggled to his feet, a semi-naked mob swarmed over his canopy.

"Hey," he called, "what you do?"

"Mifors," the children called back, and went on with their parachute rolling. By the time he had unhooked himself from the harness and checked his Car-15, they had stuffed his parachute into an aviator kit bag. He fished in his pockets for Vietnamese dong, found none, and looked up to see a kit bag with legs making its way past Blek and off the drop zone.

"Hey! Where go my parasol?"

"Go turn-in point," Blek laughed, "so can get coca cola."

"Congratulations, Jumpmaster," St. Cyr extended his hand.

"Good, hunh?" Blek beamed. "I like!"

"Damned good!" St. Cyr confirmed in English as they paused to watch the second aircraft deliver the final pass.

McElroy's grim face was waiting at the assembly area. Eight men had suffered injuries which would require their being left behind. Nearly an entire squad.

"Saville ain't g-gonna like it," Mac mumbled. "I told Campbell we needed more than three days for Jump training."

"It was my choice," St. Cyr countered. "Next retraining we'll go back to marksmanship and live fire exercises. Where's the captain?"

"Up at An K-khe with Major Regter. The NVA c-cut the road. Word is that's our next mission."

"Clearing roads?" Biloskirka scowled. "Bad mission for MIKE Force. Specially with so many new men."

"That's what the major went up to tell 'em, Boris. B-but that's the mission if they say it is. Your second jump's been cancelled. M-major Regter said you can pin jump wings on the new men now."

After a quick check of the turn-in point, St. Cyr drained his canteen and ambled over to a group of young women standing in the shade of a nearby tree. Rahlen H'nek's eyes smiled into his own. He was pleased to see she'd worn a blouse.

"Well?" he asked. "What you think of parasol jump?"

"I see before," she teased. "Will you come into my long house tonight?"

Her companions tittered and looked away as his eyes wandered across the outlines of her body and up to her eyes. The wind blew her hair across her face.

"Cannot," he said. "Must stay in compound."

"But you are commander..."

"Yes, and I must set example."

"I will not see you for many days."

"As many my men will not see their wives..."

"Then come for evening meal with Blek and Mac."

"For that, I will come," he smiled.

As he turned to go, she stopped him with a touch. "G'hlen, I like you very much."

"Yes," an empty sensation in the pit of his stomach reached up to stifle whatever mechanism drove his voice. "I...like you too," he stammered.

"Then," her lips returned a curious smile, "share my mat, one more time, before you leave to die."

He paused, uncertain of what he had heard. "Before what?"

She looked deep into his eyes. "Before you leave to die."

"I don't intend to die"

"Silly, those are words from the saga of our great hero. Someday, G'hlen, I shall have it sung for you. Blek signals. It is time to return to your men."

He stepped away, and caught sight of a figure at the edge of the drop zone whom he sensed had been watching. When the figure removed his helmet, he recognized Rchom Jimm.

Regter and Saville returned just before dark. In the wake of heavy losses at Tet, there had been a major troop reshuffling between the Viet Cong and NVA. Now numbered among their old foes from the 1st and 2nd NVA divisions of the B-3 front was the 325C NVA division and independent regiment 101D. Elements of these last had been detected around Ben Het, Polei Klang, and north of Kontum, where the 4th Division was too tied down to effectively secure national route 19, the highway to the coast. Three days earlier, a convoy running from Qui Nhon to Pleiku had been hit west of the Mang Yang pass. Air strikes, air cavalry, and 4th Division elements airlifted in from Kontum had driven the attackers off, but during the night sappers had returned to cut the road. Several got caught in a 4th Division ambush. Documents recovered from the bodies identified their unit as the K-19 special Independent Engineer Battalion, which was supposed to be operating under 101D. The enemy appeared intent upon drawing the 4th Division away from Ben Het and Polei Klang, but First Field Force (IFFV) suspected that no more than a battalion was operating along the highway.

Saville's battalion would recon national route 19 in force, between the Dak Ayun and Dak Katung rivers, to locate and destroy enemy in zone. A Troop from the 2/1st Armored Cavalry would patrol the highway proper while the MIKE Force ranged further into the bush, ready to react if the cavalry engaged anything larger than a few platoons.

This was not the light infantry ambush and strike mode the MIKE Force trained for, but somebody had to keep the road clear. They would be operating within range of U.S. Artillery with attached forward observer teams and a forward air controller overhead.

To make sure all went well, Regter would collocate with Jed Saville's command post. He felt no great confidence in IFFV's assessment of the situation, and if the MIKE Force bit off more than they could chew, he intended to limit his losses as best he could. He stayed long enough to congratulate the new jumpmasters, leaving Saville to issue orders, hand out the Intel packets, and send the company cadres off to work.

At 0200 the next morning, St. Cyr dragged himself into the BOQ to find all dark and quiet. Behind closed doors, some performed last minute checks on rucksacks, harness, and weapons, while others caught a few hours' sleep. He was surprised to find Moshlatubbee gone when he opened their door. To allow room for a small desk and chair, they had bolted their two bunks to the wall with hinges, and secured the outer side with chains hung from the rafters. Stark by stateside army standards, the room would have required field grade rank in the 4th Division. His last luxury would be a hot shower, unless the water had been used up. He dropped his last garrison clothes for a month into a laundry bag, wrapped a towel around his waist, and made his way down the darkened corridor to the showers. Since the new XO's arrival, lights-out was strictly enforced. He found the water still hot, and was nearly finished when Moshlatubbee walked in.

"Hey Frenchy, that you?"

"Yeah."

"At least," Moshlatubbee called *sotto voce*, "I know you're not slimin' the floor like someone else who showers in the dark!"

"Fuck you, Blanketass." Ferris's voice called from his room.

"What makes you sure I'm not sliming the floor?" St. Cyr laughed.

"Who're you kiddin'? Hey, I'll be in the Team house. You've got one hour."

He was pondering the meaning of that when he pushed open his door. The sexy figure in the shadows was definitely not Moshlatubbee.

"*Swas'm lai*," he greeted.

She smiled, holding her finger to her lips. Even in the dark, it was obvious she filled out a tiger suit as tautly as she filled out a skirt. His fingers unbuttoned her shirt while she pulled off his towel. Then he wrestled his mattress to the floor while she brushed her nipples across his back. She nibbled his earlobe as he pulled her down.

They were still tangled in each other's arms when the rockets started coming in. St. Cyr cocked an ear to the sound of the motors, and confidently whispered that she needn't worry. H'nek giggled and rolled over to position herself on top.

"Everybody out to the bunkers," called the new XO's voice from the hallway. Toller protested that Charlie was shooting over, but his Majority prevailed. Seconds later, there was an urgent bang on their door, followed by Chart's angry growl: When he ordered people to their bunkers, they'd goddam better get there. What the hell was going on in there anyway? St. Cyr was still trying to disentangle himself from a snickering H'nek, when he heard Moshlatubbee call from the latrine.

"Frenchy's down in his company area checking bunkers, Major. Anything you want me to pass along?"

Under his breath, the XO cursed the fact that nobody ever told him anything. The sound of his boot steps faded, leaving only a dark humid stillness broken now and then by muted gasps, sighs, giggles and whispers, punctuated by the odd distant thundering explosion.

Chapter Fourteen

THEIR CONVOY DIDN'T CLEAR Pleiku until late morning. The trucks had arrived without the required sand bags in their beds. If a mine went off underneath, you wanted a few layers of sandbags between you and the blast. So the men set to filling sandbags while Saville paced back and forth, answering angry calls from the convoy security commander standing by outside Pleiku. To the lieutenant's biting assertion that his name was Abrams, in case that meant anything, Saville scathingly replied that he certainly hoped the rank of captain did. They were still exchanging angry words when the convoy rolled out amid waves and calls from the Montagnard wives and children lining the road. Not all eyes observing their departure were friendly. Viet Cong agents among passing townsfolk noted the convoy's size, content, and direction.

Romah Dat watched with particular interest. "How convenient," he smiled to his deputy. "Brothers Bloom, Jimm, and Blek are in field while I remain here."

Glan Perr merely nodded. His once voiced opinion that Me Sao's appearance could be favorable to their cause had triggered such a hostile rebuke, he now kept his opinions to himself.

That evening, as B Rob Ya sat in the interpreter's shack recording airborne qualifications in the new men's records, he felt a presence behind him. Turning, he found two burly newcomers in the company of Romah Dat. Leaping up from his chair, he snapped to attention.

"Lieutenant B Rob Ya, at your orders, my Colonel."

Romah Dat flashed a cynical smile. Sitting on the edge of the desk, he picked up Rob's cigarettes, lit one with Rob's lighter, offered several to his companions, and casually dropped the pack and lighter into his own pocket.

"We were unaccustomed to such luxury in Iron Brigade. You not mind I take?"

"No, my Colonel."

"You lie well, Lieutenant B Rob Ya, operations-adjutant of Ede Brigade of FULRO army." Romah Dat paused to take a deep pull on his cigarette. "A grandiose title for a minor clerk who scribbles meaningless papers which Meerika stuff into boxes, no?"

"Sir, I am soldier. I obey orders."

"You do?" Romah Dat exhaled his smoke into Rob's face. "Then obey mine. Who is this Me Sao who has taken to calling themself by name of that Ede scum?"

"My Colonel, Me Sao was a great warrior!"

"To my ancestor, he was just a bit of tasty liver."

"Sir, he was killed by the French."

"Spare me the legends, Lieutenant! It is who this new Me Sao?"

Rob gulped involuntarily. "I know not, sir."

"You know not?"

"Sir, I swear as Christian..."

"Ah yes. One of those who have abandoned the spirits and tombs of their ancestors to spiritually fornicate with this Jesus Christ and Virgin Mary. Like our esteemed president Y B'ham."

"Sir...," Rob's voice dropped to a whispered growl. "This first time I ever heard one Dega so criticize the spirit beliefs of another."

"It is?" Romah Dat's own voice dripped with acid as he switched from French to Rhade. "Then why not swear as Dega? Who are you to presume that as Jesus follower, you possess higher truth whose oath carries more weight than that of brother tribesmen?"

"Sir, as Dega, I swear I know not this Me Sao."

"A lie." Romah Dat exhaled the last of his cigarette into Rob's nostrils, and flipped the butt at his feet. "Answer me now, or I will have you..."

There was a sudden banging on the door, which grew more demanding as his bodyguards called for them to go away.

"Security!" one announced. His companion stepped back into a corner as the door burst open. Rahlen Blir's lively eyes peered in. Glancing carefully around the room, he sauntered in with four guards carrying M2 carbines at the ready. Ignoring Romah Dat's presence, he studied Rob's eyes.

"Lieutenant! I think everyone go home. New Meerika major see light. Ask I check."

"We are finished here." Rob drew himself back to a position of attention. "Good evening, my Colonel."

"Not just yet," cautioned Romah Dat. "Brother, I must speak to this lieutenant alone. You will wait outside?"

Blir looked at Rob, who nodded.

Blir's men herded the two bodyguards out. When they were alone, Romah Dat leaned closer to B Rob Ya and switched back into French.

"My lieutenants, Monsieur adjutant-operations, are real lieutenants, who have commanded real sections, killed men, and suffered much to earn their rank. They do not write papers with which certain 'Meerika' wipe their ass. And I have many more such as these on the way. You have until tomorrow night to identify this 'Me Sao.' If not, I take punitive action, understood?"

"Yes."

"Good. It would desolate me to lose an officer who can read and write Meerika, a talent of value. Oh, and many thanks for the cigarettes. And the lighter, that was truly gentlemanly of you."

And with a smiling sneer, Romah Dat strode out the door.

When they were sure he had gone, Rob and Blir strolled back to the security company's new quarters.

"Guard call when see they go in," Blir explained.

"Then I am fortunate. They would have killed me. Now I live until tomorrow."

"We knew risk when we vote to support Me Sao. This is K'pa Doh's doing. We must take care."

"You will get word to Me Sao?"

""Yes, but Me Sao not here."

Rob slowly shook his head. Even in the dark his anguish was visible. The decision to support Me Sao had been made in headier days, when FULRO leaders had risen up to control key MIKE Force positions. As young Rhade, Jarai, Koho, and Bahnar found themselves working together with the Americans, their sense of pan-tribal solidarity had grown. And with it, the realization that they were acquiring a power that rested upon the loyalty of the MIKE Force alone. Together, they were building a military force far greater than the one pieced together in Cambodia in the wake of the September '64 revolt. Now, with K'pa Doh's people fresh in from their sanctuaries, the day of reckoning had come.

"Then Uncle," mumbled Rob, using the honorific, "Romah Dat spoke truth. I am dead."

"Not while I live, my Lieutenant." Blir reached over to squeeze Rob's bicep. "The security company is behind you. You will be safe in this compound and within our village. When Me Sao returns, things will be arranged."

Departing the interpreter's shack, Romah Dat and his bodyguards found their way to a large rough hall bearing the sign: *Montagnard Hilton*. Inside, an attractive female bartender served canned American beer to soldiers from the security company, while banks of tables in the room filled with Iron Brigade recruits anxious to spend their 5,000 dong partial pay. Offside from the bar, several LLDB cadre played Chinese cards at a better quality table.

As his bodyguards hung at the entrance, cautiously eyeing the Vietnamese, Romah Dat passed from table to table, shaking hands and sharing words with his men.

Better than their last village, they laughed, even though Three-fingers had done his best to see that air H'Meerika kept them in beer. Things would be even better once they finished training and brought in their families.

True enough, agreed Romah Dat, but they must remember that their last village had been in friendly territory. Here, they should guard against the Tiep-zap. As Romah Dat finished his rounds, hostile eyes followed him to the door.

"That one Highlander," snorted Sergeant Thuan, "pretend he lieutenant colonel."

The short husky Chinese to his right carefully folded and covered his cards before looking up. "That one Romah Dat. He try come Eagle Flight when I command Nung Company in 1965. American throw him out."

"Why American not throw one dirty Moi out now?" sneered Thuan's companion.

Long looked carefully around the room. "Better to guard one's tongue, Trung-si. Tiger fresh from jungle sometimes forget he is in cage."

"China boat people," snorted Thuan's companion, "always talk riddle. Take more than riddle to make one sage."

"Ah," Long snorted back. "Then I speak as to a fool. If you wish call our Highland compatriots savages, you will do so outside this establishment."

"Our friend," chuckled Thuan, "safeguards his investment. A wise choice."

Thuan's companion merely glared. With a resigned sigh, Long gathered up his money. "Not just investment, Trung-si. This innkeeper graduate Whampoa Military academy before you born. Come back this country 1949 with Kuo Ming Tang division. When I command Nung Company in Eagle Flight, I learn it best to keep friends among our Highland brothers. Their friends live longer lives. Treat them as men, and they will fight to death beside you."

"They're dog shit," scoffed Thuan's companion, "and so are you. If you had anything to teach, you would yet be masters in China. Instead, you suck blood of Viet Nam."

Long stepped over to the bar, handed his daughter his winnings, and signaled for her to call the LLDB duty officer. Then, turning to Thuan's companion, he balanced himself on his feet.

"Why speak of dog shit? Is that what your mother ate while she whored for the French?"

The sergeant's face turned pale. He pushed himself up from the table.

Thuan grabbed his companion's belt. "Not fight Mr. Long. Bring trouble."

"Why not? Just dirty boat person who go-fucked his mother," his companion snarled, striking Thuan's arm away.

He rushed Long, anxious to close in and knock him to the floor. Long feinted his upper body to the right, stepped inside to the left, and swept the leading foot as his right fore-arm came up under the sergeant's shoulder. The LLDB tumbled, held out a hand to cushion his fall, and landed hard on his wrist. Warning pains flashed as he rolled back to his feet. His eyes flashed hatred. Spit flew out with each breath. As he positioned himself for his next attack, Long's practiced eye caught signs of a sprained wrist.

Thuan's companion glanced past Long's poker eyes into a wall of grinning Montagnard faces. "You think I fear you, you stupid Chinese? I fear neither you nor these fucking *Moi* monkeys!"

The word *Moi* whipsawed through the room. Long gave a resigned shrug, and moved cautiously back. Rather than abandoning the fight, he was making room to spot the weapon or grenade that experience had taught was not far away. At a bank of tables, an extremely large Montagnard with a broad face, wide lips, and flat nose, stood to push his way forward. A laughing sneer passed through the room. Ro'o Mnur was a 17-year-old kid from outside Cheo Reo who stood just over six feet tall. Christian in a society that had a low tolerance for Christians, he had learned to fight while being evicted from village after village following his mother's death in a missionary leprosarium. The Iron Brigade had become his home, and he viewed himself its champion. Unhappily for Thuan's companion, *Moi* was among the few Vietnamese words Ro'o Mnur understood, and the MIKE Force had recently added 'fucking' to his English vocabulary.

"Tell Tiep-zap monkey this *fucking Moi* will fight him," grunted Ro'o Mnur to a companion noted for his ability to speak Vietnamese. While his comrade grinningly translated, Ro'o Mnur removed his shirt and stepped forward.

If Ro'o Mnur's height had been cause for alarm, the sight of his thickly muscled chest and shoulders gave Thuan's companion definite pause. He reached instinctively for the small .32 caliber automatic in his belt.

"At ease!" Major Ngoc's voice cut through the room.

The sergeant's hand rested on his pistol.

"This Moi," he sneered, "would attack a Trung-si of the Luc Luong Dac Biet."

Ngoc pushed his way through, followed by Long's daughter. "Then," he smiled, "you must teach him the error of his ways. Give me your pistol."

The sergeant hesitated, then handed over his pistol.

Fixing the multitude with his eyes, Ngoc continued. "I am Major Ton That Ngoc, commander of MIKE Force. MIKE Force is unique force where Highland people and Viet Nam people serve together with America and Australia people. No man can serve here who is not willing to put aside differences for good of nation. And no man can serve who is not willing to fight." He glanced around. "This not place for fight. I apologize to Long Syen-sheng. Outside is proper place. When I give order, everyone go outside. Trung-si Thuan?"

"Yes, Thieu-ta."

"Form everyone in a circle around streetlight, now!"

Thuan's barked orders were rapidly translated into Jarai. While the mob streamed outside, two men slipped off in search of Rahlen Blir.

The mob formed a circle around the edge of the light. Ngoc stood in the center, holding his watch. These would be combat rules, he explained, but no eye-gouging, blows to the throat, or bone breaking would be permitted. When Trung-si Thuan blew the whistle, fighting would commence. When he blew it again, fighting would stop. Anyone who continued to fight after the whistle would be shot. To emphasize his point, Ngoc brandished the chrome-plated pistol. He then asked if the two men were ready.

"My Major," replied the LLDB sergeant, "I think wrist mine broken."

"Unfortunate," Ngoc agreed, as he motioned to Thuan. "But, such can happen in combat."

At the whistle blast, Ro'o Mnur lunged forward swinging his arms like hammers. Thuan's companion took evasive maneuvers, dodging and skipping to avoid the chopping blows. He succeeded, at first, but as Ro'o Mnur caught him on the shoulder, and then the face, he threw caution to the wind. The enraged LLDB stepped in and delivered his own punch to Ro'o Mnur's chin. A flashy blow, it carried no weight and brought him within reach of Ro'o Mnur's arms, which immediately locked around his neck and wrestled him to the ground, where Ro'o Mnur pinned him down and sat on his chest. Now in position, the big Montagnard began hammering the sergeant's face with telling blows. After several punishing strikes, the whistle stopped him cold.

"Get him on his feet," Ngoc ordered.

As Thuan stepped in to help his companion, Ngoc held up Ro'o Mnur's fist. "This MIKE Force champion," he declared. "He has defeated one Trung-si of Viet Nam Special Forces!"

A wild cheer erupted from the crowd. Back in the rear, several Roundeyes arrived to watch the action.

"You are called how?" Ngoc asked. Someone translated from the sidelines. Ro'o Mnur threw out his chest and stated his name proudly.

"Ro'o Mnur, you are champion fighter. MIKE Force need champion fighters. Can you beat one old Thieu-ta of Luc Luong Dac Biet?"

As he listened to the translation, Ro'o Mnur flashed Ngoc an insolent look and grunted two syllables which his translator was intelligent enough to phrase in the polite conditional.

"Excellent," said Ngoc as he handed Thuan the pistol. "Same rules. Blow whistle."

Thuan hesitated, then blew. This time, Ro'o Mnur showed more speed and sureness of foot. But every time he came close to cornering his quarry, Ngoc managed to slip away and deliver a strike or two in the process. They were not bone-breaking blows, but they stung. With the calls of his comrades urging him on, Ro'o Mnur charged directly at Ngoc with the same hammer-like blows. But again, Ngoc feinted with ease, this time sweeping Ro'o Mnur's feet. As the big Yard fell, a few laughs amid louder expressions of wonder from onlookers, hurt his pride. It was time to finish this. He backed off to catch his breath, then abruptly charged in a grappling pose.

This time Ngoc stood his ground. His hands clamped down on Ro'o Mnur's wrists, his boot snapped up under his chest, and Ro'o Mnur somersaulted through the air to land on his back. Dazed, he rolled over to rise as a boot sole lashed in to emit a loud snap just millimeters from his nose. Though it never touched him, Mnur felt its power.

"You see?" Ngoc's voice was controlled. "With that, I can kill you. Though you are stronger than myself."

Ngoc signaled for the whistle. Reaching down for Ro'o Mnur's hand, he pulled him to his feet and examined his eyes.

"You OK, not so?"

Ro'o Mnur recognized his second English word, shook his head, and grinned. "OK, Thieu-ta."

Ngoc raised Ro'o Mnur's hand in victory again. "MIKE Force champion," he called. "Great courage, great strength. But still can learn from old warrior like myself. Everyone back inside to drink one beer. That Trung-si there," Ngoc sneered at Thuan's companion, "buy beer. Then everyone return to barracks."

As the boisterous mob crowded back inside the Montagnard Hilton, Ngoc led Thuan and his companion to the LLDB headquarters. As soon as they were through the door, Ngoc ripped off the sergeant's beret, grabbed a handful of long hair, and backed him up against the wall to place the snout of his own pistol under the sergeant's nose.

"You putrid gob of dog shit! How dare you disgrace Luc Luong Dac Biet? Who gave you authority to insult Long and call Highland people *Moi*?"

"My Major, that is what they are. This one also pretend he lieutenant colonel."

Ngoc pushed the muzzle of the revolver further into the sergeant's nose while slowly releasing his hair. The tone of his voice turned cold, as he cocked the hammer and carefully moved his face outside the muzzle-blast fan.

"Thieu-ta! Not kill. Please!"

"Why not kill?" hissed Ngoc. "You lack courage. You disgrace Viet Nam Special Forces before *Moi*. Better you die here!"

"Sir, my God!"

Ngoc's thumb shot up to catch the hammer just as he pulled the trigger. The sergeant slumped against the wall, a hot wetness spreading down his pant legs. Ngoc sniffed disgustedly, his voice calm and cold.

"You will never use word Moi in this army camp again. Inside this army camp, I am only one who make use of this word. Understand?"

"Yes, my Major."

"Go clean up. Stay confined to army camp until I say otherwise."

As his companion slunk off, Thuan braced for his turn. Surprisingly, Ngoc smiled and invited him to sit while he eased himself into a chair.

"Trung-si Thuan, this your first time with Special Forces. I see you come from Parachute Battalion Three. Why volunteer for LLDB?"

"Promotion, my Major. In Parachute Battalion Three I am squad leader. Here I can be platoon sergeant, maybe even warrant officer."

"But glory is in Airborne Division."

"For officers, my Major. For other ranks, too many friends mine die."

"So you came here to live?"

"Not for myself." Thuan looked down at the floor. "My mother lives with us. She is old."

"Do not be ashamed. We all fear for wives and families. Frankly speaking, the sight of war widows working as maids, bootblacks, and prostitutes for American troops, in order to feed their children, does not give one confidence in future. Let me ask of you one question. You despise these Highland people, not so?"

"Not so, Thieu-ta. My own mother's mother was Khmer. They are like all prescient beings. But one who think he one officer, I do not like."

"You do not fear that they will eat your liver?"

"I do not believe such..."

"And if I tell you such is true?"

"Then such is true, Thieu-ta, though I thought it child's tale."

"Not child's tale. True! And among Highland people present tonight are men who have eaten livers of Viet Nam people. Not from hunger, but hate. Do you yet wish to stay?"

"I will honor my oath, Thieu-ta."

"Even if I place you in command of some certain people who only months ago would have killed you and eaten your liver?"

"Yes, Thieu-ta. If such is my mission."

"And if I tell you that this one Moi who think himself officer were to be your commander?"

"Then I must leave, Thieu-ta."

"You will not serve under Highland people?"

"Not under highland people who wear loincloth while I long time in army."

"And of Highland people who wear red beret while you still child?"

"Those, Thieu-ta, have earned their swords. If there is one such, I would serve under him."

"Good night Trung-si," Ngoc smiled. "And welcome to Luc Luong Dac Biet. There was one time when we were warriors, not politicians. That time shall come again."

Relieved, Thuan turned to leave. Ngoc's voice stopped him at the door.

"Trung-si. One must choose friends with care, and beware fools who gratuitously style themselves such."

"True, Thieu-ta. I will take more care."

Out in the darkness, three cigarette tips glowed in the distance.

"Who is more dangerous, my brothers? Meerika major, or this Tiep-zap major?"

"This Tiep-zap," Romah Dat's bodyguards agreed.

"Yes," mused Romah Dat, "I thought otherwise. Now, I agree." But to himself he thought: *That was exactly what Glan Perr had said. Why would these agree with Glan Perr?*

Chapter Fifteen

Western Bahnar country, An Tuc District, Binh Dinh Province, Vietnam:

THE FOREST LOOMED DARK and still as tiger-striped figures moved up from the riverbed. The cool waters had been temporarily refreshing, but a prickling humidity soon returned. The point men moved cautiously, M16s at the ready. M79 gunners followed, the stubby snouts of their launchers covering the scouts out front. Fifteen paces behind the last man of the point squad came the first man of the second. He took care to keep the point squad in sight, while his eyes searched the uphill sector to his left. Should the forest erupt with gunfire, he would push in and form the pivot of the assault.

The men wore simple canvas harness with canteens and ammunition pouches, over which each slung two cotton ammo bandoleers. An expendable item for holding clips and belts of ammunition, these had been converted into carriers for extra magazines. Most toted a simple light indigenous rucksack, but the radio operators and Montagnard cadre humped the heavier U.S. tubular frame packs. Some wore tiger-striped bush hats, their brims trimmed to reflect each owner's personality, others tiger-striped berets pulled down straight over the skull to resemble tight tribal turbans. All wore U.S. issue jungle boots, the lighter Bata boot common to camp strike forces being unfit for MIKE Force operations.

Although the NVA normally sprang prepared ambushes from uphill, the men also watched their downhill side. Crossing a clear river or stream stirred up sediment, which roiled some distance downstream before settling to the bottom. Enemy scouts who observed that sediment would know someone was upstream.

Ryan clambered up the bank, mentally cursing the wet squishing in his boots. He had long since trained his feet to go without socks, but a week in wet boots had given them a sickly purple ashen jungle fungus hue.

Ahead, broad-leafed plants shot up from the forest floor through the remains of last year's foliage. This was the dry season, but it had rained late every afternoon for eight days. Not the bone-crushing monsoon rains, but enough to soak everyone down for nightfall's chill. Ryan hated that chill, and envied the units that had drawn search and destroy missions down on the sunny Darlac Plateau.

He had volunteered to take the recon platoon while Toller was in Taipei, and walked five paces behind Jimm, who in turn shadowed the point squad. In the beginning, Ryan had tried to set the lead, as he did in his own platoon, but Jimm kept pushing ahead. At first, he thought his pace wasn't up to recon standards, but it soon became obvious that Jimm viewed himself as dominant. This irritated the young medic. Jimm accepted his role as Toller's shadow without argument. The fact that Ryan was younger than Toller did not mean he was tactically inferior. So Ryan would pass Jimm, Jimm would pass Ryan, and the platoon's pace would grow erratic. At length, St. Cyr's acerbic tone would cut over the radio, reminding Ryan that the recon platoon was supposed to be in the reconnaissance business. The advice did not improve his disposition. Exasperated, Ryan finally pulled Jimm aside.

"Platoon Leader," he said, flicking a thumb at his chest, "I take the lead."

"Jarai platoon Leader," Jimm retorted, wagging his finger in an arc. "Jarai platoon. *Bac-si* Medic best stay where can treat wounded."

Having abandoned his platoon leader duties in previous firefights to treat casualties, Ryan found an inner voice agreeing with Jimm. With an irritated shake of his head, he signaled for Jimm to take the lead.

The newest Recon cadre member, Trung-si Pham Van Xuan, hung back to the rear. Spam was equipped like the Americans, except for his LLDB-pattern camouflage fatigues and a small brass whistle looped through his shirt buttonhole.

"Did you get a load of Spam's whistle?" Ryan asked Cohen during a meal break.

"Yup. Think he's gonna direct traffic on the Ho Chi Minh trail?"

"Either that," chuckled Ryan, "or he used to be an MP."

"Shitheads," Boris muttered. "Whistle is for tactical control. Makes it easier to direct fire and movement during contact." He went on to explain that whistles had often been used in the old Indochinese Paratroop Companies for immediate reaction maneuvers.

Ryan and Cohen were unimpressed, and clung fondly to visions of Spam, replete in spit-shined boots and a polished Arvin QC helmet, directing traffic on the Ho Chi Minh trail. Too many kids were in Special Forces these days, groused Boris. They needed more time in the infantry.

Or the MPs, sniggered Cohen.

The company was breaking brush in a northwesterly direction to intersect a trail which showed on old French maps, but not the new. The forward air controllers couldn't find it, but given the lay of the land and village settlement patterns, St. Cyr was sure something connected the area east of Plei Bon with the Dak Ayun river and national route 19. People didn't just haphazardly cut across country as rough as this. His arguments convinced Boris, but Ryan and Cohen figured that any such trail had long reverted to jungle. Most villages east of Plei Bon and south of Mang Buk had been abandoned in recent years.

The troops sweated and heaved along, keeping a sharp eye on the trees. Rather than Viet Cong snipers, they were watching for particularly vicious weaver ants that constructed fragile-looking leaf nests in the branches. At best, knocking down a nest brought multiple stinging welts that later filled with pus. At worst, an allergic reaction to their venom brought on muscular seizures and death. Any and all trees containing such nests were given a wide berth.

As Jimm's lead scout ghosted through the forest, he heard a distant shout. His raised arm sent the point element to earth. As the signal was passed back, Jimm inched up to the lead squad. The point man, they whispered, had heard a shout and was checking it. Jimm whispered a report back to Blek. Moving on, he found his pointmen awaiting the lead scout's return.

An itching sweat clamped down on the company as everyone settled in. Fifteen, then 20 minutes passed. As Jimm signaled the platoon to move up on line, his lead scout slithered back into view. Jimm motioned for everyone to stay put as the scout whispered his report: North Vietnamese army ahead, digging in positions overlooking a trail. One had knocked down an ant nest. Men were cursing and frantically jumping about, while others looked on and laughed. The scout estimated at least a platoon, maybe a company. Jimm gave a quick translation to Ryan before passing it up to Blek on the indigenous net. To his surprise, St. Cyr's voice answered his transmission.

Blek, St. Cyr, and their forward observer moved cautiously forward to confer with Jimm and Ryan. Jimm figured the enemy to be 200 meters ahead. St. Cyr advised Blek to bring the remaining platoons up on each flank to form a wedge. Once in formation, Jimm's platoon would lead out. Particular attention had to be paid to their flanks. With contact imminent, they had to be able to react in any direction.

While St. Cyr passed his report to battalion, the artillery lieutenant plotted fires behind expected enemy positions and called the Forward Air Controller. St. Cyr cautioned that the FAC should fly somewhere out of earshot until contact. These instructions brought the FAC's sarcastic voice up on the company net.

"Ah, no shit, Shakespeare. Like to come up and give me some pointers on how to fly the plane?"

Ryan smirked. St. Cyr shot him a glare as Jed Saville came up on the battalion frequency to question his concept of the operation. Shouldn't recon check things out first?

"They have," St. Cyr insisted. "We need to hit them while they're still digging in, before they're in prepared positions."

"Roger. Wait, out."

Damn! St. Cyr toyed with his handset. They had to move fast. It was an instinct. This would be more than a platoon—likely a company. And their backs lay facing his direction of attack. Once Clyde was dug in, he'd have supporting positions. It wasn't often you caught him with his pants down. Now was the time. Before some Yard wandered off the trail to take a piss, and stumbled into the inevitable trail watcher or listening post.

Move out! St. Cyr motioned to Ryan and Jimm. *We'll trail you.*

Jimm took his platoon forward another hundred meters, halting momentarily to bring the men on line. He ordered his 3rd squad to follow in the center, prepared to reinforce as directed. Trung-si Xuan took charge of this reserve. Only after his squad leaders had confirmed visual contact with men from Biloskirka and Cohen's platoons, did Jimm motion them on.

Selector switches clicked to full automatic as the troops moved out. Senses alert, they scanned for telltale signs of movement and anything out of the ordinary that might signal a booby trap or mine. In the quiet hum of the forest, equipment thumped with obscene clarity. Sweat stung the corners of their eyes. Boots clumped on stones. Branches and twigs snapped. As they drew ever closer to the brilliant green light at the edge of the forest, they heard fragments of voices and the slice of entrenching tool blades biting into earth.

A ragged sputter of bursts to their left sent an echo rolling under the jungle canopy. Jimm noted that it was M16 fire as he pushed his men into a rush. Ryan moved to his right. An AK-47 sounded from the left, followed by a muffled explosion. The entire platoon now opened up, firing wildly into anything that moved or flashed. A mad popping sounded to their front. Branches snapped overhead and around them. Thunks ripped into a nearby tree trunk, showering Jimm's party with bark and splinters. A crash sounded close by. The grenadiers were in action. A deadly chattering ripped off to the right.

Static hissed over the radio as Biloskirka reported heavy contact. A company medium machinegun had them pinned down. The bunkers, someone screamed, get to the bunkers and consolidate. The thoughts were Jimm's, but the voice was Ryan's. Whooshes arced above the jungle canopy, followed by shattered explosions to the far front. Too far to do any good, but now the sonuvabitch knew they had artillery.

Jimm pressed his magazine-release button. Pocketing the empty magazine, he slapped in another loaded with pure tracer. These were marking rounds for directing his men's fire. Screaming for the men to keep together but maintain some distance, he leapt over a downed tree trunk and fired into a vague movement to his front. Ryan took cover behind a nearby mound and fired short bursts in behind Jimm's tracers. The radio operator stumbled after them. With sudden clarity, Jimm noticed fresh earth spread carefully about the area.

"There!" he called in Jarai. Reaching down to tap Ryan and alert him that he was going by, Jimm was suddenly thrown forward, slamming his head on an exposed tree root. Blood and sweat ran hot and wet down his temple.

Ryan scrambled around the mound to face Jimm's rear, enemy rounds stitching into his rucksack as he stripped it off. Jimm flattened into the earth as RPD rounds tore into the root above his head. Gritting his teeth, he waited for the round that would smash his skull. *Not the face*, he thought. *Please, Ai Die, not the face.*

A whistle sounded, followed by a long burst. Then two short blasts on the whistle, followed by more bursts. From his vantage point perhaps half an inch above the earth, Jimm caught sight of a slight movement in the mound they'd passed. An RPD gunner was searching for the whistle. Reaching up to his harness, Jimm twisted off a grenade. Sweaty fingers wrestled with the tape and pin. He didn't bother to count. He had to get the grenade off before the muzzle of the RPD swiveled back. Rising up on his left arm, he hurled the grenade. It thumped down five feet short of the bunker. Jimm flattened himself to earth and tensed for the explosion.

"Ai Die damn that sonuvabitch!"

Startled by the thump, the RPD gunner swung the muzzle back to Jimm. The explosion momentarily obscured his vision, but he was an experienced gunner. He blinked rapidly to clear the dust. Even with his eyes closed, his finger tightened on the trigger. He didn't have to see to kill; that was the genius of aiming stakes.

Tet, you Moi bastard. I will repay you for Tet! The RPD muzzle searched, then steadied. The gunner wedged himself hard up against the roof of the bunker, straining to drop his angle of fire. He could barely see his sight. He squeezed out enough of a burst to get a green tracer that tore into the root mere millimeters above Jimm's head. *The damned bipod!* In a flash, the gunner pulled the RPD back in the bunker and collapsed the bipod. But as the muzzle pushed back out, something smacked in.

There was a muffled explosion, followed by a near-simultaneous louder secondary explosion that threw the RPD and gunner's arm out through the aperture. As Jimm scrambled over to Ryan, Spam ambled casually past to pop another round into his M79 grenade launcher. One long and two short blasts of the whistle later, Spam's squad rushed up on line. Jimm stood and called for his radio. The operator limped sheepishly over, a gash cut in his leg. Two rounds had passed through the radio. It was his stumble that had thrown Jimm forward. Pulling out the antenna on a nearby squad leader's indigenous radio, Jimm turned to Spam and extended his hand.

"Trung-si, today you are my brother."

"Lik jakk'a eh," replied Spam in his only Jarai. Then, in Vietnamese: "You too are my little brother."

St. Cyr moved in long minutes later to consolidate the objective. It was quiet, he noted, or thought, or said. Too quiet. Sweat ran from every pore in their bodies. Something moved up ahead. Heavy firing erupted from Biloskirka's side to which the artillery and tactical air replied. Just as suddenly, it tapered off. The company tensed, cursed, and waited. Boris tried to push his men forward, but they seemed glued in place. The new men refused to budge, and the older hands held back, waiting to see what would develop. None save the recon platoon were moving. St. Cyr called around to gauge the temper of his men, and cautioned Boris to wait for the counterattack. It never came.

They had killed five enemy for two of their own: Men from Biloskirka's platoon caught in the open by the first machinegun burst. Numerous blood trails marking the route where the NVA had withdrawn were ignored in the final count. They'd seen too many men bleed profusely, and survive, while others bled hardly at all, and died. Guesses were best left to war tourists hot for awards and promotion. The bodies of their own were lifted out with the wounded on a medevac chopper.

It wasn't much of a victory in terms of body count, but the series of positions dug along the trail told their own story. Built to conceal a company, they were sited to engage a larger force. Along the trail itself, the tops of the trees to each side had been lashed together, rendering it invisible from the air. Hunched over the battalion situation map, Jed Saville plotted the bun-

ker locations carefully. He then drew Regter's attention to where the unmarked trail should meet the road. This was where Charlie had intended
to cut it. When the MIKE Force reacted, he would have withdrawn up the
trail, chewing them to pieces in a series of carefully laid ambushes.

"You're right, Jed. Galen was lucky to have stumbled across that trail."

The young Aussie flashed a wry smile. "A bit more than luck, wouldn't
you say Major?"

"You think Galen's got a feel for the terrain?"

"Finding that trail was his idea."

"Once is lucky. If he does it twice, I'll agree it's more than luck. Meanwhile we've got a NVA battalion in the area that knows we're on to them.
What'll they do?"

"You're asking me?"

"Why not? You did pretty well last time."

"Right. Well it depends on their mission. Charlie will either hold one
company out as bait to draw us into a fight. Or he'll pull back, wait for us
to leave, and then move in to cut the road."

"OK, which is it?"

"I'd opt for the second myself. He's still recovering from Tet, so I'll
wager he's reluctant to risk any heavy losses now. Unless, of course, he has
another well prepared ambush site we haven't found."

"And that," Regter nodded, "is what worries me. If we engage a battalion in prepared positions, we're going to take heavy losses."

"Yeah, well you might try telling that to IFFV."

When Regter did, the harried lieutenant colonel running the IFFV
tactical operations center was unimpressed. Five bodies was too small a
count to base any conjecture on. Regter argued that the extent of the preparations was what counted. The MIKE Force had located the enemy, and
uncovered his plan. What they needed to do now was to patrol deeper into
the forest, away from the road. The MIKE Force could act as a tripwire,
but when the shit hit the fan, it was the 4th Infantry Division or 173rd Airborne who needed to move in for the kill.

The colonel disagreed. What the hell good were Special Forces if they
couldn't do the missions you gave them? If they did find a battalion, and it

dug in to fight, the MIKE Force would take them on. Hell, that's what they got paid to do. That way, they'd have Gooks killing Gooks...

At the word *Gook* Regter lit up. The staff colonel's CIB was painfully new, and to Regter only Korean veterans had any right to say *Gook*, a term borrowed from the Korean language. He stormed out demanding to see the deputy IFFV commander, but the general was too busy. Two days later he was ordered back to Pleiku. While Regter and Cox argued, the companies slogged up and down the hills above route 19.

Saville's assessment coincided with that of a 95B regiment battalion commander. In documents sent to the B-3 front, he reported that the severe losses his unit had inflicted upon Puppet Ranger troops had forced the Americans to withdraw to the relative safety of the road. Protecting the road would tie them down while his battalion prepared for the coming midsummer offensive.

Back in Pleiku, there was no relative safety for B Rob Ya. Each day brought a mortal fear that bored deeper into his soul. Romah Dat's deadline had passed, and the young Rhade's every movement was observed by Romah Dat's men, who made no secret of their intentions. Restricted to the safety of the compound, he had become a hermit. He avoided the mess hall, stayed away from the Montagnard Hilton, and worked under the protection of a bodyguard. After two weeks, the fire in his stomach had become constant. It was one thing to be willingly used as bait to flush out Me Sao's enemies, but quite another to have no idea of what was going on.

Rob had never seen Me Sao, and refused to speculate on the FULRO leader's true identity. Superiors, especially ruthless ones, were best left undisturbed. Rob well remembered Bloom's exhilaration at being raised to the rank of lieutenant colonel, and his anguish upon immediately being ordered into the Rhade country to carry out an uncle's execution. Oh, Me Sao would avenge Rob Ya, as he had Ko'pa Jhon, but that was a shallow triumph for a corpse. Perhaps this front within a front hadn't been such a good idea. Maybe they should have consulted the Iron Brigade before brashly announcing at the Bu Prang conference that MIfors commanders must be consulted in military matters. At the time, Ney Bloom and the others had counted it no small victory that they had walked out alive. And that, reportedly, was only due to the intervention of Siu Dot and Blek's sister. That should have tipped Rob Ya off as to the strength of their position.

He needed an escape, however short, from his enforced solitude. Straightening his olive drab jungle fatigues, the status symbol of a senior interpreter, Rob opened the door of his room.

"We go," he nodded curtly.

Today's bodyguard was a young Raglai nicknamed Cowboy, who had transferred up from A-502 to follow his 'lieutenant,' a young medic. When the American had been medevaced for wounds, Cowboy moved over to the security company to await his return. He was tall, well built, slightly hare lipped, and forever wearing the western boots his mentor had given him.

As loyal as a dog, thought Rob, smiling at the simile. Though related to the Rhade and Jarai, the Raglai were demeaned as dog-people by their more advanced cousins. Living close to the Vietnamese, said the Rhade, had accustomed the Raglai to being treated as dogs. In point of fact, the Vietnamese feared the Raglai as human liver-eaters, and enough mutilated corpses had been found over the years to endow the legend with substance. That, mused Rob, could explain why the Raglai were somewhat slow-witted.

With the sun dipping into its late afternoon quadrant, they ambled across the helipad on the trail to the dependent village. Unlike other bodyguards, who followed behind, Cowboy walked at Rob's side. Every odd number of paces, he would quick-draw his .38 from its western style holster to engage imaginary gunmen. Intended to boost his charge's confidence, Cowboy's flashy speed merely increased Rob's sense of depression. His fate was in the hands of a clown.

"You play *bi ya*," Rob asked, hoping for a good game of billiards.

"Ooagh," grunted Cowboy.

"Good. We go China Market."

Nestled just below the dependent village, China Market was owned by a retired Nung from the Eagle Flight. Wedged into his small establishment was everything that any villager would ever need or want. Meat cleavers, sharpening stones, sewing thread, and cooking pots of all sizes and shapes competed with large earthenware jugs of *mnam pay* and tribal tools and implements. To the right side, on a concrete slab floor hemmed in by green walls constructed from salvaged mortar round crates, was the China Market's latest addition; a beer garden of sorts, complete with billiard table and overhead neon lighting.

Billiards was becoming popular with off duty MIKE Force troopers and Vietnamese alike. Rob chalked his name up on the scoreboard, and invited Cowboy to a beer. The owner's wife brought two cold Tigers and deftly pocketed Rob's 100-dong note.

The sight of Montagnards drinking premium beer triggered angry comments from a handful of Vietnamese Rangers slouched behind a corner table drinking Beer 33, called *ba-muoi-ba*. A scar-faced senior corporal swaggered over to chalk his name up over Rob's. Cowboy glared at the ranger, who sneered in open contempt, but Rob merely shrugged.

"Not worth to die over game," he told Cowboy in Ede. "They are jealous. Trooper in MIfors earn three times what senior corporal receive in Viet Nam Rangers."

"Then they should show respect," grunted Cowboy, playing his fingers lightly across the butt of his revolver. The ranger slouched back on his bench to rest his hand on a regulation .45, and glare arrogantly back.

"Not worth to die," repeated Rob. "Keep hand from pow-pistol."

Cowboy grunted a pidgin-English obscenity, but wrapped his gun hand back around the beer. The scar-faced corporal shot them a contemptuous grin as he swaggered over to pick up the cue.

The Rangers dragged their game out until early evening, when Rob finally got his chance to play. He was into his fourth or fifth beer, and the crowd of Montagnard patrons had grown. Cowboy knew a little pool, but nothing about billiards, and Rob soon gave up any hope of teaching him. Fortunately, several Vietnamese C Team interpreters happened in who knew the game. They started out playing for 100 dong, and quickly upped it to 500.

The play was evenly matched. For a while Rob would be the clear winner, but then his protagonist would move ahead. An alarm in the back of his mind warned him to return to the compound, but this was the first good time he'd had in weeks. Even his indigestion had subsided. Mindful of Blir's instructions, he promised to quit when two games ahead.

He had just moved up even, and was lining up the shot that would give him a one game lead, when a commotion broke out.

"Let me pass," shouted an angry Jarai voice. "No man cuckold me while I go field."

Cowboy grinned. Someone, likely from the headquarters, was in trouble. He glanced around for the culprit. Back in the village you got fined for such indiscretions. Here in MIfors, you could get killed. He didn't want to miss the action, but first he had to use the latrine. As Cowboy dashed off to the outhouse, numerous brows in the room furrowed, wondering if the voice belonged to the husband of someone they knew.

Rob tapped his cue nervously on the edge of the table, wishing the fool would shut up. He had a difficult shot to make. Sweat ran down his forehead. Heat and nervous tension had prompted him to remove his shirt. His dog tags swung forward, as he leaned out to study the path of his shot. There was pushing and shoving somewhere across the table.

"You, B Rob Ya..." shouted a wild-eyed Jarai.

Rob stared up into the muzzle of an M2 carbine.

"...you fornicate my wife!"

Righteous anger flashed in Rob's eyes. As he straightened to deny the charge, something slammed him in the chest. In shock, he fell back into a support beam and slumped to the floor, the carbine's report ringing dimly in his ears as China Market broke into pandemonium.

Cowboy crashed in through the back, brandishing his revolver. The assassin ripped off a short burst as Cowboy dived to the floor, his finger frantically working the trigger. Women screamed from the adjacent shop while tiger-striped pool players melded desperately into every nook and corner. Seconds later, China Market was deathly quiet. Cowboy leapt up, ejected his spent shells, and was nearly to the door when Rob's faint call reminded him of other duties. Miraculously, no one else had been hit.

Regter was putting on civilian clothes for dinner with Cox and Ngoc at Colonel Khanh's when news of Rob Ya's shooting came in. His adjutant made it sound like an Old West gunfight. The good news was that Rob's dog tag had deflected the deadly shot, and he was recovering in the 71st

Evac hospital. But Harry Perkins wasn't around to give him the back-story. Harry should have been back from Bu Prang by now. And since Harry wasn't really at Bu Prang, it was time for Regter to call in a favor.

Chapter Sixteen

THE FOUR HUEYS THAT lifted off before first light from an airstrip nestled among rubber and coffee plantations east of Ban Me Thuot differed from their Army brethren. Their twin engines made them look squatter, and they were flown by older, more experienced Air Force pilots from the 20th Special Operations Squadron. Still, control of the insertion was in the hands of a 32-year-old recon platoon sergeant, acting as launch officer, seated in the command and control ship. This was followed by a first gunship, an insertion helicopter, then a second gunship.

The insertion slick carried a team of four Montagnards and two Americans, all armed with Car-15s. If this mission deviated from standard insertion flights of four slicks and four gunships, Recon Team Durango's name likewise deviated from the standard snake and state names used by MACVSOG reconnaissance teams. As the first team leader, or One-Zero, Staff Sergeant Henry 'Snake' Espada had been told he could choose the name. Since Colorado was taken, he opted for the name of his home town. Riding along as the team One-One was Specialist Five Mario Guilliani, known as the 'Gootch,' Espada's radio operator and second in command. The four Rhade team members were led by Y Char Nuu.

The team toted standard recon equipment: large U.S. nylon rucksacks packed with a prescribed load of ammunition, spare radio batteries, signaling panels, morphine, blood expander, IV kits, and pyrotechnics. Where RT Durango differed from most teams is that they went in heavier on food and relatively lighter in ammunition. Espada believed that strength and nutrition were key to any team's survival, so they also went in heavy on water. Besides two standard canteens, each man carried two 2-quart canteens. The radio was a standard PRC-25, since they relied upon aerial relay for reporting. Y Char Nuu and another Indig team member carried black box HT-1 hand held radios. Forty minutes southwest of Ban Me Thuot, the choppers abruptly turned westwards and dropped down to tree-top level, signaling that they had passed their release point and were inbound to the landing zone. SFC Roberts, in the lead helicopter, called off the check points. Though this was supposedly a gravy run, everyone felt that familiar twitching in the pits of their stomachs. Y Char Nuu's eyes were impassive.

The C&C ship broke into a climb. Forest gave way beneath them as grass-covered slopes appeared. The lead helicopter dipped down into a clearing for the briefest second, then abruptly shot up to join the tail. Above, Sergeant Roberts tensed as the formation cleared a grass ridge-line. The grassy knolls appeared deserted, but Roberts knew that tracers could erupt at any minute. A tight turn, and the infil chopper dropped abruptly down to feather at the still. As the two gunships passed overhead, the infiltration bird pulled up to rejoin them. Impossible to observe were the six forms crashing into a thicket at the near edge of the landing zone.

For Roberts, this was the hardest part of his mission. Espada would wait 15 minutes before clicking in to confirm a successful insertion. Any voice transmission now meant something was wrong. Had he heard one, Roberts would have called for immediate extraction. But AK-47 rounds could silence a radio, and the enemy had long since learned to direct their fire to the team member with the telltale antenna—silence was not always golden. One misty Cambodian highland morning, Roberts's twin brother had taken a team in, only to disappear into the silence. No tracers. No flares. No transmission. And no trace of his team had ever been found. Roberts was not a kind soul when it came to prisoners.

Down in the forest, RT Durango huddled 15 meters from the edge of the landing zone, waiting for the rattle of an RPD, or some other sign that un-invited hosts were waiting. The silence was only partially encouraging. The Viet Cong often seeded potential LZs with two-man teams whose only mission was to pick up and track CCS recon teams. As bird sounds returned, Espada pulled out his map, oriented it to the surrounding terrain, and checked his azimuth. It looked like the right LZ, but pilots and launch officers could make mistakes. He checked his watch. When the minute hand touched 06:37 he gave his handset three quick clicks, waited for five seconds, and then gave two short clicks followed by a five-second squeeze.

Thirty seconds later, he had the responding click squeeze click from Roberts.

He had just folded his map when thrashing noises sounded nearby. The muzzles of their Car-15s swept up. Anxious eyes looked to Espada, whose eyes followed Y Char Nuu's gaze. A series of short choppy animal grunts later, Y Char Nuu's face crinkled into a smile.

"Gaur," he whispered. "Man-gaur boom-boom lady-gaur."

Espada nodded. "We wait?" he mouthed wordlessly.

Y Char Nuu shook his head. He pointed to the noise, signaled listen or hear, indicated themselves, and pantomimed an enraged Gaur rushing towards them. Espada nodded his understanding and signaled 'commence mission.' Y Char Nuu motioned for his point man to move out.

No VC, thought Espada. Not yet, anyway. At least that jived with what the Intel pukes said. This insertion was a little too late after daybreak for his liking, but both Intel and Lieutenant Gonzoni had insisted that the area was clear of all but local VC, and perhaps the odd Khmer Rouge or two. But what did Benzino Gasolino know? That asshole spent all his time in the compound. With eight months ground time in Command and Control South, Snake Espada was one of the best recon men in the business, ranked up with Phil Amatto and Jerry 'Mad Dog' Shriver. Eight months in Recon was a lifetime. One week, you could go in and walk around like you owned the place, maybe even taking time to kill a deer. But the next week, a follow-on team launched into the very same area might land smack in the middle of a North Vietnamese regiment. Hot extractions were hairy enough, involving the commando company reaction force and what seemed like the entire United States Air Force, but it was marathons that Espada feared.

Sometimes, Charlie let you insert, then ran you off into deep forest away from your planned extraction zones and into ones he had prepared. You literally ran for your life, playing out the agony of your physical and mental deterioration over obscure radio frequencies with soft handed, pasty-faced midgets whose company you shunned back in the compound. A man could run for days with a couple of hundred VC on his tail, only to die in the splinter ripping, tracer pierced inferno of a hot extraction. So RT Durango had two commandments: One, that the entire team came out together or they didn't come out at all. Two, that you ate full rations in the field. For if worse ever came to worse, Recon Team Durango planned to forego extraction and walk out. And they would do it together.

Paralleling an animal trail, they found the stream some 200 meters beyond the clearing that the maps had promised, another sign that confirmed their position. A trail cut across the stream 500 meters up, which wound its way 14 kilometers north to an abandoned Rhade village. Near that village, at a leper's hut, they were to meet up with a Montagnard with blue eyes. Espada glanced at Y Char Nuu. They'd had a laugh about that. Who the hell had ever heard of a blue-eyed Yard? Somebody named the Man Bear. Y Char Nuu had heard the name. It belonged to a sergeant with the MIKE Force.

After confirming the trail, they crossed the stream and fanned out on both sides to take up a hasty ambush position. If there was a VC watch team, now was when they'd show. Long minutes passed, and nothing happened. Y Char Nuu looked to Espada, who nodded in the direction away from the trail. Seconds later, they were gliding through the shadows of the underbrush.

The march to the village took more than a day. Race-car fast by recon standards, Espada would have liked to make it slower. That all signs were encouraging just made Espada worry more. So-called easy missions bothered him. When some staff puke thought it was easy, they didn't invest the required care in piecing a mission together. Back in Ban Me Thuot, after he and Roberts had finished their recon flight, he'd scoped out all possible danger areas on the map—areas which might hold enemy forces or expose his team to danger. He took extra care on those, bypassing them if possible, but otherwise sending out the point team first. Durango always worked in groups of twos, providing mutual cover. Poor security was what had killed Che Guevara, as Espada knew from personal experience. The worst part of this mission was the village, which sat exposed on a knoll.

Early the next morning, they began to pick up signs that it was occupied. *Benzino Gasolino had done it again*, Espada cursed. One of these days, he was going to beat the piss out of that squirmy little slug. He could scrap the mission, and claim that the blue-eyed Yard never showed, but RT Durango didn't work that way. Down in the forest below the village, Espada reported his location code word to Roberts in a whisper which was answered by the familiar click-squeeze-click.

While Espada and the Gootch scoped out the village with field glasses, Y Char Nuu stripped down. Whoever was in the village was taking care not to advertise their presence. If the NVA had picked up this blue-eyed Yard, they'd be waiting for the team to walk in. Crackling sounds to their rear sent Espada and Gootch to earth. Y Char Nuu walked by carrying a bundle of branches. Barefoot, dressed in a faded tribal shirt and old loincloth, he looked exactly like a wood gatherer. Minutes later, he struggled up the hill under a load of firewood.

As Y Char Nuu disappeared into the village, the team tensed. If they heard shooting, or Char Nuu's grenades, they'd allow him a few minutes to reappear. If he didn't, Espada must decide if they would execute their official escape and evasion plan, or adhere to RT Durango's commandments. It was his call, and it all hinged on a snap judgment as to whether Char Nuu was alive or dead. Minutes creaked by. Gootch and the Yards kept glancing back at Espada, who kept checking his watch. It was mid-afternoon, and unbearably hot. The cicadas' singing buzz annoyed him. Finally, Y Char Nuu appeared at the top of the knoll. This time instead of firewood, he was carrying a blue, red, and green flag. The Gootch sighed with nervous relief.

"I'll go in first," Espada whispered. "Cover me."

The Gootch nodded. Y Char Nuu's distant call reached their ears. Y M'dra flashed a gap-toothed smile. "FULRO," he whispered, meaning they were among friends. Espada's glare silenced him, as he motioned for Gootch and the Yards to stay back and cover him. Then, he ghosted up the hill towards the solitary leper's hut, Car-15 at the ready, where Y Char Nuu sat with another Yard.

"I expected you guys yesterday," greeted Harry Perkins.

Espada stared in disbelief. The short, bare-chested burly bronzed figure with extended earlobes, ivory ear plugs, and mahogany face with sparkling blue eyes, looked at home in his tattered loincloth. Obviously an American, but even the way he sat hinted of a tribal elder.

"We get here when we get here," Espada snapped. "Who the hell are you?"

"This Man Bear," interrupted Y Char Nuu.

"Yeah? What's your real name?"

"I'm Harry Perkins, the MIKE Force S-Two. And you guys are here for me, aren't you?"

"Yeah. What the hell're you doing over here anyway?"

"Visiting my family..."

"Your family?" Espada was incredulous. "They launched us over here to pick up some asshole who's visiting his family?"

"Watch your mouth," warned Harry, reaching a friendly hand for the shoulder of a tall boy who emerged from the hut carrying a man's cross-bow. "My adopted son's learning English and I don't want him picking up the wrong kind."

"Sorry," muttered Espada. "I was just wondering why the hell you couldn't have walked out. You obviously walked in. You and Gonzoni buddies or something?"

"No, but our commanders are. You're here as my insurance. My hosts would prefer I didn't leave. You guys are proof that I can. Let's get inside the village. Out of sight is out of mind."

Espada waited for the Gootch and the Yards to catch up. As they walked through the supposedly deserted village, he took note of the numerous troops lounging in longhouse shadows. Despite the friendly voices that called out to Y Char Nuu and others on his team, Espada felt nakedly exposed.

"Is this the so-called Iron Brigade?"

"What's left of 'em. Notice the American weapons?"

Numerous M2 carbines were slung from pilings, but it was the M16s and occasional M60 machineguns that caught Espada's eye.

"Yeah. Where they gettin' this stuff?"

"Right out from under our noses. These are better armed than the ones who showed up at our compound a couple of weeks back. They had everything from Moisin-Nagants to Arisakas and MAT-49s. But the interesting part is their tribal affiliation. They're all Jarai."

"What're Jarai doing this far down in Rhade country?"

"Actually, it's M'nong, and that's why you're here."

Harry Perkins ducked to enter a longhouse. Inside, women squatted around pots on the hearth. Sleeping mats lay along a ledge which ran the full length of the house. He paused to exchange sniffs with a woman who rose to greet him, and invited Y Char Nuu to make himself and his men comfortable. Then, he led Espada and the Gootch to a compartment in the rear.

"You see, FULRO's having a little internal dispute. When do we leave?"

"Extraction is first light tomorrow. We need to get moving. It'll take a few hours to get to our remain-overnight position."

"What," Harry chuckled. "You don't trust our friends' hospitality?"

"Hey, FULRO's great and all that shit, but everybody in the world I trust just walked in with me. I quit trusting my mother the day I went recon."

"Good," agreed Perkins, relieved that he hadn't drawn a team prone to hole up in the false safety of the village. "Let's go over the route out. Once it gets dark, these guys shoot up anything that moves. Oh, I'd like to take my two boys along to watch the extraction."

Espada flashed a pained look. "Hey, Sarge, I know you out-rank me, but over here I'm in charge. No way."

"OK," agreed Perkins in an amiable tone, "you're the boss. But if I ever have to extract my family, you guys'll probably be the team that's coming back to get 'em. Might be handy if they got to do a dry run first."

"Shit!" Espada thought that over. "OK, Sarge, but if they slow us down I'm cutting 'em loose. Dark or not. Otherwise, they stay with us until we lift out."

"No problem," said Harry. "They travel quieter than you guys." And they did.

The choppers snatched them up early the next morning when there was barely light enough to see. An hour–and-a-half later, Harry Perkins was in the CCS compound debriefing their commander and intelligence officer on the latest developments in FULRO. By noon the following day, he was sitting in Regter's office going into greater detail. Then, back at his type-writer, he hunt-and-pecked his report for intelligence channels, giving himself a fictitious source name with a B-2 history of accuracy. No reason, he thought, to tip of the MACV J-2 that a mere Sergeant had violated their directives governing the conduct of operations in Cambodia.

FULRO was on the verge of a civil war. K'pa Doh had shown up at Y B'ham's headquarters to demand a reassessment of their plans for an August revolt, and an open rift had developed. Y B'ham wanted specific highland towns temporarily seized for the purpose of punishing corrupt Vietnamese officials and underlining their demands for Highland autonomy. K'pa Doh, citing assurances that the Viet Cong would not interfere, wanted all major highland towns taken and held, and action as far afield as Nha Trang, with demands for nothing less than full independence.

When Y B'ham insisted that K'pa Doh had no authority to confer with the Viet Cong. K'pa Doh countered that he was well aware of Y B'ham's secret communications with Paul Nur, the Vietnamese Minister for Highland Affairs. That was hardly new, Y B'ham argued, and as Vice president, K'pa Doh had been informed. Which brought their argument to the crux of the matter; Y B'ham's recognition of the Mike Force upstarts. Under what authority had Y B'ham granted this person a military rank equal to K'pa Doh's? And who was Me Sao? Under his authority as president, Y B'ham had replied, and Me Sao's true identity would be known in time. All that presently mattered was that Me Sao would provide forces at the proper time and place. Then, came the reply, let him do so as a Major.

Such a Major, Y B'ham noted, commanded a force many times larger than the Iron Brigade.

That sent the FULRO vice president into a rage. The Iron Brigade was unpaid, badly fed, and poorly armed compared to the tribal mercenaries of the MIfors. Yet it was loyal. How loyal would this MIfors be when the Vietnamese offered them positions in their own army? Don't bother to answer, K'pa Doh sneered, their loyalty had been proven the minute they had begun dictating to their superiors. Storming out of the communal longhouse, K'pa Doh had ordered his troops to "take all necessary steps to ensure the president's protection." Y B'ham was now a prisoner of FULRO's most radical elements and the situation was tense.

Regter sat in his office and reread Perkins' report by the glare of a neon lamp. Out in the darkness, the front door slammed. Boots scuffed along the cement slab floor. He continued staring at the words as Harry's burly form barreled into view.

"Well, boss, what d'ya think?"

Regter shook his head. "I wish there was some way I didn't have to send it, Harry. But it's got to go to Group. A revolt is bad enough, but if FULRO splits into a shooting war, there isn't a camp in the entire Highlands that won't be effected. The problem is that once Group sees it, they'll send it to MACV. And a FULRO civil war may be just what the MACV J-2 would like to see."

"You think they'll try to help it along?"

"No. But they'll pass it on to the Vietnamese, who sure as hell are going to do everything they can to get it started."

"Maybe, but Y B'ham seemed determined to resolve this peacefully. He sent word to the A Camp at Bu Prang that their troops were not to interfere."

"It's not Y B'ham I'm worried about. The wild cards in this equation are Me Sao and Romah Dat, which doesn't leave me much choice. I want Romah Dat out of the compound immediately. Also, alert the Security and Training companies that anyone who goes with him leaves their weapons and ammo behind. And get that new warrant officer of yours down to see me. He must have some idea who Me Sao is by now."

Regter had signed off on the report, shut down his office, and was back in his room curling weights when Harry Perkins knocked on the door.

"Boss," Harry grimaced. "No one's seen Romah Dat since early afternoon. And, ah...there's one thing that didn't go into my report."

"Spill it, Harry." Regter motioned Perkins to his chair.

"Y B'ham hinted that Me Sao is receiving advice from an American, who...ah...holds a FULRO commission."

"Well, that's either you or McElroy. So I guess it's Mac?"

"Y B'ham wouldn't say. The only one I can think of is Mac. But I'd like to believe that if he knew who Me Sao was, we'd know."

"I'm not so sure, Harry, not since Ko'pa Jhon's wife died. Mac put his honor and prestige on the line to guarantee she'd get medical treatment. I think he feels personally betrayed by the State department, not to mention the Department of the Army."

"Maybe. Mac's been telling me for years that they'd offered him a commission. If I remember correctly, he took it just after she died. Still, it's only honorary. He can't be taking it seriously."

"Are you speaking as my S-Two, or using me for a sounding board?"

"Both, I think. I mean, my gut feeling is that Mac's involved, even if I don't want to believe it. The question is why? He always wanted to be an officer, but that stutter kept him back. Still, there isn't an NCO in Special Forces who isn't qualified to be an officer, so that rules out ego. So why would Mac take a FULRO commission seriously? I've been wondering about that, and all my guesses bring me back to the Rahlen clan. If an American is really advising Me Sao, it has to be Mac. And if that's the case, Me Sao has to be from their clan. The problem is who? It sure as hell isn't Blir, and Blek's a great kid and a fine company commander, but he's no Me Sao. So who is it? About one out of every ten Jarai in this compound has some blood connection to the Rahlens. It could be any one of 'em. Ney Bloom or B Rob Ya makes more sense. At least they're Rhade, like the original Me Sao, but they appear to be working for this new Me Sao. Anyway, Boss, that's all I know."

"It's a start. What can you tell me about the Rahlen clan, Harry?"

"Not much, other than the fact that they're originally from Cheo Reo, and that Blir's branch is from Plei Djereng. Mac's our resident expert on Jarai clan histories."

"So," Regter nodded. "It all comes back to Mac."

Chapter Seventeen

Near Plei Djereng, Pleiku Province, South Vietnam:

THE BURIAL GROUND lay an hour west-southwest of Pleiku, off a road that started as pavement, turned to dirt past artillery hill, and degenerated into a single lane trail some 20 minutes from the hardtop. Behind a FULRO flag taped to the Jeep's windshield, Rahlen Blir drove cautiously, a worried look furrowing his brow. To his right, Romah Dat lounged in the shotgun seat, staring vacantly into the distance. Rahlen H'nek sat wedged between two young bodyguards in the rear.

Past an abandoned tea plantation, they spotted the small knoll. Tombs lay scattered across it, many surrounded by wooden walls some three feet high and 10 to 15 feet long. Carved burial poles represented family, friends, and the deceased at various stages of their lives. Weathered roughhewn faces gazed vacantly at the intruders. These tombs had once been masterpieces of Highland art, lovingly carved and woven-thatched to provide adequate lodging in the afterlife. Now, time and termites had taken their toll. All that remained of the village that had built them was a semi-bare hillside in the distance.

"There," H'nek indicated to Romah Dat as Blir ground to a halt, "up behind the great tomb."

Romah Dat stepped out and pulled up his seat to allow H'nek to dismount. His guards clambered over the sides, scanning the surroundings, M2 carbines at the ready.

"You," Romah Dat indicated to one, "stay and cover Jeep. And you, walk behind and cover me at all time. If any shooting, kill these two first. Understood?"

The guards nodded as Rahlen H'nek led Romah Dat towards the knoll.

"Do you remember this?" she asked.

"I may have been here once." He marveled, taking in the muscle rhythm of her tight thighs and buttocks flashing under a black sateen skirt as she climbed.

"The Tiep-zap forced us to abandon this village. They took our land for Northern refugees, who now inhabit Pleiku as most clans who lived here inhabit Plei Djereng. At least they respected our tombs."

Romah Dat shrugged. Though the Jarai moved their fields every four to seven years, their villages were more permanent. The Ngo Dien Diem years had been hard. After the refugees came the strategic hamlet program, which pushed even more Dega off the land. The woman was frightened, hence the small talk common to her sex.

"Do not worry little sister. If all goes well, you will not be harmed."

Watching the sunlight play between her legs, Romah Dat imagined the pleasure they would offer once he finished with Me Sao. He had known women who could be thoroughly aroused by violence. And others so relieved at escaping harm, they became frantically compliant. If would be nice if H'nek was either. He had never forced himself on a woman, but he intended to possess this one before he placed her beyond her Frenchy's reach.

"It is women's habit to worry," H'nek admitted. "Do you recall Rahlen H'lam of Plei Djereng? You once took her to the lover's house. She remembers you."

"So," smiled Romah Dat, "you are from H'lam's branch of the Rahlen."

"She is my mother's sister. And that," H'nek nodded at the approaching tomb, "is my mother's grandmother's tomb."

Alone among the other tombs, the teak lined walls and large roof resembling a vertical tomahawk blade had withstood the ravages of time. Despite thoughts of pulling H'nek's skirt free, and some small concern over meeting Me Sao, Romah Dat marveled at the structure's size and grandeur.

"I have never seen such tomb for women. It is worthy of a P'tao."

"As it is worthy of a great Po Lan."

"You speak of po lans as if they have power beyond that of family council. Among my own clan, our po lan merely walks the earth."

"This Po Lan," snorted H'nek, "had duties other than marking clan lands. She guided family councils of all her clan. It was something she learned among the Ede."

"Her brothers must have been women to permit their sister such airs. What of her husband?"

"His tomb lies within. He was so taken with grief, he died not long after. Among the clans here, it was famous story. I am surprised you have not heard. She was Me Sao's daughter."

Romah Dat's hand instinctively dropped to his pistol. H'nek's eyes bored into his own.

"Does the renowned Romah Dat fear a woman," she challenged.

"Little sister," he sneered, "I fear neither you, nor this Me Sao. Otherwise I would never have come. Glan Perr warned me, but he is too cautious. Which is why he will always be deputy, never commander."

H'nek shrugged, and turned to resume her climb. Romah Dat paused. The glint in her eyes had disturbed him. He was older, but still handsome. Something in those eyes that should have coyly parried his own made him uneasy. She had gazed upon him as an equal. He looked up to watch the rhythm of her climb. So, he thought, as our little sister draws nearer to Me Seo, she becomes arrogant. It will make our coupling sweeter.

H'nek was pulling ahead, so he ordered her to slow down. Hooking his thumbs into his web belt, he pushed on, carefully checking his surroundings. Romah Dat expected a trap. Me Sao would do no less. But guts, good shooting, and his legendary *baraka*, good luck, would pull him through. His reputation had been built on an uncanny ability to size up an ambush or fight in a single instant, and unerringly do that which would throw his enemies off balance. This graveyard didn't allow much room for error, but neither had many others. He brushed H'nek from his thoughts as his mind raced ahead.

This self-styled Me Sao was dead just as soon as he showed. He had promised such to K'pa Doh, and Romah Dat had never failed an oath. He would buy time with words, until sure that this was truly Me Sao, and then he would strike. One shot to the lower stomach, and one to the head at point blank range while his guards handled Me Sao's men. Another

FULRO schism healed, he smiled to himself. Then he would take this girl on her own ancestor's tomb, willing or not.

Just below the knoll she turned. "We wait here," she said.

"I did not come to wait, little sister. Me Sao is where?"

"Near. First, listen..."

"Little sister, I treat only with Me Sao. Not a woman, no matter how desirable her loins."

"And what if Me Sao has desirable loins?"

"Pah." Romah Dat's lips curled in contempt.

"Romah Dat," H'nek did not return his mocking smile. Her voice now had a sharp edge. "My skin you have seen, my eyes you have searched, but you have not listened to my words. Listen now. You tried kill my lieutenant! Now it is our turn. We can kill you, but rather would we make you an ally."

"Your lieutenant?" Romah Dat's eyes narrowed. His thumbs edged up from inside his belt. Facing the distant woodline, he called out. "Me Sao, this is Romah Dat. I will not treat with a woman. Show yourself."

H'nek's hands slipped down to the knot of her skirt.

"Little sister," he said under his breath, "if this is a ruse, I will kill you here."

"Then do so. Me Sao speaks only through me."

"Through you?" Romah Dat's voice was edged with contemp. "I treat only with your father, little sister. Yes, him. We know this Me Sao. How cunning. One leader whose body is never recovered is reported dead, and an old legend rises magically in his place. Well, you certainly fooled the Meerika and Tiep-zap." Romah Dat's hand flashed up to point his cocked pistol at H'nek's head.

"Ko'pa Jhon, my old friend," he called out. "I have come to treat with you, not kill. But if you do not show yourself, I will kill your daughter. In five. Five..."

"Not my father," H'nek whispered hoarsely as her supple fingers undid her skirt, "whose spirits do indeed wander these High Lands..."

"Four..."

"Romah Dat, will you not be our ally?"

"Three..."

H'nek stepped slightly back to remove her skirt and lift it over her shoulders, a black satin flag in the highland breeze. Romah Dat's gaze wandered over her pubic fold, up across her flat dusky stomach, breasts, and brown nipples to her lips, nose, and hypnotic eyes.

"What game is this, little sister?" His finger tightened on the trigger.

"No game," she flashed an enigmatic smile.

Something was wrong. He could not feel his *baraka*. Ko'pa Jhon had to be close by. He would not allow his daughter to die. Her eyes stared coolly into his own. His vision wandered back down to her silken pubic fold, whose heat he could feel in his souls. He wrenched them free, casting quick glances into every nook and shadow. She now had a glint in her eyes he recognized. One he had often felt in his own.

"You...?" It was an exclamation of wonderment. A light breeze carried her skirt away.

"No," she murmured in an unconscious plea to stop an act in motion, rather than deny any fact. She winced as the sniper's round exploded through Romah Dat's face. The simultaneous crash of his pistol sent her reeling back. Above the deafening ring in her ears, she heard an RPD chatter a short burst below the hill, followed by a singing silence.

H'nek lay still for long moments before clambering up to recover her skirt, wipe her blood spattered face, and retrieve Romah Dat's pistol. Only then did she wave to Blir. Turning to the blood and brain spattered tomb, she uttered a silent prayer for forgiveness. Had this been a lesser man, some steeled specter within might have termed it a fitting sacrifice. But Romah Dat had been no lesser man. In the dark days following the French withdrawal, his name had inspired terror among those Sedang and Bahnar inclined to raid Jarai villages, and among no few Viet Minh. He had fought long and honorably in FULRO's cause. Her prayer complete, she rewrapped her skirt, stooped to recover his pistol belt, and carefully avoided looking at his head. Nausea hit before she had taken many steps. Squatting, she shuddered until it passed.

Further down the hill, she found the second guard lying on a patch of blood-stained earth. The first sat timidly in the Jeep, covered by Blir, who now brandished his carbine. From the brush line, figures in mottled camouflage sauntered towards them.

"This one," Blir nodded, "would swear fealty to Me Sao."

"As he once did," she snorted, "to Romah Dat?"

Blir stared at the instrument panel. "He did surrender. The decision is properly Me Sao's."

"Then Me Sao's instructions are clear. Not one to be left alive who can name him."

"I cannot name him," protested the guard. "I saw no Me Sao."

"You saw," H'nek insisted, "and did you not swear an oath to defend and avenge Romah Dat's life with your own?"

"True," he murmured, cautiously eyeing the lead FULRO soldier, who approached carrying an American sniper rifle. "But I had no choice."

H'nek motioned for the guard to dismount and let her up. As he did, she took the front seat.

"Nor do I," she said in a voice turned hard. "Oaths taken must be honored." She nodded to the FULRO sniper. "Bury Romah Dat and dead guard with military honors. Sacrifice a pig. This one's body, you can leave for Sir Tiger."

As the sniper herded the guard away, Blir started the engine. "He surrendered his weapon," Blir protested, "when he could have killed me."

Maneuvering the Jeep through a tight turn-around, he felt H'nek's hand settle over his own. Blir pushed in the clutch and waited.

"Mother's-brother," H'nek's soft voice had returned, "in duel between a sharp sword held in resolute hands, and an equally sharp sword held in wavering hands, which sword triumphs?"

"Why, the resolute sword. I have heard such words before. Where did you hear them?"

A single shot sounded from the brush.

"In my dreams," she replied. "Our ancestor said them to me. You see, Uncle, the safety of our movement is my greatest concern. While that guard lived, we were not safe. We are not yet strong enough to show mercy."

As they drove back to Pleiku, dark clouds rolled in.

Further north, along the Dak Ayun, heavy rain rolled down a poncho suspended between two trees by parachute cord. Beneath it, St. Cyr, Blek, and Biloskirka huddled over their midday meal. The operation had ended, but extraction was delayed by a swollen stream.

"Some dry season," St. Cyr grumbled.

"Warning rains," shrugged Blek. "Spirits show what lies ahead."

"Better it rains," said Boris, as he held out a canteen to catch water pouring off a broad leaf. "In '54, it was so dry we nearly died of thirst."

"You were here in 1954?"

"Yes. We spent Christmas '53 up in Laos, then went to Nha Trang and Tuy Hoa for big amphibious operation, then here. Viet Minh kept cutting the road between An Khe and Pleiku."

Mac's voice crackled over the handset.

This is Fox Warden Two-six," St. Cyr replied.

"Two-six...this is Three. What's your situation? B-break. I've got choppers standing by...Over."

"Roger, Three...the water's going down...Break...estimate two hours to pickup...over."

"Roger... If you ain't there then, it'll be tomorrow. Break. B-be advised we got problems in Pleiku. Out."

It was a bone-tired mob that yomped into Pleiku four hours later to find a somber Regter waiting at the gate.

"Inventory all weapons, ammunition, grenades, and mines immediately." Regter instructed. "Supply will take charge of cleaning. I want your men paid and out of the compound by sundown. They've got five days stand-down."

St. Cyr noted the red-rimmed eyes. "Yessir. Ah...we had a sacrifice scheduled for tomorrow."

"Reschedule it. The FULRO leader who came in from Cambodia a few weeks ago is missing, along with some of his men. Like I said—out of the compound by sundown, and I want your Indig cadre back here tomorrow. Tell them they're going to be talking to the Two. And pass the word: only Roundeyes, LLDB, and the security company are authorized to carry weapons inside the compound until further notice. Any questions?"

"Nossir."

As St. Cyr saluted and turned, Regter stopped him. "Galen." something of a friendly sparkle had returned to his eyes.

"Yessir "

"Your men did a good job out there. Tell them the Americans were impressed. We'll throw a party for their families when this business is over."

"What business is that, Sir?"

"A little internal house cleaning in FULRO, or the beginning of a revolt."

From inside the LLDB building, Ngoc watched Regter and St. Cyr with vague interest as he fingered a 'Very Reserved' message from his G-2, responding to his earlier report of an apparent split in FULRO over the disappearance of Romah Dat. The message advised him of a corresponding split in the national FULRO leadership between Y B'ham and K'pa Doh. He was to now take active measures to destroy the MIKE Force FULRO leadership, beginning with the man they had identified as Me Sao.

Ngoc shook his head in disbelief. He was under no illusions as to how this target had been selected: The LLDB high command Intelligence chief, under pressure to provide a name, had pulled it out of his ass. They had the wrong man, but Ngoc had the mission. It was clandestine because General Quang wanted deniability if it resulted in any American dead, and it was 'active' because the G-2 wanted Ngoc's testicles hanging in the line of fire if anything went wrong. That didn't disturb Ngoc. In clandestine operations, it was the way business was done. You used your enemies to destroy your enemies, and if you couldn't use your enemies, you sacrificed your friends. Ngoc's objection was purely professional. Ney Bloom was ambitious, which meant he could be dealt with. And he was too obvious a candidate to be Me Sao. Of that, Ngoc was absolutely sure, but orders were orders.

A passing shadow alerted him to someone approaching the door. He stepped inside his private office, placed the message in his field safe, and looked up in time to receive his adjutant's report that Mr. Long had arrived.

"Ah, Long Syen-sheng, Ngoc smiled. "Happy to greet you, my friend. Please come in."

Long accepted the outstretched hand with a perfunctory shake. "Thank you, Thieu-ta. I came as soon as I could. I trust things are well with your family."

"Indeed! As I trust in the Empress of Heaven that all is well with your own. Your youngest daughter now works for Americans as interpreter, not so?"

Long filed the Empress of Heaven reference in the long list of reasons he despised Ngoc. The arrogant little martinet didn't even know he was Catholic. Outwardly, he beamed and nodded.

"Just so. With U.S. 4th Division Civil Affairs. Such allows her to return home every night. As you know, my house in Cholon was destroyed in Tet fighting. Though Pleiku is provincial, I prefer to have her here, where I can safeguard."

"As is every father's duty. Tell me, how succeeds the Montagnard Hilton?"

Long suppressed a frown. He was already passing Ngoc one third of his profits. With Regter breathing down his neck, there wasn't much space for fudging the books.

"Not so good, Thieu-ta. Business is off."

"What, with new battalion in training? You misunderstand, Long Syen-sheng. We appreciate your monthly contributions to our Families Beneficence Fund. Truly speaking, it is not our intent to seek any higher payment. Rather, I would pass along to you information which might protect our mutual interests."

Long smiled. So he wasn't being shaken down. Not yet, anyway.

"In particular," Ngoc continued, "one fact. That bodies of some certain Romah Dat and his bodyguards have been recovered by Vietnamese Army forces. He has been murdered, we believe, on order of Ney Bloom. Be aware that some certain Moi will start killing other Moi soon, so take precautions with your family in this army camp."

"So FULRO is close to civil war."

"Appears so, for which reason I give you warning. You have forever been our friend. You will note from actions of Americans that they are aware of this, and still I doubt that they have told you. Not so?"

"It is so, Thieu-ta. You have the gratitude of my family. May the Goddess of Mercy favor your own."

As Long left, smiling with relief, Ngoc noted the laterite dust blowing across his floor with mounting irritation. Most Americans managed to steal air conditioners for their command bunkers, bedrooms, and offices, but Regter was far too strict. Everything the MIKE Force stole, or traded, ended up in their teamhouse or the dependent village, and most went into civic action projects that cut into the profits of local businesses. Was it too much to ask that some small portion end up in the office of the Vietnamese MIKE Force commander?

"Thieu-ta," his adjutant's legs moved into his field of vision. "Trung-si Hu'u is here."

"Right," Ngoc looked up. "Send that dog shit in."

Thuan's former companion strode stiffly through the door and saluted. Ngoc left him standing at the position of attention.

"Trung-si Hu'u, your uncle the colonel on the presidential staff has been kind enough to inquire about a certain nephew's health. Naturally, I have assured him that this one nephew has been assigned very confidential duties in this army camp, and is not required to go to field. I have not told him of your barracks arrest, or that you were beaten in a fight with a Moi. Are you prepared to erase the blot that stains your family honor and that of Viet Nam Special Forces?"

"Yes, Thieu-ta."

"Good! There is a 'very reserved' mission which you will undertake. It will be known only to one certain Trung-si and this Major. You understand, no?"

"Yes, Thieu-ta."

"Good!" Ngoc reached down under his desk to deposit a Schmeisser MP-40 wrapped in heavy canvas on the table. Beside it, he lay a photo of Ney Bloom.

"You have four days to familiarize yourself with this weapon and study habits of your target. You will brief me on plan of action on fifth day. Between fifth and eighth days, you will carry out your mission. Most importantly, you will make his death appear the work of other Moi. You understand, no?"

A smile creased Sergeant Hu'u's face. "I understand, Thieu-ta."

Ngoc made a pretense of going back to the papers on his desk. Hu'u did not make the mistake of leaving. Presently, Ngoc glanced up.

"We will see if you truly are worthy of the Luc Luong Dac Biet. Your carcass smells of dog shit. Get out!"

It was well after dark when a small Honda approached the dependent village, shutting off the headlight as it came within range of the gate. Guards walked out, M2 carbines at the ready, peered at the driver, and waved him through.

The driver parked his motorcycle under the communal longhouse, then made his way down rows of bare wooden single story dependent quarters to knock on a door. It opened to reveal two Rhade women sitting near an oil lamp set on the floor. The younger was breast feeding a baby.

"Long Syen-sheng," Ney Bloom voiced genuine surprise. "It is an honor to receive you in my house. I only wish that this was my wife's clan longhouse."

"Cannot enter," stated Long flatly. "You must come out."

"Certainly. Can you wait?"

"Yes."

Minutes later, Ney Bloom stepped out into the darkness. Long led him away from the house, his voice barely rising above a whisper.

"Ney Bloom, my brother, you served me well in Eagle Flight, and I never betray old comrades. Your life is in danger, as is my own if Thieu-ta Ngoc learns I have warned you."

Chapter Eighteen

Big Marty's Bar and Grill, Pleiku, Vietnam:

> *Maryanne Barnes is the Queen of all the acrobats,*
> *She can do the tricks that'll give the guys the shits,*
> *She can shoot green peas from her fundamental orifice,*
> *Do a triple somersault and catch 'em on her tits,*
> *She's a great big sunovabitch, twice as big as me,*
> *Got hair on her ass like the branches of a tree*
> *She can shoot, ride, fight, fuck, fly a plane, drive a truck,*
> *She's the kind of girl that's going to marry me,*
> *She's Special Forces, Ranger, Airborne Infantreee,*
> *And MIKE Force, tooooo"*

HOARSE VOICES RATTLED the screens in Big Marty's Bar and Grill. The Superjew and Ryan took the lead as beer cans banged time to the MIKE Force anthem on rough wooden tables. For this party, the Superjew was dressed in his formal attire: a tiger stripe yarmulke, a small gold *mezuzah*, and a See Israel First T-shirt depicting a column of Israeli tanks in a desert backed by pyramids and the sphinx. A similar yarmulke graced Ryan's head. Their eyes gleamed like demoniacal rabbinical students in some strange corner of Hell. Nearby, a Filipino band sulked, waiting for their cue. The sooner they got started, the sooner they could collect their pay and get out. The hard looks coming their way made the female singer and back-up dancers nervous.

With three companies fresh from the field, and three others standing by to lift out in the morning, Big Marty's was jammed. Hoa frantically mixed drinks, deftly slicing lemons between splashing pours with a butcher knife she drove into the bar top for storage. None but the brave complained when their rum turned out bourbon, or vice versa, and the brave took care to stand out of range. Tonight was Open Bar, and the liquor flowed freely.

In a room behind the teamhouse kitchen, the medics had set up a hasty OB/GYN clinic where each girl was carefully and politely examined. Some 25 had been contracted for the night, and the deal was straightforward. Forty dollars for all night doing anything, with anybody, anywhere they wanted. There was a free ride in, a free ride out, free breakfast in the morning, and a free exam for venereal diseases. If any were turned away, they'd get free medication and an escort to the gate. As the medics examined each girl, they stamped her hand. No stamp meant no inspection, and no guarantee that this was Grade A prime chicken. The heat and hollers emanating from Big Marty's warned that the natives were restless. After the last girl had been inspected, they were directed through the swinging doors to a deafening reception.

St. Cyr, seated with Spam, Moshlatubbee, and Toller, couldn't help but smile. Now he saw why Cohen and Ryan had been so anxious to play cheerleader. Being up front when the girls came through the doors gave them a decided advantage at first pick. Several attractive candidates were ushered in their direction. Cohen nudged a teenage girl with mocking eyes and a shy smile towards him.

"Trung-oui, this one's for you."

"Thanks, but I'm on my good behavior."

"Yeah, and right on yer," Toller winked as he reached for the girl's hand. "But I'm single."

"C'mon Laurie," Ryan held her back, "you just got back from Taipei."

"All right," agreed Toller. "What about Spam?"

Spam shook his head.

"OK, Laurie," Cohen shrugged. "She's yours."

"Right nice of you, Mates." Toller pulled her into his lap while Ryan scrambled for the doorway. He emerged from the kitchen minutes later with a triumphant smile, and a demure, dark, stunning beauty.

"Trung-oui, meet My Lei. Quarter Cambode, quarter Vietnamese, and all woman."

"What's the other half?" St. Cyr wondered.

"Afro-Caribbean French. Her dad was from Martinique." Ryan guided her into a chair across from Toller while Cohen leaned close to St. Cyr's ear.

"My Lei's not one of the 'girls,'" he whispered. "She's a stripper who works the American clubs from here to Nha Trang, which means she'll be at the Bamboo Bar tomorrow. You won't want to miss her act."

"Yeah," grinned Toller. "Give you a bloody heart attack, she will."

Up front, the loudspeaker system popped, squealed, and whistled as Regter stepped up to the microphone. As his eyes swept the room, noise dropped to a whisper. His spiels were short—lauding the men being bid farewell, listing the highlights of their combats, and dropping an occasional embarrassing moment or joke at their expense. While the crowd cheered, clapped, and stomped, each departing man took the microphone. Some gave rousing speeches, some choked on the memory of lost comrades, and some merely mumbled through bloodshot eyes. One apologized for going home. He had a wife and children, and felt he was betraying the Yards by leaving, but he had to go. Otherwise his plaque would end up on the wall under Hoa's tender loving care, and no offense, but he sure as hell wanted to see his kids again.

In the embarrassing silence that followed, Toller gave out a hearty "Good on yer, Mate," which filled the club with cheers and applause. After downing Hoa's goodbye drinks as a group, they swaggered or staggered back to their tables. Regter closed the formalities with a reminder: Everyone was to have a good time. No fights or weapons. What started here, stayed here. If anyone had any unfinished business in the morning, the Sergeant Major would be happy to referee. As Regter stepped away from the microphone, Cohen sprang to his feet to lead another round of singing.

Regter was leading Ngoc to the door, silently thankful that no one had unleashed the word 'Slope,' when Ngoc caught sight of Spam. His eyebrows knit together.

"Trung-si Xuan," he fired in moderate staccato, "I see that some certain little brother has been accepted by these long-noses."

Spam shot to attention as the girls looked away in shame. "Yes, Thieu-ta. Such is my mission, no?"

"Just so," Ngoc took care to retain his smile and pleasant tone. "But not appropriate for sergeant of Viet Nam Special Forces to consort with long-nose foreigners while they fornicate women of our race who have fallen upon misfortune. Stay perhaps half hour and drink, then leave. I am understood, no?"

Such were my intentions, Thieu-ta."

"Excellent." Ngoc extended a handshake to St. Cyr. "It pleases me that Trung-si Xuan does well in your company. He is good soldier."

"Hey," cut in Ryan, "Spam's better'n good, Major. He's the goddam best!"

Regter winced at Ryan's belligerent tone, but Ngoc merely nodded and continued to the door. Regter chuckled. Though he'd never learned enough Vietnamese to really speak it, he knew Ngoc's pet terms by heart.

With the brass out the door, the party kicked into high gear. The band started off with rock and roll and then slowed down to ballads more appropriate for groping. Some dragged their girls to the dance floor, others pulled them along to their rooms, while one carried his protesting date off for a good time on the pool table. Friendly disputes started over which company was better, which degenerated into who should have done what in past firefights, which at times turned acrimonious. Songs sprang up to compete with the band, and sporadic toasts punctuated the din.

"Hey Boris," called St. Cyr over the noise, "Where's your girl?"

"Not to worry," Biloskirka confessed, "I have someone waiting."

Cohen glanced up from nuzzling his date's breasts. "Would this be anybody we know?"

"Maybe."

Cohen flashed Ryan and Spam an evil grin.

"Anything to do with a sweater?"

"Esshole," Boris's face flushed. "That is not your business."

"A sweater," St. Cyr wondered.

"Yeah," grinned Cohen. "Hoa knit Big Boris here a sweater while we were in the field. Whatsamatter, Boris? You didn't wear your sweater tonight."

"Hey, no big deal," St. Cyr retorted. "I thought maybe Boris was married."

"I was, once," said Boris, taking his cue, "to German girl who stayed back in Berlin when I got sent to States."

"Any kids?"

"Sure, a daughter. Also, I have son...here." The big Ukrainian's voice trailed off. "His mother worked in field brothel. When she was pregnant, the Madame tried to make her have abortion. But, she run away instead. So! I have a son I haven't seen since he was baby."

"What happened to him?"

Boris shrugged.

"Aren't you going to try and find him?"

"Find him?" Boris flashed St. Cyr a quizzical look. "Buddy, this is Asia. Here, to fuck is fun. Everybody does it like rabbits. But to have baby whose blood is not pure is very great shame. Girls who have such babies run far away. If they are lucky, baby looks Vietnamese and they can claim to be war widows. But if baby looks half something else, is great misfortune. Sometimes they are killed. Sometimes they are kept. Most times they are given away and raised as someone else's. To find him now would do him no favor."

"Goddam." Cohen slid his fingers under his date's panties, "you people need to lighten up. C'mon sweet thing, let me show you my room."

"Speaking of rooms," St. Cyr grinned. "I'd better get out of here. See everybody in the morning."

As he stepped out the swinging doors into the cool night air, St. Cyr's eyes adjusted to the darkness. A hundred-odd Montagnard bodies were wedged up against the screens, watching the party inside. Like Mac said, it was life in a fishbowl. Thinking of Mac, he wondered why he hadn't heard a familiar stutter. Pushing his way back to peer through the doors, he eyed the rows of faces to confirm his hunch. Strange, with the Rahlen clan up at Plei Djereng, Mac should have been at the party. Crossing to the nearby BOQ, a distant pair of eyes watched his departure with satisfaction.

"You see," she nodded to her companion, "with Tiep-zap women at his bidding, he sleeps alone."

"He should sleep alone always," hissed her companion. "You need to find a Dega."

"Perhaps I have."

In a darkened barracks at the far corner of the compound, with two low-burning oil lamps providing their only illumination, the FULRO cadres waited. Guards were positioned at all approaches, and observers at key points kept an eye out for any Vietnamese. In response to a light rap on the door, Blir opened it to allow Rahlen H'nek and Siu Dot to enter. Both were wearing tiger fatigues.

"Lieutenant Colonel Bloom," said H'nek, "your report."

"Po Lan, all cadres from MIKE Force and Iron Brigade are present."

"Excellent," she nodded. "I greet you on behalf of Colonel Me Sao, who cannot be present," her liquid dark eyes flashed over the assembly. "With me is Captain Siu Dot of the disciplinary committee. If anyone has doubts about brother Dot's identity, I will ask that he display his hands."

The silence was reassuring.

"Good," she continued. "I am Rahlen H'nek, sister to Rahlen Blek, niece of Rahlen Blir, daughter of Ko'pa Jhon. My blood is Jarai, but the great Ede warrior Me Sao was an ancestor. Those who know that name will recall that his daughter, my mother's grandmother, freely chose to remain among us as a Jarai. For this reason, I speak for colonel Me Sao, whose identity will be revealed in time..."

Pausing, she caught a murmur.

"...we came to hear Me Sao, not some girl in men's clothing. One wonders at what other service she renders..."

As H'nek's eyes honed in on the mumbler she nodded to Siu Dot, who stepped out from behind an upper bunk to reveal a silenced Sten gun.

"We were told there were to be no arms," protested the mumbler.

"And better there not be," barked Siu Dot. "The rule does not apply to disciplinary committee."

The mumbler nodded a cautious assent.

"So," continued H'nek, "you object because I am woman? Tell me. Does the Po Lan of your clan wear testicles?"

Snickers rumbled through the tense darkness.

"Among my people," countered the mumbler, "Pau Lun is a term of respect. But she is only a Pau Lun. She walks the lands, and guards the earth. She does not mingle in men's affairs."

"Only a Po Lan? Tell me, does your father inhabit your mother's house, or does she inhabit his?"

"Stupid question, everyone knows..."

"What? That land and houses are ours? And when men sit within family or village councils, are there any among them whose wives are not Po Lan?"

"None...but Pau Luns have age and wisdom!"

"Yes! And if these old and wise women choose a younger Po Lan, cannot such a woman's voice be heard at this council? Can you not listen to one who carries a message from another far wiser?"

"Not...not...correct," insisted the mumbler, his voice strengthening in the belief that he had found his argument.

"Not correct, Brother? If we entrust to you a message to carry to K'pa Doh immediately, how do you it get there?"

"I must walk many days."

"Why not take 'otobus' if we give you money?"

"You would do so?"

"Of course. Or we could loan you 'moto.'"

"Hah," snorted the mumbler. "Tiep-zap would demand my identity papers. As they would your very own."

"Agreed," nodded H'nek. "But what if my papers say I am wife to Tiep-zap soldier. Or even Meerika officer? Or say I work for Meerika as interpreter? After all, I am only one woman. Would they not let me go?"

"Perhaps," nodded the mumbler.

"No, not perhaps. Certain," said H'nek. "And hear this: Although we are a united front, divisions exist from which our enemies profit. Tiep-zap wish to divide us. Meerika would see us divided. And among we here tonight are some who would chance war among ourselves rather than accept the will of majority.

"Major Romah Dat was one such person. Acting on orders of persons who dispute leadership of President Y B'ham, he attempted to assassinate Colonel Me Sao. Romah Dat failed, and paid with his life. Now the Tiep-zap say that a certain Rhade murdered him. Such is not true. Romah Dat was executed by brother Jarai on orders from highest authority. I myself was present. Which among you is senior?"

A compact, muscular figure with salt and pepper hair rose to his feet, bowed, and spoke in French. "Captain Glan Perr, at your service."

"A kinsman," smiled H'nek, "from the Ho'drung branch."

Glan Perr nodded.

"Then, kinsman, I would ask that you accept Romah Dat's pistol. It was an arm he honored with many years struggle in our cause. His death does not diminish our respect for his sacrifice."

Glan Perr took the belt and pistol. Turning his back to Siu Dot, he withdrew the pistol from its holster and examined it in the dim oil-light. At the click of the slide lock, the room tensed. A faint bronze glint shone from the top cartridge. He depressed the magazine lock, the magazine dropped down, and the slide slammed home.

"It is indeed," he noted with satisfaction, "the pow-pistol of Romah Dat."

As Glan Perr took his seat, Rahlen H'nek launched into a plea for unity among all FULRO cadres, noting that division only aided their enemies. Her voice carried the soft and seductive nuances of a lover's whisper, then cajoled and pleaded with the intimacy of a favorite sister, and finally turned hard, ringing of fire, and war, and retribution to those who would, even unintentionally, aid or abet their common enemy. And as her voice rose and fell with the strength of an aria, it dawned on many that beneath the soft, supple, taut curves that any man would gladly bed, stretched the bone, muscle, and will of a warrior queen.

Sweat glistened from her body as she finished to a deathly quiet room. There was nothing more to say, she murmured. The time for words had passed. Pacing slowly back and forth, her eyes strangely luminous, she stopped before Glan Perr.

"Captain Perr, may I have Romah Dat's pistol"

Glan Perr rose and handed her the pistol. With deft motions, she re-seated a round in the chamber, placed the weapon in Glan Perr's hands, and lifted the muzzle to touch her breast.

"Brother Dot. Whatever happens, you will not kill Glan Perr. Understand? You will take no revenge."

Siu Dot nodded a cautious assent.

"Brother Perr. I am Me Sao's agent. You can only reach him through me. If you wish to avenge Romah Dat, it is myself who must be killed. I alone carried out Me Sao's order."

"Little sister," whispered Glan Perr, "I swore an oath to Romah Dat."

"As I," H'nek murmured back, "have sworn an oath to my two peoples. No longer will our blood be shed in useless feuds or foreign causes. No longer will we walk our own High Lands as strangers."

Glan Perr moved the pistol slightly below the cleavage of her breasts. "I would not see you suffer," he whispered softly.

"Thank you," her eyes did not waver. "But we will suffer whether you kill me or not."

As his finger tightened on the trigger, the muzzle wavered.

"To destroy such beauty is a great sin against such children as you would have borne. May their spirits forgive me."

His eyes searched hers for the slightest sign of doubt or fear. But even in the dark they glistened with a strange glow at once sad and certain. Something in them triggered a long buried memory.

"If I live," H'nek continued, "in my time the many shall be one. We Dega will once again rule these, our own High Lands."

The pistol abruptly spun and rose to Glan Perr's own temple. H'nek's hand flashed up to wedge her forefinger between the hammer and firing pin just as Glan Perr pulled the trigger. She winced as the hammer mashed down, but her hand remained locked on the pistol. Her voice shifted from dreamlike to husky and low.

"Captain Glan Perr, we need soldiers in service of a cause, not warriors in service of leader. Just as we need your experience and wisdom. Join us, and Romah Dat's spirits will welcome your own when your time has come. The decision is yours." She pulled the hammer back to release her finger.

He dropped the hammer to half cock as he lowered the pistol.

"Po Lan, leave us. Those who support you will stay with MIfors. Those who cannot will leave. There will be no more bloodshed among we Dega here. We have enemies enough to kill."

She found her companion waiting in the shadows of an adjacent barracks."You had success," he smiled with relief. "I heard no shots."

"The Iron Brigade is with us," she murmured, "Their leader is now Glan Perr. He has accepted the authority of Me Sao, but I am unsure of how he will serve us. He has worn triple bars of a captain for many years."

"Perhaps he will accept command of this new battalion. Many of its troops will be his own."

"Is it possible," she asked, climbing up on the motorcycle behind him. "Otherwise I fear conflict between himself and Rchom Jimm."

"It depends on Meerika Major," muttered her companion, as he kicked the engine into life. "I will find a way to suggest it."

Back in his room, St. Cyr had given up his attempts to write home. After the standard salutation and best wishes, he couldn't find much to say. He tried launching into a detailed description of various Jarai customs, but the sight of Misses February and April, coupled with sounds of squealing springs and frantic gasps and sighs from adjacent rooms, drove him out into the night air. Filling his highland pipe with American tobacco, he meandered through the compound.

Raucous twangs and throbs still sounded from Big Marty's, but the Montagnard throng had dispersed. A solitary light shone in the square near the Conex containers. He wandered down the company street, and cut back through the indigenous barracks to walk the defensive perimeter. He had a sense of being followed, and as his walk continued that feeling grew. Warning voices, countermanded by a mocking inner self, sounded in his brain. You're unarmed, they warned, too far from the barracks. We can kill you now, and no one will know. Fears, he scoffed, more appropriate for a green lieutenant in the 4th Infantry Division than a MIKE Force company commander. This was home. If he stumbled across some VC sapper coming through the wire, he had only to raise his voice to bring the entire compound running. Like hell, retorted the panic. You'll be lucky if they remember to look for your body in the morning. And then as suddenly as they had come, his paranoid thoughts subsided, to be replaced by a more palpable desperation. God, why did she have to be in Plei Djereng?

From the darkened interior of an indigenous barracks, two pairs of eyes watched him pass.

"I should kill him now," one murmured.

"Then do so. Why just talk about it?"

"Because I will not clear the path to H'nek's long house for you, little brother Jimm, while I suffer exile in Nha Trang."

"Exile? I would take pride to command company in Nha Trang MI-fors."

"Said because you are here. No, if this Meerika angers me by amusing her, at least he has barred her long house door to you. Someday I will thank him, before I shoot his testicles away."

"Such bitterness," chuckled Jimm, "from one so young."

In the darkness, Siu Dot reached up to tap the base of Jimm's neck with the muzzle of his Sten gun. "Do not mock shortness of my life, little brother, unless you would feel the centipede's sting. I have nothing to lose but that which is lost already."

"Then…" Jimm's jawline tensed, "pull the trigger, fool!"

The pressure of the Sten Gun's muzzle subsided.

"I believe," mocked Siu Dot, "H'nek's performance has affected us all tonight. Does she still hear voices?"

It was well after midnight when St. Cyr headed for the BOQ. He had stumbled across two departing captains who insisted that he step into their room for a drink. Both were bachelors, but both had left when the party turned wild. While Parry disputed that Jack Kerouac had ever been a poet, Jordan popped the corks from his remaining wine collection and introduced St. Cyr to New York jazz.

Both were career soldiers. Now on the eve of returning to the regular army, they voiced fears that they would never fit back in. The war, the Highlands, the Montagnards, and their American and Aussie comrades had marked them forever. Parry, or perhaps Jordan, put it best.

"What you're seeing, Galen, will never be seen again in our time. You take the right commander, like Charlie Regter, the right NCOs, the right

allies, and the right young troopies, and give them tribes of mountain warriors to turn into airborne rangers, and then cut them loose with the mission to go anywhere or do anything as long as they're killing the enemy,
and you have a legend in the making. Something they'll be talking about
for as long as we've got Special Forces."

"So, why leave?"

A curious agonized look passed between them.

"Because there's a time for everything, and if we don't leave now, we'll
never get out of here. Not in any configuration that would make us fit for a
career. Have you looked at our casualties?"

"I got here at Tet."

"I didn't ask if you'd seen them. I meant have you ever looked into
them. And the answer is no. Eight months ago, neither one of us would
have considered leaving. Now, there're only two of us left out of the six
company commanders we had then. Do you know how many medics
we've sent home in the past year? Zero. Take a good look at your medic,
Galen, because chances are he's going home in a box. And take a good look
at yourself. A year from now, you stand a damned good chance of being
dead, or wired together in some hospital."

"I've been wired before."

"Then you should know better. Look, we love this goddammed MIKE
Force so much it hurts. When we walk out of here tomorrow, it's going to
be like a large piece of our souls has been ripped out. But we are walking
out, Galen, and we're walking out alive. And I pray to God that I don't get
stupid and end up back here. We've done our time. Now, we're going to
take our experience back to the real army." He paused to take a long draw
on a bottle of pinot noir. "An army that values staff service in the rear more
than combat service in Special Forces. Oh, we get the sexy 'green beenie'.
But the others get the fast track jobs and promotions. You know, not too
long ago, we were just like you. Wanting to be part of a legend..."

"Who said I want to be part of a legend?"

"Galen, you're in the MIKE Force!"

"Yeah, but..."

"But nothing. You joined the MIKE Force because it's everything military wet dreams are made of—the self-selected chosen few, the impossible

mission, the staggering odds of an anonymous death versus everlasting glory. That's why you joined Special Forces, and when you didn't find it there, you came to the MIKE Force."

"Are you wrong," St. Cyr chuckled. "I was going to be an investment banker, working in Hong Kong. I only joined Special Forces because I was being drafted and wanted to spice up my resume. Otherwise, I'd have spent two years as a pay clerk. And I only came to Vietnam because my team got sent here…"

"Galen," Perry's voice was incredulous, "you were proud to be on that team…"

"Of course."

"And you were really proud the day they pinned the Combat Infantryman's Badge on your chest."

"Yeah, but…"

"But nothing, Galen. They flicked that pretty little fly out there, jiggled the rod a few times, let it float down past you. And wham, they had you hooked. So instead of an investment banker, you're now an infantry officer. And the dangerous part is you're a damned good one. You're no different than us, Galen, so shut up and listen. If you make it through the next six months, get the hell out and go home. Whatever debt you owe your dead will have long been paid. Save something for the living, because you owe them something too."

With those words ringing in his ears, St. Cyr made his way past a deserted Big Marty's. Hoa was closing down, and he glanced in just as she shut off the lights. Biloskirka's huge frame was waiting in back. Boris was wearing her sweater. They sauntered out into the moonlight holding hands like teenaged lovers. Embarrassed, St. Cyr stepped back into the shadows and waited until they were out of sight.

Chapter Nineteen

Binh Dinh Highlands, west of the Bong Song plain:

BIG MARTY'S WAS A DISTANT memory when Cobra gunships from the 17th Cavalry barreled across the landing zone at tree top level, mini-guns and rockets raking possible enemy positions. Seconds behind, strings of Hueys slipped in to disgorge a company of the 503rd Parachute Infantry. The newly renamed 212th MIKE Force company followed in them, trailed by a second rifle company. Once again, he was commanding Americans. A platoon from the 503rd Infantry had been attached to them in exchange for Toller's platoon, now with the Americans. A red headed Cuban-American lieutenant headed up this platoon, which counted so many Latinos that the unit's few Blacks and Gringos joked that they had been shanghaied into Fidel's army.

The Cubans wore their flag in a full color patch on the right shoulder, and had a low tolerance for anyone suspected of being communist. Lieutenant Sanchez set about his cordon and search duties with particular relish. After several reluctant villagers were manhandled into the square facing the communal longhouse, an open disagreement broke out between the two lieutenants. When the fiery Cuban demanded that St. Cyr accompany him outside to fight, St. Cyr ordered Sanchez's men out of the village.

Cohen's men were brought in to conduct the search. No weapons or caches were found, which Sanchez took as a sign of criminal neglect. The row started up again. Disgusted, St. Cyr radioed the young Cuban's company commander. He found an angry captain demanding to know why Toller's men had ransacked their target village. A quick check with Toller confirmed that there were problems. These particular Bahnar liked neither Jarai nor FULRO, and had made their displeasure known. The discovery of several chunks of ivory triggered the looting.

The 503rd Infantry civil affairs S-5 officer flew in. As the afternoon wore on, the Battalion S-5 gave way to Brigade G-5, and St. Cyr received an acerbic ass-chewing from the 503rd's battalion commander, delivered over the command frequency for everyone's benefit. No less a personage than the deputy 173rd Airborne Brigade commander flew out to "see what the hell was going on."

After this last ass-chewing, Boris clapped a friendly hand on his shoulder.

"Buddy, you don't look so happy."

"There goes our great mobile guerrilla operation," St. Cyr mumbled, "straight to hell in a hand-basket."

"Bullshit!" Boris's forehead wrinkled with joy. "We could not have planned this better. Helicopters everywhere. Radios crackling. Staff weenies running around. Higher commanders demanding to know what in hell is going on. This looks like major operation! If we had asked the hundred-and-seventy-third to do this, they would have refused. Now we are getting circus for free!"

"Yeah? Well by tonight this circus will probably have a new ringmaster."

"Hah! You think it is accident Regter is MIKE Force commander? Shit, Buddy, he knows what is going on. Trust me. He gets paid to do his job end take his ass chewings just like you. Important thing is that when this is over, every VC within miles will be up in the hills and no one in villages will move until they are sure we are gone."

"Just like we planned it, huh?"

"Buddy, Marshal Zhukov couldn't have done better."

It wasn't just the circus that dragged at his spirits. As soon as they laagered for the night, his thoughts turned to H'nek. One night he had been sitting with Blek in an empty longhouse, drinking beer and going over their plans. And the next, the longhouse had returned to life. He could feel its spirits quiver as she glided across the floor to hand him his dinner. They exchanged furtive, then cautious, and finally, bold glances which sent Mac away grumbling as they hurried to the lover's house to tear and fumble with each other's clothing until she moaned and writhed beneath him, and his toes and fingers clawed the floor.

When it was over, they ceded the lover's house to walk through the village under the light of a waning moon. He did not return to the compound that night, nor she to her long-house. They passed their time in fevered bouts of lovemaking, interrupted by long walks in moon shadows. That next afternoon, Blek had come up from the village to hand him a thick bronze bracelet with intricate designs hammered into its face.

"My sister would have you wear this."

"I am honored," he replied in his most formal tone.

Proudly sporting his bracelet, he had trudged down to where Biloskirka was putting the platoons through an obstacle assault course. Mac had stopped by to check on training. Catching sight of the bracelet, he shook his head and walked off muttering. St. Cyr merely shrugged. Mac was Mac; some of his best conversations were with himself. In any event, the bracelet wasn't Mac's business. It was H'nek's decision, and St. Cyr was aware that they were now engaged and had the right to sleep together in the clan longhouse.

Imperceptibly, there were other changes. As they passed under the gate's arch in trucks bound for the Camp Holloway airfield two mornings later, he caught sight of Brock. Here was someone drawing parachute and combat pay just like himself, spending his nights back in Pleiku.

"I c-can fix it with the major to make you S-Four again," Mac growled. "Or even S-Two, since you speak Yard. No need to be out bustin' your hump in the boonies, like the rest of us. You're special."

He had deserved that remark, and now kept such comments to himself.

After days of cordoning off and searching villages, the 173rd Airborne departed with a fanfare equal to their arrival. Under cover of darkness, St. Cyr's men moved into deep forest. Morning found them filing south by columns. Despite good weather, a relative absence of leeches, and a fairly clear route of march, his inner hunger continued to gnaw at him.

Beneath the forest canopy, they moved in relative silence. Radios were turned to 'listen only.' Absent contact, no one was to transmit for the next 48 hours. Since MIKE Force companies carried more radios than either the Viet Cong or ARVNs, their signature was noticeable once anyone keyed a mike. And as Harry Perkins had noted at their final briefback, a Viet Cong radio intercept unit had been uncovered in Binh Dinh province. Once they transmitted anything but code, they should assume their presence was compromised.

They kept a lookout for trail watchers. Bases like the 803rd Independent Battalion's would be covered by a series of trail watcher units, local Viet Cong who moved through areas adjacent to U.S. Activity to observe and track. The higher number of Viet Cong sympathizers found among the eastern Bahnar demanded increased counter-measures.

Each platoon had selected its best trackers and hunters. As the columns advanced, these small teams would break off and go to ground. If no trail watchers appeared, they would back-track to their units, alert for any evidence that their presence was known. St. Cyr, who expected discovery at any moment, was forced to assume that continued silence meant success.

They closed on Area of Operations Leech late the fourth day. Despite its relative dryness, it soon lived up to its name. On the plus side, their coded messages to McElroy, functioning as liaison to the 173rd Airborne, were acknowledged in follow-on messages. A ration resupply took place two days later, courtesy of a C-130 which dropped cluster bomb loads into selected spots of jungle before their resupply packet came down under guise of a faulty load. By this time, they had picked up evidence of a Viet Cong presence. St. Cyr canceled a follow-on resupply mission, and ordered everyone to tighten their belts. Ryan was quick to question his decision.

Regter was reviewing reports from the companies when he looked up to find Harry Perkins' anxious face.

"Boss, are you in the mood for some speculation?"

"Concerning?"

"Our friend, Me Sao."

"Sure. Go ahead, Harry."

"Well, when Mac told me I should recommend this Glan Perr to you as the Fourth Battalion commander, I did some checking. Mostly, it's the standard stuff. Glan Perr was one of the first Jarai to start working with us in sixty-two. He was involved in the sixty-four revolt along with Romah Dat, and he accompanied his boss into Cambodia. Six months later he showed up to join the Eagle Flight under a different name. He worked for a Lieutenant Jacobelly, who's back in country but apparently down in some division. I did manage to find Clyde Sincere, Jacobelly's old boss, who's now up at Kontum with Command and Control Central.

"Clyde tells me that Glan Perr was fired for issuing orders in Jacobelly's name. Apparently they had some disagreements over how the Eagle Flight was being used, and in one of them Glan Perr claimed that he'd been a lieutenant in the French Army."

"Yeah, well the French created a lot of paper lieutenants, sort of like Ney Bloom and Jimm. Real combat command, but no official recognition."

"That's what I thought. So I asked my LLDB counterpart to pull up the old G.C.M.A records. The problem is that the Vietnamese have some of those, but they don't have them all. Frankly, sir, the Frogs are pretty good at keeping secrets. Remember that French major who visited us in Korea?

"Trinker, or something like that?"

"Yeah, Trinquier. Well he just published a book and the LLDB S-Two has a copy. He loaned it to me. Trinquier mentions visiting Korea, but claims that the Americans didn't have any special ops going on. At least none that he saw."

"Well, you've got to admire his operational security."

"I do, but my point is the Frogs don't lightly blabber secrets. Good from their perspective, lousy from ours. But every army staff has got to have its logs and charts, and sometimes the left hand doesn't get the word from the right hand that it's not supposed to record certain things. And it happens that whoever was the S-One of the GCMA compiled a list of their cadres. And being both a Frog and an adjutant, he was real picky about categorizing people by the type of commission they held."

Perkins stopped to let his point sink in.

"Harry, I've always hated playing poker with you. Get to the point."

"Well, Boss," Perkins smiled, "like I said, the old GCMA records don't do us much good. The Vietnamese were only interested in going back north, so they only got the records associated with guerrilla networks up there. The GCMA adjutant, however, probably thought their request was too trivial to bother with. So he just sent a copy of his latest personnel roster. Lucky for us, it contains the names of all GCMA operatives in north, central, and south Vietnam as well as the high plateau. One of those names is so-called Glan Perr."

"So Glan Perr was in the GCMA."

"To be exact, Boss, a person called Glan Perr. It's a pseudonym. And just our luck, the space with his real name had a big inky fingerprint on it. But this *dit* Glan Perr held his commission as a lieutenant, *a titre francais*, which means his status was that of a regular French officer. Now, why would anyone who could have gone on to a career in the French army choose to stay in Vietnam as a second-class citizen?"

"Tribal loyalty?"

"Maybe. But Trinquier's book lists a Meo highlander who held a similar commission. In fact, they're the only two Indig on that list who held commissions *a titre francais*. And that's Vang Pao."

"Colonel Vang Pao, over in Laos?"

"The one and the same."

"So what're you telling me, Harry?"

"Well, suppose the French set up some stay-behind operations when they pulled out. After all, they'd had so many changes in governments since 1945, it was entirely possible some future government might order them back to Indochina. And if that happened, stay-behind operations could pave the way. Now the guys they'd want running those operations wouldn't be your average captain or lieutenant. They'd be natives who the French could trust. Someone *a titre francais*, if you know what I mean. I suspect that Vang Pao was one such stay-behind operation, and that FULRO grew out of the other. Y B'ham was in the GCMA, as were some others we know. But the trick is, by French standards, Glan Perr was senior. And that ties in with something that Mac told me about the Rahlen clan. Certain branches of the Rahlen clan can claim descent from Me Sao. And it just so happens that Glan is a derivative of Rahlen. He's a fellow clansman..."

"So you believe he's Me Sao."

"I think there's a chance he might be connected."

"It's a good theory, Harry, but it doesn't explain the fact that Me Sao was here before Glan Perr."

"Was he? Or was he merely working through an agent, maybe somebody from his clan?"

"You mean like Blek or Blir?"

"Why not? Blir was in Glan Perr's Eagle Flight platoon when they were with Jacobelly. But all Blir will admit is that he knew him. In a way, it's a double shame that Pappy Green got killed when he did. With his contacts, we might have nailed this down."

Regter sat back in his chair and unconsciously reached in his desk drawer for the cigar that wasn't there. After several minutes of digesting Harry's theory, he remembered something Pappy Green had said.

"Harry, you've been working pretty hard lately. How'd you like to take a little R&R?"

"Sure, Boss. Any place in particular?"

"How does Singapore sound? Pappy Green had a friend down there from his French army liaison days."

"From the GCMA?"

"I believe so. Anyway, it's worth a try."

"Goddam, Boss, throw me into that briar patch! When do I leave?"

"As soon as possible, but let me check with Ralph Johnson first. I want to make sure we're not stepping on the Company's toes."

On the 12th day, deep into their area of operations and still undetected, Ryan stumbled across a trail. He had found several trails, but this worn path promised results. It lay on the down slope side of a mountain chain where all streams flowed into the Kim Son River.

Under cover of a squad, Ryan crept forward to examine it. He found several types of boot prints, a phenomenon that had piqued his curiosity ever since it had been reported at a previous night's squad leader's conference. Prominent among prints of familiar Ho Chi Minh sandals were the prints of Chinese sneaker-boots and others of an unknown origin. And if the variety was unusual, their pattern was even more intriguing. The Ho Chi Minhs walked in file, carrying some heavy cargo judging from the way their heels and outsteps dug in. The sneaker-boots moved in and out in a haphazard fashion. The unfamiliar prints, however, moved into column only when travel was restricted.

In his mind's eye, Ryan could recreate a fairly accurate picture of their activity, but he wanted to make sure. If he was right, this was not Independent Battalion 803. Carefully masking all signs of his inspection, he made his way back to the squad. After whispered instructions, they moved cautiously back to their patrol base.

Throughout the afternoon, the humid forest hummed and sang with insects and birds. Butterflies flitted through thin beams of sunlight that pierced the shadows. A troop of monkeys swung by overhead, disturbing a flock of lorikeets, who registered their displeasure with a raucous din. Once, he thought he heard the growl of a tiger or some other large cat, and prayed he was mistaken. If Sir Tiger moved into their area, the platoon would turn trigger-happy.

While Ryan fretted, Dung lay back in his hammock asleep. That irritated Ryan. Dung should have been out with a patrol, just as he should have been switching patrols daily. But Dung was no Spam. He was just was along for the ride. At least he was careful not to throw his weight around. Still, his inactivity angered the young medic, who chafed at his own passive role. Whenever the patrols came in, they found Dung and Ryan together. Ryan felt that he was being judged guilty by association. But the patrol base had the radio, which was where he had to be. He damned sure couldn't trust Dung with it.

If that wasn't enough, the leeches had also found their base, and that didn't seem to bother Dung. Ryan wondered if there was some genetic trait among Vietnamese that made it harder for mosquitoes and leeches to target them. On many Vietnamese it was difficult to locate veins for drawing blood. And even the leeches preferred Ryan. They were so thick he developed a fetish about defecating at night. In the daytime, he would look down and see the repugnant little critters weaving and swaying as they tried to reach up and attach themselves to his bared buttocks and testicles. Night was much worse. Maybe this was how Boris had gotten his famous leech. Ryan kept soaking his hammock rope with insect repellent, but the effect only lasted until the liquid evaporated, which wasn't long in this heat.

And he had to be careful not to use too much, or the scent could carry downwind.

Kevin Ryan was not happy, and the fact that every other Roundeye was suffering the same frustrations did little to ease his pain. At least he'd found something, even if it wasn't the 803rd Battalion. As he prepared a message calling for a platoon leaders' conference, K'pa Blan came back to motion him under the poncho tent. Inside, Blan leaned close to Ryan's ear.

"Eight, maybe nine stretcha," he said. "Two *bac-si*, two, mebbe three *Y-ta* nurses. Altogether two-five, two-six VC."

"What wear?"

"Black pajama, black and blue uniform. Bac-si wear green uniform."

"Type pow-fusil?"

"SKS, AK-47. One bac-si wear pow-pistole."

"Where go?"

"Up mountain. Same other track."

"How long ago?"

"Mebbe half hour." K'pa Blan pointed to his army-issue wristwatch to emphasize the point. Teaching everyone a western concept of time had been one of Ryan's contributions to the company.

"Good," Ryan told him. "Pull your people back. I have to go to company CP."

Ryan motioned for K'pa Blan to step out of the tent while he checked the radio frequency and slipped on the earphones. Checking his watch, he gave the mike the long, short, long squeezes indicating that he had a message to send. He waited for five long minutes with no answer, and repeated the process. A short, long, and three short keys came back. Cupping his free hand around the mike and his upper lip, he breathed the words "Two. Chisholm. Victor Hotel..." and waited. Up at company, St. Cyr would be thumbing through his brevity codes to decipher "Hotel."

After five minutes of required transmission delay, he heard a series of short clicks telling him to repeat the message. He half wished for the rattle of small arms fire that would blow all these precautions to hell, but patience was vital. Five minutes later, he repeated his message, switching to the alternate frequency to do so. Five minutes after that, he heard three long keys followed by a long, short, and long. After a short delay, the expected words "CC now" followed.

Against his better judgment, Ryan left his PRC radio with Dung. He would rely upon the HT-1 if they ran into trouble. Three men from his best squad accompanied him the six hundred meters to the company CP, where Cohen and St. Cyr were waiting. They waited a little longer for Biloskirka. Toller sent Rchom Jimm in his place. With everyone assembled, Ryan went over his findings: Unlike other trails, this one showed signs of frequent use. Enemy went up, but there was no evidence of anyone coming down. In Ryan's judgment, the lighter use on other trails was probably tied in with operational security. People moved up one trail carrying stretchers and supplies. After delivery, they dispersed into small groups and left. On a guess, more people were going in than coming out. As Ryan figured it, they had stumbled onto a Viet Cong field hospital, probably guarded by up to a company.

"A hospital?" St. Cyr had been hoping for something more spectacular.

"That's right, Trung-oui. A hospital."

"The 803rd Battalion could be collocated with the hospital."

"Yeah, but if we just mine the trail, we'll never know. We need to recon up instead."

St. Cyr frowned at the commanding tone of Ryan's voice. "That's my decision. Boris, I need to see you for a few minutes."

Ryan shot St. Cyr a contemptuous glare as he pulled Biloskirka away to go over the map.

"Asshole thinks he knows everything, doesn't he?"

"Hey," needled Cohen, "lighten up on the Trung-oui. He's OK."

"That's what you two keep telling me, but so far he hasn't shown me shit."

"Speakin' of shit, what do you think of this?" Cohen pulled a small instant coffee bottle from his rucksack pocket. It contained a leech between six and eight inches long. "A little present for Boris."

Ryan shot Cohen an angry glare.

"Goddam," murmured the Superjew. "Everybody's losing their sense of humor around here. And after all the careful feeding I've been giving this sonuvabitch."

"You've been feeding it?"

"Well, trying to. This one seems to have had enough, but every other leech around here keeps latching on to me. I'm going to name her Sergeyevna."

"Sergeyevna?"

"Yeah, Sergei's daughter in Russian. When we get back to Big Marty's, we'll pour a little formaldehyde in the bottle and put her up behind the bar. Maybe we can do up a little cartoon. You know, a leech in a bikini with big red lips, crooning, 'Oh Boris...you are soooo big!'"

Jimm chuckled first, then Ryan, who muffed his mouth as convulsions shook him and tears filled his eyes.

Their mirth was cut short by St. Cyr's return. Effective the next morning, he explained in clipped tones, they were reorienting their efforts to Ryan's trail. The platoons would regroup, ready for action, while Jimm's reconnaissance people scouted up both sides. Boris's platoon would move up on the right, Cohen on the left. Ryan's platoon would close up from behind, paying particular attention to their rear. Platoon nets would be on listening silence with minimum traffic on the company net.

"So," said Ryan acidly, "we're going to attack a hospital."

"Yes. Have you got a problem with that?"

"The Geneva Convention does."

"That's for the lawyers to decide, and I'll bet you this one's not clearly marked. Our mission is to kill as much of the security force as possible, capture or kill the medical staff, capture or destroy as much equipment and supplies as possible, and take the patients prisoner."

"Lieutenant, can I speak to you in private?"

"Sure, why not?"

St. Cyr led Ryan to his own poncho shelter. Once inside, Ryan let loose, fighting to control the volume of his voice.

"Lieutenant, that's a great fucking mission back at Fort Benning. Or maybe in the Fourth Foot. But it isn't worth a shit here. These are Yards! They're going to kill every sonuvabitch they find, wounded or not..."

"You got a problem with that?"

"You're goddam right I do. I'm a medic..."

"You're not a doctor..."

"The hell I'm not! Out here I as much a doctor as any sonuvabitch back in the world. And not killing the wounded is what the Geneva Convention is all about."

"You're also a goddam platoon leader, so it's your job to see that no patients get killed."

"That's easy to say, Lieutenant. Let's see you stop it once it starts..."

"Stopping your men is your business. Are we finished?"

"No. I want to know why Jimm's platoon is taking my mission."

"Because they're the recon people, that's their job!"

"Recon's a fuckin' title. My people are as good at recon as they are. What's more, we found that goddam trail."

"Is that what's eating you?"

"There's a lot of things in this company that're eating me, Lieutenant. This is just one..."

"Then maybe you need to move to another company, Sergeant. When we get back to Pleiku, I'll see what I can do."

There was a subdued silence as they rejoined the others. Ryan avoided St. Cyr's eyes.

"Sergeant Ryan," he noted for their benefit, "has expressed concern about the wounded. You all know the Geneva Convention. No wounded will be killed, unless they're offering armed resistance. Once we've secured the area, we'll call in choppers and evacuate the patients back to the 173rd Airborne for interrogation. Prisoners are a priority. Does everyone understand that?"

Silent nods indicated that they did.

"Good. Make sure your people do. Jimm, I need to see Toller first thing in the morning."

A pert Chinese secretary ushered Harry Perkins into the French commercial attaché's office on the upper floor of an old colonial building overlooking Fort Canning. His U.S. Army uniform caused some discomfort among the consular staff, and he felt equally ill at ease.

Once inside Patrick Bonnelle's office, however, Harry felt right at home. Bonnelle was a powerful, wiry man in his late thirties or very early forties who stood 5'10" and had the sky blue eyes and blond hair on suntanned skin that only France produced. Perkins guessed, incorrectly, that he was Norman. A paratroop statue graced his desk, and pictures from Indochina and Algeria lined the walls. His friendly hawk eyes went straight to Harry Perkin's chest.

"Ah, the Vietnamese *Croix de Vaillance* and you are a master parachutist. We have something in common."

Harry took the extended hand and noted the strength of the grip with satisfaction. Bonnelle might be a former paratrooper, but the stamp of his early profession rode proudly under the blue blazer, cuff-linked shirt, and carefully knotted silk tie. Even the tread of his moccasin shoes carried the authority of someone who had thrust himself out aircraft doors. Harry also guessed, this time correctly, that Bonnelle's civilian pursuits centered on scuba and sport parachute activities.

"I know the purpose of your visit," said Bonnelle, "but first let me express my profound sympathy at the loss of Captain Green. He was a fine soldier, and deeply respected by those of us in the GCMA. I cannot say the same for the other American you sent us. Tell me, did you ever serve under him?"

"Yessir, in Korea..."

"With the Partisan forces?"

"Yessir."

"Then I am doubly honored to meet you. Unfortunately, I am not the best qualified. You really need to see Hentic or Thebault. But for that you would need to go to France, so I'm afraid I will have to do. That is, unless your command wishes to send you to our parachute-ski competition..."

"Nossir. I have a week here for R&R, and it may be a wild goose chase anyway. It's just a theory that keeps rolling around in my head."

Bonnelle invited Harry to sit at a nearby small table and called for coffee. Not as good as what they used to get in Ban Me Thuot, he noted, but it too would have to do.

Harry smiled, and placed the package he had been carrying on the table.

"Sir, I believe you'll find this to your satisfaction."

"Ah," Bonnelle accepted the package with a smile. "I see that they've prepared you well for your visit."

"No one's prepared me," countered Harry, "but a planter down in Ban Me Thuot named Simard told me that the French were nuts about Ban Me Thuot coffee. So on a guess, I thought you might like some. My boss suggested that I trade it for some of that Armagnac."

"Done. But I'm afraid it won't be of the same quality as that I sent Captain Green. Anyway, that's not why you're here."

"Nossir. As you've guessed or heard, I'm looking for information about some of your old GCMA operations, and you were in the GCMA."

"Yes, but I wasn't what you'd call an old GCMA hand. It was my only tour in Indochina. In truth the GCMA preferred old Indochina hands like Loustau and Fournier. Because of my relative inexperience with the natives, I was posted to the commandos. GCMA commandos were parachute trained forces used for long range raids and penetration operations. Mine was commando six-ten. You don't have any equivalent in your own army."

"As a matter of fact, sir," Harry tapped the MIKE Force pin on his right breast pocket, "we call 'em MIKE Forces. Were your troops Montagnards?"

"No. Central Vietnamese and Nung. Montagnard troops were usually found in the Colonial Infantry battalions, though there were some with other commandos. My commando was incorporated into the reformed 5th Vietnamese Parachute Battalion after the old one was destroyed at Dien Bien Phu."

"Well," said Harry with a note of dejection, "I guess I bothered you for nothing. I was hoping that you could give me some information on a Jarai called Glan Perr."

"Glan Perr? It doesn't ring a bell."

"Too bad. He was commissioned into the French army as a lieutenant."

"A Jarai? That's not possible, not in the French army. Though we did have a lieutenant Pierre who was half Jarai."

"Pierre? We have a Pierre, but he's a Koho and too young to have been with you guys."

"Not the same man. Our Pierre was the *Métis* son of a sergeant in the Colonial Infantry. In fact, he was commissioned from Saint Maxaint, which is for active duty reserve officers, many of whom went into the Colonial Infantry."

Perkins' ears picked up. "Then he was a Frenchman?"

"Oh absolutely, though one couldn't tell. I'm afraid his mother's genes were dominant. He resigned his commission in Algeria, I believe in 1960, just after his unit was disbanded. In any event, Pierre was the family name. His Christian name was Jean-Marie. He's likely back in France somewhere, because the Vietnamese certainly didn't like him."

Harry shook his head in disgust. "Sir, you've shot my theory all to hell. Well, thanks for your time." he reluctantly rose to go.

"Not at all." Bonnelle leaned back in his chair. "And, what was this theory of yours?"

"Oh, that maybe the GCMA left a few stay-behind operations in Indochina. Maybe even one under the command of this Glan Perr."

Bonnelle rose to turn and stare out the window. "You understand, Sergeant, that even though my military attaché has told me you are cleared, I cannot discuss any but the most general details of our GCMA operations. Even if I knew them."

"Yessir, but I thought as one soldier to another, you might possibly give me enough information to save the lives of some of my own soldiers."

"Yes. Well, Indochina is your war now. Enough of your countrymen stabbed us in the back when it was ours."

"Yessir, and many of those same sons of bitches are stabbing us in the back now."

There were several moments of silence. Then, Bonnelle motioned for Perkins to sit down.

"Sergeant, may I call you Harry?"

"I'd be honored."

"Harry, you can never understand what Indochina and Algeria did to us. We had the finest army in the world in Indochina. Not the French army as a whole, but the Colonial army. And by that I mean anybody who had volunteered to be there, whatever the color or design of their buttons. And it bled us dry. Our finest officers and NCOs died in Indochina, but those of us who survived went on to win in Algeria. It was the one consolation we could offer our fallen comrades. That we had learned from their sacrifices, and we had won. Only to be sold out by the very people who had rolled over in 1940. None of us, not even those like myself who have made their peace with the government, can ever forget that. Nor can we forgive. Nor can we ever betray the trust of the oath we took..."

Bonnelle paused for a few moments of heavy silence.

"You know, one advantage of being with the commandos was that you heard bits and pieces of everything. Not the specifics, of course. Our operations were very compartmentalized. But in the messes, and in the field, one heard stories and rumors. Most of our efforts were concentrated in the north, between Laos and Tonkin. But we had small missions among the Hre and Bru. Have you ever heard of 'Hre Doc Lap'?"

"Nossir."

"It was Hentic's brainchild. An independence movement that would have made the Hre country independent of Vietnam. It failed, of course."

"Of course."

"I heard of a similar mission among the Jarai. There were several, but only one took hold. As I recall, the leader was a woman."

"A woman?"

"Yes. Some kind of Amazon queen. I'm not sure of what they called her. In any event, I heard the story from Loustau. You see, Lieutenant Pierre was pulled from Loustau's commando and parachuted into the Jarai country at the specific request of Captain Hentic. It seems that this woman and Pierre's mother were from the same clan. Do you know how our maquis were organized?"

"As I recall, you trained up your guerrilla bands under the authority of some local political leader, and then parachuted them back into their area of operations along with a French cadre."

"Yes. Of course, it didn't always work out that way. At least, not in this case. The Maquis chief's name sounded like something from the musical scale. Fa Do, Do Re, something like that. In any event, after we parachuted him in with Captain Hentic, the locals refused to work with him. It seems he got on the wrong side of this tribal queen. That's when they sent for Pierre. He was pulled from the Condor mission and sent in as her military counselor. He went in under a code name.

"That's all I know, or rather, all I heard. You have to understand, there were many stories in Indochina in those days, some about Amazon queens. Usually from old colonial soldiers who'd spent too much time in the bush. You learned to take them with a grain of salt."

An hour later, Harry Perkins strode out into the sunlight with a confident step. He had found Glan Perr. He was sure of it. The pieces fit too perfectly to explain otherwise. A Jarai *métis* who looked full Jarai. An officer in the French army who had served in a special project to establish an independent Jarai country, and then left the Highlands to fight in Algeria. Someone who had returned to the Highlands after the formation of FULRO. Someone who knew K'pa Doh, but had to play second fiddle to a Jarai outlaw and cattle raider named Romah Dat. Someone with a connection, however tenuous, to the Rahlen clan.

The only question was: had he found Me Sao? At first he was sure he had, but after changing out of his heat-wilted khakis into a sports shirt and pants, and ensconcing himself in the long bar of the Raffles Hotel, something Bonnelle had said gurgled back into his mind. *There was a woman. Some kind of queen. One had to take it with a grain of salt. There were many stories of Amazon queens floating about Indochina in those days.*

"Captain Bonnelle," said Harry *sotto voce* as he raised his glass in salute to his reflection in a recessed mirror, "I take it you've never heard of a Po Lan."

An attractive young Indian woman down the bar smiled shyly in his direction. "I'm sorry, were you speaking to me?" The accent sounded slightly British with a hint of French.

"No, Miss. I was just making an observation that Singapore certainly has some very attractive ladies. May I buy you a drink…Miss…"

"Mohini, and I would be delighted. It's a bit early for my date to show."
Harry flashed his friendliest smile and ordered her a gin and tonic.

"I'm sure it's no fault of his own. If you don't mind, I'd like to keep you company until he shows up. Where are you from?"

"India," she laughed delightfully. "I was born in Pondicherry, but Singapore is now my home."

"Pondicherry. Wasn't that a French colony?"

"You know it, then?"

"Not really," Harry confessed. "But it's always interested me. Here's to you, Miss Mohini."

As they raised their glasses, Harry thought to himself: *Bonnelle, you sly bastard you.*

Well, there was no reason to disappoint.

Chapter Twenty

LAURIE TOLLER WANDERED in to the company CP just after first light to find St. Cyr and Blek heating coffee over a pinch of plastic explosive. Boris was hunkered down near the PRC-74 radio, a notepad at his knee. Alone among the Roundeyes, Toller had taken the trouble to shave. St. Cyr repeated his instructions that there would be no killing of unarmed patients. When he was finished, Laurie hung on.

"Leftenant, mind if I offer some advice?"

"Concerning?"

"Concerning the employment of my platoon."

"Go ahead. Unlike some around people here, I don't consider myself the final authority on tactics."

Toller gave an uncomfortable shrug. "No worries, Mate, but we do have a slightly different way of doing things in Aussie. Take your plan. Essentially it's much the same as our own would be, but I do note one minor difference."

"Go ahead." St. Cyr stirred some powdered coffee into his canteen cup and offered it to Toller, who took a sip.

"Well, as I understand it, Recce's job is to reconnoiter the camp, report back to you on the layout, and provide a forward screen while the assault elements move into position."

"That's it."

"Well, have you given any thought to stop parties?"

"As a matter of fact."

"And?"

"And I prefer to keep things simple, Laurie. There's a good chance we'll be picked up moving into position. Then this plan of mine's going to degenerate into a hasty assault."

"Quite likely, if we all move up together. But my mob's good at this. We can get in, get the layout, and report back without getting caught. Better than that, we can slip around the bastards and set up stop parties along probable routes of escape. As I see it, once the shooting starts, their security's going to react like a kicked ant's nest. They'll fight a delaying action while the medical staff picks up and takes off, carrying what patients they can. The rest, they'll leave to our tender mercies."

As St. Cyr mulled this over, Biloskirka handed him a note confirming that Mac had received the previous day's situation report. When did they want the aerial relay up? Mac had helicopters on call to evacuate any prisoners.

"Tell Mac to put the aerial relay up at 1000 hours, but make sure the pilot knows not to overfly the area until contact."

"If it's FAC, he knows."

"Yeah, but if it's some chopper jockey he'll want to come down and take a look. All right, Laurie, we'll do it your way."

Toller broke his recon platoon down into two elements. Scouting teams moved parallel to the uphill side of the trail, close enough to keep within sight or hearing, but far enough into the brush to remain covered. His reaction force followed some fifty meters behind. The rest of the company followed Recon's axis of march, keeping clear of the trail, and moving only at St. Cyr's command. After days of radio silence, the occasional FM transmission sounded obscenely loud. By late afternoon, the tension and frustration were palpable. A small VC patrol was spotted on the trail just before nightfall, and Recon had uncovered several booby traps. Instead of laagering in a company position, St. Cyr ordered everyone to ground in their respective locations. No fires, no hot rations or coffee, and no smoking.

Sometime after two in the morning, Toller heard voices. As he drifted back to sleep the realization hit him with a cold chill; they'd been speaking Vietnamese. A hand tapped his shoulder. Staring up into the blackness, he made out the forms of Spam and Rchom Jimm. Jimm crouched close to his ear.

"VC," he whispered. "Wake up Trung-si Spam. Say time to go on guard."

Toller eased himself up. Around him, prone figures lay like bodies in a kill-zone. On the ground, decayed twigs had turned phosphorescent. Picking up a twig, he checked his watch by its glow.

"Get everybody up," he whispered, "but no movement until I say so. And for God's sake, don't let anybody wander off."

St. Cyr was squirming under his poncho liner, trying to find the right position to relieve some shoulder pain when his radio gave a slight hiss. Fumbling for the headset, he pulled it over his ears.

"Go," he croaked.

Laurie's low murmur informed him that Recon was either in or just outside of the hospital perimeter. In an instant, St. Cyr's shoulder pain was forgotten. He alerted the platoons for action. Listening silence would end at first light. After rolling and stowing his poncho and poncho liner, he sat back to chew his lip.

First light brought the smell of distant cooking fires, reminding everyone that they were hungry. Toller reported that the trail swung abruptly to the right, just forward of his last position. Bunkers commanded both sides of the trail, but the enemy's security appeared spread out in fighting positions. The security force probably doubled as work parties. He estimated a company sized force, no larger. No heavy weapons were visible. Hootches inside the perimeter served as quarters for the medical staff and camp mess. A large roof-like structure lashed under living trees was probably the patients' ward. They also had a generator, and on a guess their surgery was dug in nearby. The area inside the perimeter was exceptionally clean and well policed. Toller had left guides, and was moving around to position his stop parties.

Reorienting the company to this new line of advance, St. Cyr ordered Cohen's people up around the trail. Blek had just started moving their own people forward when there came the sudden pop-pop of an AK-47, answered immediately by an M-16 and an explosion.

Blek charged forward, screaming instructions to Biloskirka's platoon. As St. Cyr took the mike from Ro'o Mnur's hand, Cohen came up to report that he had taken fire from two enemy in a listening post. The jungle went ominously silent. Somewhere, St. Cyr heard a whistle. Biloskirka had

placed two squads on line in assault formation and was holding the third
and an M60 machinegun in reserve.

The men rushed forward around tree trunks and over small irregular-
ities in the earth until the undergrowth thinned out and the forest erupted
with the crash of automatic weapons, grenades, and mines. For long
minutes, everyone went to earth. Then, as their volume of fire grew, they
made small dashes forward, diving to ground to pour fire into anything that
moved, jerked, or flashed.

Biloskirka and Blek raved like madmen, shouting in three languages.
St. Cyr kept calling Mac on the battalion frequency, but only got static. Beyond the lead squads, the cleared area of the hospital perimeter came into
view. Blek, holding an HT-1 radio to his ear, gestured wildly to their right.

"Tiep-zap! Move up," he called in Jarai. St. Cyr had just ordered Ryan
to take their flank when heavy automatic weapons fire ripped into the trees
above their heads. He dove to earth, and looked up to see Blek kneeling
nearby, a single knee touching the ground. Moving up to a crouch, St. Cyr
pulled Ro'o Mnur down as branches and wood splintered just above the
young Yard's head. "Where the hell are our M60s?" he screamed over the
microphone. Seconds later he noted their responding bursts. As the splin-
ter-shower subsided, Blek rushed ahead. St. Cyr and Ro'o Mnur followed
close behind. An explosion set the roof of the ward on fire. Men screamed
for the medics as rounds tore through Ryan's platoon. Snatching an M79
from a nearby gunner, Blek fired two quick rounds into a hootch. Then,
pulling his radio operator aside, he motioned to St. Cyr.

"I go with Superjew."

The FAC's voice came over the radio. St. Cyr reported contact with
an estimated enemy company. Did he want gunships? Only on stand-by,
as the pilots wouldn't see anything but smoke. The FAC had the smoke in
sight. What about medevac? He'd need medevac, were there any clearings
in the area? None that the FAC could see, but an F-4 with a couple of five-
hundred pounders could fix that. Negative on that, at least at present.
Friendlies were all around. All right, the FAC was putting them on standby.

To his right, St. Cyr spotted Ryan moving through the far side of the
small depression where Recon had stowed their rucksacks. Cohen had
cleared the bunkers to the left of the trail and was now moving into the

camp. The NVA had disappeared. Distant firing erupted in short furious bursts that contrasted with the general confusion in the camp proper. Cohen was hit, light, nothing to worry about. Ryan's radio operator was down. Where were the indigenous medics? A muted explosion to his left front was followed by sustained bursts of M16 fire.

"Captain Blek," grunted Ro'o Mnur, "kill VC bunker."

They were into the clearing. Small orange flashes sputtered amid shadows and smoke. Crumpled figures in black, blue, and tiger stripes dotted the ground. Then as suddenly as it had started, the firing fell to occasional spurts. The men pushed on, taking cover where they could, firing precautionary rounds into any prone enemy they passed. After this came a second wave, the muzzles of their weapons carefully sweeping the terrain around them. Behind these, St. Cyr advanced. The heat from burning hootches was intense. To his left, Blek sauntered forward with an HT-1 radio in one hand and his .30 caliber Ruger revolver in the other. St. Cyr grinned in amazement. Blek had replaced his bush hat with a cadre-officer beret whose jump wings appeared shined for the occasion. Blek called for the medics to assemble the wounded.

"My brother," grinned St. Cyr as Blek strode by, "you have what is called 'command presence' at Officer School."

Blek acknowledged the compliment with a slight nod, his eyes sweeping the area for trouble. Ryan hurriedly set up his medical kit in what looked like the camp mess, and got to work on the wounded. After Toller had limped in to report that he had all his platoon back, St. Cyr called for the airstrikes and medevacs.

Mac came up on the net to bitch that he wasn't getting reports. St. Cyr explained that he was assembling the wounded and would get back with a body count after he set was up for the counterattack. But Mac was unrelenting. While Blek took charge of their defenses, St. Cyr radioed in his reports. Mere numbers and ciphers. Something the adjutant back in Pleiku would post to a typewritten page, file in an anonymous manila folder, and forward to some faceless staff weenie more concerned with making the Group commander look good than in recapping an anonymous firefight so distant from the Nha Trang Steam and Cream.

St. Cyr glanced over at Ryan, frantically pumping a young Montagnard's chest. Dirty tears coursed down his cheeks. "My radio operator," Ryan murmured. "Kid's been with me a long time...ricocheted off the femur...must've cut the femoralis vein. I didn't see the blood...didn't have time. I need more albumin, the kid's going into shock."

St. Cyr reached for Ryan's kitbag, but the indigenous medic beat him to it. The mike sputtered with Mac's voice. St. Cyr stepped away to hear better. "God fucking damn!" Ryan agonized. St. Cyr recalled his labored instructions to spare all enemy wounded. An inner voice muttered that, patients or not, they could kill all these commie scum. No prisoners were the best prisoners. But the words never passed his lips. Toller's voice came up on the net, just as Jimm dragged in a skinny Vietnamese girl whose hands were bound with parachute cord.

"One prisoner," Jimm grunted as he pushed the girl down at St. Cyr's feet. The girl stared through his legs at the scene in the mess shed. Sergeant Dung, who St. Cyr couldn't remember seeing during the fight, swaggered over to draw his pistol. The girl's voice pleaded frightened incomprehensible words. St. Cyr glanced back at Ryan, frozen in agony over the body of his RTO. Let Dung blow her away, an inner voice hissed.

"She nurse," Jimm said in Jarai. "Say please not kill. We cut loose, she help."

The FAC's voice cut through the mike. F-4s were inbound. Was everyone clear of the target? Dung screamed something at the girl and pointed his pistol. Jimm stepped between them. St. Cyr shoved Dung back with the barrel of his Car-15. Dung shot them both a venomous glare.

"Cut her loose," St. Cyr told Jimm, "but keep an eye on her." As he answered the FAC, Dung stormed off in a cloud of Vietnamese expletives. Looking back, St. Cyr noted the girl hooking up an IV next to a young Montagnard Ryan was bandaging.

The counterattack never came. Perhaps the airstrike had driven it off. More likely, the hospital security company was too busy getting the survivors away. In truth, the enemy had done extremely well in light of their own early advantage. Subsequent conversations with the girl revealed that he was a Viet Cong senior captain named Minh who'd had constant run-ins with the colonel doctor over his insistence on frequent evacuation drills. Nine members of his company and the hospital staff had paid with their lives, and only Miss Nguyen Le Tu had been taken prisoner. Yet he would likely be disciplined for losing the new bone surgery kit, whose grisly ant-infested implements were discovered in their half buried hiding place.

St. Cyr was preoccupied with evacuating his own dead and wounded. The action had cost three killed and four seriously wounded, and Blek recommended that they evacuate nine others whose light wounds would heal faster in Pleiku. Cohen had taken a nick which sliced a light groove in his thigh. He'd given more blood to little Sergeyevna, he joked, but it was worth a purple heart. Boris didn't appreciate the reference, and demanded to be let in on the joke. When Cohen finally tracked down his rucksack, to display his trophy leech for all to see, little Sergeyevna was cut up in a mash of crushed glass. Only Ryan smiled at his suggestion to amend the casualty report to include one friendly leech dead of wounds.

Toller was anxious to get on the trail of the hospital staff, but St. Cyr had other ideas. After turning the evacuation of wounded over to Ryan, he pulled Boris and Laurie aside.

"Boris, if the hospital were our target, what would we be doing now?"

"Easy. After good sweep, we would call in slicks to get out of here."

"What are our chances are of exfiltrating out of here undetected?"

"Hah, not likely. This commander will have sent back trail watchers once he broke contact. They're probably moving in now."

St. Cyr nodded as pointed to his mapsheet. "Laurie, how long will it take you to recon this hill mass if you stay off the trails?"

Toller leaned forward to check the coordinates before studying his own map. He paid particular attention to the contour lines about three kilometers to the south.

"Well, if the jungle is as open as what we've been seeing, and if that river's not too deep, I might make it back by nightfall. That's pushing it."

"What if I want you to select an area up here for a company base? A tight one, all platoons grouped together. Somewhere we can lay low for a couple of days. Can you do it, and send back a patrol to guide us in?"

"You're asking me to split my platoon? Could be hairy, that. Especially if that Eight-Oh-Third Battalion decides to come have a look."

"Yeah. I was thinking that either you or Jimm could come back to lead us in. If we're careful, we can move in at night. We'll get an ammo and ration resupply late this afternoon, then lay low for a couple of hours. After dark we'll move out guided by your people. We'll limit FM transmissions this afternoon to the Roundeye net, and impose listening silence on the Indig net. After the resupply, radio silence goes into effect. We lay low for two days, then go back into the mobile guerrilla mode. What do you think?"

Boris and Laurie looked at each other.

"You want my honest opinion?" said Laurie.

"I do."

"Right. Well it's not a bad idea, but under the circumstances it's a waste of time. What you're proposing is that we go back into the mobile guerrilla mode. We just got away with that. Fat chance we'll get away with that twice, moving just three kilometers in this terrain. Now, if it were a good fifteen to twenty kilometers, we might."

"Sorry, Buddy," Biloskirka nodded. "I'm with Laurie on this."

"All right, you two put your heads together and come up with something else. I'm going to check on the medevac."

He found Blek near the landing zone with Ryan and the prisoner, who was toting Ryan's medical kit bag. She was pointing out a series of narrow furrows which dipped between rows of trees.

"The hospital cemetery," explained Ryan. "She says they're buried head to foot. Must be over two hundred. The hospital's only been here since Tet. That's when they recruited her from a village outside Tuy Hoa. She's fifteen years old."

"Was that the medevac I heard going out?"

"Yes, sir."

"So what's she doing here?"

"Trung-oui," Ryan looked down."You need to discuss that with your counterpart."

"My brother," Blek looked St. Cyr in the eye, "she is not communist."

"She is prisoner. We must send back."

"She has treated our wounded."

"So? She is prisoner."

"So we send her back, Tiep-zap put her in prison camp. She is too young. Tiep-zap prison camp very bad place."

"I cannot make that decision."

"My brother, FULRO cadre has discussed this. They would ask this of you. She will be taken her back to Pleiku and live in our village until old enough to live alone. Maybe she be nurse in Montagnard hospital..."

The radio sputtered with Mac's voice. Where the hell was their POW? The 173rd Brigade G-2 was all over his ass. Blek and Ryan gave him an expectant look. Ro'o Mnur handed him the microphone.

"Ah...Green Bandit Three-alpha, this is Bandit Two-six. Regret to report that Papa Oscar Whiskey was KIA...repeat Kilo India Alpha...trying to escape, over."

"Goddam," Mac muttered at the other end of the airwaves. "If you assholes were going to b-blow the sonuvabitch away, you shouda just done it in the first place."

After their resupply choppers had lifted out, they moved into their new area, remained overnight, and resumed active patrolling the next morning. Other than a few trail watchers and local VC, they made no further contact. The 803rd Independent Battalion had either departed, or was playing it cautious. Their one mine victim was a barking deer. Days later, they lifted out of a recently cleared ray. Virtually invisible in the midst of the tiger-striped mob that clambered down from the Hueys at An Khe was a skinny Vietnamese girl carrying a medical kit bag. Within the ranks of her bitter racial enemies, nurse-trainee Nguyen Le Tu had found a home.

Chapter Twenty-One

THE ROLLING PLAINS OF Pleiku had turned green. Even as the C-123s taxied off the runway, rain moved in to soak the airfield. Montagnard troopers were soon trudging up both sides of a puddled road, drawing awed stares from passing American airmen. Clad in a faded tiger suit and bush hat, Miss Nguyen Le Tu stumbled along beside Spam. Her first ride in a helicopter, and now an airplane, amazed her only slightly more than her presence in the heart of the enemy's stronghold.

Over the past week, Spam had checked the girl's story. 'Autumn Tears' was the last child of an elderly couple from a Viet Cong controlled hamlet near Tuy Hoa. Her father had served the Viet Minh against the French, as her brothers now served the Viet Cong. Coming from a guerrilla-controlled area himself, Spam knew the system well. The most overt Viet Cong presence would be idealistic young rebels and field commanders who took pains to win over the peasants and embody the noblest ideals of National Liberation Front propaganda. Once these combatants took control of an area, agit-prop teams of equally young and idealistic kids moved in to organize the villagers in patriotic song fests, pageants, and morality plays. When you witnessed the National Liberation Front's soldiers cum song and dance teams, you could not help but feel an intense pride which swelled your heart to the point of tears. You thanked God and the Merciful Buddha that you had been born a son or daughter of Viet Nam. But beneath the lilting beauty of poetic words, and handsome features of youth, lay a more sinister presence; that of the Viet Cong disciplinary cadres. Hard men with harder souls who only emerged from the shadows to lecture, tax, or kill. The Front seldom demanded. Requests phrased with Confucian politeness appealed to that sense of neighborly cooperation that had forged the greater *Dai Viet*. But no matter how many times you assisted their cause, the moment you expressed the slightest doubt or disagreement, you had signed your death warrant. Under cover of darkness, or in brazen daylight, the black-clad mongoose would come. Theirs was not indiscriminate killing, the chance of war, but murder premeditated to induce terror.

The Viet Cong shadow government knew how many children lived in any given hamlet, and paid particular concern to those approaching military age. When cadres had shown up one night to tell her father that the Front had a desperate need for nurses, Spam knew what the only answer could be. He had been smuggled out of his own hamlet, to live with an uncle in a government controlled town, by a father who had paid the ultimate price. In his heart of hearts, Spam hated the Viet Cong to the point of crippling insanity, but he knew who the true Viet Cong were. This skinny Autumn Tears was not among them. Like himself, she was their victim. Spam's own father, whose headless body lay in an unmarked Mekong Delta grave, had not raised his son to be a soldier.

In the heat of battle, the girl's first instinct had been to take cover. Only later had she helped with the wounded. The shock of combat and the sight of the dreaded Moi had traumatized her into a passivity from which she was desperate to emerge. It was this reaction that had laid her soul bare to Spam. As he watched her face register revulsion, he could read her thoughts. Moi! They would rape her, fire a bullet into her brain, and leave her body for the worms. Worse, they might eat her flesh. As a child, whenever she had wandered too far, her mother had filled her head with dire warnings of the Moi. Certainly the brown hands that had pinned her to the ground and spread her legs and arms for a rough search had not given much room for hope. Yet, when it was over, she was still a virgin. The Moi leader who delivered her to the American had been gruff but gentle. When it became clear that she might not be killed, the need to reassert herself had broken through the shock of capture.

"Not worry, little sister," the Moi leader had told her, "If not true Viet Cong, you have no reason for fear."

The mean-faced Vietnamese, on the other hand, had left little doubt as to his intentions. If she could prove herself a nurse, perhaps they would spare her. Hadn't Captain-Doctor Thieu himself said that medical staff were noncombatants? Poor Thieu, he had steadfastly refused to wear his pistol. Yet in the end, his vaunted noncombatant status had failed. When the brush exploded, he had knocked her to the ground to shield her body with his own. A Trung person like herself, he would have been amazed at how close she had drawn to these Moi. To her surprise, they were not cannibals and ate rice like humans. Once accustomed to the distracting gaps in their smiles, she even developed a frank liking for their faces. Honest, open faces that wrinkled when they smiled, or laughed, or cried, as two had done for a dead comrade. Stepping into the aid station just after she had removed an IV, they had squatted down to chant some strange incantation which could only have been a prayer for the dead. Then, the older had reached over to tug at her sleeve.

"Little sister," he said in halting Vietnamese. "He my village, my family. Die so far his home. Never find way. You beware. His spirits angry."

Which was when her own tears came, as much as for this dead brown boy soldier as for herself. "I want go home," she sniffed. "I want see mother mine."

The Moi had draped a friendly arm over her shoulder. "Not worry, little sister. We protect you that Tiep-zap."

"Tank," she sniffed. "What tank?"

The Moi nodded towards the scowling Dung. "That mound of shit," he spat.

In the days that followed, she became Ryan's shadow. Moving in and among the Moi, she learned to call them Dega, their own word. They gave her a uniform, and rice, and showed her forest plants which could be used to supplement their meager rations. At a meeting of their leaders, she was called forward and questioned about her life with the Viet Cong, after which they bickered and argued. When it was over, they promised to take her to Pleiku. She found it strange that these puppet rangers, as the National Liberation Front called them, could dictate terms to their American master. She would become a nurse, they told her, but she would have to live in their village. Only there could the United Front for the Struggle of Oppressed Races protect her from the Vietnamese. It no longer seemed incongruous that they were referring to her own people.

212th Company lumbered through the gate to the catcalls of other battalion troopers, who had lifted in from Ban Me Thuot a day earlier. Joking references to stolen wives and lovers prompted humorous but pointed replies. While they cleaned weapons and turned in all munitions and arms, St. Cyr met with Harry Perkins to schedule the cadre debrief.

It was early evening before he sauntered over to Big Marty's. As he stepped through the doors, a raucous cheer went up and Jed Saville pushed out a chair.

"First," called Saville, "a toast to our lost company. Despite a lack of detailed guidance from battalion, they managed not to botch the mission. IFFV informs us that the Viet Cong are in a fit over the loss of a field hospital."

"An easy target," sneered Knuudsen. "Docs and nurses aren't hard to kill."

"Hey, asshole," glared Boris, "how many VC you get this month?"

There was a short silence which Saville took advantage of to clear his throat to remind everyone who was in charge. He then raised his glass.

"To First Battalion. We hit them in Binh Dinh, and we hit them in Darlac. Well done!"

Cheers rang out as everyone raised their glasses. Hoa stopped passing out drinks long enough to clasp her arms around Boris's neck and give him a nuzzle. Saville rapped on the table with his glass. "

"If we can have some order, there's a little matter of a presentation. Galen, I believe you're acquainted with a certain Leftenant Colonel Love?"

St. Cyr nodded.

"Right," Saville continued, "Attention to orders!" Everyone climbed to their feet. "By unanimous acclaim of his brother Roundeyes, Galen St. Cyr is hereby presented with the Love Memorial Award for Faithful Service above and beyond the Call of Duty."

Moshlatubbee pulled a leather dog collar from his pant-leg pocket which Saville fastened around St. Cyr's neck to friendly cheers.

"What's this? I'm his puppydog?"

"Read the inscription," grinned Moshlatubbee.

He removed it to read the small brass plate: "Scout, Official Mascot, Second Brigade, Fourth U.S. Infantry Division."

"And," added the Choctaw, placing a plastic wrapped bundle on the table, "we even smoked you some of the meat."

"You ate a dog?"

"Not just any dog."

"The Fourth Division mascot?"

"Better'n that."

It had been a long and frustrating operation with only fleeting contact. And when Jed Saville walked out of the airfield control shack at Ban Me Thuot, he was not smiling.

"Bloody wankers! They've white-anted our airlift."

"What?" Ferris's eyebrows knit together.

"Our airlift," repeated Saville, "the Fourth Division's stolen it."

"Shit," grumbled the Choctaw, "they're shuttling troops up to Pleiku just like we are."

"Quite true," agreed Saville, "but it appears an American colonel trumps an Aussie captain, even if we laid it on. I'm going over to see if there's anything we can do. Otherwise, its C-123s tomorrow, provided they don't nick those. Care to come along?"

The 2nd Brigade's bunkered, concertina-ringed, sand-bagged command post lay on the far side of the airfield. Approaching the entrance, they were met by a German shepherd who tensed, crouched, and rushed forward growling as his leash snapped taut. The trail end was firmly anchored to a husky young MP. "Easy, Scout," he said in a soothing tone.

They stopped to flash their identity cards. Passing through the entrance, Moshlatubbee squatted down to hold his hand just out of reach of the dog's muzzle.

"I'd be careful," cautioned the handler. "He only likes Americans."

"What part of Oklahoma you from?" asked Moshlatubbee, recognizing a familiar accent.

"Ponca City."

"You gonna tell me a Choctaw from Ada isn't a thousand percent American?"

"Hell no, Lieutenant!" grinned the trooper. "Got some Cherokee blood myself. But Scout here belongs to the Brigade XO. He thinks all real Americans are White-Eyes."

"He does?" chuckled the Choctaw. "Well we'll just have to teach him better. Easy, boy." He moved his hand into range to let the dog sniff it, then caressed its chest before moving up to pat its neck.

Outside the operations center, they were accosted by a young lieutenant colonel in creased starched jungle fatigues and spit-shined boots. His camouflage helmet cover shone unnaturally clean, totally devoid of stains or frays. Even his web equipment gave off a fresh, dull glow. His face was neatly shaven, the white of his skull visible beneath a fresh haircut.

"Who the hell are you people? And why haven't you shaved?"

"Captain J.E.D. Saville," Jed saluted and extended his hand. "Australian Army Training Team. That's my MIKE Force battalion at the end of the airfield. Is Colonel Fay in?"

Love ignored the hand. "He's out with the battalions. I'm Colonel Love, the Brigade XO. Are you the same Green Bandit Six who told me to get the hell out of your AO last week?"

"I am if you're Red Ivy Five."

"Just where in the hell do you come off ordering me out of my own TAOR?"

"Well, Colonel, it wasn't exactly your Tactical Area of Responsibility. IFFV had assigned it to us. You can take that up with my commander if you wish. Major Regter, in Pleiku."

"Pleiku MIKE Force? Do you have a lieutenant St. Cyr?"

"In this battalion as a matter of fact, but just now Galen's operating in Binh Dinh province."

"That figures. Captain, if you want to see Colonel Fay, get yourselves cleaned up and looking like soldiers."

"Colonel, we're just out of the bush!"

"Exactly, and we have a PX tent that will sell you soap and razors. So until you get cleaned up and looking like soldiers, you can get the hell off my airfield. Captain Williams."

A harried young captain hurried over.

"Escort these gentlemen from the CP. And tell those damned MPs to start screening people. No one's allowed in who isn't shined, shaved, and looking like a soldier. Do you think you can handle that?"

An anxious look flashed across the captain's face, while a flinty glare crept into the Choctaw's gaze. Heeding the warning, Saville edged between Moshlatubbee and Love.

"We can find our own way out, Colonel. Thank you for your courtesy and time. Your welcome was in the very finest traditions of the American army. I hope we can do the same for you someday."

Captain Williams walked them to the gate, mumbling half-hearted apologies for Love. He could save his breath, grumbled Moshlatubbee. Everybody had their assholes. Once through the gate, the Choctaw pointed to a rubber plantation beyond the airfield control tower.

"If you care for some beer and dinner," he said, "come on over tonight any time after seventeen-hundred hours. Ever had Montagnard chow?"

"No."

"Well come on over. You might like it."

"Montagnard grub," wondered Saville after the captain had left. "You don't mean PIR rations?"

"Nossir. The boys are going to hunt up a little real meat. Sort of an early-American-Montagnard dish, courtesy of colonel Love. You'll see."

Captain Williams showed up at the MIKE Force perimeter later that evening, explaining that he'd been tied up in a briefing. Moshlatubbee led him to an area where jugs of *mnam pay* purchased from a nearby Rhade village were set up. Pots fashioned from large cooking oil tins, suspended by commo wire from tri-poles, held several varieties of local tubers stewed with chunks of fresh meat. Saville introduced him to Ferris, Ney Bloom, and the rest of the cadre, and invited the captain to sit. A bearded Aussie tossed over a lukewarm can of Foster's beer.

Despite the MIKE Force's ragged appearance and overpowering smell, Williams felt at ease. The Aussies joked about the Americans, the Americans poked fun at the Yards, and the Yards good naturedly poked fun at the Roundeyes. The stew was so good that Williams accepted seconds. The beer was followed up with a turn on the *mnam pay* jug. In his two months in country, he confessed, this was the first time he'd eaten Montagnard goat. In fact, this was the first time he'd ever eaten goat. And to tell the truth, this was the first time that he'd met any real Montagnards or Vietnamese.

"*Con chaw*," said a grinning Vietnamese sergeant, as he dug into his canteen cup of stew. "Good."

Williams grinned back and repeated the words. "What's he saying?" he asked Ney Bloom.

"Oh," Ney Bloom flashed an open smile, "Sergeant Dinh from Hanoi. Say this first time he eat this meat in very long time, but is good."

"You can say that again. Better'n what we get in our mess hall."

As Ney Bloom translated the remark, laughter rippled through the clearing. Later, Ney Bloom formally presented Williams with a bracelet to mark the occasion. As it was clamped about his wrist, he suddenly noted that his hour off had passed. As he rose to leave, Moshlatubbee tugged at his harness.

"Say, Captain, how well do you get along with colonel Love?"

"He's my boss," shrugged Williams, "so what can I say. Ours not to reason why. He's been under a lot of strain lately, waiting to see if he's getting promoted and going back to the states to command some training brigade. With luck, that'll be the last we see of him. Who's this St. Cyr? Love spent the whole afternoon badmouthing him."

"Someone probably very much like yourself," the Choctaw grinned. "Used to be one of Love's company commanders, until he saw the light and came over to us."

"God, how'd he get that lucky?"

Williams saw them again, early the next morning, as their C-123s taxied in. He was looking for Saville, but zeroed in on Moshlatubbee.

"Hey Choctaw, Colonel Love wants to know if anyone's seen his dog."

Moshlatubbee passed this on to Y Mlo, who called it out in Ede. The Montagnard ranks broke into grins and laughter.

"What's so funny?" Williams asked suspiciously.

"Just a little Montagnard humor," grinned the Choctaw. "But if you run into any Vietnamese and you want to ask them about a dog, the word's *con cho*, pronounced '*chaw*.'"

"Wait a minute, you don't mean..."

"Yeah, I do."

For a moment, William's face turned pale. Then, he cracked an evil grin. "Not Scout?

"None other."

"Damn, Choctaw. Scout's the only thing anybody likes about Colonel Love. Tell you what, I'm gonna wait until you guys clear the airfield before I give him the news."

"We'd appreciate that. Tell him if he wants the pelt back, it'll be up on the wall in our club. Just look for a sign that says 'Big Marty's Bar and Grill'."

"So," chuckled St. Cyr, "he had a dog."

"Very good dog!" cut in Ney Bloom, rolling his eyes and patting his stomach.

"Tasty dog," added the Choctaw, "and that's the first one I ever ate. We go more for beef back in Oklahoma."

"Here's to scout," St. Cyr lifted his glass. "He deserved a better master. Rat-atat-Tat, Rat-atat-Tat, Mow Those Bastards down..."

The table erupted in song, beer cans and drink glasses banging time to the tune. From the bar, Hoa shouted sexually explicit warnings as to what would happen if anyone broke a glass. Major Regter walked in, and stopped to clap a friendly arm around Jed Saville and Ney Bloom's shoulders. He stayed long enough for a rare drink, then took off to wrestle with his latest crisis with Ngoc, and meet with Harry Perkins, who had just returned from Singapore with an even wilder theory about Me Sao.

The next morning, Regter was up for his run. A late night rain had soaked the earth, but as the rising sun, wedged between mountains and orange-fringed purple clouds, sparkled off rain flecked blades of grass, he jogged down through the compound and out the gate. Thirty minutes later, he had the satisfaction of catching a bleary eyed Cox just outside the C Team.

"Morning, Charlie! How're things going?"

"Sir," panted Regter, not yet cooled down, "I need to bring you up to date on my counterpart. Are you aware that he's fired all my Montagnard civilians and replaced them with Vietnamese?"

"No, but camp administration's an internal matter. I don't intend to get involved. That's between Ngoc and Khanh."

"It was probably Khanh's idea, but that's not my point. I've told Ngoc that the camp is his. He can do with it what he damned well pleases, but physical security of the Roundeyes is my affair. I think you need to be aware that when these Vietnamese women show up for work, they're going to be subject to search by my security company."

"Male or female?"

"We're recruiting some females."

"Then there shouldn't be a problem." Cox abruptly turned and strode off to wish Colonel Khanh a good day.

As bosses went, Regter mused, Cox wasn't bad. Their relationship had improved since Tet. But Cox lived in an American compound, worked in an American-staffed office, sited across from a totally Vietnamese wing of the building, and had never mentally left the United States. The fact that Vietnamese women were going to be searched by female Montagnard guards on orders of an American officer couldn't help but offend the Vietnamese. But Regter would be damned if he backed down from Ngoc on this issue.

Back in his own compound, he found Rahlen Blir instructing the new female recruits in the intricacies of drill and ceremony. Readily identifiable was the shapely figure of Blir's niece. Montagnards might be a different race, Regter chuckled to himself, but Asia was Asia. It's not nepotism when our guys do it. The girls giggled as he stopped to watch. The few words he caught, before Blir's bark silenced them, were Jarai slang for "dirty old man."

Payday and the sacrifice went smoothly. The troops stepped up to one of four tables, received their monthly wages of about $55.00 in Vietnamese *dong*, then passed on to a single table staffed by K'sor Tlur, Blek, and St. Cyr. Here, those who had been absent, late, or otherwise shirked or incurred K'sor Tlur's wrath, paid their fines. This month another collection had been added. It was costing 60,000 dong, more than 500 dollars, to keep Sergeant Dung quiet about the girl. Many grumbled. Word had spread that 'Jimm's Tiep-zap' Spam had refused any pay-off, and Dung had the bad grace to be present while the troops were being paid. Two of the company's rougher characters walked uncomfortably close to him and called out an oath that they would eat his liver. K'sor Tlur quickly sent them on their way.

At that afternoon's company sacrifice, a white buffalo had materialized as promised, drawing half-jealous, half-admiring complaints from the other companies. That he was albino showed in his eyes, but Boris had taken the precaution of having him liberally powdered with rice talcum. There was no such thing as too white a sacrificial buffalo. Regter opened the sacrifice by challenging everyone to a morning run, then bowed out after drinking the perfunctory two measures.

Regter was surprised to find Biloskirka up and ready the next morning. When he remarked on it, the big Ukrainian merely noted that it was Camerone. Probably some Orthodox feast, thought Regter. In deference to the sacrifice, he kept the workout light.

Following a shower and shave, Boris made a final check of his uniform. On rigidly starched and tightly tailored U.S. jungle fatigues, he had affixed his traditional green and red Legion epaulets. French para wings shone above the right pocket, while the left sleeve bore his old rank insignia of chief corporal above a reenlistment chevron and legion grenade. A green and yellow Theater of Operations *fourragere* hung from the left shoulder, and full sized U.S., French, Soviet, and Vietnamese medals were carefully arrayed on the left chest. Centered on his right breast pocket was the small silver triangular dragon of the 2d Foreign Legion parachute battalion (BEP), while the left bore the green MIKE Force dragon. Carefully zipping his uniform into a garment bag, he checked his kepi hatbox. Then, almost furtively, he loaded his equipment into the truck. Machetes, a shovel, folding chairs, a long metal folding table, and two footlockers of miscellaneous items were packed into the three-quarter ton. Cohen staggered from his room just as Boris was finishing up.

"Hey, Boris. What'cha up to?"

"Nothing, Buddy. A little work detail."

"On standdown?"

"I volunteered."

Minutes later, Boris pulled up in front of the indigenous mess hall and blew the horn. A senior Nung cook named Tang climbed up into the cab while two assistants manhandled several boxes into the back of the truck. When they were seated, Boris made a short stop at the security company to collect his work detail. Then he was out the gate for one final stop at the Vietnamese dependent quarters near Corps, where they pulled up next to a small stucco duplex. At the sound of the horn, Company Sergeant Major Huynh's head peered out.

"Did you get it?" Boris asked in French.

Huynh's grizzled face wrinkled in a smile. Sidestepping into full view, he snapped a MAS-36 rifle to present arms, taking care to dip the muzzle forward. Affixed to the barrel was an embroidered satin facsimile of the 2nd BEP pennant.

"A true *adjutant-chef*," marveled Tang in his singsong French.

"And what of you?" Asked Huynh.

"The best boudin never tasted! Me I make myself with cooked pig's blood and rice."

"Excellent," noted Huynh as he climbed up to sandwich Tang in next to Boris.

Pleiku's French cemetery lay on a small knoll just south of the city's center, not far from the CMA hospital. Originally an open area, villas and shacks were intruding. The grass, which burned off in the dry season, had sprouted up in the recent heavy rains. After some minutes searching for the military section of the cemetery, Boris put the detail to work, joining in with a machete to assist, while Tang and the cook detail got busy. Mildew and fungus had stained the once white stones, making them appear much older than they were. After the weeds had been cleared away, they set to work with bleach and whitewash, paying particular attention to Rolf Müller's headstone.

It was nearly noon before they finished. Boris invited everyone outside the cemetery gate for a beer at a nearby Chinese store. A raincloud passed overhead, but loosed nary a drop. When it was gone, the assistants set to work under the sparse shade of a flame tree which sat back from the edge of the cemetery. While Huynh supervised the setting of the table, Boris and Tang cleaned up and changed into their Camerone uniforms.

Sometime around 1500 hours, Monsieur Chantpique of the S.E.U.F. electric company passed by. The military truck inside the cemetery gate caught his attention. This was the French cemetery, and a military truck was unusual. As he slowed down, his nose caught the smell of roast pork. Really, these damned Indochinese had no respect for European dead. Slamming on the brakes, he had the presence of mind to lock his Willis Jeep steering wheel before barreling into the cemetery. The sight of a linen covered table set at the far edge of the military section stopped him cold. Three legionnaires sat at the table, two kepis and a white beret set meticulously across from their plates. He noted it was set for full service with a bottle of red wine at each place. Facing the table and legionnaires was a tripod of stacked rifles, one of which carried a pennant of sorts.

Chantpique could not restrain himself.

"Messieurs, this is what? The Legion departed Indochina in 1956."

The face of the Caucasian fixed him with an intense glare. "You have fooled yourself, Monsieur," he gestured at the headstones. "The true Legion is...here."

"So you were a Legionnaire…"

"As were my comrades, and today is Camerone."

Chantpique's eyes took in the eight settings and three ex-legionnaires. "Where are the others?"

Boris nodded back at the headstones, singing as he did so. "*The most handsome soldiers...in all of France...are those you see before you.* My comrades, good Buddhists and Confucians that they are, insist on setting servings for the dead. Won't you join us?"

"I cannot. I was not a legionnaire. I've not even done my military service. Only because I was overseas, you see."

"But you are French?"

"Of course. With the electrical power commission. My wife is buried here."

"Then join us, for today we are French too. Not by the blood we were born with, but by the blood we shed."

They rose to accept his hand while Boris called for another place to be set with blood sausage and wine. After Chantpique had been seated and drank a healthy toast to the Legion, Boris asked if he had ever heard of Camerone. He had not.

"Then Sergeant Major Huynh, who despite that ugly mug is the youngest man here, will speak of it. Kindly pay attention, because once he has finished you will be held accountable for recalling certain facts."

The sun had dipped low over the horizon before Chantpique took his leave to stagger out, pausing briefly to say a short but still coherent prayer at the edge of his Sophie's tomb. As he passed the gate, he noted a solitary Vietnamese officer watching the group within. A metal French parachutist badge shone from above the cloth Vietnamese wings on his pattern 47/51 camouflage smock.

"You should go in, Major. They would welcome you."

"Thank you, but no. I believe this is a purely private affair"

And a purely private affair was just what Colonel Khanh had in mind when Ngoc returned to his headquarters.

"An insult," thundered Khanh. "That some certain Moi have temerity to search person of Viet Nam army dependent when she is leaving your army camp."

"But Trung-ta," protested Ngoc. "Security is domain of Long-noses. There is little I can do. Besides, some certain dependent had temerity to place one Long-nose's money inside her panties."

"Agree, not correct. Still, this certain dependent is poor and Long-noses have so much."

"True, but recommend we not protest at this time. There is still matter of taxing one meat supplier. We need those funds to meet our contribution to Corps' fund. To protest now is to risk their non-cooperation when Long-noses hear of that. I believe we should keep silent for sake of harmony."

"Harmony?" Khanh lit up a cigarette and fumed in silence for long seconds. "This all that damned Phu's fault...," his voice tapered off. The Northern Mafia was a slumbering beast about which successful Southern officers tiptoed lightly. As a member of the Ton That branch of the royal line, Ngoc would have friends in both camps. "Of course," Khanh continued, "with national economy in such state, who can blame her? Yet the temerity of that Long-nose major to call in national police infuriates me. We have lost face with Phu! That woman is dependent of a Trung-si on his staff."

"Major," Khanh paused for more nervous puffs. "Pay particular attention to Long-noses actions. Inform me immediately when any one of them violates our laws. We shall see who loses most face!"

"Of course, Trung-ta."

"Good. Tomorrow morning, when I meet with colonel Phu, you will accompany me."

It was just after supper when Harry Perkins stuck his head through the door to St. Cyr's room.

"Hey, Trung-oui, I thought you'd be in the village by now."

"I would be, Harry. But while we were in the field my betrothed decided to join the CIDG. She'll be off when they finish checking these new maids. Did you hear about the money she found?"

"Yeah. Hey, forty dollars isn't much to us, but it'll feed a family of five over here for almost a month. And these new maids are all ARVN dependents or widows. Their paychecks don't go very far these days."

"I hadn't heard that, but Toller wouldn't agree with you on the money. It was his, and the Aussies don't get paid like we do. They make just slightly more than our interpreters."

"Which is a lot more than the Arvins. Anyway, that's not why I'm here. Superjew says you speak French."

"Northern Maine Acadian. Got any Canucks you want me to interrogate?"

"No. A Jarai named Glan Perr."

"Hell, we can do it in Jarai. I have learned some since I've been here."

"Brother," replied Harry in Rhade. "If I want talk him Dega tongue, I talk him Dega tongue myself. I wish use French talk."

"French it is."

"Good. Now when I start popping the questions, this sonuvabitch is going to start lying through his teeth, so this is what I want you to do..."

It was dark when they got to the S-2 shed. Glan Perr was waiting outside. After a polite handshake and the formalities, Harry guided him in and poured everyone a cup of coffee, taking care to sweeten Glan Perr's with a generous helping of condensed milk.

"I should like to conduct this interview in French," said Harry in passable French, "as it appears you served with the Autonomous Mixed Commando Group of the French army."

"Of course," replied Glan Perr in flawless French that carried a hint of regional dialect. "I told Special Forces that when I joined in 1963."

"Yes," said Harry, through St. Cyr this time. "But you served under French title, meaning you were a French officer."

"Myself never," said Glan Perr. "I was solely a partisan."

"But you were a chief of partisans."

"Yes, that is why the French recruited me."

"And you attended St. Maixent Military Academy."

"St. Maixent? Not possible. That is in France!"

"Then you attended the Dalat military academy, or the Special Course at Cape Saint Jacques."

"Never."

The responses were what Perkins had been expecting. He slowed down, letting the caffeine take effect, and focused on Glan Perr's hands.

"Did you ever know or hear of an officer called Jean-Marie Pierre?"

"But of course. He was killed in the Bac Phi country..."

"You mean Algeria?"

"Wherever the Bac Phi come from. You know, Bac Phi is Vietnamese word. We ourselves call them K'sor Bani. The French had a war there."

"You've never been there yourself?"

"How would a Jarai get there? Can one walk?"

"Lieutenant Pierre was there, and he was Jarai."

"Him, never! He only looked Jarai. He was French!"

"He was half French, and your mother and his were from the same clan."

"The Glan clan is not small. Ask your own Rahlen Blir."

"But he was a kinsman from your own subgroup..."

"Only until he betrayed us by leaving to fight for the French."

Harry paused to fill his pipe. "You know," he said offhandedly to St. Cyr in English. "We may have to wait until those records come in from Pau. I can't get the old GCMA records, but the files of all former French officers, as well as foreigners who served in the French army outside the Legion, are kept in a central bureau there. And it just so happens I have a friend who can get us a photo..."

Glan Perr's right hand twitched into a fist, then relaxed.

So," continued Harry in carefully rehearsed French, extending his hand, "Thank you, my Captain."

"It was nothing, *Adjudant*," snorted Glan Perr, as he accepted Harry's hand in a perfunctory grip.

"Well," grinned St. Cyr, after Glan Perr had left, "you drew a blank, Harry."

"Think so?" Perkins smiled. "The trouble with you Canucks is you're too informal. Did you notice what happened when I called him Captain?"

"Sure. He said 'It's nothing, First Sergeant,' and left."

"No cigar for you, Trung-oui. You missed the most important point. He said *adjudant*, not *mon adjudant*. He addressed me as an inferior. Shook my hand like one, too."

"Captains outrank adjudants. You've been over here too long, Harry."

"Maybe, but I'd wager he was addressing me as a former colonial infantry lieutenant, not a FULRO captain. French senior NCOs didn't get addressed as inferiors in the colonial army, especially by indigenous officers. Unless, of course, they were bona fide French officers. The trouble with you, El Tee, is that you haven't been here long enough."

Chapter Twenty-Two

ST. CYR WAS CHEST DEEP in muddy pond water, holding one end of a net, as Ryan approached and squatted down behind several crones in the shade of a clump of banana plants. Six to eight paces away, Blek maneuvered the other end of the net. The crones ignored Ryan to puff away on their pipes, studying the water's ripples. As the men raised one edge of the net, the water boiled with panicked fish. In an instant, the old women were in to claim their fish. St. Cyr barely had time to grab a 15-inch carp up behind the gills.

"Careful," warned Blek, as he lifted up a larger carp by its eye sockets, "these fish stick."

"Hey, what's a little gill-stick between friends?"

"This fish not friend," warned Blek. "Bad pain, maybe get infected."

Threading their catch head first into a fish basket, Blek pushed it back underwater and reached for more.

"Hah," chortled the women, "Meerika bring good luck!"

"Lieutenant," interrupted Ryan, "can I talk to you?"

"Sure," St. Cyr threw a friendly arm around Blek's bare shoulder. "I return in few minutes, Brother."

As he climbed out of the pond, muddy water ballooned from the bottom of his pants.

"Good way to pick up leeches," observed Ryan.

"In this country, what isn't?"

Reaching the shade of a mango tree away from the pond, Ryan turned around. "El Tee, I hear you've been talking to Moshlatubbee about trading medics."

"Yes, as I told you I would. You're not too happy with the way I run the company, maybe you'll be happier someplace else."

"OK," Ryan fought to keep his temper under control, "but why didn't you ask me first?"

"What for? So I could hear about how you were in the company when I was in Officer Candidate School? Or how Dick Grey was the only real commander this company's ever had? I'm tired of hearing it. Look, no decision's been made, but we are considering it."

"Is this the way you did things in the Fourth Foot?"

"No. In the Fourth Division, my first sergeant would have handled this."

"Because I'm enlisted?"

St. Cyr nodded.

"You know," anger crept into Ryan's voice. "A few weeks ago you told us how we aren't really enlisted men, though we are, but really officers, which we aren't, because we're platoon leaders. Even though we're not officers."

"That is your significant other duty."

"So if I'm a platoon leader," Ryan's voice rose, "why haven't you asked me if I want to change companies? After all, I'm just one level below you. Besides, I have a real fuckin' skill. I've trained every medic in this company. I mean, if we lose you, you're just another officer. We can always find a replacement. But it takes years to train up a medic with my skills. So, my question is: Is this the way they treat officers? You just decide whatever the hell you want and I'm supposed to salute and say yessir? If that's the case, fuck you!"

Ryan's anger triggered St. Cyr's own.

"When the hell have you ever acted like an officer? Oh, I'm the medic, I'm special. Yeah, right. And the senior medic on any team is an E-7. That's a platoon sergeant in the real army, Junior. Second to the platoon leader. Let me tell you something else. The mere fact that anyone's an officer doesn't mean he can go around criticizing his commander. Officers who do that get fired. So, just because you're the best medic I've seen, and a competent platoon leader, doesn't mean I'm going to put up any greater ration of shit. Fuck you too!"

The words had no sooner passed St. Cyr's lips, than Ryan's fist snapped into his face. He felt a crunch in his nose, and staggered back as pain shot into his brain, triggering his rage. He shook his head, deflected Ryan's next punch off his shoulder, and got an arm around Ryan's neck.

They grappled. Ryan managed to slip his head free, but St. Cyr's left forearm slammed into his chin while his right fist hit Ryan's ribs. Ryan grabbed St. Cyr's wrists and held on. They wrestled and tumbled to the ground. St. Cyr's wiry strength surprised him. Twisting one hand free, St. Cyr soon had Ryan partially pinned down, pounding his head with his fist. Ryan gave nearly as well as he got, but being on the bottom weakened his blows.

Blek arrived to pull St. Cyr off. Ryan scrambled to his feet, his fists clenched. He hung back as Blek shoved St. Cyr away.

"This Meerika business," St. Cyr hissed. "Let me go!"

"This company business," retorted Blek. "Come, brother, we take fish and go."

"I have to settle this."

"Later," Blek glanced at Ryan. "You go. Get out." Ryan hesitated, then stormed off.

"Everyone awaits us," Blek murmured to a heavily breathing St. Cyr. "Come…"

"I can't, Blek. Tell H'nek I'm sorry. I'll see everyone tomorrow."

He drove back to the compound in a rage, stopping off at Big Marty's to put a bottle of rum on his tab. Happily, his room was empty. He should have kicked Ryan's arrogant-little-prick head in, he fumed to himself. After all, Ryan had thrown the first punch. But the fact he'd hit an enlisted man weighed on his mind. It was not something that Regter would condone. He'd have been smarter to walk away, to put Ryan up on charges. To let the system, with its Article 15s and courts martial, handle. That's what any real officer would have done. But, he shook his head in frustration, he couldn't. For all Ryan's carping, he had bled for his country and performed duties far above those of a low ranking enlisted soldier. Even with his annoying I-know-better-than-you attitude, Ryan had St. Cyr's respect. And fact that Ryan so obviously disrespected him hurt his pride. And it was his problem, at least for the next few months. As St. Cyr washed the blood from his tender nose, he resolved that any dirty laundry between them would be washed in house. It was no one's business but their own.

After two painkillers, he fell asleep to wake in the wee hours of a chilly Highland morning. Wandering over to the Teamhouse, he heated up a stale pot of coffee, drank a cup, stared at his swollen nose in the latrine mirror, and staggered back to bed. He was dimly aware that his Jeep was gone, and that the Choctaw had come home with a date. He woke again just after 0600, but feigned sleep until Moshlatubbee and his date were ready to leave.

"Hey, Choctaw, can I borrow your Jeep?"

"After I drop Brenda off. Where's your company Jeep?"

"Probably down in the ville with my Roundeyes."

"I'll be back later. If you're not here, I'll leave the keys on my bunk."

A few hours later, St. Cyr crawled out of bed still tipsy from the rum. After a long shower, he stopped by the Teamhouse where several Aussies had prevailed on the Nung cook to prepare a stockman's brekkie of steak and fried eggs. With that void in his stomach filled, he steeled himself for the inevitable and knocked on Ryan's door.

Knapp was the only one home. Ryan hadn't been back since the previous evening. St. Cyr returned to his room to find Moshlatubbee's keys on his bed. He barreled out the gate, but Ryan was neither at Blek's nor Madame Binh's. He did find Cohen, who mentioned that Ryan had a place he rented when My Lei was in town, and drew St. Cyr a map.

Ryan's night had been no easier. After cleaning up, he went by the Bamboo Bar to wait for My Lei, where Boris and Cohen found him sometime after 2000 hours. Neither was happy to hear about the fight. He expected Biloskirka to side with the El Tee. After all, Boris was a career NCO. But even Cohen took up St. Cyr's defense, and insisted Ryan should cut him some slack. Worse, even My Lei weighed in. She had listened to him unwind, but as he started repeating himself, she lost her temper.

"You hit you lieutenant, you stupid! He OK. Everybody make pass at me, OK? But he don' make no pass at me. He know I you girl. That 'cause he respect you. You wan make love me, then make love me. Othawise, you talk all you bullshit by youself, I don' wanna heah."

They argued for about an hour, when he finally gave in and pulled her over to him. She was angry and reluctant at first, but surrendered to the vixen within. They fell asleep in each other's arms, where he stayed until daybreak. Then he slipped into their postage stamp-sized kitchen and brewed himself a coffee. His time in the MIKE Force was over. Whatever St. Cyr did, and as an officer he could only report it, Sergeant Major Slover would the one to decide the issue. Ryan would likely be sent down to Nha Trang for the few months he had remaining, essentially throwing him out of the MIKE Force. All because he'd let the El Tee get under his skin. Since things couldn't get any worse, he squeezed into their small table and began going through his stack of unopened mail.

Just after 1100, while My Lei was in the shower, Ryan heard a knock. He cracked it open to find a slightly grinning St. Cyr with one eye swollen and a nose still out of joint.

"Hey asshole," St. Cyr threw his fists up in a fighting stance. "You ready for round two?"

"Sure," Ryan couldn't help but grin, "Where're the MPs?"

"Probably handing out traffic tickets."

Ryan pushed the door open. "Care for some coffee, El Tee?"

"Already had some…"

"Not like this. My Lei likes her *café sui* Vietnamese style."

"Sure. Got anything I can pop for my nose?"

"Yeah, but we need to run up to the dispensary and re-set it."

"I'd appreciate that. But seriously, if you really want to take another shot at me, this is your chance."

"Look El Tee, I took all the shots I needed yesterday. Besides, it wasn't supposed to happen like that. Anyway, I like Moshlatubbee. If you've worked out a trade, I'll live with it."

"We only discussed it. Look, to tell the truth, I'd hate to lose you. But I'm sick and tired of the shots you keep taking at me. It got on my nerves."

"Lieutenant, I didn't mean it personally. Look, Dick Grey was my commander, my brother, and next to Superjew and Boris, my best friend. And when I got back and found you here, well, it pissed me off. I mean, you just rolled in and took over, like he never existed."

"Bullshit," insisted St. Cyr, knowing as he said so it was true. "I've done my best to keep Dick Grey's spirit alive in this company, but it's my company now. Mine and Blek's. We have to sink or swim with it, and the very least we can expect is the loyalty of our right hand men."

"Sir, you've got my loyalty. I swear! But maybe just every once in a while, I might want to whip your ass."

"And when you do, you'll get your chance. Until then, this never happened."

Ryan stared down at the floor. "I appreciate that, El Tee, but there is one thing that grates on both me and the Superjew. Look, when you give orders to Blek or Boris, you always ask their opinion. I mean, we understand that. Blek's your counterpart and Boris was fighting wars before we were born. And you take Toller's advice when he offers it. But with me and the Superjew, it's just: Do this! Make sure you do that! I mean, no offense, but is that the way you were treated when you were enlisted?"

"Are you saying my leadership style is autocratic?"

"It is when you deal with us."

"Ouch," grimaced St. Cyr, "Maybe I learned more from Colonel Love than I like to admit. You're right. At Tri Chuc I always got respect, even though I was only an acting sergeant. And Jerzy Jacowiecz went out of his way to teach me how to run recon. And he did it in such a way that I always thought of him as an older brother instead of a Sergeant First Class. I'll try to do better."

"We'd appreciate that, El Tee. I'm getting out in a few months anyway, but I'd like to stay with the company until I do."

"Any word on medical schools yet?"

"As a matter of fact," Ryan retrieved two recently opened envelopes. "Both Tufts and Harvard have accepted me. Now all I've got to do is get the army to give me an early out."

"You just got the word?"

"Sort of. I've had the letters since we got back, but I was afraid to open them. This morning I figured: what the hell."

St. Cyr pumped Ryan's hand. "Congratulations, Kev! Boris and the Superjew will be damned proud to hear it. Next year in the...?"

"Black Rose, sir. March Seventeenth."

"It's a deal. Now, I've got other fish to fry."

"No so fast, El Tee. We need to run up to the dispensary and fix that nose. It looks bad enough as it is, and the longer we wait; the harder and more painful it's going to be."

They drove back to the compound and ran into Mac near the dispensary. Mac smiled at seeing them together, and tagged along to watch Ryan reset his nose, grinning all the time.

That evening, St. Cyr arrived at Blek's to find everyone waiting. Spam had brought his wife, who peered nervously about the longhouse. H'nek left the cooking to lay a clean pallet in the guest area for Ba Xuan, complimenting the beauty of her blue and gold Ao-dai as she did so. Then, noting Ba Xuan's attempt to mask her disapproval of bare breasts, she ducked back into her compartment and emerged wearing a lime colored sateen blouse. Squatting by the fire, she signaled to H'pak, who likewise excused herself to dress.

"If Tiep-zap woman does not like your breasts," St. Cyr whispered, "she can leave."

"Idiot," H'nek whispered back, "she is guest."

St. Cyr would have joked that Ba Xuan was jealous, but wasn't sure how much Jarai Spam had picked up. H'nek had surprised him with her Vietnamese. He was even more surprised when the door slid open and Rchom Jimm stepped in, leading his sister and Miss Le Tu. After hasty introductions, during which Le Tu seemed to regard Mrs. Spam with absolute dread, the girls excused themselves to help with the cooking. Following a whispered conversation, H'nek instructed him to give money to Le Tu for the purchase of sauces. Jarai cuisine did not use Vietnamese sauces, and the girl was concerned that Spam's wife might not like the food.

Dinner was rice flavored with bitter melon slices and fried fish. Normally eaten with fingers and spoons, Le Tu had thought to buy several pairs of chopsticks for the guests. Ba Xuan complimented Le Tu on her *nuoc mam* sauce, and H'nek asked for the recipe. They finished the meal about an hour before curfew, when Spam excused himself with the explanation that they had to get back to town. Toller insisted they stay longer, and loaned them the keys to Mac's Jeep.

"Just make sure you lock it g-good," Mac warned them. "I don't want no sonuvab-bitch stealin' it."

"Right," laughed Toller. "Be a shame if the poor bugger you stole it from, stole it back."

Spam promised to guard the Jeep with his life, to which Toller retorted that Mac could always steal another. After they had gone, Le Tu murmured something to H'nek.

"What she say?" St. Cyr wanted to know."

"She say wife Trung-si very nice. High class Viet Nam woman. Know how talk and act around Highlander."

"She'd better," snorted St. Cyr in English, "or we'd throw her skinny ass out."

There was a ripple of assenting laughter which H'nek ignored.

"G'hlen, Viet Nam government is enemy, but not all Viet Nam people are enemy."

"True," Jimm was quick to add, "as not all Meerika are friends."

"Ya know," drawled Cohen in his best John Wayne imitation, "Sure would be nice if folks could talk a little English around here."

With the switch back into English, the Roundeyes moved out on the porch. Toller uncapped his long-hoarded bottle of Bundaberg rum, and passed it around.

St. Cyr saw them off at midnight. Exhausted, he staggered back to their compartment to blow up the two air mattresses he used for their bed. After carefully arranging the sleeping bags and poncho liners over the air mattresses, H'nek came in to douse the lamp. The brush of her nipples across his stomach drove the dull pain from his nose. He was soon erect and throbbing with energy. She passed soft kisses over his neck, chest, and navel before dipping lower, her kisses turning wet. He lay back in anticipation when, with a low throaty laugh, she suddenly rose up to pin him to the floor. He slipped his wrists out from under her hands, wrestled both arms up around her waist, and tried to roll her over, but with his nose like it was, she was strong enough to keep him pinned. So in the end, he let her slide down over him.

They untangled themselves to lie back on the deflated air mattresses and listen to the muffled laughter coming from Blek's quarters. Her fingers tweaked the hair on his chest.

"G'hlen, when will you leave?"

"Leave? You mean leave Dega Highlands?"

"Yes."

"Know not. Warrior-Band says I shall leave in Month eleven, but perhaps I stay."

"Month eleven?"

"Yes, when rains stop."

As if to emphasize the point, a light patter sounded on the roof. It grew into a deafening rush before tapering off as quickly as it had come.

"And if I am not here?"

"I know not. I go where Warrior-Band sends me. You know, we could marry..."

H'nek sat up to wrap her arms around a raised knee and stare off into the darkness.

"I could follow you?"

"Yes. Back even to my own country. I would be proud to take you to my clan."

She turned her face away from his. For several moments, she was silent, then: "Were I my aunts, we could do so. But I cannot. A Po Lan can never leave her lands. It is bad enough that I am here at Pleiku, so far from my own rays. But my ancestor has work here."

"Your ancestor?"

"My third spirit. Sometimes, when I sleep, my spirit shows me dreams. Strange dreams. Dreams of things happened long ago, and of things before they happen. This is why in my clan, all agree that I will be Po Lan. I was born a seer. And among we Jarai, seers are respected."

"What sort of things does this ancestor show you?"

"Last night he show me Ban Don. But people live there not Ede, they Lao. Come buy elephant from Ede. One Lao, he buys best elephants, paying much gold. Then, while Ede return to Tieu Atar, he has men kill them to take back gold. But my ancestor learns of this, and he hunts down and kills these Lao. For this, French are angry. My ancestor must flee. On his way, he buries Lao gold facing east gate of Cham temple."

"Cham temple?"

"Yes. The Cham built a temple at Ea Suop. You have never seen it?"

"No."

"I have, in dreams. When we were allies of Cham, they built temples and towers to worship Yang Prong, and to tell Khmer, Lao, and Thai people whose lands these were. You will see it when you journey to Tieu Atar."

"Tieu Atar? Am I going there?"

"You will. Sometime."

"H'nek? If you see things before they happen, why ask when I leave?"

In the darkness, she shook her head.

"G'hlen, some things I see, I see before happen. Not all things. Understand? I even know where Blek dies. There are two hills, one taller than other. Many Tiep-zap are on smaller hill. They fight hard. Blek has many warriors, but he is killed. Another leader takes his place, but this face is blurred. He leads our warriors up to slaughter the Tiep-zap. My own beloved is there, for I can feel his presence. But I do not see him. I know not if it is you. I know not if warriors are MIfors, or FULRO, or Viet Nam Warrior-Band. I know only that such will happen."

"Does this hill have name?"

"Of course. But unspoken, it is a dream. To speak such a dream is to give it flesh. I should not have told you even this. You see," a velvet melancholy slipped into her voice, "that which I speak becomes truth. And sometime, that which I do not speak also becomes truth. And sometime I dream dreams which are not spirit dreams, and they are most beautiful dreams of all. But they can never become truth. Like you. I have had beautiful dreams of you."

"Those I will make come true."

"No, G'hlen. Would that such be so, but they are only dreams."

In the coolness that had come with the evening rains, he pulled her down to cradle her in his arms and fluffed the poncho liners around them. Minutes later, he was asleep.

H'nek fought off sleep as long as she could, but it finally overcame her. She stirred several times in the night, as dark images flashed beneath her eyelids, but she did not see the twin hills. Instead, she saw Maine. Broad rays of sweet potato stretched out to tall forests where large barking deer roamed under strange trees which smelled of Dalat pine, while wondrous white crystal flakes sparkled down from the skies.

They were walking through a town much like Pleiku, where pale, thin people stared at her breasts. The air was cool and people wrapped themselves in great red and black checkered blankets, but she and G'hlen wore their tribal finery. In his best ceremonial loincloth, his buttocks and legs shone muscular and tanned. Everything was strange, yet familiar. They were laughing, enjoying themselves, but somewhere out beyond the crowd of gawking, friendly faces, was a familiar menace. At first she did not recognize him, but then he pulled in closer. In the field of red-and-black-checkered blanket shirts, he was the only one wearing tiger-striped fatigues. His was the only Jarai face, and his hands the only claw hands clutching a Sten gun. At first she thought he had come for her, but his eyes were locked on G'hlen. Her shudders and moans awoke him. He stirred.

"G'hlen," she whispered.

"Yes, my cub tigress."

"Beware of Siu Dot. He will hunt you."

"Maybe Siu Dot should beware of me."

"No, you beware. He will come when you feel safely among your own."

Trung-si Dung staggered angrily out the doors of the Cafe Saigon. Once reserved for Vietnamese, the damned long-noses were taking over. Worse, many were nguoi My Den. Ugly, frizzy-haired, smelly animals even more offensive than the pale long-noses. After a week of drinking, whoring, and gambling, Dung's funds were low. He had used some of the money to buy his wife a ticket to Saigon, where she insisted on visiting her sick sister. He had also made a down payment on a new Honda, but the rest had vanished in a streak of bad luck.

He had saved his last 20 dollars for a tumble with the beautiful Lan, but a damned My Den had come in. Lan, from Cam Lam district down on the coast, was young and new enough to her trade to do anything a man wanted for 20 dollars. Twenty dollars for 20 minutes to an hour that made your whole body shudder with pleasure.

Piqued at his bad run at cards, Dung's sole consolation was that after a half hour of tumbling Lan there would be seconds when he really wouldn't mind. But the muscular young My Den had offered his 20 dollars in military payment certificates. Vietnamese currency, protested Dung, was just as good. But when the slut translated this, the boy abruptly threw out another five dollars in MPC. Twenty-four hundred dong wouldn't even get Dung back into the game. Incensed, he stormed out. He needed more money, and it just so happened that he knew where to get it.

It was late when Dung got back to the compound. Carefully avoiding the LLDB headquarters, he slipped past the interpreter's shack to the indigenous barracks area. The lights were on in 212th Company's barracks. St. Cyr and Biloskirka had just left when Dung swaggered in to find Bloom, Blek, Rob Ya, and Rchom Jimm crowded about a small plywood table in a cadre room.

"Ah, Trung-si Dung," greeted Blek. "My brother says we will patrol Darlac, south of Tieu Atar and north of Ban Me Thuot…"

"I not go," snapped Dung, "wife's sister very ill. Need more money for operation!"

"No more money until next payday," said Blek, noting Dung's drunken belligerence. "Company fund spent on sacrifice."

"Then, you stupid Moi, get more. I need sixty-thousand dong."

The word *Moi* sparked angry glares. Bloom silently signaled for caution.

"This Highlander cannot grant such request," said Blek in his best Vietnamese. "I will discuss with my brother."

"Then do so. If I not have money, some certain Thieu-ta might learn of your prisoner."

"I'm going to kill that pile of shit," hissed Jimm, as Dung stormed away in a stream of curses.

"Yes, but wait for right moment," cautioned Bloom. "We have worked too hard to compromise ourselves. Everyone agreed? Communications exercise will occur eleventh day."

One by one, they nodded their assent.

"Good. Brothers," Bloom clapped a hand around B Rob Ya's shoulder. "The day approaches when not even the Meerika can stop us."

Chapter Twenty-Three

Northwest Darlac Province near the Chu Prong Massif:

THE C-7 CARIBOU ANGLED into a steep descent as it aimed for the leading edge of Tieu Atar's dirt runway.

"Way to go to war, eh Leftenant?" Laurie Toller called above the engine roar.

St. Cyr braced as the C-7 abruptly pulled out of its dive. He clung on to the rucksack cradled in his lap as Toller's ruck slammed into it. For a brief second, they were weightless. Anxiety flashed across the nearly 40 Yard faces strapped into seats or sitting on the floor. Older hands clutched the nearest aluminum seat tubing to keep from sliding about. The Caribou bounced once, then twice. The men felt themselves pulled forward as the aircraft reversed its engines and slowed to a bumpy crawl. Craning their necks to stare through the half opened rear ramp, they could see the distant mountain through billowing red dust.

"Chu Prong," called Toller. "Pity we didn't come by helicopter. I'd fancy a closer look at the Ia Drang, wouldn't you?"

"Sure," St. Cyr grinned. "But not on my stand-down time."

"Easy for you Yanks to say. You take all this for granted. I'll never have another chance to see war on this scale."

Laurie had spent the last of his stand-down time strap-hanging with a fighter pilot from Pleiku Air Base. Five days earlier he'd been in the back seat of a T-28 which took anti-aircraft fire over Laos. A photo of a grinning Laurie and the pilot, pointing to a golf ball-sized hole in the fuselage, now graced his hootch wall.

"If it'd been up to me," Laurie continued, "I'd have been a pilot with the R.A.A.F."

"So why didn't you join the Air Force?"

"Yeah, long story that. Hadda quit school at fourteen because me dad couldn't afford the fees. And with six younger brothers and sisters to feed, he apprenticed me out to a neighboring cattle station. After that..."

Toller's voice disappeared in the rev of engines, as the aircraft spun around and dropped its ramp. The cadre were immediately up and off to guide the troops away from the propellers and around to the assembly area. As rucksacks and equipment were being wrestled off, a second, then third Caribou touched down at the edge of the runway.

St. Cyr surveyed the gently rolling hills and distant forests. Tieu Atar, at the northern edge of the Rhade highlands, was a famed elephant hunting village. Massive log fences lined the approach to the village's capture pens. Ban Don, Vietnam's major elephant market, lay seventy kilometers south, where resident Laos trafficked newly tamed elephants into Laos, Cambodia, and Thailand. As the C-7s engines idled, a Jeep driven by a short, mustachioed captain pulled up. While he signed for his team's mail pouches, the team sergeant, a tall Czech named Tadeus, welcomed them to Tieu Atar.

"Damned glad to have company," he said with a grin. "Where's Big Boris?"

"Honchoing the next lift. They'll be in shortly," St. Cyr called above the engine noise.

"I'll wait. I haven't seen Boris since we were on 'Det A' in Berlin."

"Well, it'll be short reunion. As soon as Boris gets here, we're moving out. Captain Saville and his crew are the ones bunking with you."

"Yah," Tadeus shrugged uncomfortably as his captain spun the Jeep back and fish-tailed off in a cloud of dust. "There's been a change of plans. Your CP is going in to the old camp at Buon Ya Suop. We'll have a chopper in the morning to lift them in."

"When did that change?"

"Yesterday, when the captain got back from the States. He claims the last time you were here, we had trouble in the village."

"I don't know of any last time were here."

"Neither do I, but he's the captain."

The lift carrying Boris, Cohen, and Ryan touched down some ten minutes later. Boris and Tadeus had an enthusiastic if short reunion.

Tadeus had brought a photo of his own kids playing with Boris's daughter. Twenty minutes later, they were moving southeast. Late that afternoon they forded the Temot River and went into night positions on a small bluff over-looking a ford further upriver. Night passed without incident, and they were on the move before first light.

The flat forests and gently rolling plains were fairly easy terrain. In some places they could have covered thirty kilometers a day, but St. Cyr kept a cautious pace. After the third day, they began to find abandoned villages. Though well to the west of National Route 14, the freshly abandoned villages were an ill omen.

Built by the French to open the Highlands to logging, rubber, coffee and tea, Route 14 began in the red earth country of Tay Ninh, hooked northeast past Dong Xoai, Bunard, Song Be, and Duc Lap to reach Ban Me Thuot. From the Rhade capital, it shot north past the Ia Drang and up to Pleiku, on past Kontum, then skirted southern Laos to degenerate into a two rut track just beyond Ben Het. Past Kham Duc, Route 14 became a road again, turning east to join the coast below Danang.

Its southern quarter had been a major avenue of French reconquest in 1945 and 1946. Jacques Massu's tanks and half-tracks had thundered up to retake Ban Me Thuot, then driven east to the coast, where they hooked up with the 6th Colonial Infantry at the Dien Khanh citadel. Once Massu's armored columns had rumbled away, its plantation towns and tribal villages slipped back into obscurity. Compared to North Vietnam's hard fought campaigns, and the occasional unpleasantness of Central Vietnam's 'Street without Joy,' Route 14 was a backwater, unless you were travelling between Pleiku and Kontum on the wrong day. Ominously, the last major French disaster, the destruction of Mobile Group 100, took place around Route 19's Mang Yang pass, connecting Route 14 to Qui Nhon on the coast.

During the Second Indochina war, Route 14 came into its own. Its rosary of Special Forces camps strung along key points facing the Ho Chi Minh trail, had a habit of exploding from obscurity into the headlines. By 1968, the North Vietnamese army was looking to control the highway itself.

Saville's battalion was searching for two battalions of North Vietnamese infantry and the K-47 artillery regiment. This last reportedly equipped with mobile batteries of 120mm mortars and 85mm and 105mm artillery, and supplied with delayed fuses which could send rounds eight to ten feet into the earth. As Harry Perkins had explained, if true, the war was going to get uglier. Camps would have to be dug in deeper, resulting in more sophisticated defensive works, which would be harder to retake once lost. Under such a threat, camps would become strict military encampments, devoid of families. And as the Yards drifted off, Vietnamese garrisons would move in. The future MIKE Force might well be a nomad band of Yard survivors wandering in and out of Maginot Line-like pockets of alien Vietnamese.

Under the open forest and wide savannas of western Darlac, Harry's nightmare echoed from the cold hearths of deserted villages. Ominously, many had been recently abandoned. There was an odor of fear upon the land—a feeling that hostile spirits were about. Spirits cold, abandoned, and vengefully dangerous. It settled over the company rank and file.

Early one morning, just after St. Cyr had finished his orders group meeting with the Yard and Roundeye leaders, he stepped outside their perimeter and answer nature's call. A week of breaking trail had resulted in a single battalion kill. One of Ferris's people had got off a snap shot at a moving shadow. A local VC trail watcher was the battalion's sole success. Credit went to a cook turned infantryman who claimed he had smelled the VC. That had been good for a few laughs.

Given that they'd seen no real enemy sign, St. Cyr waved Ro'o Mnur away. There was no reason for more than one nose to suffer. He found a spot of soft earth and set to work on his cat-hole. Glancing up across a narrow streambed, he spotted a clump of shivering dwarf bamboo. At first he thought it a small animal, and warned himself that it could be one of the Yards. But the bamboo shook even more violently, and he spotted a flash of black. Almost automatically, his Car-15 swung up to the ready, tracked a blur of fleeing movement, and fired off a short burst which sent something crashing to the ground.

The forest went silent as Biloskirka, Blek, and Ro'o Mnur came running. Weapons at the ready, they fanned out to flank the dwarf bamboo.

"Buddy," chortled Boris, "that is one VC that won't be stealing any more honey."

212th Company's first confirmed kill of the operation was a medium sized honey bear. Ryan and Cohen immediately took to calling him 'Bearkiller' on the company net, and the call sign quickly spread.

Days later, he received a cryptic call from Toller requesting that Bearkiller come forward. Moving to the recon platoon's position, he was met by a grim faced Laurie and Rchom Jimm.

"Leftenant, we're being tracked."

"By the NVA?"

"Local VC's more likely, but it's the same thing. Jimm and I've suspected it for the past few days. Screwed up, I'm afraid. Put a claymore out for him last night. Moved the platoon out this morning like we were leaving and then doubled back. I'm afraid he's got the mine. Whoever it is, he bloody well knows the terrain."

"Montagnard VC?"

"Jimm thinks so. Some Rhade and Jarai went north back in fifty-four. The North Vietnamese gave most of them political training, but some were trained for just this type of work. When you add that to an already considerable amount of jungle lore, you end up with a pretty formidable opponent. Have you ever tangled with a Rhade VC?"

"Not that I know of."

"Well if you had, you'd know. We'll waste more time and effort bagging this bugger than we will searching for a whole bloody battalion. I'd wager a case of Fosters on it."

"Not a hard bet. No one's found any trace of these battalions yet."

"And we won't, either. Not with this bugger on our tail. At least, not until they want us to. By then, it'll be too bloody late. Five to one says him and a couple of others like him are keeping Charlie informed of our whereabouts."

"That would explain why we haven't found anything despite all that supposedly hot intel."

"Yeah," snorted Toller, "well I *might* have learned a thing or two in my time."

Ryan and Cohen had their doubts, but accepted Toller's judgment. After all, said Cohen, the claymore could have ended up in FULRO's inventory. Boris, on the other hand, had sensed an unseen presence for days. Toller kept his plan simple. The company would remain in place for longer than usual, while Recon ostensibly went on ahead to check the trail. One squad would then peel off to select and occupy an ambush position, which the company would move through. If they were successful, a carefully prepared ambush site would draw in their tracker.

Over the next few days, they tried this and other variations with zero results. Toller grew exasperated, Ryan and Cohen grew skeptical, but Boris and Blek remained convinced that the company was being tracked. That was enough for St. Cyr. Though he had yet to spot one of Toller's ambushes, their unseen tracker seemed to do so with unerring accuracy. On the fifth day, the game turned deadly. Under cover of darkness, Toller had sent ahead his four best men. Inside a stand of spiny bamboo near a stream crossing, they had painstakingly set their ambush. Both the platoon and company main body stumbled through without a single man detecting them.

Toller had dropped back to so inform St. Cyr when they heard a distant explosion. Rushing back to the crossing, Toller found two of his men dead and two seriously wounded. The blast of the mine amid razor sharp spiny bamboo had increased its lethality. While Ryan administered morphine and cautioned his Yards against giving water, Toller called for a medevac. Forty minutes later, when the medevac had lifted off for Ban Me Thuot, a third man had died from internal bleeding.

"Bloody bastard," cursed Toller. "Well he might be laughing his arse off now, but I'm going to kill this bugger if I have to do it myself." As he squatted to confer with Rchom Jimm, Boris pulled St. Cyr aside.

"Buddy, got trouble."

"The tracker?"

"No, Dung just took off with the medevac."

"Was he sick?"

"Sick of jungle, maybe. Sonuvabitch has been sniveling like a rat eating onions since we started."

"Well, that's one less pain in the ass."

"Or one more. He's been trying to shake down the Yards for more money to keep quiet about the girl."

Toller motioned for St. Cyr to join him. "We're going to try a counter-tracker."

"A counter-tracker?"

"Righto. This bastard's far too dangerous to leave mines out for, and he has an uncanny sense of picking up our best-laid ambushes. Heard of cases like this in Malaya, though I never saw one. There's some can spot an ambush by its feel, you know, by a smell, or a sound, or just the lay of the land. I'm not sure exactly what it is, but every once in a while you'd hear of it."

"And you think a counter-tracker will work."

"It might. The 10th Gurkhas had some success with them. The question is: Are our Yards as good as Gurkhas? I'd wager that some of them are, at tracking and ambushes at any rate. And right now, it's the only option we've got."

"Then do it."

"Not so fast, Leftenant, there's a little matter of extra pay."

"Extra pay?"

"That's right. The best tracker in the company is Ko'pa Kchel. Now Kchel may be our best, but he's not necessarily better'n this bugger. Tracking's like a muscle; you've got to keep it exercised or it gets rusty. So there's a certain amount of risk in this, if you catch my drift, above and beyond. What we propose is that he get an extra twenty-five dollars for taking on the job, and another twenty-five when he gets his man."

"Coming from the company fund?"

"Where it comes from is your business."

"All right, give it a shot. If the company fund can't pay for it, I will."

Recon took the lead again as the company moved out. Several hours into the march, as they dropped into the brush for a break, Ko'pa Kchel removed his boots and rucksack. Taking only his web harness, machete,

and rifle, he wandered off into the woods in search of a spot to relieve himself. When the company resumed their patrol, Ko'pa Kchel was gone.

They continued west southwest, moving towards Cambodia across a series
of small rolling plains divided by rivers. Though experience told him otherwise, St. Cyr half expected some sign of contact. Toller, for his part, was
unconcerned when Ko'pa Kchel failed to show by twilight.

"Isn't he coming in?"

"When the job's done. With luck, maybe tomorrow night."

"Tomorrow night?"

"Or the day after. These things take time."

They waited all night. Sometime after midnight, they were assaulted
by a troop of monkeys who pelted them with seedpods and excrement. To
St. Cyr's relief, the troops held their fire.

Early into the next morning's march, the company emerged from the
forest into a grassy valley peaked by yet another deserted village. After
searching the longhouses for signs of VC habitation or use, they crested a
low wooded ridgeline to descend into a forest of spiny bamboo so dense
that it took the rest of the day to chop their way through.

The next morning's thunder-shower gave way to mid-morning heat,
which gave way to an afternoon thundershower.

On the fourth night of Ko'pa Kchel's absence, they took up positions
in a driving rain which chilled the night with deathly cold. Huddled under
a poncho shelter, inside his hammock and another poncho which had been
rigged as a sleeping bag, wrapped in two poncho liners, and wearing his
jungle sweater, St. Cyr was miserably cold. Staring at fingers which glowed
chalky white in the darkness, his thoughts went out to a soaked barefoot
man, with no poncho or sleeping hootch, who hadn't eaten a full meal in
days. All for an extra fifty dollars, or five trips to a low priced whorehouse.

The following morning dawned under cotton wet clouds which
promptly lived up to their threat. As the lead platoon groped its way up a
slippery trail, there was a loud shout followed by calls of greeting.

Toller's voice crackled over the company net for St. Cyr to come forward. At the head of the column, a grinning Ko'pa Kchel clutched two
Montagnard heads.

"One hundred dollah," he beamed.

"My bloody arse," countered Toller. "The deal was fifty."

"Hokay. American dong, not Vietnamee."

Toller glanced at St. Cyr, who nodded.

"You want?" Ko'pa Kchel asked in Jarai, proffering the heads to St. Cyr.

"Not want."

Nonchalantly, Kchel flipped the heads into the brush as he chattered a staccato burst of Jarai at Rchom Jimm.

"What's he saying?" asked Toller.

"He says they were tracking us from the front," answered St. Cyr.

"No mean trick, that," marveled Toller.

"Yeah, but there were also some Vietnamese. They weren't there when he killed the trackers."

"Probably the runners, reporting on our location."

"That's my guess. Question is: who were they reporting back to, and how far away are they?"

"…and how big."

Saville and Mac were going over possible landing zones for inserting Ferris's company three valleys upcountry from St. Cyr, when Sergeant Magnuson handed them a terse message from Regter: 'St. Cyr report Pleiku immediately.'

Regter had returned from another IFFV meeting a few hours earlier to find a contingent of national police holed up in the Montagnard Hilton, surrounded by a screaming mob of Montagnard troops. Unsurprisingly, neither Ngoc nor his staff were in sight. As Regter approached, the mob quieted and opened a path for him. The door immediately opened, and several squads of White Mice emerged, two of whom were trundling a skinny screaming Vietnamese girl by the hair.

"What the hell's going on?" Regter demanded.

A police first lieutenant detached himself from the phalanx. "Thieu-ta. She VC. Hide in MIKE Force."

"VC! How the hell did she get in here?"

"Not know, Thieu-ta. Only know someone say she here."

"Who?"

"Not know. Superior officer say come get."

Minutes later, as civilian White Mice Jeeps sped from the compound, Regter caught a flash of movement down by the bunkers. Two Montagnard troopers were hastily loading a belt of ammo into an M60 machinegun. Before he could shout, the gunner snapped the weapon to his shoulder. As he took aim, the Jeeps barreled past a long line of Montagnard women and children trudging up the road. The gunner held his fire, then cursed as the Jeeps disappeared into the dip in the road. By the time they reappeared, Regter had arrived to disarm them.

The more Regter asked about the incident, the less anyone knew. Mister Long had some clues. Lieutenant St. Cyr had asked him for a job for a Vietnamese peasant girl who had recently married one of his Yards. On St. Cyr's word, Long had hired her. That she was well known to 212th company was obvious. Yet Long could not remember seeing her husband. He guessed that she lived in the village, because she came in every afternoon with the female Montagnard guards. Regter's attempts to find Ngoc proved fruitless. Ngoc was off somewhere with Khanh, and his staff denied any knowledge of the girl. With nothing more to go on, Regter ordered his adjutant to notify the C Team duty officer. Cox would get a complete report when he had more information. In Regter's experience, the first report was usually wrong, and the hardest to live down. Yet the incident set off alarm bells in his subconscious. When Ngoc showed up early the next morning to disclaim any knowledge, Regter sent for St. Cyr.

Miss Nguyen Le Tu squatted naked in the far corner of a cell that reeked of urine, excrement, and fear. Sleek cock-roaches darted from the single hole in the middle of the floor that served as her toilet. As two policemen opened the door, a third stepped in to splash a bucket of water across the floor. Instinctively, she covered herself with her hands.

"Miss come," ordered one of the police, tossing down a soiled set of clothes. "Senior corporal have more question."

They led her out past the cells, through a side door, to a low windowless cement building set at the rear of the compound. Despite its unimposing exterior, her steps faltered as they approached. With vise-like grips, the guards steered her inside to where two others waited. These were the rat-faced Trung-si they called Dung, and the Ha-si Nhut—or senior corporal—with a cherubic smile, her inquisitor. They noted with satisfaction that their canary started singing as soon as she passed through the door.

"I nurse assistant Nguyen Le Tu, Cat Lam hamlet..."

"Already know," said cherubic face. "Now ask more questions. Have seat, please."

The girl glanced fearfully around. A heavy wooden seat, and a long oblong table, both fitted with straps, were set away from the walls. Two metal folding chairs and a small table stood in the corner. She looked hopefully at a folding chair, but was gently motioned to the 'mynah perch'. She sat nervously on its edge.

"Little sister," cooed the corporal, "this throne of truth. Not one who ever sit here fail to say what I want hear. Except such persons as called before Queen of Heaven. Not one! Do as this Ha-si Nhut ask, and I stay. Not do what I ask, and this Ha-si Nhut must leave. Those," he indicated the guards, "then ask question. Not," he grimaced, "very pleasant."

The girl nodded.

"Little sister, one Trung-si tell me you go-fuck with long-nose Trung-oui."

"Not so."

"Also see you go-fuck with one Moi leader."

"Also not so." Although her tone was barely audible, the corporal detected a hint of iron creeping into her voice.

"Must be so, little sister. Some certain Trung-si say he see with own eyes. Naturally," he cooed, "girl from good Viet Nam family never do such certain thing because want do. Must be rape, not so?"

"I not go-fuck American. I not go-fuck Highland person. I not go-fuck any certain person, ever..."

As she spoke, the corporal placed the straps around her wrists and forearms. As the first strap tightened, her body shot up. Despite her diminutive size, fear had increased her strength. Long minutes of grappling, grunting, and stumbling ensued before they had her legs strapped to the chair.

"I want go home," she screamed, "I want see mother mine!"

Red faced and now scowling, the Ha-si Nhut leaned in to tighten the straps. The muscles in the girl's arms and legs jerked in spasms as she strained. Finally, she slumped back to sob bitter tears.

"Little sister," he hissed, "that certain Trung-si say you go-fuck American. You say you never go-fuck any certain person. Some person lies. Here...," he snapped a typed sheet bearing inked and embossed stamps at her face, "...this paper say certain American commit rape you. Sign, and I send to nice cell with bed and blanket. Not sign, and I must leave while some stupid girl's virginity is made test by very unpleasant means. Little sister never see Long-nose again. Why protect barbarian? He kill friends yours!"

"I not go-fuck American," she wailed. "Trung-oui American not go-fuck me."

The corporal could hear her muted screams as he trudged across the compound for his morning coffee. He liked it thick, sweetened with a large spoon of condensed milk. He also liked flirting with the teenaged widow who'd set up her coffee business in a ramshackle kiosk just outside the gate. A shame that this morning's coffee break would be so short, but he had to get back before those idiots abused his prisoner.

"Rape," thundered Cox, waving a sheaf of papers at Regter from the other side of his desk. "It's bad enough that a company of yours captures a goddam Viet Cong agent that they fail to turn in, but your goddam lieutenant can't wait to get back to a whorehouse."

"I doubt that, sir. And she's hardly an agent..."

"You do? Well Group headquarters has no doubts. In fact, they're convening an Article Thirty-two investigation the day after tomorrow, and that sonuvabitch had better be there..."

"Isn't that short notice? I just had him pulled from the field. He has a right to consult an attorney."

"Well he'd better goddam get down there and consult one, because the Deputy Group commander himself is chairing the investigation, and it's not your old buddy Green."

Out in the C Team hallway, St. Cyr paced back and forth as shouted demands and threats filtered through the door. From their tone and intensity, Regter's career was hanging by a thread. Two passing majors registered a frosty disdain as they glanced at his name tape. Only Lieutenant McKechnie, the C Team civic action officer, had a friendly word.

"Uh woudn'na worry too much, Galen," he burred in barely intelligible Glaswegian, "The old Man's allus callin' up the divil when Group gets on his arse. He gits uver it."

Regter stepped out a few minutes later, looking grim. "Lieutenant, report to the C Team commander."

If his session with Cox proved less painful than expected, it was because Regter had taken most of the colonel's venom. Cox's questions were cautiously phrased. He almost seemed anxious to hear some official version of the events which he could report back to Group. Still, the session left St. Cyr in a somber mood. He had done what he instinctively felt was right, as had Blek and the cadre, only to be betrayed. That Dung had fingered him was no surprise. Indeed, it had been expected. Charges of rape by the girl, however, came as a shock. They had been played for fools by a fifteen year old Viet Cong slut.

"Maybe it'd be better," he mumbled, as they walked out of the building, "if I just blew my brains out."

"Listen, asshole," Regter grabbed the back of his collar, "can the graveyard jokes. Blowing your brains out is Charlie's business. Meanwhile, ponder the fact that you failed to keep me informed. We'll take that up later. For now, get down to Nha Trang, get this shit settled, and catch a ride back to Ban Me Thuot. I want you back with your company as soon as possible."

As they approached the MIKE Force, a new motorcycle sped into the compound. Recognizing the two officers, Dung was careful to pull around to the rear of the LLDB building, out of sight.

"Well," muttered St. Cyr, "there's where some of the money went."

They stepped into the headquarters to find that the adjutant had laid on a flight to Nha Trang in the back of an O-1E, which even then was standing by. Following a rushed ride to the airfield, and a flight memorable only for the thunderstorms they dodged, St. Cyr found Captain Joe Meissner in his office above the Group public affairs section.

"Hey Joe, got time for an old Jump refresher buddy?"

"Galen!" Meissner pumped his arm with a warm handshake. "That was what, five months ago?"

"A lifetime, Buddy. A whole lifetime."

"C'mon, the MIKE Force can't be that bad. You were so gung ho."

"Oh, the MIKE Force is great. Never better. In fact, my company is out killing Cong as we speak."

"So what're you doing here?"

"Looking for a lawyer. We picked up a slight problem on our last operation. And I do mean picked up."

Meissner's tone waxed professional. "What're we talking, a court martial?"

"Probably. Right now it's an article 32."

"Who's the investigating officer?"

"Shumann…Shingle…something like that. The Group DCO."

"Shungle? Oh shit..."

Regter was going over his draft serious incident report when Lieutenant McKechnie stuck his head through the door.

"Hi, Eoin, what's up?"

"Surr, uh heerrd over at C Team thut yer huvin' problems gettin' inta thuh POW compound ta see thuh girrul."

"That's right. Anything you can do to help?"

"Wull, uh been werrkin' with a captain down therr. Yuh know, gettin'm materiels furr'is proejects. 'S a deecent sort furra Slope, if yuh know what uh mean."

"Do you think he'd help?"

"Harrrd ta say, but uh have been bendin' uver backwarrds ta help 'im, so it's werrth a try. Uh brrut muh Jeep heerre, and muh secretary, Co Thuy, has uhgrreed ta interrpret fore us."

As they climbed into McKechnie's Jeep, Co Thuy looked up from buffing her two-inch nails just long enough to acknowledge Regter's presence with an imperious nod. She was not going to cede the shotgun seat to any lesser human and ruin her hair. That brought a smile from Regter, who merely climbed into the back. Had McKechnie been driving an old Citroën sedan, Co Thuy would have taken the right rear seat and put Regter up front with the chauffeur. A dangerously polished and attractive woman, she happened to be the LLDB deputy's youngest sister.

Regter's seat in the back placed him downwind of her jasmine and vanilla scent, a pleasant enough aroma, but not enough to overcome his irritation at her cooed and cadenced orders that McKechnie drive slow enough to avoid mussing her hair.

Captain Bang was pleased to see McKechnie, and more than pleased to bow and scrape before the beautiful Miss Thuy. He had strict orders, however, that no one see this particular prisoner. McKechnie cajoled, pleaded, and finally argued, but it did no good. Co Thuy rasped her nails lightly across his forearm and cooed in her sexiest voice that she would always remember some certain favor, to which Captain Bang winced as if lashed with some velvet whip. But the result was the same. Orders were orders. As they turned to go, Regter's temper flared.

"All right," he demanded, "how much?"

Co Thuy chose not to translate the question, so he repeated it in a more belligerent tone. This time, she frostily translated. Captain Bang, despite his slick appearance, was taken aback.

"How much what?" he wanted to know. Perhaps the question had been mistranslated. Even a Long-nose would know that such matters were never discussed in open terms, much less in the presence of an LLDB major's sister.

"How much goddam money," Regter exploded. "You know, dong, dollars, MPC, gold? Bribe, you know, b-r-i-b-e. How much is it going to take to bribe you and your boss to see the girl? The hell with it, we'll pay. What's the matter? You afraid we'll see she's been tortured? Shit, we're long nosed barbarians. We see that all the time."

"It don' cost you nothing, Major," hissed Bang in his suddenly acquired English. "You see, Viet Nam people not fucking long-nose barbarians. We not torture. We not take bribe, unlike American who do not know how act in my own country. I take you see her myself. You see, she attack my guard last night. Must be placed in solitary. Understan', she is Viet

Cong. Maybe she lie 'bout your lieutenant. Maybe she say that just get him in trouble. But he American. American rape Vietnam girl alla time!"

Bowing a hasty apology to Co Thuy for the sexual explicitness of his language, Bang switched back to English. "You come me."

Calling for a sergeant and the keeper of the keys, he instructed the Americans to leave their weapons behind. Then, with mincing angry steps, he led them out through the compound to a row of low concrete boxes surrounded by a barbed wire enclosure. In rapid-fire Vietnamese, he asked the sergeant how the girl had been behaving. The sergeant didn't know. She had been in there since the day shift had come on.

Miss Thuy translated the remarks in a whisper. The clack of a tumbler, the creaking of the gate, and another key was inserted into a second lock. The captain braced unconsciously. You could never tell what these people might do. He had seen emaciated fanatics rush out to attack guards with bare hands or crude weapons that they had somehow managed to conceal or forge. Just as he had seen muscled giants meekly paddle out to their execution.

The door creaked open, and a sliver of sunlight darted over an unnaturally pale and prostrate form shivering in a small pool of dried menstrual blood. Co Thuy gasped. Regter cursed. And Captain Bang ground his teeth through the inside of his cheek. Seconds later, he was screaming for the camp medical orderly.

St. Cyr was standing in the Group headquarters hallway, staring into the buffed and polished floor, when Joe Meissner opened the conference room door.

"Lieutenant St. Cyr, report to the president of the Board."

The wiry, hawk-faced, crew-cut lieutenant colonel in crisp tropical worsteds glared as he strode in and saluted. He noted the shiny new ribbon of the Distinguished Service Cross as the colonel returned his salute. *I'd be far more impressed if you'd gotten that as a lieutenant,* sneered his inner self. A second inner voice cautioned against letting too large a chip ride on his shoulder.

A Vietnamese LLDB captain sat to the colonel's left, and a female specialist six to his right. *The LLDB observer,* he thought, *and a court recorder.*

Strangely enough, the colonel and SP6 shared the same last name. He did not know that they were father and daughter. The colonel explained that he was investigating charges made against him to determine if there was enough evidence to proceed to court martial.

St. Cyr nodded that he understood.

"Do you," the colonel asked with a hint of disdain, "elect to retain captain Meissner as counsel?"

"I do."

"All right. Would you explain in your own words what happened in Binh Dinh province during your last operation?"

It started smoothly enough, and he even felt that the colonel was on his side, until he got to their assault into the objective.

"Hold on, Lieutenant. Are you saying that your men killed wounded prisoners?"

Meissner leaned in to murmur a warning in his ear.

"Nossir, my men killed wounded enemy. During any assault, we never leave wounded enemy behind. It's the double-tap principle. Once the assault's over, we take prisoners if we can, to include wounded prisoners."

"And this girl was such a prisoner?"

"No, sir. She was grabbed by the stop parties trying to exit the camp."

"But it was during the assault?"

"Yessir."

"And she was armed or unarmed?"

"Unarmed, sir."

"So, you don't routinely murder unarmed prisoners?"

"Sir, we don't routinely murder anybody. My men are killers, not murderers."

"Do you, or don't you, routinely kill unarmed personnel?"

St. Cyr paused, while Meissner whispered further warnings.

"Colonel, if you're wearing a DSC, you should know what it's like. I'm not going to sit here and tell you that unarmed Vietnamese don't get killed. They do. But when they do, you can be damned sure they're Viet Cong. And you can be damned sure that it's in the heat of battle. Hell, taking prisoners has always been one of my missions. And it's certainly been one of my commander's top priorities. Before I took command, my company hadn't taken a single prisoner in over a year."

"Yet they took this one."

"Yessir."

"A female."

"A poor scared girl, yessir."

"Why?"

"Because she wasn't VC."

"And how did they come to that conclusion?"

"By the way she acted, in conjunction with years of experience and first-hand observation that you and I will never attain."

"Did it have anything to do with the fact she was a teenage girl?"

"Yessir," St. Cyr gave a bitter laugh. "Small, skinny, scared shitless. And one of the homeliest Vietnamese they'd ever seen."

"And based on that, you decided that she wasn't VC."

"Based on that, sir. They did."

"The whole company?"

"The FULRO cadre..."

"FULRO? Lieutenant, FULRO's an illegal organization. Are you telling me that an illegal organization is running your company?"

St. Cyr looked Shungel in the eye and shook his head. Meissner leaned over to whisper another warning.

"Sir, I'm under oath to tell the whole truth. I command half an A Team of five men and one Aussie. The indigenous soldiers in my company are commanded by Rahlen Blek, a FULRO officer, and K'sor Tlur, a FULRO *adjutant-chef*. That's the way it is with every company in the II Corps MIKE Force. And that's the way it is in every camp in II Corps. Since I'm under oath, I'd like to state that for the record that your MIKE Force here in Nha Trang is also run by FULRO cadres, as is the I Corps MIKE Force at Danang... "

"Specialist, strike that from the record. Lieutenant, you will only address issues that you personally know to be true. You will not venture any opinions unless asked to do so. Do you understand?"

"Yessir."

"Where were we?"

"Sir, I believe we were working our way to the part where the Slope..."

The LLDB captain's eyes shot up from doodling on his legal pad to lock St. Cyr's in a glare of unrelenting hatred.

"Do you mean the Vietnamese?"

"Nossir, I mean 'slope.' Sergeant Dung's not fit to be called Vietnamese. He's the one who tried to murder her after she'd surrendered. When she was alone and unarmed. He was nowhere to be found during the firefight, but he damned sure showed up when it was over. And he'd have shot her in cold blood if one of those supposedly non-FULRO Yards and I hadn't stepped in. Dung's the same Slope who took five-hundred dollars to keep his mouth shut. My other LLDB is Trung-si Pham. Spam's Vietnamese, and one of the finest soldiers I've served with. But Dung's a slope. I wouldn't walk across the street to piss on his corpse..."

"Lieutenant, you will refrain from using racial pejoratives."

"Sir, with all due respect, you told me to state the facts in my own words."

"All right," the colonel's jaw muscles tightened. "Go on!"

The next hour was spent reviewing his attitude towards the Vietnamese. Where had Dung's and Spam's names come from? Had he ever slept with any Vietnamese women? How had he felt about the Vietnamese when in the 4th Infantry Division? And when was the last time he'd had sex prior to the operation, and with who? As the investigation turned to sexual questions, which Meissner kept objecting to, St. Cyr asked for a short recess which the colonel seemed relieved to grant.

They were standing in the hallway, waiting to go back in, when the colonel was called to his office. Five minutes later, he instructed Meissner to stand by while he talked to the Group Commander. An hour passed before he returned to reconvene the board. This time, the LLDB captain did not return. No sooner had it opened, the Board was declared closed. All charges were being dropped at the request of the LLDB high command. As St. Cyr turned to go, the colonel fixed him with an earnest stare.

"Lieutenant, you were lucky. I hope you've learned your lesson."

"Colonel," it was St. Cyr turn to glare. "I've learned a very valuable lesson. Never trust anyone outside your immediate chain of command.

They're just out to cover their asses. All they care about is their next promotion and phony award."

The colonel started, as if stung. "Do you have anything personal you want to say to me, Lieutenant?"

"Nossir, he doesn't," Meissner cut in forcefully, as he pushed St. Cyr out the door.

Chapter Twenty-Four

Nha Trang, Vietnam:

FOR HIS ATTORNEY'S FEES, St. Cyr treated Joe Meissner to the *Fregate*, where they dined on spiny lobster washed down with a bottle of unoaked French Chablis. Afterwards, they hung around the bar with the locals. One was an ex-legionnaire who had served on the armored train. Neither had ever heard of *La Rafale*, so the locals explained its history. Built when Nha Trang had been home to the 2nd Foreign Legion Infantry, it had been vital in keeping south Central Vietnam's scattered coastal garrisons supplied. The camaraderie and armored train tales defused some of St. Cyr's anger. When he mentioned Boris, the former trainman was ecstatic. He had served with a similar giant on the Rafale, a Hungarian. And had known a few Ukrainians, good legionnaires all.

They stayed long past curfew, drinking the owner's best stock in a small courtyard away from the street. When it was time to go, the owner insisted on driving them out to the 5th Special Forces compound in his Citroen sedan to get past the MP checkpoints.

He awoke with a hangover's nervous hunger just in time to make it to the Logistical Support Complex ramp at the airfield. A gaggle of Nungs and Vietnamese were loading pigs, chickens, and a cow into a C-7 Caribou.

"Hey, Lieutenant!" hailed a grizzled warrant officer wearing an 11th Airborne Division combat patch. "You the one going to Tieu Atar?"

"That's right, Chief," he replied. "I'm manifested on the Twin Otter going to Ban Me Thuot."

"This bird'll get you into Tieu Atar long before the Otter gets to Dalat."

Beware gratuitous advice. It was late afternoon, after stops at An Lac, Gia Nghia, Buon Blech, and Duc Co, that the Caribou began its descent into Tieu Atar. Through a round window, he marveled at the enormous log enclosures. One now contained elephants. He found the Team medic piloting the Jeep, waiting to pick up his vaccines.

"There's a chopper coming in to pick you up, Lieutenant. Just wait here."

Some 20 minutes later, a Huey touched down. He clambered aboard and sat back to enjoy the ride. The pilot followed a smaller river south, then cut across to the larger Ea H'Leo. As they approached Buon Ya Suop, the crew chief signaled for him to look out the side.

There, on the bank of the river, stood the remains of an ancient square building. He nodded. Ten minutes later the chopper set down next to two others in a field guarded by regional forces from a nearby village.

"Did you see the temple?" the crew chief asked as he climbed out.

"Is that what it was?"

"Yeah, a Hindu temple. Some French planter said it dates back to seven hundred A.D."

As he stepped away, St. Cyr remembered H'nek's words.

Trudging up a trail to the abandoned Special Forces camp, he spied Mac's brooding form among several strikers perched atop a small mound near a 292 antenna. They were cooking something in a stone lined hole that had been with covered logs and wet leaves.

"B-bout time ya got here," Mac greeted, "and ain't it a coincidence yer just in time for chow."

"Thanks, Mac, but I'd like to get back to my company."

"Too late today, Trung-oui, you'd only compromise their position. We'll g-get ya in first thing in the morning."

He found Jed Saville below in a bunker.

"Hullo," Jed smiled. "Wasn't expecting you back so soon. Mac's been drawing up plans to spring you from the Long Binh jail. A three company combat drop. FULRO said they'd support it, but he's not sure the Air Force would go along. I'm half-kidding, of course."

"About this time yesterday, I was beginning to think I'd need it."

"Learned your lesson?"

"Yeah. Don't take prisoners."

"You're not bloody serious?"

"No. But after all we tried to do for the bitch..."

"The girl never made any such charges, Galen. Major Regter sent a copy of his report. I recommend you read it. She refused to sign the witness statement even after they deprived her of her virginity. The pity is, if she wasn't a VC when you picked her up, she sure as hell is now."

"So who made the charges? And why me?"

"I've no idea. Harry Perkins suspects it was a plot by Ngoc to get Major Regter relieved. You were just the handy target."

"It still doesn't make sense. They could have charged me with something related to not turning in a prisoner. Why rape?"

Saville shrugged. "Well for one thing, failing to deliver prisoners is a military charge. A strictly internal Fifth Group matter. Rape, on the other hand, gets the Vietnamese authorities involved. Did you ever stop to think that they're firmly convinced that you did have sexual relations with her?"

St. Cyr gave a dumb stare.

"Put yourself into a Vietnamese mindset," continued Saville. "Here you have a company not known for taking prisoners; composed of Moi savages, who aren't exactly renowned for love of their lowland brethren, commanded by an American, and we all know how horny and ill-mannered you Yanks are, suddenly decide that it's going to adopt a fifteen-year-old female Viet Cong that they just happened across in a firefight. Quick, in five words or less, tell me what service she's performing for the entire company."

For long moments, St. Cyr was silent. "Well, I damned sure I know who their witness was," he said weakly.

"Right," agreed Saville. "Don't expect to see Dung again. And I suspect Spam's in hot water with Ngoc. Which brings me to another point." His voice lowered as he looked around to see who was within earshot. "They're still piggy-backing off our communications. Blek knew about the girl as fast as we did. And shortly after that, we got word from Pleiku that your company sergeant major's wife was deathly ill, and that he should get back immediately. If the two are connected, I need to know."

"You don't think Tlur's wife is sick?"

"She very well could be. But we've had a rash of sick wives lately, and right after we lifted Tlur out, Mac started referring to Sergeant Dung in the past tense. Hardly a hopeful sign."

"Serve the sonuvabitch right!"

"I agree. But FULRO piggy-backing off our communications is a serious matter. What we do know is that they're not simply switching frequencies. Try to find out how they're doing it. Now let me bring you up to date..."

Saville gave him a quick rundown on battalion operations while they agreed to split the night-watch. Mac had been burning both ends of the candle, Jed noted, and needed a night off. While Magnuson relieved them at the radios, they walked out to try some of Mac's pit barbecue.

St. Cyr didn't realize that it was first light until Mac threw up the poncho covering their bunker entrance the next morning.

"Everything OK, Trung-oui?"

"So far. Commo checks were on time. Moshlatubbee may need a medevac. One of his Dega got bitten by what they think was a centipede."

Mac walked over to shine his flashlight on the map. The Choctaw's position was surrounded by green shaded contour lines cut by the thin blue line of a river.

"No p-place for an LZ. They'll have to c-cut it."

"Yeah, but the Choctaw says there's a bald spot up on the hill, so maybe they won't need to."

"Ain't no such thing as maybe," Mac grumbled. As if in reply, Moshlatubbee came up on the radio to confirm they needed a Dustoff. While Mac called Ban Me Thuot for a medical evacuation helicopter, St. Cyr switched the backup radio over to 211 Company's frequency. Warrant Officer Rayne's clipped Aussie voice was advising the Choctaw to wait up until the other platoons got across the river. Knuudsen was some 20 minutes away, having run into a thick stand of bamboo. He was going to have to backtrack to the river.

Rayne repeated his advice to delay the medevac. "Can't," growled the Choctaw, "the kid's going into shock."

Up on the battalion frequency, Moshlatubbee wanted to know about the medevac. "On its way," Mac replied. Roger, they were moving to the LZ now. Down on the company frequency, Moshlatubbee passed this to his platoon leaders. Silvers, his medic, advised him to wait. They would be across the Blue Line soon.

"Can't wait," replied Moshlatubbee.

"What're they d-doin' split on both sides of the river?" Mac's bloodshot eyes looked accusingly at St. Cyr.

"They ran into problems on the crossing last night. The river rose as it was getting dark. After they almost lost two Yards, Moshlatubbee ordered Rayne and Silvers to hold in place until morning. Said he lost a Roundeye about eight months ago."

"Pollack," Mac affirmed, "drowned up near Dak Seang. Still, you don't ever split your p-platoons to where they can't support each other. You shoulda..."

The crash of automatic weapons over the radio mingled with the hiss and pop of static.

"Six...this is One-six...contact...contact...over." An edge of concern had crept into the Choctaw's voice. The firing was close.

St. Cyr grabbed the microphone. "This is Two-six. Correction, Three X-ray. Roger, standing by. Over."

Mac had grabbed the mike from the radio set to B-23's frequency and demanded the medevac now, along with some gunships.

"Ah, Bearkiller," wheezed Moshaltubbee. "Thought that was you. Contact with estimated VC squad—maybe trail watchers—scared the shit outa me when they blew their claymores. Russian I think. Sited 'em badly...but opened up with everything they had. Break...ah, I've got a squad movin' up after 'em...ah..."

Mac's eyes locked into St. Cyr's.

"Sunavabitch's hit." Mac gritted his teeth.

Moshlatubbee's voice ignored them. "Snoopy suits one-six-three, what's your position, over?"

"Just across the blue line," answered Rayne.

"Ah, roger. Six-three, sending up a cluster. Can you identify? Over."

"Negative. Estimate four hundred meters from where we heard the firing, over.'

"Roger. Three-six-mike...where are you?"

"At the blue line," Silvers responded.

"Roger. Need you ASAP. Ah, Bearkiller," Moshatubbee's voice wheezed unnaturally. "Appears bad guys have broken contact. No known enemy casualties. One Yard KIA...one badly wounded...still need medevac. One Roundeye WIA…right lung..."

The medevac ship came up on the battalion net. Mac passed the co-ordinates and advised that they had an American with a sucking chest wound. The medevac advised that they were about 15 minutes out.

Silvers' voice instructed the Choctaw to stay on his feet as long as possible. He'd have the chest tubes ready. Rayne was closing in. A burst of fire to Rayne's flank signaled where Knuudsen's people had run into the ambushers.

Moshlatubbee's face was ashen and bloated when Rayne arrived on the scene. Y Diet Kpor and two Yard troopers were propping him on his feet. His radio operator lay dead beside him. Moshlatubbee clutched a radio handset while his left hand clamped a field dressing to his heaving chest.

"It's sucking in," he murmured hoarsely, "but it ain't blowin' out."

Rayne ordered his Rhade platoon to clear the trail ahead and establish the landing zone. He'd be along shortly.

"Feel like a goddam balloon," gritted Moshlatubbee. "I shoulda waited, like you said. Cost me...two good men."

Rayne looked away. "You didn't know."

A half smile showed through Moshlatubbee's pain. "For once in my life, I wish I was five feet tall…instead of six."

"Does tend to make you stand out, Leftenant," mumbled Rayne as he prepared a morphine syrette.

"No drugs, Ray. Not 'till...Silvers gets here."

St. Cyr's voice came up on the battalion net to request a status report. The medevac was on station. Rayne reached for the microphone, but Moshlatubbee cut him off.

"Ray. Let me run this. Snoopy suits Three x-ray, this is Three-six…ah… We hear the bird—break—should have our people up there in one zero. Over."

While St. Cyr confirmed with the medevac, Moshlatubbee went back to the company net to check on Silvers' progress and verify that Knuudsen had no friendly casualties.

By the time Big Knute reached the perimeter, Moshlatubbee could no longer stand. When they tried to lift the hastily assembled poncho-stretcher, he ordered them to put him down. Silvers would be along any minute, said the Choctaw, and could he talk to Rayne and Y Diet alone?

After giving both a warm Montagnard handshake, he looked Rayne earnestly in the eye. "Ray…I need you to…do me a favor. That's why I asked Knute to…stay back."

"Right, Mate. Anything."

"Get me a…grenade."

"What for," Rayne winced.

"Ray, I thought I…was going to make it, but I'm not. Let me do it …my way."

"Can't do that, Mate. You'll make it."

"Like hell…then shoot me…"

Rayne blinked and looked away. "I can't do that either."

Moshlatubbee's arm reached up to grip Rayne's harness. "Ray…my people don't…let our enemies…kill us."

"I understand, Mate, but back in Aussie we don't kill our mates, even if they want us to."

Moshlatubbee pulled the dressing from his chest.

"Wasn't you that… killed me, Ray," he rattled. "Take care of Y Diet. Tell Knute…Silvers goodbye. Take care of the company…"

Rayne fought back the urge to grab the dressing and clamp it back down on the wound. Though he knew this was what his friend wanted, it would haunt him for years to come. The wheezing and sucking stopped. Moshlatubbee appeared to melt onto the earth. Rayne, famed throughout the army for his salty language, repeated a simple Lord's Prayer as he reached up to close the Choctaw's eyes. They rolled back open. As Rayne tried again, he felt Y Diet's hand.

"He eyes should be leave open," murmured Y Diet, "so can see *Ai Die.*" Rayne wasn't sure who *Ai Die* was, but he understood. Minutes later, as Silvers rushed in, tubes, decongestants, and IV at the ready, Moshlatubbee's face and neck had returned to normal. Back in the battalion command bunker, St. Cyr pushed his way past Saville and Mac. Out on the berm, he choked back tears of rage and sorrow.

It was late afternoon before Regter finished his report on Moshlatubbee's death. He ordered Saville to terminate the operation and return to Pleiku. With 12 companies rotating through what had been a six-company compound, Regter was turning into the one thing in the army he despised: a manager. With luck, he would soon ship the 4th Battalion to Kontum, leaving him three battalions and a reconnaissance company to command while the 5th Battalion began training. Ngoc stopped in to express his regrets, and inform Regter that the Vietnamese government was awarding Moshlatubbee the Cross of Gallantry and Special Service Medal. He would appreciate Regter passing them along to his family. Though the Americans often joked about Vietnamese awards, Regter was pleasantly surprised. Ngoc also mentioned that four Montagnards had been selected to attend the Vietnamese officer candidate school at Tu Duc. The names were another surprise; all had known FULRO connections. If this was visionary, Regter was tempted to offer Ngoc some of Pappy Green's Armagnac, but his cynical side prevailed. If the LLDB were sending FULRO members to officer candidate school, they had something up their sleeves besides the usual poisoned darts and daggers. Still, it put him in the mood to stop and bid Ngoc a good evening on his way out the door. He stepped out just in time to see sergeant Dung roar by on his new motorcycle.

With the approach of night, traffic grew light on the Pleiku road. Passing rains had cleared the dust from the air, and the open sky darkened to a blue translucence. As Sirius pierced the horizon, shadows lengthened to blur the images of brush and *tranh* grass. Distance became suspended in a crystal clarity that made the far appear near, and the near appear closer. At the edge of the MIKE Force perimeter, whose low buildings faded deeper into the red earth with the coming of night, two troopers shook out a mattress with studious precision. As they did so, Dung's motorcycle raced by on the road below. It became a speeding blur that grew smaller as it raced downhill. It disappeared for a few minutes as the road dipped down, then rose to join the national highway. The driver shifted in his seat, glanced back over his shoulder, pulled his bike up onto the main roadway, and throttled it into a burst of speed. Dinner, some cold *ba-moui-ba* beer, and a chance to relax and give his wife good news were only minutes away. As Dung zipped down the highway, Sirius hung momentarily overhead, reflected through the shifting ionosphere, across the round, polished, invisible melted sand surface which propelled the star's light back through a tubular void to the cornea, lens, and retina of K'sor Tlur. Tlur took a deep breath, ordered his body to relax, took up the slack in his trigger, and squeezed. Muscle, nerves, wood, bone, and metal melded together to concentrate on a sphere some 7.65 millimeters in diameter; the only one of its kind in the entire universe. A foot kicked Tlur's boot just as the rifle cracked. While the motorcycle sped away, an enraged K'sor Tlur spun to find the muzzle of his Moisin-Nagant sniper rifle pointed at Rahlen Blir.

"Idiot! You ruin my shot!"

"Orders," said Blir, hunching down. "Me Sao say too dangerous now. We wait."

"I kill now."

"Me Sao says not yet. That is order."

An hour later they were playing billiards at China Market, where K'sor Tlur had good-naturedly lost to several Vietnamese Rangers. They chided him about the semicircular cut under his eye. Dirty old man. Obviously, he'd been staring through a telescope at some girl's treasure when she'd abruptly closed her legs.

Of course, laughed K'sor Tlur, and would they like another *ba-moui-ba*? They would. He ordered the beers, and stepped back to calculate where best to drop his grenade. If he couldn't get Dung, he'd kill other Tiep-zap dogs. No one would be the wiser. As he reached into his canvas mapcase, B Rob Ya walked in. The American Montagnard had been killed, Rob told him. A loss, agreed K'sor Tlur. A true loss. He'd been one of the good ones. Tlur's fingers caressed the grenade, then moved on to a wad of bills.

"Mow those Vee Cee down, boys, mow those Vee Cee down, the only song we ever sing is mow those Vee Cee down. Vee Cee in the bushes, Vee Cee in the grassss..."

Ryan swaggered stiff-legged into the B-23 club. He wasn't drunk, just angry. He motioned for Cohen and Silvers, busy teaching the lyrics of "Mow Those VC Down" to a captive Thai band, to shut up and sit down. The mob at the tables weren't in a singing mood anyway. He edged into a seat next to Toller and Rayne, across from St. Cyr, Blek, and Biloskirka. Knuudsen glowered in their direction from the far end of a long table.

"These assholes," Ryan mumbled under the staccato beat of drums. "They still have Moshlatubbee's body at the morgue."

St. Cyr turned his head. "What's that, Kev?"

"Moshlatubbee, Trung-oui. His body's still down at the morgue. The sergeant major sent me down to identify him."

"Is that where you've been?"

"Yeah, but it ain't right! They shoulda had him outa here yesterday."

"Righto," agreed Rayne. "But it does allow us to pay last respects."

"A-fuckin'-men," said the Superjew.

Ryan nodded a humorless grin, and stood to glare across the dance floor at Ferris.

"Hey, Ferris!"

Ferris's face froze. His eyes narrowed to red slits. "You lookin' for an ass-whoopin', Sergeant?"

"That's Staff Sergeant as of this month, Cap'n."

"Yeah? Well you ain't going to live to sew 'em on, Fuck-head."

"Maybe not. I thought Moshlatubbee was a friend of yours."

"You're goddam right he was, *Specialist*."

"Well, *Captain* Ferris, *sir*, they still have his body down at the morgue. Whad'ya say we give him a wake?"

Fifteen minutes later, Staff Sergeant Tyson, the junior B-23 team medic, heard a loud banging on his door.

"What'dya want?" he called.

"We need the keys to your ambulance," growled Knuudsen. Tyson recognized Big Knute's voice. It was not one to be ignored. He cracked open his door to a wall of grim faces.

"Who got hurt?"

"Lieutenant Moshlatubbee got killed. We're gonna give him a wake."

Minutes later, B-23's front line ambulance rolled out the gate.

"You can't take it," insisted a skinny spectacled specialist four, in charge of the Ban Me Thuot morgue by virtue of being the only man on duty. "I'll get in trouble."

"It ain't an it," growled Boris. "He's a him. And if we don't get him, you'll be in worse trouble with me."

"Come on, Buddy," pleaded Ryan. "We'll have him back in a couple of hours."

"Look, you've got to get out of here or I'll call the MPs."

"With what?" said Boris, stepping over to the telephone.

The door opened, and Knuudsen, Rayne, Silvers, and Ferris filed in.

"Took a wrong turn," growled Big Knute. "Now where's the Choctaw?"

The specialist looked up into Big Knute's eyes. "Uh, follow me, gentlemen."

By the time they got back to the B-23 club, the Tuesday night crowd had thinned out. Boris and Cohen manhandled the stretcher from the rear of the FLA while Knuudsen scouted ahead. Spying an uncluttered length of bar-top, Big Knute asked its patrons to move over. Two did so. The third took offense.

"Who the hell do you think you are?" protested a young lieutenant in fresh jungle fatigues.

"The MIKE Force," growled Big Knute, "maybe you've heard of us." Knute's hand swept the lieutenant's drink off onto the floor.

"Hey, asshole!" The lieutenant jumped up, all five foot eight inches quivering with indignation as he glowered at Big Knute. The more seasoned patrons stared off into the distance. A lanky Vietnamese girl giggled, and settled her bottom more firmly into her date's lap.

"Looks like our new club officer," someone said softly, "is about to drop his ass into a sling."

St. Cyr stepped through the door just in time to spot the problem. "Hey Knute! I'll handle this. Why don't you give Boris a hand?"

Knuudsen hesitated.

"Knute," Ferris called. "This is officer business."

As Big Knute stepped away, St. Cyr turned to search the lieutenant's chest for a nametape. "Hey, Maloof." St. Cyr held out his hand. "What're you drinking?"

"Nothing you're buying." Maloof ignored the extended hand. "Who's the asshole?"

"Big Knute? Someone not known for being friendly. I'd watch my mouth."

"Like hell! This is my club. Get him outta here. Sonuvabitch smells, and so do you. Haven't you assholes heard of showers?"

"Lieutenant," Ferris leaned over into Maloof's face. "Notice the pretty little captain's bars I'm not wearing? If you don't like the smell now, I suggest you leave."

Big Knute pushed a table and chairs away to make room for Boris, Silvers, Tyson, and the stretcher.

"It's my club, Captain. I'm responsible. Hey, what's wrong with him?"
"He's dead."

Maloof's eyes widened. "He's what?"

As they hefted the stretcher up onto the bar, Knute unzipped the body bag a quarter of the way down and tenderly folded back the sides covering Moshlatubbee's head and shoulders. The Vietnamese girl shot up from her boyfriend's lap while noses and lips curled.

"Jesus Christ, you're not kidding. What the fuck's he doing here?"
"Being waked," snapped Ryan. "It's an old Irish custom."
"Well, this isn't goddam Ireland."

"Yeah, and it's not Africa, South Carolina, or Oklahoma either. But he's being waked here. Or we're going to kick your ass so bad, you'll be up there with him."

Maloof's eyes narrowed, his nose quivered, his lungs filled with righteous indignation, and an overpowering odor he'd never smelled. His next words disappeared in a gagging rush to the door. He made it out just as supper's Swiss steak, mashed potatoes, peas, and gravy came up. When he looked back inside, the club was nearly deserted, the Thai band was desperately seeking to escape, and only the poker players seemed unconcerned.

"Goddammit, Lieutenant," growled his six-foot-two-inch Intelligence Sergeant, "can't you do anything to stop that shit?"

"Yeah," gasped Maloof, "I suppose I could find some master sergeant and order him in there to pull rank on those two gorillas."

"Who, Big Boris and Big Knute? It ain't gonna be me, El Tee. It ain't gonna be me."

"My point exactly. Where are all those green beret heroes when you need them?"

"The real ones are at that wake, El Tee. I'll be in my room if you're in the mood for a bourbon and coke."

RAT-ATAT-TAT, RAT-ATAT-TAT, *Mow those bastards down, UUNGH! Oh what fun, it is to have...* Drunken voices floated through the compound as Lieutenant Colonel Ramon 'Black Arrow' Williams' Jeep rolled through the gate. He glanced over at his sergeant major. "I hear the MIKE Force back in town. I thought I told Maloof that I wanted the club quieted down on weekdays."

"Don't blame the lieutenant, sir. Probably turned out too much for him to handle. I'll settle 'em down."

"No, Sergeant Major. I'll handle this."

Cohen was just switching into "My Mother's a Montagnard Sergeant" when a tall, lanky Black edged through the swinging doors. The dim lights barely picked up the silver leaf on his beret, or gold and white embroidered insignia on his tailor made, skin-tight, black HALO suit. But there was no mistaking the stamp of command on his demeanor. His eyes immediately darted to Big Knute.

"Knuudsen, what the hell are you doing in here? I barred you from this club months ago."

Big Knute rose uncomfortably from his chair. "Sir, I came for the wake."

"The wake?" Williams' carefully cadenced footsteps carried him over to the bar. His nostrils flared and the whites of his eyes flashed momentarily wider as he peered inside the body bag. Disgust and sympathy twitched under his facial muscles.

"This would be Lieutenant Moshlatubbee. So, who's the senior man?"

St. Cyr sat back to watch the confrontation, and suddenly realized that he'd last seen Ferris locked in some earnest conversation with the female Thai singer. Clearing his throat, he rose to his feet. "I guess I am, sir."

"What do you mean, you guess?"

"What I mean, sir," St. Cyr glanced around the club for Ferris, "is that I'm it."

"And you're…?"

"Lieutenant St. Cyr."

"So, you're responsible for this...wake." The words were carefully metered, but there was no doubting their razored edge.

"Uh, yessir."

"That's what I wanted to hear. Outside, Lieutenant!"

Out in the cool darkness, Williams paused under the entrance awning to sniff at the night air. "What do you suppose that smell is, Lieutenant?"

St. Cyr dutifully took a whiff. God, this man had a nasty way with the word 'lieutenant.'

"Sir, it smells like someone puked."

"Smells...like...someone...puked?"

"Yessir." He could feel Williams' eyes burning into him from the darkness.

"And why would anyone puke? I mean, it's just a body up on my bar. The stench of death all over my club. Why in the hell would anybody puke?" Williams' fingers tugged at St. Cyr's pocket flap. "MIKE Force, hunh?"

"Yessir."

"And you guys are baaad, right?"

"Charlie seems to think so."

"But not so bad that one of you can't get greased."

"Colonel, getting greased is part of what we do. And Moshlatubbee was one of our best."

"I know that, Lieutenant. Now look," Williams' stare softened, "I know what the MIKE Force is, and I know what you do. You don't have to prove anything here. I also know how it feels to lose a friend, because I've lost enough of my own. But that's not Lieutenant Moshlatubbee in there. Not anymore. That's a hundred and seventy pounds of bone and rotting meat. Legally, it's a moveable good. And it belongs to his family. You've got no goddammed right to go dragging it around like it was some kind of personal amulet, understand? No matter how good a friend he was. So get the hell in there, drink up one last drink in his honor. Then get that body back to the mortuary. Do I make myself clear?"

"Yessir."

"Good. You've got ten minutes to be out of my compound!"

St. Cyr threw a snappy salute and stumbled back inside. As Williams walked across the quadrangle, he met his sergeant major.

"Any trouble, Colonel?"

"None at all, Sergeant Major. Just the MIKE Force conducting a wake."

"A wake, sir?"

"Yes. Haven't you heard of a wake?"

"Yessir. But don't they need a body for that?"

"As a matter of fact, they provided their own. The lieutenant that got killed two mornings ago. I expect we'll be getting a call from the morgue. They've got ten minutes to clear this compound."

"Well, Sir. In that case I should be there."

"You sure you want to be? I'd be quite happy to check on it myself."

"Nossir. As senior enlisted man, I should be there for the last drink. Besides, Big Knute and I go back a ways."

"Then they're all yours, Sergeant Major. I want them gone in ten minutes."

"Yessir." As the sergeant major walked off, the Black Arrow's voice trailed after him.

"Sergeant Major, make that within ten minutes from whenever you decide to call it."

Chapter Twenty-Five

Pleiku, Vietnam:

"WE HAVE A VISITOR," noted H'pak as H'nek stepped into the longhouse. "He awaits your return."

Within the dim interior, H'nek made out the form of Glan Perr. "We are honored, Kinsman. But Blir not return before sundown."

"Not come see Blir," beamed Glan Perr, "but his niece. I need speak with Me Sao."

"H'pak, procure our guest wine. I shall sit with him."

H'nek settled in on a mat across from Glan Perr. "So Kinsman, speak."

"Will you not take me see Me Sao?"

"I cannot. Me Sao not present. But I will convey your words to him."

"Do you not find such strange? Me Sao's presence is forever in MIfors, yet Me Sao never here. I find such strange."

H'nek shrugged her shoulders in her best imitation of a guileless young girl. "Kinsman, it is not this woman's place to ask. It is by such means that Me Sao's identity is kept hidden. Look at your own Romah Dat. He who would have killed Me Sao, discovered his identity only too late."

"That is past," Glan Perr nodded sadly. "As are many other events. Last month-eleven at Bu Prang conference, certain MIfors commanders swaggered in to state that they took orders only from Me Sao. There were six MIfors companies then, with six leaders. Today there are ten in Pleiku and three in Kontum. Soon, three companies my own battalion ready. Would you not think Me Sao ready to reveal herself to another her commanders?"

"Her? Me Sao is no woman."

"Yet Rahlen H'nek is very much so. To credit of her female ancestors, who can only take pride in such beauty."

"It is their gift," she acknowledged, "but such gifts exact their price."

"Like talent, beauty is never without pain."

"My ancestors' experience has been that beauty blinds to talent. Which is why Po Lans must forever walk obliquely. What true Jarai warrior would see fit to accept battle orders from a woman who teases his loins?"

"Battle order! Where have you heard such words?"

"Me Sao said them."

"Do you know meaning?"

"Of course."

"And you would yet tell me that you are not Me Sao?"

"How can such be? I am merely the woman you see."

"Yet, there is one way."

"How?"

"I think you know. When I was with French, I parachuted into Plei Djereng. This was when Viet Minh had extended their empire into our country. French controlled the road as far as An Khe, but where not present with troops, Viet Minh roamed at will. We had been sent to stop that, my captain and I. Myself, chosen because my mother was Jarai. Our captain's idea was that we Jarai were a warrior people who would constitute a web of maquis. Do you understand?"

"This *maquis*. Was it like field of grass-spider webs? Each spider cast his own web. As Tiep-zap came within edges of web, they were caught and killed. But those who skirted around, escaped. Except that in the end, Tiep-zap returned like warrior-band ants, tearing away the grass that supported the webs."

"Exactly," Glan Perr nodded. "Me Sao explained this to you?"

"Yes..."

"In dreams?"

"Why you say in dreams?"

"Because when Captain Thebault and I were at Plei Djereng, there was this certain Po Lan who died. She had a grandchild girl of perhaps five years. And on that night this Po Lan died, girl-child had strange dreams in which she sat up while asleep and talked of things that had happened long before she was born, and of things to happen. Such were neither a child's words, nor a child's dreams. Nor were they those of any Po Lan. Your sorcerers feared some male ancestor. I tried to have them tell to me this child's name, but they would not. She had not yet reached that age for her true name. But they did let me hold this girl-child. Do you remember?"

"No. I have been told of that night, but I remember not. Those dreams are gone."

"You said in a great country of sandy forests with no trees, I would descend from the sky on spider's silk to hunt with tiger-men. And as I hunted with these tiger-men, it would be revealed who my true people were. And that though Jarai, my chief would be a famous Ede warrior who controlled my destiny. Under him, I would return to my true people to lead a warrior band."

"Perhaps some other girl-child told you this..."

"Perhaps," Glan Perr lapsed unconsciously into French, "but this I know, little sister. Me, I left the Dega highlands thinking that I was returning to *la belle France*, a land mine by birthright. The land of my father's family, which I had seen only when I had gone to France for military school. But my father's family shunned me. As my own mother had died, he had taken another wife. This wife was French, and he had two children by her, who his Po Lan, my Grandmama, considered her own. Perhaps I was too dark for Breton tastes, but there was still the army. I was sent to Algeria to serve with a company of Indochinese, mostly Rhade and Jarai, that Captain Simon had smuggled out.

"Algeria was foreign to us. A dry country as you had said. And as this war raged, they needed commandos, so our captain volunteered us. We became parachute Commando Thirty-Five, but we called ourselves 'Dam San' after the Rhade legend. One night, we parachuted into east Algeria, near a land called Tunisia. And as we were running through this land of sand, bare rock, and scrub trees not much higher than my head, my souls awakened. Our unit symbol was a tiger's head. We wore battledress striped like Sir Tiger's. And I realized that 'motherland' in French is much like 'Po Lan's domain' in our own tongue. And I knew that you had truly dreamed this.

"That day, I ceased to be French. I took the name of my mother's clan, and the one she had called me, and left their army to come home. Except the Viets would not permit my return. So I entered through Cambodia, and joined K'pa Doh, who sent me to Romah Dat. And then, I heard that a certain Me Sao had appeared in the MIKE Force. I wanted to return then, but Romah Dat would not permit it. Yet the fortunes of war placed me here. And so, I began to look about. And I have looked about long enough to know that you speak for Me Sao even when Me Sao not here."

"Why you not so inform Romah Dat?"

"Romah Dat was my brother in arms. But I was a parachutist officer in the French army when he was stealing cattle. Much we shared together, and with my military training, much there was that I could do through him. But in truth, much I had learned that I had to unlearn. At times, he would refuse my advice out of simple jealousy. He was no more prepared to accept advice from a *Metis* than he was from a mere woman."

"As you are prepared to do now?"

"Little sister, if what I suspect is true, I shall gladly die for you."

"And this truth is?"

"That you fall into deep sleeps and hear voices which are not your own. And among those voices is that of Me Sao. Which is why no one suspects you. You are a woman." Glan Perr paused to lean in close to H'nek, his eyes staring intently into her own. "Tell me, what was the name of Me Sao's daughter?"

"Fawn Eyes."

"Yes," Glan Perr nodded with satisfaction. "It is not Me Sao who lives within you. It is his daughter. But he commands you through her. I would ask that you give proof positive that Me Sao truly commands H'nek's soul and therefore your body. That he does not just steal into your dreams."

"And this proof would be...?"

Glan Perr switched back into Jarai. "It is well known that you have betrothed yourself to this Meerika, Saint Cyr." as he said the name, Glan Perr's lips curled in distaste.

"Such betrothal is my affair."

"The loins of Rahlen H'nek are indeed her own, until she carries child, when it becomes her clan's affair. But Me Sao has no loins, and he belongs to all clans. It is Me Sao who must be consulted."

"You do not approve of my betrothed?"

"It is not for me to approve. Consult Me Sao! But consider this: Me Sao's descendant must soon stand before MIfors and call them to war. On that day, if Me Sao is speaking through a woman, that woman must be above all men..."

"I have yet to see a warrior who was above all women."

"Little sister. I tell you how it must be, not what you wish hear. You yourself have wondered how woman can give battle-order to true Jarai warriors. I know not. But I do know that if you are to give battle-order, then no man whatever his race can have you. For if one man has you, then others who do not will resent such. Worse yet, he who has your body, will not respect your commands. Lose respect of one man, and you lose respect of all. Resentful warriors do not easily follow commands of men. Much less some supposed Po Lan who has yet to undergo pain of giving this world her first descendent. In this, you are fortunate to have chosen a Meerika. When gone, he will be forgotten. Consult Me Sao, and give me his answer. Then, and only then, my loyalty is yours."

"Provided Me Sao's advice is as your own."

"Not so," Glan Perr rose to go. "Only that it be truly Me Sao's voice I hear."

"Kinsman, one question."

"Ask."

"You dislike my betrothed. Why?"

Glan Perr's eyes turned hard. "Him," he replied in French. "He takes such pride in stating that he is American him, not French. Yet look at his name, and how he speaks this language that he calls our own. I have buried too many French brothers in these jungles and paddies to allow such insults to pass. Yet, for my mission, I must."

"Then it is an affair purely personal."

Glan Perr's eyes softened. "It is an affair of honor, little sister. You speak the Front's language well. Please understand. After these our Dega Highlands, I love France and her races more than anything else in the world. The spirits of those who were my brothers will always be with me. As you hear voices in your head, I see their faces in every night's dreams. And every morning, with the rising of the sun, I salute their spirits. Consult Me Sao. Do as Me Sao commands, and I will be your brother, your closest uncle, and your slave."

That night's dreams came as vividly as H'nek had feared. Once again she was alone on the path to a village which stood on a great, lonely knoll. Dark foggy forests loomed in the distance. Broken and decayed tombs littered her pathway. Cautiously, she wound her way past the spirit gate to a circle of run down longhouses. Child-like voices called out. Voices that whimpered, cried, whispered invitations, or mirthlessly chuckled and laughed. Inner councils warned her to ignore them. One could walk the spirit world, but to mix haphazardly with its inhabitants was to invite danger. A great longhouse dominated the village center. She entered this looming, dark structure to pad softly across a dark purple floor. Black-green and gray-shadowed walls wavered at the edge of her vision. A single great piling thrust up through this floor. Nearby, two empty stools were set behind a great jar of *mnam pay*. Making the spirit sign, H'nek approached the stools and prostrated herself before them.

Glan Perr, said a female voice, has been too long among these French. As his skin is Jarai, his heart remains theirs. He sees in Fawn Eyes that woman-warrior whom French revere as a goddess. Such accords with their own spirit beliefs, and their cult of virginity, but not with our own that the more natural state is marriage. Man and woman must be united in order to constitute the whole.

Of course, thundered the male voice, yet Glan Perr speaks true. Woman's way is to push and pull from behind, never to stand out front. Our traditions reserve such for men, who must then bear the shame of error. Which is why living men distrust women. For a living woman to direct men, she must be unique. And what could be more unique among our people than a beauty whose loins belong to no one...

No. She should take a Jarai husband. A warrior. This Rchom Jimm...

Agree! But not at present. I myself thought that she should take an Ede, but I was wrong. To take a warrior in these times is to tie herself to that warrior's fate. Better her task be done alone...

Alone, yes, but not unmarried. She cannot be respected...

With Glan Perr beside her, she will be respected and obeyed. He is a kinsman, but not so close as to be seen a Rahlen clan tool. And, she has our blood and our counsel.

H'nek awoke in the gray rainy dawn with a throbbing head and snatches of ancestral arguments rolling through her subconscious. They had debated, argued, reasoned, and bickered, until their thundering words had propelled her from their longhouse into the present. She sat up, shivered violently in her blanket, and wiped away her tears. There was one point upon which there had been no disagreement: The words that Glan Perr was waiting to hear.

Late that afternoon, as she made her way to the compound, she spotted Glan Perr with two American sergeants as they watched one of his companies run an obstacle course. The Americans did not disguise their stares as she approached. She avoided their eyes, and motioned for Glan Perr to join her.

"*Swas'm' lai,*" he greeted.

"*Swas'm lai.* I have dreamed, kinsman."

"And?"

"And when I return from Plei Djereng, I shall send away my lover and not take another."

Glan Perr drew himself to attention. "My battalion is yours to command, Po Lan."

Moshlatubbee's wake was a hangover when the next sun thundered up over the Darlac plateau. As Saville assembled the companies, he checked the Roundeyes to ensure that they were shaved and cleaned up. He was in no mood for confrontations with ranking officers. At the airfield, their C-123s arrived just after 0800. By the time Love's Jeep barreled up to the airfield control building, the MIKE Force had lifted out.

Back in Pleiku, the troops were quickly off and moving up the road, anxious to begin the cleanup and turn-in that would see them in their villages by nightfall. As they marched through the gate, H'nek was on hand to receive them.

In lieu of her tiger suit, she was dressed in a familiar black silk skirt, a reddish purple sateen blouse, and a black turban wrapped tightly around her head. Her greeting was reserved; no obvious delight, no public display of intimacy. She merely nodded in St. Cyr and Blek's direction. The sheen of the skirt across her hips and thighs made St. Cyr nervously anxious to begin stand-down.

Up in the quadrangle bordered by Conex containers, Blek turned the company over to K'sor Tlur. He and his brother, Blek grunted, would return later that afternoon to see how cleanup was progressing. St. Cyr charged Biloskirka with checking on pay and the sacrifice. Then, after a public handshake with Trung-si Xuan that was as much for the company's benefit as Major Ngoc's, they ambled over to H'nek.

"We must leave for Plei Djereng tonight," she informed Blek. "It is time to abandon our mother's tomb."

"So," Blek's voice was hopeful, "There is a new Po Lan?"

"A new Po Lan shall attend the ceremony," she agreed. "G'hlen, I must speak with you. Will you walk with me?"

Out past the gate, he reached for her hand. She let it drop away. He tried again. She accepted with hesitation. Despite the exciting aroma and heat of her body, the iron of some inner self noted the rebuff.

As Regter and Ngoc watched the couple go, Ngoc was reminded of epic poems recounting lovers' vows and warrior's deeds. His Nguyen ancestors had not been blind to the beauty of Highland women, and had even taken concubines from among the tribes. Indeed, one of his own female ancestors had been Jarai. Regter's thoughts were more pragmatic. With Harry Perkins getting so close to ferreting out Me Sao, he didn't need another American getting too involved with the tribes.

Out in the field past the helipad, H'nek looked up into St. Cyr's eyes. He ached to draw her body in to his, but too many eyes were watching.

"G'hlen," she murmured, "I missed you."

"As I have missed you. God..."

"G'hlen, I must ask something of you, and tell you something as well. Will you come Plei Djereng?"

"It will be an honor."

"Even if, when we return, we must stop to be lovers?"

"What?" In the silence that rushed in, he heard the sounds of grasshoppers and crickets above the singing in his ears.

"When we return, we must cease our betrothal..."

Ignoring the eyes of several nearby busybody crones, he pulled her in to sniff gently at her nose and lips. "So says which person?"

"So say my ancestors."

"And this?" He held up the bracelet on his right wrist.

"G'hlen, my heart is yours..."

"Yet," his tone accused, "we can no longer be betrothed. Then this—we—mean nothing."

"Not so, G'hlen. There are certain things I must do. I told you from day you accepted my bracelet that I am to be Po Lan. Just as I know that you must someday leave these Dega Highlands."

"Someday, but not now! I want marriage. I wish to take you with me."

"Cannot..."

"Why cannot?"

"You are not...Jarai."

"But I am accepted as Dega."

"Yes, but we Jarai are a jealous race."

"You knew such when you sent your bracelet!"

"G'hlen, do not curse me! Come to Plei Djereng. Abandon my mother's tomb with me. Let her souls see yours."

"Why?"

"Because it is important to me. And because, I pray that her spirits can change my ancestors' will. If not, it will be our last time together."

"If not?"

"Yes..."

"Tell you what, Honey," he shot back in English as he stalked angrily away. "I'll goddammed think about it."

She neither called after him, nor attempted to follow. Po Lans of great clans did not chase after lovers. But then, every other Po Lan in Jarai history had been married.

When Mac and the Rahlen clan left Pleiku that evening, St. Cyr was not among them.

"I have no time," H'nek snapped, "for fools and slighted lovers."

Nor did she have much time for abandoning a tomb, whose logistics and protocol were largely left to her younger aunts. H'nek and her older aunts were busy convening an event that was the first of its kind since Trung Trac had summoned the Khmu and Muong, among other northern tribes, to oppose the Chinese two millennia earlier.

It became known as the meeting of the matriarchs. The Romah, Rchom, Rahlen, Ko'pa, K'sor, Ro'o, and Siu clans spoke for the Jarai, while the Blo, Nie, Mlo, Nguu, Eban, K'pa and H'dok represented the Ede. There were also respected and withered crones from the Koho, Sedang, Bahnar, Rengao, Jeh, Katu, and Chru peoples, though these were patriarchal tribes. Together, they sat under a great roof prepared specifically for the occasion, and dropped clan and tribal differences to discuss the war and their future.

Their message was the same. The Viets had taken control of the Highlands. Villages were being destroyed with the rising of each sun. Sons, brothers, and husbands were going off to the camp strike forces, the MI-fors, the Iron Brigade, from where many would come home in coffins, or maimed and unable to work the family rays, requiring more of a wife's attention. Those who stayed were being taken off by the Viet Cong, who also took the women, since there were not enough men to defend the villages. Clan riches were being squandered in multiple sacrifices to the dead which were as much an honor, as a bribe to keep the spirits friendly.

Perhaps it was time to leave the Highlands to the warring Tiep-zap; the government in the cities, which had now become Vietnamese, and the Viet Cong in the forests. FULRO promised much, but where was their great liberation? Or they could move into Cambodia, whose eastern mountains were no more Cambodian than the High Plateau was Vietnamese. Maybe in Mondolkiri and Ratanakiri, they could survive the darker days that were surely coming. The Meerika meant well, but how long had they been here? And how long would they stay?

Within sight of a U.S. Special Forces camp, Rahlen H'nek pleaded, cajoled, threatened, wept, and whispered. Who was this girl, the matriarchs wondered. The great-grand-daughter of Me Sao. Now there was a name to be reckoned with. Another Me Sao was needed, not the posturing fools hiding above Bu Prang who styled themselves a Montagnard liberation movement. To be fair, such men were trying, but when elephants war, even Sir Tiger steps aside. Me Sao's great-grand-daughter. But she was Jarai?

Yes, but Ede Ad'ham blood flowed in her veins, as did that of the Rahlen clan. By Ai Die, there was a time when that name was feared among the Viets.

On the third day, after many buffalo and pigs had been sacrificed, Rahlen H'nek asked them to assist in abandoning a tomb. An up-away from Pleiku had arrived carrying a Meerika officer who boldly walked beside H'nek's brother. Her lover, it was whispered. Pah, that was her affair. Certainly he was handsome, but what of her own blood? A clan cannot live without descendants.

Her clan, she told them, would be the Dega nations. And as proof of her word, she would even send away this handsome Meerika, though it tore her heart out to do so. Such was her love for her Dega people. Glan Perr would have applauded. Many a matriarch wiped away tears.

A cold, windy rain was blowing when they returned from Plei Djereng. Mac helped St. Cyr carry his belongings, which H'nek had packed into carry baskets as per tradition. Against tradition, they spent a final night together, shaking the longhouse floor with their passion. But when morning dawned cold and rainy, she stepped out onto the porch, crying for all the village to hear.

"My betrothal to this Meerika is broken. He has agreed to pay sacrifice demanded."

The sacrificial fine was stiff. One steer, two pigs, numerous chickens, and 50 jars of *mnam pay*. But the hardest sacrifice was yet to come.

When the Jeep drove up to take him away, its driver was Rchom Jimm. They drove back to the compound in silence, where Jimm pulled up in front of the Teamhouse. "My Lieutenant," said Jimm, "I would be honored to have worn her bracelet."

St. Cyr said nothing. The feeling that Jimm might wear it yet grated on his heart. He spent the day writing long overdue letters home, but by early evening he could no longer stand his room.

Limiting himself to a minimum amount of drinking money, he wandered into Big Marty's. To his surprise, there was a new bartender, whose svelte, sexy beauty contrasted pleasantly to Hoa's squat presence. Easing himself onto a stool, he eyed long sensuous legs that ran down from a short miniskirt that fell even with the bottom of her panties. Large almond eyes, accentuated by high cheekbones and waist length ebony hair, eyed him suspiciously. Her skin shone like brushed gold.

"Either Hoa's had one hell of a cosmetic surgery job, or I've died and gone to heaven," he smiled.

"This here's Tiger, Trung-oui," grinned Silvers, "and I'd watch my mouth. She's got an even nastier disposition than my favorite bull dyke."

"Speaking of which, where is Hoa?"

"She and Big Boris went down to Nha Trang to the beach. Should be back tomorrow."

"The beach?"

"Yeah, ain't love grand? And that ain't all. Big Boris is takin' her down to Cholon next month."

"Cholon?"

"S'truth," added Rayne. "She's going to help him find some kid of his down there."

Silvers shook his head disgustedly. "Don't know what going on around here, Trung-oui, but we figured it's your fault."

"Mine?"

"Yeah. You started all this goody-goody romance shit with Blek's sister."

"Ancient history, my friends. What're you drinking?"

He spent the next hour trading war stories about Moshlatubbee, and eyeing Tiger's skirt, which lifted just enough to expose some very tantalizing thighs whenever she leaned or turned. But by some perverse design, it never managed to rise any higher. When Silvers and Rayne took to needling him with pointed questions on H'nek's sexual performance, St. Cyr bowed out.

"Well," winked Rayne as St. Cyr departed, "What d'ya think, Mate?"

"Like I said," sneered Silvers, edging a hand across the bar-top towards Tiger's half exposed breast, "Ain't love grand!"

Tiger proved even quicker than Hoa, but Silvers' hand cleared the bar-top before the knife drove home.

"Miss Tiger," he grinned, "I love you too many."

"Humph," she grunted, pulling the knife out of the wood. "Next time I doan miss. Who that Trung-oui?"

"Saint Cyr? You don't want nothin' to do with him, sweetheart. He sleeps with Yard women."

Yahd? You mean Moi?"

"We call 'em Yards around here."

"Hmm. He too cute for Moi woman."

"My thoughts exactly, sweetheart." Silvers shot Rayne a sly wink. "Now you take me, for example..."

Chapter Twenty-Six

BIG MARTY'S BAR AND GRILL thundered back to life with the company's return. Cohen and Ryan recounted grotesque versions of wild nights in Nha Trang. Boris passed around comically formal tourist photos of himself and Hoa at the Cham Tower and Buddha. Laurie Toller confessed to an enjoyable few days with an American nurse from the 8th Field Hospital. Her name had his fellow Aussies choking on their pints.

Laurie's allegedly shy companion turned out to be a rippled amazon of epicurean sexual hungers and a taste for anything Australian. Under cross-examination, he confessed to dubbing her 'Brumby,' not from any equine features, but the condition she left their bed in.

The illusion of good times was welcome. But each night, before he rejoined the team to hear standdown's lies retold in the raucous warmth of Big Marty's, St. Cyr would wander out to the back bunker, smoke his Montagnard pipe, and stare at a distant village. Wild sexual fantasies of what he could do with Tiger, if given half the chance, failed to fill the void. And it was becoming apparent that he might get more than half a chance. From time to time, in the middle of someone's joke or story, he would glance up at the bar to find Tiger observing him with a wary but appraising eye.

"Psst," Hoa whispered one evening. "Tiger like you. She say you han'some. You don' say her I tol' you so."

Instead of thanking her for this bit of intelligence, he theatrically clanged his bracelets on the table in a gesture that said, "I already have a wife," and went back to drinking.

"Hunh," Hoa sneered. "wha' wrong wi' him?"

"Highland malaria," shrugged Boris.

Their time on reaction-force duty, standing by to be delivered anywhere in II Corps by helicopter or parachute, was plagued by drizzle and rain. Despite an ambitious training schedule, his days dragged. Too soon, they were back in northern Darlac province where he now regretted a standdown and retraining period that had ended too soon.

In a firefight south of Tran Phuc, camp strike forces killed several NVA from the 66th regiment. One had a notebook, a diary really, where penned between poetic lines evoking a fatherland of sacrifice and valor, were pointed references to greater sacrifices to come. IFFV wanted more information. While battalions from the 4th Division made a major patrolling effort west of Highway 14, the MIKE Force operated close to the border, beyond the range of friendly artillery. Between the two ran the 4th Division's LRRP, or Long Range Reconnaissance Patrol company—commonly called 'Lurps.'

"They're turnin' us into a battalion of g -goddam legs," was Mac's constant comment. He had been otherwise pleased ever since St. Cyr had vacated H'nek's longhouse.

On the third morning of the operation, Staff Sergeant Knapp of Ferris's company stepped out to pull in his claymore mines. An old mobile guerrilla hand, Knapp used mines as his insurance policy, covering all approaches into his position. They not only they increased his defensive firepower, but their simultaneous detonation provided cover under which his platoon could withdraw in heavy contact. Lately, Knapp had been mixing command detonated mines with booby trapped mines. Now, with Ferris demanding that he move out, Knapp was having trouble finding his last mine. Ahead, on the trail, one of his Yards suddenly appeared, hurrying to catch up after a quick morning dump.

"Freeze," Knapp called.

The young Yard flashed a grin of recognition and quickened his pace.

"Stop!" Knapp repeated in Rhade. His agonized tone slowed the kid down. "Can't find the damned claymore," Knapp mumbled. The word claymore froze the young Yard in place. Knapp studied the bush to his front, and took a cautious step. He blinked his eyes. He'd been having trouble focusing lately, and an annoying ring sounded constantly in his ears. He felt a slight pressure touch his pant leg. *Aha.* He bent carefully down, his fingers searching for the metallic tautness of wire. They felt dew wet leaves, twigs, a small vine, and then ever so lightly, the wire. His frown relaxed as he eased the wire out from under a small shrub. *Strange*, he thought, *I don't remember putting it out this far.*

The explosion pitched Knapp sideways. For long seconds he lay stunned, hearing and feeling nothing while his lungs fought for air. Then, catching his breath, he twisted, pushed himself up, and tried to stand. Something was wrong. As hard as he tried, he wasn't rising.

Y Blo Eban, his fellow platoon leader, was first on the scene. The horror on the young Yard's face was all Knapp needed to see. For a split second, he remembered his pistol. He reached down to find it at his side. All he had to do was to draw it, pull the hammer back from half-cock, and squeeze the trigger. His mother, his wife, his son, would never have to see him like this. But another Knapp was taking charge. A Knapp who had the guts to face the very worst life had to offer, provided he moved fast enough.

"Get my bag," he called, "and get men here to hold me up."

While Y Eban radioed a report to Ferris, who had started moving when he heard the explosion, Knapp tied tourniquets around the bloody stumps that had been his legs. Wiping his blood stained fingers on his shirt, he untangled a bag of blood expander from its container and set about lining up the needle with a vein. He congratulated himself for a rapid and patterned response, while an instructor's voice deep in his memory warned that the real shock was yet to come. He felt a rising nausea and uncontrolled dizziness. He was slipping away. "Save my legs," he called. "I want them."

Kilometers away, St. Cyr squatted by the handset with an anguished Ryan.

"Damn," Ryan grated his teeth, "medics get all the bad luck. Me, Knapp, and Silvers all took medical training together."

"Officers don't do much better," offered St. Cyr. "Medics and officers are our highest casualties. I wonder why?"

"It's not hard to figure out, El Tee. When the shit hits the fan and everybody ducks for cover, what's the first thing you hear when anyone gets hit?"

"Medic!"

"Amen! All Charlie's got to do is sit back, listen, and watch for movement."

"What about the officers?"

For a brief moment, Ryan's black humor flashed through. "That's easy. Officers are supposed to be in charge, but they're usually the last ones to know anything. So whenever the shit hits the fan and somebody screams 'Medic,' guess who's the next guy to stick his head up for a look around? That radio antenna close by doesn't help much either."

"So, medics get greased doing their job, and officers get greased being stupid?"

"Hey Trung-oui, don't take it personal."

"Yeah, well we're going to beat those odds."

"Sure," the thousand-yard stare crept back into Ryan's eyes, "so was Knapp. And he's one of the most carefully coordinated medics and field soldiers I know. Cool like you wouldn't believe. Maxed out all the tests and practical exercises on operating room procedures back in Training Group, and in Dog Lab we had no doubt his was going to survive, no matter what they did to it."

Ryan kept to himself for the rest of the day. Though Dustoff 90 got Knapp to the 71st Evac Hospital in time, his maiming cast a pall over the operation that matched the feeling they got each time they passed another village. Though these were occupied, they were met with barely concealed hostility.

H'nek and Blir were finishing their evening meal when Glan Perr arrived. Blir stayed long enough to share the wine jar, then excused himself. He was unhappy with Glan Perr's recurring visits. Powerful visitors, he told H'nek, could only draw the wrong attention. She replied that while security was his responsibility, the direction of their movement was hers alone. Since being named Po Lan, she had become decidedly autocratic. Respected po lans, Blir reflected aloud whenever he had the chance, ruled from the background.

"What brings you to our hearth, Kinsman?"

"I thought, perhaps, I could offer certain counsel."

"Your counsel is always welcome."

"Then I shall speak frankly. You have given thought to our revolt?"

"Certainly."

"So we can expect soon battle-orders?"

"At appointed hour. Not sooner."

"Such efforts require preparation."

"Forgive me, Kinsman, but we have been preparing this for two years already. You came to question judgment of our United Front?"

"Never! But may I speak without reservation?"

"As commander, such is your right."

"Then," Glan Perr unconsciously looked around, "I must tell you I fear this revolt will fail. It will expose the fangs and claws of our movement for the Tiep-zap to tear out."

"Our decision was not lightly taken."

"No, and in Month-nine Nineteen Sixty-Four, such a revolt would have succeeded. Viet Nam army had only one paratroop brigade, few helicopters and many enemies. Meerika had not brought forces into Viet Nam, Tiep-zap Rangers were still small..."

"We had not our present strength, and certain Meerika betrayed us," cut in H'nek

"Me Sao said this?"

"No. My father said such, as does Mac."

"Then, little sister, hear voice of one who has seen Tiep-zap army from very beginning. One who has fought with as well as against them. This revolt will fail for reasons which owe nothing to any betrayal by Meerika. We can seize some towns, and attack pitiful Tiep-zap soldiers of highland garrisons, but our real reckoning will come when red berets move against us. The red berets are warriors who will gladly die to kill us..."

"You speak as if you fear them.

"I respect them, little sister. More importantly, they are now an entire division, far better equipped than ourselves."

"So, you would tell Y B'ham and K'pa Doh that MIfors will not obey their orders?"

"Never! We must execute their orders as received. But there must be a back-up strategy."

"I would hear it."

Glan Perr nodded, relieved that his intentions had not been misinterpreted, and amazed that this girl understood him.

"If the Tiep-zap and Meerika move against us in force, we should move into Cambodia. Not as refugees, but as a military force. Their highlands are poorly garrisoned; their *Chasseurs Cambodgiens* fit only for bartering favors of young ladies. Their paratroop demi-brigade counts just two battalions. Even in French war, it saw little combat. Except for ruby diggings at Stung Treng, which we should leave to them, their roads are poor and their army moves best by river. Of importance, recognition of our government's presence there might be in interests of both Viet Nam and H'Meerika."

"You have given this much thought."

"Of course. Such lands are as much ours as is Pleiku. It would give us a country to hold before the world. Within Viet Nam borders, I would accept autonomy from Tiep-zap..."

"You would accept Mondolkiri and Ratanakiri for Ban Me Thuot, Pleiku, and Cheo Reo?"

"Only until the many could be made one."

"And this would be when?"

"When the elephants have ceased their war, and the jungle once again safe for tigers."

"You can write me this plan?"

"In French or Jarai?"

"In the language of our United Front."

"But of course," he replied.

"Then do so, and give to B Rob Ya who will forward such to Ney Bloom for comment before we courier it to President Y B'ham."

"Ney Bloom?" Glan Perr's eyebrows knit together.

"Ney Bloom, Kinsman, is senior MIfors military commander, as B Rob Ya is chief of staff. Me Sao has forwarded your name to central committee at Bu Prang for confirmation as lieutenant colonel. But until approval, Ney Bloom is yet your senior. These are Me Sao and Y B'ham's instructions."

Glan Perr rose to draw himself to attention. In the darkened interior of the house, he saluted Rahlen H'nek. As he turned to go, she stopped him.

"See B Rob Ya, Kinsman. He will provide you details of our preparations."

As Glan Perr departed, H'nek turned to find Blir staring at her from the shadows.

"Yes, uncle?"

Blir said nothing. But he too drew himself to attention, and saluted.

Late into 212th Company's third week, they had still not found any enemy, though there were signs. The villages they passed were sullen and fearful. Villagers cited persons who had gone out, only to be killed. They believed that Americans were responsible, but when pressed for details, fell silent.

St. Cyr reported his findings to battalion, but similar incidents were not noted by the other companies. Whatever malaise was on the land appeared confined to their area. Since they were the furthest east, Mac checked with the 4th Division, who denied having any forces nearby.

Late one afternoon, the company crested a knoll to find the spirit gate of yet another village closed. St. Cyr and Blek dutifully waited outside. When no village elder appeared, he sent Rchom Jimm's men around the back. They returned with an angry village chief who minced no words about their presence.

"Why kill my people?"

"We have killed no one," St. Cyr replied.

"Lies!" choked the old man. "Two suns ago you kill three people from this village. Peaceful people who had mean you no harm!"

"Two suns ago we not here."

"More lies, Y Ang Enoul see with very eyes! Meerika!" he spat. "Kill my son-in-law! Kill his brother and nephew! Meerika with pow-fusil who wear tiger cloth like you! Men who had gone for collect honey from bees. Carry no pow-fusil, no pow-karbin, not even crossbow."

While St. Cyr forwarded the report to battalion, Blek and Jimm prevailed upon the village chief to show them the site. Reluctantly, he agreed. As they passed behind the village, a matriarch rushed out screaming curses.

At first, she was merely pathetic. But as they moved past her, she pulled a small utility knife and slashed at St. Cyr.

Loaded down with his rucksack, St. Cyr was barely able to dodge the blade. It glanced off the sheathed survival knife taped to the top of his harness, and cut a slight gash in his shoulder. When Ro'o Mnur grabbed the old woman's wrist, it took all his strength to pry the knife from her bony fingers. By then, it was getting late. Blek wanted the company bedded down before nightfall and asked permission to billet the company in the village. The village chief refused. As a sign of good faith, they agreed to bed down elsewhere, but they wanted the village chief to point out where his men had been killed.

By 1030 the next morning, the old man had led them to a small stream bounded by tranh grass and broad-leafed trees. A blackened swatch blotted the grass.

"Claymore," said Cohen, whose platoon was in the lead.

"So," sighed St. Cyr. "Everyone's got them."

"Maybe, El Tee," Cohen stooped for a brass casing. "But not everybody uses these."

St. Cyr glanced at the 'L.C.' stamped on the cartridge base.

"Lake City arsenal," continued the Superjew, "five-five-six."

"So? There's also a lot of U.S. weapons in the wrong hands here."

"If it was anything but 5.56mm, I'd agree with you Trung-oui. But Clyde would have taken the trouble to police up his brass. And he wouldn't have wasted so much ammo on three honey-gatherers."

"You're saying this was U.S.?"

"I don't know for sure who it was, Trung-oui. But I damned sure know who it wasn't."

"What you think, my brother?" St. Cyr asked Blek.

"Maybe bandit. Maybe Tiep-zap deserter. Probably Meerika soldier."

"Meerika soldier," St. Cyr insisted, "would not do so unless these Dega were armed."

"Armed?" snarled the village chief. "Too dangerous carry weapon here!"

"Maybe Russians," shrugged St. Cyr.

While Ryan disinfected the slight gash on St. Cyr's upper arm, he passed his report to Saville, who alerted McElroy for a trip to the 4th Division.

As Mac's Huey touched down on a landing pad outside the bunkers of the 4th Division's Tactical Operations Center at Ban Me Thuot, he jumped down to walked around to the pilot's door. "Pick me up in 'bout three hours," he called over the turbine whine. "Should b-be ready then."

The pilot shot a thumbs-up sign as Mac peeled away, bent forward at the waist to avoid the rotor blades, and holding the young Yard by his harness to make sure he did the same.

At the TOC entrance, Mac flashed his ID card for the MPs, who called ahead to make sure that the S-3 would allow such a scruffy figure in.

"You're a master sergeant?" asked the young MP, as he looked Mac over for some sign of rank.

"Yeah, why?"

"Hard to tell, Sarge."

"S'posed ta be. We don't wear rank in the field. Keeps Clyde g-guessin' when he g-greases us."

"Clyde?"

"Yeah, the VC."

"All right, they say you can go in now."

"Thanks, guys." Mac started out of the gate with the young Yard in tow.

"Hold up, Sarge!"

"What?"

"The Gook's gotta stay here. He ain't allowed in the TOC."

"He ain't a fuckin' G-gook, asshole. He's a Yard, and he's my bodyguard."

"Don't matter. He ain't allowed in the TOC."

"K'sor," Mac said in Jarai. "Stay here. Smoke all their cigarettes." To the MPs, he asked: "You got any smokes?"

"Sure."

"Well you might wanna g-give him some. K'sor here don't like people calling him a G-gook. Pisses him off. Know what I mean? And he ain't had a decent cigarette in days."

"No sweat, Sarge. Hey—didn't mean nothin' by it."

Inside the tactical operations center, Mac found the S-3 tied up with some division staff and the brigade executive officer. At the sight of Mac, Colonel Love's eyes narrowed. "What's your unit, soldier?"

"The MIKE Force," Mac growled back. "And the rank's Master Sergeant."

The Brigade operations sergeant major jumped in to steer Mac away. "The colonel's all right," he whispered, "but he's hell on uniform violations."

"Too b-bad he ain't hell on war violations," Mac grumbled. "Somebody's b-been massacrin' our Yards."

Together, they went over Mac's field map, verifying 4th Division unit locations off the map in general directions and kilometers. Occasionally, the SMAJ would nod to a map hanging behind the cluster of officers. Mac noted that Love kept staring up from his visitors to glare at his Sedang midwife necklace. He regretted being unable to get closer to the situation map, but the SMAJ was adamant in his belief that there were no 4th Division troops anywhere near 212th Company's area.

"What 'b-bout yer LRRPs?" Mac wondered. "Don't they wear tigers?"

"Sure, but we don't have any Lurps within ten kilometers of your area. They're workin' to your east."

"You g-got locations?"

"The S-Two does. He just gives us the general area they're in. He and the Three keep gettin' in a pissin' contest over who controls the LRRPs. The S-Two's got their locations, but he won't tell us where they are. Just where they ain't. Secret Squirrel OPSEC shit."

Mac looked back up over Love's head to the situation map. "Opsec's sp-posed to fool the enemy, not your friends. What're all those diagonal lines on the map?"

"Free Fire Zones. Where the Lurps work."

Mac nodded. In most of Vietnam the use of artillery was tightly controlled. Before a unit could fire a mission, they had to call up to clear it with higher U.S. and Vietnamese authorities. A Free Fire Zone was an area where a commander could make immediate use of all supporting weapons without any approval from the higher ups. All he needed was an identified enemy target.

"Yeah. Well, any of your LRRPs g-gettin' lost?"

"You mean wanderin' into your AO? I doubt it, Sarge. Those kids are pretty good at land navigation. Too bad I can't say the same for some of the officers here."

"Know what'cha mean," Mac laughed. "Well, I'll see you, SMAJ."

Mac was almost to the gate when Sergeant Major Dawkins called him back.

"Hey, Sarge, I just got the latest sitreps from the LRRPs. The S-Two's been sittin' on 'em."

He handed Mac a clipboard of situation reports with a red Secret cover. Mac flipped through it. Down under pages of small-scale enemy movement and no-change-to-previous-situation reports, he found a single page referring to three enemy killed. Two men and a boy. No weapons recovered. The coordinates of the contact had been carefully blacked out.

"Looks like our honey gatherers. Where c-can I find your S-Two?"

By the time Mac found the S-2, the S-2 couldn't find time to talk with him. He had barely managed to talk the S-2 NCO into sitting down with him when a burst of fire sent everyone scrambling for weapons.

"Hey, Sarge," called Dawkins, "you're wanted at the gate."

Two young MPs stood at attention, staring straight ahead as Love paced back and forth spewing verbal venom into their faces. Several junior officers and NCOs sulked nearby. K'sor looked sheepishly at Mac.

"Sergeant," demanded Love, "what the hell's this man doing here?"

"S'my bodyguard!"

"Your bodyguard? Well the next time you come to this TOC, you leave your bodyguard behind. Is that clear? That goddammed Gook nearly killed me!"

"He ain't a Gook, he's a Yard!"

"Sergeant, when you address me, you do so by my rank or 'sir.' Is that understood?"

"Yessir, and he ain't a fuckin' Gook, sir."

Having made his point, Love stalked away screaming for the adjutant. Where the hell was the idiot responsible for TOC security? As Mac walked out to the helipad, K'sor explained that the MPs had questioned him about his carbine and his ability to hit anything with it. Since they'd been nice enough to share their cigarettes, he'd obliged by letting loose a short burst into some birds in a distant tree. Unfortunately, the Meerika Colonel and several others had been standing directly under his line of fire. K'sor didn't understand why the Meerika was so upset. The rounds had passed at least 10 or 12 feet over their heads. By the Master of the Sky, he'd even checked to make sure no one was in the line of fire beyond the tree.

"You frightened him," Mac chuckled. "Meerika who pretend be great warrior not like that fright show. Next time, do not shoot when persons near target."

"Unless Tiep-zap," K'sor amended.

"Unless VC," Mac agreed.

"Well?" asked Jed Saville when Mac had returned.

"Well," Mac shrugged, "It's gotta be the 4th Division LRRPs."

"You're sure?"

"No. Could be bandits, Khmer Rouge, VC, or anybody else in this country runnin' 'round with g-guns. But the Yards say the killers are American, and the Fourth Division LRRPs are claimin' three VC KIA that look like our honey g-gatherers. What'd'ya say I g-go out with the company for a while? I'd like to see it on the ground before we start makin' accusations."

"Yes, you'd better," agreed Saville. "Eating their mascot is one thing, but making careless accusations of a massacre would bring real trouble."

The air inside the briefing tent was stifling. While Lieutenant Rose and Sergeant Swift went through their briefing, the patrols of company E, 58th Infantry (Division-LRRP) (Airborne) scribbled on notepads and maps.

They would insert into AO Gold by helicopter to determine and report on the strength, disposition, organization, and movement of enemy forces in zone. The operation would last five days. Their mission was re-connaissance, Rose emphasized, not combat. But they knew the rules. This was a Free Fire Zone. Anything moving inside was enemy. He wanted solid recon results, or he wanted bodies. There was a week's in-country R&R waiting for the patrols that produced the best reconnaissance results and highest body count. Right now the platoon up at Kontum seemed to have the edge on Recon, but theirs was ahead on kills. After a few more rah-rah statements about his Lurps being the best in the army, Rose took his seat while Swift went into the meat of the mission, noting specific patrol areas, call signs, frequencies, emergency signals, landing zone locations, insertion times, and miscellaneous matters. Among these last, Swift noted that the MIKE Force was working the area to their west. That meant that they needed to be careful. Special Forces, in his opinion, weren't very good at map reading. He didn't want any of his men being shot up by so-called friendlies.

Map reading and land navigation were Staff Sergeant Swift's strongest skills. Service as a private in an armored cavalry troop on the Czech border had been followed by a subsequent European tour as a LRRP. On patrol, Swift had few peers. It was hard to believe that he had been dropped from flight school for shortcomings in navigation.

The instructors, Swift said, had been out to get him. But the real cul-prit was something no army doctor had found. Swift suffered from a rare inner ear disability. When engaged in aerial flight, the 4th Division LRRP's recognized genius at finding himself on any piece of terrain on earth could easily lose his sense of direction. No matter how hard he concentrated, a few unexpected twists and turns was all it took to disorient him. And trying to read a map in the vibration of a helicopter only made it worse. Aware that any failure in his vision would cost him his career, Swift downplayed the problem and tried to get his lieutenant to do as many insertions as pos-sible. But the lieutenant would have none of it. His talent was standing in front of a map with a pointer, looking military, and rattling off canned briefs for visiting VIPs. The Lurps called him 'Brinkley' after a well-known news anchor.

Their choppers lifted out just after first light. After a heated argument between the pilots and a junior patrol leader over the locations of two insertion points, Swift was back in time for coffee and chipped beef on toast with the Brigade Sergeant Major.

212th company had swung east to enter a stretch of forest running between Trang Phuc and Buon Brieng. Tieu Atar had come under mortar and recoilless rifle fire the previous night, and Saville believed that these might be elements of the merged artillery battalion that intelligence was trying to pin down. Villages were few and far between, but their reception hadn't changed. Someone was killing the locals. Mac had been with the company for three days, and was getting on St. Cyr's nerves. Every time they came to a village, Mac was quick to take over. When St. Cyr pulled him aside to demand the courtesy of letting him run his own operation, Mac tactlessly pointed out that he was the Battalion S-3.

"Then get back to your Three shop," was St. Cyr's curt reply. Accordingly, Mac lay on a chopper for first light of the following morning. An hour later, feeling a bit apologetic, Mac dropped back to request St. Cyr's permission to accompany the recon platoon.

"My brother," St. Cyr commented to Blek as Mac walked away, "sometimes very concerned about this father yours."

"Uuangh," Blek grinned, rapping his knuckles lightly against his skull, "like certain commander my brother, very hard head."

"It's nothing personal," advised Boris. "When I got here, Mac was standing in your boots, advising Ko'pa Jhon."

Late that afternoon, after Toller's men had gone ahead to check out a company patrol-base position, there was a distant burst of firing. Ten minutes later, shorter bursts sounded from the same direction. As St. Cyr and Blek pushed the platoons to the sound of firing, Toller's disturbed voice came up on the net. Advising St. Cyr to come up quickly, and keep the other platoons back.

It had started just after recon crossed a small stream. Footprints showed two adults and three children, all carrying loads.

"Women," said Jimm, pointing to the adult prints. Laurie studied the heel-toe pattern and instep before nodding in agreement. An explosion and firing in the near distance drove Jimm's lead squad to earth.

They held their fire, waiting for Jimm's signal. Twigs fell as patters sounded in the treetops. The firing ceased as abruptly as it had begun. Toller motioned the platoon into assault formation while Jimm led the first squad ahead. Mac quickly joined Jimm's squad and positioned himself behind K'sor Blo, the squad leader. Blo grinned a quick "hello" while his eyes swept the terrain to their front and sides.

"Blek's father," he whispered, "we hunt Tiep-zap again."

"As always, my Brother. You think I too old?"

Blo merely grinned.

Up where the trail left the woodline, Mac heard a low murmur of voices. The squad ghosted forward, weapons at the ready. Mac waved for them to stop. Blo signaled back to Rchom Jimm, who motioned for the platoon to stand by. Mac whispered that he was going ahead on his own. Carefully edging up to the brushline, his M16 at the ready, he heard the hissing sound of a radio breaking squelch. A voice exclaimed that they really didn't have any hair on their pussies.

"What the fuck's going on here?"

Four startled Lurps jumped up to face Mac, the muzzles of their weapons covering him. A fifth looked up from his task of parting a small wisp of pubic hair for a photograph.

"Jesus Christ," called a young sergeant clutching a radio handset. The muzzles of the LRRPs' M16s twitched nervously. "Who the fuck're you? What are you doing here?"

"You're in the MIKE Force AO. Our AO!"

"The hell is it, man..." countered the Sergeant.

"Fuck me," muttered a Chicano PFC, "that goddam Swift got us lost again."

The Sergeant glanced at the PFC, who continued. "You know it, man. That's why the goddam river wasn't there."

"It's a stream. They dry up..."

"Not this time of year, they don't."

Mac wasn't listening. His eyes had focused on the torn bodies of two women and three children. Kindling wood lay spilled where they had fallen. Callused footpads pointed out from akimbo positions. The young sergeant keyed his handset, trying to raise a relay station. Pops and static answered. He tried again. The amateur photographer held his camera two feet from a woman's splayed legs, bobbing back and forth to get her vagina in focus.

Behind him, Mac heard movement in the bushes. K'sor Blo stepped up beside him. Angry voices sounded from behind. The sense of nervous panic that jolted the LRRPs strangely bypassed the photographer. The Sergeant's voice had a concerned edge as he threw another call across the airways. Mac glanced over his left shoulder to where the LRRPs were staring. K'sor Blo and Rchom Jimm's eyes had widened. Glimmers of hatred, shock, and loathing rose up under their faces. More Jarai heads appeared. Rifle muzzles zeroed in on the LRRPs. Toller's voice came over the HT-1, demanding to know what was going on. Mac noted the Chicano PFC nervously fingering a claymore clacker whose wire ran down past his feet and out into the grass.

The Sergeant's radio sputtered: He was coming in broken. Could he change positions, over? The Chicano kid's fingers tightened around the clacker. The photographer was now looking up, stunned, as Mac's M16 muzzle tracked the movement of his face. Then someone yelled: "Kill 'em!" in Jarai.

The crash of firing sent Toller's trailing squads to earth. Then, they were up, rushing forward, to join Mac and the lead squad. But it was too late...

Shock was on Toller's anguished face as he reached out to keep St. Cyr from moving past him.

"Leftenant, you don't want to see it."

"See what? What the hell's going on?"

"We...we've killed some Yanks."

"Yanks?"

"Yessir. 4th Division LRRPs is my bet. Apparently the ones who've been killing our Yards."

"What the hell…" St. Cyr tried to push past him, but Toller's iron grip held him back. "Leftenant, you'd better let me explain first. It looks like some 4th Division LRRP's ambushed a wood gathering party of two women and three children. No weapons. Totally unarmed civilians. That's the shooting we heard and came up to check out. I put the platoon on an assault line and sent the first squad forward. Mac was with the first squad. He claims they were approaching the LRRPs when they heard a burst of fire. When they got there, the LRRPs were dead. I don't believe it."

"Why not?"

"It's the way they're acting, Leftenant. I'd be careful up there."

"You think they'd turn on us?"

"I reckon they already had, but Mac beat 'em to the punch. Like I said, be careful up there. I'd bring Ryan's platoon up here to cover us if I were you."

"Why Ryan's?"

"He's got the most Bahnar."

"No, Laurie," St. Cyr shook his head. "These are our people. I'll handle this."

As St. Cyr pushed by, Toller dropped back to cover him and motioned for Ro'o Mnur to do the same.

They found Jimm hunkered down beside the Dega bodies, going through their carry-baskets. Blek squatted off to the side, whispering intensely with Mac. The recon platoon was standing about in groups of threes and fours, staring at the bodies. The eyes that met St. Cyr's were not friendly. A few were openly hostile, but most merely gave a guarded stare. He'd seen that stare before. It was the one Jarai reserved for outsiders. A voice inside his head warned that the Jarai did not treat outsiders kindly. For the first time, he felt pangs of being alien and alone. Toller's assessment was on the mark. As of now, the recon platoon was a danger to all Roundeyes except, perhaps, Mac. Hunching down between Blek and Mac, he looked into McElroy's red-rimmed, glazed eyes.

"Mac," he kept his voice carefully cadenced, "tell them that this was an accident. A bad accident. An ugly accident. But it was an accident. We don't know why it happened. Perhaps Yang Brieng Pong, or some other evil spirit, blinded these Meerika so that instead of sticks, they saw arms.

We don't know. But we do know that the Meerika are no enemy of the Dega. That's why we're here. After that, tell them we're going to send the Meerika bodies back to their people and take the Dega to their village. Is that understood?"

Mac looked away.

"Sergeant," St. Cyr repeated, "is that understood?"

"This no accident," Mac replied in Jarai.

"Speak to me in English, Sergeant."

"This murder not accident," Mac repeated in Jarai, "and I speak only Jarai tongue. My tongue. Tongue of my Dega people."

St. Cyr stepped away to take his handset from Ro'o Mnur, who was carefully watching the recon platoon. Minutes later, he vaguely heard his own voice telling Saville that they had discovered some ten bodies, apparently killed in a Viet Cong ambush. Five were local Rhade villagers, and five were American. He had only their dog tags to go on, but the uniforms and equipment suggested 4th Division LRRPs. Mac could explain it to him in detail, because Mac was headed back to battalion on the next available chopper. After things settled down, he'd come in and explain it further.

Saville came back to suggest that they might be a MACVSOG recon or roadrunner team. Highly unlikely, St. Cyr replied. The only Indig were the two women and three children.

When he had finished, he casually walked over and fired a short burst into the LRRP radio. The platoon jumped. Hands nervously jerked weapons into the ready position. Distant eyes glared into his own.

"Such," he said in Jarai, "explain why no radio-talk message heard."

A subtle current passed through the platoon. The charged atmosphere lifted. Just as suddenly, he was no longer a stranger. *If that's what it takes*, he thought, *so be it*. As an afterthought, he picked up the small 35mm camera. Then he glared at five Americans he was fully prepared to hate. A face now freezing in death jolted his memory. The name was forgotten, but it was a face he'd seen before. Grinning, joking, and trudging along under a helmet and heavy pack in Delta Company, 1st Battalion, 35th By God Infantry. A Hispanic kid from Albuquerque, if he remembered right. Gonzalez, Morales, Perales, something like that. A great kid and a good soldier. A kid who had always wanted to be a Lurp.

Chapter Twenty-Seven

As THE BODIES WERE lifted out, Saville radioed to confirm that they were 4th Division LRRPs and ordered St. Cyr to take up night positions nearby. The 4th Division would investigate the site the following day. The Roundeyes huddled for their evening meal and orders group in silence. Toller was the first to break the huddle, muttering on the need to be with his troops. Mac tried to tag along, but St. Cyr ordered him to stay. For once, Mac accepted without comment. He had wrapped himself in a brooding depression, and avoided looking anyone in the eye.

Helicopters clattered in and out the following day. Saville was the first to arrive, and took Mac back with him after a quick look. He was plainly baffled, but everyone's story checked out. They had heard an explosion followed by an intense burst of small-arms fire, followed by silence, then a second burst of fire. Moving to the gunfire, they had stumbled across the bodies. The LRRP platoon leader and company commander showed up, trailing an NCO who insisted that he had put the team down some way to the east. They were followed by the brigade commander and a deputy division commander, who loudly berated the LRRP captain.

While they bickered, St. Cyr had his own worries. The almond eyes observing the outsiders were not friendly. Blek and K'sor Tlur kept the troops under tight observation. To prevent anyone from hosing down a helicopter in revenge for the villagers, Recon was sent out to select that night's positions.

"Are we imposing on you, Lieutenant?" demanded the colonel, piqued that St. Cyr's attention appeared to be focused elsewhere.

"No, sir. But this area's not secure."

"That's why it's your job to secure it."

"Yessir, but all this air traffic is bound to attract attention. If we get hit by anything bigger than a company, it'll be more than we can handle. Getting you and the general would be a feather in their cap."

"If they're stupid enough to hit us now, their asses are mine. I've asked division to give me this area and another battalion, so we can find the bastards who did this. I've also asked that your company be attached to us. We'll put a firebase on that hill five kilometers south to provide supporting fires."

Just what we need, thought St. Cyr, *more dead Yards*.

"You know," continued the colonel, "if we can get some civic action teams into these villages, we should be able to dig up information on the VC infrastructure here. Civic action is the key to these operations. You've got to have the support of the population. Otherwise, you're pissing into the wind."

St. Cyr nodded sagely. *You might get more support*, he thought, *if you'd quit killing them*. While the colonel radioed back to check with his S-3 on his new operational area request, his S-2 studied the bloodstains.

"I don't understand it," the major confided to St. Cyr. "LRRPs are supposed to be better than this. Where the hell was their security? And what were they doing all mixed in with Yards? It doesn't make sense."

"Maybe they were trading for a little pussy."

An angry glint flashed in the major's eyes, but he merely shrugged. "What, with their kids along? I wouldn't put it past our grunts, but the LRRPs are serious about their work. You say you heard two separate firefights?"

"That's what it sounded like."

"And it took you how long to get here?"

"Maybe twenty minutes. You know how it is when you're running to the sound of guns; it could've been more, it could've been less."

"Less is more likely. Charlie didn't take time to police up their weapons. That's unusual. And something else is strange."

"What's that?"

"The brass. It's all U.S. And all 5.56mm."

"That's what we've been finding. Our battalion should've sent you some reports on it."

"Yes. Now that you mention it, they did."

Regter heard more about the massacre from General Rock, who had flown into An Khe for IFFV's semiweekly briefing. Rock had been tied up in MACV headquarters, trying to live down a flap in the press about sending soldiers to forward combat bases for failing to salute. Discussion of the massacre tied up the first 20 minutes. Rock was taken to task for having his LRRPs outside their AOR, but his plan to hunt down the LRRP killers was vetoed. Any spare battalions he had could be redirected to Kontum.

He did not take that kindly. There would be a new LRRP company commander. He thanked Regter for the MIKE Force's quick response. As the IFFV intelligence officer briefed that the enemy was preparing a Highland wide offensive for early or mid-August, and that the 2nd NVA division was building up around Kontum, Rock's *aide-de-camp* entered the meeting to hand the general a message. Rock scanned it, then motioned for Regter to see him when the briefing was over.

Regter waited an additional half hour while Rock tried to convince General Peers that he could spare a battalion to hunt down the LRRP killers and still respond to developments north of Kontum. When General Rock came out, he appeared to have forgotten Regter. But as Regter turned to leave, Rock called him over.

"You know, Major, the funny thing about communications," he handed Regter a barely legible copy of a teletype message, "is that you can be five kilometers from the transmitter and not hear anything, while a station well beyond your range picks it up. What do you make of this?"

The message was from the LRRP base radio station in Pleiku, notifying their base station in Ban Me Thuot that they had intercepted a message from Lima Tango 352 Delta. At 231520 July they had initiated an ambush in AO Gold. Results of ambush appeared to be a local wood-gathering party. Two females and three minors KIA, no weapons or documents found. The party appeared to be carrying wood for village cooking fires. Extraction was not—repeat—*not* requested at this time.

"They certainly didn't mince words, did they General?"

"No, they didn't. The coordinates are wrong, but that's our team. I'm going to look into this from my end to find out what the hell we're doing running around ambushing civilians. I want you to look into it from your end. My aide tells me that we found only U.S. brass on site."

"That's my information. I'd double check on that. Sir, are you suggesting my men killed your LRRPs?"

"They damned well could have, Major. By accident or on purpose. Look, I'm not assigning blame. Hell, it's not your fault the LRRPs were in the wrong AO, and I've had enough publicity lately over this ridiculous saluting affair. All I'm saying is that I'm going to check into this from my end, and I expect you to do the same from yours. Whatever action I take will be low key, but you can expect that justice will be served."

"All right, General. I'll check my end. You have my word that I'll take whatever action is required."

"What was all that about?" Cox wanted to know as Regter boarded the chopper.

"The Lurps, sir. General Rock wanted to talk about the Lurps."

The LRRPs were soon forgotten. Gutted, embalmed, and packed off in metal coffins, they went home in the cargo holds of the same aircraft that brought in their replacements. Division's attention shifted north, where red enemy symbols began cluttering the maps around Kontum's northwestern outposts. But back in AO Orange, the LRRPs were not so easily dismissed. Cohen and Ryan sided openly with Mac. So what if Recon had wasted the LRRPs? The sonsuvbitches had been greasing women and kids. They got what they deserved. So fuckin' much for the mighty 4th Division LRRP. Besides, the people who had pulled the triggers weren't even American. Hell, they weren't even South Vietnamese. And being tribal irregulars, they weren't subject to any code of military justice.

It wasn't the LRRPs' fault, St. Cyr insisted. These were kids who a year ago had been back in high school, or on the block. Only a small percentage had the meanness to be murderers. The majority killed as required. Kids volunteered for the LRRPs for the same reasons that career NCOs volunteered for the MIKE Force: To be out against the enemy on their own terms, away from the institutional discipline and petty harassment common to conventional forces. When a unit killed indiscriminately, leadership was at fault.

Boris voiced a similar opinion. The problem with the American army was that they were fighting a war while pretending that it wasn't, rotating draftees and first-time enlistees in and out of faceless units for a single year. Kids who had barely memorized their general orders were now making life-and-death decisions.

Even Blek got into the argument. Recon had done no more to the LRRPs than the LRRPs had done to the Dega. What was important was company had held together. There had been no desertions. They were still unified. They were still a team.

Toller's response was more introspective. "When we get back," he said softly to St. Cyr one night, "I'd like to transfer out."

"To another company?"

"No. Out of the MIKE Force. Reckon it's time I went back to RAR."

Over the next week, they fell back into the rhythm of patrolling. To the south, Ferris's company ran into elements of the 66th NVA regiment. Following a two-hour firefight, the enemy withdrew. On a hunch, Saville lifted 212th company into an area northwest of Ferris, with instructions to move southeast.

The terrain was marked by rolling hills and wide stretches of grassy plain, interspersed with forest. Movement was fairly rapid. *Too rapid*, worried Boris. The NVA could cover 50 kilometers across such terrain in a single night.

At a ford near a small river, St. Cyr called a halt. After a careful study of the hill behind them, the bend of the river, and a flat apron of grassland at the far side, he called for his platoon leaders. This was where 212th company would bed down for the night. Instead of their standard laager procedures, he opted for a more defensive posture. Cohen and Ryan would position their platoons forward, to each side of the ford's exit, and cover it with interlocking bands of machinegun fire. Biloskirka's platoon would be halfway up the hill behind them, providing overwatch. Recon would set out observation and listening posts to their rear and flanks. Their single mortar was to be just behind the crest of the hill.

The men set to work digging hasty fall-back positions around the hill, while their squad leaders walked their routes in from the ambush positions. Just before nightfall, the indigenous platoon leaders emphasized noise, light, and fire discipline with their troops. St. Cyr settled in with the grim premonition that the night would not be quiet, though Ryan and Cohen had their doubts. As the last of the insect repellent wafted away, the mosquitoes mobbed them for an uninhibited feast. Under a waning moon, intermittent banks of clouds moved across the sky. Except for claymore mines and the single mortar, they were on their own. The FAC wouldn't arrive on station until first light, but a single Spooky gunship on stand-by. After conferring with Boris, St. Cyr moved forward to locate with Cohen.

Radio silence was in effect. Civilians who might be out, and enemy in singles, twos, or threes, would be allowed to pass. Small enemy patrols coming from the river would pass through into Boris's ambush. The decision to trigger that ambush would be his. Recon would continue to provide security until ordered to withdraw, when they would reassemble behind the hill and stand by for orders. Jimm wanted a squad on the far bank, but St. Cyr vetoed it. If Spooky did arrive while a fight was on, he wanted it to have a clear field of fire.

Shortly after midnight, Boris reported a string of lights moving down a distant ridgeline. Cohen flashed a nervous smile. "Well, El Tee, that's twenty bucks I owe you."

St. Cyr took the handset from Ro'o Mnur to whisper into the battalion net. Magnuson's voice confirmed that Spooky was on strip alert at Ban Me Thuot, and A-6 Skyraiders were available from Pleiku at first light. St. Cyr's doubts began to gnaw away. Without artillery, and with Spooky a good 20 minutes out, what if this turned out to be a battalion? The river wasn't much of a barrier. Maybe 70 meters wide, it was barely waist deep. If this turned into a real fight, they weren't properly dug in. He'd have been smarter, a nagging voice insisted, to have set out a single platoon ambush under the protection of a company defensive perimeter based on the hill. Accustomed to the shadows of the forest, the open sky made him uneasy.

An hour later, three figures slipped into the water from the far bank. As they waded across, the muzzles of their AK-47s swept the darkness. On reaching the near bank, two hung at the water's edge while a pointman moved forward at the crouch. After checking several clumps of grass on both sides of the trail, the pointman gave a low whistle and went to earth. A second figure now moved past to check the trail beyond the first. St. Cyr lay ten meters back from a clump of tranh grass being probed by an NVA bayonet, and prayed that Ro'o Mnur had remembered to switch the radio off. All they needed now was for someone to break squelch.

When this NVA had signaled, the pointman motioned the third man into action. He passed through to check the area beyond the second. With that done, they huddled by the trail for a whispered conference.

The pointman lit a cigarette and passed it around. So much, sneered St. Cyr, for vaunted NVA discipline. The assholes were taking a smoke break in the middle of an ambush. For a brief second, he considered taking them out, but every movement and gesture hinted of a larger force behind. He glanced at Blek, staring at the three NVA with studied amazement. The pointman flipped the half-smoked cigarette away. Seconds later the NVA were moving rapidly out.

Blek was up, whispering instructions into his radio. "Signal," he murmured, "cigarette signal. VC not cross here, cross..."

Blek's voice was interrupted by Toller's hoarse whisper. "Bearkiller, I've got a major element crossing the river upstream, about a hundred meters out. Looks like a platoon, and there's more behind them."

"Break," cut in Ryan's excited murmur, "I've got movement downstream. Too far away to be sure."

A short burst from Boris's area took out the pointmen. In the heavy silence, St. Cyr keyed his microphone in a low calm voice and reported contact. He wanted Spooky launched immediately. Sergeant Magnuson's voice came back to ask as to the size of the enemy element. An estimated company, he was told. What time did it start? Start? Goddammit, it was starting now! Funny, Magnuson said. He didn't hear shooting. What about casualties? Casualties? There weren't any yet! What about Spooky? Yeah, Magnuson agreed, just as soon as he got his report filled out. Report? Where the hell were Mac and Saville? Goddammit, thought Magnuson, what was wrong with this lieutenant? No shooting, no casualties, and he thought he had contact?

Seconds later, the sounds of firing overrode both the transmit whine and St. Cyr's voice.

Contact, exulted Magnuson, as he nudged a nearby sleeping Yard. "K'sor, get the Captain."

Minutes later, Saville ducked into the bunker, followed by Mac and Ney Bloom. "Where's Spooky," he asked.

"Sonuvabitch is up," grunted Magnuson, "but Fourth Division's got 'em. Got a contact somewhere."

"Great," muttered Saville. "All the bloody artillery in the world, and they grab our gunship. Get B-23 immediately—the Black Arrow himself if you've got to—and get that Spooky back."

Saville picked up a handset and glanced over at Mac. "Well? Going to stand there with your thumb up your arse, or are you going to give us a hand?"

Mac said something in Jarai.

"He say you do hokay," translated K'sor. "No need."

"Bloody fucking great," muttered Saville. "Now I need a Yard to speak to a Yank... "

The sound of Saville's voice at the other end of the ether may have been reassuring, but at that moment there was another sound on St. Cyr's mind. It was the first time he'd ever heard bugles.

The distant whoosh and crackle of a green star cluster above Cohen's position was followed by the thunderous clap and flash of mines, and the angry explosion of a platoon firing full automatic. Seconds later, the area to Ryan's front and flank erupted in fire. Toller came up to report that two platoons were on their left and that the cluster was his signal for Recon to reassemble on the hill. St. Cyr looked at Blek, who had tied on his company scarf and was checking the cylinder of his Ruger revolver.

"Better get down," St. Cyr called.

"In fight," Blek flashed a morbid grin, "commander best stand! Better to be seen."

Sheepishly, St. Cyr stood. When Ro'o Mnur did the same, St. Cyr ordered him down.

Cohen's platoon poured fire into dark shadows and muzzle flashes. Explosions lit the darkness. Whooshes sounded above their heads as B-40 rockets arced by. Boris's position exploded in a raging crackle of fire. The radio kept cutting out as everyone transmitted at once. Minutes later, the company frequency fell strangely quiet.

Back in his bunker, Jed Saville glanced at Ney Bloom, who had just tuned their backup radio to the company frequency.

"Three hours and forty-one minutes to daylight," noted Saville.

"Blek do OK," Ney Bloom assured him. "Too busy to report now."

"Right! Well just to be on the safe side, I'll alert Ferris he's lifting in after first light."

"They're trying to get behind us," St. Cyr called to Blek. Into the mike, he ordered Toller to stand by to reinforce as ordered. Bugles sounded to their front. Across the river, a heavy machinegun shattered the night with green tracers. Ryan reported that the movement to his front had dropped off.

"How 'bout bugles?" St. Cyr wanted to know.

"No bugles, no movement. Just the occasional whistle."

St. Cyr and Blek looked into each other's eyes. The same thought flashed between them. "Uuangh, my Brother, we go."

Pulling along Ro'o Mnur, they rushed to Ryan's position while St. Cyr told Cohen to prepare to pull back to the hill. As Cohen answered, there was a deafening crash of small arms, rockets, mines, and grenades to Ryan's front. Under the wavering light of a dying parachute flare, the grass moved in waves as dark lines of enemy rushed forward. Ryan's men poured fire into their ranks while the young medic screamed instructions to fire low. The surging enemy seemed unstoppable. Suddenly, in ones and twos, his men began pulling back. Blek arrived and waded in, waving his revolver.

"Who runs, dies," Blek shouted. "Everyone hold!"

A B-40 rocket fishtailed in to explode next to a young Yard trooper. Involuntarily, he recoiled and rose.

"You stay!" Blek slammed the barrel of his revolver into the trooper's chest. "Fight Tiep-zap!"

The young Yard spun back into a crouching position, and emptied his rifle in a wild burst of fire. Blek kicked him in the buttocks. "Reload. Shoot low. Keep shoot pow fusil!"

While the trooper changed magazines, Blek fired aimed shots into the rushing shadows. "Grenad," he called, "where pow-grenad?" As if on cue, a telltale kapunk sounded nearby. Seconds later, a distant explosion flashed amid moving shadows.

St. Cyr and Ro'o Mnur were too busy emptying magazine after magazine into surging enemy ranks to hear the radio. A parachute flare popped up to their right, streams of red tracers crisscrossed their front. A thunderous crash of automatic fire signaled the arrival of Boris's platoon on their flank. St. Cyr didn't remember calling for it. There was a tap on his shoulder as Ro'o Mnur handed him the handset.

"Bearkiller Two-Six, this is Spooky. I am over your position now...break...where do you want it? Over."

"Roger Spooky, give me some light...break...and how 'bout hosing down the far side of the river? Over."

"Roger, Bearkiller. Understand you're up to your ass in alligators, but...which far side...over."

"Ah...side south of the green star cluster. Over."

"You got it. Just send up that cluster..."

He no sooner let go of the handset than Ro'o Mnur handed him a polished aluminum tube. "Green," grunted Ro'o Mnur.

Popping off the cap, he seated it over the base to slam it home. The shock of the detonation jerked his arm down as a stream of sparks whooshed by his face. Goddamn, somebody back at the factory had double charged this one. His hand throbbed dully as he grabbed the handset and ordered Boris and Cohen to send up green star clusters.

"What the..." he shouted as Blek jerked him away him by his harness.

Rockets slammed into where he had been standing. 82mm mortar rounds now crumped up the hill as Spooky made his flare pass. The night lit up with an eerie yellow light. Spooky banked sharply, then sent a moaning red torrent of fire hurtling earthward.

Cohen reported that the enemy had bypassed his positions. He was falling back to help Toller at the hill, where a raging firefight and bugles could be heard.

No, St. Cyr ordered, Cohen was to hold in place. As he let up on the push-to-talk switch, he noticed their own sector had fallen quiet. Blek approached, kicking the soles of troopers' boots and shouting orders that they were to fire only when they saw the enemy up close. As he looked into St. Cyr's eyes, another thought passed between them.

"Too quiet; something's up."

"Uangh," Blek agreed.

On Ro'o Mnur's PRC-25, Spooky cut off Saville's voice, which had been demanding a status report. St. Cyr checked with the platoon leaders. They had two killed and five wounded seriously.

The sudden silence was unnerving. They had either hit a company on an independent mission, or the lead company of a battalion. If the latter, the enemy commander was sending his own assessment back to battalion and awaiting further orders. Now was the time to pull back to the hill. A quick check with Toller confirmed that Recon had been facing no more than a platoon. Spooky reported that he had just hosed down the area where he had spotted mortar flashes. St. Cyr pulled Blek over.

"We hold until Spooky shoot far bank. Anything try to cross, we kill. When Spooky finish, we pull back to hill. OK?"

Blek nodded his assent. St. Cyr passed orders to the Roundeyes while Blek passed word to his indigenous platoon leaders. He then let Spooky know they would be moving just after his pass. They would make their stand at the hill, with Spooky flying cover. With luck, they could hold till the A-6s got on station.

Spooky's reply changed his plan in an instant. "Bearkiller, Bearkiller, this is Spooky. You've got major, I mean major, movement off your left flank. Look like ants all spread out."

St. Cyr rogered the transmission while Spooky went into a tight spin, miniguns blazing. He cancelled his previous order and ordered everyone to fall back immediately. As he and Blek moved to the rear, they met the Superjew's men.

"Goddam, Trung-oui! Who the hell's running this contact anyway?" Cohen's eyes had a distant stare.

"Anybody who can see what the hell's going on!"

Toller was on the hill. Everybody else was moving. The Yard platoon and squad leaders were doing their best to keep panic to a minimum. Blek moved back and forth between Cohen and Ryan's platoons, waving his pistol and encouraging the men. Spooky reported that he was getting low on

ammo, and suggested that he rake their old positions with miniguns on order. As Cohen's lead elements reached the skirt of the hill, a deafening
crash of AK-47 and RPD fire sounded from their old positions. When Blek
called for reports from the delaying element, Trung-si Xuan's voice came
up to report they had cleared their old positions and were dragging a few
wounded with them. No one would be left behind. Blek tapped St. Cyr on
the shoulder.

"OK, fire Spooky."

"Who say so?"

"Trung-si Xuan."

St. Cyr agonized for long seconds. Spam's shrill whistle sounded in
the distance amid heavy bursts of firing, St. Cyr's wet palm kept slipping
on his handset. He could be killing his own men. But Spam's word was one
he trusted. He squeezed his push to talk button. "Spooky, this is Bearkiller.
Hose 'em down. Over."

Spooky's 'roger' drowned in the thunderous buzz of miniguns and
static. Seconds later, Boris's voice came up to report that he had linked up
with Toller below the bare knob of the hill. An unnatural silence followed
in Spooky's wake, punctuated by the muffled sounds of clomping feet, the
exhale of labored breaths, the rattle of gear, and the occasional hiss of a
radio.

Spooky hung on for another twenty minutes, hosing down suspect areas while they regrouped around the military crest of the hill. After a medevac ship touched down to take out the dead and seriously wounded,
Spooky departed to rearm and refuel. Despite sporadic bursts of fire to test
their positions, no further attacks came. Just after first light, the A-6s
showed up on station.

Jed Saville arrived after dawn, just as their remaining wounded were
medevaced. He took St. Cyr up for a quick aerial reconnaissance, and cancelled Ferris's lift. The still beaten patterns in the grass told a graphic story.
In one chewed up and blackening area, they found a burst mortar tube.
The enemy had taken time to evacuate the other tubes, but the building
stench made it clear that Spooky's guns had ground up its share of ant-
morsels. Two bodies found near Biloskirka's old position identified the
unit as the 209th NVA regiment.

"NVA?" exclaimed Toller, "well the regiment might be NVA, but I'll wager that this company were VC regulars."

"Why's that?" St Cyr wondered.

"Well for starters, Leftenant, by the way they fought. Hitting us on one flank with bugles to make us think they were larger than they were, while their main effort moved against our other flank. Your average NVA doesn't have that much experience, not these days, anyway. Tend to do things rather straightforward, they do. Down in the Aussie Task force, it's VC regulars who fight like this."

St. Cyr nodded in agreement, remembering the pointmen.

"You know," Toller said to St. Cyr, after Saville had lifted out, "we did rather well."

"Yeah, it could have been a battalion."

"It probably was a battalion, but what I meant was that the men did rather well considering that they're irregulars. I'd like to see some of your American units stand their ground like mine did. By the way, you do award medals to Vietnamese, don't you?"

"If they deserve it. Why?"

"Well, from what Boris tells me, Trung-si Spam earned himself a *Mention In Despatches* last night. Our MiD is the equivalent of your Bronze star for Valor."

"Not a bad idea. I'll see what Blek thinks."

After he had finished discussing this and other items with Blek, he wandered over to Boris's platoon and found the Roundeyes bunched together for the morning meal. He refused the offer of a first cup of coffee, deferring that honor to Spam, and then added some of his own water and coffee to Toller's canteen cup, calling for Blek to join them. The conversation was at first reserved, but turned animated as the caffeine kicked in, reliving the surprises and anxieties of the night's battle. He concluded by going over his concept for the day's operations, which would kick off just as soon as they finished sweeping the area, and everyone took a good bath in the river.

As he stood to go, Boris glanced up.

"Buddy, that was good job last night."

"RAR standards," mimicked Cohen, affecting his best Australian accent.

"Yeah," added Ryan, "Almost as good as Dick Grey would have done."

"It wasn't my doing," he confessed. "All I did was run around with a handset to my ear. It was you guys, and Blek, and the Dega, and Spooky who did the fighting. Hell, Ro'o Mnur did more than I did."

Still, he felt a warm glow inside that had nothing to do with the coffee.

Toller said nothing. But then, he never said anything more about leaving the MIKE Force either.

Chapter Twenty-Eight

ST. CYR'S EUPHORIA LASTED as long as it took to lift in to Pleiku, where they found an angry Regter waiting. They followed him to his office, where he leafed through a sheaf of papers, before flipping a single sheet to Saville, who gave it a quick glance and passed it to St. Cyr.

"General Rock gave me that at the IFFV commander's brief last week," said Regter. "As you can see, it was the LRRPs who killed the Yards. My question is: Who killed the LRRPs?"

"Sir," St. Cyr's hand remained steady, his voice controlled. "I really don't know. It could've been local VC, or FULRO..."

Regter leaned forward in his chair to stare intently into St. Cyr's eyes. His tone was angry yet calm. "Or your Goddam company? Galen, I didn't call you in here to hear any bullshit. You'll notice that I didn't take the trouble to read you your rights under Article Thirty-One, but that doesn't give you the right to jack me around. Now I'm asking you as your commander. The man who gave you your job. The man who stuck with you when my own commander wanted you court-martialed and hung out to dry. The man you once told that if some sonuvabitch could have the balls to go around calling himself a professional, then he could damn sure start acting like one. I want to know what the hell happened out there. You've got twenty-four hours to get a complete report on my desk. I want it in your own handwriting, I want it signed, and I want the truth. Now, get the hell out of here!"

Back in his room, St. Cyr stared at the yellow writing tablet. He'd filled in the heading and a long paragraph on the fight at the ford. But when he went back to the LRRPs, his pen froze. He'd scribble out a few lines, rip up the sheet, and then start again. Finally, he closed his eyes and saw the kid from Albuquerque. Gonzalves. His name had been Gonzalves, from some remote Galician ancestor who'd marched up from Mexico with Oñate. The kid had been proud of that. American since 1592, he used to say.

And with the name, the pages wrote themselves. He poured out every detail, concluding with a statement that he had been responsible for everything his company had done or failed to do. Then he rummaged in his rucksack for the camera, and ducked out to the latrine to clean its smear of dried blood away.

When he got back, Saville was waiting.

"Galen, is there anything you want to tell me before we see Major Regter?"

St. Cyr passed him the legal sheets. Saville read them, his eyebrows knit together in a frown. Finally, he looked St. Cyr in the eye.

"So, you have no idea who actually pulled the trigger."

"Captain, I have a very good idea, and why. But it's my opinion, not proven fact."

"Regter's not looking for proven facts. He's looking for the truth."

St. Cyr held up the camera. "It may be in here. The rumor in the company is that they were taking pornographic trophy pictures when they were killed."

"So your men did kill the LRRPs."

"I'm sure they did, but I can't point out any man in that platoon and say with absolute certainty that he was one of the triggermen. All I know is what they've told me, and what I've heard them say among themselves. I do know that when I got there, that platoon was within a hair of killing me and going over to the enemy.

"Jed, I've been shot out of the sky. I've found many a bullet hole in my sleeves and pant legs after a fight. I've stood next to a fellow officer when a mortar round dropped in to kill him and wound several others around me. And that fragging that made me a company commander in the Fourth Division damned near took me out. But I've never been as close to death as I was when I walked in to where those LRRPs were.

"My men were pissed. They wanted revenge and we were the closest thing at hand. We had become the enemy, and they would have killed every one of us, though I had a strange feeling that Mac was being counted as one of them. And in a split second, I changed that. I lifted some invisible tent flap and brought them back inside. Our firefight the other night proved that. It was the biggest engagement we've had since Tet, and those same men stood with us and fought. It cost five American lives, one of whom I knew, but that's the price of war."

The resolve in St. Cyr's voice reminded Saville of someone else he'd known: A young SAS lieutenant who'd taken his men deep into Indonesian territory to destroy a base for cross-border operations. That too had cost lives, Indonesian lives. Still, the flap had almost ended his career since Australia wasn't legally at war. Jed Saville sat in silence for several minutes, then picked up the camera.

"I'll have Sergeant Perkins develop this. In the meanwhile, we're to see Major Regter tomorrow, the first thing following lunch. And I must say, Galen, I see no option but to replace you."

"Captain, you do what you think is right. I did."

After Saville left, St. Cyr set to tidying up his report, as if grammar and diction mattered. Then suddenly it didn't. He stood up and stared vacantly out his screen window. He'd failed in Malaya, and he'd hardly been a success in the 4th Infantry Division. Now, he'd failed in the MIKE Force. This time, five Americans were dead because of it. Though he never intended to make the army a career, St. Cyr desperately wanted command. Combat command, real command, was the major reason he'd reenlisted to become an officer in the first place. For the captains, lieutenants, and young sergeants who commanded in Vietnam were America's warrior kings. They made the life-and-death decisions, reaped the reputations, and paid the price in flesh, bone, and nightmares. Everything in Vietnam, from the largest ships, to the heaviest artillery, to the most modern combat jets, existed to support that company commander or platoon, squad, or team leader in contact. Whether operating independently, as in the MIKE Force, or under some battalion, brigade, or division commander, they were the only element who truly mattered. Everyone else managed, directed, followed, or supported.

Kapunk! St. Cyr looked up to see sparks shoot through the teamhouse roof. He hit the floor, his arms wrapped over his neck and head, and waited for follow-on explosions. When none came, he was up and running for the teamhouse. He reached the kitchen door just as Cohen crashed out in a plume of acrid smoke and dust. Moans cries and shouts came from within.

A flashlight beam sliced the darkness. Biloskirka called for the medics while Ferris shouted orders to get the ambulance.

"The dispensary," Cohen choked. "We need stretchers!"

They sprinted down a row of Montagnard barracks to the dispensary. Battering open the locked door, they grabbed an armful of stretchers, and ran back to the teamhouse, prepared to hit the ground when any explosions signaled the arrival of the main salvo. Their luck seemed to hold. Dumping the pile at Ferris's feet, they unfolded the first stretcher and elbowed their way inside. Smoke and dust blinded and choked them as they bumped through the darkness to a flashlight beam below Biloskirka's voice. Ryan's barely visible arms were frantically tying a tourniquet.

"It's Silvers," Ryan wheezed. "Get him out fast."

With furious seemingly stop-action motions, they wrestled Silvers up on the stretcher. As they lifted, St. Cyr slipped and fell, banging the stretcher against the wall. Silvers emitted an agonized but feeble groan as St. Cyr wobbled back to his feet.

Frenzied seconds later, they lurched out of the choking tunnel of smoke and dust into the clear night air. It was startlingly cool. As he fought for breath, a front line ambulance pulled up. Behind them, Toller and Rayne crashed out with another stretcher victim. As soon as the two stretchers were strapped in place, he banged on the rear and called, "clear!"

As the ambulance sped away, a three-quarter-ton truck pulled up. More stretchers were thrust up into its bed. Magnuson ran over with a radio.

"It's on the medevac freq," he told St. Cyr. Before he could key the set, Ferris's voice called out that the 71st Evac Hospital had been notified and was standing by.

"That's the last one," Knuudsen banged on the side of the truck. "Get going!"

As the truck shot away, horn blaring, St. Cyr looked at Cohen. "Think Silvers'll make it?"

"Trung-oui," Cohen's eyes glistened in the darkness. "He was dead when we threw him on the stretcher. I don't think Grant'll make it either."

"But I heard Silvers groan."

"That was you."

"Me?"

The lights flashed, then dimmed, then flashed again. St. Cyr looked down at his soaked trousers, tee shirt, and hands, and discovered it was blood. Nearby, Ryan stared off into the distance through stupefied eyes as he talked quietly with Ferris and Regter.

"It was a grenade, sir. One of the guys started to play with a grenade. We told him to put the sonuvabitch down, but he pulled the pin and said that we were going to separate the men from the boys. After that, he passed it to Grant, who passed it to Silvers. Silvers said that this was enough bullshit, and tried to put the pin back in. It slipped, and we all heard the pop. Silvers called for everyone to stay down, and tried to run it out of the building. When he saw he wasn't going to make it, he doubled his body over and screamed for everyone to take cover. That's when it went off." Ryan choked, dirty tears coursing down his left eye. "Goddammit, sir, that's two of us this month. Medics always get the bad luck."

As Regter turned away, Ryan shouted after him.

"Major, Silvers' brother's coming down tomorrow. He's a Marine up in I Corps. They were going to Australia on R&R together."

A pained look passed between Regter and Ferris.

"Sir," said Ferris, "As Silvers' commander, I'd appreciate it if you let me handle it."

"All right," Regter nodded, "but send him in to see me afterwards." Then he was off to notify Cox.

Ryan was standing under the shower fully clothed, staring at the bloody water running down the drain, when St. Cyr stuck his head through the latrine door.

"Hey, Kev, is what Boris just told me true?"

"You mean my early out?"

"That's right."

"Yeah, it's true."

"So you won't be making this next operation."

"The hell I won't."

"The hell you will. You can't come out of the field and report in to medical school some three weeks later."

"Who say's I can't?"

"I do. You need to get back to the states as soon as possible."

"Hey, no offense Trung-oui, you're OK, but fuck you."

"C'mon Kev. It's in your own best interest."

Ryan stared at the water tumbling down the drain. "El Tee, I decide what in my own best interest. Understand?"

"Silvers'd want you to leave..."

"He'd want me to do my job. You didn't see him leaving. Shit, he already had eighteen months in country and was getting ready to extend another six. Besides, you assholes need me out there."

"We've got medics in the CIDG Hospital just waiting for a company."

"Well, one of 'em's going to have to wait a month longer."

Big Marty's was somberly quiet when Regter returned. All eyes watched as he strode up to the bar and ordered a bourbon straight up. Then, turning to the crowd, he lifted his glass.

"To Mervyn Silvers, and all our dead!"

"Mervyn Silvers," came the muted echo.

After a brief rundown on the status of their wounded, Regter motioned St. Cyr and Saville outside.

"Jed, I'm tied up tomorrow. Can I get that after-action report now?"

"Galen will get it for you, sir. But there are some photographs you need to see when you read it."

"Photographs?"

"Right. A camera belonging to one of the LRRPs was recovered on site."

"By who?"

"By one of my men."

"When can I get them?"

"Harry Perkins tells me he can have them by noon."

"All right, Jed, get them to me." Regter motioned St. Cyr away and lowered his voice. "I've got a newly promoted captain coming down from CCN. He worked for me up in the Hornet Force, and he'll fit in well with your gang. He's taking a month's R&R, but once he's back, I'm sending him down to get a feel for how you operate. After that, we'll see where he goes."

"Very good, sir. But there is one other problem."

"What's that?"

"Sergeant McElroy. He was with Galen's company when the LRRPs were killed, and hasn't spoken a word of English since. I thought he'd come around, but he hasn't. Earlier this evening, I found him sleeping out behind the barracks."

"Behind the barracks?"

"Yes, sir. Out in the open. And he's been defecating into cat holes he's digging not twenty-five feet from the latrine. "

"All right. Have the adjutant get hold of the Group Surgeon. I want Mac on the next flight to Nha Trang, and I want him mentally evaluated. They must have a shrink at the Eighth Field Hospital."

When St. Cyr returned with his roll of tablet sheets, Regter merely took them and turned away. As he did so, St. Cyr felt an overpowering urge. It might have been the alcohol, or the weight of the evening's events.

"Major..."

Regter's head turned.

"I'm sorry I let you down, Sir. I, ah, want you know that."

"Lieutenant," Regter said sharply, "I've never doubted your loyalty, your competence, or your motivation. But your judgment worries me." Regter's hands rolled the legal sheets tighter. "I'll get back to you after I've had time to digest this."

St. Cyr awoke late the next morning to the sounds of thumps and scuffles. Peering over the side of his bunk, he found a young kid with dirty blond hair opening Moshlatubbee's old locker.

"You St. Cyr?"

He reached out from under the mosquito netting to take the extended hand.

"I'm Dan Balden, here to take 213th company."

Pushing back the mosquito net, St. Cyr sat up. His clearing eyes took note of Balden's CIB, combat patch, and cavalry brass. "173rd Airborne, hunh?"

"As a recon platoon leader. Before that I was a radio operator down in III Corps with the Mobile Guerrilla force. Hey, how's this Captain Saville? Any good? Or is he all bloody dress-right-dress?"

"You've never worked with Aussies before?"

"We had one in B-36, but I never went to the field with him. And the 173rd had a battalion of 'em back in sixty-five and sixty-six, before I got there. Been too busy killing bad guys to watch our gallant allies on parade."

"I wouldn't tell any of them that until they get to know you better. Saville's question will be: How good are you?"

"Hey. Four mobile guerrilla ops with Bo Gritz, and the Herd wasn't able to kill me off. Not that they didn't try…"

Wow, four whole operations, St. Cyr thought sarcastically, *you should be a real asset to the MIKE Force*. But as Balden turned, St. Cyr caught sight of the fresh scar tissue on his neck and shoulders.

He spent the morning checking on the company sacrifice, ate lunch in the indigenous mess hall, and then reported into the Head Shed where Saville informed him that Regter was tied up with Cox, Khanh, and Ngoc, but Harry Perkins had gotten the photos to him.

With his afternoon free, he decided to try a few letters home. But the same pen that had finally dashed off the LRRP report was blocked again. Balden's questions were getting on his nerves when Boris saved the day. He and Hoa needed a lift to the Air Vietnam terminal. After a quick stop to pay their respects to a young Marine, they were out the gate.

He waited until Boris and Hoa had boarded their flight to Saigon. Then the Jeep guided itself to a distant Jarai village. To his surprise, there were guards from his own company around the village, armed with M2 carbines and BARs in lieu of their recently issued M16s. More uniformed troops were visible inside the village.

"*Swas'm la'i*," he greeted the pair at the gate.

"*M'nam Lu'u*," they smiled back. "K'sor G'hlen, you are not expected."

"No. Let me pass," he winked. "There is woman I must see."

"Ha, a woman" The gap-toothed smiles widened. "Certainly you will pass. But first must get permission."

"Permission," he wondered aloud. "But I am commander!"

The guard shrugged uncomfortably. "My commander, you cannot pass until permission has been received. There is council..."

"FULRO?"

The guard looked away to watch a third guard hurry to H'nek's long-house, step up the male ladder, and disappear inside. Minutes later, the guard emerged to flash a series of hand signals.

"Apologies, my commander, you must return when council finish."

"But, it is just a woman I wish see..."

"My commander, such are orders."

"Then I shall return," he grinned. "Certainly it ill omen when hard fighting warriors such as ourselves cannot see their women when come from field."

The guards grinned their appreciation, giving a friendly wave as he backed the Jeep into a circle and pointed it back down the road.

Fifteen minutes later, he was spinning through a tight turn into the gate of the compound when he spotted Harry Perkins.

"Hey, Harry!"

Perkins turned.

For a second, St. Cyr hesitated, but Regter's last words rang in his mind. "Been down to the Jarai village lately? Some kind of conference going on. They're not letting anyone in."

Glan Perr, Ney Bloom, B Rob Ya, Rchom Jimm, Blek, Blir, Piere, Elvis, Y Mlo, and a host of other commanders sat in the great room of Rahlen H'nek's longhouse, notebooks in hand.

"...The general uprising decision will take place as promised," H'nek continued in French. "But there is change from the strategy announced at Bu Prang. President Y B'ham has concurred with Me Sao that we not take Pleiku. Our Jarai capital can be taken, but not held. Too many Tiep-zap and Meerika will contest us. Too many lives will be lost. Our principal goal is now the liberation of Ban Me Thuot..."

An angry murmur sounded among the non-Ede cadres. She let it die down, then raised her hand. "Me Sao entrusts this task to Y Bloom Nie's 1st Battalion, whose Jarai, Ede, Koho, and Bahnar will liberate the Ede capital. This Meerika," she referred to Regter, "has done much to divide us.

Ban Me Thuot will prove he has failed. President Y B'ham has tired of Viet intransigence, and will restore unity to our Front. To Meerika, Ban Me Thuot is merely a village. If we signal them pacific intentions, they will perhaps not move against us. Even so, they will not direct artillery and planes into the city to support the Viets. Your mission, Colonel Bloom, is to seize the radio station so that proclamation of President Y B'ham offering the Tiep-zap peace in exchange for autonomy can be heard throughout Dega Highlands. Only then will you move against province headquarters and 23rd Viet division. Captain Piere, as of this date you are Major. Your battalion will cut the highway between Pleiku and Ban Me Thuot at Buon Blech. Now that they have taken Blek's father, you must move on foot. In the south, camp strike forces at Duc Het will rise to attack the Viets at Dak Mil district headquarters and block Highway Fourteen. Lieutenant Colonel Glan Perr, you command the reserve. Your mission will come from Me Sao himself..."

"And Kontum?" demanded Elvis, who as a Sedang had some interest in the town.

"Camp strike forces must take it. Our objective is Ban Me Thuot."

"And Cheo Reo," demanded another voice, "Cheo Reo is key."

"Enough!" H'nek ordered. "Who here is the woman? You have all received battle orders. Operations commence when the next new moon rises. Captain Rob Ya, what is that on the calendar?"

"Eighth month, twenty-eighth day," he replied.

"There," she said, "an auspicious number. Brothers, you must seize and retain your objectives until the Viets grant us autonomy."

"But Duc Het," protested a voice in Sedang. "We there last month. Duc Het camp strike forces cannot seize and hold their own wives..."

"They will be assisted by MIfors companies of Captain Y Nu'u of Nha Trang..."

"Nha Trang? What of the Cham?"

"Enough bickering," ordered Glan Perr, standing to take his place beside H'nek. "You have received your orders. Much you cannot know until the hour."

"This," proclaimed Elvis, rising to glare at Glan Perr, "not what Sedang and Bahnar agree to at Bu Prang."

Ney Bloom, Jimm, and Rob Ya rose to take their places beside Glan Perr. Below the glaring threats, H'nek's words sounded soft and clear.

"Brother Elvis, Siu Dot not with us now, but he can be summoned if necessary. Our centipede yet has a fang or two."

Elvis raised the back of his hand to display the cobra-head tattoos marking his status as a sorcerer. "Even with fangs, your centipede has reason to fear me."

"What can you do to Brother Dot that Master of the Sky has not already done?" cooed H'nek. "Shall I send him your message?"

"Do so. I not fear Siu Dot." As Elvis sat back down, there was a challenge from the rear of the longhouse. A guard called in that the Man-Bear wished entrance.

"So much for this revolt," sneered Elvis, noting the concern on most brows. "Even the Meerika know."

"Bid him enter," called H'nek.

The door slid open, and Harry Perkins stepped in wearing a French military jacket over an old loincloth, his head covered by a black Basque beret.

"When cadres such as ours meet," said Harry in Rhade, stressing the plural possessive, "is best that commander responsible for security stay with his men. Otherwise, unexpected visitors might approach."

"You," H'nek agreed, "were not expected."

"Yet I hope I am not unwelcome. I came speak with Me Sao."

"Late already," cut in Glan Perr. "He has departed."

"A misfortune," mused Harry, "I wished see this Jarai with an Ede name."

"You," H'nek nodded to Ney Bloom, Piere, and Glan Perr, "will remain when others leave. As will Man-Bear."

Harry sat on a mat they had placed for him in a far corner of the room. Ney Bloom, Piere, and Glan Perr sat between himself and the door. H'nek paced back and forth behind them.

"I can send you see Me Sao now, if such you wish, but better to allow time to arrange your trip."

"Where to?" smiled Harry. "A certain burial ground near Plei Djereng?"

"If so you wish." H'nek did not return his smile.

"Not wish. I would see Me Sao here, where many eyes and tongues would see and speak of my death."

"Why speak of death? Even I must travel great journeys to speak with Me Sao. Always there is risk."

"But, you said you can send me see Me Sao now."

"Merely," smiled H'nek, turning girlish, "one form of speaking."

Meaning, thought Harry, she had decided not to kill him. Not yet.

"Is important," he continued, "that Me Sao hear me. Can you give him my message?"

"Certainly."

"Then tell him this: Any revolt now will fail. There are too many Viets, and too many Americans, whose enemy are too many Viet Cong. My commander, long a friend to the Dega, advises this; help us win, or stay out of our way, but do not fight our allies. You have many friends and brothers among us who wear Green Beret. We do not wish to fight Dega. But we are warriors. If revolt comes, and our leaders order us fight, then fight we must. Whoever they say to fight, even our brothers!"

H'nek stopped pacing to lean gently forward and snag her finger under Harry's numerous bracelets. Her eyes stared into his.

"Even against brothers from clans whose spirit signs you wear? Such is what your oath is worth?"

"I will not. But those like me will be sent away. Replaced by steel-hat soldiers who have never seen Dega people. These will come in great numbers and be told only that you are enemy. Viet Cong! Your revolt will not last five suns. You will not take Pleiku. You cannot hold Ban Me Thuot. You will be run into Kampuchea, where Viet Cong will make you slaves. Time has changed in these Dega highlands since Me Sao was a warrior. Indeed, much has changed since I was with Y B'ham at Bu Prang. Please tell this to Me Sao. Now, with your permit, I leave."

As Harry rose to go, Ney Bloom and Piere looked away. Only Glan Perr looked to H'nek for instructions. She nodded her head. As Harry reached the door, he turned back.

"You have here competent military advisors. Listen to them. Convey their judgment to Me Sao."

"He has reason," mused Ney Bloom in French after Perkins had left, giving voice to all their thoughts. "But we too are soldiers, and soldiers must obey."

Lieutenant Colonel Cox had just been raked over the coals by the deputy group commander for fiscal shortcomings in two camps out of Qui Nhon when Regter slipped quietly into his office and closed the door. Cox shot Regter a steely-eyed glare, which Regter ignored as he eased himself into a chair.

"I'm busy, Major."

"Yessir, but we've got to talk."

"Dammit, I just told you I'm busy. By the way, that was a fine ceremony your people put on for General Phu's promotion the other day, but we could have done without the FULRO scarves. If it had been anyone but Phu, we'd both be in hot water."

"Minor stuff, sir. I've got hotter water."

Cox did not appreciate subordinates telling him how hot the water was, but something in Regter's demeanor urged him to listen.

"Go on."

"It may have been my people that killed the LRRPs."

"What?"

"One of my companies..."

"Are we talking about Yards?"

"We're talking about Yards and Americans. One American in particular. Master Sergeant McElroy, who appears to have been there when it happened."

"Regter, are you telling me an American NCO was in on killing the LRRPs?"

"That may have been the end result."

"What the hell do you mean 'may have been'?" Cox slammed his fist on his desk. "What does McElroy have to say about it?"

"He can't say anything, sir..."

"What? He's got a lawyer already?"

"Nossir. He hasn't spoken a word of English since he got off this operation. He spends his nights sleeping on the ground outside his room, and shitting into cat-holes instead of using the latrine. My interview with him was just conducted through an interpreter."

"So he's playing crazy?"

"He's not playing anything, Colonel. He's gone over the edge. I've taken the liberty of notifying the Group Surgeon. Mac will be on a plane later today, headed for the Eighth Field Hospital. Depending upon what they find, he'll likely be sent back to the States."

"What are you up to, Regter? Getting him off the hook for murder?"

"With all due respect, Colonel." Anger flashed in Regter's eyes. "Mac was out behind the lines back when you were a cadet. He taught me the ropes of this business, and he damned sure taught whoever it was that taught you. I've seen him kill his share of men, but he's never murdered anyone."

"And what the hell would you call the LRRPs?"

"Under the circumstances, an accident of war."

"That's for a judge and jury to decide."

"Sir, are you going to prefer charges?"

"Major, I don't like your goddammed tone. What the hell else would I do?"

"Well, you might first discuss this with General Rock. He's had his share of bad publicity lately, and may prefer that we handle it in-house."

"Regter, get the hell out of here! I've heard enough."

Regter rose from his seat. He would have saluted, but Cox had already turning to reach for the phone.

The strains of 'Maryanne Barnes' echoed through the late afternoon compound as Harry Perkins knocked on Regter's door. As he entered, Regter lay down a book: Liddell Hart's study of T. E. Lawrence and the Arab campaign.

Harry glanced up at the rough olive-drab bookshelf. Past a dog-eared copy of Larteguy's *The Centurions*, Hickey's *Eaters of the Forest*, an army pamphlet on minority groups of South Vietnam, Hemmingway's *For*

Whom the Bell Tolls, and *Field Manual 31-21: Special Forces Operations,* was an unopened bottle being used as a bookend.

"I don't know about you, Boss, but I could use a drink."

Regter nodded. "So," he grimaced as Harry mixed the bourbon and waters. "The news is that bad, huh?"

"I don't know, Boss. The news may not be that bad at all. In fact, it might not even be news. And then, it might not even be true. On the other hand..."

"Dammit, Harry. Don't get convoluted on me. I've had enough of that from Mac and St. Cyr. What the hell are you trying to say?"

"Boss," Perkins gritted his teeth. "I believe I've found Me Sao."

"All right, who is it this time?"

"Ouch," Harry winced. "That hurts, Boss, and this ain't going to be any easier. I think its Rahlen H'nek."

"Blek's sister?"

"The one and the same."

Instead of a scornful laugh, Regter nodded thoughtfully. "That's not as stupid as it sounds, Harry. What happened to Glan Perr?"

"He's her military advisor..."

"And Bloom, Jimm, Piere, Rob Ya..."

"Her underlings. They all take orders from H'nek."

"Who the hell put her in charge?"

"Apparently, Me Sao."

"You just said she was Me Sao..."

"She is, and she isn't. From what I can piece together, Me Sao is a voice she hears in her head. She's descended from him."

"Who the hell's going to believe that?"

"For starters, every Yard in this MIKE Force, though most of them think there's a real Me Sao waiting somewhere out in the bush. Hey, it's all mumbo jumbo bullshit to us. But to a couple of hundred thousand animists who believe that each person has three souls..."

"It makes sense, Harry. We should have seen it coming. Now, we've got an even bigger problem." Regter sat back to take a sip of his bourbon.

"Yeah," Perkins agreed, taking a healthy sip of his own. "Namely, who the hell's going to believe us? I wouldn't have believed it myself until today.

There may even be a real Me Sao somewhere out there, but she's the one calling the shots."

"You're absolutely positive?"

"I sat there and watched her decide not to kill me. Don't let those big eyes, tight ass, and sweet tits fool you. This girl's a tough cookie. The question is: Who's she working for? And the only guy who really knows the answer to that is on his way to the loony bin. Although, we still have Lieutenant St. Cyr…"

"Had, Harry. He's on his way out of here. He didn't play straight with me on the LRRPs."

"Boss, from what I've heard, if I'd have been out there, it wouldn't have been any different. Those assholes got what they deserved."

"They were American soldiers, Harry."

"Sir, 'were' is exactly right. With all due respect, they quit being American soldiers the second they knowingly killed unarmed women and children. Besides, being American doesn't make them a protected species. They get to live and die just like the rest of us. But that's not important right now. What is important is that other than Blek and Blir who're under her control, St. Cyr is the only connection we have to Rahlen H'nek."

"So you're telling me not to fire him."

"Boss, he's the one who tipped me off that something was going on down in the village. And he's the one who told me about the voices in H'nek's head. Firing him's the worst thing we could do right now."

"Just like you told me not to fire Romah Dat."

"If you had, we wouldn't even know he was dead."

"You know," Regter's voice took on a dejected tone, "up until a few days ago, I thought he was one of the best company commanders I'd seen."

"Then trust your instincts, Boss."

Regter pondered that in silence, then raised his glass in salute. "You win, Harry. I just pray to God you're right."

"So do I, Boss. Now, there's just one other little item…"

"What's that?"

"The Broken Bow report. We've got to send one out."

"You think we're that close to a revolt?"

"They weren't down there discussing next week's square dance."

"What do your sources say?"

"That everything's peachy-keen. The revolt is months away, if ever."

"You don't believe your own sources?"

"Not after what I saw today."

"OK, draft it up and I'll sign it."

"It's already drawn up. I just need that paragraph about how we've co-ordinated with our LLDB counterparts and considered their assessment of the situation."

"All right," Regter gave a distasteful shrug. "I'll see Ngoc in the morning."

"Yessir. By the way, the lights are on in their building. All sorts of activity going on."

"Dammit, Harry," Regter stood and put on his shirt. "I guess I'll see him now."

"Just a suggestion, Boss."

Chapter Twenty-Nine

THE MONSOON RAINS pummeled Pleiku with barrages that left drizzle and fog in their wake. Late each afternoon, as bone-tired men in mud caked boots and soaked fatigues clumped through the gate, their thoughts turned to private escapes.

Cohen and Ryan still hung together like twins, but Boris and Toller had withdrawn into their own worlds. Boris spent every off-duty hour with Hoa, while Toller hung with Rayne and his other Aussie mates. The malaise extended even to the Yards. St. Cyr found himself drinking with Balden and Ferris, while invitations extended to Blek, Rchom Jimm, and Ney Bloom were politely declined

On a bright note, he had returned to his room on the night before the company sacrifice to find a Jarai shirt and ceremonial loincloth on his bunk. No note was required. The richly colored threads and pearled beads above the long fringe were instantly recognized. H'nek had ordered them on the day after their betrothal. He decided to wear them to the sacrifice.

Y Thak met them at the village gate, but his eyes lacked their usual sparkle. In lieu of extending his hands in welcome, he sniffed and glared at the newcomer. Whatever malaise was upon the land had penetrated even Y Thak's souls.

"Him," he nodded at Balden, "take clothes and burn. They bring evil spirits!"

"What's the old coot talking about?" Balden wanted to know.

"Your clothes. They have evil spirits and have to be burned."

"My ass. Who the hell does this old coot think he is?"

"Two-thousand Yards think he's the MIKE Force chaplain. If he says your clothes have evil spirits, then we have to burn them."

"You and what army?"

"Buddy," Boris clasped a huge arm around Balden's neck, "choice is not whether they are burned, or not burned. If you want to command here, this is important. So take them off, or go back and pack. One bad word from this old coot and no Yard will ever follow you out the gate. Understand?"

While Knuudsen drove back to the compound to get Balden a fresh set of clothes, the Roundeyes retraced their steps to a spot designated by Y Thak. Here, Balden stripped down while a grinning Toller dowsed the offending clothes with gasoline, stepped back, and tossed in a match. As the flames jumped up, Y Thak squatted close in to study their form. Satisfied, he ordered the still naked Balden to walk backwards to the village. Just forward of the spirit gate, Thak ordered a halt. After sniffing at the scars on Balden's shoulders and chest, he motioned Blek aside and whispered.

"Well?" St. Cyr asked in Jarai.

"I'm freezing my ass off," Balden cut in. "Get this goddam show on the road."

"Thak say no can smell," grunted Y Diet K'por, "but believe still have bad spirits. We decide. We want, he can enter. Y Thak say better send away."

"He's a new company commander; we can't send him away. I don't think the major is ready to replace him just because of bad spirits."

"Then he stay." K'por didn't sound terribly enthusiastic. Ten minutes later, after Big Knute had returned with a new set of clothing, Balden was led to the longhouse.

"It was easier with the Cambodes," he griped. "All I had to do was run around and bite the Buddha every time we got in a firefight. Shit! I nearly choked to death the first time I got hit. Bit right through that sucker."

The *mnam pay* improved Balden's disposition, but did little for Y Thak's. He had his assistant clasp Balden's bracelet on, and hurried away as soon as the invocations were over. Despite the inauspicious start, the younger troops in Balden's company mobbed the mnam pay jars. But after the required two measures had been drunk, many older hands slipped away. After numerous turns on the straw, Balden was bundled into a Jeep which Knuudsen pointed precariously towards the MIKE Force compound.

"Starting today," grumbled Saville, "no more sacrifices on any day preceding an operation. I'll be feeling this tomorrow."

"Uuangh," agreed Blek. "Come our longhouse. Eat!"

Inside the darkened interior of Blek's longhouse, everyone dug greedily into chicken and taro root. St. Cyr kept looking for H'nek, but she emerged only to serve the men and, once, to compliment him on his shirt and loincloth.

He returned to the compound after nightfall to find Balden sprawled on the lower bunk, still dressed and snoring loudly. After carefully folding and hanging his loincloth, St. Cyr grabbed his toilet kit and headed for the showers. Familiar laughter came from the far end, where Hoa's wet head was snuggled up against Boris's ribcage under rushing water.

"Hot water's out in our building," Boris explained.

St. Cyr discretely chose the furthest shower head and turned his back to them.

Balden was still slumbering when St. Cyr returned. After checking his Car-15, rucksack, web gear, ammo pouches, and map case, he climbed carefully over the end of the bunk to slip under the mosquito netting. He had almost fallen asleep when a soft knock jarred him awake.

"Who is it?"

The knock was repeated. He climbed deftly out from under the netting, and lowered himself over the side, taking care not to step on Balden.

Twisting the knob, he was bumped by the door as H'nek rushed in. Her lips met his as she wordlessly unbuttoned her tiger fatigue shirt. He nodded in Balden's direction, but she simply grasped his hands and pulled them to her breasts. They kissed, and sniffed, and caressed until he passed small biting kisses down her neck, across her shoulders, and over and between her breasts. She pushed him down. His tongue tickled around her navel, as his hands hooked in between her knees to cup under her buttocks and lift her up to taste her. Seconds later, she slid down over him to lock her ankles behind the small of his back. As she glided up and down, their tongues explored the recesses of each other's mouth and throat. Sweat streamed down their chests and stomachs. The darkness throbbed with heavy breathing. Then, he withdrew to hoist her up into the top bunk as quietly as he could. After he had slipped back in, their lovemaking grew bolder as each thrust and quiver passed unnoticed by Balden below. Within minutes, the bed was rocking with wanton abandon.

"G'dam arclights," came a voice from the darkness. "Whasa hell going on?"

H'nek silenced a giggle as Balden lurched to his feet, pulling at his clothes.

"You OK?" St. Cyr asked with forced innocence.

"*Mnam pay's* n-nassty sh'shit," grumbled Balden. Losing his balance, he fell as he was pulling his shirt free. Staggering to his feet, he swayed as he fumbled with his trousers. His skin glowed with an unhealthy pale luminescence.

"M'towel, where's m'towel?"

"Hanging from your locker."

"M'locker?"

"Straight in front of you, to the right."

"Goddamn! where's 'lights?"

"It's lights' out."

"Liess sout?" Balden staggered forward to snatch St. Cyr's still wet towel from the back of the chair. As he slammed the door shut, St. Cyr threw back the mosquito netting.

"Did you enjoy?" He let out a long breath. "God, I've missed you."

She nibbled his chest in response. "As I miss you, G'hlen. But I must go."

"So soon? We can go out to the back bunker."

"Cannot!" Her eyes widened in the darkness. "I would be seen!"

"So? Jimm will do nothing. We are friends. And this Siu Dot? He has not been here for much time."

She put her finger to his lips. "G'hlen, I have told you. We can be neither betrothed nor lovers. I must go."

He helped her down from the bunk and into her clothes, cupping his hands over her thighs, buttocks, and breasts as he did so. "You do this to see me suffer," he cooed.

"I would so see you suffer every night of my life," she whispered, rising up on her toes to sniff at his neck, and mold her body next to his. "G'hlen, I will not be here when you...return."

"Then I shall go to Plei Djereng."

"I not be at Plei Djereng. G'hlen, I love you." As she tried to slip out the door, he caught her wrist.

"You will be where when I return?"

"Not Pleiku! Not Plei Djereng! G'hlen, you will not see me again."

"You will be where?"

She pried her wrist free with a strength that belied her grace. "You cannot know, G'hlen. You betrayed us once already. Take care. Beware of enemies who wear skin of friends!"

"I betrayed you? When?"

"Not myself. My ancestor. It matters not. May the spirits guard you."

And she was gone.

Down past the indigenous mess hall, Rahlen H'nek slipped into the barracks area. At the third barracks she drew up against a screen window near the corner.

"Blek?" She paused. "Blek?"

A shadow stirred within. "Sister, what do you do here?"

"What I should not. My brother, take care."

"I always take care."

"Then take more care. Brother. Do you know that H'pak is with child?"

"She is not certain."

"You will have a son, my brother."

"You have dreamed this?"

"I dreamed him as a man, handsome and strong. You will be truly proud."

"We must drink to this son," said Rchom Jimm's voice from the darkness. Raindrops began to patter on the zinc roof.

"I go, my brother. H'pak awaits my return. Do not worry about your son. Jimm?"

"Woman," Jimm's voice joked. "You are a bother. It is good we never married."

"We will, Jimm. Protect G'hlen for me. If you do so, when this has passed, the Rahlen clan shall send your sisters my bracelet."

"Worry not. He is my friend and commander. Besides, Blek is his shadow."

"Yet he will need your help. Ai Die be with you my brothers."

The rain broke as she stepped away. Ignoring her motorcycle, Rahlen H'nek strode through the gate, her tears washed by the raindrops streaming down her face.

The night before, she had lain in the darkness, turning and thrashing as the whites of her half-closed eyes shone with dreams. While the rains whipped the thatch of the longhouse roof, her inner eyes were blinded by sunlight. Two hills rose in that sunlight. Two hills that dominated fingers of lower hills covered with forest and coffee plantations. And across the face of these hills, tiger striped figures swarmed and fell among explosions as Hong Klang swooped in to claim their bodies. Her nightmare even had a name. The M'nong called these hills *Duc Het*, the Brother Houses. A harmless enough name, but its sounds evoked that of air being parted by a cane knife with the rendering chop of a blade meeting flesh and bone.

For brief hours the next morning, 212th Company escaped the monsoon. While Ferris and Balden's men loaded out of Pleiku on C-130s bound for Ban Me Thuot, Saville and 212th Company boarded C-123's bound for Duc My. A cold hour's flight later they descended into a verdant valley surrounded by gentle hills. Ninh Hoa lay to the east, and the Cung Son Special Forces camp was somewhere nearby. As the troops deplaned to reorganize for helicopter lift, bright sunlight burned away the Highland chill.

"Damn," St. Cyr chortled to Boris, "we might have decent weather after all." Light hearted Montagnard voices agreed, but Boris shook his head. St. Cyr unfolded his map.

"What you looking for, Buddy?"

"Duc My. I don't see it on the map."

"Is not on that map. We are near ARVN Ranger Training Center, maybe fifty kilometers northwest of Nha Trang."

They trudged past a small flight operations building to find a helicopter apron with a mere two choppers standing by.

"Not our birds," grunted Saville, "but get your company organized for lift-out."

Twenty minutes later, 212ᵗʰ Company was lined up by chalks. While the Roundeyes and cadre conferred, Vietnamese women hawked fruits and foodstuffs from the road. Language barriers and barbed wire aprons proved easily overcome where trade was concerned. Most had barely finished bargaining when an armada of Hueys thundered in. An hour later, they were back in the fog and drizzle. Duc My wasn't even a memory.

That climb towards the headwaters of the Krong Pach was the hardest trek he'd ever made. Through heavily forested valleys and hills, they moved in old-growth forest. Trees shot up over 120 feet into the air. Strangler figs and mace vines, whose thickness rivaled pine tree trunks in Maine, spread everywhere. Under the dark forest canopy, nothing dried. Climbing meant trudging up and down, crossing streams whose slippery rocks and rushing waters could quickly carry a man away. Every few hours brought another waterfall. Up over one spur, they reveled in the sight of fields set on the sides of the hills. Each field was crowned by a small crop-guard hut, but neither villages nor crop-guard huts were occupied by anyone they could find. Over the next spur, they moved back into old-growth forest. By night, a large cat prowled nearby. *A panther*, thought Blek. No one ventured outside the perimeter to find out, and the cat was smart enough not to venture in.

Days later, they descended into a narrow valley and ran into their first booby traps. Two men had to be medically evacuated by jungle extractor, a task that tied up hours. By late afternoon they were again clomping upwards in a long snaking column.

Progress was measured in hours per kilometer. Yet the harder they climbed, the more his feet, bones, and back ached, the more certain he was that this was some divine personal destiny. On their short and more frequent breaks, he would glare up into the mist covered mountains and mutter dark curses to the Viet Cong regulars of Regiment 95. Moshlatubbee, he promised them, was a name they'd hear in hell.

At two hours past midnight the day after the medevac, Staff Sergeant Mike Dudley of the Duc Het Special Forces camp tired of his duties on radio watch and stepped out of the teamhouse for a chew. In an effort to quit smoking, Mike had recently switched to chewing tobacco. After spilling a spit cup over a carefully drafted cartoon, he had learned to take his chewing outside. Cartooning was Mike's lifelong hobby, and his satirically drawn views of Special Forces life in Vietnam had gained a loyal audience. Several published in the *Army Times* had been so well received, he was considering a career as a cartoonist.

Out in the darkness, he wedged a damp wad of Red Man into his cheek. As he felt the nicotine rush, he looked up in amazement to find the sky clear for the first time in weeks. For brief seconds, he enjoyed the unparalleled view of a sky totally cluttered with stars. Then, remembering that starlight had military uses, he ducked inside for his starlight scope, pausing to turn up the volume of the radio before stepping back out. Climbing up on the bunker's roof, he flicked on the switch, gave it several seconds to warm up, and then glassed the hills that dominated the Duc Het basin. Things appeared quiet to the west and south, but he spotted a small string of lights moving down a mountain behind the French coffee plantation to their northeast.

Local VC, he thought, or perhaps something more ominous. If he could get clearance from the Vietnamese at district, he'd call down a fire mission to the camp's two 105mm howitzers. That would get a reaction, not the least from the plantation's French manager.

As he climbed down from the bunker, he glimpsed flashes in the west, followed seconds later by rumbling as mortar rounds dropped into district headquarters. Dudley took off running for the teamhouse. As he crashed through the door, he ran into Master Sergeant Brady.

"Get everyone up, Top. They're hitting district."

"See what you can get from the radio," Brady called out. "I'll get the Trung-oui."

"Hey, Top," Dudley grinned, "You don't suppose it's the big push?"

"Yeah," Brady chuckled, "wouldn't want the El Tee to miss it."

Brady knocked once on Lieutenant Delier's door before pushing it open. Delier was lacing up his boots.

"That you who hit the alarm, Top?"

"Yeah. District's getting hit. This might be it."

As Brady pulled his head out of the lieutenant's room, there was a crashing explosion from the far end of their bunkered teamhouse. Smoke and dust boiled down the corridor.

"Everybody into their positions," Brady screamed. "Childers, follow me!"

Brady and the youngest team medic pawed their way through choking dust and smoke to the radio room. Under the beam of Brady's flashlight, they found Dudley's mangled body pasted with his latest cartoons. An 82mm mortar round had penetrated the bunker roof directly above the radio.

"Get the hell out of here," Brady ordered.

They had no sooner cleared the building when a salvo of mortar and rocket fire rained into the camp. Up in the command bunker, Delier huddled with Captain Bao, the new LLDB camp commander, who was screaming Vietnamese into a radio handset.

"It's district," Delier explained to Brady, "they need help."

"What's Bao telling 'em?"

"Check's in the mail. We'll give 'em fire support for now, but we're short troops. I need a headcount from the companies before we launch the alert company, and send Rodriguez down to the gun crews. They're going to need supervision.

"Got it. El Tee?"

"Yeah?"

"Dudley's dead. Make sure they watch the northern edge of the perimeter. The Dude spotted something in the plantation." As Brady turned to go, Captain Bao waved frantically for him to stand by.

"Sumnabitch," Bao snarled, "Two company go recon in force desert last night. Go FULRO! Trung-si Duc just walk in Dak Song district. Say they take his gun and boots."

"What about Tavares and Heglund?"

"They OK. No boot, no gun, stay at Dak Song. Go pick up tomorrow."

"So," Delier shook his head. "We're down to two companies. D'ya think it's our guys that hit district, Top?"

"Not with 82mm mortars firing support."

The Black Arrow was sitting in the B-23 radio room when word came through Vietnamese channels that Duc Het district had all but fallen. A-293 so far was reporting only mortars and rocket fire. He checked with Delier to confirm that no heavy firing was coming from district, then took his first sip of coffee as the phone rang. The senior MACV advisor wanted to know when A-293 would relieve district.

"Colonel, from what I'm hearing, its only stand-off attacks."

"Well, my people say that district is under ground attack as we speak!"

"That's not what A-293 is reporting. Look, I'm going down just as soon as it's first light. Care to come along?"

"I can't. I have a meeting in the morning."

"Yessir. We're providing fire support." The Black arrow gave a disgusted shake of his head. "That's all we can do for now. Yessir, I'm well aware that they're vitally important...Nossir, I can't, no." The Black arrow's voice turned hard. "Colonel, that A Team has two companies out on operation, and two back in camp. All understrength. I'm not ordering anyone to reinforce district until I know what's going on. Yessir, I'm fully aware of what that decision means...As a matter of fact, we do have other options. It's called the MIKE Force. You go to your meeting, and I'll keep you posted."

"Something about maps," murmured sergeant Major Lusk as he took the telephone from the Black Arrow's hand, "makes everyone a goddamn general."

"Yes," Williams acknowledged, "until they get on the ground." He paused to listen to agonized squall of Delier's voice spilling over his radio handset. "I need to talk to Colonel Cox, Sergeant Major, but first get me through to Charlie Regter."

The voice at the other end of the line was groggy. When Lusk identified himself as the sergeant major of B-23, the voice was suddenly alert. It had to be important if the SMAJ was calling. As Regter came on the line, Lusk handed the receiver to the Black Arrow.

"Charlie, Ray Williams down here in Ban Me Thuot. I don't have much time, but we're calling Cox for help. Duc Het's being hit by mortar and rocket fire. Worse, they've kicked this off using delayed fuses. The team's senior radio man was the first man killed. This could be another harassing attack, or it could be the real thing. Right now there're only two understrength companies inside the wire. Two companies outside the wire deserted. I'm being told they deserted to FULRO, but could be they picked up rumors of this attack. Frankly, Duc Het's strikers aren't very aggressive. I need at least one company to sweep around the camp and clear any mortars they find, and I might need more. Better get your people ready."

As Regter hung up the phone, he looked to his adjutant, who'd been pulling watch duty.

"Have the Two and Three meet me in the C Team Ops Center with the latest company status figures."

Captain Stan Nowinski and Harry Perkins were still rubbing sleep from their eyes when they stumbled down into the Ops Center to find Cox and Regter pouring over maps. Despite the early hour, the TOC was abuzz. Vietnamese and Americans traced out red pennants on the mapboard while radio operators scribbled furious notes. Regter interrupted his conversation with Cox to mumble an aside to Nowinski.

"Stan, give me a recommendation as to who we can commit to this operation. Assume we'll employ at least a battalion. Right now, airlift's the problem. They have to be prepared to move into Duc Het as soon as possible. Harry, get some map sets put together, and check your order of battle with B-23's."

The duty NCO pointed Nowinski to an unoccupied desk and telephone. Within seconds, he had his notebook out, scribbling notes as he talked to the aviation duty officer. A half hour later, he pulled Regter aside.

"What'cha got, Stan?"

"Sir, I recommend 1st Battalion. Anything else we need can be pulled out of 3rd Battalion starting with 232nd Company. If we need any more than that, I'd recommend the new battalion."

"Why 1st Battalion?"

"Galen convinced Saville they'd find some VC battalion base, but so far they've only had contact with trail watchers. 2nd Battalion's pretty important up near Mang Buk and Plateau Gi right now. If Charlie's decided to hit Duc Het, he might also move against Plateau Gi or Dak Pek. Airlift's the other factor. Camp Holloway can only give us enough lift for half a company because they're committed to the 4th Division and 23rd ARVN. 155th Aviation down at Ban Me Thuot is much closer to 1st Battalion; they can only lift a bit more than half a company, but their turnaround's faster."

"Do it," snapped Regter, "and get with the Black Arrow's S-3. Ferris will take the mortar hunting mission, but if this turns into anything more, I don't want those companies sent in piecemeal. Any reinforcement's got to be a package deal."

"That shouldn't be a problem, sir. We've got the airlift."

"To lift in half a company? Listen, Stan, all that can change two minutes into any combat assault. You make damned sure that Williams and his S-3 understand that if this snowballs, I want those companies inserted together, even if it means airdrop. Is that clear?"

"Yessir," Nowinski swallowed hard.

Regter glanced across the TOC just in time to see Ngoc and several LLDB NCOs arrive. Ngoc gave a friendly nod in his direction before reporting in to Colonel Khanh.

Chapter Thirty

Upper Krong Pac'h Valley, Eastern Darlac Province:

ST. CYR LAY SEMI-COMATOSE between sleep and exhaustion in the pre-dawn darkness. Days of clomping up and down forested hills had reduced his feet to dead weights. Residual raindrops from a late night thunderstorm beat a slow rhythm on the poncho stretched above his hammock.

Lifting his hand to push the poncho up and drain the water, he felt an ominous movement. Something coiled and living was draped over his lower legs. Chills crawled across his neck and shoulders.

"Blek."

"Uaangh?"

"Snake on my feet is venomous?"

Blek inched the edge of the poncho up with the barrel of his Ruger. A dark form drew its head back into the recesses of its coils.

"White lipped viper. Maybe take shelter from rain."

"Tell him stand-to. Time to go home."

Blek grinned and murmured to Ro'o Mnur, who handed him a stick. He tapped it on the hammock a few times, and gently prodded the snake. "Stay calm," he cautioned St. Cyr. As it tensed to strike, St. Cyr fought his rising sense of panic. Blek waved he stick slowly back and forth like the motion of a cobra, then drew it back. The snake slid rapidly to the ground, paused for a brief second, and then took off. Almost immediately, Ro'o Mnur decapitated it with a machete. Smiling in triumph, Mnur raised the still writhing form.

"Morning meal. I fix."

While Mnur set to expertly skinning the snake, St. Cyr climbed out, stretched, and staggered off stiff-legged to join his fellow Roundeyes for a quick cup of coffee.

"Hey, El Tee," Cohen grinned through a week's growth of dark beard. "Got my bottle of Crown Royal?"

"No. And I've still got two days."

"Yeah, but remember; not just contact, it has to be with a battalion from 95 Regiment."

"And don't forget my Hennessy," added Ryan, whose own beard almost matched Cohen's. "That's Hennessy XO, not the cheap VS stuff the PX sells."

"The Hennessy's on the way, Kev." St. Cyr glanced at the date window on his Rolex. "Should get here today. A nurse I met at Camp Zama's bringing it in. She's being reassigned to the Eigth Field Hospital in Nha Trang. But so far, that Hennessy's mine."

"Only for two more days, El Tee."

"This nurse," Laurie's eyes lit up, "did you two...you know?"

"She's a friend, Laurie. A pretty little Cajun girl from East Texas who's saving herself for marriage."

"Only because she's yet to meet a handsome Australian," Toller winked.

Toller's vision of another Nurse Brumby was interrupted by Ro'o Mnur, who stepped in to hand everyone a sliver of bamboo with freshly roasted viper.

"Where's Spam?" St. Cyr asked.

"Having brekkie with Sergeant Thuan."

"How's Thuan working out?"

"OK," cut in Ryan. "I think he's offended he's not up with you and Blek, being senior Trung-si Nhut and all that. At least he's not some racist shithead like Dung. The Yards seem to like him. He keeps wondering why you put him with me."

"Did you explain that you're our only Roundeye medic?"

"Yeah, but he still thinks he's supposed to be with you."

"Well, that's not going to happen. Ksor T'lur was a sergeant in the colonial infantry when Thuan was just a corporal."

"You're comparing Army and Marines," Boris smiled. "Thuan has no doubt he is the more experienced soldier. He was a Senior Corporal in the Indochinese Provisional Battalion. That's like a Marine Buck Sergeant. And he made Trung-si Nhut in Airborne Division, who are as good as anything we have."

"Maybe," St. Cyr agreed. "But as long as I command this company, Dega leaders keep their seniority."

The other Roundeyes nodded in agreement, but Boris shook his head. "Buddy, like it or not, Vietnamese must take over."

Once the meal finished, they were back on the move—a longer, legged species of viper cautiously winding through the shadows of cathedral sized trees whose lower branches erupted in clouds of iridescent blue white and black butterflies. While the men marveled, St. Cyr agonized. A unit from 95 Regiment would choose its battleground wisely, but it couldn't leave a total lack of sign. While trail watchers might ghost through old growth forest, infantry companies left inevitable signs of passage. Cohen and Ryan were likely to collect on their bets.

As the head of their column topped a ridge, Saville's voice broke radio silence: "Bearkiller, this is Boomerang. Change in mission. Break. I have a chopper inbound to your location, over."

He found Saville, Ferris, Balden, and Bloom at a small village south of Buon M'drak, guarded by Raglai tribesmen in regional forces uniforms. Sergeant Major Lusk had flown in from Ban Me Thuot with a roll of maps, and was briefing Saville on the developing situation. Jed's normally friendly expression had been replaced by a worried frown. Ney Bloom kept casting dark glances into the eyes of his fellow Montagnards.

"Sorry about all your hard work, Galen, but that battalion from 95 Regiment will have to wait. The Duc Het Special Forces camp and district headquarters got hit with 82mm mortars last night, and 122mm rockets this morning. The A Team reported movement, but until two hours ago it had only been harassing fire. That's when an F-4 fighter that was bombing suspected mortar positions was shot down. B-23 has asked for a company to sweep around the camp and clear anything they find. Ferris has the mission, but we'll be standing by in case anything develops. Once Ferris is on the ground, Balden and you lift out for Ban Me Thuot in that order."

"How're we fixed for close air support?" Ferris wanted to know.

"Fighters and gunships will rake the target as you go in," Lusk replied. "With luck, any VC will keep their heads down until you've cleared the LZ."

"That goddammed F-4 wasn't luck," Ferris glared. "How'd they knock it down?"

"We don't know," Lusk confessed. "Could've been a stray round, a B-40 rocket, or a .51 cal."

"Or it could have been a friggen rock. When you get back, Sarge, how about kicking that worthless S-2 Sergeant of yours in the ass. We like to get the answers before we have to ask the goddamned obvious questions. What about the pilot?"

Lusk held his temper. He didn't like Ferris, but he did respect tactical competence. "Both the pilot and navigator got picked up, and no one fired at the rescue bird. From what I heard, the aircraft nose-dived into a rice paddy. Nothin' left but the hole. If you touch down to the northeast, like you're supposed to, you should do OK."

The Sergeant Major's assurances made Ferris's sphincter muscles twitch. There was a brief, painful silence.

"Right," coughed Saville. "Now you know as much as I do. If there are no further questions, get back and get your companies ready to move."

While Ferris pulled Lusk aside, St. Cyr's eyes focused on Ney Bloom, who had gathered the Montagnards for a hushed conference. From their pained looks and animated gestures, something was up.

"Galen?" Saville's tone was piqued. "Any questions for me?"

"Nossir. But, ah, anything wrong with the Yards?"

Saville shrugged and glanced back over his shoulder. "They've been like that since this operation started. Maybe they've got the jitters."

"I doubt it's the jitters, Captain. Ney Bloom's an old Eagle Flight hand. From what I've seen, he doesn't spook easily."

"No offense, Galen," Saville's eyebrows knit together, "but I think I know Ney Bloom a bit better than you. We all get nervous on occasion."

"True, but something's not right."

During their flight back, St. Cyr had the distinct impression that he and Blek were in different worlds. As he assembled the platoon leaders, Blek pulled the Dega cadre aside. After a whispered conversation, they rejoined the group, directing wary stares at Sergeant Thuan.

St. Cyr passed out the map sheets he'd been given, and explained their mission. Ferris's flight to Duc Het would take some 50 minutes. If the pickup zone was clear of enemy, the choppers would be back an hour after that. Under optimum conditions, it would be five hours before their two remaining companies would be in Ban Me Thuot.

"Beats walking," Boris shrugged.

The Roundeyes nodded, while the Yards merely stared.

"Shit," muttered Cohen. "Where's everybody's sense of humor?"

They backtracked to a small patch of valley covered by waist high tranh grass. After felling a number of trees with C-4 explosive and the odd claymore, they had an adequate landing strip. There was no sign of enemy presence, but the explosions made everyone nervous. Even the radios were working well.

St. Cyr and Blek huddled at the edge of their PZ, monitoring Ferris's lift. As Saville's voice clicked off checkpoints and pre-landing warnings, St. Cyr's mind flashed pictures of a LOCH shuddering down into FARP Last Chance. Emptiness gnawed at his insides. His mind's eye saw frantic tiny figures scrambling about. He gripped his radio handset with white knuckles. Blek tapped them gently, lifted a wagging finger, and brought St. Cyr back to the present with a wink.

The voices in his handset droned on. Duc Het was under bright sunlight. Jet fighters hosed down the LZ with miniguns, then peeled away as the gunships made their run. Troop slicks slid in behind the gunships and dropped to earth. Ferris' people scrambled from the choppers and charged for the wood line.

The gunships circled around to come in from a flank, ready to unleash more rocket and minigun fire. Ferris reported incoming sniper rounds, but soon called a cease fire. He had zero casualties and was pushing his men toward the high ground to his east to over-watch the LZ and await his remaining platoon. Saville alerted Balden that the choppers for his first lift were on the way.

An hour later, Ferris's remaining platoon was on the ground. The choppers were half way back to Ban Me Thuot when Ferris ran into a bunker complex near the crest of the hill. Despite heavy fire, he had one only man killed and several wounded. As he pulled back, Phantom jet fighters screamed in with 500-pound bombs that sent everyone diving for cover. The bunkers were well built and camouflaged, Ferris raged. They may have been invisible from the air, but they lay within sight of the camp. There was "no way in hell they'd been constructed in a goddamn day." He was going to personally punch out the lights of the goddam Det Commander and Team Sergeant.

Saville ordered him to screen between the bunkers and the landing zone, and alerted the battalion that they were now bound for Duc Het. Balden would go in next, followed by Bearkiller. Ferris would be in command until Saville got on the ground.

As Balden's first lift went in, St. Cyr's men huddled around the radio. "Piece of cake," Dan reported.

"Too easy," Boris muttered. "Little commie assholes are up to something." When Ferris reported a small group of NVA on an elephant observing them, Boris grimly shook his head. "Just like old times," he said, rising to return to his platoon. "And I don't mean good ones."

As Saville climbed aboard Balden's second lift, he was interrupted by a call from the Black Arrow, who needed to see him. While Saville diverted to Ban Me Thuot, Balden's second lift thundered off to Duc Het. There, the lead gunships were met by a hail of medium and heavy machinegun fire and occasional B-40 rockets. One exploded in a fiery ball, as did a second when it circled back to check for survivors. The trailing slicks took hits, but managed to touch down and disgorge their troops. As they pulled away, two more F-4s lumbered in to drop 500 pound bombs on the bunker complex. Both took hits, and one aircraft went down after its crew ejected.

Once Ferris linked up with Balden, they pulled back to the west. Despite anti-aircraft fire, there was little ground contact. Balden's few dead and wounded had been quickly loaded out. The ground was relatively open, and progress was rapid. Soon, they formed a crescent moon-shaped perimeter over-looking what would be St. Cyr's LZ. With an hour of day-light left, they had just started digging in when Lusk's helicopter slipped over the ridge behind them to drop off an ammo resupply. As Ferris was expressing his rare thanks, Lusk cut him off.

"Save your breath, Captain. There's lots of movement on the other side of that ridge. You're in for a busy night."

As Lusk lifted off, Ferris called Saville. "Bushranger, this is the Wheel. I need Bearkiller now."

"Righto, and Bearkiller needs lift. We're working on that. Out."

Back at St. Cyr's position, Boris flashed a sardonic smile. "Well, Buddy, we goddam sure won't have to go looking for the bastards now."

The damage to Balden's lift had cut down the number of slicks to less than enough for two platoons. Saville fired off a status report to Regter, and informed Ferris that St. Cyr wouldn't be in until first light.

St. Cyr's men began lifting out as the sun dipped towards the horizon. It was after dark when he touched down with his last squads at the 155th Assault Helicopter Company airfield on the edge of Ban Me Thuot.

"Took your time," Lusk greeted.

"Had to make sure there was still a Roundeye on the ground in case things got ugly, Sergeant Major."

Lusk nodded his approval. "You go in early tomorrow morning, El Tee. Captain Saville's back with the Black Arrow right now, going over the latest intel. You're to stand by. Word on the street is that you may go in by chopper, but it could be a drop. It all depends on what the 155th Helo's repair crews can do tonight. Major Regter has two C-123s laid on for the jump, just in case. They'll bring the parachutes with them. Anything I can do?"

"A 292 antenna and an extra radio and some batteries would help. I need something to monitor the action. Also, I'd like to get in and take a look at your situation map."

"I'll get you the commo equipment, but I recommend you stay here. Captain Saville will have all the information you'll need. Anything else?"

"That'll do."

Jed Saville arrived a short time later. After sticking his head into the airfield control shack, he called everyone in.

"The good news is that the jump is cancelled. Additional helicopters are on the way. We should get most of the company in with the first lift. The bad news," he tapped his finger on his map, "is that they've got a battalion somewhere nearby. Neither Ferris nor Balden were able to get into the camp, and more of 95C Regiment is on the way. The Black Arrow has called for the Nha Trang MIKE Force too, but we'll be the first in. We have to get into the camp, reinforce the defenders, and hold until the rest of the MIKE Force gets here. Our problem is their perimeter. It's mined, and entry is through a single gate near the airstrip on the west side." Saville dropped an aerial photograph on his map, and tapped it with a finger. "So, at first light Balden and Ferris move out, and we lift in. Balden covers our LZ while Ferris pushes down to the camp airstrip. Once he's in place, they clear as far as Duc Het's northwestern perimeter while you cover their northern flank. A striker will meet us at the gate."

Satisfied that everyone understood the plan, Saville was off to find his battalion headquarters. He returned an hour later with Sergeant Magnuson in tow.

"Galen, have you seen Ney Bloom or the other Yards?

"No, Sir. I've been looking for Blek and my own Dega platoon leaders."

"Bugger of a time to go walkabout."

"Something's going on, sir. Blek and K'sor Tlur should be here."

"So where in bloody hell are they?"

"Your guess is as good as mine. But Ney Bloom's father is chief of some village near here. Maybe they went over for a visit."

"Any idea where?"

"No, Sir, but it can't be hard to find. Bloom's family is well known."

Saville was back in five minutes with a Jeep. On a thought, St. Cyr asked the military policeman at the airfield security gate for the nearest Montagnard village. He was directed across the highway to a bombed out gasoline station.

"There's a whorehouse a hundred Yards down that road," said the MP. "Go past it until you see a gate with a big 'Off Limits' sign manned by some Yards in Ruff Puff uniforms. They don't normally let people through, but if they do, the village is just past the gate."

The blacktop ended at the whorehouse, where business was in full swing. A team of American and Vietnamese MPs checked ID cards and waved them on. After a short, bone-jarring ride to the gate, they found it unmanned. Saville leaned on the horn.

"Nice thing about Asia," he grinned, "everyone pays attention to cars."

A flashlight was soon making its way towards them. Two old Montagnards in plain green pants trudged up to the gate. Only one was wearing a shirt, both were armed with M1 carbines.

"We seek Ney Bloom's village," St. Cyr called out.

While the shirtless Montagnard opened the gate, his companion stood back, carbine at the ready.

As the Jeep reached this second Montagnard, St. Cyr motioned for Saville to stop.

"Which longhouse belong clan of Ney Bloom?"

"Cuoi will show for you. When wish leave, beep horn."

Ney Bloom's clan longhouse was the only one in the village with a 292 radio antenna. As they pulled up, Saville spotted two young Montagnards from his security detachment lounging on a nearby porch,

"What in bloody hell's going on?"

As the two miscreants jumped to attention, hurried movement could be heard within. The door slid open. K'sor Tlur's face peered out.

"Captain Savvy, please come in."

Saville shut off the Jeep, climbed out, straightened his uniform and pistol belt, and with short choppy steps made his way up the male ladder and into the house, with St. Cyr trailing.

An older powerfully built Montagnard introduced himself as Y Jhon Nie. Despite an elaborate loincloth and tribal shirt, he sported a western style haircut and prescription aviator glasses. Giving Saville a formal handshake, he smiled.

"I believe you know everyone here."

"I certainly do." Saville glanced around at Ney Bloom, Rchom Jimm, Rahlen Blek, K'sor Tlur, and nodded curtly. "And whilst I understand a desire to see their families, we have a mission very early in the morning and I need them back at the airfield now."

No one moved. Y Jhon Nie flashed an earnest smile. "As I need them here, Captain. We have grave matters to discuss."

"That's all well and good, but I'm their commander."

"Not here. Here, I command!"

"Perhaps in this village…"

"Not 'perhaps,' and not just in this village. I govern this province of Dega Highland Plateau of Champa."

"So, you're the FULRO province chief?"

"At your service."

"Then this is not some family dinner."

"My son is here, but this is a council of war. After they have done what is required of them, they may return to you."

"They may?"

"Or they may not. If not, you will not have a battalion."

"It's a bit late for that. Two companies of their comrades are already in the fight."

"And depending upon what we decide here, they can leave Duc Het by simply walking out."

"In that case, I'd like to discuss it with you."

"No. You will be taken below and guarded until we finish. But you may leave Lieutenant Ksor G'hlen to speak for you."

"Ksor G'hlen?"

St. Cyr quietly cleared his throat. "Me, sir."

"You? You're bloody FULRO?"

"No, Sir. I sympathize with them, but I think they're offering to let me argue your case."

"Against what?"

"Against a revolt."

"Right! Well I need to speak to you in private. Mister Jhon, the leftenant will return to you shortly. "

As Saville turned to go, Y Jhon reached out to grasp his arm.

"Captain, before you leave, we drink toast to Ostralya. Five years ago, I work with Captain Petersen. You know him?"

"Barry Petersen? No, but I met him once in Borneo. He came out to visit our patrol base."

"Ah! I work with Ba-Ri in Truong Son Force. Very good officer. He like drink Johnny Walker Black."

"Did he? I'm afraid all we had was beer. He liked that well enough."

Y Jhon Nie handed a glass to Saville. With a respectful, "Ostralya: oi, oi, oi," he clicked it against his own.

Saville took a sip, and found it to be the real thing. Then, following his host's example, he tipped the bottom up. The whisky took the edge off his anger. Strange country, he reflected, as St. Cyr led him out. A tribal chief who looked very much like a Borneo head hunter, drank Johnny Walker Black, and was on a first name basis with Australia's foremost guerrilla warfare expert, who was also the army's leading black sheep. After some whispered angry instructions to St. Cyr out on the porch, Saville trailed off after his guards.

"How is it possible," Y Jhon Nie addressed St. Cyr in French, "That you knew we were here?"

"I didn't. I knew only that Ney Bloom is from Ban Me Thuot, and that his father is chief of a village. Since everyone had disappeared so rapidly, they had to be somewhere nearby. So I looked for the nearest village, and asked. And here we are. It wasn't truly difficult, that."

"And what do you know of our plans?"

"I know that: One, you have orders to liberate the Dega Highlands some days from now. And two, the enemy has moved on Duc Het. Given Duc Het's location, I presume that this is in support of your own plans."

"It is not! Perhaps this is just a harassment attack."

"Harassment? You've been listening yourself. Is not that radio set to the frequency of Duc Het? Does it have a speaker?"

"No, but if we turn it up, you can hear over the *micro*."

"Then turn it up. Let's listen."

Y Jhon nodded to his assistants. As they turned up the volume, distant panicked voices flooded the silence.

"You hear that? What is left of the camp strike force is falling apart. We have heard rumors of your revolt for months. But we've also seen reports of an NVA offensive. Either someone in FULRO has betrayed your plans to the enemy, or this is a rare coincidence. Either way, Duc Het must be defended."

"It will be," said Ney Bloom, "by their camp strike forces."

"Camp strike forces, my Colonel? From where? Bao Loc? Gia Nghia? An Lac? They have their own camps to defend. Only the MIfors can save Duc Het."

"We have our mission, they have theirs. Others can reinforce them."

"Who? The 23rd ARVN division? The 4th U.S. Division? Neither will allow any enemy to block the major artery from Saigon to Ban Me Thuot, just as neither can allow FULRO to attack Ban Me Thuot."

"We are not America's enemy."

"True. But the people in Saigon and Washington don't know that. They will see only that when the NVA took Duc Het, FULRO attacked Ban Me Thuot. Obviously, you are part of an NVA offensive plan. Unless, after Duc Het, the NVA move on Ban Me Thuot. Then you will have to fight them street to street, as we did in Pleiku. Only this time, you will not have our support. You will last only as long as your basic load of ammunition. And even if they leave Ban Me Thuot to FULRO, you lose. Because when the Americans and Viets retake the city, and retake it they will, you will be forced to fight us and become communist allies. You have no choice."

"But we do have choices" retorted Ney Bloom. "If we succeed: That of an independent and non-aligned Dega Republic."

"Independent and non-aligned?" St. Cyr was careful to avoid a scoffing tone. "As Cambodia and Laos are independent and non-aligned?"

"Whatever they are," Bloom cut in, "they have their own armies, their own schools, and control the number of foreigners allowed in their countries…"

"Only in regions not controlled by the NVA." Under St. Cyr's gaze, Bloom averted his eyes. "Yes, they have only as much independence as is useful to the Tiep-zap. Did you not tell me that the National Liberation

Front views the Dega Highlands as part of *Dai Viet*? Great Viet Nam? That if they win, you will be strangers in your own lands, within your life times?"

"True," spat Ney Bloom, switching into Ede, "but we are become strangers even now."

"Then you have no choice, my friends. You must defend Duc Het."

Ney Bloom's hand moved down to rest on his pistol holster. From the corner of his eyes, St. Cyr noticed other weapon muzzles moving, fidgeting. He felt his stomach muscles tense, as they had when he was back with the recon platoon, standing by the LRRP bodies. He had always considered Bloom a friend, but now?

Bloom twitched uncomfortably, adjusted his web belt and holster, and settled into a more comfortable position. The pain of his dilemma reflected in his eyes.

"The spirits have betrayed us." Blek whispered to Y Jhon Nie.

"Not spirits..." Y Jhon Nie's voice was bitter, "...but certain brothers who are tools of the Communist's so-called National Liberation Front. While a finger points to revolt, the hands prepare an offensive. The MIfors is the largest, best equipped, best trained army we have ever had. How convenient that at the very moment we would use it to force the southern government to recognize our rights, the northern government moves against Duc Het. Ksor G'hlen has reason. They are forcing us to join them, or be destroyed fighting. Just as they intend to kill every man in this longhouse who does not join them. Make no mistake, my sons, from this day forward we are marked men. Perhaps our best course is to go to Duc Het, fight as we must, and do our utmost to limit our losses."

"Limit our losses," Bloom looked to his father. "How?"

Y Jhon glanced at St. Cyr. "We'll speak of that later."

"So you would have me abandon our revolt?"

"I am telling you that this can be no revolt. It is a betrayal. The masters of those who demanded it have decided for us. We should have called it off after Tet. Now, our fear of being seen as weak will see us labeled as traitors."

"Then myself and those with me are truly dead! And our shame is that Blek's own sister will order kill us all, and our own men will carry out that order with reason. Our names will not be spoken by our descendants for shame!"

"Perhaps," Blek agreed, "Me Sao will order us killed. But while my sister hears his voice, and listens, it is her own counsel she keeps."

"Then K'pa Doh will surely have us killed."

"We have always had to watch for K'pa Doh's assassins. Besides, was he not the one who assured President Y B'ham that the Viet Cong would not interfere?"

"And what of our men, whom we have been preparing for this? What will they think? Perhaps they will kill us here with the Roundeyes."

"My company follows me, my Colonel, as this battalion follows you. There are no betrayers here."

The others nodded in agreement.

Bloom turned to St. Cyr. "You understand that there are those within our own ranks who disagree. What of those who wish to leave?"

"They can take their packs and any personal weapons, but their military arms remain with us. No grenades, claymores, explosives or ammo can be taken. I will recommend to Captain Saville that we not alert anyone as to what has happened until after we are at Duc Het. You have my word on that."

"And what of we who stay?"

"That is Captain Saville's affair. I would like for him to leave you in your commands, but I cannot promise that. He must report this..."

"Ksor G'hlen," Y Jhon Nie interrupted. "You are dismissed. We must vote in council."

St. Cyr departed with two guards in tow to join Saville below an adjacent longhouse. Over the next hour, they caught snatches of distant voices: Voices raised in anger, anguish, and despair. At times, their guards' glances turned hostile.

In the end, the council agreed to cancel their revolt, bitter with the certainty that they would be labeled traitors and marked for death. After Bloom passed a series of code words over the radio, they descended the stepped ladder in grim silence. Blek announced their decision by simply throwing an arm over St. Cyr's shoulder and saying: "My brother, together we live, together we die."

Sometime after 0300, Duc Het degenerated into a mad struggle. Under the flicker of illumination flares, NVA assault troops moved in from the west and south. As distant shadows crawled through barbed wire entanglements, orange pinpricks flashed and rumbled from the trench lines. Two long columns of green tracers arced up the northern hill. Red tracers arced down. Brilliant flashes erupted, followed by waves of enemy soldiers pouring up through breaches in the wire and into the trenches. From their positions on a hummock two kilometers northwest of the camp, Ferris and Balden watched the attack unfold through their binoculars. They were too far from the camp to support by fire, and more concerned with their own defense.

Under hastily erected poncho lean-tos at the edge of Ban Me Thuot, the cadre of 212th company listened as Duc Het's agony played across two nets. Some 30 minutes later, Ferris and Balden's voices joined the melee as they beat off probing attacks into their own perimeter. The voices dueling across the frequencies sparked echoes of everyone's own worst fights, and the slumbering Montagnard bodies draped about the grass seemed an ill omen.

"We should've gone in today," grimaced Cohen, his face illuminated by Boris's cigarette. "They could have dropped us in."

"Yeah," agreed Ryan. "Better'n waiting around here. They could've put us down right on the airstrip."

"Nah," disagreed Boris. "Maybe it worked at Dong Khe, but not here, not now."

"Dong what?" Ryan's ears pricked up.

"Dong Khe. Up near China border. Viet Minh took it once. Next day, French dropped colonial paracommandos right next to camp. Big surprise, so they got it back. One year later, Viet Minh took it again. French sent in 1st Legion Para Battalion with brigade of Moroccans. That time, Viet Minh were ready. Of five hundred men who jump in, only twenty-nine made it out."

"Thanks for the confidence builder, Boris. Why'd they get the shit kicked out of them the second time?"

"Lot of reasons, Buddy. First attack was a test, to see what French would do. Second attack was serious one. More soldiers, better training, and they came prepared for airborne insertion."

"Sorta like Duc Het," Cohen drawled sarcastically. "Damn, Boris, that raises my morale."

"What's your problem?" Boris flipped his cigarette butt out onto the grass. "Ryan asked, I answered. Maybe you worry your time is running out? Shit, Buddy, all our time is running out. Maybe you survive Duc Het, and you go home to get run over by truck. End of story. At least here, you are dying for something besides crossing street. Here, you die among men. Men who remember their comrades. You don't want risk death? You shouldn't join goddam army. Does it matter if it is Dong Khe, or That Khe, or Nghia Lo, or Dak To, or Duc Het?"

"Damn, Boris," marveled Ryan. "How do you remember those names?"

"Makes 'em up," snorted Superjew. "Pulls 'em right out of his ass and floats 'em up in front of us. Trouble is, we can't tell the bullshit from the real thing."

"Assholes! For enemy, everyone was step on ladder. Every time, he learned. Every time he got better. In eighteen months, Mike force has come to Duc Het three times. Every time we run him off. Every time he comes back. And always he is larger and better organized. Listen to that shit," Boris nodded at the radios. "What you are hearing says this time he thinks he is here to stay, just like last time."

"Yeah, whatever," sneered Cohen.

"Essholes," Boris ducked out from under the poncho shelter and stalked towards the perimeter, his voice trailing off. "Once you been here six months, think you know everything."

"Shit," muttered Cohen, "I didn't mean..."

"You cobbers would've been smarter to listen," counseled Toller from a darkened corner beside the radio.

"Maybe," agreed Cohen, "but Big Boris gets on my nerves. All that Frenchy shit. What I wanna know is, if the Frogs were so goddam great, how come they lost the war?"

"Maybe for the very reasons Boris just mentioned," mused Laurie. "I don't know why they lost either, but I do know it cost Boris a lot of good friends. I suppose that's why he's here."

"What, reliving the good old days?"

"Oh, I'd wager it's a bit more personal than that. My impression is he's paying off debts to dead mates. Problem is; there's only one way to pay off debts like that. Did he ever tell you about his leftenant up at Dien Bien Phu?"

"Ha," snorted Cohen, "Boris wasn't at Dien Bien Phu."

"Right you are. He got hit between Kontum and Pleiku just before they pulled his battalion back north to drop it in. But his leftenant was. Didn't he tell you?"

"I don't remember..."

"That's the point, Mates. And you've known Boris a lot longer than I. Maybe you just didn't want to hear. Anyway, the same leftenant that pulled Boris out of the ambush up near Kontum, got hit pretty bad at Dien Bien Phu. And when his men kept getting themselves killed trying to reach him, he blew his brains out to make them stop. Reminds me a bit of what Rayne said about Leftenant Moshlatubbee. Anyway, you don't go through that without accumulating some serious blood debt."

In uncomfortable silence, Cohen climbed to his feet. "Gotta take a piss," he growled, and ambled off towards Biloskirka's dark distant form.

Chapter Thirty-One

USSF Detachment C-2, Pleiku:

COX WAS IN HIS command post, explaining Duc Het to some lieutenant colonel in painfully new jungle fatigues when Regter walked in.

"Sir, can I see you for a minute?"

"Sure, Charlie. Wait in my office."

Regter had spread some opaque sheets on Cox's desk by the time the colonel joined him.

"Sir, I took the liberty of having some Red Haze and Side-Looking Aerial Radar missions run west and north of Duc Het. If my Intel sergeant's right, and was assisted by a competent analyst, there are two main lines of communication running just north of Duc Het towards Buon Bu Diri, where they swing west into the Nam Lir Mountains."

"Sounds like a good area for a B-52 strike."

"Yes Sir, until you consider their frequency of use."

"What do you mean?"

"What I mean is that they're being used to resupply a regiment around Duc Het and Dak Mil, and ferry back the wounded and dead. Bomb them, and the NVA will simply move around. But put a battalion in at key points between them, and Charlie will have to divert forces from Duc Het to deal with them. When they do, we can employ B-52s and artillery."

"Have you discussed this with Williams?"

"Generally. I didn't get down to specifics."

"And what did he say?"

"He'll go for anything that makes the NVA pull back from Duc Het."

"And what's your plan if the camp falls?"

"I'd let them sit there for a day or so while we plaster them with arc-lights and artillery. After they've been chewed up fairly well, we can go in, clean up the remnants, reoccupy the camp, and hold it until Ray Williams recruits a new camp strike force."

"You surprise me, Charlie. I expected a more aggressive approach from my MIKE Force commander."

"Colonel, the fact that taking camps back is part of our mission doesn't mean it has to be done by frontal assault."

"Then what the hell do I have a MIKE Force for?"

"For independent light infantry missions in the enemy's rear, or in zones controlled by him, or in zones he's contesting. Yes, reinforcing camps in danger of being overrun is our mission, but that statement was drafted three years ago when Main Force VC battalions were our greatest threat. Under present conditions, I'd suggest that the MIKE Force is an *in-extremis* force. If there's nothing else available, send us in. But as long as the 4th Division's not tied down, I don't see this as an in-extremis situation. They're far better equipped for this type of combat than our Yards are."

"As a matter of fact, General Rock's been in touch. He's positioning his forces to intercept the enemy when they pull back. That's if they're needed?"

"If they're needed?"

"Yes. If it's something that neither we nor the 23rd Arvins can handle." Regter shook his head. "That doesn't sound like Rock."

"That's because you haven't seen the latest guidance for American commanders, Charlie. Abrams has been ordered to do everything in his power to keep U.S. casualties to a minimum. I just got off the phone with Colonel Aaron. He's alerted the Nha Trang MIKE Force for Duc Het. As far as Aaron is concerned, Duc Het is *in-extremis* situation, and the MIKE Force is our first option."

They were interrupted by a light rapping on the door. Cox's operations officer stuck his head in.

"Sir, they've been beaten back from the smaller hill, and all major actions seem to be petering out. Williams has called off the B-52s."

"All right, call Aaron and tell him we want those Nha Trang MIKE Force companies committed tomorrow morning, if possible, and tomorrow afternoon at the latest. Regter, I want your two other companies standing by."

"Yessir," Regter mumbled as Cox made for the door.

"Ah, one more thing, Charlie. That was Mac McClellan I was talking to. Mac just got in country. He's going to take the MIKE Force when this Duc Het thing is over. I'll get with you so we can set up a date for the change of command. Will you be in your office?"

"Until morning. I have a chopper laid on to take me down to Ban Me Thuot."

"Why Ban Me Thuot? Williams has everything under control."

"Because if I'm going to have five companies down there, I'm damned sure going to have some say about how they're employed. Besides, Ray needs somebody to take command on the ground if his XO gets hit."

"That's not your job, Regter. That's what Williams gets paid to do."

"With all due respect, Colonel, Ray Williams is a fine officer—but he's a territorial commander, and he's thinking like one. He piecemealed two of my companies in there today against my specific advice because that was all the lift he had. He should have held them back until he got the lift and launched them all together, or dropped them in. Now he's going to piecemeal another three of my companies in. Not because he's a bad commander, but because he's desperate to relieve the people he has in contact. That's why I need to be there. I'm not sending those companies in alone. They'll go in together, and they'll go in with a plan, or they won't go in at all."

"That's Ray Williams' decision."

"And it will be. But I want to make sure he hears it from me, if he hasn't thought it up himself!"

"Regter, just who the hell do you think you are?"

"Colonel, I think I'm the II Corps MIKE Force commander. That's the job you gave me, and that's the job I intend to do."

"You know damned well I didn't give you the job. But I've kept you there. Don't push me, Regter. Or by God, I'll replace you now!"

"Yes, Sir. Can I have a few more minutes of your time?"

Cox checked his watch, and nodded.

"Colonel, I don't know why you've picked this McClellan for my job. Hell, he might be the best commander the MIKE Force has ever had. But I do know why I was picked. I was shoved down your throat because I know the MIKE Force's limitations as well as its strengths. So I strongly recommend that you consider this: If we go in there like conventional infantry, we're going to take heavy casualties. We'll lose quite a few Americans, an Australian or two, and more importantly, take heavy casualties among the Yards. That means that we'll have a lot of Yards quit when this is over. It'll take months to build us back up to where we are now, and in the meanwhile, all the other missions they want us to do will suffer. We've got the fourth battalion trained up and a fifth battalion will be ready in just over a month, and besides Duc Het, we do have one other small problem."

"Your Montagnard revolt."

"It's not exactly mine. The sonuvabitch has been brewing for quite some time. And now that we know who Me Sao's main contact is..."

"A fifteen-year-old girl."

"More like eighteen or nineteen, Sir, but it doesn't matter. She's Jarai. They don't keep the same calendars we do."

"All right, an eighteen-year-old girl. Regter, that's it! I didn't want to do it this way, but you leave me no choice. First, one of your companies brings back a VC nurse. Then there's the LRRPs. Then you start telling Ray Williams how to do his business. And now you tell me that your main FULRO agent is an eighteen-year-old honey who screws one of your lieutenants. Charlie, get real. There is no FULRO revolt! It's all griping and scheming from the same malcontents who've been sniveling since sixty-four. Face the facts: These people are mercenaries. They do what they get paid to do. You've been over here too long, Charlie. Green forced you on me, and when this is over, it's time for you to go home."

"Sir, I'd love to go home. But until I do, I'll do what I get paid to do."

"Only for as long as I want you to do it, Major."

"Yessir."

"I'm glad you agree."

Regter drew himself to attention. "Sir, if the Colonel will excuse me, I need to get down to Ban Me Thuot to help Ray Williams in any way I can."

"All right, but only if you stay out of Ray Williams' way and don't do anything he doesn't specifically tell you to. Also, Colonel Khanh informs me that Major Ngoc has trained up a tactical command post group for situations just like this. You've got two companies on the ground, and three more either standing by or on the way."

"Yessir."

"Chop control of those two companies still here to Major Ngoc. They'll function as a provisional battalion under his command. We have to get the Vietnamese involved sooner or later, and now's as good a time as any."

"I'm not sure my people on the ground will see it that way."

"I don't give a damn how they see it. You'll do everything in your power to see that Ngoc succeeds. Third, take McClellan along. He'll be a straphanger with zero authority, unless you get killed or medevaced. He might as well start learning your job now."

"Anything else, sir?"

For a brief second, Cox surrendered to a well-hidden sense of humor. "No. I think I've screwed you enough for one night," he half smiled. "Sorry about that, Major, but it's what I get paid to do."

"Yes, Sir. I hope the kids in the body bags see the humor."

"Regter," Cox's eyes hardened. "Get the hell out of here."

Regter's helicopter touched down at the 155th Assault Helo airfield just as St. Cyr's men were lining up their *chalks* for lift-out. He climbed down followed by McClellan, Sergeant Major Slover, three indigenous radio operators, two U.S. commo NCOs, and a Jeep's load of equipment. A trailing helicopter carried Major Ngoc and his CP group with two Vietnamese radio operators. McClellan pushed past Regter as soon as he spotted the Black Arrow.

"Hello Ray, I'm Mac McClellan, the deputy MIKE Force commander."

Williams' handshake was perfunctory.

"Welcome to Vietnam, Mac. I understand you were a classmate of Aubrey's at the Point."

"Yes. We're good friends. Major Regter and I are prepared to take command of the MIKE Force if and when you deem necessary. Two additional companies will be here tonight. When they move out tomorrow, they'll be under the command of Major *Knox*."

"Right. Charlie, make sure Ngoc understands that he takes his orders only from you or me. I want confusion kept to a minimum."

"No problem, Ray"

"Ray?" McClellan's eyes narrowed.

"Charlie and I didn't make it to the Point," Williams smiled, "but we do go back a long way. Any questions, Charlie?"

"When are you launching 212th Company?"

"As soon as I can. Right now my XO's in the camp, and your units on the ground are working for him. Nha Trang's sending in a Captain who'll run their companies, but they won't get here until late. Besides 95C regiment, elements of the 66th and 24th NVA regiments are moving this way, so this could get bigger. As I see it, Major Greely fights the camp defense battle.

"Charlie, once we've relieved the camp, you take command of all MIKE Force units outside the wire and clear any enemy as far as Dak Mil district. Your subordinates will be your own Captain Saville, this Captain Truffle from Nha Trang, and Major Ngoc. Khanh's pushing Cox to place Ngoc in overall command, but I'd like keep him under you. You can phase Ngoc in as this winds down. That way, he'll be standing by to grip and grin when the press and VIPs arrive, and take his bows as the MIKE Force commander. Mac, your job is to give Charlie all the help you can. You've got zero authority except as regards Major Ngoc. If he has any problems taking orders, your job is to collocate with him and summon up as much command presence as you can so that has no doubts his orders are coming from a higher ranking officer."

"Ah, I'd rather remain with Charlie and observe how he handles the MIKE Force."

"That's up to Charlie. Consider anything he tells you as coming from me. Is that understood?"

"Understood. Hopefully this Major *Knox* won't give us any problems."

The Black Arrow choked back a cough. "Mac, I'm sure it won't be anything you can't handle. Good luck, Charlie, and I'm glad to have you on board. Oh, Mac, one more thing. If we do send you down to deal with Ngoc, be careful how you handle him. Ngoc has personally shot two subordinates, and I don't want him shooting any Americans."

As Williams climbed into his helicopter, McClellan leaned over to Regter. "He was kidding about *Knox*, right?"

"Well, he hasn't shot any Americans I know of, but he did kill a friend of mine back in Fifty-Seven."

"Nineteen Fifty-Seven? Wasn't that a training accident? Faulty explosives or something? I remember reading about it in our alumni newsletter. You've got a good memory, Charlie."

"Mac," Regter flashed McClellan a patient look, "I was the officer Cramer replaced. And the official report did rule it an accident, but those of us who knew Ngoc had serious doubts."

Regter led McClellan over to where Saville and 212th company were making last-minute checks. While Saville called Regter aside for a private conversation, St. Cyr gave McClellan a quick brief of his plan as turbines whined into action and troopers started for the choppers.

"Sounds good to me, Lieutenant," McClellan beamed. "What's your…"

He was interrupted by Saville, who pulled St. Cyr aside.

"Major Regter says that was a damned good job last night, Galen. He needs to know how many days you think he's got."

"That depends on what happens at Duc Het. I don't think we'll know until three to five days after. Intel needs to look for false Team situation reports that mimic our own."

Nodding a "sorry, Sir" to McClellan, Saville rushed off.

"What was that about?" McClellan's warm voice had turned neutral.

"Internal business, Sir."

"Ah," McClellan nodded knowingly and extended a tepid handshake. Blek signaled from the choppers that all were aboard. "Thanks for the briefing, Lieutenant. Remember, what you're learning here will stand you in good stead once you get back to the real army."

"Yes, Sir," St. Cyr grimaced. "I've always wanted to command a company in some fucking leg division."

"Now you listen here…"

McClellan was interrupted by a flight-suited major who motioned for St. Cyr to get on the chopper, and for McClellan to step away.

While St. Cyr double-checked Ro'o Mnur and the radio, Spam shot Ngoc a salute. Ngoc snapped to attention, bent slightly forward, and nodded back. Cohen's lip curled at what he saw as Ngoc's arrogance, but Spam's spirits soared. The Nguyen armies and their Highland allies were lifting off to battle, and its Lord had just acknowledged his worth.

Twelve slicks rose into the mid-morning air to join the gunships and scouts.

Once the choppers cleared the rubber plantations on the eastern edge of Ban Me Thuot, they turned due south for Buon Trap. Sooner than anyone wanted, the waters of Lak came into view on the left side and they hooked westward. Past Dak Sak, the fleet dipped down to hug the treetops. St. Cyr ignored the checkpoints flashing beneath them to focus on the sequence of actions he would take on the ground. The choppers dipped lower, then climbed up over a low range of jungle covered hills to barrel down into a narrow depression. From his right side, St. Cyr could not see the two hills dominating the depression's southern quadrant that gave the camp its name.

His ears rang with the roar of door guns while the choppers shuddered down to earth. As men clambered off the decks and struts, St. Cyr tugged Ro'o Mnur behind him. They landed knee deep in paddy mud, buffeted by muddy rotor wash as the slicks lifted off. As they trudged forward in the heat and naked light, Cobra gunships thundered overhead to unleash rockets on a distant tree line. Glancing over his shoulder, St. Cyr spotted a hamlet with tiger striped figures clustered around a radio. Balden's voice squalled from the handset.

"Bushranger Two-six, this is Three-six. 'Bout time you got here. Break…assemble your people on the blue smoke."

St. Cyr passed down instructions to assemble on the blue smoke, where he found a grinning Balden waiting for them.

"Boy, are we glad to see you. It damn sure got lonesome out here last night."

"There's more on the way. Any trouble with the Yards?"

"Other than the fact that their assholes are puckered up under their Adam's apples, they seem OK."

"Keep an eye on them. There was supposed to be a FULRO revolt in the next few days, but they almost called it for last night."

They were interrupted by Ferris on the radio. A mob of tiger suited figures accompanied by women and children was making its way down the southern hill and away from the camp.

"There's your revolt," grinned Balden.

"More'n likely some camp strikers and their families bugging out." St Cyr was interrupted by word that their second lift was five minutes out.

"You're on your own, Galen," Nodded Balden. "Where's Saville?"

"On this lift. He was reading Major Regter in on the problems we had last night."

"Hey, go FULRO, ungh!"

St. Cyr's retort was stifled by a call from Ferris. Concerned that they had too large a gap between them, he ordered Balden to close up immediately.

"Wilco," Balden responded. "Hey Galen, Saville's supposed to collocate with me. I'll leave Big Knute with a squad to bring him in."

"I'll give him your regrets."

"No need, old chap. I'll present them myself at this afternoon's tea."

"Only a week, and you're startin' to sound like a bloody Pom."

"Righto," Balden winked, his voice now nasal, "Mister Rayne did entertain us with a few tales of young Jed in Malaya."

The second lift touched down without incident. Though Saville tripped into the paddy, he emerged with his sense of humor intact and hooked up with Big Knute. After looking over the terrain from the ground, he opted to stay with Galen's men. Big Knute walked off grumbling while St. Cyr positioned his platoons within sight of Balden's flank.

Saville moved them forward by bounds, occasionally calling a halt while he glassed the distant camp and its surroundings through binoculars.

By early afternoon he could see the forward slope of a distant plantation. At first, he doubted what he was seeing, but Blek confirmed it.

"Black Arrow Six X-ray, This is Bushranger. I've got a small group of NVA observing us from the coffee plantation."

"Roger Bushranger," Greely's voice answered. "Are you sure they're NVA?"

"Hard to tell. The uniforms look pea green enough, but I can't see any helmets or hats. Request a fire mission, over."

"Nix on that fire mission, Bushranger. That could be our lost patrol."

Saville ordered everyone to spread their men out. They pushed cautiously forward, ears straining to hear the expected crump of mortars. As Balden and Ferris reached the bottom of the slope, the men began to drag. A cornfield lay beyond the far side of a small stream. Enormous tree trunks, felled to clear the airstrip, were laid end to end along the cornfield's southern edge to Ferris's far right. The saddle between the camp's two hills was visible above the cornstalks. Balden and Ferris pushed their men across the stream and down the cornrows. Further up, under cover of light forest, St. Cyr's men carefully searched for bunkers.

A loud explosion to their right triggered a firestorm in Balden's area. Sporadic fire from Toller and Cohen's platoons was quickly brought under control. Toller reported that he had received no incoming fire, but some of his newer men had panicked. Saville's calls to Balden went unanswered. Ferris was receiving fire from several RPDs and at least one company medium machinegun. Coming after the explosion in Balden's area, this had spooked his newer men. The sight of them streaming by, combined with the heavy return fire from those engaged, prompted others to run. A good half of Ferris's men were back across the stream. While he was busy trying to sort them out from Balden's company, Knuudsen broke into Ferris's transmission, calling for Saville to move to his location.

They found what was left of Balden and several Yards crumpled up in a mud-swatch of blood, as if riddled by an enormous shotgun. Big Knute and Warrant Officer Two Rayne looked grim.

"Chinese claymore," said Big Knute. "They let the lead platoon pass and must've detonated it when they saw the El Tee and his radio. Killed four Yards. The newer men all took off. We're still rounding them up."

"Right. We'll return for the dead later. We can't lift them out just yet."

"We'd figured that out for ourselves, Captain," interjected Rayne. "We called you over here because: First, they're monitoring our transmissions. This has all the earmarks of a hasty ambush, and I'll wager they were gunning for you. Second, by rights, I'm senior man, but as the only Australian in this company, that needs a decision from you."

"Is that a problem, Sergeant Knuudsen?"

"Not as long as it's only temporary," grumbled Knute. "I figured you'd see it his way."

"Look, we don't have time to explain, but Mister Rayne was at one of Australia's key fights at Kapyong in the Korean War. So if this turns really bad, I'd like to have someone who's faced human wave attacks before."

"Captain, I have no problem working with Ray. But when we get back to Pleiku, I want Major Regter to make the final decision."

"Right. And out of respect for you, Knute, I'll tell him that I have no preference. Fair enough?"

"Fair enough."

"Anything else?"

"Don't forget," Rayne reminded. "Once we're through the wire, we need to change call signs and frequencies."

A Cobra gunship whuppered by overhead, its minigun buzzing angrily. Spent cartridges rained down through their position. As it finished its run, a salvo of 82mm mortar rounds dropped into the distant saddle, followed by the sounds of firing.

Saville dropped back as Ferris and Rayne got their men moving. He urged them across the cornfield with "all due speed," but the troops continued to drag. Frustrated, Saville glared over at Bloom, chattering into the indigenous net.

"See what your bloody revolt has done!"

"No." Bloom shook his head. "First, Lieutenant Dan had bad sacrifice, now first man killed. Men fear his spirits have brought Hong Klang among us."

"Well, if we don't get in that camp quickly, they may bloody well be right!" Saville fumed a few more minutes, then placed a friendly hand on

Bloom's shoulder. "I know you're doing your best, Bloom, and I appreciate your loyalty." And with that, he was off to check on St. Cyr.

212th Company was keeping a deliberately slow pace in light of their security mission. Trailing Toller's men, St. Cyr kept Rayne's flank platoon in sight. As the forest opened to where they had a better view of the cornfield, he spotted conical bundles of cornstalks as he studied the northern hill.

Their supporting gunships had left to rearm and refuel, leaving only the Forward Air Controller on station. As Rayne's men approached the cornstalk piles, heavy automatic fire ripped out, cutting down the lead men and driving the rest into cover. The FAC swung into a wide arc, and came back to fire his sole remaining marker rocket down into a middle cornstalk cone, which erupted in fire and smoke. Long minutes later, the gunships returned to rake the cornstalks with miniguns. On their second pass, large green tracers reached skyward. Both gunships took hits, but stayed in the air.

Rayne, busy rounding up and regrouping his men, asked for permission to shoot deserters. Saville nixed that. While Rayne and Knuudsen bullied their more reluctant souls forward, Saville ordered 212th Company to assume Rayne's mission.

St. Cyr and Blek moved their men down in a wedge formation with Toller in reserve. As they neared the cornfield, Blek passed among the platoons, waving his revolver and threatening to shoot deserters. As the gunships worked the cornfield over from a safer distance, 82mm mortar rounds bracketed Ferris' company. Within minutes, he was back with Rayne and Knuudsen, sorting his own men out while a U.S. Staff Sergeant and two new Australian warrants held in place with the small, hard core.

"Bushranger, Bushranger," Saville fought to keep his voice calm. "You will hold forward of the blue line. Repeat, the blue line. Bearkiller, belay last mission. Report to me. Acknowledge."

St. Cyr found Saville with Rayne, urging a group of men forward.

"Galen, change of mission. Get your company back to the far side of the creek. Verbal orders only, no one is to reference their location in the clear. Move south, policing up everyone you come across, and get next to those logs along the airfield. When I give the order, you will do everything in your power to push through to the camp. Pay no attention to your flanks. Duc Het has to be reinforced today, and we will accomplish that. Any questions?"

"Where will you be?"

"Behind you. But first I have to finish here."

Twenty minutes later, they pulled back to the creek. Movement was rapid only because many believed they were abandoning the fight. To maintain control, St. Cyr grouped his platoons together, a bad but necessary tactic for control. Once across the creek, he called a temporary halt while Toller moved Recon into the lead.

As they moved south along the far bank, they picked up stragglers. K'sor Tlur took charge of these, massing them into a separate group between Toller and Cohen with four of his meanest corporals in control. What started as a squad became a small platoon, then a larger platoon. As they reached the bottom of the slope, where the creek swung west, their rate of movement slowed. The men were stalling, waiting to see if they were moving away from the fire, or closer to it. When Recon crossed the creek again, they had their answer. It took a few minutes to reorganize. Toller took the right, next to the log windrow, with Cohen in the middle, Biloskirka on the left, and Ryan's platoon behind Cohen. St. Cyr was advising Blek to divide up the stragglers between the lead platoons when K'sor Tlur intervened.

"*Mon Capitaine,*" he addressed Blek. "Better to place them in front of the line as skirmishers. When they run, easier to shoot."

"Do so," grunted Blek.

K'sor Tlur nodded to his four corporals, who herded the straggler platoon forward.

"Collect their hats!" Tlur ordered.

As the corporals waded through the stragglers, pulling hats off, K'sor Tlur called the indigenous platoon leaders on his HT-1 radio:

"See men run, no wear hat, you shoot. Shoot kill! Tonight, those alive get back hat!"

St. Cyr said nothing. It was an order that would have cost Spam his life, but the Yards were willing to accept it from their own. He made a mental note to include that in his after action report.

While St. Cyr radioed Saville, K'sor Tlur spread the platoons out. At a nod from Blek, he ordered them forward. Automatic weapons fire and occasional mortar rounds sounded from the left, but Blek and K'sor Tlur kept urging speed.

Saville advised St. Cyr that he would soon join them. Across a drainage ditch and up into the cornfield, they came under light automatic weapons fire and occasional B-40 rockets. The men answered with scattered fire from the skirmishing line and heavier fire from the platoons. Blek moved among them, waving his Ruger in one hand and holding an HT-1 radio to his ear with the other.

"Keep fire. Keep men moving," he called.

The company stumbled forward, then hit the ground as scattered 82mm mortar rounds exploded nearby. St. Cyr felt his stomach muscles tighten, recognizing ranging rounds. The barrage would follow shortly. Saville radioed for A-293 to take the 82's under fire. More rounds fell, this time to their front, drawing screams from the skirmishers. The distant crump of the camp's own mortars sounded. Ryan's report that Saville was with his platoon was drowned out by the excruciating screams of a disemboweled skirmisher. Bareheaded men fell back to mix in with the rest, panic written on their faces. The better squad and team leaders berated their men into facing the general direction of the enemy and firing their weapons. Some did so. Others cringed in fear.

Ro'o Mnur aimed vicious kicks at two who were frozen near his feet. Reluctantly, they rose to fire a few wild shots. K'sor Tlur approached with an unholstered .45 automatic to grab St. Cyr's arm and point back to the far end of the cornfield.

"*Mortiers, Mon Lieutenant,*" he screamed above the din. "Call in *mortiers* there."

"Chef, that's behind us!"

"*Mais oui!* 82mm, 81mm *mortier* same same. Vee Cee shoot behind, company go ahead."

For split seconds, St. Cyr weighed the danger of placing his own company between two mortar barrages. It was insane. He looked into K'sor Tlur's eyes. Where some would have seen insanity, he recognized the genius of experience.

"Bushranger six, this is Bearkiller, fire mission, over."

"This is Bushranger, pass it to Dirty Letters yourself."

"Roger, but need your approval, over."

"All right; send it."

Saville reacted, saying, "Are you bloody sure?"

"Bushranger, I've got a crazed Montagnard first sergeant stomping on my chest to get that fired ASAP."

"Tell 'im he'll have to wait until my arse gets just a bit closer, but it's on the way."

Minutes later a barrage of mortar fire fell to their rear. K'sor Tlur and the Yard platoon leaders were up like madmen, screaming "Vee Cee," and pointing to their rear.

In an instant, the men were up, sprinting forward and firing as a mob. K'sor Tlur and Blek screamed for the platoon and squad leaders to keep their men under control, but only Toller and Biloskirka's men maintained tight cohesion. Halfway across the cornfield, RPDs chattered to their left. The men would not be checked. After an M60 burned off a belt of ammo in their general direction, and M79s peppered them with grenades, the RPDs fell silent. Past now shredded cornstalk cones and the smell of burned human flesh, the men sought shelter in a sandbag-edged drainage ditch running between the airfield and the camp's northern hill.

While Blek and K'sor Tlur sorted men out and reformed the platoons for a hasty defense, Toller sent a squad to check the camp gate. They were barely out of sight when an explosion sounded. Toller rushed over, expecting the worse, but found his squad safe.

The lead man pointed to two NVA bodies that had been shredded by a mine. Alerted by the bodies, the squad had tossed several rocks into the area to check for mines.

"Good thinking, mates."

Seconds later, Saville showed up with St. Cyr in tow.

"What's it like, Laurie?"

Toller pointed through a break in the clumps of tranh grass. "Their mine fields are supposed to be further up. Reckon the rains washed some down. It'll be bugger all to find them."

"Right," agreed Saville. "Well get to work clearing them."

"Cap'n, these mines won't be in any pattern. Some will be upright, whilst others will be on their sides or upside down. It'll take hours. Why not simply go around? My guess is the area to avoid is this wash to the left. All that sand appears to have traveled downhill. The far side should be safer."

"That exposes the men."

"Yeah. Mines, bullets, or mortars. Not much of a choice if we want to get in there now."

"You're right. But if they hit us with automatic weapons on that far bank, we'll never get the men moving."

"Your call, Cap'n. I'll move my platoon around to the gate. Any word as to whether it's open?"

"Greely has someone there now. I'll tag along with your blokes to take a look."

"It's your battalion, Cap'n," Laurie shrugged.

As Saville trailed off after the squad, Toller leaned close to St. Cyr. "Makes me nervous him coming up front like that. All these radios mobbing about, know what I mean?"

"He wants to show us he's willing to take risks."

"Cawr! I've been watching him take risks for the past half year. You mark my word—his luck's going to run out."

Back in the drainage ditch, Ryan was washing off the intestines of a wounded skirmisher. Two morphine syrettes were pinned to the man's shirt collar, and below the armpits his shirt had been cut away.

"Talk about luck," marveled Ryan. "The shrapnel sliced his stomach open, but didn't even nick his intestines. If we can get him to the camp dispensary and properly cleaned up, he'll recover."

Ryan had two Yard assistants lift the man up while he wrapped a poncho around his midsection. After it was firmly secured, he instructed the bearers to carry the patient with his stomach up.

"Was that our screamer?"

"No, his buddy. The same shrapnel that nicked this guy nailed him in the vitals. Blood, bile, and shit everywhere. I gave him one syrette, but he only lasted a few minutes."

As St. Cyr looked up, Blek flashed him the five-minute signal. St. Cyr nodded, and Blek radioed the platoon leaders to get their men ready to go. K'sor Tlur was busy redistributing the surviving stragglers among the platoons when a rash of fire sounded from the gate.

St. Cyr grabbed his handset. "Bushranger Six, what is your situation, over."

The only reply was static. As he repeated the call, Toller's voice cut him off.

"They've got bloody NVA on that hill! The incompetent bastards failed to tell us that there are enemy on the hill. And the farkin' gate is closed!"

Ryan rushed up with his medical kit. Toller's men stopped him at the wash, warning him of mines and that the far side of the ditch was exposed to automatic weapons fire. When Ryan tried to push past, Jimm grabbed his kit bag strap.

"Bac si, wait!"

Jimm motioned to a striker, whose comrade made a sudden movement, then ducked for cover. RPD rounds snapped overhead to ricochet off the far bank.

"See?" Jimm said. "When I say, you go! OK?"

Ryan nodded.

Farther up, Toller's point squad hunkered down behind the near embankment of the narrow road which ran from the airstrip to the camp. While several loosed long bursts in the general direction of incoming fire, one lobbed a hand grenade. When it exploded 25 meters out, they heard Saville's angry shout. As the grenadier prepared to toss another, his team leader frantically motioned 'No.'

RPD rounds peppered the far bank where Saville had last been seen. A Cobra gunship swooped in to hose down a nearby target with its minigun. As it went into a tight turn directly above him, Saville crabbed frantically back towards the point squad.

St. Cyr, Blek, and K'sor Tlur seized the same opportunity to push the company up the ditch. They were supposed to move by bounds, the platoons covering each other with fire. But once movement started the men proved impossible to stop.

Saville rejoined the point squad just as they received word to pass under the culvert and come up on the far side near the gate. With his radioman nowhere to be found, Saville limped along, lugging his AN-PRC 74. Minutes later, a lone camp striker emerged from a small shack and dashed down to open the gate. While the gunship made another pass, sending hot spent brass raining down, 212th Company poured through the culvert, up through the gate, past the camp dispensary, and into the trenches of the southern hill.

Major Greely was overjoyed at their arrival, but excoriated Lieutenant Delier for failing to tell him that NVA were still on the northern hill. A-293's Team members offered no excuses. Between manning trenches, firing illumination, adjusting mortar fire, coordinating air strikes, resupplying ammunition, treating the wounded, evacuating Dudley's remains, restringing wire, reseeding mines, trying to keep strikers and their families from deserting, and answering Greely's numerous demands for information, they'd had no rest. So they entrusted the defense of the smaller northern hill to their Vietnamese counterparts, and accepted their word that the hill had been cleared. Greely wanted guarantees that it would be, and called for a commander's conference in the camp bunker. Since he couldn't trust Delier's men, the mission would go to the MIKE Force.

Saville got the call from Greely as Ryan was wrapping his left forearm and wrist with a field dressing. An RPD round had punched through his radius bone just above the wrist, leaving part of it protruding through the skin.

"You should've sent me a spotrep," Ryan chided. "I could've gotten killed."

"A spot report? Listen, Kev, I'm bloody left-handed. Couldn't lift my head without the bastards firing at me, and I had bugger-all switching the damned frequencies!"

"Apologies accepted," gritted Ryan with mock severity. "Just don't let it happen again, Captain. Now drop your drawers…"

As Ryan administered the penicillin, Toller stopped in to offer encouragement.

"Young Cap'n, you and I need to have a serious talk. You get killed on my watch, and my bloody reputation in the Team will be buggerall. The Regimental Sar'Major will have me fronting him, demanding to know how I allowed my officer to get killed playing point man."

"Mister Toller," Saville jerked his pants up, "you're no bloody Yank, and my proper title is Captain. Is that clear?"

Toller's friendly grin faded to a flinty stare. "Clear, Captain. My apologies…"

They were interrupted by Greely's call that it was time for the commander's conference. Saville dashed off after instructing Ney Bloom and his radioman to remain behind.

"So," mused Ryan, "We're bloody Yanks."

"Yeah. Did you give him anything for the pain?"

"No, he refused it."

"Well, that'll bring out the pommy in any officer."

"The pommy?"

"Yeah, tut tut, cheerio, and all that dress right dress rubbish. Give him a shot of painkiller when you can and we'll have our ol' cap'n Savvy back forthwith."

Saville found A-293's command bunker at the top of the hill, dug in under the camp's emergency evacuation helipad. Sited between the U.S. And Vietnamese team houses, its sole above ground entrance faced the northern hill, within sight of trenches occupied by the remaining NVA.

Greely convened his meeting with a request for status reports. The two FULRO companies that had deserted earlier were somewhere outside the wire, too far out of range to help. The two companies in the wire had a combined strength of 84 men, and that included wounded. Jed Saville reported that he had 163 men in the wire, to include his own small battalion CP, and another 200-plus men somewhere near their previous night's positions. These were working on a plan to reach the camp from the southern edge of the airfield. The third person to speak was a large, bald, Prussian looking American warrant officer. He had not been introduced, nor did he mention his role in the camp. He merely went over the enemy order of battle, cited a judgment that both the north and south hills would be hit that night, and that future enemy fire might include 130mm howitzers as well as 122mm rockets.

With that cheery news, Greely tasked Saville with clearing the remaining enemy from the northern hill. Saville countered that in light of the late hour and the chief's intelligence, his men might be better employed improving defenses on the southern hill. If the LLDB still had any men on the northern hill, he'd be happy to support by fire.

Greely shot him a disgusted look. "I don't need support by fire, Captain. I need you to get down there and clear it out."

"Right," Saville's voice was tense. "Might we have some of Captain Bao's men for liaison?"

Greely looked at Bao, who nodded back.

"Good," continued Greely. "Now let's go up top and I'll show you how I want this attack conducted."

"What," Saville said, startled. "Upstairs?"

"Yes."

"In full view of the enemy?"

"Captain, I wasn't aware that the Australian Army was so timid."

"Timid?" Saville was more surprised than angered. He waved his bandaged arm. "Major, there's timidity, and there's stupidity. And standing around in full view of the enemy, whilst you point him out, strikes me as imbecilic."

"There can't be more than a squad or two left, captain. You wait here while I take the *men* upstairs. I'll sketch it out for you when we get back."

"All right," Saville's eyes hardened. "I'll be here."

With Greely leading, the group clambered upstairs to cluster around the entrance. Waving a section of antenna, Greely pointed out the opposite trench lines where no pith helmets could be seen. As he waxed over what Captain Bao's men should have done, Saville wandered from the bunker over to the team house via an underground conduit. He was on his way back when an explosion sounded. Men clambered down the stairwell as voices screamed for a medic.

Greely was manhandled down and laid up on the map table. He'd taken B-40 rocket shrapnel in the chest and neck. As the team medic worked to clear the wound and stop the bleeding, Saville pulled Lieutenant Delier aside.

"Who's the ranking man after Greely?"

"I am, sir. This is an American camp."

"Right, I've no time for argument. I'm placing my company in a three-sixty degree defense around this hill. I'd recommend you get every man you can spare over to the northern hill. I'll be back to set up a small CP."

"There's no room here, Captain. But there's a bunker near the flagpole that's got a table and field telephone."

"We'll take it."

As Jed Saville worked his way down the hill, firing erupted from the northern hill. It took only a few minutes to brief St. Cyr and his crew. Then, with Toller's platoon taking the twelve o'clock position, the remaining platoons spread out through the trenches while Saville and Ney Bloom made a quick tour of the perimeter. The trenches were in moderate shape. Ominously, the Yards were digging in as deep and as fast as they could. By the time they got back to their CP it was evening twilight. Heavy firing raged on the far side of the northern hill while small ragged mobs of defenders streamed up the saddle into the MIKE Force positions. As Saville and Ney Bloom watched, the same thought passed between them.

"Where the bloody hell's their camp mortars? Bloom, get Laurie Toller up here as fast as you can."

At the Nha Trang Special Forces Operational Base, that same twilight had now turned to darkness. Inside the MIKE Force compound, two companies mustered for movement to Duc Het, while a third was standing by. Coincidentally, these were Rhade, Jarai, and Cham companies, which was hardly news to the scruffy figure brooding at the end of the B-55 MIKE Force bar.

"Hey Mac, you heard the news 'bout Duc Het?"

"Been there," grumbled Mac, hefting another shot of 151 proof rum. "Even got the tee shirt."

"Yeah, well we ain't there. Not officially, anyway. Check this out. Truffle got it over at the Group briefing tonight."

Mac picked up a message copied off the wire services. "South Vietnamese commandos poised to retake beleaguered Special Forces camp," read the headline.

"Ain't nothin' new," grumbled Mac. "We do the dyin'. They get the credit."

"Politics," sneered Estrada. "Truffle says MACV wants the American public to think the Slopes can fight."

"Funny thing," said Mac, "some of 'em can. And they'd have a whole lot more if they'd let us shoot about three quarters of their generals and colonels. Only problem is; we'd hafta shoot 'bout half our own."

"Got that right. Say, Mac, you feelin' OK?"

"Sure, why?"

"I dunno," Estrada shrugged, wondering what had happened to Mac's stutter. "You sound funny, that's all."

"Maybe it's the pills they've got me takin', or the fact I'm headed back to the States."

"The States? You? You're kiddin'. You been here since Christ was a corporal. When ya goin?"

"Catch'n a flight Tuesday."

"You're gonna miss the fun."

"I ain't missin' nothin'."

"Yeah, well—did ya know a guy named Balden?"

"New kid. Got in just as I left."

"Well, he got greased today. They had'da leave the body. Group commander's pissed! Say's he's gonna fire some El Tee named St. Cyr for pullin' back and leavin' the body..."

"St. Cyr?"

"Yeah..."

"What're they blamin' him for? Saville's the battalion commander. And if they left the body, you can bet they were in deep shit. The Trung-oui's a lotta things, but a coward ain't one of 'em. That's my battalion."

"Hey, Mac, gotta run. See you when I get back to the states."

"Yeah. Hey, what time you guys pullin' out tomorrow?"

"Lift off's at oh-eight-hundred; why?"

"Oh, I was sorta thinkin' of straphanging. Got a weapon and some web equipment you can loan me? Mine's already turned in."

"I don' know, Mac—could get me in trouble."

"What're they gonna do? Put you in the infantry and send you to Vietnam?"

Chapter Thirty-Two

Duc Het Special Forces Camp:

As THE LAST OF THE northern hill's defenders scrambled up the saddle, K'sor Tlur called for his cadres to keep them moving and away from the men. Fear could be contagious. Spooky 41 came up on the net to report an estimated NVA company on the hill.

The enemy had timed their reinforcement to coincide with nightfall, when close air support dwindled. Saville asked Spooky to hose down the hill's trenches and reverse slope, but Delier called a check fire. Some of his strikers could still be there. Saville argued the point, but Delier was adamant.

"Sir," St. Cyr stepped into Saville's bunker. "You sent for me?"

"Yes. Delier tells me most of his mortar crews have been killed or wounded. Gone walkabout's more likely. We need illumination and supporting fires. Send Mister Toller down to see what he can do."

"Sir, Big Boris is heavy weapons qualified."

"Yes, and he's the most experienced man here in defending and taking back bunkers and trenches. I'd prefer you keep Big Boris. Just in case…"

"In case of what? I get hit?"

"We don't come with guarantees, Galen." Saville waved his bandaged arm. "Have Laurie get with Master Sergeant Brady. "

Toller found Brady at the camp's mortar pits, grouped together on the southern military crest of the hill. Numbered stakes around the rims of the firing pits marked predesignated targets whose direction, elevation, and charge settings were noted on the plotting board table of a nearby bunker.

"What do you think?" Brady asked.

"Not too much to think, Sarge. There's no way our Yards are going to learn this in a few hours, but they can fire illumination."

"That'll do. When you need fire support, I'll get some Roundeyes and maybe a few LLDB down here."

"Got any sixty-millimeters?"

"There's a few in the arms room. If you want 'em, they're yours."

Toller reported back to Saville that they had enough illumination for five to six hours. With Spooky on station, that would be enough. But as far as fire support went, they'd have to rely on hand-fired 60s. While Laurie busied himself with the mortars, Biloskirka walked through everyone's positions, checking that sandbags were properly filled and laid, automatic weapons properly sighted, and claymores were out. Ryan and Cohen split their time ransacking A-293's supply bunkers, paying particular attention to C rations, canned grapefruit sections, and anything else that might contain liquid, which they divided among the platoons.

The camp water tower had taken a hit, and now tilted at a 65-degree angle. Its remaining water dripped into the red earth from B-40 rocket holes. A check with the American bunker revealed that they had water enough for themselves, and would share whatever they had. The LLDB bunker curtly brushed their enquiries aside.

"They have," gritted Spam, "but no give anybody but them. Maybe me and Thuan a little."

"Yeah," Cohen sneered, "with friends like them, who needs VC?"

"Camp LLDB," Spam protested, "not same same 91st Aibohne Ranger LLDB."

"Were you 91st Airborne Rangers?"

"Uagh," Spam grunted.

"Little Buddy," Cohen threw an arm around Spam, "If I ever come back, I'll ask for the 91st Airborne Rangers."

By 2100, the companies were settled in. A kilometer away, Ferris and Rayne had dug in near their previous night's position. Aerial reconnaissance reported a battalion sized heat signature fifteen kilometers southwest, just inside Cambodia. The Black Arrow called for an arc-light, declaring a tactical emergency. Saville, St. Cyr, and Bloom, doing a walkthrough of their positions, paused to watch the strike rumble and flash in the distance. The ground beneath them trembled.

"First time I've been this close," Saville marveled. "Let's hope that's one less battalion we have to face."

"Maybe," Ney Bloom's brow furrowed, "less elephants."

A barrage of 82mm mortar rounds sent them into the nearest bunker. Firing erupted from the opposing trenchline. Biloskirka and Jimm's platoons responded with withering fire. Movement along the lower flanks of the saddle prompted some of the stragglers to pull back. Blek rushed in to pistol whip several back into position as his M-79 grenadiers shifted their fire. His platoon leaders cautioned everyone to conserve ammunition. It was going to be a long night.

Sometime near midnight, a barrage of 122mm rockets hit the lower southern slope, killing or wounding nine camp strikers, tearing gaps in the wire, and collapsing sections of trench. Brady sent his engineer sergeant off to restring what wire he could, while K'sor Tlur led a detail down to repair the trenches. As Blek and Ney Bloom moved among the platoons, passing encouraging words, St. Cyr convened a quick Roundeye conference.

"Boris, what are they up to?"

"Buddy, they're keeping us busy with the smaller hill, while they get ready to hit us right up this one."

"Where the one-twenty-twos just hit?"

"Exactly."

"What about the east and west flanks?"

"One they will leave open, so strikers can escape. West side is closest to village, so expect a supporting attack through plantation to our east."

"Anyone have any different ideas?"

Toller didn't, and nodded his agreement.

"All right," St. Cyr continued, "considering that last night many were ready to desert us for the revolt, we've done pretty well. As I see it, we have a good forty or fifty hard core who will fight through to the end, and I count Blek, K'sor Tlur, and all your Indig platoon leaders in that group. Add to that another forty who'll follow those because of clan allegiances, and that's as many men as I had on a good day in the Fourth Foot. The rest will fight, or not, depending upon how things go, but that's Blek's department. Whatever you do, don't shoot or threaten to shoot any Indig. Push them, shove them, berate them, but leave the physical measures to the Yard chain of command."

"The FULRO chain of command," nodded Ryan

"Exactly," St. Cyr nodded. "Anything else?"

Ryan reported that the camp's dispensary had been relocated to a bunker near the mortars, and medical supplies were adequate. Severely wounded CIDG would be held there for medevac in the morning. Severe Roundeye casualties would be held in the Teamhouse.

Toller had scrounged four 60mm mortar tubes and would send one to each platoon. He suggested giving the tubes to their best M79 gunners. Later on he'd be down to show them how to fire it by hand.

Cohen had scrounged a case of radio batteries, which were being shared.

Biloskirka chimed in that they needed more machineguns. To St. Cyr's querying look, he added that the camp arms room had a surplus of Browning .30 calibers and ample ammunition. Firing the older and heavier M1919s from the trenches would save M60 ammo, and give them greater firepower in the defense.

St. Cyr lauded everyone's initiative and added that Ferris and Rayne's men would break through in the morning. All they had to do was hold through the night. When he dismissed them, Ryan hung back. Fishing in his pant-leg pocket, he took out a small packet of green and white capsules.

"El Tee, if you're get too tired, these can help."

"What are they?"

"Amphetamines, Green Hornets. Take one every four hours to stay awake. Just don't take any more than four in a twenty-four hour period."

"Thanks, Kev. If it gets too much, I just might have to pop one."

Sometime between 0130 and 0200 next morning, 82mm mortar shells rained down as corridors of green tracer raked the main hill between its southern and southwestern quadrants. For long minutes, everyone took cover. Then St. Cyr heard the .30 caliber's respond, assisted by M60s on the southern slope. Fire discipline seemed good until Toller reported movement from the northern hill. As Toller's mortars sounded, St. Cyr dashed out to check the trenches. Blek rushed ahead of him, waving his revolver. It was enough to get most reluctant souls engaged, but some still huddled in their trenches. The sensation of having Blek's pistol barrel jammed into their heads convinced most to stand and fire, particularly when the hammer cocked. But one young straggler simply closed his eyes and trembled.

Blek holstered his pistol, grabbed the boy by his harness, pulled him to his feet, and slammed him into the trench wall. Grabbing the kid's M16, Blek crouched below the parapet, snapped up to squeeze off several fast shots, then dropped back into a crouch to look across at the trooper.

"See? Stay down, jump up, fire, get back down. Look, see target in head. Jump up, fire, get down. Not stay down long! Stay down not safe. VC come up hill, they kill you. Up down, up down, you do, OK?"

The wide-eyed kid nodded. With that, Blek thrust the M16 back into his hands and manhandled him into position. At Blek's order, he jumped up, squeezed off a few rounds with his eyes shut, and dropped back down.

"OK," Blek screamed. "This time, eye open!"

Again, the kid popped up and fired with his eyes closed. Blek moved to the right of the kid's firing position, and drew and cocked his pistol.

"Again," Blek screamed.

Again, the kid shot up. This time he jerked off three rounds with both eyes open, flinching visibly every time he pulled the trigger. For good measure, Blek squeezed off a round of his own at some distant target.

"Remember," he patted the kid's shoulder, "no stay down long. I see you hide, must shoot!"

With that, they made their way to Cohen's position, where Blek pulled his Jarai platoon leader aside for an ass-chewing and sent him off to make sure that his men were shooting back. He wanted every straggler paired with an experienced trooper, and passed this back to K'sor Tlur, who was making his way through Ryan's trenches in the opposite direction.

They returned to the company CP just as another mortar barrage fell. Had the NVA set their fuses for airburst, or the camp's base soil been harder, casualties would have been heavier. But Duc Het's twin hills were nothing more than accumulated top soil. With no underlying rock, mortar rounds dug themselves in before exploding, pock marking the hill with shell-holes.

St. Cyr advised Saville that his men were holding up well. Saville passed this to Delier, who was busy passing all reports on from deep in his bunker. Minutes later, Bangalore torpedoes tore gaps through the wire that Brady and his crew had just managed to re-string. As a full battalion moved against the bottom slope, Delier called for the mortars to cease firing. Spooky was now on station.

The heaviest firing came from Ryan's positions, where a horrendous explosion shook the hill. Dust shot from the rafters of Saville's bunker. In the eerie silence that followed, Saville was up and running to the Team Bunker. He found Delier in a bewildered state, and Greely in a moment of lucidity. A mortar round had hit the camp's 105mm howitzer position, penetrating the ready ammo bunker. Since the gun crews had deserted or been killed earlier, the ammo's loss effected no one. As Saville wound his way back to his own bunker, Ryan and Cohen called for help.

"Spooky Forty-One," Saville keyed his mike, "this in Bushranger. We need fires on our southern slope below the red flares, over."

"Roger, Bushranger. Where are the red flares? Over."

"On their way, out." and with that, Saville called for Ryan and Cohen to mark their forward positions with flares.

The sight of NVA troops pushing into the lower trenches sparked panic among the camp strikers. Some leapt out to flee, only to be cut down, while others abandoned their sectors to bunch up where firing was less intense. The lower trench sections were not interconnected, save for one or two narrow communication trenches running to the middle trench line. The middle trenches were interconnected and, given the higher ground, could be held if panic remained in check. To ensure that it did, K'sor Tlur made a quick run through, directing automatic weapons fire, tossing grenades into enemy occupied sections of the lower trenches, and exhorting the surviving strikers below to stick together and fight back.

While St. Cyr berated himself for not switching Boris's platoon with Ryan's, Boris and Jimm beat back supporting attacks from the northern hill. Yet the southern slope remained the critical fight. As St. Cyr cursed his own stupidity for having heard Boris, but not listened, Master Sergeant Brady showed up.

"Lieutenant, where do you need the most help?"

St. Cyr's red-rimmed eyes gave Brady what old troopers called the 500-Yard-Stare: Not yet over the edge, but halfway there.

"What've you got, Top?"

Brady called over in camp striker with a tank strapped to his back. "We've got two German flame throwers. All we've ever used 'em for was burning grass back from the airstrip. With enough pressure, they'll reach those lower trenches."

"Good enough. Get 'em down to Sergeant Ryan's platoon. He needs the help."

Fifteen minutes later, Ryan was hunkered down next to Brady as his striker sent a wall of flame into a trench filled with NVA. Men screamed: Several leapt out, flailing, rolling, and trying to douse the flames. Brady, temporarily blinded by the flash, didn't see them. But he did feel something snap by his head and jerk the flamethrower out of his hands. Reaching down, he found his striker, a gurgling choking sound coming from his throat. As Brady and Ryan positioned the striker so the blood would run out, the kid choked uncontrollably and died.

"Sorry, Top," Ryan mumbled.

As .51-caliber machinegun rounds thudded into the rise behind Brady, Ryan rushed off to screams of "Bac-si."

An eternity later, Duc Het fell strangely silent except for the occasional outgoing mortar round. They'd lost seven killed and five seriously wounded—a testimonial to deep digging. Since one was Ryan's indigenous platoon leader, St. Cyr declared him a Roundeye and called for a medevac. When the medevacs touched down on the camp helipad, Ryan added his most seriously wounded to the lift. As the second medevac pulled away, two camp LLDB rushed over to scramble aboard over the wounded men.

"Goddam slope bastards," Ryan sputtered in rage.

"*Ungh.*" Trung-si Thuan spat in agreement. "I see again, I kill."

With the medevacs gone, Duc Het fell silent. B-52 arclights, Spooky's miniguns, Brady's flame thrower, and the ability of Toller's ad hoc mortar-men to put steel on target, had paid for a few more hours of life. As fatigue set in, St. Cyr and Blek moved up and down the trenches, prodding the platoon leaders to keep the men busy with ammo resupply, first aid, cleanup and repairs.

Everyone needed water, but there was none. Already bone-tired, thirst was making the men listless. Despite the platoon leaders' best efforts, many dropped down to nap as soon as anyone was out of sight. Biloskirka ordered all empty canteens gathered up while he scrounged for plastic tubing in the camp dispensary. What he found was too small to be of use, but there was a roll of neoprene hose in the supply room, and some five gallon sized cans. With this, he and Cohen, and several assistants, made their way to the water tower.

It was a simple concrete cube on reinforced columns erected on the southeast quadrant of the hill, just past the LLDB Teamhouse. Connected to a network of PVC pipe, no one had ever dug a trench to it. Its shattered support column tilted at an angle that prevented any remaining water from reaching the output valve.

"What's the plan, Boris?" asked Cohen.

"Simple, Buddy. You stay here. I scale tower, remove access hatch, climb in, and run hose out through RPG hole. Then you siphon water and fill all cans and canteens.

"Hey," Cohen flashed a sly grin. "Why are you the one climbing up? You looking for a medal?"

"Shit, Buddy! You think you can lift that access hatch?"

"How much does it weigh?"

"Concrete? Mebbe thirty, forty pounds."

"I can handle that."

"You sure?"

"Sure I'm sure."

"OK, you go."

Cohen stripped off his harness, passed his Uzi to his Yard radio operator cum bodyguard, slung the coiled hose across his shoulder, and dashed to the tower. The bent rebar steps set into the column proved an easy climb for the first 12 feet, but six feet above that, where the column had shattered, the steps lay at a sharp side angle.

He leaned out as far as he could, until his feet swung free and he was forced to pull himself up and across one rung at a time. A sick feeling gnawed his stomach as a burst of medium machinegun fire cracked below his dangling feet. An inner voice berated his bravado. *You knew they'd have the tower covered*, he told himself. *Hell, the fact they'd hit it in the first place was no accident.* His feet bicycled, and came in contact with the tower. Silence warned him that the NVA gunners were fine tuning their elevation. Their next burst would be on target. Grasping the last rung by his left hand, he swung his right around to grasp the bent rebar that formed the handle of the access hatch. Green tracers thunder-cracked past his left ear. He almost let go, but held on. His intestines knotted tighter as he swung around.

Out of the line of fire, thank God. But now he had to get inside. No longer dangling, he still couldn't let go without sliding off. He angled his body to where he could get his lower right leg over the top edge of the tower, then stretched up to where he could grasp the edge with his right hand. A single round pinged somewhere behind him. *Shit*, he cursed, *a sniper.* He tugged at the high end of the rebar handle but the hatch barely moved. Another round pinged off the roof, then another. Cursing his weaker left arm, Cohen pulled himself up on the edge of the tower and moved his right hand to the rebar handle. Pulling and pushing just enough to tilt the hatch out, he pushed it away. As it grated off the roof, his right foot gave way. He slid down but managed to get his arm through the hatchway just in time to break his slide.

Cohen scrambled in. Falling into the water, he unrolled his hose and threaded it out through the nearest RPG hole. Knowing that the longer he stayed inside, the greater the chance of an incoming RPG round, he began dipping and raising his end of the hose into the water in an attempt to kickstart the siphoning process. Long minutes later, Boris tugged on the hose.

Though an occasional burst rattled the tower, no B-40 rockets hit. Too early for congratulations, Cohen warned himself, he still had to get out. An eternity later, Boris called up that they were finished. Bracing himself for the worst, Cohen clambered up to the hatch, pulled himself through, grabbed the edge of the tower, felt for the rebar rung, and pulled himself over. Seconds later he was on the ground and into a shell hole, gasping heavily.

"OK, Jewboy," Boris grinned, "that was worth a Bronze Star!"

"Bronze Star my ass! Maybe for you, you're a lot taller and stronger. For me, that was a Silver Star."

"Shua," Boris agreed. "For you is Silver Star."

"You're kidding."

"No. I write it up myself when we get back. Now everyone has water. More important, come morning, everyone will get a bit of coffee."

"Coffee?"

"Yes. While I am scrounging, I also find coffee, big pot, clean socks, and gas burner. Everything we need. At first light every men gets small shot of fresh coffee. Good for morale, you'll see."

Chapter Thirty-Three

As FRESH HOT COFFEE was being ladled out in the trenches of Duc Het, trucks rumbled out the Nha Trang MIKE Force compound gate. Dark clouds ringed Grand Summit mountain, but the sun rising over the South China Sea bathed the great Buddha dominating the valley in a brilliant white light—the color of death in the Orient, and resurrection and purity in the West. The omen may have meant something to the few Buddhists and Christians present, but the majority of men were Animists. They took it as a sign that the spirits inhabiting Nha Trang were pleased. The spirits at Duc Het would be a different matter. As the trucks approached the dependent village, gaggles of women and children rushed out from bare wood structures set on concrete pads to wave through the wire at the passing troops. Some would be widows and half-orphans this day.

Wedged in among the Montagnard troops was a scruffy mustachioed American in a faded tiger suit, tattered indigenous rucksack, and worn-out harness. Except for a shiny new M2 carbine and his Sedang midwife's necklace, Marvin McElroy was all but invisible. Captain Truffle didn't spot him until they were loading up on C-123s for their flight to Ban Me Thuot.

"Hey, Estrada! Who the straphanger?"

"That's Mac, Cap'n. Ops NCO of the Pleiku MIKE Force battalion at Duc Het. He just got back from R&R last night and asked if he could ride in."

Truffle took in Mac's demeanor, bracelets, and necklace. "OK," he scowled. "But next time you want to add a strap-hanger, check with me first."

"Sure thing, Cap'n."

Truffle recalled their extra passenger in Ban Me Thuot, when the Pleiku MIKE Force commander came out to check their frequencies as they transferred to Hueys, but graver matters demanded his attention. According to B-23, enemy fire was too hot to touch down near the camp. They'd

have to land two kilometers south and move up through a coffee plantation. Back in his command ship, Truffle wondered why the straphanger
hadn't greeted his boss. When the pilots pulled pitch, it no longer mattered.

Ferris and Rayne had lost communications sometime after 0400. With B-
52s and Spooky in the air, that was a serious matter. Despite a change of
handsets, they remained out of contact. From broken transmissions, they
knew that the Nha Trang MIKE Force was expected. Just before first light,
Ferris and Y Mlo Duan Du sat down for a hasty conference with Rayne and
Y Diet Kpor.

Ferris was down to 97 men. Rayne had just over 100. When Ferris
asked if this was part of the revolt, both Montagnard leaders shook their
heads no. On the plus side, casualties had been low, and many missing men
were already inside the wire.

Now, Ferris emphasized, they were doing it his way. Their only real
choice was another shot at the camp gate, but this time they'd move
straight across the airstrip. To speed them up, each man would carry only
mission essential equipment; ammo, grenades, water, and a single meal.
Everything else was to be dumped. Rayne's company would lead, while
Ferris followed in reserve. Once in position, Rayne's company would cover
Ferris's men as they rushed across the landing strip to the narrow wash on
the far side. As soon as they made the wash, Ferris's company would cover
Rayne's crossing. All grenade launchers were to concentrate their fire on
any automatic weapons.

As Ferris and Rayne closed on the airstrip, Regter radioed Saville the
latest intelligence and passed along his warning order for clearing NVA
forces from around the camp. Minutes later, Ferris's radio reappeared on
the net as he advised Saville that he and Rayne were moving. While Saville
congratulated him, Ryan entered the bunker. Lifting Saville's useless left
arm, he sniffed it, cut away the sleeve, carefully removed the bandage,
sniffed it again, and wrapped it in a new bandage. Then, he motioned for
Saville to drop his pants. When Saville ignored him, he motioned again.

"Sergeant," Saville's voice was agitated. "I'm busy."

"Captain, necrosis is setting in."

"What the hell's that?"

"Gangrene. If you don't get on the first medevac ship and get the hell to a hospital, you're going to lose that arm."

"Look, Kev, I've got a war to run."

"If you don't want to run the next one without that arm, you'll do what I say. They're going to have to debride it anyway, and the longer you wait, the more tissue they'll have to cut out. I'll give you another penicillin shot, but as long as you keep banging your arm around, the gangrene's going to keep spreading."

"I'll leave when this is over."

"Your choice, Captain. Drop your drawers and bend over."

As Ryan jabbed the needle in, he pushed hard on the plunger.

"Ouch, Kev!" Saville flinched. "Don't look for my name on your patient list when you open your practice."

Ryan flashed a weary grin. "Cap'n, it's a price I'm willing to pay."

Ferris and Rayne's companies were on the move. Despite several sharp exchanges with NVA reconnaissance teams, the men followed willingly enough, though fatigue and fear made them skittish. Whenever they bunched up or held back, the cadres pushed them harder. Nearing the airstrip, Rayne advised Ferris that their companies should cross together. When Ferris insisted they stick to the plan, Rayne cut him off.

"Look, Captain. I know what they teach at the Infantry School. But right now it's the best course of action."

"Says who?"

"Says a farkin' Warrant who's been carrying a rifle since Nineteen Forty-Four."

Ferris's protest was cut short by a call from Saville. Gunships were inbound. Once they were through the gate, he wanted an immediate assault on the northern hill. Ferris countered that first they had to get their stragglers back and reorganized. When Saville insisted that time was of the essence, Rayne's voice cut in, advising young Jed to listen. Saville agreed, but the mission was still theirs.

Though Delier was working on a plan to retake the hill, Saville had no intention of waiting. Delier had yet to come up out of his bunker to check the situation for himself, while Greely kept slipping in and out of consciousness. With more NVA on the way, they needed that northern hill back before the next major ground attack.

While Saville ground his teeth over the northern hill, call sign 'Crossbow' called for Delier. After several more unanswered calls, Saville replied. The Nha Trang MIKE Force was inbound, where did he want them? Saville advised Crossbow that he was to take orders from Bushranger, and to put down as near the southwest edge of the camp as possible. He was then to move around the camp's southern edge, and come up on the east flank, clearing any NVA remnants and ready to support an attack on the northern hill.

Truffle rogered this and reported that Duc Het was in sight. Motioning his Montagnard radio operator to follow, Saville stepped out of his bunker and made his way to the trenches behind the Teamhouse. In the distance, Huey gunships were plastering a facing hill in the coffee plantation across the valley. Golf ball sized green tracers zipped up to riddle the first two, sending them into fiery crashes. The next two gunships fired volleys of rockets into the tracers' point of origin, then raked the area with miniguns before peeling away. As they did so, the slicks thundered in to dump lines of helmeted troopers into paddy fields and tranh grass.

Up near the teamhouse, Toller stood by his mortars as Saville advised pilots not to overfly the camp airstrip. With that, Toller's crews aimed their tubes at various points along the airstrip, log windrow, and cornfield, and began dropping in rounds. At the first audible crumps, Ferris and Rayne's men dashed across the airstrip in a single mob. Once across, the cadres sorted them out as they pushed on to the camp gate. Ferris took the lead, with Rayne's company in tow. There were short firefights with outlying NVA, but no serious opposition. Twenty minutes later, 213th Company was in the wash. Toller called off the mortars as gunships swooped in to rake the northern hill's near slope. Ferris led his lead element to the gate, dispatched the lock with an M79 grenade round, and urged his men up into the trenches. As Rayne's company passed through, Saville watched a second lift of helicopters deposit more Nha Trang troopers in the distance.

Down in the trenches, a wave of euphoria swept Roundeyes and Yards alike as they greeted each other with joking insults and handshakes. Any illusions that the siege of Duc Het had ended were quickly dispelled by a barrage of NVA mortar fire. Ferris, searching for Saville's bunker, barely had time to take cover in St. Cyr's.

"Welcome to Duc Het," St. Cyr grinned.

"Yeah," Ferris grunted. "Beats getting hit by this shit out in the open. I had a helluva time getting our guys to dig in last night. But once that first mortar round fell, all you could see was assholes and elbows. Some were still digging in at first light. I should'a done like Rayne."

"What'd he do?"

"Walked around using a folded entrenching tool for a swagger stick. Anybody that wasn't digging fast enough, or deep enough, got a taste of it."

"I wouldn't try that."

"Neither would I. But I guess his wrinkles give him some status among the Yards. Hell, even my guys were doing whatever he said. Hey, where's Saville's CP?"

"Straight up that trench. Cohen'll get you there."

"Ta ta, Mate. Sorry we don't have time for tea. Isn't that what y'all drink up there in Massachusetts?"

"Maine. And where I'm from, we drink coffee."

"Whatever. One of those damned Yankee states." And with a friendly clap on the shoulder, Ferris was off.

Saville was hunched over his field desk glaring at Ryan when Ferris stepped in. He motioned for Ferris to wait outside.

"You had no bloody business going over my head to Major Regter," Saville barked.

"Sir, I'm the senior medic, and like it or not, your health concerns Major Regter."

"I bloody well disagree! You go through Leftenant St. Cyr to me. That's the proper chain of command."

"You're both officers, sir." Ryan did his best to look contrite. "Once you told him that your arm was OK, that would have been it."

"As well it should have been."

"Look, Captain, your arm's not OK, and it was my job to tell the major. So, excuse me, but I've got other patients."

Ferris stuck his head back in as Saville was sniffing at a discarded dressing. He recognized the faint but foul odor.

"You wanted to see me, Jed?"

"Yes. Once Nha Trang is in position, we're going to take back that hill. Your and Mister Rayne's companies will conduct the assault with Galen's company in reserve and supporting by fire. Do everything in your power to keep moving and fight through. The Nha Trang battalion will be outside the wire, covering our right flank. They'll kill or capture anyone trying to escape, and meet any reinforcement or counterattack from that direction. Once we've cleared the hill, per Major Regter's orders, you're to assume command of this battalion…"

Saville paused, while Ferris's heavy eyebrows knit together.

"How long can I expect to remain in command, Jed?"

"Given my time here, permanently. I'll likely be reassigned upon leaving hospital."

Ferris extended his hand. "It's been good working with you, Jed."

"Yes, well I wish it had been longer. Once you've retaken the hill, one company will remain here to hold the camp and support you with fire, whilst you and the two Nha Trang companies assault the bunker complex you ran into on day one. Expect Major Regter to arrive and be in overall command. Now you know as much as I do. Questions?"

"What's this Task Force Ngoc?"

"Two companies under Major Ngoc. He's placed LLDB officers in both."

"And he's commanding them?"

"Personally, as a provisional battalion."

"That'll be a real screw-up."

"Right. Well Ngoc's a prickly enough bastard. Did you know he's a member of the royal family?"

"He's just another dink in my book."

"Hardly. His father was first cousin to the emperor…"

"I thought you Aussies didn't give a shit about royalty."

"We don't. But with Ngoc's money and family connections, he could be sunning himself on the Riviera right now, diddling some very fine looking young French sheilas. Instead, he's out here with us. So much for the view that all ARVN officers are from the bottom of society. My point is, if Ngoc ends up in charge, and you end up working for him, do you very best to cooperate."

"Jed, I've worked with a lot of assholes. Ngoc will just be another name on that list."

"Well that's good to hear. After all, command's not a popularity contest. G'day and Good luck."

Ferris returned to find that WO2 'Blue' MacBride and Y Mlo Duan Du had moved the men into Jimm's area and positioned them for an assault across the upper half of the saddle. Rayne's company would take the lower half. As Rayne's people would run the greater risk, Ferris decided to weight his attack on the higher right wing, so he could hook around the crest and hit the reverse slope trenches from the side. But, as he checked his men, he sensed a palpable fear. In Korea, he'd have given anything to take on the communists like this, and never doubted how his attached Korean KATUSA troops would perform. He liked Yards far more than he'd ever liked Koreans, but he had no illusions. They were ambush and long range patrol artists; masters at tracking and living off the land. Seizing and holding terrain was not one of their strong points. As he and Y Mlo walked the trenches, they emphasized the need to get everyone up and moving when the order came. Casualties were to be left where they fell until the attack was over. Nothing was to stop their momentum. A quick check with Rayne revealed that he would attack with three platoons on line, with his Recce platoon in reserve. Rayne had put an M60 machinegun team in every squad, as was Australian army practice, and was counting on that heavier firepower to keep his men moving. Ferris was going forward with two platoons on line. The hook platoons would follow, ready to swing around the hill once the lead platoons reached the upper trenches. The hook would be led by MacBride, a West Australian, and Staff Sergeant Jimmy Johnson, the army cook turned infantryman.

Upon hearing that Nha Trang was nearing their jump-off point, Saville led Ney Bloom, his radio operators, and bodyguards to the A-293 Teamhouse, where he would control the attack from just beyond the steps where Greely had been hit.

A narrow trench had been dug from the steps to the forward slope, with several layers of sandbags facing the northern hill for added protection. Greely, who was lucid for the moment, shot Saville a thumbs-up as he passed by. Saville returned Greely's wan smile with a friendly nod.

Under an early afternoon sun, Saville made radio checks while Ney Bloom opened cans of grapefruit. With the arrival of Ferris and Rayne, water was again critical. They needed to clear the northern hill, if only to bring in water.

As Nha Trang reached their jump-off point, gunships raked nearby targets with rockets and miniguns. There was a moment of panic when one Cobra made a tight turn to barrel down on an isolated Nha Trang platoon. While strikers scattered, Mac fumbled for his strobe light, switched it on, and prayed. The Cobra thundered overhead, made a tight turn, and flittered away. As the platoon reassembled, the young Buck sergeant gave Mac a friendly nod.

"Quick thinking, Sarge. Thanks."

"It's nuthin'," Mac grunted. "Just glad the pilot recognized the strobe. Kid's got good eyesight and nerves."

With Nha Trang in position, Saville nodded to Bloom, who fired a green star cluster skyward as St. Cyr's .30 caliber machineguns raked the opposite slopes. Ferris and Rayne's troops loosed war cries and popped up and down in their trenches. The ruse was Saville's idea, and was quickly rewarded with volleys of 82mm mortar fire that saturated the saddle. Saville's command group hunkered down while he and Ney Bloom glassed the northern hill and distant forest. As Air Force jets swooped in to his known and suspected targets, streams of green tracer reached skyward. Once the jets had cleared, Toller's 60mms laid a short preparatory fire on the reverse slope of the northern hill, while Rayne and Ferris urged their men forward.

To the credit of the Montagnard leadership, the men were up and moving under a stream of .30 caliber machinegun fire cracking inches over their heads. They surged down slope with illusory precision. As they crossed the access road and began to climb, the opposing trenches filled with sun-helmeted heads firing AK-47s and RPDs on full automatic. Saville's trained eye picked up lighter colored sun-helmets, probably senior NCOs and officers, moving back and forth. He ordered St. Cyr to concentrate his machineguns on these. This was passed to K'sor Tlur, who gave a Gallic shrug. His gunners were well trained. They'd figure that much out for themselves. Still, he rushed from gun to gun, checking on his men and directing their fire.

The initial surge down was now a crawl up. While small groups moved forward, others huddled in the road's drainage ditch, or in shell-holes or small folds in the hill. Most still fired at the enemy trenches, but some began scrambling back. St. Cyr stared in nervous anticipation. Those falling back weren't his problem, but they could panic his own ranks. He prayed that his mission would be anything other than reinforcing Rayne at the bottom of the saddle.

Saville watched a stream of green .51 caliber tracers reach out. Not skyward, but bound for their own positions. His first thought was for the Nha Trang companies, but the tracers passed well above them before burning out. Now invisible, they drooped into a sharper arc to crack down the saddle, tearing flesh, smashing skulls, and sending Ferris and Rayne's stragglers into a paroxysm of mind-numbing fear. Some screamed, others wailed, most clutched the earth in abject misery.

Rayne ordered his men to ignore the fallen and drive those remaining forward. While his reserve platoon raked the higher trenches with fire, his lead platoons closed on the lower trench line. It was hardly a wave. Here, there, small groups made it in, where they engaged the NVA at point blank range. As Ferris and Knuudsen drove their own men for the trenches, Knuudsen collapsed. Big Knute was too big a company institution to ignore. Ferris grabbed his new medic and rushed to Knuudsen's side. A round had broken Big Knute's hip, but the femoral artery had been spared. They dragged him into a nearby trench, where Vandermeer did his best to stop the bleeding and bandage the wound.

Knuudsen's loss and the sight of men streaming back, prompted Saville to order St. Cyr into action. Laurie overheard the call, and rushed to the Teamhouse to find Brady.

"Sarge, I have to go forward! Got anyone who can spell me on the mortars?"

"Who's there now?"

"Trung-si Thuan. He knows his mortars well enough, but no one can understand his English."

"I'll send someone when I can."

"Your word?"

"My word."

"Ta, Mate." Toller gave Brady a crushing handshake, rushed back to strap on his web equipment, and made for his platoon. Jimm greeted him with a wide smile as Toller squeezed his shoulder.

"No way you're going out there without me, Mate."

Spam flashed Toller a beaming welcome.

"You either, Spam," Laurie nodded. "You're part of this bloody team"

"Farkin' right, Mate," Spam shot back in Australian. Familiar dark bronze faces flashed Toller nervous smiles.

"Goooooo, Fullllro, Uuuaaannghhh!" Toller chanted.

The troops stared into Toller's crazed eyes. Recognizing the challenge, Jimm took up the chant:

"Goooooo, Fullllro, Uuuaaannghhh!"

The nearest troops smiled. Others looked doubtful. Then Spam took up the chant. "Goo, Furro, Uaaannghhh!"

Smiles cracked through the ranks. Here was a Tiep-zap chanting for FULRO. In seconds, the entire platoon took up the chant.

Blek called Jimm on the HT-1 radio and ordered him to move out. Jimm glanced at Toller, who nodded. With Jimm and Biloskirka's platoons in the lead, 212th Company moved up behind Ferris. Biloskirka's men allowed the stragglers to stream on by, but Jimm's ordered them to join their ranks. Two who tried to run away were gunned down.

Toller trailed close behind Jimm, keeping his eyes and ears alert for signs that his mortar crews were busy. He was no longer in charge. Jimm and Spam were leading this attack. Toller was now a true combat advisor. As they crested the east flank of the hill, Biloskirka's men took up the FULRO chant.

Back at his CP, Saville fought back the urge to key his mike. The attack was underway. However messy it looked, it was moving, and Saville meant to keep up that momentum going. He called for Toller to shift mortar fires, and was surprised to hear a heavily accented Vietnamese voice answer his call.

"Who the hell are you?" Saville demanded.

"Trung-si Nhut Thuan," answered the voice. "Who hell you?"

"Your bloody battalion commander," answered Saville. "Where's Mister Toller?"

"Oh, too busy now," Thuan responded. "Kill beaucoup VC!"

"Right on him," Saville responded, unsure as to why. Where the hell was Toller anyway? No matter. He called for more fire on the trench above Rayne's men, and was gratified to see mortar rounds pepper the area. These were answered with a rash of 82mm mortar bombs that raked the crest of the saddle.

Cohen's platoon, below the crest, dove to earth as the rest of the company scampered over. When barrage ended, Cohen was up and calling for his men to move. He hadn't gotten four steps when a thunder clap cracked past his head. He stumbled to ground under a stream of .51 caliber rounds. Glancing down the saddle, his mind registered the boot sole of his radio operator.

A light kick brought no response. Cohen crawled back down. The kid's eyes were alive, but there was no pulse. The blood pouring from a gaping .51 caliber exit hole in the upper ribcage was being emptied by gravity. Cohen pushed the kid over, wrestled the radio off his body, and cut away the left rucksack shoulder strap near the gaping exit hole. Wiping his bloody hands on his shirt, he keyed the handset and reported that they were pinned down. Dragging the radio, he crawled to where his shaking interpreter still hugged the earth.

"When machinegun *pow-mitrayoor* stop fire, must move," Cohen screamed.

The interpreter mumbled and nodded. Cohen grabbed him and pulled him close. "When *pow-mitrayoor* stop fire, must move," he repeated. The interpreter's eyes looked into his own.

"We move," he nodded.

Boris's voice advised Cohen to stand by. Saville had called an air strike on the .51 caliber and a FAC was overhead. Once the strike went in, Cohen was to clear the saddle and close on Biloskirka. Cohen told his interpreter to pass word to the squad leaders. The interpreter stared into his eyes. "You me go!"

"OK," Cohen nodded back. "You me!"

Together they crawled down slope. The interpreter screamed for his squad leaders to get their men ready. On order, they would rush over the crest. As the men tensed, Cohen picked up the sound of a fighter bomber slowing down for its run. Seconds later, a loud explosion sounded in the distance.

"*Pung tee Y now*," Cohen screamed to make them move. "*Pung tee Y now!*"

The nearest men stared. Clutching his Uzi and radio rucksack strap, Cohen rose and ran bent over. A gaggle of men followed, then more. Rounds snapped by, fired from trenches where the NVA were still trying to drive Ferris and Rayne back. Over the crest of the saddle, Cohen spotted Biloskirka's men in a middle row of trenches, firing into a higher trench. He barreled straight for them with his platoon strung out behind. As the F-4 made another run, Cohen passed the radio to his interpreter.

Boris clapped an arm around Cohen's shoulder and pointed to the upper trench.

"Buddy, keep those assholes busy while we push down, OK?"

"No prob..."

Boris knocked Cohen back, ducked to pick up a grenade, and flipped it downhill. "See," he winced as it exploded, "you haf'ta keep these bastards busy."

Cohen nodded, fired a few bursts from his Uzi at the upper trench, and began spreading his men out. By his best count, he was down to 23 troops, not including himself. Most took to firing at the upper trench in earnest, but one young Yard trooper gave him an eager smile and unslung a LAW anti-tank rocket.

"You want I shoot?"

"No. Shoot pow-fusil."

Cohen moved down the trench with the would-be LAW gunner in tow. Every time he looked back, the gunner would repeat his question. Exasperated, Cohen agreed. To his surprise, the LAW gunner extended the tube and released the safety with a fair amount of precision. Popping up to face the upper trench, he gave the rubber covered trigger a steady squeeze. The explosion shook several nearby riflemen, but the smiling gunner shot Cohen a thumbs up. The rocket plowed into a sandbag, where its explosion audibly slowed the enemy's fire.

"Now," Cohen ordered, "stay here, shoot *pow-fusil.*"

As Cohen joined Biloskirka in his own position, heavy firing broke out farther up the trench. A call from St. Cyr advised Boris that Jimm and Ryan were blocked by heavy resistance. Could Boris get around?

Only if St. Cyr wanted to lose men. The mortar fire didn't appear to faze the upper trenches, which appeared to have better bunkers with overhead cover. Saville called for St. Cyr to give Rayne and Ferris more support.

"Stay here until I tell you to move," Boris ordered Cohen. "Keep your men spread out and firing."

As Cohen moved back among his men, snap shooting with his Uzi, he felt a tug at his harness and looked back to find the smiling gunner with another LAW.

"I shoot?"

"How many have?"

The gunner held up two fingers. Cohen was seized by an idea. Insanely sane, he told himself. He tapped his interpreter on the shoulder. "Follow me!"

Trailed by the gunner, he moved down the line, breaking the men up into teams of two and spreading them out with instructions to keep firing. At times, Cohen would tap a particular man and motion him to follow. He only remembered one or two names, but their faces were familiar as men reliable in past fights. The fire storm continued from the far end. Ryan couldn't get his men moving. Jimm's lead elements couldn't lift their heads up, and were busy tossing back grenades that kept dropping in. St. Cyr pleaded for mortars, but Rayne and Ferris needed them more.

As Cohen reached his last man, he cast a quick glance at the opposite trench. No fire was coming in, it was all going out. Either there were no NVA there, or they were scared shitless and hunkered down. He was betting there was a gap. He couldn't risk his whole platoon on it, but he was going to find out.

Gathering his volunteers, he made a conscious effort to slow his speech. Comprehension was critical.

"You," he pointed at his interpreter. "You stay here. Keep men fire *pow-fusil, pow mitreeyoor*. You, you, and you. We go there." He pointed to the upper trench. "You," he pointed to the LAW gunner. "You shoot time one. Wait short time. Shoot time two. Understand?"

As the interpreter repeated the instructions in rapid Jarai, the gunner's eyes shone. He reached down, rummaged through his indigenous rucksack, and pulled out a choking gas CS grenade.

"Then I throw. Yes?"

"No throw! I take."

The gunner reluctantly handed over his CS grenade. The last thing he needed, thought Cohen, was some clown setting off a CS grenade in his own trench. He slipped it into his assault pack. After checking his grenades, star clusters, and smoke grenades, he tugged on the interpreter's harness.

"Green smoke, bring platoon! Bring quick! No green smoke, you tell Captain Blek! OK?"

The interpreter nodded, and called for everyone to get a full magazine ready. Then he looked into Cohen's eyes and nodded again. Cohen motioned to the gunner, who raised the LAW to his right shoulder. Once the gunner had a steady aim, Cohen tapped his left shoulder.

"Fire."

Chapter Thirty-Four

THE ROCKET SLAMMED into the parapet of the opposite trench. Too intent on sprinting forward to look back, Cohen heard another bang as the second rocket whooshed by to explode just behind the first. He hit the ground and shot a glance back at his four volunteers. Fumbling with a grenade, he pulled the pin, forcibly slowed his breath, counted three hippopotamus, and lobbed. It hit the edge of the trench to tumble in. He winced as it exploded. Then they were up, across, and in, firing short bursts into prostrate forms. One or two might have been wounded, but the other four were already dead. His team's eyes stared wide-eyed into his own. They had to move quickly. He pushed the nearest man down the trench. M16 and 60 rounds snapped over their heads. Turning the corner, they found a small group of NVA busy firing on the MIKE Force. Squatting, Cohen and his lead man opened fire close enough to see the hits. As one NVA spun to fire, rounds slapped his chest and abdomen. Momentum carried him down. Cohen put a final round into his head, then pushed his wing-mate to the front and motioned the others to follow. As the point man reached the last NVA, he stripped away the web magazine carrier and passed Cohen his M16. After slipping on the magazine carrier straps, he jammed an NVA sun helmet over his boonie hat and grabbed an AK-47. Cohen nodded his approval.

They edged cautiously up to an adjacent trench being raked by heavy fire from the MIKE Force. Cohen's NVA took a quick glance around, and flashed his hand three times.

Damn! Fifteen men or more. Two squads at least. They had to move before anyone came up behind them. Cohen signaled for everyone to check magazines and ready their grenades. Putting his Uzi on safe, he collapsed the stock and slung it behind his shoulder. Borrowing some M16 magazines from the others, he nodded that they were ready. The point man flashed a nervous gap-toothed smile and held up three fingers. "Kapow three time, you come."

Cohen nodded, hoping he understood. His mind was racing: three shots or three bursts? Doubts pro and con played in his mind. He gazed into the eyes of his men. The point man waited. Once the NVA were firing everything they had, he shot up, loosed a quick high burst in the direction of the MIKE Force, and slipped around the corner. He fired a second short burst over the MIKE Force.

"Lower, shoot lower," screamed a nearby NVA.

Slamming a new magazine into his AK-47, he spun to fire into the speaker and his comrades. Seconds later, Cohen's M16 joined in, targeting a tall NVA in a faded sun helmet. Cohen's bursts punched into his upper chest, tore away the lower jaw, and sent the sun helmet flying. The NVA crumpled forward while the point man directed short bursts into those farther back. More M16s joined in to chop up further targets. No-jaw pushed himself to his knees, retrieved a nearby AK-47, and fired two wild bursts. Then, he staggered up. Two more rounds tore through him, but he made it to a crouched stance and jerked the trigger.

There was a sickening click. Blood poured from his mangled tongue and the gaping remnants of his mouth. He jacked the bolt back to eject a spent cartridge. It hung on an empty magazine. His eyes flashed surprise, then disgust, then a glare of unrelenting hatred. He reached down, swiveled the bayonet into position, and lunged forward with visible effort, blood spraying behind him at every hit. He managed four steps before he collapsed; the stuff of nightmares and legends. He had bought enough time for two wounded comrades to make it into the neighboring trench and shout a warning.

Cohen leaped over his body, pulled the pin from a grenade, rose, and tossed it after the escapees, spotting a line of green helmets bobbing in their direction as he did so.

Biloskirka saw Cohen rise, cursed, and called for his men to fire at the bobbing heads. They slowed, but kept moving. Boris gave a quick warning over his radio, but got no reply. The sound of Cohen's grenades confirmed that he already knew. He was either too busy, or had left his radio behind.

Left behind? Boris grabbed his own radio operator and several men, and took off for Cohen's platoon muttering: "Goddam, Jewboy, I am Master Sergeant. You disobeyed my order. When this shit is over, I am going to kick your ass."

St. Cyr radioed Cohen for his position. Boris replied that Cohen was in the upper trench. By the time St. Cyr was asking why he hadn't been informed, Boris had found Cohen's interpreter.

"Buddy, he's up there on his own. I repeat, on his own. Out."

Boris glared at the interpreter. "Goddam! Why you not move up? Get goddam men moving!"

"Wait for smoke!" the interpreter protested. "Must wait for smoke."

"Smoke my ass! Get moving!"

An 82mm mortar round exploding behind them sent everyone ducking for cover. The parapet absorbed most of the shrapnel. A short salvo bracketed the area. Someone screamed for the "Bac si." Boris stood back up, noted a shrapnel slice across his shoulder, and gazed over at the opposite trench where a second line of sun helmets was moving in from the left.

"Too late, Buddy. Too goddam late," he agonized. Fighting back the urge to scramble across, he cancelled his last order, set the interpreter to directing his men's fire, and passed the news to St. Cyr.

In the rush of adrenaline, Cohen had forgotten his platoon. Now, pulling back to the first trench section, he readied a green smoke grenade. In sight of his own positions, he tossed it over the parapet. AK rounds snapped past his ear. Spinning, he fired a quick burst at the far end, and clambered over NVA bodies to retreat around the corner. He motioned to his point man that they had enemy coming from the right. The point man motioned that they had enemy coming from the left. Cohen nodded, and readied his CS grenade.

With NVA pouring down both sides of the upper trench, Biloskirka rushed between Cohen's platoon and his own, directing fire. A medium machinegun firing on them from the summit was momentarily silenced by Thuan's mortars. Saville called for St. Cyr to get around to Rayne's flank, but both were under heavy attack. A storm of fire sounded from the upper trench. Boris pulled some of his own men down to help Cohen's. Those who had jumped out on the green smoke now desperately hugged the ground, machineguns slicing air inches above their shaking forms. Boris fired streams of tracer into the opposite trench, pummeled Cohen's men to do likewise, and rushed back to check that his own men were keeping up the fire. There was a flurry of grenade explosions, followed by a rash of mixed M16 and AK-47 fire, which popped to a stop amid a cloud of acrid gray smoke.

In the deadly lull, Boris gritted his teeth so hard a denture broke. The rush of sharp pain jolted him into total awareness. Ryan's anguished call to Cohen on the radio was answered by silence. Above that silence, Cobra gunships thundered over to rake the upper trenches and bunker. Biloskirka set both platoons to recovering ammo and water from the dead and seriously wounded. After keying his mike and choking several times, he passed word to St. Cyr that they had one probable Roundeye KIA. Minutes later, St. Cyr arrived with Spam in tow. A red eyed Boris gave him a quick rundown on Cohen's actions, to which St. Cyr gave a cold nod, leaving Spam in charge of Cohen's men.

St. Cyr got back to Blek and Ro'o Mnur just in time to hear firing from below. The Nha Trang MIKE Force was clearing remaining pockets of enemy from the base of the hill. Truffle reported he had two companies with him, minus a platoon he'd sent off to take out the .51 caliber. Mac had tagged along with this platoon, as several Jarai from his old 25th Company were with it.

With 212th Company in the middle trenches, Truffle's arrival pushed the NVA below the hill into a running fight around its base. Near its northernmost point they ran into Rayne's Recces. Met with heavy M60 machinegun fire and a shower of grenades, they pulled back into a partially finished communications trench along the bottom of the hill. Where it ended, they struck out for the forest a half kilometer away. Rayne alerted Saville, who called in the Cobras. Guided by swaths trampled through the grass, the gunships made a single pass as the NVA scattered. When the Cobras swung around for a second pass, golf-ball sized green tracers zipped by, prompting them to break contact and clear the way for fighter-bombers. As they did so, the survivors scrambled into the forest in bits and pieces.

Minutes later, Montagnard troops in steel helmets piled into the trenches near Spam. Friendly calls flew back and forth between Pleiku and Nha Trang troops, but the newcomers glared at Spam. Boris noted their hard looks as he moved in to brief Staff Sergeant Franke.

"Hey, Frankie—your men Jarai?"

"No, Rhade with some Koho. Estrada's company's Jarai. And the Cham Company's standing by to lift in."

"How well they get along with LLDB?"

"Same as all the rest. If the VC don't kill your Slope there, one of them just might.

"Boris jabbed a firm finger into Franke's chest.

"Look Buddy, Spam's no slope. He's OK."

"Boris, if you say so, he's gotta be damned good. But they don't know, and they don't care. Been acting real funny these past few days. Tell your man to stay out of their gun sights."

Back among his own, Biloskirka called St. Cyr to recommend they split Cohen's men among the other platoons and send Spam back to Recon. Having just received Saville's attack order, St. Cyr nixed that idea, but sent K'sor Tlur over to keep an eye on the Nha Trang troopers.

Truffle called St. Cyr to ask for a quick coordination meeting. With Blek, K'sor Tlur, and Ro'o Mnur in tow, St. Cyr made his way back to Cohen's platoon. Despite the 101st Airborne combat patch, Truffle greeted Blek and K'sor Tlur with a Montagnard handshake and a friendly "*Swas'm lai.*"

"Been in the MIKE Force long?" St. Cyr wondered.

"Since June. I had B Company, Second Bat of the Five-Oh-First at Hue."

"Must've been rough."

"This don't look a whole lot better. What's the plan?"

"We're the hammer. Rayne and Ferris are the anvil. Saville's going to put as much fire as he can into the trenches facing us. On the red and green star clusters, we push up into those trenches as fast as we can. Once we're in, I go to the right. You go to the left. And when either of us hits a communication trench, we push up to that bunker on the crest and clean it out."

"Got it. How've they been using their mortars?"

"We've been hit with eighty-deuces, but the fifty-one cals have been our biggest problem. The air's been keeping the mortars off our backs."

"Not for long, El Tee. They'll be saving everything they have for this last trench and bunker. What do you know about the bunker?"

"It's a bunker."

"Yeah? Well listen up, Junior. It's two buried conex containers with pierced steel planking and timbers covering a space in between. That means it's got three chambers. Make sure whoever goes in knows that."

"Hey, Captain, thanks for the intel. We weren't sitting on the beach in Nha Trang when we got the call. We'd been humping heavy bush for more than a week, had a small FULRO revolt, and were lifted in here taking casualties from the start. And you're looking at the only company that made it through the wire. So, with all due respect, fuck you!"

Truffle managed a smile. "That's fuck you, Sir! Hey, Frenchy, what's your real name?"

"Galen."

"Look, Galen, it's the way I talk. Don't take it personal. When this shit's over, I'll buy you a beer and give you the chance to whip my ass. But get your head in the game. When Saville lifts that fire, send this platoon up first. I'll send Franke's. The rest can support by fire. Just soon as they reach that trench, we push up the rest. That way, there's less confusion. Just make sure your men keep up with mine. What's the password?"

"Go FULRO!"

"Whose bright idea was that?"

"Mine. They're two words that every Yard we've got will recognize, even yours. I'll get word out that your men are wearing U.S. helmets. Most of mine are in boonie hats. My call sign's *Bearkiller*, Ferris is *Wheel*, and Rayne is *Simo*."

"What the hell's a Simo?"

"No idea. He's new, but this is his fifth war. He's an old SAS and Commando hand who just came out of a provincial reconnaissance unit.

"Shit, why isn't he the hammer?"

"Probably," St. Cyr flashed his own tired grin, "because he was smart enough to suggest us."

Truffle took a handset from his radio operator. A voice told him that his companies were positioned and ready, except for the platoon still searching for the .51 caliber. Truffle rogered and looked back at St. Cyr.

"OK, Galen. Any questions for me?"

"Yeah, who's your Yard counterpart?"

"We don't have them above platoon level any more. The LLDB fired them all a few weeks back. I sent mine down to Estrada's company, but he's pissed about the demotion. A really great kid named Johnny."

"Johnny! Siu Dot Jhon Nie?"

"Just Johnny, I guess. We've got a couple of those. Hey, gotta run. Remember to keep your guys up with mine. Good hunting!"

As Truffle trudged away, Blek cautioned K'sor Tlur to stay close to Spam and keep an eye on any Nha Trang troops in their sector. As they moved back through Boris's platoon to position themselves between Boris and Ryan's men, St. Cyr felt the knot tightening in his gut. Firing had died down, but everyone was tensing up. Biloskirka pointed to where fresh earth marked new or improved trenches up near the bunker.

"They know what's coming," griped Boris.

"Not too hard to figure out."

"Well, Buddy, if I see the Jewboy I give him your regards."

"If I see him first, I'll do the same."

"Good!" Boris flashed St. Cyr a look of genuine affection. "Otherwise, next year in Black Rose."

"In the Black Rose," St. Cyr called back, as he pushed off to rejoin Blek and Ro'o Mnur while Thuan's mortars peppered the upper trenches and bunker. Once the mortars fell silent, Cobra gunships whuppered overhead. A .51 caliber opened up somewhere. Wedged in between Ro'o Mnur and Blek, St. Cyr prayed. One moment's faulty judgment by a 19-year-old warrant officer pilot busy dodging small arms fire and .51 caliber rounds, and the plaques over Big Marty's bar would have plenty of company.

He winced as aerial rockets slammed around the bunker. Blek flashed him a "gotcha" smile. Then, the miniguns cut loose. The troops covered their heads with their arms to protect against the rain of hot brass. As a second pass went in, St. Cyr popped his head up and spotted the green and red star clusters. He was about key his mike when Boris's voice came up on the company net.

"Trung-si, *di len di!*" Get going up, go!

Blek keyed his HT-1, shouting orders in Jarai while everyone fired on the upper trenches. Few were taking aim. Spam and K'sor Tlur were up and moving, followed by seventeen or so troopers. In the opposite trench, heads were bobbing. Spam had no time to look to his left and track Truffle's men. He blew his whistle, and his men hit the ground, firing at any movement to their front. Behind, Biloskirka's group leapt out of their trench. A few brave NVA lifted their heads to fire, and were quickly taken out. The more cautious threw grenades. Spam called for grenades from his own men. Several flew in. One was tossed back. As soon as the last explosion sounded, Spam and Tlur were up, driving their men into the trench. There was a quick rash of firing from both ends. Tlur signaled that Truffle's platoon had made it. Spam passed the report to Blek and set about positioning his men.

Low-firing RPDs in Boris's sector had forced his men into an even lower crawl. Leading forward under green tracers snapping just above them, he kept calling "crawl and fire, crawl and fire" while his M60 machinegun crew and grenadiers back in the trench tried to cover them.

"Bearkiller," Boris called over the radio from a shell hole. "We're almost in. Get moving!"

St. Cyr had busied himself with the radio, jiggling his ankles nervously. The crash of small arms and the sound of Boris's voice drenched his soul with fear. His eyes wandered from Boris's men to Blek, who had unholstered his Ruger single-action and was shouting into an HT-1 radio. Blek nodded back, his vision fastened on the upper trench. Toller reported that Ryan and Jimm's men were moving. Spam's whistle sounded in the distance. K'sor Tlur radioed that they needed more men. Fire from the upper trench was building.

A voice that sounded like his own screamed for everyone to get moving. He forced himself up out of the trench and after Blek. His feet moved like lead weights. An eternity of maybe ten to fifteen seconds out of the trench, it was crawl or die. The better men crawled and fired, and prodded those in front of them forward. Many lesser heroes froze. Green RPD tracers snapped down from their front while invisible .51 caliber rounds lightning-cracked from the side. St. Cyr froze. Assessing the situation, he told himself, but an inner voice sneered otherwise.

To his left, Boris and a small group inched forward under the tracers. Five meters from the upper trench, Boris lobbed a grenade. As it exploded, he crawled rapidly behind it and rolled down into a trench slippery with blood, ground organs, and bodies. Seconds later, Nur Liet and a few others joined him. Two badly wounded NVA were quickly dispatched. To get the rest of his men moving, Nur Liet tossed an inert NVA grenade back behind their prostrate forms. Some started crawling, but others stayed glued to the earth. Nur Liet rummaged through an NVA rucksack and found several more grenades. These he lobbed back as fast as he could arm them. The explosions sent his men crawling frantically forward. As they reached the trench, an irate Nur Liet manhandled them into position.

With Ryan's men pinned under RPD fire from a small bunker in an adjacent trench, Boris had no time to look for the Superjew. He motioned for Nur Liet to stay in place, and for a fire team to follow. Spotting the bunker, he hunkered down. Searching his pack, he found a white phosphorous grenade. Best saved for the command bunker, he told himself. His index finger touched his last hand grenade. With his eyes locked on the nearest aperture, Boris pulled the pin, released the handle, counted two seconds, then rose and lobbed it in.

There was a brief second of silent panic, then one-two explosion set as his grenade set off a louder secondary explosion. Ears ringing, Boris pushed his men into the adjacent trench. As Nur Liet's face bobbed into view, Boris grabbed his harness.

"Liet, where is everyone?"

"Sergeant Bori, everyone who come. Here. Other come later!"

Boris glanced up and down the trench. At best, he had just over 20 men. "OK," he nodded. "We need *pow mitreeyoor* here, also grenadiers. Now! Everyone stay with squad. No buddy-ganging. Keep fire on main bunker, and next trench. Make sure we keep contact with…Trung-si's men."

He'd choked the Superjew's name back just in time. Naming the recently killed invited bad luck.

While Nur Liet set to work, Boris dragged the bodies out of their bunker, and squeezed in to look for St. Cyr and Blek. Seconds later, K'sor Tlur crowded in to peer over his shoulder.

"What you do here?" Boris demanded in French.

"Check my captain. Sergeant Spam does well. I tell squad, if anything happen to him, I shoot them all."

Boris peered out to where Blek, St. Cyr, and Ro'o Mnur were pinned under streams of .51 caliber fire. Though it passed mere inches above them, frontal fire from RPDs and AK-47s was a greater threat. The trenches had to be cleared quickly. Rchom Jimm's voice over Tlur's HT-1 radio reported that they had taken their sector and that Toller was leading a squad towards the communication trench. Boris asked Jimm to send a few men his way as he and K'sor Tlur led their men toward the adjacent trench. The lead man stepped into the corner only to be cut down. The men behind him dropped to the trench floor as grenades rained in. Boris set them to throwing the grenades back.

K'sor Tlur readied a U.S. grenade and peered above the parapet while a second Yard trooper edged cautiously around the first. Holding his M16 sideways with his left hand on the butt, he nodded to Tlur, who released the handle, counted, and threw the grenade. As it exploded, the rifleman stuck his M16 around the corner to blindly spray automatic fire. Several more explosions signaled that the grenadiers had shifted their fire. As K'sor Tlur pushed a fire team in behind the gunner, Boris snapped up, threw a grenade into the farther trench, and rushed in behind Tlur. In a short, sharp firefight, and they lost one killed and two seriously wounded before they reached the far end. Picking up a discarded NVA helmet, K'sor Tlur draped his tiger striped beret over the visor and inched it around the corner. AK-47 rounds shredded the visor.

"Grenade," he called. The men shook their heads. They were out. "Get grenade Tiep-zap bodies," he ordered.

No one moved, reluctant to touch men they had killed only moments before. A pineapple grenade thunked off the nearest man's harness and dropped to the floor. In an instant, K'sor Tlur picked up and threw it out. It barely cleared the parapet before it exploded with a deafening concussion. Ignoring the dull throbbing in his head, Tlur popped up to fire a burst from his paratroop M2 carbine while screaming for his men to get around the corner.

If the NVA had intended to follow the grenade up with an assault, the return fire must have changed their minds. A nearby trooper, rummaging through the canvas tote bag of a lighter sun-helmeted corpse, discovered a half dozen RGD-5 grenades which he passed to K'sor Tlur.

After positioning two grenadiers ten feet apart with instructions to toss all their grenades, he moved back to where the men had bunched up to watch the M-16 gunner fire around the corner. Several more men straggled in. For once, buddy-ganging was in their favor. Vile curses spread everyone out. While Boris put a few to firing at the adjacent trench, Tlur led his assault group forward.

Northeast of the camp, Snake Estrada's detached platoon was working its way to the smaller hill. They had taken out a .51 caliber with the help of gunships, and were halfway back when a second .51 opened up. McElroy studied the men pinned under its fire. Falling back to the young sergeant leading the platoon, Mac asked him to switch his radio to Saville's frequency. Saville's unanswered calls for Bearkiller told Mac all he needed to know. He prodded Sergeant Walker to ask Estrada for a change of mission. When Estrada refused, Mac grabbed the microphone and added his own weight to the argument, but Estrada needed to recover his platoon.

Mac detained Walker long enough to call a new .51 caliber target for the gunships, then barked orders to the men in Jarai.

"Hey, Sarge, what the hell ya doin'," Walker shouted as men began to cluster around Mac.

"Borrowin' some of your troopies."

"Ya can't do that.'

"I can if they follow me."

To Walker's amazement, nearly half his men formed up around Mac. Mac had them kneel while he issued his attack order in rapid-fire Jarai. As Walker fumed, Mac looked up.

"You got any air recognition panels?"

"Yeah, Sarge. One."

"I need it."

"I need it myself."

"You got a PRC-25. All we've got are HT-1s. If you don't want your men mistaken for NVA, give me the panel. And tell any inbound jet jockeys to keep an eye out."

"Estrada's going to whip my ass."

"He's gonna whip mine too, but it's gotta be done."

Walker, a strapping coal miner's son from Harlan County, Kentucky, didn't like being undercut like this. But he'd seen enough of Mac to confirm the stories he'd heard. Rummaging through his radio operator's rucksack, he handed Mac the bright orange panel.

"Thanks, kid. I'll buy you a beer when we get back to Nha Trang."

"After I whip your ass."

Mac flashed a sardonic smile. "I'm probably as tough as your dad."

"You're gonna get the fuckin' chance to prove that, Sarge. But this ain't the time and place."

"No, it ain't. And you got a deal."

While Walker led his remaining squads to the northern hill, Mac pushed off. He tied the panel to his rucksack, and prayed that any inbound aircraft would recognize it in time. Cobras thundered in the distance. The .51 caliber continued to rake the hill below the upper trench line. As the cobras made their attack, both took hits from company medium machineguns set up at right angles to the .51. Mac marveled at the thoroughness of the NVA's fire plan. Whoever had dreamed this up had no small amount of experience. This .51 was going to be dug in much better than the last, likely with only a firing slit exposed. As Mac pushed his men towards the sound of its firing, 82mm mortar rounds fell to their left. Someone had spotted them. The cobras peeled off to go after the mortars. As they fell silent, Mac rushed his men to the wood line. As they neared it, the rattle of an RPD sent everyone diving to earth. Split seconds later, company medium machineguns tore through the tranh grass like a giant scythe. Mac crawled into a small clearing and rummaged in his rucksack for the binoculars he'd hoped to get home. Rising up enough to glass a small hill just inside the wood line, he spotted a .51 caliber muzzle blast as it shook the grass and surrounding vegetation. Dust flew up from a Cobra gunship's pass. It appeared to be a direct hit, but the .51 was back in action a few seconds later. Mac watched several passes, until a sniper round nicked ear. Dropping into the grass, he crawled to the nearest squad leader.

"Can talk Sergeant Walka?"

"Uangh."

Mac took the HT-1 and instructed the Jarai platoon leader to pass his radio to Walker.

"Walker, Tell Estrada there's two fifty-ones left up there—one's a little further back behind the first. When one stops firing, the other takes it up. They're dug in. It'll take at least a five-hundred-pounder to take 'em out. Tell Estrada to pass that to the FAC."

"OK, Sarge. When the hell do I get my men back?"

"As soon as that air strike goes in. Over."

"Roger. I'll meet you at the break in the wire."

Mac was betting it wouldn't be long before the 82s started up again, and at least an enemy platoon was headed their way. So he pointed his men back towards the northern hill, which erupted in a frenzy of firing and explosions, and waited for the sound of that 500 pounder.

K'sor Tlur cast one last glance over the parapet as he readied his men for the assault. Another line of green helmets was moving down from the upper bunker. Blek, St. Cyr, and Ro'o Mnur were inching forward.

"Go," Tlur yelled.

The grenadiers tossed their grenades as a new M16 gunner emptied 30-round magazines down the trench. After counting five explosions, K'sor Tlur physically pushed his men ahead. The first two were hit, and fell, but kept firing until their comrades stepped past. Despite having been trampled, one managed to limp to his feet and follow.

Out under the .51 caliber fire, St. Cyr looked into Blek's eyes.

"My brother," Blek smiled grimly, "we must show them. Ready?"

Time was running out. A rash of firing from the far end of the trench signaled opportunity. St. Cyr cast a glance at Ro'o Mnur, who was wiggling out of his radio harness. Smart decision, he thought. They could recover the radio later. A jet thundered somewhere above. A loud explosion sounded in the near distance.

St. Cyr glanced at Blek, gritted his teeth, and nodded. He wanted to crawl, but if Blek got up, he would too. Ro'o Mnur crawled past, firing his M16 single-handedly and pulling his radio by its web straps. An overpowering fear clawed at the pit of St. Cyr's stomach.

"We go," Blek grunted, rising.

St. Cyr flinched, desperately trying to rise, but some traitor in his souls was pushing him down as hard as he tried to push up. Blek inched up first. As he went into a crouch, St. Cyr managed to rise just enough to fire a burst into the trench. He had no target and was firing only to kill his own fear. His eyes locked on Blek, two steps away. Everyone was crawling forward in seeming slow motion when the dreaded lightning cracks sounded again. An invisible sledgehammer smashed into his chest. He was knocked sideways. For long seconds, he couldn't breathe. In an instant, he was a child on his Aunt Marthe's farm down in Ste Agathe, where he had climbed her apple tree. Up and up, until the branch he was perched on had snapped, and all the terror of having disobeyed rushed into his juvenile soul while he dropped 20 feet to the ground, landing squarely on his back. As he fought for breath, instead of cousins and parents, Blek's face came into view.

"Faster. Must move faster!"

Sweat and blood ran down his chest, and still he could not breathe. *God, please, no!*

As Blek's hand grasped St. Cyr's harness, his head mushroomed into an obscene pink balloon, spraying St. Cyr with bone, jelly and blood. St. Cyr didn't hear the second jet, or its explosion, or see Ryan's men rise and scramble into the trench. The deadly lightning cracks ceased, but fire rained down from the bunker at the crest of the hill. He tried to move, but each motion wracked his chest with pain. He lifted his arm to find his Car-15 receiver had been smashed.

Ryan called from the trench, asking where he'd been hit, but St. Cyr couldn't reply. The men's firing was ragged, uneven. Ryan's voice called that Bearkiller was down. K'sor Tlur was screaming for more fire on the bunker, demanding to know where the M79 grenadiers had left their testicles. Firing from the trench up to the bunker grew louder.

Seconds later, Ryan and an indigenous medic dashed out to manhandle him over the parapet and into the trench. The movement and shock of being dropped brought fresh sharp pains, and a gasp. He was on the point of passing out when fresh air exploded into his lungs. His shirt was ripped open. Ryan's fingers probed the bone and muscle under his chest. Electric pain waves flashed along his ribcage.

"Your sternum's probably cracked, but not broken," Ryan shouted. "You should be able to stand."

Heavy firing sounded nearby. Toller dropped down, placed his finger on St. Cyr's jugular vein, and took a quick count.

"Leftenant, you're in shock! Snap out of it. We've got work to do."

St. Cyr reached a hand up to his face to wipe away some grey jelly. "Where's Blek?"

"Dead! You need to get up, or we'll be joining him."

The image of Blek's head exploding under the impact of a .51 caliber round flashed dimly in St. Cyr's subconscious.

"Dead?"

"Goddammit, El Tee," Ryan flashed him a disgusted look. "You're the commander. Get your ass moving. We've got a lot of people in much worse shape. Get the hell up on your feet!"

Taking Ryan's extended hand, St. Cyr pulled himself up, wincing as a light cough sent pain coursing through his chest. After some carefully spaced breaths, he looked around, his voice a course whisper.

"Get Jimm up here. He's the Dega commander now. Mister Toller, return to your platoon. Where's my radio?"

Toller called for Ro'o Mnur, who came limping up. One round had sliced him vertically across the upper back, another had creased his thigh. Ryan had his indigenous medic slap a quick dressing on Ro'o Mnur's thigh, and went back to his platoon.

As St. Cyr keyed the microphone, a firestorm broke off to their left. Truffle's voice demanded to know what the hell had happened to Bearkiller. Answering fire poured down from the bunker. There was no plan now. If Truffle's people were assaulting the bunker's far side, there was only one way out. They fired at every aperture they could see, and any flash of movement near the bunker. Toller reported a gap between his men and Rayne's. Ferris reported that Truffle's men were falling back. Where the hell was Bearkiller? He was interrupted by a barrage of 82mm mortars bracketing the hill.

Everyone hunkered down in the trenches or crowded into bunkers. No one seemed to mind bodies now. As soon as it ended, Biloskirka was up, calling for K'sor Tlur. The men's' eyes were wide with fear.

"Get up and get firing," he called. Some did, but many stayed down. "Nur Liet, get them up and firing." Boris moved down the line towards K'sor Tlur's last position, firing bursts as he went. The third time he rose, deafening green-tracers cracked by his ear.

"Sergeant Bori!" A nearby trooper pointed to his own ear. "You hit."

Boris reached up to his left ear to find part of it missing. The machinegunner was tracking him.

"Ear OK," he called to the anxious trooper. Pulling back to his right, he rose to fire a longer burst, dropping down just before another stream of green tracer arrived. Pushing on to the next trench section, he found a gaggle of men bunched up below a communications trench, staring vacantly at him.

"Where Nur Liet," he demanded. No one answered. The mortar fire had stopped. With only the bunker and communication trenches left, the men were losing their drive. As soon as the bunker was taken, they reasoned, the fight would be over. Who wanted to be the last man killed?

"Get up and fire," Boris raged, manhandling men up as he moved down the line. Some did, while others crouched back down. "Grenade. Who have grenade?"

Several men produced grenades. Boris collected them. Moving to the communications trench, he picked up an NVA pack. Swinging it in front of the trench entrance brought a short AK-47 burst. Someone was up there. He swung it out again, but his opponent wasn't fooled. It could be a fire team or a whole damned platoon. Boris was guessing it was close to the latter—waiting for the order to push down and drive his men back, or up into the machinegun fire.

He took a quick glance at the firing aperture. Where the hell were his M79 grenadiers? It was too far to chance his only white phosphorus grenade. Smoke wouldn't bother a gunner with marked fields of fire. But WP fragments and smoke inside the bunker would drive the occupants out, and maybe touch off a secondary explosion. But he had to get up close, and he needed covering fire to do that.

Boris prepared two grenades, and tossed them into sections of the communications trench. Then he took off at a run, keeping as low as he could. A ways past the communication trench entrance, another machinegunner picked up his movement. Boris could feel the bursts cracking by just above his spine. He found Nur Liet directing fire in an adjacent trench section, stopped to chew his ass for not moving among all his squads, and brushed past into Cohen's men, where he found K'sor Tlur and Spam near a few helmeted Nha Trang troopers. For split seconds, Boris weighed taking Spam with him. Spam could work wonders with an M79, but he was busy directing Cohen's men, who hadn't been trained to react to his whistle.

Grabbing K'sor Tlur, Boris explained his plan in short words. Tlur was to take half of Boris's men up the communications trench as close to the bunker as possible. Close enough to where the machinegunner could not swing his gun around. Boris would take it from there. Nur Liet's job was to spread the other half out and keep them firing in support, with any M79 gunners concentrating on the machinegun's aperture. As soon as Nur Liet saw Boris come out of his trench, the M79 gunners were to cease firing at the aperture.

K'sor Tlur and Nur Liet set to work organizing their men. Tlur passed out Boris's grenades among his own, while Boris stole another glance at the bunker. He was no longer the lithe 17-year-old with hungry wolf reflexes. Twenty-three years had added weight and muscle: Good for humping overweight rucksacks long distances, but it slowed you down. Mentally, he gauged his best angle of approach and how long it would take to cover the ground. If only the Jewboy were here.

Once K'sor Tlur had his men organized for their rush up the communications trench, he nodded to Boris.

Boris fished his neck chain out and kissed the small gold Orthodox cross next to his dogtags. *Well, Jewboy, here's hoping I don't see you today. No offense, but I would see my son first. Rolf, put in good word for him.* Glancing at K'sor Tlur, he nodded back and signaled 'go.'

At K'sor Tlur's first signal, his M60 machinegunner began hammering away from Nur Liet's position. At Tlur's second, the men he'd armed with grenades pulled the pins, counted down, and tossed them at sections of communications trench ahead. His third signal pushed his riflemen forward as Nur Liet's men opened fire. Boris placed himself in the middle of the assault group. NVA grenades rained back; some falling outside the trench, some falling in. Men screamed in rage, fear, and panicked pain as fragments and rounds found their mark. Boris stole two glances at the aperture. Pink dust spurts amid the muzzle flashes told him that some of Liet's people were aiming. The bunker sandbags were old, the red earth inside them packed and sunbaked.

As one fire team bogged down, K'sor Tlur pushed another forward. As he crouch-sprinted, Boris side-stepped the wounded and dead to push on. Both sides appeared to have run out of grenades. They made it two thirds of the way to where small arms fire raged back and forth around a commanding turn in the communication trench. Boris grabbed another peek at the aperture. It had to be 50 feet away. An M79 round smacking five feet above the aperture sent rivulets of dirt cascading down. It wasn't much of an opportunity, but Boris decided to chance it.

"Tlur," Boris called. "Have the men keep VC heads down."

Tlur signaled he understood, and screamed instructions to his troops. With that, Boris stripped off his equipment, retrieved his white phosphorus grenade, and slithered over the parapet as Tlur rushed to and fro among the men, directing their fire.

It was a quick and hard slither, then a crawl on knees and elbows. Incoming fire passing over him petered off as approached the aperture. He didn't have long. Experienced gunners would know what that drop in fire meant. Up against the bunker wall now, he pulled the pin, slithered forward another three body lengths, and tossed it in when he figured he had two seconds left.

Boris didn't plan on hanging around. A quick turn about and he was crawling straight away, praying he'd clear the bunker before any serious secondary explosions. There was a muffled explosion. He did not look back. Whatever the result, he had to get to the communications trench in time to get the men moving.

The sound of the explosion and smoke pouring from the aperture brought one young M79 gunner to his feet. With a weary smile, he pointed his still loaded weapon single-handedly at the aperture and fired his last round. The smile disappeared as he saw it bounce off the ground, glance up to hit the bunker, then ricochet back to where the big Meerkia was crawling.

The round thumped down three feet in front of Boris's face. In an instant, he understood. *Buddy*, irony flashed in his eyes, *you were not supposed to fire*. Then it exploded.

The sight of smoke billowing from the bunker reenergized the troops. Ragged at first, the volume of fire built rapidly. As Ryan and Toller pushed their men up another communications trench bit by bit, Spam grabbed any and all M79 gunners he could find and kept them firing. Men rushed, skidded, fell, rolled, and screamed. As other bunker apertures fell silent, small groups from the trenches rushed out and up, taking shelter in bomb craters to pour in fire and grenades wherever they could. Helmeted Nha Trang MIKE Force troopers now mixed with Pleiku's boonie hat crowd.

"Who your commander?" K'sor Tlur called as several rushed into his position.

"Rahlen Blek's father," came one reply.

"'Bout dam time you here!" K'sor shot back in English. Mac flashed a grim smile and pushed on. Tiger striped figures poured out from the trenches.

"What the hell's going on?" St. Cyr rasped as Mac approached in a swarm of Nha Trang troopers.

"Thought you might need some help," Mac called back. "Where's Blek?"

St. Cyr choked up, and just shook his head. Mac paused, then pushed towards the heaviest firing with the look of a man who had scores to settle. Heavy small arms fire broke off to Toller's flank as the NVA tried to force the gap between Toller and Rayne. Fire from both companies dropped many, to include a few friendlies.

As gunships raked distant targets of opportunity with rocket and machinegun fire, the bunker's tottering resistance triggered a terrible psychosis. If the men within had ever harbored illusions of survival, these were now gone. Cursing and hating, they waited as the MIKE Force surged towards them with panic, terror, hatred, and revenge coursing through their bones. From trench to trench, and up to the bunker, tiger-striped packs of men rushed, ducked, crawled, and shot their way through, leaving dead, dying, and screaming comrades and enemy in their wake. Amid the screams and fire, an insanely low throaty growl of desperation and revenge was heard. Go, FULRO, Uangh! Whispered, chanted, murmured, and screamed until even Spam took it up.

Somewhere past the upper trench line, where he crouched heaving under a merciless sun next to a dying Ro'o Mnur, the psychosis entered St. Cyr's soul.

"Go FULRO!" He tottered out of his trench to stagger forward. At first halting, then somewhat quicker, then at a run. He screamed and frothed at the mouth, wild, wild-eyed, and mortally shamed. Men rose as from the grave. Among the familiar silhouettes of Rchom Jimm, Spam, and K'sor Tlur were helmeted Dega he'd never seen. Around him, bullets spewed wildly from the muzzles of guns as men rose to kill or run. And then they were on them. These arrogant, twig-limbed, scheming, lying, backstabbing, murdering, invading yellow slime. The bastards who'd killed Grey, Moshlatubbee, Balden, Blek, the Superjew, and Ro'o Mnur. He picked up a smashed RPD by its still hot barrel, and swung it like an ax, searching desperately for that fear he so wanted to see in their eyes. Aching to feel the crunch as it broke into their skulls, screaming a belabored and hoarse "Go FULRO", he smashed his macabre war club into both the living and the dead, until he stumbled and fell. Spasms of choking pain flashed through his chest and heart. He struggled to rise, just in time to meet an enraged but dying North Vietnamese, who banged an AK-47 receiver into the side of his skull.

He lay stunned in a trench, breathing with labored difficulty, until a panicked feeling that his chest was caving in drove him to push the dead NVA's body away and struggle to his feet, gasping for breath as if emerging from a deep free dive. Under a merciless sun, he gazed about the twin hills of Duc Het, Dak Min district, in the Dega High Plateaus of Champa, amidst a victorious FULRO army. The silence overpowered his ears as singing tones subsided.

"Care for some water, Leftenant?" Laurie Toller's face came into view. He took the proffered canteen and drank greedily, each gulp sending spasms of pain through his chest.

"I'll tell you, Mate," Laurie continued. "I'm damned glad I never got on your wrong side."

He wasn't sure what that meant. "Where is everybody?" he rasped.

A dirty tear trickled down Laurie's cheek. "You and I and Ryan are what's left of the Roundeyes. Helluva fight. Best I can figure, we've about sixty-eight dead or missing."

"Where's Blek, Boris, and the Superjew?"

Toller glanced at the gash in St. Cyr's head, and nodded. "We need to get you medevaced."

"What happened to Cohen?"

"His attack was what cleared our way into the upper trenches. Haven't found his body yet, but he's in here somewhere. Boris got killed at the bunker. Spam's hit, took some rounds through the thigh and forearm. I sent him down to get medevaced. That new man Thuan's with him. With all these strange Yards around, its better they stick together, if you know what I mean."

Toller was shirtless, except for a heavy bandage around his shoulder. The late afternoon sun dipped low over the horizon. They were standing by a trench at the top of the hill. Laurie had picked up a radio and was talking to someone.

"Medevac's inbound. If you'll excuse me, I'd like to make sure that Spam gets out on this one. We'll get you out later. Jimm, you're in charge. You might remember, Leftenant, Jimm's commander now."

His eyes focused in on Rchom Jimm and a sea of Dega faces. Tired apprehensive faces with distant pained stares in their eyes. Some wore the dragon patch. Others wore the blue shield and red crossbow of the Nha Trang MIKE force. Friends.

"Swas'm lai," he flashed a weak smile, sending currents of pain slashing through his chest and ribcage. "Go FULRO..."

A few gap-toothed smiles replied. Others murmured. Most merely stared through him. Something in that look stirred a faint memory, but he couldn't recall what it was. He couldn't see his own thousand Yard stare. Jimm stepped away to confer with several nearby Dega leaders. St. Cyr was having trouble breathing. His passageway was clear, but each breath sent spasms of pain through his chest. Panicked voices inside urged him to get to the medevac, but a stronger voice ordered them to shut up. He was commander, and commander best stand in a fight. He would go out on the last medevac, after formally turning the company over to Toller.

The faces around him warmed as they heard him speak Jarai. Voices sounded off to his left. He turned with difficulty. A new Dega leader had arrived: A handsome young man who swaggered as he passed friendly words with his men. They laughed. He was carrying a Sten gun with a thick barrel—a silencer. The new arrival gave him a strange look, and an even stranger smile. It was then that he noticed the hands, like claws, lifting the Sten gun. His eyes focused on this young Dega's battle jacket, which bore the Pleiku MIKE Force patch on the right shoulder, and the Nha Trang MIKE Force patch on the left. As he looked into Siu Dot's eyes, the muzzle of the Sten gun steadied, and clapped two short bursts. Loud claps. He could actually see the copper and green hornets spit from the ugly black muzzle and race towards his chest, as if in stop-gap motion. There was a cry behind him, and an answering crash of gunfire as he crumpled over into a searing pain that wracked his whole frame. Above him, Rchom Jimm was still pointing Blek's revolver at the now prostrate form of Siu Dot Jhon Nie.

Jimm's foot clamped down on the Sten gun's barrel as Siu Dot gasped and clutched his own chest, his voice an angry, hoarse whisper.

"Me Sao's orders!"

"Perhaps," said Jimm, staring coolly over the iron sights as he casually advised everyone to stay calm. "But I too have orders. From H'nek."

"H'nek? But…Me Sao… "

"A family dispute, Brother Dot. H'nek's clan has offered me her bracelet."

"You?"

"Yes, myself. At least you no longer need fear the rot." And with that, Jimm pulled the trigger.

Minutes later, St. Cyr was being helped down the hill. One of the faces was Mac's. Ryan had put the chest tubes in, and was carrying the albumin bottle that had been hooked up above his left wrist. A familiar Dega face was to his left.

"Take it easy, Trung-oui," advised Ryan. "They're going have to do a little digging, but you'll make it."

"Won't be anything I haven't seen before."

"C'mon, El Tee, you can't fool an old combat medic." Ryan flashed a wan smile. "Every time's new."

They helped him up into the chopper. He looked over to find Saville, who gave him a friendly wave. As he lay back into the webbed seat, the last words he heard were Mac's, spoken in Jarai to some young trooper.

"He was warned," said Mac, "that too many wished to make her their betrothed. He would not listen…"

As the chopper lifted off, he turned his head to try and catch a glimpse of Blek and Ro'o Mnur's bodies. But all he could make out before exhaustion overtook him was smoke, and tranh grass, and the twin hills of Duc Het, and finally, a solitary anvil-shaped mountain brooding in distant Cambodia.

Epilogue

EVERY BATTLE DESERVES a glorious ending. Something to salve wounds, dull pains, and blur memories. Duc Het was no such battle. After-action reports from the 5th Special Forces Group, the Australian Army Training Team Vietnam, and the Luc Luong Dac Biet General Command all trumpeted Duc Het as the first time the MIKE Force had ever taken back a Special Forces camp by itself. But more such fights were in the wind.

If the battle's Free World participants were unaware of Duc Het's true purpose, the B-3 Front was not. Under cover of manning a border surveillance post, A-293's attached Army Security Agency signals intercept specialists poured over B-3 Front communications, and reported their contents directly to MACVSOG. Some 27 miles away at Bu Prang, another Special Forces camp, A-263, served as a MACVSOG launch site. So while the Roundeye survivors of Duc Het dulled their pains and brains, 95C Regiment's surviving officers limped around a terrain mockup, rehashing key moments of the battle before 66 and 42 NVA regimental cadres.

Prominent among them was a scarred senior captain who felt no reluctance in criticizing his superiors. Their movement to contact had been too predictable, he railed. It massed too many men, making them too easy to find and vulnerable to gunships, artillery, and B-52 strikes. They needed to split up in multiple smaller columns, approach the target from several directions, then mass to hit its most vulnerable points. In short, they had to move to their target like sappers, mass to hit it like infantry, then withdraw like commandos to hunker down in previously prepared bunker complexes and wait out the inevitable B-52s.

This point of view did not go unnoticed, and Duc Het underwent a frenzy of construction. Months after St. Cyr limped off the twin hills, the NVA launched another attack. Dak Min district was obliterated in hours. Duc Het would have suffered the same fate, but the NVA only sent a small deception force there, while they moved against Bu Prang.

McClellan grabbed the not-yet-reconstituted 1ˢᵗ Battalion, and shuttled them in. Ferris was killed in the first night's fighting. As the battalion disintegrated, its dwindling companies overrun, Warrant Officer Rayne took over. Amid this confusion, McClellan lifted a new 5ᵗʰ Battalion into the exact same landing zone. It took heavy fire going in. While Rayne battled on with what was left of the 1st Battalion, 5th Battalion's Lebanese-American commander recognized a lost cause. Abandoning his orders to clear any NVA in zone. He set about establishing a defensible perimeter to which Rayne's men could withdraw. Over the next three days, the two mangled battalions managed to beat off every attack, thanks mostly to artillery and the U.S. Air Force. But their forces kept shrinking. Many Yards simply walked away. Major Ngoc's attempt to establish LLDB command over the task force ended in a similar disaster. He went in accompanied by a slice of the Recon Company and never made it off the LZ. To his credit, Ngoc stayed on the ground until the majority of men had been lifted out, and died fighting as the LZ was overrun.

St. Cyr, meanwhile, had got on with life. At Nha Trang's 8ᵗʰ Field Hospital, they removed 9mm slugs from his shoulder and lung. They also found small chunks of some strange alloy peppered into his chest muscles that drew the doctors' attention. From X-rays, they verified what he knew already, that his sternum was cracked. It was a simple but painful fracture, and required tubes to keep his fluids drained. He also had a hairline crack along the left side of his skull that gave him splitting headaches, and various intestinal parasites. Other than the fact that he was down to three quarters his normal weight, and hooked up to all kinds of tubes, everything was fine. Most of the Dega medevaced from Duc Het had hardly fared so well.

The Nha Trang MIKE Force had several of their own in hospital, and made a point of stopping by. On his second night, he awoke to find a familiar shadow in the dark recesses of his ward.

"Mac?" he could barely hear his own voice. The shadow stirred, but didn't answer. Maybe it wasn't Mac, for there was only silence and the friendly patter of a nurse as she changed his IV.

A few days later, Regter stopped in to say goodbye. It was an awkward moment for both. Regter wished him well in civilian life, and then as he was leaving, said: "If you ever decide to come back in, Galen, you can work for me anytime." As a farewell speech, it wasn't much, but St. Cyr treasured those words for the rest of his life.

Nurse Jeanne-Marie Beauchamps was now with the 8th Field Hospital. Their reunion was not as either wished, but her smile and cheerful 'hello Cuz' kept his soul from plunging into darkness. He had her place the bottle of Hennessy XO at his bedside for Ryan when he came through, but Kev never made it. The bottle had only been there a few days when he was sent to Hawaii for further treatment and therapy. The doctors were concerned about an old injury to his spine. After a long and painfully boring flight, he was in Tripler Army Hospital.

Sometime that month, or maybe the next, he received a long and garrulous letter from Brock, now the adjutant, who brought him up on the latest MIKE Force news. Cohen and Biloskirka had been recommended for Distinguished Service Crosses. There had been talk of recommending the Superjew for the Medal of Honor, but Cox had nixed that. Perhaps Cox was right. Much of the sentiment to award Cohen the 'Big Bluie' came from the sight of his mangled testicles. The Superjew had fallen into NVA hands alive, and some worthy had attempted to castrate him before a gentler soul fired a bullet into his brain. All in all, the Superjew's men had probably killed 40 NVA before going down themselves. Ryan, Ferris, Balden, and Knuudsen had received Silver Stars. Neither Saville, Toller, nor Rayne received anything for Duc Het, but Rayne was up for Australia's highest honor, the Victoria Cross, for his later fight at Ben Het. This was the first that St. Cyr had heard of any fight at Bu Prang or Ben Het. Jed Saville had been recommended for a Military Cross by Headquarters, AATTV. But that had been vetoed by some faceless Brigadier on the grounds that Jed's twin brother, a captain with the 1st Australian Task Force, had previously received an MC. The Brigadier was not of a mind to give two brothers the same high award. Considering that most of the awards were posthumous, or to people in hospital, there was little ceremony to bother with.

As for Boris's remains, the Department of the Army had not honored a clause in his will that he be interred in Vietnam, nor had anyone thought to simply dump him in a mass grave with his opponents and report him missing. Brock had no idea where Boris's official resting place lay, but the two kids running the Pleiku mortuary had been kind enough to pass the parts they normally destroyed to the MIKE Force. Wrapped in plastic and placed in a child's coffin, they were interred in the military section of Pleiku's French cemetery, along with Boris's old kepi, beret, bush hat, wings, and shoulder boards. They owed this favor to some ARVN sergeant major up on the Corps staff who knew Boris from his Legion days. A local French civilian had donated the plot and paid for the headstone. One of the Nung cooks had even seen to it that Boris got a sendoff befitting a former member of the 2nd BEP, while the survivors of his platoon sacrificed a water buffalo to speed Boris on his way.

Weeks after Boris' death, Hoa had committed suicide in the liquor storage room next to Big Marty's bar. Brock had been in hot water with McClellan for having loaned her Boris's pistol to shoot what she said was a large rat. He'd been waiting for the Article 15 punishment that would end his career.

Brock had no news of Major Regter, whose name was on the latest lieutenant colonels list. He was supposed to be with the 8th Special Forces in Panama, but while awaiting his flight home at Cam Ranh Bay, he'd been rushed off to Bangkok for some kind of interview. Rumor had it he was up in Laos on some special project.

As for LTC McClellan, he had angered the old hands with a wholesale transfer in of newbies, and had let one of the new battalions walk out of the compound under the command of Glan Perr and Rahlen H'nek, who led it into Cambodia. The final straw came when Cox found McClellan playing volleyball while Rayne's people were fighting off annihilation at Bu Prang. Cox may have been a friend, but he recognized a mistake. The MIKE Force was under the temporary command of an Australian major while they looked for a replacement. Major Brendon's first action had been to call Brock in, chew his ass out over the pistol, and tear up papers that would have ended his career.

As for Rahlen H'nek, now somewhere in Cambodia, no one in the MIKE Force was supposed to know what was going on, but Ralph Johnson from the CIA's Montagnard Training Center kept showing up to see Harry Perkins. Rumor among the Yards was that the Highland Republic had been declared in Ratanakiri province under Y B'ham and Me Sao. As for

Marvin McElroy, some claimed that he was back in the states in a psycho ward, while others swore that he too was in Laos. Brock believed that Mac was in Cambodia with Rahlen H'nek, a hunch based upon the fact that the latest Yards to come in had told tales of two Americans working with a FULRO column. A common enough rumor, but one of the Yards produced a penciled note requesting that McKechnie, the C Team S-5, airdrop a couple of carefully packed bottles of 151-proof rum on his next Cambodian leaflet run. Unfortunately for Mac, or whoever wrote the note, the coordinates were smudged, which may have been quite fortunate for McKechnie.

St. Cyr kept that letter for years, occasionally taking it out to read, as if stepping back through some secret door in time. But as life passed, it got buried in deeper recesses of his boxes and drawers and went missing. It was all rumors and daydream anyway, mixed with just enough fact to make it dangerous. On his third month in Hawaii, some visiting general stopped in to pin a Silver Star on him, along with another Purple Heart. He accepted, if only to avoid unpleasant explanations to people who neither understood nor cared. He spent his last months in the army combing the coasts of Oahu in search of isolated beaches, and found none. You could not be alone on Oahu.

He took an early discharge in December, which factored in his convalescent leave, and returned home to Maine. This time, it was more an exile than a return. Madawaska, the town founded by his ancestors in 1785, was now his prison, peopled by fellow inmates whose vague exteriors masked former relatives and friends. When his mother insisted that he move in to his old room, in order to save money for an eventual marriage and house purchase, he did so. Still, he looked for jobs outside of Maine.

In March 1969 he traveled to Boston to interview with an investment firm. Arriving a few days early, he scouted out the Black Rose. On St. Patrick's Day he was there when it opened, and left only after it had closed. An entire day spent anxiously scanning every arrival for a familiar Black face had produced nothing. The following day, he called Harvard medical school. A Kevin Ryan had been accepted, but had failed to show. That news depressed him. He woke up the next morning with a hangover, and missed his interview.

Instead of banking, he took a job teaching economics at the local high school, where he met a girl from Scowhegan who taught at Fort Kent State College. His mother rejoiced in this proof that he was home to stay, and welcomed Evangeline Everett into their home. She was pretty enough, and from an old Yankee family. Soon, he was looking at rings.

Their marriage plans did not survive the Cambodian invasion. She sat before the television screen with clenched white knuckles, cursing Nixon for her powerless inability to stop the war. His eyes carefully scanned the news footage, cursing for entirely different reasons. Among the caches un-covered in Cambodia, a 1st Cavalry Division soldier joyously waved a FULRO flag. After Kent State, she mailed back his ring.

He responded by driving down to Caribou and signing up for the army reserve. It was a clubby civil affairs unit filled with distinguished mid-dle-aged men who stood in awe of his combat record. They did their an-nual training in Germany, supporting fall maneuvers, so he got some travel, and hopes of an eventual retirement out of it.

But he could not get the Highlands out of his souls. Often that winter, he would tiptoe downstairs and watch in the darkness as the wind whistled between the house and barn, driving snow snakes across white carpeted potato fields. If he stared long enough, he would see a Highland wind whip-ping through the tranh grass. One night, as silent tears of shame and grief coursed down his cheeks, he heard his father come up behind him.

"What is it you see there, my son?"

"Duc Het," he choked, turning his face away.

"For me, it was always Italy, Nineteen-Forty-Three, Casa Berardi. What were their names?"

"Rahlen Blek, Boris Biloskirka, Myron Cohen, Ro'o Mnur—and who knows, maybe Kevin Ryan. And a young lady named Rahlen H'nek."

"Ah, mine were Dionne, Paradis, Gagnon, and Michaud. Him, Michaud, I loved him like my own brothers. And Moriarty, an Irish kid from Montreal. He wouldn't speak English him. Me, I never met no young lady for long. And your commander, this Regter?"

"The finest damned officer that any army ever produced."

"Yes, like our own Capitaine Triquet. He looked like some silent movie star him, but when it came to fighting, he had guts."

For long minutes they fell silent. And then he felt his father's arm curl around his shoulder.

"Welcome home, my son. Thank the good God, but you had us worried. Especially your mother. If you had been killed, it would have made her die too."

As he hooked his own arm up over his father's shoulder, he saw the first tears he'd ever seen his father cry. And so they stood, staring out the window together, gazing beyond the distant forest into the stars and aurora borealis, saying nothing, in the most meaningful conversation of their lives.

About the Author

SHAUN DARRAGH served over 27 years in the U.S. Army before retiring to take a civilian intelligence position, first with the Joint Special Operations Command, and then with the U.S. Embassy in Mexico City, the U.S. Army South in Panama and Puerto Rico, and the Eighth U.S. Army in Seoul, Korea, before retiring to write. *MIKE Force*, his first novel, is based on his experiences on both a Special Forces A Team and in the II Corps MIKE Force in Vietnam. It 2010, under the title of *The Dega*, it took 1st Place in the Unpublished Historical Fiction category of the Florida Writer's Association Royal Palm Literary Awards competition. He speaks Spanish, French, Portuguese, Dutch/Afrikaans, and Vietnamese with varying degrees of fluency, and is currently working on a novel set among the ethnic Cambodians of the Mekong Delta.

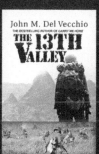

Made in the USA
Coppell, TX
18 May 2021